THE SUGAR CANE CURTAIN

Historical novel

ZILIA L. LAJE

GUARINA PUBLISHING

Copyright © 1991 Zilia L. Laje, "The Bagasse Curtain"
Spanish edition, "La Cortina de Bagazo", 1995
English edition, "The Sugar Cane Curtain", 2000

All rights reserved. No part of this book may be reproduced in any form or by any electronic or mechanical means including information storage and retrieval systems without permission in writing from the author, except by a reviewer, who may quote brief passages in a review.

P.O. Box 45-1732
Shenandoah Station
Miami, Florida 33245-1732

Library of Congress Catalog Card Number: 00 091110

ISBN: 0-9646224-1-6

To my son Alberto Luis and
the children of the Cuban exiles.
May they always have a Homeland.

PROLOGUE

The Sugar Cane Curtain is an account of different experiences lived by any average non-political Cuban citizen in her struggle during the first four years of the communist regime in Cuba and exile in the United States, compiled into the creation of an imaginary character and told in the form of a historical journal within a genre framework in as dispassionate a way as I have been able to. All the main characters in the foreground are fictional and any resemblance to actual persons living or dead in names or physical descriptions is purely coincidental, the only real persons being the many public figures, mainly political, artistic and international, whom the reader will readily identify, all in the historical background, linked to events in news taken from newspapers, magazines and non-fiction books, listed in the bibliographical reference. The names of some persons involved in events of public interest, as well as a singer and a television character, have been changed to protect their sensitivity. Fictitious names have also been used for some companies, hotels, towns, farms, stores, restaurants, organizations, automobile models, publications, a bank, sugar mill, building, club, gym, clinic, travel agency, market, metal plant and news agency.

I wrote the manuscript originally in English, then translated it into Spanish and published it as *"La Cortina de Bagazo"* in 1995. I read about fifty books and consulted countless history, geography, botany and zoology books, encyclopedias, atlases, road maps, street maps, directories, newspapers, travel guides, weather reports, calendars, poetry anthologies and dictionaries; watched videos; wrote to libraries, weather bureaus, magazines, tourist commissions and companies; called librarians, writers and historians, and tired friends, relatives, coworkers and acquaintances with my queries for over ten years. I felt a *need* to tell the story.

I found it especially difficult to recall the sequence in which the (newsworthy) events took place. Fictional liberties have been taken with weather conditions, schedules, programs and so forth.

I want to give special thanks to Mrs. Justine F. Postal, of the Palm Beach County Public Library, Mr. T.I. Bradshaw, of RCA, Jorge González, of the foreign language department of the Miami-Dade Public Library, Luis González Lalondry, of the *Diario Las Américas*, show-business columnist Rosendo Rosell, and Jaime Rico Salazar, of the Musical Studies Editorial Center, for their valuable help, and to everyone who in any way has contributed to this novel.

I'm very grateful to my son, Alberto, who read the manuscript for syntax and punctuation, and to Anita Leiser and Georgina D. Carretero, who acted as editors pointing out typographical and vocabulary errors.

§

TABLE OF CONTENTS

Chapter   Page

PART I - THE LAND WE LEFT BEHIND

1. Liberation from the Dictatorship 1
2. Pride in Being a Cuban 42
3. Revelation of Communist Take-over 96
4. Apathy to the Events 120
5. The Agrarian Reform Under Way 135
6. Good-by to Traces of the Good Life 160
7. Witnesses to the Destruction of the Country 190
8. The Education Campaign 242
9. The Freedom Fighters 304
10. On Leaving the Homeland Behind 333

PART II - EXILE

11. Landing on Free Soil 381
12. Getting Settled 416
13. Planning Campaign 442
14. Hope of Return 451
15. Organization Campaign 471
16. Acceptance of Expatriation 514

Prologue ii
List of Characters iv
Popular Dishes v
Epilogue vi
About the Author vii
Bibliographical Reference viii
Works Quoted ix

❖

PART I

THE LAND WE LEFT BEHIND

CHAPTER 1

LIBERATION FROM THE DICTATORSHIP

> *"Hora de triunfo en que el pueblo,*
> *al sol de la independencia,*
> *dejó libre la conciencia*
> *rompiendo la oscuridad."*[1]
> *("A La Patria",* Manuel Acuña)

It was New Year's Day. She woke up to the loud voice of the newscaster on a television set heard from the air shaft. The deaf lady in the apartment upstairs always turned the sound up as high as it was possible. But it seemed loudest on Saturday mornings, or on holidays, when Ana could otherwise afford the luxury of sleeping late. The night before, she had gone to greet the New Year dancing with Dany, and her cousin Norma with her boyfriend. She went over the evening now. They had first been at "El Chico", which was pathetically deserted except for two other bored couples, and they had then gone to the "Rancho Luna", which, although far from crowded, had been fairly full, considering that many people were adhering to the "Campaign against the Three D's" (no dinner, drinks or dance) during the holiday season, launched against Batista's government, and others were afraid of terrorism. There was no band, so they had danced to the record player. They had dined late, on roast suckling pig, with Spanish farm cider – the boys had had Scotch whiskey, – and at mid-

---

[1] Time of triumph in which the people
set their conscience free
breaking the darkness
in the sunlight of independence.

night they had eaten the twelve fortune grapes. And an idle photographer had taken their picture at the table, four happy faces under paper hats, hands in the air rattling noise-makers. It had been a wonderful evening, despite the lack of holiday spirit. She must have gotten home about 3:00 and was still sleepy. She tried to bury her head deeper in the pillow, but the voice from the television wouldn't be shut out and she couldn't go back to sleep. She listened and made out what the newscaster was saying.

"The President didn't want any more blood to be shed." What *could* he be talking about? "Batista's son, Papo, made a statement from abroad", the announcer went on. "This is Channel Twelve. We caution, don't go out on the streets, avoid the crowds. We repeat, our leader doesn't want any more bloodshed."

There was no doubt, that *was* what he was saying. Ana María sat up on the bed, wide awake now. What could it be? Could the Rebels have taken Channel 12? But how could they have? It was on O Street, in the Eda Building, right in the middle of Vedado. Had there been a revolt? Why was Batista's son making statements from abroad? Where was he? She looked at her wristwatch on the nightstand: 11:15. She turned her radio on. And then she heard the whole startling news. Batista had been deposed by Castro's rebels and had left the country in the sunrise hours. Maybe he had already left when she had gotten home? She got up and dressed hurriedly. She still couldn't believe what she had heard. The apartment was quiet. Her parents had gone out. Did they know yet? Why hadn't they awakened her? Her head felt stuffy from the cider. She crossed the living room and stood at the open door of the apartment. She heard the janitor's voice from the upper floor.

"Felipe!", she called. And, when the colored man came down, Ana asked him, already knowing the answer, "What happened?"

"Batista was toppled", he answered without elaboration. His big feet shuffling, his thin arms dangling, he seemed excited as about any unexpected event, but not particularly affected, almost unconcerned, about what it really meant to them all. She was speechless now. A lump had formed in her throat, and she only looked at Felipe blankly. He apparently expected more of a reaction. Somebody upstairs called him back up, and Ana went downstairs without stopping to lock the apartment door and stood at the top of the steps to the building entrance. Realization really hit her fully then, and excitement began to bubble up in her and would not be contained. Finally Cuba

Liberation from the Dictatorship

was free from the dictatorship of almost seven long years! Girls were walking around laughing, in red and black clothes, the colors of the Revolution. Several convertibles sped by with the tops down, people sitting on the folded tops, yelling merrily. Ana was smiling broadly now. She ran upstairs and called Dany on the phone. Ignacio, his father, answered. She knew his voice.

"Danilo, please", she asked, excitement letting impatience show through in her voice. He also would know who it was.

"Wait a moment." He was always curt to her. She could tell – anybody could – that he didn't like her. His mother was more polite to her. She could now hear Dany's voice talking to somebody as he neared the telephone.

"Hello".

"Dany, have you heard?", she asked, excited.

"My sister just woke me up to tell me. Mamá had tried to when they heard it earlier, but I guess I was too fast asleep.

"Are you coming over?", and the thought immediately struck her. "Do you have the car?" He lived in Almendares, over three miles west from Havana across the river.

"I have the car, but we have no gasoline and Sonia says the service stations are closed. I'll see if I can later. Maybe I can borrow my uncle's if he has gas. All right, darling?"

"All right ...", a little disappointed. "I love you."

He threw her a kiss before they hung up.

She brushed her teeth and changed into a black blouse and a red skirt. Her parents were probably at her brother's around the corner, but this event deserved recording. She took her camera from her wardrobe and ran downstairs, this time locking the door. The excitement was building up in her. She walked down 17th Street to L, then up L Street to wide 23rd, where the Habana Hilton, some thirty-odd stories of blue and plate-glass newness, stood on the busy corner, its doorman in his plume hat. People were hurrying by, rushing nowhere, talking loudly, laughing happily, congratulating each other, their repressed emotions suddenly unleashed. There were Rebel soldiers everywhere. She walked to a little open-front restaurant and bought a roll of film at the cashier's counter just as they were closing for a general strike, and put it in the camera.

There were American tourists, in the city for the holidays, walking down L and 23rd Streets. Their eyes were wide with amusement. Some were taking pictures. Ana wondered what it all seemed to them. She felt proud, felt like saying to them, "See? We finally did it, we're freeee!" She walked to 25th Street and snapped pictures of the soldiers obligingly posing for her lens on the sidewalk with their rifles, and of jeeps going by full of jubilant rebels. They all had beards and long manes grown on the hills, and wore wide-brimmed hats or black berets. Some of them were very young. Many looked ill at ease, maybe the first time they had ever been in Havana. Tears were welling up in her eyes and then spilling down her cheeks, and she sniffled and smiled happily. An American walking near Trader Vic's in slippers and no socks surprised her by talking to her in English, and a man called to her from a doorway, "Congratulations!"

"To you too", she called back, smiling at the stranger. And the lump came back up in her throat.

She hadn't had breakfast. She walked back home behind a mist of tears, and found her mother carrying an avocado and a bowl of radishes out from the kitchen.

"Where were you?", she asked Ana.

"I went to take some pictures of the rebels." Ana held up her camera in one hand and squeezed her mother's shoulders with her other arm. "And you?"

"We went to Gustavo's. We hadn't heard the news yet when we went out. We heard it on the street. Imagine!, at ten, and the man had been gone since dawn. They were downstairs. You were sleeping when we left and it was still early, so I hadn't wanted to wake you up. You came home *so* late!...", she added reproachfully. – So she *had* been awake. – Ana conveniently ignored the remark.

"Why didn't you call me?"

"Well, Blanca wanted to, but, since I had to come to get this anyway", she indicated her full hands, "Gustavo said, if you were still asleep, this news over the phone would startle you needlessly, and your father thought I should tell you. And I came to get you, but I've been here half an hour."

"The television of the deaf woman upstairs had woken me up."

"They want us to have lunch with them. This caught me without anything in the house and the grocery stores are closing... And the restaurants." They had planned to go out to dinner today. "Blanca already called. Let's go." Ana went into her bedroom to leave the camera on her dresser. "The soldiers didn't mind the pictures?", her mother asked.

"Mind? Oh, no! Most seemed to enjoy it. Many of them look

like country men."

"Well, they probably are, but just think of what they've just done, they've pulled the chestnuts out of the fire for us 'city people', and don't start finding fault with them so soon."

"I wasn't. I just meant they seemed to enjoy the attention."

"I have to take this to Blanca", her mother said, unnecessarily, as they went down the stairs. "Have you talked to Dany?", she asked as they went out of the building. Her parents didn't especially like Dany much either, because he was a year younger than she and still going to college – her mother claimed they would probably have to wait three years before they could get married, – but they suppressed their objections politely, on the psychological theory that, if they set themselves openly against him, they would only draw them closer together. Ana was aware of this.

"I called him, but they don't have any gas and the service stations are closed too."

They hurried up 17th Street, as if a party awaited them, and turned down I Street to where her brother lived. They could see him now, leaning back against the balcony railing, his back to the street, smoking, and her father sitting on a canvas chair looking down at the Rebels going by and the people rushing around excitedly.

"We thought you were going to sleep the whole day", her father called down to her.

They walked up the flight of stairs, and Blanca, her brother's wife, met her at the door with a hug and brushed her cheek with a kiss.

"What, happy?", she asked her.

"Sure."

"And you dressed in red and black." She slapped her on the abdomen, and Ana whirled around to model. Blanca then turned back to her task of trying to get little Gustavito, not quite two and a half, to eat what looked like ground beef and mashed *malanga*. He kept turning his chubby face away, laughing nervously. He was wriggling in his high chair, the family's excitement having transmitted itself to him, not aware of what was going on, but excited just the same.

Ana prudently passed him by and went on toward the balcony. A natural Canadian Christmas tree stood in a corner of the living room, a Nativity scene arranged under it.

Her brother asked her, "What do you think of this, *Basurilla*?" He always called her "Little Rubbish" and she always ignored the nickname, which he intended to annoy her, but she secretly liked it. It made her feel very young and protected, sheltered.

"Wonderful!", she answered him. "I still can't quite believe it."

Teresa left the avocado and radishes on the table and walked to the door from the living room.

"I know", Gustavo said soberly, "it took us by surprise". He was twenty-six, an accountant, with their father's height and their mother's dark looks.

His lunch finished, Gustavito jabbed his finger on the tray, repeatedly saying "Ping!" and accidentally stuck it in the sweet potato pudding. He was startled for a moment, looked at it in surprise and then started laughing contagiously until they all joined in.

"After seven years", said their mother, "I thought Batista was there for life."

"It took us four centuries to free ourselves from the Spanish", reflected Gustavo.

"It had to come, Tera", said their father. "Things had gotten much too difficult this last year."

Ana María Méndez hadn't personally experienced the difficulty during Batista's government. She was aware of the fear in the people, but she couldn't identify herself with the atrocities the people claimed the government inflicted. She knew there had been a constant struggle for the last five and a half years to overthrow the regime, but they hadn't had any relative involved in the revolution or any friend caught in subversive activities. The most active area had been the easternmost province of Oriente and this had contributed to make the activity seem remote.

> The opposition against General Fulgencio Batista was led mainly by university students and followers of deposed President Carlos Prío, now in Florida. The Triple A group was headed by his right-hand man, former Minister of Education Aureliano Sánchez Arango.
>
> The most significant event took place when Fidel Castro, unknown to the Cuban people until then, led an abortive suicidal attack on the Moncada Military Fort in Santiago de Cuba, the provincial capital of Oriente, in the early morning of July 26, 1953, with about 120 men and two girls, Haydée Santamaría and Melba Hernández Rodríguez, where they knifed 18 soldiers in the barracks, and it resulted in the death of 69 of the attackers. Abel Santamaría Cuadrado, who was second in command, had his left eye taken out by the army and people said Haydée was presented with her brother's eyeball. Her fiancé, Boris Luis Santa Coloma, was castrated and mur-

Liberation from the Dictatorship

dered. Constitutional freedom guarantees were suspended in Oriente province.

Monsignor Enrique Pérez Serantes, Archbishop of Santiago, intervened to end the execution of prisoners, and obtained a promise from Army Colonel Alberto del Río Chaviano, commanding officer, that their lives would be spared if they gave up. Dr. Felipe Salcines, Rector of the University of Santiago, interceded to save Fidel Castro's life. Monsignor Pérez Serantes delivered Castro to the army. He was tried in the Boniato jail in Santiago in October. In the oral proceeding, he promised that, if they won, they would uphold the Constitution of 1940 and hold elections within a year, and he said he'd nationalize all public utilities. His five-hour self-defense was later published under the title "History Will Absolve Me", the words with which he had ended his speech. He was sentenced to a 15-year term and sent to the National Reclusory on Isle of Pines, but he served only 18 months and was released from prison, on a general amnesty granted by Congress, in May of 1955.

Castro had been nominated as a Cuban People's (Orthodox) Party candidate for Representative to the House for the June, 1952 elections, which were never held. He had married Mirta Díaz Balart in October of 1948 and they had one son, but she divorced him shortly after he came out of prison.

A plot was discovered for an army uprising to take place on April 4, 1956, headed by Colonel Ramón Barquín López, *attaché* in Washington. Lieutenant Colonel Manuel Varela Castro was head of the tank corps, with Major Enrique Borbonet Díaz in charge of the paratroopers. Barquín, who had chosen Dr. Justo Carrillo Hernández to be president, was arrested, tried, convicted and sentenced to six years in Isle of Pines.

The Montecristi group, which was not connected with Castro, was headed by Dr. Carrillo, who had been President of BANFAIC (the Cuban Bank of Agricultural and Industrial Development) under Prío's office. On April 28 the Montecristians and a small group of Prío's organization led by Reinol García García, attacked and tried to capture the Goicuría Army Installation in Matanzas. Eleven died.

Colonel Antonio Blanco Rico, chief of SIM (the Military Intelligence Service), was shot to death in Montmartre nightclub in October. The joke went around, "Would you rather be poor black or Blanco Rico (*'rich white'*)?"

There was an uprising in Santiago on November 30, led by

Frank País García, Secretary General of the movement, in which they burned down police headquarters. Haydée Santamaría Cuadrado, who kept active revolutionarily, eventually married Armando Hart Dávalos, and they were both in Santiago at the time of the uprising. The revolt of Frank País was going well.

An 82-passenger expedition from the blue and white yacht "Granma" landed on the morning of December 2 at Belic on the muddy Las Coloradas beach, below Niquero, near Cape Cruz, on the southwestern coast of Oriente. Airplanes strafed the rebels in Alegría de Pío, and seventy were either killed by Lieutenant Julio Laurent in Ojo de Buey or captured. Twelve escaped, including Fidel, his brother Raúl Castro, Argentinean Dr. Ernesto Guevara, Camilo Cienfuegos, Universo Sánchez, Ramiro Valdés, Juan Almeida, Faustino Pérez, Ciro Redondo, Efigenio Ameijeiras, Calixto García and Reinaldo Benítez, and survived to reach their goal, the Real del Turquino Peak, 6578 feet high, to the east in Manzanillo, in the towering Sierra Maestra. Twelve men were on a mountain top on Christmas of 1956. But the expedition was not taken seriously by the people in Havana. It stirred little interest in the public.

All the news travelled, unconfirmed, by word of mouth. "*Radio Bemba*" ('Radio Thick Lip'), as the people had come to call the rumors, was the rebels' only network for disseminating news.

The bullet-ridden bodies of young boys were found, who the people claimed had been killed in the police stations. It was said that wives were ravished before their husbands.

One proven case of torture which had become public was that of school teacher Florentina Pedrayés Chelín, who was arrested and horribly tortured by Captain Evaristo Saco at the Ninth Police Station, where Colombian Ambassador Juan Calvo accidentally found her later.

The army killed fourteen-year-old William Soler Ledea in Santiago on January 2, after breaking his arms, legs, ribs and nose by beating him. They castrated him, fired a bullet into his head and left him on a roadway. In protest, 300 women dressed in black staged the "March of the Mothers" on January 4 in Santiago with banners that read, "Cease the murders of our children!"

Castro was believed dead by most until, less than three months after their landing, The New York Times' Herbert Matthews interviewed him and took pictures in the Sierra. The interview appeared in the Times on February 24, 1957, turning him into a national hero

Liberation from the Dictatorship

with international edgings. Matthews became an advocate of Castro. Catholic Father Guillermo Sardiñas arrived in the mountains to join Fidel.

Ana had seen clandestine newspapers which published photographs of people shot by the army, there was whispered news of men hanged from trees in secluded places, a favorite one being the Havana Country Club Park lagoon, and people rumored that many times, when the government agencies officially released the news that a revolutionary had been shot while trying to place a bomb, it was actually a frame-up, where they had first killed the person and then placed the bomb in his hands for the press photographs. It did seem improbable that the bomb never exploded when the man was shot. The people seemed to live in fear, they dreaded the army and were cautious with the police. They talked about the tortures inflicted especially by the SIM and the Fifth District Garrison. So, when it was known that Castro was in the Sierra Maestra gathering forces to overthrow the government, most of the people they knew had nursed the hope that they would succeed, but it seemed far away.

While Fidel was ensconced in the rugged Sierra Maestra, terrorism against Batista flared. University students carried out acts of sabotage.

José Antonio Echeverría, Faustino Pérez and Armando Hart were the leaders of the underground in Havana. On March 13, a four-hour attack was launched on the Presidential Palace by members of the DER (Revolutionary Student Directorate) and Prío's Cuban Revolutionary (Authentic) Party from a florist's truck in the garden. The plan was plotted by Echeverría and led by Hart. They got up to the second floor of the Palace, the elevator operator switched the power off on the second floor and a locked iron grille stopped them. José Luis Gómez Wangüemert and Menelao Mora Morales were killed, along with twenty-three others. A group of students headed by José Antonio Echeverría, president of the FEU (University Student Federation), simultaneously crashed into and captured radio station CMQ in Vedado, seized the transmitter of "*Radio Reloj*", and shouted on the air, broadcasting to the country. Many were shot down by the police outside. José Antonio was killed on Jovellar and L Streets by a squad car.

The next day an Army sergeant assassinated the president of the Ortodoxo Party, Dr. Pelayo Cuervo Navarro, with a submachine pistol at the Havana Country Club Park lagoon.

On April 20, four young members of the Revolutionary Student Directorate were shot by the police in the apartment building at Humboldt Street, #7.

The yacht "Corinthia", purchased by Prío, with a 29-man expedition led by Calixto Sánchez White aboard, from Miami, ran aground on May 19 in Cabonico Bay, east of Nicaro, in Mayarí, on the north coast of Oriente. They were surrounded by the army, gave up to Captain Pino and were machine-gunned.

Frank País had been killed by the police in Callejón del Muro in Santiago the day before new United States Ambassador Earl T. Smith arrived on July 31. Two hundred women dressed in mourning gathered along his route to welcome him, protesting against "the kingdom of terror", carrying banners reading, "Don't kill our sons" and shouting "Freedom, freedom!", and they staged a demonstration in front of City Hall while Smith was inside. The day of País' burial, a workers' strike closed down the stores and industries in Oriente and Camagüey.

Oriente province has two million inhabitants, and in 1957 it was shut off from Havana.

On September 5 of that year, there was a naval uprising in Cayo Loco station in the southern city of Cienfuegos. Colonel Carlos Tabernilla Palmeros ordered the air force to bomb the city. A leader, Second Lieutenant José Dionisio San Román Toledo, was tortured and murdered. Sixty were killed. Escaping participants fled to the Sierra del Escambray to the east of the city.

Students of the Revolutionary Directorate and members of Prío's Auténtico Party formed a second front in the Escambray range, the chiefs of which were Faure Chaumón and Víctor Bordón. The Directorate was represented by Major Eloy Gutiérrez Menoyo. William Morgan was second in command. Their outfit grew to two-thousand strong. In the Maestra range, Cristino Naranjo, Huber Matos, Celia Sánchez, Haydée Santamaría and Vilma Espín were with Fidel.

Twenty-six men were rounded up in Holguín on December 24 and found in the outskirts of the city on Christmas Day, shot or strangled. Army Colonel Fermín Cowley Gallegos, military chief, was killed by the underground.

On February 22, Oscar Lucero and Faustino Pérez, of Hart's team, kidnapped Argentine car driver Juan Manuel Fangio, who was in Havana to run in the *Grand Prix* race, from the Lincoln hotel.

Liberation from the Dictatorship

The rebels had the *"Cuba Libre"* underground newspaper. *"Revolución"* was the publication of the Twenty-sixth of July Movement, which took its name from the date of the Moncada attack. *Radio Rebelde* began broadcasting on February 24, 1958, operated by Luis Orlando Rodríguez. It was heard, "Here Rebel Radio broadcasting from the Maestra Range, free territory of Cuba."

Castro stated to The Chicago Tribune's Jules Dubois in May that the movement would not nationalize the industries, they fought for free enterprise and would hold elections in one year.

His brother Raúl led his troops into Sierra Cristal, near their home town, in Mayarí, in the northern part of Oriente, and established his headquarters there. In June they kidnapped 45 Americans in the hills of Oriente as hostages, including 27 Marines and sailors from Guantánamo Navy Base, thirteen American civilians and three Canadians from Moa Bay in Baracoa.

American movie actor Errol Flynn went into rebel headquarters on the Sierra Maestra for three weeks to write a book. American television host Ed Sullivan went up into the rugged hills for an interview with Castro. Dr. Manuel Urrutia, who had been relieved from his post as judge in January of 1957, was the statesman for the movement.

By October the rebels had cut all transportation between Santiago and the rest of the island. Three columns fanned out, led by Raúl Castro, Camilo Cienfuegos and "Che" Guevara. The one led by Guevara joined the Second Front of the Escambray. Castro bribed Colonel Alberto del Río Chaviano, who was in charge of the military force in Las Villas province. Armando Hart was in the Isle of Pines prison.

The regime of the native of Banes worked prisoners to death in the Zapata swamps in the southern peninsula. The outrages of Senator Rolando Masferrer's private army of 1,500 *"Tigres"* drove decent elements into the Castro movement. Freedom bonds were sold for $1.

At SIM informers were paid $20. for reports. The Bureau of Investigations headquarters was on 23rd and 32nd Streets, on a steep hill overlooking Vedado.

On November 3 of that year Batista held rigged elections, fixed in favor of Dr. Andrés Rivero Agüero. Only 15 percent of the population voted — the Méndez family hadn't voted, — and his handpicked candidate was elected by a landslide.

On November 18 the rebels blew a bridge in Guisa, Bayamo, the Army's nerve center of communications for Oriente province. In late November the water supply to Guantánamo Navy Base on the south coast was cut off by Raúl Castro.

Camilo and "El Che" were fighting west of Santa Clara, the provincial capital of Las Villas. Major Rolando Cubelas Secades trained men with William Morgan in the Escambray mountains.

On December 17 Ambassador Earl Smith asked Batista to resign.

Cubelas smashed at the Army squadron headquarters in Santa Clara. By Christmas Day Guevara had seized the city of Sancti Spíritus in Las Villas. Santa Clara was captured late in December. On December 30, 1958, El Che took an armored train carrying arms.

To the people Fidel was a legend, not a reality. It seemed so impossible. The last few months the rumors had grown and a few people had been sure the end was near, but it was still hard to believe and they couldn't help feeling it was nothing more than talk.

The leaders of the Communist party, founded in 1925, Dr. Juan Marinello Vidaurreta, its President and life-long electoral candidate; Blas Roca, Secretary General, and Lázaro Peña, syndicate leader, were out of the country. The Communists' leader on the Island was Carlos Rafael Rodríguez.

There was no celebration New Year's Eve, the streets were empty.

Several names stood out among the others in the government. General Francisco Tabernilla Dolz was the chief of staff of the Army. General Eulogio Cantillo Porras was in command of Fort Moncada. Havana's chief of police was Colonel Pilar García. Colonel José María Salas Cañizares was Santiago's chief of police. Colonel Esteban Ventura Novo was head of the secret police. Lieutenant Colonel Joaquín Casillas Lumpuy was in charge of Santa Clara. Captain Andrés Pérez Chaumont commanded the Moncada barracks. General José Eleuterio Pedraza Cabrera, Colonel Conrado Carratalá, Senator Rolando Masferrer, Major Jesús Sosa Blanco and Colonel Roberto Fernández Miranda were other notorious names.

As Batista's rule came to an end, it was said 19,000 people had been murdered, 20,000 had fled into exile, 300 men had been castrated in Havana, there were many tortures and mutilations, and

Liberation from the Dictatorship

women were raped. It was proven that torture chambers were used.

The street below could be seen from the living room door, where Ana and her mother were standing, and, as they looked, the architect's family across the street got into their car, waving at them and yelling something they couldn't make out, and drove away in a rush of cries.

Blanca had finished feeding Gustavito and put him in the playpen with a bottle of milk for his afternoon nap. The Pomeranian pup was spinning in the living room trying to catch his tail, perilously close to the Christmas tree.

Ana looked from the open door of the bedroom at little Blanquita in her crib under the picture of the Guardian Angel. She was falling asleep and looked up at her briefly from under heavy eyelids. So Ana abstained from turning the television set on. It was 1:00 in the afternoon and they hadn't had lunch yet.

Ana María Méndez Bermúdez had a full mouth, light brown eyes, almond colored − her irises seemed outlined in a darker brown, − black, thick eyelashes and naturally wavy, light brown hair, filbert colored, which she wore brushed back from her forehead with the barest insinuation of a curl over each temple, swept up from her neck in the back and brushed forward over her ears. Her fair skin was creamy and smooth, and her nose straight. Her central incisors receded ever so slightly from the row of her other teeth, lending her smile a hint of mischief, like a "wink". Her long, dark lashes seemed to rest flittingly on her high cheekbones when she blinked. She had a tendency to thinness, but her hips flared out in the typical characteristic passed down from generation to generation of Cuban women.

She went to the dining room, where her sister-in-law had started setting the table, and she helped her with the dishes, silverware and glasses.

"Leonor didn't show up today." Although Ana could never keep track of their names, she supposed Blanca was referring to their current maid. "I guess she had no way to get here. The buses aren't running, are they?"

"I don't know, I guess not."

"You know, I never really thought this could happen."

"And so unexpectedly."

"And quietly, too; no riots", Blanca marvelled.

"Yes, I guess not many people have been killed."

"They will", Ana's father predicted fatalistically from the balcony.

"Let me help you", Teresa said to Blanca.
"You be still, Teresa. Ana is helping me. And there isn't that much to eat, anyway, believe me."
"The people in the street are happy, like at Carnival time", said Ana.
"But now will come the personal vendettas", said Gustavo.

Trying to judge impartially what good things Batista's government might have done for the country, Ana reminded herself that many government buildings, plazas and highways had been constructed by it. The Tunnel of Havana was built under the harbor to join the capital with the eastern part of the province. The big Monumental Way, across the Bay from Havana, was an eight-lane highway. The Civic Plaza was built around the huge marble-covered 370-foot pentagonal Martí obelisk, with the Palace of Justice, the Court of Accounts and the Palace of Communications surrounding it; and further away in the area were the National Library, the National Theater and the new Bus Terminal, all beautiful modern buildings erected by the government. The seventy-acre Sports City, the new Rancho Boyeros International airport building, the tunnel of Línea under the river to Miramar, the East Havana development and the connection of the six-lane Vía Blanca with the Central Highway had all been built by Batista's regime. And many foreign companies, lured by long-term tax exemptions, had built factories in the little towns around Havana and offered jobs to the country men who had been working in the sugar and tobacco plantations, or opened their offices in Havana because of the tax advantages that they enjoyed in Cuba and hired office workers who had held poorly-paid Ministry positions. The Cuban companies had raised their own salaries to retain their employees. And Cuban companies were also building factories in the surrounding towns. The automobile company where Ana had been working for almost a year and a half, Wayne Motor Corporation, had set up their international sales office in Havana two years before to avoid the heavy taxation in the States. It was a period of economic prosperity. The tourist industry flourished. Yet, Ana's father had contributed to the underground collections taken up to buy weapons abroad for the revolution, and Ana herself had bought a few $1 freedom bonds.

Blanca went to the balcony. Two years Ana's senior, she had very black, straight hair, down to her shoulders, which made her face, narrow at the cheeks, appear longer.
"Let's have lunch."

Liberation from the Dictatorship

"I'm starved", said Gustavo. He had gone into the accounting office with his father about four years ago. Before, he had taught bookkeeping at a boys' school. He had married Blanca almost three and a half years before, with everybody's approval, just two months after Ana had graduated from business school, and Ana had been a bridesmaid along with a cousin of Blanca's. They had Gustavito and Blanquita, nine months old. He was intelligent, reserved and, although Ana admired him, she didn't feel close to him, but felt shy with him. Perhaps because she considered him intelligent, he could sometimes make her feel very foolish. She knew he loved her, though, in his own undemonstrative way.

"Is it all right if I turn the television on?", asked Ana, anxious to learn the details of the news.

Blanca looked into the bedroom. "Go ahead, she's asleep now."

Ana turned the television on and they sat down to eat. There was ground beef, white rice, fried ripe plantains, the avocado and radishes Teresa had brought, and orange shells with cream cheese. Hardly a meal for New Year's Day, but they had probably been planning to go out to dinner today, supposed Ana, as they had. The men had "Tropical" beer. And Gustavo's usual cry went up, "Don't pour it smack in the center of the glass", at the same time tilting the glass for Blanca, to make the spurt run down its inner side.

"Your mother does the same to me", commented Carlos, their father, feigning resignation.

Blanca looked at Teresa and rolled her eyes in mock suffering; Teresa shrugged her shoulders.

They could see the television set from the table and turned to it, avid for news. Two newscasters, one of them a woman, sitting behind a long counter, were alternately reading the news from the releases on the table in front of them. Regular programming had been suspended. They were relating, repeating it who knew for how many a time, how the end of the deposed government had come about.

In the early morning Batista Zaldívar had turned the government over to General Eulogio Cantillo and fled with his family before 4:00 in his private plane "Guáimaro" for the Dominican Republic. Left behind was his Finca "Kuquine" with his gold chamberpot — Ana and Dany had driven past Kuquine. — For some reason, they called Cantillo a traitor.

Colonel Esteban Ventura, Prime Minister Gonzalo Güel Navarro and president-elect Dr. Andrés Rivero Agüero had left with Batista.

General José Pedraza and Colonel Conrado Carratalá had also gone to Santo Domingo. General Francisco Tabernilla and Colonel Pilar García had reached Jacksonville. Rolando Masferrer had fled by yacht to Miami.

The Secretary General of CTC (the Cuban Confederation of Workers), Eusebio Mujal Barniol, had fled to an embassy when Batista fell.

"Do you know what the colors of the Twenty-sixth of July Movement armbands stand for?", Gustavo asked his sister, pointing to her clothes. The armbands read, "*M 26-7*".

"No. I know they're the colors of their emblem, but I don't know why."

"Red stands for freedom and black for death."

"How gloomy!"

The underground seized control of the police stations.

By 10:00 in the morning, mobs had begun gathering downtown.

They occasionaly showed Army soldiers and Rebels shooting in the streets, and "myrmidons" — this new word was being used often lately — being carried by their arms and legs into patrol cars. The houses of some of the deposed leaders were being ransacked. People were shown carrying pieces of furniture away with them, or smashing and burning others. Ventura's house was emptied out onto the front garden and furnishings were burned. On top of the smoldering pile was a broken picture frame with a photograph in it, which caught Ana's attention — a wedding picture? — Others were shattering slot machines and crap tables in the Deauville hotel. The gambling casinos of the Sevilla Biltmore, Plaza and St. John's hotels were wrecked. Only American actor George Raft's "Capri" casino in Vedado was left untouched. They attacked Shell service stations. People were smashing parking meters and coin telephones.

Their conversation during lunch excluded any topic other than the event.

After lunch, Blanca's mother called on the phone. Her parents lived on San José Street, in the downtown district.

"Mamá says there is shooting from the roof of the Manzana de Gómez." Blanca joined them in the living room, sitting next to Gustavo on the sofa, one leg bent under. "It seems Masferrer's Tigers are fighting the rebels off. And my brother wanted to go."

"Oh, God, no!", Teresa cried.

Ana welcomed the call and, as soon as Blanca had hung up the

Liberation from the Dictatorship

phone, she used the pause that followed to call Dany. He hadn't gotten gas yet nor his uncle's car. She felt terribly lost, not knowing when she'd see him.

The puppy was on the balcony, barking at the people going by. Blanquita woke up crying, and Ana picked her up — she smelled of violet water — and kissed her on the bridge of her nose; and the child yelled in delight. A pink celluloid sphere doll hung over her crib. Her yells woke up Gustavito, who climbed out of the playpen and immediately yanked the pup's tail, the former yelling, "Wow, wow!", the latter yelping. The boy was quieted down with a glass of Maltina.

Gunfire was heard all over the city.

Colonel José Rego Rubido at the Moncada Fort and 5,000 soldiers in Santiago surrendered, as did Major José Fernández Hernández.

Castro started out from Palma Soriano. He chose Dr. Manuel Urrutia Lleó for the presidency. In Céspedes Park, before the Cathedral of Santiago, he proclaimed the city the temporary capital of the nation and called a general strike throughout the Island, with the exception of electric, gas and telephone services, until Urrutia reached Havana. Urrutia, who had been a judge of the Urgency Court of Appeals in Santiago, took the oath in that city. Colonel José Rego Rubido was named chief of the Revolutionary Army by Urrutia.

"Do you think you could go get Leonor?", Blanca asked Gustavo.
"She lives on Pasaje Giquel."
"It's on Xifrés. She said it was an 'accessory house' a block from Infanta."
"It *is* a block from Infanta", said Teresa, "but it's on Ciprés."
"I still think it's on Giquel", insisted Blanca.
"And I think we had better wait until you find out", concluded Gustavo.

When she and her parents went home, Ana and Dany called each other several times during the day.

Truckloads of rebels from the Escambray mountains rolled into Havana.

Major Faure Chaumón Mediavilla headed the Revolutionary Directorate; the Second Front was headed by Major Eloy Gutiérrez Menoyo, a Spaniard, and second in command was American paratrooper William Morgan, which served to inflate Castro to world recognition.

Ana and her father walked the ten blocks to the Vedado Secondary Education Institute, which had been taken over by the Second Front and turned into temporary quarters. Not a business was functioning. The grocery store high on the corner with its trimmed little trees in planters and its "Foodstuffs and Liquors" sign painted on the wall had its corrugated metal doors rolled down. They took pictures from Medina Park across the street from the Institute.

Cars were overturned, some blazing; there was broken glass, smashed furniture, gutted stores, broken shutters and the distant rattle of gunfire. The vigilant police of the Communist-dominated FONU (United National Labor Front) broke up the fights that burst out. Even the Boy Scouts were directing traffic.

Two thousand American tourists, come for the holidays, were stranded in Havana.

Colonel Ramón Barquín was liberated from prison at 8:00 on the night of the 1st and flown to Havana, where he took command of Camp Columbia. He arrested General Eulogio Cantillo there and put him in prison on Isle of Pines.

Dr. Carlos Prío Socarrás, leader of the Auténtico Party, flew to Havana from Miami on New Year's night.

And so ended January 1st, the first day of their liberation. That moon-less night, in the cool darkness, Ana fell asleep with the taste of freedom in her mouth and a smile on her lips, thinking a whole new future lay ahead for Cuba with the new year.

Camilo Cienfuegos and Che Guevara marched to Havana from Santa Clara.

Raúl Castro was named military commander and became the commanding officer at Fort Moncada. On January 2 Fidel visited the Fort.

Prío appropriated offices in the Radiocentro building in Vedado. Major Gustavo Iglesias took charge of the Habana Hilton Hotel on the 2nd.

As Castro marched west, moving up the Central Highway through the eastern provinces, with the troops in jeeps, trucks and tanks, nearly the country's total population of six and a half million celebrated.

It was two days before Dany could get to Vedado to see Ana. On Saturday, Teresa answered the door and, when Ana came out of her room, she found Dany standing in the living room and was gladder than ever to see his dear face. After having expected him all day Friday, she was surprised to have him drop by today.

"The Old Man got some gas and needed to come to Havana", he smiled, "so I asked him to bring me by", he added a little awkwardly, because Ana's parents were standing by in the dinette area, looking at him.

Danilo Gutiérrez Núñez had very dark brown, slightly wavy hair, which he parted on the left, and big coffee brown eyes with a deep look, which crinkled at the corners at his ready smile. His full lips drew Ana's glance as he talked, and his teeth, perhaps a trifle big, were very even. His forehead was wide and a few unruly strands of hair escaped the part. He had a straight, strong nose and his jaw had a slightly square outline. His shoulders, wide and very straight, seemed to have a curious movement independent from that of his chest or waist.

"Sit down", Ana said anxiously.

"I can't stay, *mi vida*." He looked so sorry. "I just wanted to see you. My father is waiting for me in the car."

"Why don't you ask him up?", Teresa invited.

Ana didn't give him time to reply. She didn't want to give his father the chance to turn them down. She went to the door and walked him to the stairs.

"I miss you", he said, taking her hand.

"Oh, I do too ... so much!"

"Service stations will start operating", he patted her hand, "and everything will go back to normal as soon as Urrutia gets here."

She smiled feebly. There were footsteps on the stairs and her door was open. They couldn't even kiss.

Teresa had managed to talk the corner grocer into selling her a few groceries to hold them over for three or four days.

A rebel soldier was posted on the roof of their building and the families of the nine apartments took turns having him for meals. Ana took his picture on the balcony with his rifle. He was a good-looking young countryman. And over the light lunch, he told them of their encounters with Batista's army in the countryside.

"They didn't know it, but we were fewer than they. So, whenever we could, rather than fight, we hid. And we heard them yelling and shooting. At what I don't know, it must've been at the rocks, because us they couldn't see..." He reflected, "They also tried to avoid meeting us", and concluded, "We had few fights face to face."

Cienfuegos and Guevara arrived in Havana on the 3rd of January. Ernesto Guevara took charge of La Cabaña Fortress and prison. Camilo Cienfuegos took command of Camp Columbia.

On Sunday Castro talked from Camagüey. He said they were disarming the Army barracks along the island as they advanced west. He promised elections in sixty days. He looked so sincere, so natural and unaffected, his hands behind his back, rocking back and forth as he talked. He had a straggly beard. His nose had no bridge indentation; his profile seemed to run in a straight line from his wide forehead to the tip of his Roman nose, and his eyebrows slanted up at the insides in what appeared to be a perpetual invocation. He was tall and heavy; he wore a medal of the Virgin of Charity. It was the first time that Ana had seen his full figure; she had only seen a few bust photographs in the magazines and newspapers. She particularly remembered one in "*Bohemia*" magazine, beardless then, when he had been in jail over four years before. He had been a phantom figure to her. He was 32 years old and his brother Raúl only 28.

The BRAC (Bureau for the Repression of Communist Activities) was invaded by rebel soldiers and its files taken to La Cabaña.

Business activities came to a standstill for those first four days. The city was paralyzed. For lack of something else to do, Ana went over to her brother's often. Twice, while she was walking, there was shooting. Once it was at a car that was speeding away. It was the first time Ana had heard gunshots other than in the movies and she didn't realize what it was − it sounded so much more compact, solid − until a passer-by shouted at her urgently, "Get under cover!", and she had run to the nearest tree, without talking to the man, who had himself run behind another tree. The other time it was between a rebel and a civilian. She had lived 21 years without hearing a shot, and now it was becoming commonplace.

She had always gotten along well with Blanca, especially because she saved her words for when she had something to say and didn't feel obligated to talk just for the sake of talking; ҫ most of the time they shared a companionable silence and they had lunch, which for Blanca, on a drastic diet, consisted of a glass of *"Carrugán"*[17]-soured milk. And Ana helped her care for Blanquita, who was her goddaughter. Blanca Xiqués Monzón had been working at the electric company for over five years. Her grandparents were Aragonese, and her father was a pharmacist. Ana's aunts had felt they had a right to express a view about what Blanca did. When, a year after they

[17] a Swedish diet powder

married, she had the baby, they criticized the obstetrician she picked. Ana always defended her. She put herself in Blanca's place and imagined how it would annoy her if her husband's family censured her. At first Blanca had tried to get her older brother Lorenzo, who had been a classmate of Gustavo's in school, interested in Ana; but, probably because she was his friend's younger sister, he hadn't paid much attention to her, and Blanca had finally given up. He had gotten married over a year and a half before to a teacher.

Fidel Castro's victory march from Santiago de Cuba moved along a 601-mile route. Thousands blocked his path to shower him with flowers.

Ana spent a lot of time watching television with her parents and reading. She felt blue in the house most of the day, and very much like crying. There was a strange atmosphere. For some reason she couldn't understand, it somehow seemed dusty to her, with a strange brightness, as if after a hurricane. She felt she needed Dany terribly.

Dany was an accounting clerk in charge of payroll deductions at the same company where she worked as secretary. They had been working together for over a year when they had started going out together, almost by accident. That Wednesday afternoon almost three months before, she had left work with Elsa, the receptionist; Ramiro, the quotations clerk of the Transmissions Sales Division, and Salvador Conde, another quotations clerk for Glass, in Salvador's three-year-old car, and Dany had been along, because he and Salvador lived close by in Almendares and they took turns driving to work and dropping each other off home. Salvador had suggested stopping at "El Cortijo", below the "O y 25" Hotel, for a drink before going on home. Elsa, who was always enthusiastic for a good time − nobody knew whether she had a boyfriend, or anything about her private life, − had readily agreed. They had done it two or three times before. Ana had had a pink lady and Salvador had asked her to dance. She had danced with him once, but, because he was married, she didn't particularly want to, and didn't want to give the others a wrong impression either. She remembered she had taken a bobby pin from her hair and Salvador, clowning, had put it in his shirt pocket, patting it in a mockingly sentimental gesture. She had queried about the colored lights by the wall and he had unscrewed a blue bulb from the planter near their table. Ramiro had been dancing with Elsa, and Ana had taken Dany's hands and asked him to dance, pulling him to his feet. She had thought she felt his arms tremble as he held her. And

Dany had kissed her, not too unexpectedly. She had enjoyed it then and kissed him back, but had thought nothing more would come of it. Salvador had never suggested stopping for a drink again. Dany was twenty and she usually called him kiddingly the *"Benjamín"* of the company − although the office-boy was actually younger, but he had started working after Dany had the nickname. − He attended the Masonic University in the evenings, for public accounting, and was one of the most serious boys in the office. She had thought him handsome, but too young for her. She liked men around 26 who were through with college. She had not been interested in such a young boy.

Thursday had passed without any sign of acknowledgment of the day before from either side. And Friday, as Ana was clearing her desk, Dany had come over and asked her out for Saturday. She felt that, if she gave him the impression that she had taken him seriously, she would only make a fool of herself in his eyes. So she had said there was no reason why they had to go out together after work, and had walked away to the supplies room to put away a mimeograph stencil. She was pretending. He had followed her, persisting, and she had given in, "to show him they didn't really like each other", she had told him. And herself. She had quickly summoned her cousin Norma that afternoon and she had come to accompany them with her good-natured new boyfriend of one month. Dany had been late, a trait of his personality to which Ana was to grow used, and they had all gone to the "Atelier", where she and Dany had written their names on a lamp shade with her lipstick and she had, unawares, leaned against a scrawled wall and gotten black and red smeared all over the back of her aqua dress. They had then gone to the "Pigalle" and gotten home very late. That Sunday they had all gone to the movies, to see "Operation Petticoat" with Cary Grant and a movie with Zsa Zsa Gabor, and then to "Hernando's Hideaway" for a short while. And they had been seeing each other every week-end and every evening he did not have classes − and even on some when he did − for three months now.

President Urrutia arrived at the airport on Monday, January 5. Colonel Barquín turned the Presidency over to him. Business was resumed and things went pretty much back to normal.

Ana María drew her hair back loosely over her ears and held it at the nape of her neck with a tortoise barrette, and arranged short wavy lopsided bangs over her forehead, and it didn't make her look older at all, as it would many other women, but actually younger. She had recently eliminated her part to follow the fashion trend. She was neat to the point of fastidiousness. Her nails were always the exact same length. She had her hair trimmed every six weeks, and a setting and a manicure every two. She wore little makeup, but very carefully applied. Her bottom eyelashes had been short as a child and she couldn't have been more than fourteen when she had read in a magazine that cutting their tips every four weeks would make them grow longer. So she had religiously, over her mother's protests, cut them with a pair of blunt scissors half a dozen times. And, be it by coincidence or consequence, they did grow longer. She had been considering for a while now bleaching streaks in her hair to follow the latest fashion, but had put it off. She always wore stockings.

In Ana's bedroom there was one twin-size bed, a nightstand next to it and on it a lamp with a wooden base and a blue lacy shade with a yellow ribbon, and a blue radio; there was no alarm clock. A print of a bluebird and yellow roses hung over the bed. The double dresser with a frameless mirror and the tall double wardrobe with sliding doors occupied the other two walls. A photograph of Dany in a wide varnished wood frame stood on the wardrobe. There was a desk under the window with a portable typewriter on it, and an armless chair upholstered in blue stood to its side. A picture of pansies and a ladybug hung on the wall by the window, and between the dresser and the door to the bathroom there was a framed lithograph of Saint Joseph that her religious aunt Beatriz had brought her from Lima on her trip for her silver wedding anniversary. The furniture was *blanchie*, in simple modern lines and, when anyone showed an interest, Ana was prompt to inform them she had picked it at "Novedades" store, on Neptuno Street. She didn't know that any business had resulted from her advertising, but the store had certainly often had its name mentioned recently. The walls were painted light blue. The turned-down yellow quilted bedspread revealed a yellow bed sheet. There was no curtain on the screenless, louver-shuttered window, which overlooked the side of the building and offered the bleak view of a wall of the building next door, beyond a shoulder-high wall which separated the two narrow side alleys. A white black-eyed susan vine trailed from a yellow basket hung from the window case. It was a functional but individual room. A big white furry stuffed cat with blue glass-bead eyes and a yellow ribbon rested temporarily on the chair, soon to resume its place on the bed for the day. Beyond the alleys, a wider window offered a view into somebody's living room.

≈

They had been to Salvador's daughter's birthday *piñata* together on a Sunday afternoon. Ana remembered well the sweet torture of those first few days, when one is getting used to a new love: not being able to eat for several days, the queasy stomach, waking up at dawn, heart pounding, and waiting for it to be time to get up, the ache in the chest when the heart seemed to flip, the feverish feeling, the weakness in the arms and the constant insinuation of a headache. After a month of seeing Dany daily, one evening after the farewell party for the president's secretary at "El Cortijo", when they had had quite a bit to drink, he had taken her home in his car and they had found her parents out. They had left her a note saying they had gone to the movies and would be back about 11:45 or a little after. It was 9:30. And she hazily remembered what had happened then. When she had sat down, the liquor had gotten hold of her. He had started kissing her on the sofa. She had felt excited, but very sleepy. He had pulled down the zipper on the back of her dress and pulled its shoulders down to her waist in the living room. She had let him unhook her brassiere, with her eyes closed, had felt her breasts come free and had told him sleepily, "I want to be yours." She had not really meant it − ever since she had first been kissed by a boy at a party when she was fourteen, she had been determined she'd save her virginity for marriage at all costs, − but she had had a lot to drink, it sounded romantic and she hadn't realized the extent of her words. She thought she dimly felt herself being lifted. And then she must have passed out, because the next thing of which she was aware was lying in bed in her room and seeing Dany standing before her dresser mirror knotting his necktie. She had asked him, "Are you leaving?", and he had said, "Your parents will be home soon now." He had then walked out of the room by himself, and she had turned on her side and immediately fallen asleep again. In the middle of the night, she had woken up and found herself naked. She didn't like to sleep in the nude, so she had gotten up and put on a nightgown. She could hear her father snoring in her parents' bedroom on the other side of the bathroom. She had gone back to bed without recalling the previous evening.

The next day, when she was getting into the shower, she had suddenly remembered waking up naked and Dany tying his necktie before her dresser came back to her mind, and she wondered, alarmed, what had happened, but, alert now, she had felt no pain or any unfamiliar sensation. She had found one pink drop of what could be watery blood on the sheet. She had made up her mind to ask Dany when he came in the evening. But she had displaced the thought from her mind and, when he had arrived that evening, she had almost forgotten to question him. When she had remembered, she had asked, confident that she would get a negative reply, "What happened last night?" But, to her dismay, he had answered her with another question, "What do you think?" Apprehensive now, she had said, "I don't know." They were alone in the living room and he had come to sit on the arm of her chair. He had taken a moment to reply and then he had told her, "Everything", and she had then started crying quietly. Dany had stayed there, his arm on the back of the chair. After he had answered that, it had then seemed to her, maybe by persuasion, that she felt the pain, a strangely dry, rough sensation which had lasted a week. Ana had held back her tears when Norma and her boyfriend had arrived, long enough to get to "Johnny 88". They had sat at a table against the rear wall and, in the discreet darkness, her tears had started rolling silently down her cheeks and, when Norma and her boyfriend had gotten up to dance, Ana had let her restraint go and cried, sobbing quietly, thinking she'd surely lose him now, because that was probably all he had been looking for in a girl older than he. And she hadn't even been conscious. It had been an unfair twist of fate. It also crossed her mind that he just might be saying it only so she would now give up her resistance. He had held her cold hand in his right one and kept his left arm over her shuddering shoulders without saying anything, as she cried quietly, and he had seemed distant in thought, considering. After a while, when he had apparently thought she had released herself, or maybe when he had arranged his own thoughts, he had said, putting his cigarette out, as if reaching a decision, "We won't talk about it. It won't happen again." He had not mentioned it again and kept seeing her. For two weeks, they had avoided being alone, and had not made love again.

The front door of the apartment opened to a long expanse divided by an arch to serve as living room and dining room. The walls were painted a moss green. The floor was of tan marbled ceramic tiles. The furniture was modern Danish oiled walnut in a style named *Sjaelland* with tweedy green and blue tartan plaid seat cushions in the Scottish clan pattern Ogilve, and cane backs and armrests. There were two love seats set at an angle with a walnut table in the corner. One armchair, a low coffee table, a long walnut bookcase under a window to the air shaft, a consolette television set and a portable record player on a small table filled the living room half. The corner table held a tall lamp with a walnut base and a burlap shade, and a blue synclinal ashtray. A peaceful countryside landscape hung over each love seat, and photographs of Ana and Gustavo in their graduation gowns (with four years' difference between them) by "Leal","the photographer of graduates", high on either side of the television set. Although unapparent to the eye, the bookcase was built of the latest material in fashion, sugar-cane **bagasse** with a walnut veneer. An artificial Christmas tree sprayed white stood on it, trimmed with gold balls. Several blue throw pillows of different shapes and in different fabrics dotted the love seats and chair at random. On the bookcase, the corner table, the coffee table, there were Dutch figurines of blue and white translucent china in profusion, girls in lace caps, boys in bangs, geese, windmills, tulips, wells and sabots. There were magazines, *"Vanidades"*, *"Romances"* and *"Cinegráfico"*, on the coffee table, and the current week's *"Teleguía"* on the television set. The telephone rested on a bronze-color metal shelf on the pilaster between the two bedroom doors. The small dinette area beyond showed a mica top table and four chairs covered in aqua vinyl. A glass-front china hutch stood against a wall and a refrigerator by the door that led to the kitchen, with a philodendron in a green ceramic pot on it. A plastic woven basket on the table held a pile of smooth skinned purple star apples and a couple of rough-coated rusty brown sapodillas. Two still-life's of fruits and goblets hung on one wall. More money had gone into furnishing the living room than the dining room. The louver-shuttered double doors at the opposite end of the room opened onto a balcony. On the balcony railing, to a side, sat a Spanish jasmine in a clay pot, and the balcony looked out over the front lawn and the street below.

Then they had been to "Rancho Luna" after work with co-workers to plan the office Christmas party, they had drunk angel's tips and Dany had taken her home in his car. That evening he had told her, "We had both had a lot to drink that evening, but I had no idea that you didn't know what you were doing. I was surprised when I saw you really didn't remember. Then I thought you were going to reproach me... but you only cried. You made me feel so ashamed."

It had unavoidably happened again then, in his blue 1951 DeSoto,

Liberation from the Dictatorship 27

and almost every time they met after that. She had not asked Norma to accompany them and had even avoided her suggestions, and her parents had, surprisingly, not objected to her going out with him unchaperoned. She loved him very much. All through the fall, she had been sure of this.

This morning when Ana came out to the dinette area, her father was already sitting at the table before his cup of coffee and toasted loaf bread, his back to the balcony, dressed and clean-shaven, while her mother moved wordlessly around — she did not like to talk early in the morning. — Carlos, fifty-one, was rather tall, on the heavy side, with gray hair that still displayed some light brown on top, and a relaxed manner. Teresa, forty-nine, was of medium height, with ample hips, dark brown hair already showing a few silver threads over her forehead, and nervous movements. They had married late in 1930, in the Church of Montserrate, during President Machado's second term.

"I'm going to the Ekloh early to do the grocery shopping", said Teresa. "We need everything."

"Life goes on", observed Carlos reflectively.

Just at Christmas, Ana had started to feel bored with Dany, see him as too young, and she had wondered if she could be "falling out of love" with him.

It was a modern three-story building with three apartments on each floor and a stairway of gray terrazzo with an iron railing painted black. The varnished doors fitted with peepholes stood one to either side of the stairs across the landing and the third one facing the stairway. A window on the landing halfway between each two floors overlooked the front lawn. Only the two front apartments on the ground floor had back doors to the kitchen from the hallway. A couple of steps led down from the front door to a slab walk, lined with low-growing purple queen which bordered beds of carmine four-o'clocks, and flanked at the sidewalk by a little lamppost which displayed the house number hanging from a protruding bar.

Dany had first talked to her about marriage sitting on the low Malecón wall, their backs to the gulf, facing the "Maine" Plaza and the Hotel Nacional perched on the rocky hill. No question had been asked. Whatever doubts she might have had had vanished. They had agreed to save up enough money to start out on their own without any help from their parents.

"How much do you think?", he had asked her and gone on without waiting for her answer, "I figure two thousand. For the furniture, the refrigerator, the month's deposit and the advance month's rent, and a honeymoon." She had agreed. "It'll take us a while." She had held her breath. "I think about two years." And she had breathed again. That wasn't too long. It'd give him time to finish college.

The stores and offices were open and Ana went back to work. She had seen Dany only once since the year had started. When she got off the bus, she saw some employees from her office building on the side street, holding big signs proclaiming their support for the revolution. She walked past them, waving as she went, into the gray marble façade, seven-story "De Quesada" building, and took the elevator. The operator was not the regular man, so she called her floor to him, "Sixth." When she had graduated from business school at "Trelles", three and a half years before, at eighteen, it had taken her three months to find a job. She had finally been referred by the school placement service to an import company on Monserrate Street, where she had started working, the only girl in the office, as bilingual secretary, making $165. a month. The two partners, in their fifties, had been very nice to her and the work oscillated between an unbearable load and scarcely enough to keep her busy between breaks on narrow San Juan de Dios Street. But it was a one-girl office, there was no room for advancement and, after less than two years, she had resigned. She had been making $180. when she left. She had found this job at Wayne Motors just over a year before through an employment agency which charged her half a month's salary deducted in three thirds over a month and a-half's period of time, and she had started working as secretary to the International Sales Manager in the Parts Division at $10. more than she had been earning at the import firm. When she had completed six months' service, she had been placed on the permanent payroll and received a $20. raise, which brought her up to a good salary, especially since they got an hour and a half for lunch and she had enough time to go home. And now, less than a year and a half later, at twenty-one, with $210. a month, she felt the world was hers. She was due a month's vacation any time she wanted to take it before the end of July. And she liked the office, her work, her co-workers and the building.

Wayne Motors occupied more than half of the sixth floor. A glass wall showing floor-length green drapes bore the name "Wayne Motors International, S.A." in gold letters across the top over double glass doors opening into an impressive air-conditioned, beige-carpeted waiting room. A receptionist's walnut-colored steel desk faced the doors, a small, simple switchboard to its left. Two green and brown upholstered chairs and a low table holding a tall lamp with a beige shade lined one wall. A copy of the company's current "Moto-gram" and several automobile magazines were spread on another low table in the opposite corner, a single chair at its side. A potted palm stood in the far corner, the bare Christmas tree now leaning next to it against the beige wall, to be hauled out. And a doorway behind the switchboard led into the inner offices. A tall, thin girl in her middle twenties was standing behind the desk unplugging the switchboard night lines. She had a way of holding her ribs up in a convex curve with her shoulders thrown back, lifting her legs high when she walked and shaking her hair back that somewhat reminded Ana of a colt.

"Good morning."

"Good morning. What a way to start the year, eh?"

"Isn't it a very good way?"

"Let's hope so."

Ana was puzzled by the reply, but, then, although Elsa was very friendly with most, she was reserved and never really gave anyone much of a chance to get close, and Ana was never really sure of what she meant – she felt uncomfortable with people like that, her brother was that way, – so she went on into the office. Elsa was the only one in the office who knew Ana was going out with Danilo. They had run into her together at Flogar store. Once when she had come to Ana's home in December before going on vacation, at Ana's complaint about Dany's tardiness, Elsa had sagely advised, "Bang your head against the wall before he gets here, but once he does, greet him with a smile." She was four years older than Ana and full of prudent wisdom, but still single. Ana had never talked with Salvador about it. She didn't know if Dany had told him, but she didn't want to discuss it with Salvador. It was not quite 8:30 and the wide, long corridor that ran the length of the L-shaped office before the executives' offices and contained their secretaries' and the typists' desks in a row, was now deserted, so Ana stepped into the Accounting Department. The big, square room behind the reception room had six desks, an assortment of imposing machines, a whole wall lined with file cabinets, a low bookcase that occupied the length of a wall and from the two windows that looked out over the east, a view of the curve of the Malecón drive, the tall buildings in downtown Havana and the harbor far beyond. The janitor was still scrubbing from these windows the foam snow left over from their Christmas decorations.

"They should stop using this stuff", he announced to whoever had entered the room, without turning to look. "The way it sticks, it's impossible to get off."

Leonardo Vidal, the quotations clerk in Ana's division, just coming in, showed his large frame at the door, eyes closely set, unruly hair over his forehead, and said, "It caught you late, eh, Pablo?"

"If you hadn't smeared the windows this way, I'd have been through an hour ago."

Leonardo winked at Ana and said, "You should've started that when we closed the office at noon last Wednesday."

"Oh, yes?", the old man snapped. "On New Year's Eve? Maybe soon now you won't have me to clean the windows for you at all."

Leonardo looked at Ana, who had remained silent, and lowered the corners of his mouth and raised his eyebrows behind Pablo's back in silent mockery. The latter, unaware of the presence of a woman in the room, was swearing under his breath. Dany would probably be late as usual, his necktie in his hand, and other employees were starting to arrive, so Ana walked to her own desk in front of Mr. Kent's office.

"Well, doll", said Leonardo, "'New year, new life' is actually going to apply this year."

"Let's see if we have peace now."

"All we needed was to have 'the Indian' leave."

"Did you see the people from the building on the sidewalk?"

"And from the office. Ramiro, Dalia and Rosa joined them."

Leonardo went on to his desk in the Sales Department at the opposite end of the office.

Mr. Kent was an American, as were most of the other executives, except for the accountant. There were eight Americans in all, all men and all married except for one, an assistant manager. And there were 28 Cubans, only one of whom held a position of importance, that of accountant. Two Cubans were also the assistant accountant and an assistant manager. Ana draped her topper over the back of her chair and started her regular work day. Mr. Meyers, the Vice President who had interviewed and hired her, and all the other Americans there seemed amused today by what was going on and interested in the detached sort of way of spectators. The Americans had been taking Spanish lessons from a professor who had of late be-

Liberation from the Dictatorship

come fashionable among the executives of the American companies in Havana, and they understood Spanish well — and Ana suspected they could also speak it, — but they spoke only English in the office. Mr. Palmer, the other Vice President, appeared to Ana to be the only one with some knowledge of Cuban politics. They were now standing in the corner of the corridor in front of Mr. Meyer's office and he was talking to his secretary, Rina, a very intelligent, trilingual, rather chubby girl with upswept long, straight, black hair and vast information, who had started working the same day as she, and whom Ana admired, boss and secretary were intellectually so well matched.

"I detect this is the outcome the people had been hoping for."

"It's amazing how ignorance rides along with the tide."

"But it's what most people wanted, isn't it?", Mr. Palmer now asked her, cautiously inviting her opinion.

"Oh, it is! But then most of the people are uninformed. They're only being led by a few loud voices. This isn't the answer to any problem."

"Don't you think this will be better than Batista's government?" He wanted to get their opinions, but wasn't expressing any himself. "It's not the right way, is it?" He had finished all his sentences with a question.

"Anything will probably be better than Batista's government. And I think the way is right. It's the man that's wrong."

Ana had been listening intently and was now surprised at Rina's statement. She looked up from her desk, where she was filing away copies of the letters and memos typed five days before, and arranging the notes in her tickler calendar.

Balding, slim Mr. Palmer was listening to her, determined to stay an outsider. Short Mr. Meyers stood silently by, a non-committal half-smile on his round face, looking at and listening to everything, not seeing or hearing much.

Mr. Kent passed the group, grinned and put in, "Let's hope we Americans won't be sped on our way", and went into his office with a nod to Ana.

She moved her lips in greeting. A tall, gray-haired, blunt man of few words and no sophistication, Mr. Kent always cut through all the superfluous subtleties and went straight to the point. Others were walking in now, and the long corridor was filling with a buzzing sound.

"I strongly believe he has leftist tendencies", Rina announced with authority.

Maybe Rina had outsmarted herself this time. She wanted to show everybody that she knew something they didn't. Perhaps Ana had overestimated her. She should revise her opinion of her. Maybe she talked to listen to her own voice. Virginia, the President's new secretary of two months, shook her head in disagreement. Mr. Meyers' secretary, Lydia Dennis, of American parents, had sat at her desk unnoticed and was now wearing a smile similar to her boss'.

"There's no basis for that", countered Ramiro, arriving. "The trouble with us is that, as soon as a leader stands out, people start trying to find something wrong to pin on him. The man is the only one who did something effective."

"There were many who tried to do something", Rina answered in English for the benefit of the Americans. "It's a pity it's he who rose to the top. I hope I may be wrong, and all the people who are rooting for him now won't have to turn against him in a year."

Others were walking in, Graciela and Raquel, the secretaries to the other two export managers; Carmen Zayas, the order clerk; Elvira, the documentation clerk, and Gloria Serrano, the file clerk.

"Let's hope you're wrong", concluded Mr. Palmer, ending the argument. "The country is certainly due for a rest. It deserves a break." He said the last words as he entered his office.

Octavio Guillén, the one Cuban assistant manager, chuckled and shook his head. And the group started to disperse and occupy their own desks. Salvador Conde, arriving, walked with Guillén and Ramiro to the Sales Department, at the west end by the lunchroom. And Ana knew that Dany would be coming in now – he had probably driven today. – She remembered she needed to type a new list of foreign representatives for Parts, turned the typewriter on and tackled the chore. Dany passed her from the opposite direction, in his gray suit, late as usual, his necktie undone, taking the long way through the mail room to the Accounting Department so as to see her, tapped her desk as he went by and winked at her when she looked up at him. She smiled back and dove into her work.

The Cuban force of the office comprised the usual assortment of types found in many a company in Havana. The predominantly female staff – nineteen women to nine men – was mostly single; in fact, only two of the women, two clerks who had to do with accounts, were married. And Virginia, the one divorcée, added to the competition, openly looking for a step-father for her little daughter. On the other hand, five of the men were married, leaving a meager four eligible boys. Fat Leonardo Vidal, the Parts quotations clerk, who worked closest with Ana, was one; others were Ramiro, in the Sales Department, who had a touch of colored blood and Rolandito, the office boy, only about nineteen, who had started with the company about five months before; Danilo was the other. Only Eugenia, a typist in the pool, was rather solvent, selling a yacht or cattle over the phone – her father's, said Rina, – or buying a Mercedes Benz in her lunch hour; she had gone to school in Canada and belonged to the Biltmore Country Club, and Ana wondered why she worked. Nelia, the Accountant's secretary, also seemed to have a streak of colored blood, a fact to which nobody referred. Raquel Weiss was Jewish, something about which most joked without any awkwardness, so much so that she had taken to referring to herself as "the little Polish girl", as many people mistakenly labeled her. Elsa Toledo's mother was Colombian. Gloria Serrano, the file clerk, and Dalia, the girl who was in charge of supplies and lived in Luyanó, were both from very humble backgrounds – and they weren't even the colored ones either – and some secretly wondered how they had ever managed to get jobs in such a company. Only Dalia, the supplies clerk, was attending school in the evenings, taking journalism or some such thing. All the other girls, with the means or the ways, managed to lead social lives among the upper middle class, and indebtedness was accepted as a matter of course. They all, Virginia included, lived with their parents. The men, whatever their original backgrounds might have been, now in their late twenties and with adequate educations behind them, found themselves in comfortable situations. Mario, the assistant accountant, drove a tiny Italian Isetta. Only Danilo was still attending college.

The two married women in Accounting were the only ones who arrived at 8:30 sharp, disappeared at 5:00 and always went home for lunch. All the others gathered around the reception room before starting work, to comment on the previous evening, got together for lunch and an occasional drink in the nearby restaurants; back from lunch early, they hung around the mail room gossiping before 1:30, and waited for one another at quitting time, to go shopping or to the beach club after work.

Ramiro was dating Berta Penabad, one of the typists in the pool, but the other men in the Sales Department knew he was engaged to be married soon. Lydia occasionally dated the one single American man, Walter Butler, but, in that typically American way incomprehensible to Cubans, she didn't expect anything serious to come of it. Batten, the Export Sales Manager for Transmission and Raquel's boss, had been married three times. There were a couple of shady relationships going on between single girls and married men. Graciela, the secretary to the Glass Sales Manager, was discreetly seeing Palacios, the accountant, and Mario, his assistant, had been seen with Dalia at "El Gato Tuerto", said Virginia. And the latter one complained that with her there were those who assumed that, because she was divorced, they could "pick low-hanging mangoes".

Somebody had brought a radio and surreptitiously plugged it in the mail room, and the stirring "Twenty-sixth of July" march, being broadcast continuously, could be dimly heard over the clatter of the teletype. *"Adelante, cubanos, que Cuba premiará vuestro heroismo."*[18] Rosa, the mail clerk, and Rolandito, the office boy, spread the news:

Governors, mayors and councilmen were dismissed, and Congress was dissolved. Ambassador Earl Smith visited the Presidential Palace. Urrutia's cabinet was headed by Dr. José Miró Cardona.

At the mid-morning coffee break, from 10:05 to 10:25, in the employees' lunchroom behind the mail room, with its west view of the sea of red clay-tiled rooftops of upper Vedado extending away to the Almendares River in the distance, the conversation of the group gathered over cheese, guava and crab-shaped meat pastries, revolved around the same subject. Bernardo, the waiter from the "Concierto" restaurant next door, was dispensing the black coffee from his coffee urn on a cart, and a few sodas. Dany sat next to Ana holding two thimble-sized cups of coffee and offered her one, his pack of "Club" cigarettes on the table between them. Almost all the employees were enthusiastic. Spanish was spoken here.

"I knew it was going to happen soon", said Gloria Serrano. "I'd been saying it for the last two months. Isn't it true, Ana? Didn't I say to you, 'It won't be long now'?" Her light eyebrows, shaped like little wings, rose above the butterfly-shaped frame of her eyeglasses. She had clear, flawless skin.

"That's true, you did", Ana grinned, "but I can't say I shared your optimism."

"I know you were skeptical", said Leonardo. "You thought it was

---

[18] Forward, Cubans, for Cuba will reward your heroism.

Liberation from the Dictatorship

just a joke."

"Well, I'm like Saint Thomas too", Elsa said, "seeing is believing."

"I didn't really think they could accomplish anything", said Carmen Zayas, the order clerk, "just a bunch of countrymen up on a mountain." Her short jet-black hair swung as she turned her head.

Rosa Izquierdo, the mail clerk, burst in with her thin voice, "I'm really excited about it." She was very young and easily excitable.

"What do you think about this?" Leonardo turned to Salvador. And they were all taken aback by his answer.

"That you'll regret all this in a few months."

Ana remembered he had two brothers in the National Police force who would now undoubtedly be purged. Dany touched her ankle with the tip of his shoe under the table, and she realized they had already been over this on their way to work. They all kept quiet, not wanting to offend him, except for Ramiro.

"Sure. What can *you* say? But you're only selfishly considering how it affects your own family. How about the country people, and the poor?"

"What about them? Do you think their lot is going to change?" Salvador was sturdy, with curly light brown hair and calm manners.

"But the people want Fidel", said Gloria knowingly. She lived in Arroyo Arenas, in a small town environment, and travelled to and from work by bus.

"The people also wanted Batista."

"I can't remember when the majority of the people wanted Batista", riposted Carmen.

"You should've been at Camp Columbia that tenth of March, then, like I was, and you'd have seen the crowd filling the place shouting for Batista", he paused and waved an arm in the general direction of downtown Havana, "just like they're shouting for Fidel now."

"Those were the families of the soldiers and the policemen", said Leonardo Vidal.

"I felt crushed on the tenth of March", protested Ana, annoyed now.

"Nobody complained", alleged Salvador.

"I think this is the change the country needed", expressed Dany.

"The man had the courage to overthrow Batista", said Gloria.

"He didn't overthrow Batista", argued Salvador, undaunted. "He's never engaged in active fighting." Ana remembered the comment of the rebel at their table.

"What do you call the attack on Moncada, if not an active fight?", Ramiro demanded, agitated.

"Look, first, that was when he was... twenty-six — it's rained a lot since then. — And second, what went on there is not really known. Now, for instance, it's been five days since Batista left and Fidel's still parading himself through the towns, waiting for Urrutia to clear the way for him. You call that courage?"

"What does the way have to be cleared of?", interrupted Rosa, amazed. "Everybody wants him."

"There's always somebody left who doesn't want him. Let a 'Tiger' get his hands on him...!", he grinned. "Batista *did* have courage."

"You're right that Fidel didn't overthrow Batista", said Elsa Toledo unexpectedly. "Batista just fled like a coward. If he had just held on, Fidel wouldn't have come down." It was the first opinion she had expressed and it seemed directed against both men.

"He had courage?", Ramiro asked Salvador. "Then why did he run away the way he did? And after boasting", he thickened his voice and thrust out his chest to quote him, "that he had 'a bullet mounted in the muzzle'?"

"Because he didn't want a blood bath..."

"It would've been only his own, not a bath", Ramiro interrupted sarcastically.

"... He knew that, if the soldiers in Oriente followed Cantillo and turned against him", Salvador continued, "there'd be a civil war. He came in without a shot ... You can't deny that", he looked around at them, "... and didn't want to stay by force."

Neat Rolandito came into the room then, smelling of soap, clean shirt spotless, waving a piece of paper.

"I have the ministers. Doctor Roberto Agramonte Pichardo was named Minister of Foreign Relations", he read, "Luis Orlando Rodríguez, Minister of the Interior; Rufo López Fresquet, Finance; Raúl Cepero Bonilla in Commerce; Manuel Fernández García, Labor; Manuel Ray Rivero, who was in charge of the construction of the Habana Hilton, Public Works; Doctor Humberto Sorí Marín in Agriculture; Doctor Armando Hart Dávalos, Education; Doctor Julio Martínez Páez, Minister of Health, and Angel Fernández Rodríguez was named Minister of Justice."

Leonardo had been counting. "That's ten", he said. "And the other two?"

"Yes, Communications and Transportation?", asked Danilo.

Liberation from the Dictatorship

"Ah, I don't know." He shrugged. "That's all I got." He placed the sheet of paper in front of Leonardo on the table, now sprinkled with specks of pastry crust and stained with rings of coffee, and left the room.

"Enrique Oltuski Azacki and Julio Camacho?", offered Elsa, a bit unsure.

"What a stylish Madras necktie you're wearing!", commented Rosa to Leonardo.

He grinned his thanks self-consciously.

The interruption had served to cool off the argument and Salvador now went on in a lighter tone, "You'll see you'll agree with me in a few months. I'll give myself six months to tap you on the back and say, 'Remember when I said this was no good?' I'm not going to argue about it now."

"I'm sorry, Salvador", said Danilo, "but I really think you're completely wrong."

"Let's talk about baseball", Elsa suddenly said, and they all laughed.

"Time will tell, Gutierrito." A friend of his father's, Salvador usually called Danilo by a diminutive of his last name.

Promises reverberated. "The courts will judge the war criminals", "I won't allow gambling", "The recovery of the civil service is sealed", "Cuba will defend democracy internationally", "I'll go on in journalism", "I'll technologize the Ministry of Education", "I'm not announcing plans, I'll work", "There won't be reforms to facilitate expropriations."

The United States recognized the regime on January 6. So did Spain, England, France, Italy, Argentina, Chile, Uruguay, Paraguay, Ecuador, Venezuela and Nicaragua. The day before it had been recognized by Mexico, Perú, Bolivia, Panamá, El Salvador, Honduras and Nationalist China.

During the next three days, Rosa took it upon herself to take a poll of the employees' support. Her verdict, on Wednesday, was, "Only three out of the twenty-eight employees are against the Revolution, the other twenty-four are with it." She paused and then added, widening her eyes embarrassedly, "Well, I haven't dared to ask Palacios."

Fidel Castro Ruz was commander in chief of the armed forces. He arrived on Thursday by helicopter at the "Modelo" Brewery, in Cotorro, before going on to Havana. His entry in Havana, on January 8, was an epic. He stopped at the Presidential Palace early in the afternoon, to greet Urrutia and his cabinet. Later television showed Fidel with the President in the Hall of Mirrors, his loyal Celia Sánchez at his side. From the balcony he spoke to the crowd in Misiones Park. He and President Urrutia walked through the crowd. Two frigates greeted him with twenty-one cannon-shot salutes. The ships blew their sirens and the churches tolled their bells.

He proceeded to Camp Columbia, riding in a tank with El Che, Camilo and his nine-year-old son Fidelito. In its two years of existence, the band of rebels had become a ragtag army of almost ten thousand. They had beards and manes. Most of the soldiers wore rosaries, scapulars or amulets around their necks. The Triumphal March rolled in jeeps and trucks to the enthusiastic clamor.

The streets along Fidel's route were packed with people waving Cuban flags. Many posters stood out declaring "Support", urging "Forward", or claiming "Justice". A few intrepid young men had climbed lampposts, electric poles and monuments for a better view of their leader. The city's population of over a million celebrated.

As Ana climbed the stairs to her home, she met their once-a-week girl coming down, her day's work finished. She hadn't remembered it was Thursday, Matilde's day for cleaning. Teresa thought it was the best day, so the house would be cleanest for the weekend. Matilde was married to the janitor in Gustavo's building and did cleaning on a day basis for the apartment tenants in the neighborhood.

"Miss, did you see him?" Her eyes with their sparse lashes seemed to bulge out of her dark, bony face.

"Who, Fidel? No, I avoided the crowd to get home. I'll see it on television."

"Oh, miss!", she cried in dismay. "I rushed to finish in time to catch a glimpse of him. They say he'll be coming down Street Twenty-three."

"I don't know", Ana put a hand on her hunched shoulder, "but hurry, then." Matilde's coral drop earrings hung limply from her thin lobes.

"I want to see him in person." She rushed out, her little bundle of work clothes under her arm. "Before they shave", she added over her shoulder.

Castro climbed down from the tank at the entrance to Belén School and kissed the flag.

That evening, Ana's parents insisted that they do not go out — "The streets are too agitated", said Carlos. — So Dany joined them to watch Fidel speak from Camp Columbia. The people had turned into television fanatics since the year had been born.

Ex-President Prío, Eloy Gutiérrez Menoyo, Herbert Matthews of The New York Times and press officer Nicolás Rivero Machado were seated on the reviewing stand. The polygon was a sea of heads; nearly 40,000 people waited. Castro arrived carrying his telescopic rifle slung over his shoulder. He stated, "The revolution was made by the people", which, although a blatant falsehood, was received as a courtesy. While he talked, someone released two white doves as a symbol of peace and one perched on his shoulder, where it remained for an hour. The crowd interpreted it as a good omen. To many of the people this was a prophesy. He delivered a four-hour speech. He stated, "Weapons, for what?", and promised elections in 18 months. He had a rare gift of swaying the feeling and emotion of his audience. He renamed Columbia "Camp Freedom". It was to be transformed into a school.

"See that, Carlos?", Teresa exclaimed enthusiastically.

"Well, he's going to hold elections in eighteen months. We needed that."

"What I like best is that attitude against weapons. We've had enough militarism."

"He seems so sincere!", Ana marvelled. It was what impressed her most. "It seems as if he were willing to give his life for his ideals."

"Yes, he does seem sincere", Dany agreed.

Ernesto ("Che") Guevara Cerna was slim, olive-skinned, with slightly curly brown hair to his shoulders, soft-spoken and quiet in manner. He had a certain way of walking that made Ana feel he had a magnetic personality, but she kept her opinion to herself. Dany wouldn't welcome it. Juan Almeida Bosque, a Negro, had a black scraggly beard and mustache, and puffy bags under his eyes. Camilo Cienfuegos Gorriarán was tall and wore a gray Stetson hat, his long dark hair showing beneath; a dark, thick beard framed his face.

While he talked, Castro paused a couple of times to look over his left shoulder and ask, "Am I doing all right, Camilo?" The phrase caught on with the people.

That year, 1959, was labeled the "Year of the Liberation".

There was a women's battalion named "Mariana Grajales". The colored troops were nicknamed "Mau Maus". Twenty-five or thirty Americans had fought with Castro.

Rebel soldiers rested in the lobby and gardens of the Habana Hilton Hotel.

Raúl Castro, the younger brother, was slight and beardless; he wore his hair in a pony tail and a black beret. He had a pointed receding chin and puffed cheeks.

Major Efigenio Ameijeiras Delgado was appointed chief of police. Major Pedro Luis Díaz Lanz was made chief of the air force. And Major Camilo Cienfuegos was commander of the Army in the Province of Havana.

Dr. Juan Orta was Director of the Technological Institute. Captain Manuel Beatón was named chief of DIER (the Revolutionary Investigations Department). Major Huber Matos Benítez was commander of the province of Camagüey. Matos was one of the few who wore a regular officer's peak cap.

Carlos Franqui was the editor of the newspaper "*Revolución*". Within a few days, "*Hoy*", a communist party-line daily newspaper, reappeared on the streets, after being suspended and banned by Prío and Batista, allowed to resume publication.

On January 11, 73 assassins were rounded up in Santiago and taken on trucks to Campo de Tiro firing range in the San Juan Valley, near the city. They were tried en masse and sentenced to death. Raúl ordered their execution. Lined by the edge of a forty-four yard common grave, they were executed by machine-guns at 4 in the morning, fell back into the trench and were buried in the ditch, which was then filled, and mechanical equipment leveled the ground. The executions had begun.

Friends of the revolution, such as former president of Costa Rica José Figueres, Puerto Rico's Governor Luis Muñoz Marín and Professor Enrique Rodríguez Fábrega, Uruguay's representative to the United Nations, protested. Castro responded by inviting over five hundred newspapermen to "Operation Truth".

Dr. Joaquín Martínez Sáenz, who was President of the National Bank of Cuba, didn't see any need to escape, but he was arrested and put in prison. Dr. Felipe Pazos Roque was named President of the National Bank. Major Augusto Martínez Sánchez was appointed Minister of Defense.

The chief of the SIN (Naval Intelligence Service) in the province of Matanzas committed suicide, as had a police corporal and a rebel soldier. An army captain hanged himself in his cell at the Colón jail, in Matanzas province; another military man did so in his cell at the

Liberation from the Dictatorship 41

Manicaragua prison, in Las Villas. An army captain had shot himself with his regulation gun. These were six similar suicides, which led one to suppose that remorse had led them to execute themselves.

On January 21 Castro held a rally and the crowd gathered in Misiones Park. When asked about criminals, they yelled, "Execution wall!" The cry rose like an ominous threat.

"Operation Truth" backfired for Castro. The first trial, in the Sports City, in the afternoon of January 22, was that of Army Major Jesús Sosa Blanco, Lieutenant Colonel Ricardo Luis Grau and Captain Pedro Morejón. Before the trial, Castro had declared that capital punishment would be abolished. There were about 18,000 people jammed in the circular structure in southwest Havana. There was no doubt in the people's minds that these men deserved execution, but the way seemed to Ana a little barbaric. Sosa stood up straight and said, "This is the Coliseum of Rome!" He had voiced the feeling of many people.

Walter Butler, the blond assistant export manager in the Glass Division, and Lydia Dennis' date, came into the Sales Department one morning, amused at having been a witness to the piece of news he brought them.

"At the 'Cachet' Bar Major Iglesias slugged his colored sergeant." A note of pride could be detected in his tone, probably at being a foreigner feeding the natives a bit of their own gossip. Ana only wondered if Lydia had been with him. The "Cachet" Bar on Prado was reportedly not a proper place for women.

Newspaperman Salvador Díaz Versón, president of the Cuban Anti-Communist League, stated that the documents taken from their offices by the rebel army had been burned in La Cabaña Fortress by order of Guevara.

Fidel flew to Caracas, Venezuela, on January 23. President Rómulo Betancourt was another official friend of the revolution. Castro made public ostentation there of his friendship for Rear Admiral Wolfgang Larrazábal and for the communists. He conferred with the Machado brothers, Communist leaders. He suggested that Puerto Rico be "liberated from the Yankee yoke".

Little posters started appearing around the city reading, "Thanks, Fidel".

CHAPTER 2

PRIDE IN BEING A CUBAN

"¡Oh, Patria tan pequeña, que cabes toda entera debajo de la sombra de nuestro pabellón! ¡Quizás fuiste tan chica para que yo pudiera llevarte por doquiera dentro del corazón![2]
 ("Patria", Ricardo Miró)

They attended an exhibition of domestic products at the School of Medicine of the University of Havana, which included from raw materials to the most elaborate pieces of furniture and machinery, and filled the better part of the building and spilled on to the grounds around it. They admired the products, then, tired, sat on a bench on 25th Street to rest, talking, and later went to a restaurant on J Street for sodas.

Raúl married Vilma Espín Guillois, the revolution's "Deborah", on January 26 at "Rancho Club", in Santiago.

In commemoration of José Martí's birthday, 15,000 students marched in front of the National Capitol on Prado.

Tuesday, Ana woke up and heard her mother's predictable, familiar noises drift in from the dinette. It was cool and she drew her sheet up to her chin. The sun rays streaming through the east window painted patterns across her blue top sheet. As she lay in bed, she recognized the footsteps coming out of the kitchen, the successive beats of glass, china, tissue paper, more glass and steel on the mica table top, the slam of the refrigerator door, the thud of plastic on mica, the rustle of cellophane paper, the click of a glass bottle against a glass tumbler, followed by a spurt of liquid, the slam of the refrigerator door again, more footsteps receding and returning and the touch of steel against the table. And then absolute silence. She anticipated the next sound and a moment later heard the wet click of

[2] Oh, Fatherland so small, that you fit wholly under the shade of our flag!
Maybe you were so small so that I could carry you everywhere inside my heart!

the milk bottle set on the landing floor outside their door by the milkman, who delivered it for 25 cents a liter, and the rattle of the bottles in their wire rack, as his footsteps receded down the stairs. This often woke her up before her mother came to her bedroom door, but she always stayed in bed a while longer. They were the same sounds she had been hearing every morning for the last three years now. She turned her bedside radio on and listened to "*Radio Voz*" tick off the time every minute – it always amazed her; a minute seemed so short and still they could crowd so many news and commercials of Goyescas' "*Siete Jarabes*", princess vine, lemon grass and licorice in one! – and she gradually became so absorbed in the news and bits of trivia, that she was hardly aware of the time. At 7:00, her mother's voice came to Ana from outside her door, which she left ajar, invariably, "Ana María, seven o'clock!", shaking her into consciousness.

She pushed the sheet aside, got up while her mother brought the milk bottle in, and went through the daily mechanical routine. She went into the yellow-tiled bathroom and brushed her teeth first – while some people didn't feel awake until they washed their face or until they had a cup of coffee, she didn't feel fully awake until she had brushed the night taste from her mouth, – she then washed her face, got dressed, put her shoes on, dusted loose face powder on, combed her hair and brushed her eyebrows. The weather forecast predicted, as usual, "Cloudy and partially cloudy skies, light showers scattered throughout the whole national territory." She turned the radio off. When she went out to the dinette area, her mouth without lipstick yet, her father's arising noises were starting in her parents' bedroom. She sat at the table while her mother moved silently about, and she drank her grapefruit juice, sweetened and stirred her coffee and milk, ate her slice of toast and went back into her room to apply lipstick while her coffee cooled.

She looked at her lacquered long nails, inspected herself in the full-length mirror on her door to the bathroom, while behind it she could hear her father rinsing his mouth – she was content with her flat stomach, – and she half turned to examine her back. Tortoise barrette in place, zipper up, the skirt of her dress neatly tapered below her hips to just below her knees – her slip didn't show – to reveal stockinged well-shaped legs, she observed, seams straight and pointed shoes polished. Satisfied with her reflection, she sprayed a little "Sentiment", diluted in Cologne water to soften it for morning use, on the back of her neck, behind her ears and under her chin.

She had never bought herself a dress at the *Salon Parisien* of "El Encanto" or at "Fin de Siglo". She could only afford the smart little shop on San Rafael Street, which offered better dresses at the moderate prices she could meet and where Sandra, the owner with the deep-set eyes, made alterations at no charge, or else "Flogar", which sold many *Freddy Astors*. Favored next for her patronage were the shops along Neptuno and Aguila Streets, where she found *Sabrinas* and *Brendas*, ending her tour at "Casa Suárez" − to finish off the trip with soursop *champola* at the Bar Polar restaurant, low on Aguila and San Miguel, which featured *Elena Ruz* and *Cup Lolita*, two enigmas to Ana. − Felicia, the seamstress, lined her skirts, and sewed facing on hems and backing on belts. And she had her hair done at the little salon on Línea Street, where Claudia, the hairdresser who looked like a physical training instructor, had gotten the knack of her style.

She came out to the dinette again with her handbag on her arm. Her father had taken his place at the table, his back to the open balcony, *El Mundo* newspaper, recently retrieved from the balcony, spread before him, and he looked up at her over his reading glasses. Her mother was singing in a low voice,

"... *La sombra de tu amor y mis antojos,*
la copa de cristal que se rompió,
en ella bebí el llanto de tus ojos... "(71)

It was an old song; Ana hadn't heard it in years. The fact that it was her parents' song made her recall that they had spent their honeymoon in historic Trinidad, and they had talked to them, especially to Gustavo, countless times, about the Hanabanilla Falls, the Potrerillo Peak and the Trinidad Plain. They had moved into that old, narrow, long, high-ceilinged house on 24th Street. There Gustavo had been born shortly after the price of sugar hit bottom low at the end of 1932, and later Ana, during President Federico Laredo Bru's term. And she and her brother had attended nearby Catholic schools, and then Gustavo had gone on to business school in Nobel Academy and Ana, to "Trelles".

On Carlos Méndez's side, his father's parents had both come to Cuba, just married, from a town by the Caudal River in the Spanish province of Oviedo, in the northern region of Asturias, in the latter half of the 1870's, shortly after the Zanjón Pact had ended the Cuban

Pride in Being a Cuban

Ten-Year War, leaving behind Alfonso XII's reign, the big house in the *"cuartel"* and the steel works, the craggy, unpopulated mountains and the harsh winters, he a typical *"farruco"* in velvet pants, fiber shoes and beret. They had settled in the western town of Artemisa and named their house "*Pomar de Covadonga*", although there wasn't one apple tree within eleven miles in any direction. He had enlisted in the Spanish Crown Army, they had had four daughters and three sons with characteristically Asturian high cheekbones and slanted eyes, and raised their family in "the Ever Faithful Isle of Cuba" in the true Spanish tradition. He had been killed in battle in Vuelta Abajo at the end of the century, when their youngest daughter was seven. And Carlos' father, Joaquín Méndez, *"Joacucho"*, had become a bookkeeper in the provincial capital school, 72 miles away. A heavy man with a mustache at twenty-four, he had kept the books of a few textile and paper merchants in larger Guanajay, then with almost 6,500 people, and neighboring towns to the east.

♦

His mother's father, a Castilian who read Cervantes, had been visiting his family's tobacco plantation, *"Fresal de Aranjuez"*, in San Antonio de los Baños, on vacation from the University of Madrid, during the period of calm left after the Little War died down. He had met a local girl and married her, much to the consternation of her parents, of *Gaditan* descent going back to the 17th Century, the open but frustrated opposition of her brothers, who belonged to the Cuban liberation insurgent forces − nicknamed *"bijiritas"*(19) by the Spanish − and the disappointment of his family, who had hoped to marry him to a cousin back home. They had had three sons and two daughters. And Carlos' mother, María Miranda, *"Maruja"*, a thin, fair girl with a translucent complexion, chamomile-light hair, gray eyes, thick ankles and an iron will, had gone to work, at twenty, in the office of a little stationery dealer in town, "*Vereda*", near the Camino Real, where she had met the shy, heavy, pale bookkeeper with handlebar mustache, Don Joaquín, green visor over his brow and arm garters on his shirt sleeves, from a town to the west. She had looked up at him demurely from her downcast almond eyes through her long thick eyelashes and, heart pounding, had asked him to write on the slats of her fan, where he had dedicated to her a stanza from one of Ramón de Campoamor's poems, and she had lent him a book by Benito Pé-

(19) 'warblers'

rez Galdós. He had visited her and courted her to the music of the pianola wound by her younger sister and over the black coffee served by her mother. They had gotten married in a year and made their home in then sprouting Bauta. They served on their table traditional Spanish dishes, like Asturian butter-bean *"fabada"*, Spanish chickpea *"cocido"* or Madrilenian white-bean *"pote"*, fish *"caldereta"*, *"puchero"*, roast lamb, grouper *"cazuela"* or tripe, with red wine, and they cooked their food with olive oil. They lisped their c's and z's, addressed their parents by the *"usted"* respectful pronoun form and, true to their combined three-quarters Spanish blood, went to the *"romerías"* at Tropical Brewery Gardens in Aldecoa, listened to bagpipe and flageolet music, sang the *"ringo-rango"* and danced the *"raposa"*, *"danza prima"*, *"corri-corri"*, provincial *"vaqueira"*, *"pericote"*, *"fandango"* and *"seguidilla"*.

And Ana's father had been born, the third of five children, in the free Republic of Cuba, in a big, merry, noisy and poorly-kept house in Marianao, the front door of which was usually held ajar with a latch, where they had enjoyed the Dance of Millions and survived the influenza epidemic of 1918, and father and sons played dominoes on the porch on Sundays after Mass. They had attended Jovellanos School, frequented the Centro Castellano on Dragones and read *"Asturias"*. And Carlos had become an accountant.

On Teresa Bermúdez's side, her father's father had come, in third class, from a town in the Aguere Valley in Tenerife, in the Canary Islands, in the Northern Atlantic, leaving behind the banana plantation, in the late 1870's, just before the Little War broke out, to a climate very similar to his own, and it had been easy for him to become acclimated. He had settled in San Julián de los Güines during the rule of Spanish governor Joaquín Jovellar, and opened a hardware store, *"El Tinerfeño de la Llanura"*, on the northeast edge of town. Her father's mother had been born in San Carlos y San Severino de Matanzas, to a very poor family of second generation Cubans, descendants of *Lugueses* with Celtic looks arrived in the 18th Century. They had set out to stress the good qualities of the shopkeeper in the nearby town, and had dispelled her misgiving and married her off to relieve the poverty of the family. He had been "covered by the stain of banana"[20], and they had had three Creole sons and three daugh-

---

[20] been captivated by the land, felt at home, gotten it under his skin

ters. She had died of tuberculosis when their youngest son was only six. And Teresa's father, José Bermúdez, *"Joselín"*, had studied at the Piarist Fathers' school and become a property registrar and, at twenty-five, had opened a proctor's office in more prosperous Guanabacoa, then boasting a population of almost 14,400.

Her mother's father had been born in Asunción de Guanabacoa and her mother's mother in El Cerro, among summer vacationers' *fincas* on the slight rise, both from lines of Cubans as far back as anybody had been able to trace and very proud of it — but probably descendants of Andalusian immigrants in the 16th Century, — and they had met in childhood. Her father had opened a general store in Guanabacoa, "*Jata del Cuabal*", near the women's prison, and they had married and had two sons and two daughters. And Teresa's mother, Eva Trejo, a plump girl with dark complexion, creamy skin and her glossy black hair in a bun, who jokingly said they were direct descendants of Chief Abaguanex, had gone to work at nineteen, in white lace blouse, as a teacher-pianist at the kindergarten near the office of a proctor who wore a celluloid collar and carried a gold chain watch in his vest pocket. The piano music and the little girls' voices reached the proctor, who, his curiosity aroused, stood on the high sidewalk by the barred floor-to-ceiling window on his way to his office down the block, to look at the children, and saw the pretty teacher who led them in song. He had boldly waited for her in the afternoon, given her a pink rose and lent her a book of poetry by José Jacinto Milanés, and she sometimes, after the girls left, played a special *"habanera"* for him, Don José, which he could hear from his office. They had gone, chaperoned, to the festival of the Tutelary Virgin and frequented the Lyceum, and they had married in tricentennial Saint Francis of Paula Church. Dominoes was played after Mass in their house too, but there the similarity ended. The food on their table was typically Cuban, *"ajiaco"* Creole or black beans led their menu, fried beefsteak with lime and parsley or fried pork chunks, *"moros y cristianos"*, Oriental *"congrí"*, yucca and *malanga* with sour *"mojo"*, plantain *"fufú"* or *"guacamole"*, with Indian reed *"pru"*, corn *"majarete"* or guava shells, and they fried their food in pork lard. They hissed their c's and z's, addressed their parents by the *"tú"* familiar pronoun form and went to La Cotorra springs; they liked accordion music, their pianola played *"danzones"* and they danced the *"caringa"*. They nursed the hatred towards the Spanish kindled by the Independence War, then under way, and enjoyed chanting, "Galicians don't bathe even with *Carabagna* water."

And Ana's mother, the second of four children, had been strictly brought up as a lady in a well-kept, neat, small, quiet, warm house near San Lázaro, where Eva had taught them to read with Guiteras and manners with Carreño, and they had lived through the tidal wave of 1919 and been through the bank crash. They read *"Carteles"*, and the girls had gone to Mariana Lola Alvarez's religious school. Teresa had worked as a typist in the office of a real estate broker in La Metropolitana building for three years and traveled on the I-2 streetcar, where she had struck up a conversation with a regular passenger, a stiff blond young man with his straw hat on his lap who told her that he worked for an accounting firm on Obrapía Street.

He had considered his position solid enough to get married, but the accounting firm closed down during Machado's second term, at the same time Teresa lost her job with the realtor, when her boss neglected the business to get involved in the opposition ABC activities, before Gustavo was born. That had driven him to work as a bookkeeper for an importer of art. Carlos was not a public accountant graduated from the University, only a private accountant graduated from the old Professional School of Commerce on Cuba Street, and for the first two years of their marriage, Teresa had been tenaciously after him to go on to the University and become a public accountant, even more persistently when she lost her job. Even after Gustavo was born, she had half-heartedly insisted on it, but then when Ana was on the way, she had given up.

Ana drank her coffee and milk in big gulps, standing.

She had known both her grandmothers. Her grandmother María, wiry, pale and thin-lipped, with a square jaw, had talked to them proudly about the high zone, the regular plant and the straight-angle streets of her native San Antonio de los Baños, and the mineral water springs, the farming of tobacco and cane, the beautiful coffee plantations, the textile and tobacco industries, the dances at the Casino Español and the processions of Candlemas. She listened to the Comedy on O'Shea Radio in her old house with the high varnished wooden beam ceilings and the maroon fret along the lower half of the walls, and made a sweet, weak coffee, always tepid, in her white spattered blue porcelain enameled pot, and, when Ana was sick, she made little old dolls with chickpeas for her. Her grandmother Eva, plumpness turned to fat in her old age after bearing four children, had died only two years earlier. She had referred to her native village as "beautiful Guanabacoa with its straw city walls", talked about the festivals of the patroness Virgin of the Assumption, bragged about the stuffed potatoes and liked to quote from Juan Clemente Zenea's poem *"Recuerdos"*:

> *"... ¡Ay, aquellos*
> *tiempos de gloria y de aventuras locas,*
> *en que eran de azabache los cabellos*
> *y gemelas la dicha y la ilusión.*
>
> *¡Oh dulce juventud! Si Dios quisiera*
> *vestir de nueva pompa el árbol mustio*
> *y hacer resucitar la primavera,*
> *y otra vez calentar el corazón!"*[68]

She played the upright piano in her living room with the multi-colored fanlight and had taught Gustavo how to read before he entered school. She had lived long enough to experience the wonder of knowing her first great-grandchild, Gustavito.

Méndez put his reading glasses in the pocket of his jacket and, with his briefcase in his hand, brushed Teresa's cheek with a light kiss and offered Ana his own cheek, which she almost blew more than kissed, lest she leave lipstick on his face, and left to ride to work with Gustavo. Teresa followed him to the door.

"Will you be late this afternoon?"

"No. Gustavo is meeting Velázquez early and I'm leaving at six, when Alfonso goes home."

"Then I'm going to make the veal *'aporreado'* today and I'll leave the *'salpicón'* for Thursday. All right?" He nodded and she added to herself, "The *salpicón* takes longer."

Hardly had the door closed after him when Ana brushed her mother's cheek with another kiss and called, "Until later."

"Don't be late unless you call me first", her mother called after her and added unnecessarily, "Your father's coming early."

Ana mumbled agreement, and walked down the stairs promptly after 8:00. Apartment 4, on the other side of the stairs, was occupied by Georgina, a divorced woman who worked in a drug store, and her son, a radiologist's aid in a laboratory, and number 6, across the landing from them facing the stairs, by Villar, a middle-aged man who worked in the office of a chocolate factory, and his chattering fat wife, who worked half a session in a ministry. Aguirre, a pitifully thin man who worked in a bank, lived in apartment 2 directly below them, with his wife, a grammar school teacher, and their son, about sixteen, who attended a military school, and the other two apartments on the ground floor were occupied by a duplicating machine repairman, whose daughter worked in a nearby hotel, and a dentist. Irene, a store salesclerk, and her deaf widowed mother lived in the apartment immediately above them, which should, by order of sequence, have been 8, but deference to superstition had turned into 9, and the other two apartments on the upper floor were rented to an electric technician who shared it with an out-of-town university student and gave loud parties, and the superintendent, whose mother it was said smoked cigars. Ana only had a nodding acquaintance with most of the neighbors, except for Natalia, the girl who worked at the hotel, who sometimes walked with her for a couple of blocks in the morning.

Out on the street, she fished in her handbag for her sunglasses with her eyes closed to the sunlight, put them on and walked with her long stride to the bus stop on L Street. The doorman at the hotel called to her, "Good morning." She had noticed he was young and nice looking. She answered with a nod of her head and a straight face. A smile might be taken as flirting. And that wasn't right with a hotel doorman. The young elevator boy in the office building called to her his usual, "Ugly!" It never failed to make her grin. And she looked down at the sidewalk. He wanted to sound worldly and different in his advance, and she wondered if he actually recognized her, or maybe he called that to every girl who went by. She had once commented to her mother about it and she had said, "Well, what an unpleasant thing!" Old-fashioned, conventional, proper Mamá. Ana found it funny. She passed the drug store on the corner and checked her wristwatch against the clock on its wall. Diagonally across from it, she waited for the white bus with its navy blue stripe around that had won them the nickname of "nurses", which would be coming from the south.

In a few minutes, she flagged it down and got on the bus with the distinctive white and red sign of route V-6 over the front, northbound, her eight-cent fare in her hand, and sat down next to a boy wearing the Baldor school uniform. The driver had his cap strategically tilted over his nape. While she paid her fare to the conductor with his coin holder at the waist, she saw out of the corner of her eye the Baldor boy steal a glance at her that became appreciative as it swept down her body. She was flattered, but felt self-conscious. She met the regular people: The man who took the bus ahead of her and got off one block before she did, the woman with her orange checked gingham Virgin of Charity vow dress, the laborer on the seat in front in the coarse blue chambray work shirt with the three neat round eyelets in its back. When the bus reached 15th Street, before it turned left, she looked east past the Chinese veterans' fluted black stone column toward the little triangular park on N Street, where she enjoyed so much sitting with Dany and listening to the distant sounds on clear, still, windless evenings. The row of lampposts formed a perfectly straight line down the middle of the street. The Art-Déco López-Serrano apartment building rose to the right with its vertical shafts, tower setback and glass-roofed watchtower.

A lottery ticket vendor got on the bus and stood on the stepwell, a cardboard number stuck on his old beat-up hat and a long poster of numbers strung together dangling from his wrist, sticking to the unwritten law of vendors, of not paying a fare. "Luck is crazy and it's anyone's turn!", he yelled. "Five thousand, four hundred fifteen; fifteen that adds up to fifteen; pretty girl. The policeman, fifty; the priest, forty; pigeon, twenty-four! It's drawn on Saturday." On Saturday the boys from the Maternity and Welfare House would draw the balls publicly from the drums. The man on the first seat bought a ticket for 25 cents. A man bending his combs to show their flexibility peddled his goods, then another one selling needles and straight pins got on displaying his wares. Further on, a candy vendor yelled from the stepwell, "The honey ones for the girls, the lemon ones for the old women!" Who felt like candy so early in the morning? Somebody did. Ana let her eyes rove over the ad cards for the umpteenth time: Biarritz home food catering, Manpower employment agency, Allyn's hair straightening cream, La Gran Vía bakery, Rendell pessaries, El Sagrado Corazón school, Ingelmo shoes proclaiming themselves "a masterpiece in each pair", "*Once-Once*" socks challenging one to "try to tear them to see if you can", a jeweler and his nephew acclaiming themselves as "the jewelers of confidence", a real estate company praising their lots on Isle of Pines, a car financing agent on P Street, a driving school on Morro, the Escuela de Comercio de la Víbora, Halicrafter television sets, Dalia dyes, *Perro* undershirts, face powder, towels, a radio station, Lady Louise lingerie, a clinic. The bus in this direction wasn't too crowded in the morning, but a few passengers did start to stand in the aisle. A couple of men gave their seats to women. A woman across the aisle from Ana offered a standing man to carry his briefcase for him. The procedure was repeated around the bus and, when it had covered half its route and standees − urged by the conductor's frequent cry, "A little step forward!" − had shifted toward the front, there was an occasional ripple of motion as a passenger about to get off tried to retrieve his package over the heads of those seated. Ana stared absently out the window, as they passed before Arturo Montori School, La Terraza restaurant and the Hebrew Community Temple, until, as they passed Havana Business College and neared the Maternity Hospital, the Baldor boy stood up to get off. She drew her legs in as he looked straight at her and held her glance. Ana met his eyes briefly and quickly looked away. Not over sixteen. She was amused. She often attracted boys younger than herself. She didn't move to the window. As they passed the Vedado Parochial Church, she crossed herself.

"On the corner!", she called to the conductor when the bus approached her destination, and he gave the bell a long ring for the firm stop for women. She waited for a Teresiano school bus to go by. A man coming out of the "Concierto" restaurant said admiringly, "What great legs!"

The uniformed elevator operator, one of the regular men, knew her floor, so she only greeted him. Mr. Sterling, the President of Wayne Motors, took the elevator up with her. He greeted her with a polite smile. He was a very quiet man − Ana had only heard his voice a couple of times. − It didn't seem to her that he did anything at the office, hardly anybody ever went into his northeast corner office, he only walked silently around, and Ana half wondered if his impressive name had had anything to do with his being named president − sterling character, pound Sterling, Sterling silver, sterling qualities. − There was a man who worked on the seventh floor, in a green vest sweater, and a girl with jet black hair in a bouffant, who worked on the fourth floor. The elevator was filled with the smell of Arpège. Ana was silent.

When she walked into the office, Elsa was inspecting a stocking with a run. She spread out one hand helplessly and spoke looking down.

"These steel desks tear stockings to shreds." Mr. Sterling passed them with a terse greeting. "Why couldn't they get wooden ones?" She looked up at Ana. "Have you seen the DuPont Glass office?"

Pride in Being a Cuban 53

"No." Ana shook her head.

"They have beautiful, beautiful oiled walnut-stained desks", she said enthusiastically, "with cane woven panels in front."

"General Corporation has this same type, don't they?" Ana had applied for a job with them before.

"Yes", Elsa paused, then reasoned, "I guess these last longer." She dismissed the subject with a shrug and donned her headset.

Rosa arrived. A voice in English could be heard coming down the hall. Guillén walked in first. "Good morning, chicks."

He was followed by Walter Butler. Rosa prompted him, trying to joke, "Good morning, no? We didn't sleep together."

"Why?", he countered, squelching her. "Were we supposed to?"

Ana walked to her own desk. In the silence just before the office started humming with busy employees, she could hear the teletype, in direct line with the Wayne Motor Company home office in Michigan, clicking madly. The piped music started. She hooked the earphone of the dictaphone machine on and pulled a sheet of the stationery with the raised logo — a green W and a brown M encased in a hexagon. — The advertising campaign Wayne Motors had launched to bring the new, long St. Clair luxury model out on the foreign market had brought an increased workload down on them. Last year it had been the now popular, economical Robin compact model. She took pride in her work and did it conscientiously. It was apparent Mr. Kent was pleased with it.

In the correspondence, Mr. Kent dictated to her a memo for their superior in the main office in Detroit where he mentioned that he had learned not to load the Cuban coffee in his fountain pen.

The day went by as usual. In the lunchroom, on the mid-morning coffee break, the usual jokes were told by the usual group. "Sick" jokes were the latest, along with "foreign language" jokes.

Berta took it up this day. "A boy gets home from school crying, 'Mommy, the kids in school called me big-headed.' His mother tells him, 'No, son, you're not big-headed, stop crying. Take your cap and go get me three pounds of potatoes'." They all, Berta included, burst in laughter.

Leonardo approved, "Score one for yourself. There's a knock on the door", he told in turn, "and a woman yells, 'Who is it? I'm taking a shower.' They tell her, 'Your son was run over by a truck and he was flattened', and the woman says, 'Slip him under the door'." There was some laughter around the table.

Elsa piped in, "Some children come to the door and ask a woman, 'Can Juanito come out to play with us?' The woman asks them, 'But why do you want Juanito to play with you?, he has no arms or legs' and the kids tell her, 'We use him as a football'." "Ugh!", some reacted.

Ramiro chipped in, "A boy asks his parents, 'Can I play with grandma?' and his father tells him, 'Well, okay, but this is the last time; we've already dug her up twice this week'." "Oh, that's sick!", said Gloria.

Ana remained quiet, only laughing at the others' jokes. She didn't think herself good at telling them. Bernardo, the waiter, was also smiling silently. A flock of pigeons flew forth and back over the red clay roofs to the west.

When she came back from lunch at 1:30, she found Mr. Kent in his carpeted office, standing behind his desk. From the window behind him, if one got closer to it, the park could be seen across the street.

"See if you can please help me with this, Ana. My wife went to the electric company this morning", he explained, flustered, "to have the service connected at the new apartment and she couldn't find anybody who spoke English in the place." He handed her a slip of paper with a telephone number and a name. "Will you call this number for me and talk to that woman? Explain to her what we need and give her our new address."

Ana respectfully took the paper, called the number, asked for the lady and explained the situation to her, and she was told the company would connect the service the next morning. She thought she detected a tone of resistance in the woman's voice. Mr. Kent was still indignant.

"Do you know", he told her, astonished, "that *NO*body spoke English in that place? My wife was getting mad and she kept saying, 'Bring me somebody who speaks English' and she just couldn't get through. Oh, she was upset!"

It was just too much. Before she had time to think, Ana blurted out, "Well, has it occurred to you that our official language is Spanish and we don't *HAVE* to speak English?" Then she braced herself for his reaction. Mr. Kent just looked at her, surprised. She was just as surprised as he at her daring. "If you find somebody who speaks English", she went on, but in a half-jesting tone now, "you should be glad, not expect it."

He reflected then, "I guess we get inflexible sometimes, don't we?"

His reaction surprised Ana even more. She went out of his office, mumbling to herself in a low voice, "You're not in Puerto Rico." The Americans, ensconced in Miramar, waited on by their Jamaican maids, untouched by the outside life, sometimes forgot there was a whole country out there beyond the walls of their little colony. The children of Mr. Kent and the other sales managers attended Cathedral School, and Mr. Sterling's and the vice-presidents', exclusive Ruston Academy, in La Coronela. He had told her a couple of months before, "I want to stay here. I have a better standard of living than in the States. Back home I couldn't afford a maid."

By the time Ana left the office shortly after 5:30, Dany had already gone – Salvador was driving. – A Sister of Charity walked in front of her. As she headed for the bus stop, Ana noticed the man who got off the bus one block before she did, walking about a hundred yards ahead of her. She saw him stop at an oyster stand on the corner and gulp the contents of the small jigger in one swallow. He was nice looking, about thirty.

She was seated in the bus when he got on and, for the first time, greeted her with a nod.

Doors started to bear a sticker, "Fidel, this is your house."

Ghost employees' sinecures were removed from the public payroll.

On the Virgin of Candlemas' or Our Lady's Purification Day, Ana cut a strand of hair, as did her mother and Blanca, to make it grow longer and thicker. The custom had perhaps started with the Canary Islanders who brought their Virgin to Cuba.

The Ministry of Social Welfare was created on February 6, and Elena Mederos named to direct it. A week later, the Ministry for the Recovery of Misapplied Properties was created, directed by Faustino Pérez Hernández. Deposit vaults in all the banks were opened by the Ministry, and officials also seized expensive automobiles left by those who had fled.

For Roman priest St. Valentine's Day, Lovers' Day, Dany gave Ana a Portuguese filigree bracelet of hinged delicate rectangles about the size of postage stamps and she gave him a belt with his initials, D.G., in the buckle, and they had a formal photograph taken together, dressed up, at a studio on 23rd Street.

♪

With the university closed, Dany arrived every evening shortly before the nine o'clock cannon shot was fired from the parapets of the once named Castillo de San Carlos de La Cabaña across the harbor – a custom which endured as a memory of the shutting of the Wall gates, – and Méndez invariably checked his wristwatch against it.

They went to "El Recodo" drive-in restaurant on G Street near the sea, and to a drive-in movie near the Vento Springs. They often went dancing on Saturdays. To "El Cortijo", which had recently had its named changed to "Flamingo", with its Spanish style décor, where the colored male singer donned an absurd blond wig and skipped around the floor chanting, "¿Dónde va la muchachita, dónde va?"; the "Atelier", with its assortment of garments and other odds and ends left by patrons as mementos hanging from the ceiling over the bar and the piano; the "Johnny 88", with its high stage behind the bar, or the "Pigalle" on O Street, where the heavy blonde singer obligingly sang *"Place Pigalle"* and *"La Casa Portuguesa"* accompanied by an accordion. Other clubs favored on their Saturday outings were the dark "Turf", on Calzada, stalactitized "La Gruta", on 23rd Street, labyrinthine "Johnny's Dream", laid out like an amphitheater, across the river in Miramar, the "Autopista Club" on the Autopista del Mediodía, where a transvestite singer, Omar Ferrán, performed, the "Club 66 de Barlovento", outdoors, where they once spotted a mouse on the wooden railing near their table and Ana, a hairy spider in the ladies' room, and once to "Las Catacumbas", with its glowing painted walls, near the Virgen del Camino fountain. They danced to the music of guitar, calabash *maracas* with Indian shot seeds or dry corn kernels, hard reddish wood *claves* with their metallic sound, grooved bottle-gourd *guayo* scraped with ox horn, tall *tumbadora* drum and siamese *bongó* drums, or to the rhythm of cow bell and copper kettledrum. Their song was *"Place Pigalle"*.

Sometimes they just sat in the little triangular park on Línea and N Streets which Ana favored, with its bust of Major Enrique Collazo. She particularly liked the way the air seemed to carry the sounds far on still, high-pressure nights, and she felt very close and at the same time very removed from everything. They were most often the only ones in the park. And they watched the buses and most of the traffic turn south on L Street, two blocks west, or west on Línea Street. The INED building loomed close to the east; there was a psychometric institute to the south. Sometimes the familiar picturesque figure of the

Pride in Being a Cuban

"Caballero de París"[21] would stop at a luxurious large green house on 13th Street across from the park, which had belonged to a senator, to talk to the maid and the chauffeur, outside his customary zone of the Paseo del Prado, where he passed out poems, and they watched him, tangled white curly mane, black cape, and folded newspapers under his arm. They once crossed the street to listen to him. In a thick Spanish accent that surprised them, he stated that Fidel was Spanish and claimed he knew him from the mountains in Spain. Ana liked to listen to him and talked to him with respect, not mockery, wondering what he had been and how he had gotten to be like this, and if he had any family.

They often sat on the low Malecón wall in the evening, their backs to the Gulf — it frightened her to look at the black waters below, — facing O Street, the modern Someillán condominium building to one side, the winged FOCSA building in the shape of an open book towering behind it, and to the other, the little wood of pines below the side of the pink spired Mediterranean style Hotel Nacional, high on its privileged site, the salt air filling their nostrils and the bright stars overhead, and they planned their wedding and their future together. The light beam from the Morro Castle on the promontory pierced the darkness over the water as it revolved, and the soft waves broke against the rocks below. A Chinese peanut vendor went by, his square box filled with rolled paper cones of peanuts in their shells, which he kept hot with red-hot coals, yelling at intervals in a thin, high voice, "Peanuts!, hot roasted peanuts! Peanut vendor is going!" A corn-*tamal* vendor, his metal box turned into a brazier by a lighted wick in a hollow cube in its bottom, strolled by, "Tamales! The tamales burn and don't burn! *Tamal*-vendor!" The colored man carrying a pole displaying his multi-colored frustum-shaped *"cariocas"* arranged in circles, occasionally twirling the pole like a Carnival masquerade lantern, the snow-cone man pushing his cart along the street with the block of ice to shave and the two rows of colorful flavor syrups, the modernized ice-cream man riding his motor scooter with his mobile icebox in front filled with chocolate-covered bars, French ice cream cups, popsicles and sandwiches, and ringing his little bell which hung from the handlebar.

They sometimes went to Mass together on Sunday, at the little Saint Catherine of Siena chapel on 23rd Street. Although Dany's

[21] 'Gentleman from Paris'

father was a dedicated Mason, his mother had turned agnostic and he himself was not a Catholic, he was willing to accompany her to Sunday Mass. Prevented from attending the University of Havana by its minimum age admission requirement of 26 for Commercial Sciences, he had selected the Masonic University for its tuition, lower than that of St. Thomas de Villanueva Catholic University, rather than for any reasons of creed.

They went to Coney Island Park in Marianao. They rode the roller coaster, the worm and the whip, and had a comic photograph taken and their fortunes read by a dark woman with braids passing for a gypsy. Dany shot the target in a booth and won a little green ceramic horse for her.

Early one evening Dany took her past Jaimanitas and Barlovento, through Santa Fe, where he pointed out the club and the park, on west to Hollywood Beach, in Bauta. Two columns at the entrance from the highway revealed that it had once been a private development, and it all seemed like a different country, with winding, narrow, steep, cobble-stoned streets, high wooden houses with peaked gabled roofs, bargeboards, gingerbread and hanging eaves. It was almost deserted except for a very few cars parked near the high cliff over the water's edge. A grocery store on a corner was open, but a dim yellow light shone on an empty interior. On their way back, under the canopy formed by old Indian laurels, they drove past Batista's former *Finca* "Kuquine", to the south.

And they made love in his car, parked on C Street, or on 6th, in the haven the concealing darkness offered them. Ana felt very happy.

Captain Herman Marks, an American, was chief of security at La Cabaña, and conducted the executions at the Fortress. Guevara organized an indoctrination course at La Cabaña, the first "military culture school". Spanish Colonel Alberto Bayo, in Cuba a month, was training boys for guerrillas at Cojímar, on the north coast of the province.

Dr. José Miró Cardona was the Premier during the first six weeks of Castro's government, but Fidel assumed the post of Prime Minister on February 16, and Raúl replaced him as commander in chief of the revolutionary armed forces.

The National Lottery was suspended. And gone were the picturesque ticket vendors shouting the meaning of the numbers to 100 ascribed by the Chinese charade. The INAV (National Institute of Savings and Housing) was organized on the 17th. Its director was

Pastora Núñez González, a chubby woman familiarly called Pastorita who had been a bus conductor.

Major Jesús Sosa Blanco was executed in La Cabaña on the morning of February 18.

Philip Bonsal arrived on the 19th as American Ambassador to Cuba.

On February 24, the Baire War Cry Day, off work, Dany asked Ana, "Do you want to do something different today?" And when she agreed, "Let's go to Managua to visit the man who sells the fruit to my uncle. He lives in a hut... The longer road through Santiago de las Vegas is better, but I'm going to take the shorter route that bus thirty-eight follows."

They went through Mantilla. The potholes and bumps in the road of over six miles from El Calvario to Managua were almost enough to discourage any other driver from sightseeing down the forsaken path. But not quite them. The regal haughtiness of these weather-beaten and yet stately mansions of yesteryear held Ana spellbound and made them go on, determined not to miss a stretch of this alien road they had taken. The uneven, narrow road slowed the old DeSoto down and allowed her to look around and take in the sight. They passed Chorrera. The trees joined their branches overhead at intervals, dappling the road with shade, but between the tree trunks she still saw big houses, tall two-story houses, standing back from the road, proud in their age, looming over the unkempt lawns behind tall iron fences, lonely sentinels on this desolate land, like abandoned forts, the only standing proof of man's hand. When had these houses been built? Who lived there? Not a person was on the gardens, not a car on the road, nothing but the houses, the trees and the overgrown grass, and once in a great while, an occasional rusty swing or abandoned bicycle. Were they old summer villas?

After they had passed Guásima, Dany said, "He has a Jerez gamecock, this man. He took me to a ring once to see him fight. He takes care of him like a child."

"Did he win?"

"Oh, yes!, he won."

They drove south past barbed-wire fences held from live fence posts, which the fertile soil of the Red Plain had made sprout into vigorous mauve-pink flowering little trees. Royal palms sprinkled the landscape, standing majestically over the scene, crowned by their nine fronds.

"What a pretty view!", said Ana.

In Managua, two women, one wearing a halter, waved from the side door of a corner bar at the male passengers of the cars driving by.

They entered the agricultural zone known as the Milky Basin, which supplied milk to most of Havana. There were cows grazing in the clayish savanna at a distance from the highway. They passed symmetrical palm-lined lanes. The Marrero Range rose bluish green not far to the east.

"This man grows mainly potatoes, peanuts and vegetables..." They were about a mile and a quarter past the town, and Dany pointed to an entrance archway to the east of the road, "Near here are the ruins of an old sugar *'cachimbo'*."

"A sugar mill?"

"Yes. You can still see there how a noria grinding mill used to work, pulled by animal force."

A countryman passed them riding a tired, skinny brown horse, and touched the brim of his straw hat to them. The couple lived more than three and a half miles out of town. They took an unpaved road off the highway to San Antonio de las Vegas. After a rugged stretch, Dany parked the car under a gumbo limbo tree with smooth copper-colored bark on a dirt path leading to their hut, and the man and his wife came out to meet them. He was thin and stooped, his cheeks hollow and creased; a two-day stubble darkened his jaw; his two upper front teeth were missing, the others tobacco-stained and his neck furrowed. It was difficult to guess his age, but Ana supposed him to be about thirty. He wore a fan-palm frond hat, a dirt-stained white shirt, baggy trousers, a horn-handled machete hung at his waist in a leather sheath, and scuffed brown sole leather boots. She was fat, with huge upper arms, her skin tanned to a shine, dry brown hair in a tight permanent, and yellowish teeth. She wore a sleeveless flower print dress with a ruffled skirt, a grease stain over her abdomen, and brown sandals. Two children, lips drawn tight, brows knitted in frowns, stood barefoot a few feet behind their parents. The girl, about six, skinny, with sun-bleached straight hair in bangs, wore a faded flower print dress with no belt, which hung low below her waist, and the boy, about three, had a faded blue shirt open over his swollen abdomen and no pants. A dirty skinny dog came up to bark at them. There was an old station wagon with mud-spattered wooden sides and a running board parked in the dirt.

The man slapped Dany on the shoulder. "Lucky are the eyes that see you around here, Danilito! I wonder what star's going to fall", he said in the accent inherited from his Canarian ancestors and corrupted by generations to the present-day country inflection, and, turning to his wife, "You remember Gutiérrez's nephew, don't you, woman?"

"Of course! How're you?"

"Fine, thank you", and, as their eyes turned to Ana, "This is my fiancée."

The man shook her hand in his callous one, "Ovidio Medina, to serve you."

The woman waited to take Ana's hand in her limp one, "Much pleasure. Juana Guzmán."

Ana smiled to them and echoed, "A pleasure to meet you. Ana Méndez."

A mockingbird poured a cascade of silvery notes nearby and an olive finch sang further away.

"Come into the house", said the man. "Have a mouthful of coffee."

"We don't have much time", Dany excused them.

"Oh, no! How could you come such a long way and go away without even drinking coffee? *Vieja*, make coffee!" He put a beaten hand on Dany's back, pushing him ahead. "Come, come into the house."

A *guazuma* shaded the hut, there were two banana trees to one side, and on the other, a coconut tree and a hollowed palm-trunk trough for water, where a pig was drinking. Two oxen rested a distance away, and in the background the royal palms. Their land was probably leased from one of the dairy farms. The nearest sugar mill, "Portugalete", was about seven miles away. A chicken clucked by.

Their house, like most country huts, was built of royal palm trunk boards, the roof thatched with dry fronds — a mahoe chair with goat-hide seat stood by the door, — and tamped dirt floors. A big table covered with oilcloth was near the front door, surrounded by five chairs, and a charcoal stove against the smoke-blackened rear wall, a broom of bare palm-berry cluster leaning next to it. A kerosene lamp rested on a small table by the window with a solid wood glass-less shutter and a burlap curtain, and an old battery radio next to it played country ten-liners.

"...y hoy viene abajo el bohío
del compadre Juan Ramón.

> *Y llegan los bailadores, comay,*
> *por los camino' atasca'os...* "(72)

A corner shelf draped with yellow satin held a small plaster statue of the Virgin of Charity and a little amber glass candleholder. A bust photograph of the couple, solemn looking, lightly colored in watery blue and pink tones, hung from the wall. Flies swarmed around. They pulled the chairs out and sat around the table. The children had followed them into the house and now stood leaning against the wall near the stove, their eyes on the strangers. There was another room behind and, through the open door, an unmade, wide, low bed could be seen. There were no sanitary facilities. Ana hadn't been in a hut in eleven years, since their neighbors Leo and Carolina had taken her and Gustavo, during summer vacation, to Cayaguazal in Caimito, where they had ridden horses at the foot of the Anafe range, and drunk milk freshly drawn, still warm and foamy.

They made small talk about the weather and Dany's uncle.

"I've known him since he was little", the man said to Ana, reaching to squeeze Dany's shoulder, holding his other hand at seat level, "a tadpole." He laughed, showing the gap between his teeth.

Their coffee was served in chipped small enamel mugs – the couple's in calabashes – and, Ana was surprised to find, with the grounds in it. She contained a choked cough and pursed her lips, and her eyes widened.

"Oh, I forgot to warn you", Dany said, amused. "Around here they drink *'carretero'* coffee."

"Oh!, strain it, *Vieja*. She's not used to drinking it like that."

"Oh, no!, this is fine. It's just that I didn't expect it and it surprised me, but I like it like this", she lied politely.

"Are you sure?", insisted Juana, anxious. "I can strain it in just a moment."

"No, really, I like it." She let the grounds settle on the bottom of the mug and sipped the coffee careful not to stir them.

"There was a parade in Havana today, eh?, along the Prado", said Ovidio. "Things are going to change around here now", he said to Dany. "This is a revolution for the poor."

"I'm sure that everything's going to be better now."

The woman was still apologizing for the coffee grounds. "It's just that we're so used to drinking it always like that, that we forget that other people don't..." As she talked, she was deftly dropping cubes of pork meat into a bowl of sour orange with crushed garlic, salt and ground toasted oregano. This would later be fried in a skillet with pork fat and water. A bowl on the table was full of eight-shaped yucca crullers, ready to fry, to be later covered with cane syrup. She proceeded to slice two green plantains. They left their empty mugs on the table.

"If it had occurred to you to come three weeks ago", said Juana, "we had a little *'guateque'* for Candlemas."

"Ah!"

"Very cheerful. Eh, *Viejo*?"

"That's right."

"By this time they were already gathering. We roasted a pig. My brother plays the guitar..."

"I'm sure they wouldn't like a country party, woman", her husband interrupted her. "In Havana they have everything."

Juana fell silent, embarrassed.

"Of course we would", they assured them. The woman smiled again.

"I don't envy anybody anything", the man was saying, "but I only want to have work and earn the money we need. Mainly for the children."

"Well, that's what they're promising now, so I'm sure everybody will be better off."

"Five generations of Medina men have worked this land, miss, five ... have grown potatoes here. My great-great-grandfather started to till it when he was eleven." From the radio came the chords of the Cuban tap dance. "My old man used to have his hut just ahead there, but a whirlwind razed it seven years ago. Now he's living a little further down. This is good land."

After more small talk about Dany's uncle, his parents, his sister and the cold weather, Dany stood up. "Well, it's getting late, and I have to take her home. Thank you."

Ana stood up. They insisted they take a bunch of apple bananas. She saw Dany stick a bill in the man's hand, which the latter earnestly tried to refuse.

Ana repeated, "Pleased to have met you", the phrase echoed from the couple, and they walked them back to the dirt path where the car was parked, the little boy holding on to his mother's skirt with his clenched fist. The winter afternoon was falling and the unbelievable sadness of the country dusk had started to set.

"Don't lose the way now", Juana said. Crickets chirred.

"Come back again soon", said Ovidio as he closed the car door on Ana's side.

"We will", they assured them in duo, knowing they wouldn't. They waved at them until they could no longer see them.

On the Managua highway they turned east, passing the National Army Officers' Military School on their right. A goat was grazing on the hillside to the left near the road. They passed the tiny town of Lechuga, not more than a settlement on low land with a well in the center, to the north of the road, and the land of the "Portugalete" sugar mill with its cane fields to the south. A ground dove flew over the field, on which the shadows were lengthening.

"My uncle says that Ovidio's family's been on that land since the early eighteen forties, when they arrived from the Canaries."

They stopped at a Reca service station on the Central Highway in Cuatro Caminos to buy Cuban gasoline.

"Do you know", Dany asked her with pride, as if he were due some credit for it, "that Cuban gas has the highest octane?"

The porches of the wooden houses ran across their full width, and a stone slab from the porch to the street served to clear a ditch.

The raintrees joined their branches overhead, forming a canopy over the highway. There were a few stone walls, probably the work of Spaniards. An old concrete mixer travelled ahead of them, its drum turning. It was a shame many factories had cut down the beautiful old trees by the highway. This was an industrial zone, with rubber, steel rod and tennis shoe factories, brewery and foundry, and further south, there were sausage, copper cable, base metal, aluminum, tire, paint, glass and sanitary fixture factories. Ana had always felt such pride in being a Cuban when she saw on the "*América*" newsreel how the country was progressing!

They drove through Loma de Tierra, El Cotorro and San Francisco de Paula – Ernest Hemingway's house was on a hill nearby. – The sun was setting and Dany turned the headlights on. In San Matías, they turned west on Dolores Avenue, the last orange glow of the sunset before them. He turned the radio on. They joined the singer's voice,

"... *Hoy he vuelto a pasar*
por aquel camino verde
que por el valle se pierde
en mi triste soledad ... "[73]

From the early half of February, Ana had been pretty certain that she was pregnant. The Brazilian progesterone injections that Dany had gotten her had not worked. She went by herself on a Saturday to a gynecologist three blocks from her house that Dany had found in the telephone book. She was a member of a mutualist clinic for only a $3. monthly quota, but she hadn't wanted to go to it, because the doctor would enter it in her medical history. So she gave this doctor an imaginary name and, of course, said she was married, but she wasn't even wearing a wedding band and was afraid he hadn't believed her. And he had confirmed her fears about her condition.

"How long have you been married?", the doctor asked her. He was thin, with dull, fair skin and light, curly hair.

"Since December tenth", she lied without hesitation, and added, "two and a half months." It was only then, when her reply came out so confidently, that she realized she had subconsciously made up what she would answer. At least Dany had mentioned marriage, and that made her feel a little less guilty. But she felt afraid just the same.

He then asked her, just like that, whether she wanted to have it! She was surprised. She pretended she wasn't sure and said she hadn't decided yet, and mumbled something about having to talk it over with her husband. He simply told her then, "If you decide not to have it, come back to see me." She wasn't sure whether he meant what she thought he did.

For a brief while she entertained the wild idea of having it. But she brought herself back to the reality that she couldn't possibly have a baby now. A child was definitely out of the question. Dany's parents would never get over it and would always look down on her if they had to get married now. They already disapproved of her enough as it was. Dany had to finish his career. Of course she would go back. She nevertheless made a half-hearted attempt when she told him that evening.

"Do you think we could get married now?"

"No, *mi vida*. You know we don't have any money saved now. I told you I don't want to start out depending on anybody. And do you know how my parents would act if I left the university now?"

"You could still go to school in the evening, *mi cielo*", she insisted weakly.

"I couldn't support a home and a child and save money to buy furniture on my salary. You would have to stop working in ... how long?, seven months? No, *mi vida*. We'll have time to have children later on."

She knew he was right and had known he would answer that way, but she had hoped he wouldn't say that. What little indecision she had had was expelled. And she hadn't even had to bring up the subject to the doctor. But how would she refer to it? She made another appointment with him for four weeks later, when Dany could go with her. And now she became impatient.

The Carnival was held off that year. They missed the symmetrical conga lines of the Scorpions, the Gardeners, the Dandies, the Sultans, the Marquises of Atarés, the *Chéveres* of Belén, the Musketeers, the Mexicans, in identical costumes along the Prado on Saturday evenings with their paper lanterns, and the floats in the promenades on Sunday afternoons, which lasted seven or eight weeks every year, with disguises, masks, streamers and confetti, celebrating traditionally the day of freedom each year that once was granted to the slaves.

The first half of March was a nightmare for Ana. She had morning sickness and, although it fortunately gave her time to get out of the house, the bus trip was an agony and she was afraid the girls in the office might notice her early runs to the ladies' room. She once met Elsa inside. She was afraid she had heard her and was sure she must suspect something, but Elsa was so discreet, if she had noticed anything she wouldn't let on to Ana.

On March 4 the government intervened the Cuban Telephone Company.

The new Urban Reform rent law was announced on March 7, one of the dispositions of which reduced rents between 30 and 50 percent, and at the office they discussed it. Some had misgivings.

"Everybody is doubtful now", Guillén said, "but tonight, as soon as the man talks on television and explains, everybody will accept it and be cheering him even before he's through."

And he was right. Castro had done it before with every law they had passed in the last two months. As soon as he talked, all doubts were dispelled from the people's minds. He talked often and long, usually until after midnight, and he knew how to convince them, make them believe him. Could all that have been possible if television had not existed?

Twenty pilots and twenty bombardiers of the constitutional army were charged with genocide and acquitted by a rebel court. Castro ordered the decision acquitting them to be overruled. In the early morning of Sunday the 8th, a new court sentenced the pilots to thirty years of hard labor; redheaded Major Manuel Piñeiro Losada, alias

Red Beard, read the sentence. The first tribunal's chief, Major Félix Pena Díaz, was called to Havana, and he killed himself with one shot to his chest in his car in Miramar.

The DIER and the G-2 on Fifth Avenue were the rebel counterparts of the old SIM. *"Combate"* newspaper, the organ of the Revolutionary Directorate, saw the public light.

Saturday they went to "Rex" theater. They bought little crisp toasted one-cent meringues with the caramel-like centers from the sidewalk candy vendor with his glass case on San Rafael and Amistad, before going in for the one-hour show with its Cuban "*América*" newsreel, Spanish "*No-Do*" and American "Warner-Pathé" news, the documentary, the comedy sketch and the Disney cartoon. A grayish aqua Italian portable typewriter hung from a spring scale in a window at the entrance to show its lightness. Past the stairs to the Duplex, an usher in the lobby announced before the navy blue velvet curtain, "A little while standing." Halfway through the projection, Ana started to feel an uncontrollable longing to eat a hot pork hock sandwich. She tried to push the thought aside, but couldn't, it was too strong. Embarrassed, she asked Dany that they leave. They went to a couple of restaurants asking for it and had thought they wouldn't find it, before they finally did at the "Pullman" on Consulado. It had been her only craving.

René Ray Rivero, an official of the Ministry for the Recovery of Misapplied Properties, and brother of Manuel, the Minister of Public Works, committed suicide in police headquarters.

A Saturday in the latter half of March, Ana walked into Dr. Rodríguez's office with Dany. As they went in, she noticed for the first time the brass plaque with the caduceus on the wall by the door, "Surgeon" under his name. It made her feel slightly more comfortable.

"Good afternoon." They all turned to look at them and muttered their replies. There were several other women sitting in the waiting room: a big, older mulatto woman with a very young girl, a middle-aged one, a young one with her husband. One couple kept walking in and out to the building hallway. Ana had bought a band in a ten-cent store a few days before, which she had slipped on her right finger just before they had come in, lest it tarnish before she even got in to see the doctor. The women struck up a conversation and were talking animatedly. The older woman said the young girl was her niece. Nobody mentioned pregnancy. Ana had no way of knowing which were there for that – she couldn't bring herself even to think of the word – or just for a consultation. It wasn't obvious if any of them was pregnant. The piped music was soft. She and Dany talked in whispers, and leafed through the dog-eared old magazines, *"Life"*'s abounding, on the center table. She had been relaxed, but was gradually growing nervous with the wait. The air conditioning was cool and she started to feel chilly. Dany smoked nervously. An American woman, met at the door by a nurse, went straight in. When they realized the wait would be long, they went out to the coffee shop on the corner of Línea, because, Ana was surprised, she felt hungry. She ate a ham sandwich.

Shortly after they went back, a thin, short nurse came out and started calling them in one at a time. She gave Ana a shot and asked Dany to pay her. It was $30. Nobody asked them what she had come in for, there had been no question as to why she was there. She was told to go back to the waiting room again. She had goose pimples and had to put her topper back on. The American woman came out, on a man's arm, and left looking straight ahead. The thin nurse came out again, and asked Ana and Dany to sit in the inner waiting room with a desk, where Dany had paid her. As they sat there, they saw the doctor rush out of one door and in another, without looking at them. They weren't even talking to each other any more. The wait was becoming unbearable, both shifting in their seats, shuffling their feet, fidgeting, when finally she was instructed to go into the bathroom – which they had been facing, – and take off any elastic garments and loosen any tight ones. Nobody asked her whether she had eaten. A brunette nurse led her into the operating room, where still another young one strapped her onto the table and a male nurse gave her a shot of anesthetic in the arm. She didn't know what the first shot had been. She didn't talk. She saw the doctor come into the room. She started to feel sleepy fast, her heartbeat quickened, she closed her eyes and then felt the gas mask on her face. She started dreaming of drums and a loud, fast beat, deep color flashes were spinning around, around, she saw the doctor in her dream, and was struggling hard to understand it when, after what seemed to her only a very short time, she felt herself being lifted from the table – she didn't know by whom, perhaps the male nurse – and carried to an adjacent room, where she was placed on a narrow bed against the wall, still trying to comprehend the dream, which would haunt her for a long time. Dany was waiting for her, sitting next to the bed. She wasn't fully awake yet. He smiled hesitantly and told her, embarrassed, that she had screamed.

"I love you", she told him impulsively.

The young girl was brought in and laid on the other bed in the room, and her aunt sat next to her. Ana turned toward Dany with an effort and they crossed a surprised and understanding look, because they had thought it was the aunt who was the patient.

"Her husband didn't know it", Ana overheard snatches of the aunt's conversation with the nurse. "She's still going to school." Ana didn't believe there was a husband.

And suddenly Ana began throwing up violently. Dany looked at the older woman, apologetically. The thin, short nurse brought them a little manila envelope with a few white tablets and a slip printed with some instructions. The procedure must be frequent.

"Follow the instructions closely", she told Dany. She helped Ana up and with her shoes. And then it was all over and she was being helped out of the office, and she walked down the steps to the sidewalk on Dany's arm. The sun made her blink. She felt nauseous. It was cold and she drew her topper around herself.

The slip revealed the tablets to be ergotine. And the instructions went into gorily explicit details.

"What do you want to do?", Dany asked her gently, still on the sidewalk.

"Let's go to a movie."

"A movie?", he echoed, doubtful. "Are you sure you feel up to it?"

"Yes. I want badly to sit down, and I couldn't possibly go home like this." Her eyelids were heavy, half closed and her face pale.

She was quiet in the car on the way. She wondered if the American woman had paid the same.

"You told me you loved me", Dany said, putting his right hand on her forearm, "and I know you meant it, because you were still half asleep."

She remembered. She didn't answer. Regret had started to set in.

On Palm Sunday, Blanca took blessed palms to them from church, some of which Teresa braided and wove into little lanterns.

Monday Ana didn't dare go to work, and she feigned an upset stomach to stay home. She stayed in bed until late. Over the sound of the deaf woman's television upstairs, the itinerant peddlers' cries reached her from the street. First, the scissors sharpener's whistle, with its peculiar tune. For months after they had moved to this neighborhood, she had thought it was Greek music coming from a radio and had tried in vain to find it on her own dial, until she had quite by accident met the mustachioed Canarian sharpener on the street pushing his cart with the flint grindstone wheel and the trestle, blowing his panpipe. She had mentioned it at work and, after kidding her about it, Salvador had promised to get her a sharpener's whistle, but never had. The cane-seat weaver, "Cane weaving!, weaver!." "I tighten bedsprings!" "Furniture bought, beds and bedsprings!" "Brooms!, broom vendor!." "I exchange balloons for bottles!, bottleman!" The florist with his fragrant, snowy-white load in a shallow hamper and a bunch held high, "For a cent the butterfly lily!" "The watermelons, Castile ones, ripe papaya!, little housekeeper!" The colored man pushing his cart filled with fruit, some wedged, right palm cupped by his mouth, head tilted back, "Mango, little mango, mango it is!, sweet China orange, yellow *'malanga'*!", with his load of mamey sapote, pineapple, tangerine, custard apple, cherimoya, plum, apple, Johnson bananas, cashew, lime. "*Salfumán*[22] and *creolina*[23]!"

She could hear her mother watering the jasmine on the balcony. A canary was singing in the next building. The mailman's whistle sounded somewhere in the staircase. And the swishing sound of the soaked baize in the pail of water as Felipe washed the steps.

She listened to the radio. "Care for your life and others', drive carefully", advised *Radio Reloj*. The topic "the conquest of sidereal space" was discussed. She fiddled with the dial searching for *"danzones"* by Antonio María Romeu or Alfarona Equis and she heard *"Cadete Constitucional"*.

"... *Cabo de la guardia, siento un tiro.*
 ¡Ay!,... que estoy herido."[74]

"Kolonia with a K 1800" wished women named Pelagia "much happiness on this day", sung to the music of "Happy Birthday", for their name day. "Against ache, fever, flu and general discomfort, '*OK Gómez Plata*' tells the time..." "And drink *Materva*, the delicious soda."

Dany called her from the office at lunch time. "How do you feel, stronger?" And she answered in monosyllables.

"*Maltina*, the formula of health, the drink of the home." "Drink

[22] fuming salt, muriatic acid, hydrochloric acid solution
[23] preparation of coal creosote and resinous soaps

Kresto three times a day." She listened to *Radio Codazos*[24]. She liked its only announcer's sedate voice — in contrast with the station's name, — advertising the Edsel and the Invicta, and its soft music. *Radio Continental* promised "varied instrumental music", and *Radio Salas* acclaimed itself "the oldest station in Cuba".

> *"Tú me quieres dejar,*
> *yo no quiero sufrir,*
> *contigo me voy, mi negra,*
> *aunque me cueste morir."*[75]

"The Esso Reporter, Esso Reporter, the first one with the latest!" The music of *"Guantanamera"* in Joseíto Fernández's voice, with the dog's bark in the background, floated through to her from a radio somewhere in the building, maybe the superintendent's mother's upstairs. Country *"décimas"* didn't appeal to her.

The clinic's bill collector came by for their monthly quota.

In the afternoon, the peddlers' cries changed. "For a cent the taffy, a cent!, chocolate, strawberry and lemon!" "The tasty tamarind pulp!", the man with his little glass case. The Spanish sugar waffle cone vendor beating his steel triangle with the rod. The colored man selling pastries, a pile of trays strung on a strap dangling from each arm, arranged one on top of the other, carefully balanced not to spill the syrups, "I'm going!" The cubic Italian-ice man with his portable icebox, the vendor of translucent conic *"pirulíes"*.

The smell of her mother's cooking came from the kitchen.

On the bus to work on Tuesday, a seed of uneasiness inside her, Ana kept telling herself everything was all right again. She wondered if she looked any different. Could anybody tell?

At her desk in the early silence, doubts assaulted her. Maybe she shouldn't have done it after all, maybe if she had kept it, she thought, she would have had a better chance that he'd marry her. She tried to chase the thought away, but couldn't. She typed one whole line before she realized she had her left hand fingers over the wrong keys. And then Dany came in and tapped her desk and winked at her with his broad smile, and she felt everything *was* all right.

Wednesday evening, without the car, he came by bus. When they were alone, he confided, awkwardness in his voice, "There was a couple on the bus with a little baby. The girl had to sit in front with the baby and the boy in back. And I watched him get up and go to

[24] "elbow blows"

them several times, to arrange the receiving blanket around it and cover its feet and push its hair back from its forehead and touch its cheek, and I thought how wonderful it'd be to have been able to have ours."

His tender thought touched her. She kissed him and gave him a sad smile, and suddenly blurted, "What I'm afraid of is that God might punish us and not let us have more children when we want them."

"No, don't think that!", he said, alarmed, taking her in his arms.

That evening Teresa, armed with the excuse that he didn't have the car, took the perfect opportunity for once to ask him politely to leave early. "You had better leave before you're caught in the *'confronta'*[25]. It's eleven twenty-five now."

On Maundy Thursday, after half a day's work, they went to the Church of the Holy Custodian Angel on Cuarteles Street. They had to take the bus because Dany's sister had again needed the car. As they arrived, a procession was coming down the stone steps to Monserrate. From here, the church with its Gothic spires seemed built into the rock. Ana covered her head with her lace veil as they went in, she flexed a knee and crossed herself in the aisle, and went to kneel at one of the rear pews. Dany, in his impeccable, white linen long-sleeved plaited *guayabera* that made him look so tall, imitated and followed her. In the cozy, quiet dimness, she analyzed the custom coldly. Was this really a matter of religion? For most it was probably only a matter of tradition. The irreverent thought crossed her mind that the crucified Christ shrouded in purple resembled a bat, and she felt immediately ashamed and fearful. She didn't voice her disrespectful thought. She was suddenly remorseful that she hadn't been to confession in six years and, after what she had just done, she didn't know when she'd gather enough courage. She bowed her head and prayed.

They passed a Chinamen's fritter stand as a boy came out eating black-eyed pea fritters from a greasy paper bag, and the pungent hot lard smell of the fritters assaulted them – plantain chips, fried dough, puffed pork rinds, meaty pork cracklings, corn flour "whistles", sweet potato fritters with anise, codfish fritters.

She thought it too much to ask Dany to do the Seven Stations with her. It was their first Holy Week together. So they went to Cojímar

---

[25] reduced bus service after 12:00 midnight

Pride in Being a Cuban 73

in Guanabacoa instead. They rode on the Monumental Way. Sisal grew on the limestone by the road. They ran into Pablo on the bus. The Lent wind blew from the south. They walked down the cracked high sidewalk, going up and down the steps on the corners. A few boys played marbles squatting on the dirt off to a side, one rolled a hoop down the street, some girls played hopscotch on the sidewalk with a flattened tin can, a boy sat on a curb sucking on a chunk of sugar cane, others played *"quimbumbia"* on a side street. Bedsheets on a clothesline swelled like sails in the wind; a red kite flew high in the deep blue sky, dancing over the houses. Hemingway's "The Old Man and the Sea" took place here. They walked north across the old town and went through the park bandstand toward the beach, where the writer had his yacht "Pilar" anchored, the sand covered with pink shells, and the castle dating back to the 17th Century.

On their way back, they stopped in Havana to buy marzipan *"huesitos de santos"* for Teresa, at a bakery counter filled with glossy *capuchinos* and "little yolks", syrupy "drunk" sponge cake, sugar-powdered napoleons, caramel *éclairs*, glazed gypsy jelly rolls, candied citron, chocolate "capitols", "heavenly" confection, French toast and strawy *palmiers*.

The Méndez family observed the fast and meat abstinence on Good Friday. For two whole days the radio and television remained completely silent. But they did not listen to the Seven Word Sermon, or attend the Adoration of the Cross. Until the year before, only sacred music had been broadcast on Good Friday and many stations were off the air, so it had been possible then to get transmissions from Mexico and Panamá.

Costa Rica's ex-President José Figueres Ferrer arrived on March 21. He was a guest at a demonstration called by the CTC. Figueres spoke before half a million Cubans. Secretary-General David Salvador Manso interrupted him. Castro later said that, in the event of a war, Cuban would remain neutral. He finished, quoting Maceo, "Whoever may intend to take Cuba will only pick up the dirt of its ground soaked in blood." On leaving, Figueres said warily at the airport, "Cuba, may this revolution of today not disappoint you again."

On Glory Saturday, Dany came in a beige plaid sport shirt smelling of "Canoe", and they went through the tunnel to the Great Christ of Havana, on the east side of the Harbor. From the winding road that took them up the hill, they took a photograph of the Christ towering over them in His act of blessing the city. When they reached the top on foot, they were surprised to find a large parking lot full of cars. They had never been there before. They walked into the park and Dany was going to snap a photograph of the 54-foot tall stone statue at close range, when a soldier, white star over red and black insignia on the shoulder of his olive green uniform, approached them carrying a submachine gun.

"You can't take pictures here", he told them. "You'll have to give me the camera. Have you taken any?"

"Not yet", Ana lied quickly − Well, not up here they hadn't, anyway, − "but why?" She was curious.

"There are many Army installations around here. This is a military post and La Cabaña Fortress is close by", he thrust his head in its direction. "Well, you may keep the camera, but don't take any pictures, or I'll have to take it from you."

"We won't", Dany promised, and the man went back to join a fellow soldier. They were appalled.

They looked around to see what the military installations consisted of. But they wouldn't allow their day to be spoiled. It was warm and they went to a fruit-ade stand in the shade of a tree and had coconut drinks. They sat on the grassy slope, talking in the spring sun, facing Havana across the bay, the camera idle between them on the moist, green grass. They could see the little town of Casablanca to the southeast, sleepy in the early afternoon, and the dome of the National Observatory.

Dany talked about the coming automobile races at the Cayuga airfield in San Antonio de los Baños, and about racing cars. "That's always been my dream."

"But I'd be afraid for you", said Ana, uneasily.

"I talked to you about it when we started seeing each other... don't you remember?... and you didn't say anything then."

"I don't remember. But I guess I must not have paid much attention to it then, because I didn't care for you yet."

"Well, I warned you. I know the way women feel about it, and I wanted you to think about it."

Ana felt perversely tempted to try his response. "And if I asked you not to do it?"

"Well, now I'm too involved with you to leave you, and I'd give in... But I wish you wouldn't ask me."

She was silent. The idea upset her.

"It's still a long time away", he said. "Do you know how much

Pride in Being a Cuban 75

one of those race cars costs?"
    She didn't try any more to talk him out of it. He was right. It was only a dream, after all. It'd probably never come true. By the time he had enough money to buy a race car, they'd probably have children and other responsibilities, and he'd probably not want to.
    The cool breeze blew in from the bay. She looked across the harbor at Puerto Avenue, and the bayside parks seemed so close, perhaps because of this vantage point. They were leaning on one elbow, half-turned to each other, not touching. She felt very peaceful and very close to him. The air was clean and the sky cloudless. They could see from there the equestrian statue of General Máximo Gómez on the Circle, the remnants of the Tacón jail, the Amphitheater and La Fuerza Castle.
    On their way back, they walked around the massive hewn stone San Salvador de la Punta Castle, on Sotavento Point, the West tip by the channel to the bay, and the moss-covered Santo Angel bulwark and sentry post, remnants of the old City Wall, and took the pictures they hadn't been allowed earlier.
    Three boys were playing leapfrog, yelling as they jumped,
        "...A las cuatro mi gato,
        a las cinco te hinco,
        a las seis pan de rey..."[94]
A couple of girls jumped rope. Several boys rode bicycles, the younger ones with training wheels. On their way to the car, a shoeshine man vigorously polished a customer's shoes at the chair on the portico of a cafe. From a record player came,
        "Te vas, yo no sé qué hacer,
        la vida lo quiso así,
        que, cuando más te adoraba,
        te vas de mí..."[76]
    They passed a newspaper vendor on the corner, his newspapers carefully arranged in a huge folded cardboard which hung from his shoulder by a rope covered with fabric to ease the strain of the weight.
    "*'Mundo', 'Marina', 'Información'*! With the latest news!"
    Another one wearing a red baseball cap with the white Old English **H** of the Havana team announced, "*'Excélsior', 'El País!'* Photographs and details! Go! *'Crisol'*! With the latest event!"
    The cry of an unidentified vendor at the bus stop reached them as they drove away in the car, "Start taking away!"

On Easter Sunday, the family went to Mass together at Saint John Lateran's Church with its tall iron fence, Dany with them. Elena, Blanca's mother, stayed with Gustavito and Blanquita. Blanca took Communion, having gone to confession the day before. She had attended El Apostolado School and remained practicing. Until Gustavito was born, she had gone on retreat.

The INAV drawings began on March 29. The first big housing project was started across the Bay in East Havana.

Thousands of public employees were dismissed on March 31.

Castro dismissed Dr. Salcines from the University of Santiago, who had saved his life not six years before after the attack on Moncada.

Word reached the Cuban people that Dr. Rafael Díaz-Balart, Castro's ex-brother-in-law, had organized the "White Rose" group in New York in January of 1959.

When the revolutionary government took power, there was free medical attention available in over fifteen large hospitals in the Havana area alone, not counting those elsewhere on the Island. There was the Calixto García Hospital, interned by the University of Havana medical students; the Reina Mercedes Hospital; the Freyre de Andrade General Emergency; the Clínico-Quirúrgico Mercedes del Puerto, in Puentes Grandes, named after Mayor Pozo's mother; Las Animas, for contagious diseases; Dr. Joaquín G. Lebredo Sanatorium of La Esperanza, for tuberculosis; América Arias López Municipal Maternity, on Línea; Workers' Maternity in Marianao, for the laborers' wives; Dr. Angel A. Aballí Municipal Infantile, for children; Curié and Francisco Domínguez Roldán, for the treatment of cancer; the Police Hospital, for members of the National Police Force and their families; Dr. Arístides Agramonte Simoni Military, in Columbia, for the army; the Regla Socarrás y Socarrás National Hospital in Aldabó, the Alta Habana National Hospital, the National Orthopedic Hospital; besides "succor houses" or first-aid stations in every neighborhood. There were also four Spanish regional centers with numerous pavilions on huge *"quinta"* grounds, which had, for their $2.75 monthly quota, social ballrooms, schools and beach clubs to offer as well, and ubiquitous mutualist clinics with monthly quotas around $3.

There were six official or public universities: the University of Havana, in the capital, well over two centuries old, with thirteen schools and an ordinary annual tuition of $45., under the rectorate of Dr. Clemente Inclán Costa; Marta Abreu Arencibia Central University in Santa Clara, Las Villas; the University of Oriente in Santiago de Cuba, founded in 1947; the Ignacio Agramonte y Loynaz University of Camagüey; Rafael Morales y González Occidental University in Pinar del Río, and the University of North Oriente in Holguín, this last one recently created during the overthrown administration. There were six private ones in Havana: Saint Thomas de Villanueva in Miramar, which had been functioning for twelve years; the Methodist Chandler College, in Alturas del Bosque; the Cuban Masonic; the José Martí Technical University, on 19th Street; Saint John the Baptist de LaSalle Catholic University, in Ensanche del Vedado, and Belén Electromechanic, on 51st Avenue.

Twenty-one secondary education institutes and 18 schools of commerce operated free in the country. Three free professional schools operated in Havana, Commerce on Ayestarán, Journalism on G Street and Publicity on 2nd Street, three Teachers' Normal schools, Arts and Crafts, Fine Arts, two Industrial Technical schools, and there were polytechnic and civic-military institutes, plus municipal schools, public schools, rural schools.

A few of the 1,700 private schools in the country were Baldor, Arturo Montori, Trelles, the LaSalle Brothers, the Marist Brothers' Champagnat, Jesuit Belén, the Piarist Fathers' Pious, the Apostolate of the Sacred Heart, the American Dominican Academy, the French Dominicans, the Teresiano, the Ursulines, Our Lady of Lourdes, La Luz; Ruston Academy, the best American school; Méricy Academy; The Guardian Angel, Mariana Lola Alvarez's old school, on Carlos III; huge The Sacred Heart of Jesus in Buenos Aires subdivision; Havana Military Academy, in Jaimanitas; St. George's, María Corominas; the Oblate Sisters of the Divine Providence, for colored girls; the "*Shung Wah*", Chinese, on Manrique; the Cuban-American, Robert Wharton's Presbyterian La Progresiva in Cárdenas, plus countless lesser schools everywhere. The Dolores and Juan Bautista Sagarra schools in Santiago de Cuba were famous nation-wide.

•

When the first laws of the Urban Reform went into effect, Ana found Rina choked with laughter in the office and, when she asked her, it was all Rina could do to tell her that Virginia, Mr. Sterling's secretary, who had invested the $8,000. from her divorce settlement in a mortgage, would now lose it entirely. She apparently found it hilarious.

Ana dragged Dany to Blanquita's first birthday *piñata* party on a

Saturday afternoon in April. Blanca broke the *piñata* for Blanquita, too small to do it herself, and, after the cake and ice cream amidst the din of the children's shouts as they scattered for candy and favors that showered on the floor and the released balloons that stuck to the ceiling, Ana and Dany escaped to the movies, while Blanca swore, "Gustavito's I'm celebrating in José Martí Park".

The CTC abolished the workers' right to strike.

Castro accepted an invitation of the American Society of Newspaper Editors and went to Washington on April 14. He flatly denied to the Foreign Relations Committee that he were a Communist. He stated his government was humanistic. He toured the States and talked in Central Park in New York. He denied any plans for the expropriation of private property, declared he had no intention of confiscating foreign private industry and called for foreign capital investment. He said elections would not be held for four years, remarking "Elections, for what?" And he decorated newspaperman Herbert L. Matthews at the Cuban Embassy.

Ana persuaded Dany to give her his graduation ring from Escuela Nacional Masónica in Nicanor del Campo to wear temporarily in lieu of an engagement one, and had to stick adhesive tape to the inside to fit her finger. She put a smaller copy of the photograph he had given her for Christmas under the glass on her desk in the office, for the first time for their co-workers to see. Guillén joked that he looked like a movie actor and Salvador that the photograph had been greatly touched up, which they took in stride.

In April the University reopened and Dany went back to class. After four months together daily, Ana felt lost in the evenings, so used had she gotten to seeing him every night. She passed the time pasting in her album the photographs they had taken on the Malecón, at the foot of the Maine Monument, on the Plaza by Roosevelt's bust, behind the Hotel Nacional, by the statue of Calixto García, before the Havana Riviera Hotel on Paseo, in front of the Sports Palace, by his DeSoto, in the park bandstand in Cojímar, by La Punta Castle, before the Santo Angel bulwark and sentry post, on the little bridge by the American Embassy and in "their" little park on Línea. In the background, the opening lines of "Heroes of Justice" on *Radio Progreso* drifted up to her from the teacher's radio, "... story of the men and women who risk their lives day after day knowing that society has deposited on them its most prized treasure: living without fear. Pulled from the files of the most famed police institutions dedicated to crime repression, the FBI, the Sureté and Scotland Yard, we reenact for you the criminal cases that most..." She embroidered her parents' initials on their towels and took to reading a lot. There still were American magazines on the stands around the tourist sections, although there were few tourists now. She hadn't read much until only three years before. Her library in Spanish had previously consisted of Cirilo Villaverde's "Cecilia Valdés", "The Hundred Best Cuban Poems" and the second edition of José María Heredia's poems, printed in Toluca, Mexico, in the early 19th Century, which her mother had treasured for 27 years − a gift from an old boyfriend, suspected Ana, maybe the son of that Consul to Mexico, − dry pansies pressed between its brittle yellowed pages, and which Ana now cherished and handled carefully. And those were the only three books she kept in her room. Aside from that, she had checked books out from the lending library of the Lyceum and gone to the municipal library on Neptuno Street often to consult reference books on school subjects. And she'd been so used by then to writing and reading in English at business school, that she'd started reading, for the practice, only books in English and American magazines, which she found on O'Reilly, Galiano Street and Concordia, Animas, Infanta Street and San Rafael, La Rampa Commercial Arcade and the lobby of La Rampa Cinema. She read Rosemary Taylor's "Chicken Every Sunday", Marjorie Housepian's "Houseful of Love", Inge's "Picnic", Grace Metalious' "Peyton Place", Heath's "Violent Saturday", Chayefsky's "The Bachelor Party", Moore's "Chocolates for Breakfast", Françoise Sagan's *"Dans un Mois Dans un An"*, "The American Magazine", Compact.

Ana received her $20. yearly raise, which took her to $230. a month.

Four men aboard a Cubana plane forced the pilot to fly to Miami, where they took asylum, as did three men on a boat. Another plane was hijacked to Miami by two men and two women.

Dany had lately been taking Benzedrine to be able to stay alert in his night classes. One afternoon he left the office early feeling ill and told Ana he was going to the clinic. When she called his home, his mother told her he hadn't arrived yet. She called a second time and he still hadn't arrived.

"I'm sorry to bother you", she told his mother, "but I'm worried." She had never talked to her that much.

"Don't be embarrassed. Call as many times as you want." She sounded so much friendlier. "When he arrives, I'll tell him you called." Maybe it had been Ana's concern that changed her attitude. Surely concern for her child would please a mother.

When she called again later, he had already arrived. "He went to bed", said his mother.

"Then don't get him up", Ana said, a little miffed that he hadn't called her. "I just wanted to know he's all right."

"Thank you for your concern."

That marked the start of a civil albeit brief exchange of niceties when his mother answered the phone from then on.

A law voided all $500 and $1,000 denomination bills effective April 30.

There was a plot to kidnap Rolando Masferrer in Miami and deliver him to a Cuban firing squad, but it was given away.

By the end of April there was a line of stool pigeons at DIER headquarters, busily informing.

Walter Butler brought the implausible news that there was an advance detachment of the military mission of the Soviet Union on the street and there was part of the Red China military mission in the Habana Hilton Hotel. They didn't know whether he actually believed it himself or only wanted them to believe it.

Toward the end of April, Ana and Dany opened a joint savings account in a branch of the Bank of Nova Scotia close to her home, and started saving toward their $2,000. goal. He gave her $20. from every semimonthly paycheck and she'd add $10. to it from hers. They figured they'd have the amount in two years and five months, considering that during summer vacation Dany could contribute $35., since he didn't have the university monthly tuition to pay.

Ana took Dany to visit her aunt and godmother Cristina, Norma's mother, in Kohly, for her to meet him. Her uncle Marcos, a clerk at Sarrá druggists, made him feel immediately at ease. Norma was out with girl friends. The china hutch with the entwined initials $\mathcal{B}$ $\mathcal{S}$ etched in the glass door and the stained-glass fruit-relief shade hanging lamp were items left from her grandparents' household. Ana noticed that the left hand of the ivory goddess of mercy Kuan-Yin had been removed, probably by Norma, asking for a favor. She went into the kitchen with her aunt to give the men a chance to get acquainted. When they returned to the living room-dining room with coffee, they found them sitting by the door to the green-tinted glassed-in porch, involved in an unlikely discussion about the difference between intestinal infection and obstruction, which Marcos, well knowing his wife, quickly dropped.

Their visit to Ana's uncle and godfather Guillermo's house in Lawton didn't go so well. Her godfather, recently retired from Toledo sugar mill and a Knight of Columbus, was polite but restrained, sucking on his cigar, while Ana looked around at this house which never failed to fascinate her, in the plain, sharp, geometric Streamline style so popular in the thirties, when steamship trips to Spain were in vogue, with flat tops, rounded corners, silver-colored flat, thin ribbon-like ironwork, wall light sconces shaded with flat frosted-glass fan-shaped tulip-like petals. Her aunt Beatriz kept getting up and walking to the glossy caramel-colored sideboard under the picture of the Last Supper, to look out of the simulated porthole round window at the street, waiting for their son Jorge to appear, and hardly holding a conversation with them. "I'm watching your car", she told Dany. Ana could see Dany felt uneasy and they left early.

Their apprehensive venture to Esperanza's home on San Miguel Street, with its noisy, slow cage elevator, found her aunt alone with her two-year old granddaughter. Her uncle Augusto, a clerk in the office of a soap factory, was playing dominoes at a friend's house and her cousin Laura and her husband had gone dancing. They sat facing the upright piano, their backs to the balcony, while Ana looked up at the delicate chocolate tinted flower garlands that decorated the rim of the ceiling, a prayer card of the Virgin of Loreto over the door. Esperanza asked him his name twice — "I'll remember it, I have a good memory", — where he lived, — "That's far!", — and where they were going — "I see you both dressed up. Well, I know you don't want to be late. You don't have to stand on formalities with me." Dany liked the little girl, Lourdes.

Teresa, apparently now accepting their relationship as more official, started inviting Dany for lunch on Sundays. Roast chicken was a favored dish on those days, or else Teresa tried out television's Ana Dolores Gómez Kemp's recipes on him. And Carlos, given more of a chance to talk with him, began to show a liking for Dany. "He's very mature for his age", he'd say after he'd left, "very sober and steady. In what year of Commercial Science is he now? Third?", then nodding, "He'll have a comfortable situation while still young."

Coming out of the baroque "Arenal" one evening after seeing "A Face in the Crowd" with Andy Griffith, Dany was supposed to take the car back to his sister Sonia early. In the parking lot, he commented, "There's an advantage to having a car as old as ours. It's easy to find: Look, it's usually the tallest one."

"Eight years isn't so old."

He drove west around Nicanor del Campo, past the Tropical Stadium. When he turned off 41st Avenue into 54th Street, Ana, not knowing her way in the suburb, was lost.

"Where are you going?"

"You'll see."

After several blocks down narrow streets, she began to wonder, afraid to hope, not daring to expect it. But, as he drove along the unfamiliar streets, the idea grew in her mind that he was taking her home to meet his parents.

"Where are you going?", she asked again.

"Never mind. You'll see when we get there."

She wondered how she looked. Her dress was modest, the gray one with a white collar that Leonardo had once actually said made her look like a governess. She whisked her hand over her hair. She would dust face powder on when he stopped. Her heart was beating fast.

He suddenly stopped in front of a triangular park and her heart took a plunge. He got out of the car and walked to a group of young people standing on the gravel near the center. She saw him put his hands on a chubby girl's shoulders, talk for a moment and turn back toward her tossing the car keys in the air. The girl looked at him and towards the car for a moment before turning back to her friends.

"I can keep it until later", he said, as he turned the ignition. And Ana realized he had come to ask his sister to let him keep the car. "Well, where do you want to go?"

"Oh, I don't know", she said, trying to cover her disappointment. "To Ward's?"

"Sometimes my father is unreasonable", Dany said to her one Sunday afternoon eating a star apple after late lunch at her house, and Ana guessed he was alluding to his dislike of her, "unjust, stubborn. I don't agree with him. But I respect him. I know how much he cares for us... And I admire him. He's come a long way on his own effort, you know. He has a hardware store now and we're pretty well off, but you'd be surprised to know how he started." He hesitated. "He started selling tin mugs and glass tumblers...", and then, almost defiantly, "sitting on a portico. You know how they take up a little space on a portico and settle there everyday?" She nodded. "Well, then he started selling pots and pans, and then can openers and corkscrews... in Machado's time, newly wed... and he added on to it until he earned enough to rent a shop, in Buen Retiro. And my mother struggled along with him and helped him. I think that's how she got her gall bladder trouble. The shop did all right and he finally bought his own store and built the brick house where we live now. It took him nineteen years, but he now owns his store and his home. So I admire his determination", he finished with a proud smile.

"It *is* to be admired." She had somehow imagined his father had always had the hardware store. She wondered what her parents would think if they knew. All the time she had felt his father didn't approve of her. And he now turned out to have been an ambulant vendor. On a portico! What right did he have to disapprove of her? Who did he think he was? What did he think *she* was!... Well, maybe he had sacrificed so much for his children, that no girl seemed to him good enough for his son. Lately he had taken to talking Dany into spending Saturdays mailing the invoices out to the customers and doing the bookkeeping of the store.

"We used to live in a wooden house in Buena Vista until five or six years ago. I liked it. It was cooler. Wood is much cooler, did you know? And we had trees. I remember there was one... The branches of an Indian almond tree used to stick in through the dining-room window when the breeze blew." He stared off, remembering, and Ana tried to imagine it. "This house is modern, but I loved the other one. We don't have any trees here. The store is next to the house now."

"Oh!, I didn't know that."

"Yes, we even have one phone number with an extension. That's why the Old Man answers the phone most of the time, because it rings in the store."

What would her mother say? She wouldn't tell her. After all, he wasn't that any longer. Now he was a shop owner.

"You know, a nurse lives across the street from me and sometimes when I get home late, she's just going in."

It was odd that he'd think of telling her that. Ana got up and went to the record player. She selected *"El Madrugador"* and put it on.

> *"Y rompe la soledad*
> *habitual de la pradera*
> *una tonada sitiera,*
> *que es signo de libertad."*[77]

Dany started humming it. "I love *'guajiras'*," he said.

"Do you? So do I. And *'criollas'* and *'habaneras'*." She sat next to him again.

"I didn't know that. Hardly anybody does any more. Now most people like the *'cha-cha-chá'* and the *'pachanga'*." He tapped the ashes off his cigarette in the blue ashtray on the corner table.

"I don't even know how to do them well."

"We've never done it. I've just realized we've only danced to *'boleros'* and *'guarachas'*." He suddenly leaned forward and kissed her.

They were delighted to be still discovering new things about each other after six months.

Music affected her instantly, usually picking her up and exhilarating her, sometimes plunging her into deep despondency. She enjoyed instrumentals. She delighted in paintings, conventional ones. She liked Raphael, Michelangelo and Manuel Vega López. The sight of bright flowers made her want to breathe deeply and feast her eyes on their colors. She loved roses. And beautiful colors caught her attention and held her gaze. She liked jade green and coral. She was fascinated by woodgrain, smoky browns, copper, bare brick, undyed leather, animal skins and dry perfumes. And she liked egg *"capuchinos"* and stuffed chayote squash.

He liked drum and trumpet music, and piano solos. He admired sculptures, marble and granite. Juan José Sicre, of whose work they had a sample in his monument to Victor Hugo just two blocks from Ana's home. And poems, about war, knights and duels. The sea. Trees. He enjoyed the smell of jasmine and night jasmine, disliked gardenia and white lily because they seemed to him to smell like funeral parlors. He liked walnut and birch, and tiger and zebra skins. He only liked lavender. And *"tatianoff"*[26] and *"ponche romano"*[27]. And hated corn flour and codfish because he'd eaten it so much as a child, and frogs.

They went out to stand on the balcony, leaning on the railing, and the perfume of jasmine wrapped them, the aroma of sweet basil from the next balcony assaulted them in the limpid spring air, and the fragrance of rangoon creeper drifted to them in the early evening from somewhere further away. The sad, sad whistle of a train going by blew somewhere far in the distance.

"I'd have liked to be a young girl from about nineteen thirty-two

---

[26] chocolate torte
[27] almond torte

Pride in Being a Cuban

to... to thirty-eight", she told him. "That would've been the perfect time for me. I should have been born around nineteen seventeen."

"For the age of streetcars and corkscrew curls, long dresses and thick stockings?"

"Yes, and ribbons, ruffles, lace and bowlers. And the big bands."

"Well, yes, and also poetry and romanticism", he said, teasing. "And flat chests!"

She laughed. He wasn't being serious any more. "Where are your grandparents from?"

"*Pontevedreses* from Vigo and *Coruñeses* from El Ferrol, raised on cabbage and leek. Why?"

"Just curious. Do you have a middle name?"

He nodded, paused and drew out slowly, raising his eyebrows, "Ubaldo. The saint of the day I was born."

"Well..."

A cockroach crawled out of the rain drain, she squirmed and he stepped on it.

"Where will we live when we get married?", she asked him. "Not in Almendares, will we?"

"Why not?"

"It's so far...!"

"There are no cockroaches in Almendares."

"I bet not."

"No, there are mice, but no cockroaches", he joked. "No, I guess we'll live here in Vedado. It's closer to work."

In April the Méndez family's two-bedroom apartment, which they had rented for $65. three years before, was reduced in half, to $32.50 a month, which was only exactly one-tenth of Carlos' draw in the office.

In April and May labor syndicate elections were held.

The so-called "First May Day of Freedom" was celebrated with a parade on the Civic Plaza, now renamed "Revolution Plaza", from 11:00 in the morning till 2:00 in the morning of Saturday.

Eighty-two Cubans, who had landed in Panamá and taken a town in Colón with the object of overthrowing the government, stated on surrendering, "We were following Fidel's orders."

On May 2 Castro attended the Committee of 21, a unit of the OAS, in Buenos Aires. His slogan was then, "Freedom with justice and bread without terror." He went on to Uruguay and Brazil.

Once in the spring, Ana and Dany went to see a Russian movie,

Chiaureli's "Fall of Berlin" with Andreyev at La Rampa Cinema. Socialist films were now the ones being shown most often. They left the theater lobby, with its wallpaper in knotty pine, very shocked by the way Stalin had been portrayed mystically as a saint in the picture.

"This is Communism. There's no doubt", Dany commented, surprised and alarmed, still standing on the front steps. Ana felt afraid and moved closer to him.

Other Russian films followed, Kalatozov's "The Cranes Are Flying" and Aimanov's "Daughter of the Steppes". They found their philosophy perplexing. They went to see Jacques Tati's "Monsieur Hulot's Holiday", French, with its haunting little background tune, and Cacoyannis' "A Girl in Black", Greek, with Ellie Lambetti. And also saw Swedish movies, "The Daughters of the Horse Merchant" and Ingmar Bergman's "Brink of Life" with Eva Dahlbeck.

Back from Trinidad, Castro assured the Cuban people on May 8 that the revolution was not communist.

For Mother's Day, Ana gave Teresa a sewing chest lined in pink satin in the morning and, after her parents went to the cemetery to take flowers, she, Gustavo and Blanca, wearing red carnations, took her to the "Amalfi" restaurant with Carlos for lunch. In the afternoon, Blanca, Gustavo, Lorenzo and his wife, Pilar, would take Elena to the "Polinesio" with Mateo for dinner. It would be a day of overeating. And Dany, after having spent the day with his sister Sonia and their mother, came to see Ana in the evening, and they went to the movies.

The University of Havana, with 18,000 students in its neoclassical buildings, closed by Batista since November of 1956, for over two years, finally opened on May 10. The FEU dismissed about thirty professors.

For Dany's birthday, a Saturday in May — he was turning 21, — Ana had her portrait taken at "Argüelles" studio nearby, and surprised him giving it to him in a wide varnished wood frame that matched the one that held his on her wardrobe, planning that both would match when they set up their home together. And also a key chain with his initials shaped like two semicircles that fit together on a round holder, which she found in Hernán Fábricas on Galiano. She loved giving him things with his initials. And they went to the "Flamingo".

They often had chicken broth and fried chicken or croquettes standing at "El Caporal". And *tatianoff, ponche romano* or stuffed

Pride in Being a Cuban 87

chayote squash at "Wakamba" Chinese restaurant with water-melon juice. Sometimes they drove to "Los Pinos Nuevos" on the Rancho Boyeros highway. They ordered a toasted Polish roll and were amused when the waiter's cry went up, "A toasted Polack!"

Castro ordered the trials ended on May 15 and the executions stopped for a while, but were soon resumed.

In May, anti-Communist workers formed the Cuban Humanist Labor Front.

A navy frigate intercepted a ship near Mariel on which a group of military men were trying to escape.

Fidel promulgated an Agrarian Reform law and on May 17 signed it at La Plata, in Niquero, in the Sierra Maestra. A moderate reform had been drawn by Minister Humberto Sorí Marín earlier, but had been rejected. Several of the office employees, Ramiro, Rolandito, Mario, Dany, Rosa and Dalia, donned peasant straw hats at noon and went to lunch at the "Concierto" restaurant next door wearing them. Ana wished Dany hadn't gone. She didn't join them, but went home for lunch instead.

The law limited the land to be held by any one owner to 3,319 acres in sugar, rice and grazing land for cattle, and up to 996 acres of farm land for other purposes. The owners were to be paid in twenty-year bonds bearing $4^1/_2$ percent annual interest. Each land worker was to receive 66.4 acres. No foreigners were allowed to buy land. The INRA (National Institute of Agrarian Reform) was created, and Captain Antonio Núñez Jiménez named director.

On the 20th of May, Independence Day, Ana got up late with the prospect of a leisurely day ahead of her. Her mother went to Cristina's to sew on a dress. Her father went to the office to catch up on some work. Dany had mentioned something about the beach club where he was a member. Maybe they would go there. She struck a match in the small beige kitchen to light the gas water heater over the five-gallon mineral-water demijohn in its swinging rack. The burner didn't light. She held the waxed stiff twisted-string match to it. The holes were probably clogged. Suddenly there was an exploding noise and the match flew out of her fingers. A flame flared for an instant and singed her finger. She turned the gas off and went to the bathroom with decals of swans on the tiles. She opened the medicine cabinet, filled with small bottles, and little labels stared at her while the burn stung. Mercurochrome for cuts, iodine for pricks, arnica for bumps, methylene blue for the throat, argyrol nose drops, borated alcohol for earaches, boric water for the eyes, cocoa butter for chapped lips, Iodex for boils, powder starch for chafed thighs, camphor against germs, chlorate tablets for a sore throat, Caffi-aspirin for headaches, bicarbonate for the digestion, Jaccoud potion for faint, paregoric elixir and chamomile for stomach aches, linden flowers for the nerves, cinnamon sticks for menstrual cramps. There were more sophisticated modern medicines, but her parents stuck to the old remedies. Personal prescriptions weren't kept in the bathroom, but in a kitchen cabinet. She finally found the gentian violet toward the back of the top shelf, with the gauze, cotton and adhesive tape. There was a washed handkerchief stuck to the yellow tiles, where her mother had pressed it to dry.

There was a knock on the door. Ana had forgotten it was Wednesday and the laundress would be coming. Holding her purple index aloft, she ran gathering her underwear and house dresses, the sheets and pillowcase from her bed and her towels, and stuffed it all into the pink pillowcase filled with soiled laundry that her mother had left leaning against the yellow hamper.

Azucena walked in, a broad smile on her black face, holding the clean wash, freshly pressed and neatly folded, on her outstretched arms before her ample bosom, a towel across the top, bedsheets underneath, on brown wrapping paper. Ana had wondered how she carried it from home. She didn't know Azucena's last name, but it wouldn't surprise her if it were *Alcorza*[28], although *Tizón*[29] would suit her better. She had once known a Lirio Blanco[30] and there were white people with the last name *Negrín*[31].

"Hello, how are you, miss? It had been months since I'd seen you."

"Fine, Azucena, and you?"

"You see me, getting fatter by the day", she laughed and her gold hoop earrings swung, "although from what, I don't know." Ana took the clean wash from her and gave her the pillowcase filled with dirty laundry, motioning her to sit down. "Everything is more expensive every day. You know they won't even give one a salt *'lagniappe'* when buying sugar at the grocery store any more? We fill ourselves

[28] Sugar icing
[29] Coal
[30] White Lily
[31] Black

with 'up and down'[32]. How's the lady?"
"She's fine. She went to my aunt's today. How's your little son?"
"Lazarito's fine... big. You should see him, miss, a little bandit. I have him in a *crèche* now. He should be starting school next year. I wanted to get a scholarship for him in one of the municipal boarding schools, maybe Valdés Rodríguez."
"How's your husband?"
"Isidro's still the same, with that chest cold. Taking 'Cocillana' for the cough. Miss, take my advice, don't get married. You're not engaged, are you?"
"No, I'm not."
"You don't have a boyfriend, do you?"
"Yes", she laughed, "I do."
Azucena shook her head. "Listen to me, don't get married. You're better off alone ... and you with your good job ... than having a man lying around in the house, I'm telling you. It drives one crazy."
"I'm sure you couldn't live without him."
"No, maybe now I couldn't, but look at my older sister. She never got married, she works with a nice family who give her a roof and treat her like one of the family", Azucena leaned forward conspiratorially and placed her fingertips on Ana's wrist, "and she doesn't have a man to take care of and tell her what to do. She's a devout of the Virgin of Mercies and she doesn't miss a vigil. She's always snuck in like the milk punch." She got up. "Well, miss, I've rested a while and I'm keeping you from your things. And I have to go down to the next block to deliver some clothes." Ana didn't know where she kept these clothes.
"All right, Azucena. Until next week."
"Until next week, miss... if I see you, because you're hardly ever here when I come... and excuse my pestering. Give my regards to the lady."
"Thank you."
In the afternoon would come Felicia, the seamstress Graciela had recommended, who lined their dresses and skirts, sewed backing on belts and facing on hems, took hems up or let them down and took clothes in or let them out.
Ana left the clean clothes on her parents' mahogany bed. On the wardrobe was their wedding picture in an ivory frame. She decided

[32] coffee and milk with bread

to settle for a cold shower, took the bar of *Hiel de Vaca* soap and pulled aside the yellow curtain with white swans. She put on a white dress with red ribbons laced through eyelet lace inserts and fixed her hair in bangs over a red bandeau close to her forehead, in the style of the twenties.

Dany took the car to the Malecón to be washed near the 16th Century Caleta de San Lázaro lookout tower, and that afternoon they drove up First Avenue from near the Community House in exclusive La Puntilla section in east Miramar westward, the iodine-laden sea air whipping their hair. They caught glimpses of the sapphire blue gulf between the social beach clubs that followed one another on the north side in endless succession: unpretentious Casino Deportivo, founded by Alfredo Hornedo Suárez, with over 10,000 members; the Rosita de Hornedo Hotel, which the ex-Senator had named after his first wife and next, the huge Blanquita Theater, which in dubious taste he had named after his second one; Club de Ferreteros; Havana Esso Club, for employees of the oil company; Club de Profesionales; Balneario Universitario, for the students; Copacabana Hotel, Hotel Chateau Miramar, Comodoro Yacht Club, exclusive Miramar Yacht Club; the Cubaneleco Club, for employees of the electric company; Balneario Daughters of Galicia, for members of the Centro Gallego; Club Marino Estabias, of which Ana was a member; Balneario La Concha, a beach house open to the public for a modest admission – across from it was Chori's popular, noisy, rustic nightclub, whose owner painted his name on the curbs; − Círculo Militar y Naval, Havana Yacht Club, Casino Español and, at the end of the rotunda in Marianao, reasonable Club Náutico. About two miles further west, beyond sight, past Flores and Viriato beaches, would be the Biltmore Country Club and a little further south was beautiful, exclusive and luxurious Country Club Park, the "emperor of suburbs".

They passed before the dog race track, and in a restaurant on the rotunda, its walls papered in an ivy pattern, they sat next to each other in a booth. The menu listed rabbit as a specialty of the house, but they ordered hot chocolate.

"When... did you... first go to bed with a woman?"
"Why would you want to know *that*?"
"Just curious."
He took a while to answer. "I was about sixteen, I think."
"Where did you go?"
"Praise! To a place on Marina."

The waiter was taking a long time.

"How did you go?"

"My uncle took me. A summer after school ended. One's father is usually embarrassed", he mused and added lightly, "but there's always a 'bad uncle'."

"Marina's house?"

"Eh? No, he didn't have money for that. It was a place on Marina Street. And how did you know about Marina's house?"

"I don't know. Everybody knows about that. I think my cousin Jorge told me. I don't remember. And with a good girl?"

"That I don't want to talk about."

"I want to know", she said, not at all sure that she wanted.

He hesitated, then drew it slowly out, "The girl I was going with before you, Irma. She was divorced."

"How old was she?"

"Twenty-two, when I was eighteen."

"How long did it last?" The conversation had started objectively enough. But she had given it a perilous turn and now started to feel disturbed.

"A year."

She felt a surge of jealousy. "A year! Were you in love?"

"No."

"But it lasted a year."

"You see? That's why I didn't want to talk about it."

"Maybe you're not in love with me either."

"It's different with you, *mi vida*. The whole time, I was always only waiting for the evening to pass for the end. That was the only purpose. And I *won't* talk about it any more", he said firmly. "I want to *be* with you. All the time." He took her right hand in his left one and looked her in the eyes, and she leaned against his shoulder.

Later they walked through the streets of Reparto Náutico. They had had no idea it was so nice, they commented. They could see gracious living going on through the large picture windows often allowing a view of a living room and a lighted lively dining room beyond.

The tobacco growers in Pinar del Río protested the Agrarian Reform.

An invasion took place in Nicaragua originating from Cuba.

A police Lieutenant reached Key West as a stowaway on the ferry. Two men and two women arrived in Key West on a boat.

On May 23 the government confiscated seven airlines, including

Compañía Cubana de Aviación. Conrado Bécquer was elected Secretary-General of the National Federation of Sugar Workers. News agency *Prensa Latina* was founded on June 9.

Ernesto Guevara married a Cuban revolutionary woman.

The Agrarian Reform went into effect on June 4, and a week later six Cabinet ministers resigned from their posts. On the 12th, Dr. Roberto Agramonte, Minister of Foreign Relations, was succeeded by Dr. Raúl Roa García; Major Humberto Sorí Marín, Minister of Agriculture and author of the originally proposed reform, by Major Pedro Miret Prieto; Minister of the Interior Luis Orlando Rodríguez, by José Naranjo; Dr. Julio Martínez Páez, Minister of Health, by Dr. Serafín Ruiz de Zárate; Minister of Justice Angel Fernández by Alfredo Yabur, and Mrs. Elena Mederos, Minister of Social Welfare, was succeeded by Dr. Raquel Pérez de Miret, that Ministry thus remaining as the one headed by the only female member of the Cabinet.

On June 13 in a television speech, Castro asked if the people wanted elections. The limited studio audience shouted, "No!" That seemed to settle the question.

The Duty Free Zone of Isle of Pines was closed. The Calzada Tunnel, built during the previous regime, from Vedado to 5th Avenue in Miramar, was opened.

On Ana's birthday, a Sunday in June, Dany was later than usual. Thinking that it being a Sunday he would come early, she had been waiting for him for hours since after breakfast. She had been standing on the balcony, she had called him and he wasn't home. She'd thought something had surely happened to him, when he arrived after lunch carrying a big box. Her parents discreetly moved to the balcony.

"Go into your room", he told her, "and don't come out until I call you."

She did as he said and she heard the match be struck, but, when he called her out, she acted surprised over the cake set on the low coffee table, its top covered with *capuchinos*. He was grinning, delighted, and had the twenty-two candles lit and, for a moment before she blew them out, she was conscious of the year difference in their ages. For a mere 29 days they had been the same age. Then he produced a little box wrapped in silver-striped paper from his pocket. For a second before she noticed its flat shape, she thought it might be an engagement ring. She lifted the velvety lid without saying anything. It was a gold locket in the shape of a heart, matte, with six engraved little stars. She threw her arms around his neck and kissed him, and he laughed satisfied and put it around her neck.

"Yesterday we were together all day", he explained then, "and I didn't have time to buy you a present, and today the stores were closed. I had to go all the way to Calzada de Columbia before I found a jewelry store open, and then was very lucky they had it." He was looking at her tenderly and Ana felt her love for him surge inside her. "Do you really like it?"

"I love it." She squeezed his arm. "I'll put our pictures in it. Let's have tiny prints made of the studio ones, *Okay*?"

"What's your flower?"

"The rose."

"If I had known, I'd have liked to send you flowers."

"Which is yours?"

"Lily of the valley. But you wouldn't think of sending me flowers, would you?"

"No", she laughed. She called her parents to show them the locket and share the cake with them, and they accompanied it with lemonade.

Because Dany was out of money, they went to the Manzanares theater on Carlos III, where they were showing three very old American movies, one of them "Black Hand" with Gene Kelly about the Mafia, and they had French burnt peanuts — Ana didn't feel up to a puzzling Russian film. — American films were getting scarcer around town and one had to settle for whichever happened to be playing.

"Sonia believes in astrology", Dany mused that evening, drinking water by the refrigerator. "She reads the horoscope everyday and yesterday, when I mentioned your birthday — Oh!, she wishes you happiness — she said you were the twins, Castor and Pollux, an air sign and I'm the bull, an earth one and, according to the Zodiac, compatible with Virgo."

"And you're going to look for a Virgo girl?"

"Tomorrow."

"Do you know what I thought that night you took me to your neighborhood after the movies about a month and a half ago?... That you were taking me to your home." She waited in suspense.

"Uh? Oh, no!, not without your parents, or your mother. It wouldn't seem right to them."

"Oh!"

"Did you enjoy the day, *mi vida*?"

"It was perfect, *mi cielo.*"

A military transport plane from Manzanillo, Oriente, with 56 men, landed in the Dominican Republic, in Constanza, amidst the mountains, in the province of La Vega, while two ships with 215 men had sailed from Nipe, with the intention of overthrowing the government. Seven prisoners were captured and over 200 men died, among them their leader, a Dominican, on whom a document was found with Fidel's instructions for the invasion. The Dominican government broke relations with Cuba.

Six army men forced the pilot of a passenger plane to fly to Miami.

Pressed at work to take her vacation, Ana did so. And, to make good use of the time buying clothes inexpensively, she and her mother decided to go to Miami for four days. They first had to apply at the Department of Investigations for exit permits. It took them two days to be issued yellow authorization slips valid for 45 days. On Wednesday, Dany took them with Carlos, to the José Martí International Airport in Rancho Boyeros to see them off. They rushed south, eleven miles, past Martí, Alta Habana, Capdevilla, "Los Pinos Nuevos", Río Cristal, Topeka, Fontanar, El Retiro, Vento, Río Verde, the cement-sheltered bus stop benches, the Mazorra insane asylum, the plant to sun-test paint color chips, the agricultural equipment factory, Campeche and Consuelo − small low signs stuck in the ground at intervals showed the names of sunken ships, Andrea Doria, Titanic, Lusitania,Valbanera, Morro Castle. − It was their second visit to Miami.

They stayed at the Colonial Hotel and walked up Flagler Street from Biscayne Boulevard west to the railroad tracks in the oppressive heat, going into every clothing and shoe store on either side, and spent eighty dollars each in two days on dresses, shoes and lingerie. Clothes, although of somewhat lower quality, were so much cheaper in Miami! And they ate at a little restaurant near the hotel which displayed an ad for its *chile con carne.*

In the meantime, the first confiscation of land, 2,470,000 acres, was effected on June 25 in Camagüey, where the largest production was cattle. Four hundred farms with almost 3,680 square miles were confiscated.

They took the other two days to rest in the coolness of the hotel lobby. There they struck up a friendship with a middle-aged Cuban couple who had been living in the hotel for the last three months.

Enrique Carvajal, gray-haired, suntanned and athletic, with broad shoulders and a flat stomach, had been in the contracting business, which had come to a standstill with the revolution, and they were now undecided whether or not to stay in Miami to live. Estela was stylishly thin, with an oval face, short curly jet-black hair and a low husky voice. They had no children. Teresa exchanged Havana addresses with them and they assured her, if they decided to return, they'd look them up.

Ana took a tie clip back to Dany — how if not with his initials — and a cigarette lighter, and for Blanquita, a rubber cat. Teresa bought presents for Carlos, Gustavo, Blanca, Gustavito and the whole family. They went back on Sunday. As the plane approached the airport, the mercury-lit Rancho Boyeros highway resembled from the air a fluorescent green ribbon. Dany was waiting at the airport with Carlos to meet them.

CHAPTER 3

REVELATION OF COMMUNIST TAKE-OVER

> *"Y entonces, entre el asco de toda la mentira,*
> *de toda la cruel befa del mundo, sintió ira,*
> *ira trágica y noble de león provocado*
> *que se ha dormido libre y despierta enjaulado."*[3]
> *("Manelic",* Antonio Médiz Bolio*)*

On June 30, a surprising event took place which alarmed the people. Major Pedro Luis Díaz Lanz, Commander-in-chief of the air force, who had discontinued indoctrination in the corps, suddenly resigned and fled by sailboat to the United States, touching shore at Fort Lauderdale. Díaz Lanz was a great-grandson of José Martí.

Nearly half the office was in an uproar. Rumors were now steadily growing that Fidel was a communist. The majority of the employees sided with Díaz. For a while, Ana was shaken. Díaz's defection couldn't just be shrugged off and disregarded as unimportant. It loomed before them to be considered. She discussed it with Leonardo, and he was weakened.

"Could we be wrong?", he wondered. "Maybe this man is right."

"It scares me", was Ana's only comment. And it literally did. It gave her goose bumps just to think of the horror that its being true would mean.

Major Juan Almeida replaced him in his post. Fidel called Díaz Lanz, "Judas".

But, as human nature is strangely indolent, the effect cooled off and life settled once again to its routine.

Elsa attended a reception where she met Raúl Castro and his wife Vilma Espín, and she had an observation to share with them. "She was wearing a navy blue dress with a white collar, and she had a ring of grime around the inside of its back border", she commented with

---

[3] And then, amid the revulsion of the whole lie,
of the whole cruel mock of the world, he felt wrath,
the tragic and noble wrath of a provoked lion
that has fallen asleep free and wakes up caged.

a grimace.
Rina passed them carrying a cupcake with a little candle still unlit in the center.
"And that?", asked Berta.
"It's for *Mister* Palmer, who's been in Cuba a year today."
Former Ambassador Emilio Núñez Portuondo, Castro's ex-wife Mirta's new father-in-law, tried to get support for an invasion headed by General Eleuterio Pedraza.

☐

The details of the events during the last five years of Batista's rule unfolded for the people's knowledge:
Fidel had been a leader in the FEU during his student days. - Castro departed for Mexico in July of 1955 and acquired Rancho Santa Rosa, in El Chalco, at the foot of the Popocatépetl, to train men for an expedition. - Newark and Philadelphia were the main centers for the purchase of firearms. - Castro's force left Tuxpán, in Veracruz, and put out to sea on November 25, 1956 on the yacht bought with Prío's money. - His loyal companion, Celia Sánchez Manduley, from Niquero, had been waiting for him up in the mountains three days before he landed. - The expedition was planned to attack the city of Manzanillo, in the southwest coast of Oriente. - The guns came in cars on the Key West-Havana ferry. - Cándido de La Torre smuggled arms to the movement by yacht. - Foreign collection branches were set up for the movement in Haiti and Mexico. - When the end neared, the commanding officer of Batista's military forces negotiated as a delaying strategy to allow Batista time to escape.

-

Ana considered hers a good life. She felt such a satisfaction, enjoyed such a sense of permanence before her organized life: Having lived at the same address for three years, held the same job for over a year and a half, and finished business school, having a club membership, old friends and an apartment fully furnished, contributing $6.90 a month to the Stenographers' Security Fund, which would ensure her a pension at retirement age, and having her own desk, radio and bookcase, and clothes, books, records and even a savings account. She felt she could go on the same way indefinitely. She felt a warm pleasantness. She was content.
Dany made her happy, happy just as he was. She didn't want him

changed in any way. She had asked herself that honestly, and she'd concluded she wanted him just as he was; she felt she couldn't ask for more. But Dany belonged to the future, a future reliable and secure, but still far. Her present state would do for a couple of years without the slightest change.

She had never thought of quitting work when she got married; she'd always work. When, at eighteen, she had applied for a job at BANFAIC, she had studied the retirement plan and commented enthusiastically, "If I work twenty-five years, I can retire at forty-three. Still a chick!"

"*'A chick'*, listen to her!", her brother had reacted, making her once more feel like a fool.

They had come a long way in the last four years, after her father had expanded his accounting office on Villegas Street, Gustavo had gone to work with him and they had hired the new clerk, Alfonso. A long way from her childhood on 24th Street near La Chorrera tower at the river mouth and the iron bridge, the long house with the high ceiling, the narrow doors, the windows down to the floor with their wrought iron grilles, and no water heater; the Sunday treats to the "Ambar" theater, which delivered announcements of its coming attractions around the neighborhood, and where they turned the lights on between shows, and between features they ran fixed ads of the neighborhood schools, drugstores and drycleaners, Guiness stout and a commercial art school, and the cry often rose, "Speaker!"; the evening walks to the Chinamen's ice cream shop for chocolate frozen custard, the strolls around the park on 15th and 16th Streets, the summer afternoons at La Concha bath house; the excursions to La Polar Gardens in Puentes Grandes, with its whirligig and its slide; church on Sundays, when her father had been an underpaid bookkeeper at the art-object import shop feeding four mouths. It hadn't been a bad childhood – her memories were filled with a love that the elapsed time had helped build up, – but it had been a poor childhood; skimping and doing without had become a part of their days and poverty a fact to be accepted in their lives, as it was in that of most of those around them. She had become used to it and it had never made her feel unhappy because the others were no better off than they. They had all learned to make the best of it. And they had always had the essentials: food, clothes from "Ultra", medicines, school supplies at the start of the year from "Cervantes", books from "Minerva". Any extras went for special treats: the radio station on Sunday evenings, roast chicken at "El Salón" restaurant on Galiano Street on the children's birthdays, the *Santos y Artigas* circus, new Rita Hayworth movies at the "Astral", Carnival on Ice, the Teatro Nacional when Mexican *charro* Jorge Negrete was in Havana. And gradually, things had changed. First, when Gustavo had graduated, their father had ventured into his own office. Four years later, he had taken Gustavo, then twenty-two, to work with him. Then Ana had graduated and Gustavo had been able to get married. She had started working and contributing from her salary to the household, they had moved from the old, long house to this new, square apartment and they had bought new furniture, for which they had been paying $25. a month until only five months before. And, when Gustavito was born, Carlos had made her brother a partner, proudly having "**and Son**" added to his name painted in black letters on the glass door of his office. Ana wanted to enjoy it.

Agriculture was the basis of the Cuban economy. Farms specialized in sugar, tobacco, cattle or coffee. There were 161 sugar mills in the country. *Central* "Jaronú" in Esmeralda was the largest and most modern sugar mill in the world. Tobacco was the country's second largest export crop. Cuba also exported coffee, pineapples and winter vegetables. Since 1940, the production of coffee, fruits, vegetables and rice had been increasing.

Cuba had a big cattle industry. In 1958, it had over 5,700,000 head of cattle. There were many dairies, and butter and cheese plants. All the workers ate meat. The average annual consumption was 144 pounds per person. First-class beef was 50 cents a pound. The country had many poultry farms.

The per capita income had been rising at an average rate of 2.03 percent annually since 1950. The labor laws were among the most advanced in the world, with benefits not found even in the United States. The labor code gave Cuban workers an eight-hour work day and a month's paid vacation. Insurance was provided, as well as three months' maternity leave.

By 1958, industry employed half a million Cubans in its more than 38,300 industrial centers. Half a million sugar workers were employed during the six-month cane harvest season, January through June. The Federation of Sugar Workers was the most powerful union. The other strongest two were the Transport Workers and Tobacco Workers Federations. Mujal was the secretary-general of the

CTC under Batista.

There was no yellow fever, typhus, malaria or scarlet fever on the island.

The National Bank of Cuba was established in December of 1948 under Prío's government and the peso became legal tender. The Cuban peso was one of the strongest world currencies, quoted at par with the American dollar. The net national income had been steadily increasing at an average rate of 3.89 percent annually since 1950.

There were 32 radio stations and six television channels, one in color.

There had never been any talk of discrimination in Cuba. The island was fairly free of prejudice, except on an economic basis. Cubans chose their friends in their economic stratum. There were 35,000 Chinese in Cuba, whose ancestors had started arriving 112 years before, mainly from Canton. Three Chinese newspapers circulated, the "*Hoy Men Kong Po*", republican; the "*Wan Man Yat Po*", nationalist, and the "*Wah Man Sion Po*", commercial, all founded over two decades before. There were some 12,000 Jews spread throughout the country, mostly Sephardim arrived just before World War I, and five synagogues functioned in Havana. Two local English-language newspapers were "The Havana Post", 59 years old, and the "Times of Havana".

Prío established the BANFAIC, with Dr. Justo Carrillo as president. Under Batista flourished the BANDES (Economic and Social Development Bank), the BANCEC (Cuban Bank of Foreign Trade) and the Cuban National Finance Corporation.

The First Cuban Hydroelectric Central built a dam in the Hanabanilla River. Running from the city of Pinar del Río to La Fe, in Guane, is the section of the Panamerican Highway corresponding to Cuba.

Of the sugar mills, 73.3% were Cuban-owned and thirty-three were American. The Moa Bay Mining Company and the Nicaro Nickel plant in the north of Oriente were the biggest mining companies on the island.

The student body of the University of Havana had been increasing at an average rate of 2.53 percent annually since Castro's student days in 1945. The Palace of Fine Arts was built.

There were 42 hotels in Havana alone. The modern Habana Hilton was built in 1958.

•

Revelation of Communist Take-over

Ana pored over travelogues about Brazil and dreamed of strolling on the sand of Copacabana Beach and climbing up to the Corcovado peak to admire the statue of Christ the Redeemer towering over Guanabara Bay, taking pictures of the Sugar Loaf mountain and even going up to the *"favelas"* on the hills near Rio. She had heard on a television documentary that a code required all the buildings facing the Rio de Janeiro waterfront to be at least six stories high, to keep harmony. She also wished to walk on the wooden bridge jutting out daringly over the Iguassu Falls. And she wanted to walk up the hills, ride a streetcar and visit Chinatown in San Francisco. But, so far, she had only made it as far as Miami twice in the last three years. And that seemed as far as she could ever afford to go.

She didn't know how to wait. She wanted little in life, but what little she wanted, she wanted right away. She didn't know how to let things come as they might. Maybe they could go to one of those places on their honeymoon, if Dany's parents came to look upon their wedding with acceptance and the two sets of parents could pitch in for a honeymoon as their wedding present.

On the adverse hand, the other side of the coin showed that 22.1 percent of the population in Cuba in 1953 was illiterate. About one-fourth of the labor force was unemployed, the main reason for this being the sugar fluctuation. The "dead season" lasted six months, from July to December.

There were districts where *"guajiros"* lived in dire poverty, as the Sierra Maestra, which had 50,000 inhabitants. Two-thirds of the peasants' *"bohios"*[(33)] were built with walls of royal palm trunk boards, roofs thatched with dry palm fronds, tamped dirt floors and no toilet. Ninety percent had only kerosene lamps and only 3 percent had piped water.

As late as 1946, 8% of the landowners held over 71% of the land. Small landholders owned 39% of the farms of up to 2.47 acres, but only 3% of the cultivable land. Over one-third of the crop land was owned by 900 corporations. The entire Isle of Pines to the south, measuring 1,187 square miles, was owned by only four landlords.

Liborio Pérez, the graphic representation of the Cuban people, created in 1908 (with Canarian name and features, starched *guayabe-*

[(33)] huts

ra derived from the Andalusian *chaquetilla*, fan-palm frond hat with tri-color cockade, white drill pants and machete at the waist), was the subject of a sad old joke as to how he resembled a royal palm: "They both have to keep very straight, they feed the pigs, have their leaves plucked, and in the end, are struck by lightning."

•

When Ana got home from work Tuesday afternoon, she found her father and brother at the table going over the house plans Gustavo had drawn for the lot that Carlos had bought two years before in the Santa Catalina subdivision, among new peak-roofed houses, where the Finca Ciénaga had once been. Gustavo only had the barest notion of drafting and it was difficult for him to work out all the details, but he was trying painstakingly to please their father, drawing and re-drawing the plan once and again to follow all the changes Carlos wanted to work into the 57-foot wide lot. They all new that it would still be a couple of years before they could afford to build, but their father said, "I want to have everything exactly the way I want it on paper, before I take the plans to an architect to have the blueprint made." And had looked at the plan − *everybody* had. − She pitied her mother, with her one-day-a-week girl and that house with hallway, steps and railings, and the sunken living room, the big kitchen, the porch and extra half-bath, and even a fireplace. But her mother seemed delighted with it all, even making suggestions for still more things to be built in, like that glass swinging cafe door and the bay window with a window seat. She probably hadn't stopped to think about the housework yet. And three doors?,... with her fear of burglars! She wanted it named *"Villa Diamela"* and her father, *"San Joaquín"*. Ana thought naming houses was old-fashioned and in any case, *"Arroyo Mordazo"* would be more appropriate, but the only thing about which she really cared was that it was fairly close to the city. Santa Catalina Avenue and Rancho Boyeros highway both had bus routes. And Dany could go down Calzada de Puentes Grandes. Or, if they delayed the construction three years, maybe she wouldn't even be living with them any longer.

Deeds to the 66.4 acres of land granted to the farmers by INRA − nearly half in Oriente − were received by 21,425 peasants, which represented less than 15 percent of the more than 150,000 tenant farmers. The rest went into cooperatives or "people's farms".

The big landowners affected by the Reform were said to have had their *"siquitrilla"* (a cock's breastbone) broken, and were nicknamed

Revelation of Communist Take-over

"siquitrillados". The Reform stated nothing about machinery and cattle, but they also were appropriated. There were no receipts. No bonds were seen.

Four members of the air force made a pilot fly to Miami, where they asked for asylum.

President Urrutia spoke out in a television interview, making a statement to the United Nations against communism in Cuba. He criticized the infiltration and the encroachment in the government, and offered to resign. *"Revolución"* newspaper published a headline, "Fidel Resigns." It came as a surprise. Castro ignored Urrutia's offer to resign; he himself resigned as Prime Minister. The radio and the press announced that he would speak on television. Everybody was expectant. Friday evening, July 17 at 8:00, Castro appeared on television, addressed the people, accused Urrutia of bordering on treason and planning a ruse, and denied being a communist. "I am not a communist", he said. "Our revolution is not red, but olive green, the color of the rebel army's uniform." While Fidel spoke, a message arrived at the studio from Urrutia stating that he would definitely not resign and he wanted to make a public declaration. Castro said he wanted all the television cameras on himself while he talked and Urrutia could make his statements after he were finished. That seemed difficult, considering that Fidel usually talked until the small hours of the morning. Castro repeated he was resigning as Prime Minister, and talked for four hours. After a short while, another message arrived from Urrutia, which moderator Nicolás Bravo announced. He had resigned as President even before Fidel had finished his appearance. They felt disappointed. What could have happened in that time?

Méndez wondered, "Why wouldn't he let him talk?"

Ana liked and respected Urrutia, and she felt doubtful about accusations against him. She was so upset, she had started unconsciously to spring up and down on the seat cushion. "Why did he do that?", she kept asking excitedly, "why did he do that?"

"Calm down", her mother impelled her. "You're going to get sick!"

Dany was in classes.

"If he didn't approve of him", commented Carlos, "why did he appoint him President?"

The act closed around midnight with Fidel and the audience singing the National Anthem and the 26th of July March.

The government definitely leaned to the left. Could they really be actual communists?

Many speculations later rose as to what had happened. It would be a long time before the truth were known. The one thing which was soon certain was that the President and his wife had fled the Palàce by a side door around 2:30 in the morning. They escaped to his brother-in-law's *"finca"*, later to go into an embassy. Dr. Osvaldo Dorticós Torrado, the Minister of Revolutionary Laws, was selected to replace the President, even as Castro was still speaking on television. Dorticós decided not to live in the Presidential Palace. His wife, a teacher, would continue teaching.

The 26th of July March was played as often as the Cuban National Anthem. At the office, Raquel parodied it, "Forward, Cubans!, we come to implant communism..."

∎

Slowly, too late for them, fragments of events and information started to seep through to the Cuban people, which allowed them to piece together Fidel's background and the pattern of events which had led to the revolution and the present state of affairs, and to anticipate what was to come:

Fidel Alejandro Castro Ruz was one of seven illegitimate children of Angel Castro y Argiz, a Galician sugar planter who turned drunkard, and his cook, Lina Ruz González, raised in the mountains near Birán, in Mayarí ... His nickname at the University was "ball of grime" ... He was a member of Rolando Masferrer's gang ... He had a police record as a terrorist. He was associated with the UIR (Revolutionary Insurrectional Union), a terrorist organization, in 1947 ... In the late summer of 1947 Fidel joined recruits training on Confites Key, north of Camagüey, for Masferrer's anti-Trujillo expedition to invade the Dominican Republic ... He escaped between the train wagons in the *Ferrocarriles Consolidados* Antilla station in Oriente ... He declared in the University that he was a leftist ... He participated in the *"Bogotazo"*, the communist-supported uprising on April 9, 1948, during the 9th Inter-American Conference of the OAS in Bogotá. The purpose was to shatter the conference and topple the government. On April 3 Castro and Rafael del Pino showered leaflets with anti-American revolutionary propaganda at the Colón Theater of Bogotá, detectives took them, they didn't have visas and they had a photograph of Jorge Eliécer Gaitán, the leader of the Liberal party. A telegram was found on them announcing the arrival of a Russian.

Revelation of Communist Take-over 105

Fidel obtained a rifle from the Colombian police. Gaitán was assassinated, according to Scotland Yard, by Juan Roa Sierra. They connected Castro, Del Pino and Enrique Ovares Herrera with his murder. Castro and Del Pino were seen with Roa Sierra an hour and a half before the murder. They were in the immediate vicinity at the time of the crime ... President Grau's propagandists said that Fidel had murdered a Catholic nun from the back and five priests from a Packard belonging to the Cuban Consulate in Bogotá. A folding ID card was found in their room at the Claridge Hotel, identifying them as agents of the Communist Third Front. Back in Cuba, Castro bragged he had killed three priests ... Fidel participated in the attempted murder of high school student Leonel Gómez on Ronda Street in August 1946, and was arrested and accused of being connected with two political murders, one that of University students, Manolo Castro Campos, ex-president of FEU, and Carlos Puchol on San Rafael and Consulado Streets in February 1948, and the other that of guard Sergeant Oscar Fernández Cabral in July 1948, machine-gunned on Infanta Street at night ... Dr. Rafael Díaz-Balart claimed Fidel had killed the president of the Havana FEU ... Raúl was in Prague, Moscow and Red China in 1953 ... The attack on Fort Moncada was scheduled by communist Blas Roca, whose real name is Francisco Calderío ... They murdered bed-ridden patients at Saturnino Lora Hospital. A book by Lenin was found on Abel Santamaría ... Fidel abandoned his men at Moncada, running away when they attacked, and Boris Santa Coloma covered him while he fled for his life ... Castro's self-defense allegation ended with the very same words, "History will absolve me", as a speech delivered by Hitler under identical circumstances ... In March of 1955 Fidel lived in the same building in Mexico as communist Lázaro Peña ... One-eyed Spanish Colonel Alberto Bayo, who had located Rancho Santa Rosa, in El Chalco, for a training camp and trained the rebels in Mexico, was an expert in guerrilla warfare and a pilot of the military aviation school, had served in the Spanish Army, became a member of the Communist Party during the Civil War and lost an eye fighting General Franco ... Argentinean physician Dr. Ernesto "Che" Guevara was a professional communist agent, had been expatriated from Argentina, organized an espionage cell in Guatemala in 1955 and was director of its secret police. He had left his Peruvian wife ... Fidel had a daughter named Alina with Natalia Revuelta, the wife of a cardiologist ... Rafael del Pino left Santa Rosa when El Che arrived ... Castro was in prison in Mexico for a month in 1956 ... Teresa Casuso, the widow of communist Pablo de la Torriente, visited Fidel in jail in Mexico ... A distant maternal relative of Ana's was stabbed in Mexico in October of 1956 under instructions from Fidel ... The survivors of the "Granma" had been 22, not twelve as Carlos Manuel de Céspedes' men in 1868 ... Castro used the Chinese communist strategy in the Sierra ... The Times' Herbert Matthews had communist sympathies, was a veteran in choosing sides with communist-dominated movements, had denied Lenin were gravitating to the extreme left, had been partisan to the Loyalists in the Spanish Civil War, in the Far Eastern crisis he had been pro-Japanese, but then he defended Mao Tse-tung as a "generous agrarian reformer" ... The demonstration before Ambassador Smith in July of 1957 was staged by the "Martian Women" under Dr. Martha Frayde Barraqué wearing black, although most of them were not even mothers ... General Eulogio Cantillo had luxuries flown in for them by air force helicopter ... A man named Armando Sánchez was shot by a firing squad in the Sierra, accused by Vilma Espín of attempted rape ... Rebel army captain Francisco Rodríguez Tamayo declared to the *Diario de New York* that Fidel had kept $4,500,000. from the money collected by the underground, not accounting for that sum ... Rebels Eduardo Valdivia and Ramiro Sánchez stated to the SIM that a Russian submarine landed arms at La Chiva, Nipe Bay in Antilla, on the north coast of Oriente for Raúl, Agapito Venero disembarked from it and was executed. Pedro Luis Díaz Lanz stated before a U.S. Senate Sub-Committee on July 14 that a Russian submarine close to the north shore of Oriente delivered supplies to Raúl in January, 1958 ... William Alexander Morgan had been dishonorably discharged from the American Army and had communist sympathies ... Herman Marks, the security chief at La Cabaña, was an ex-convict ... The armored train was sold to the rebels for $600,000. ... Colombian José Antenor, who had shot SIM Lieutenant Móntez, simply disappeared ... Major Díaz Lanz said Castro had remarked, "I'm going to introduce in Cuba a system like that the Russians have" ... After Cuba, they planned to attack Trujillo in the Dominican Republic and the Somozas of Nicaragua ... The invasions to Panamá and Nicaragua were made from Cuba and financed by Guevara ... Dr. Osvaldo Dorticós was a former member of the Cuban Communist Party and had been secretary to leader Juan Marinello for over ten years.

•••

The Cocuyé Carnival of Oriente came to Havana before moving

on to Santiago for its culmination which started on St. Cristina's Day, and they went to Infanta Street to watch the *"comparsa"* lines, made up mostly of colored people, do the conga on the wide street. There were few costumes except for a few hooded masks and hardly any paper lanterns. Gone was the harmonious uniformity of old. Also missing were the streamers and confetti bits. The shuffle of hundreds of shoe soles "trampling" against the pavement produced an almost hallucinating rhythm. They sang and chanted something that to Ana, amid the turmoil, sounded absurdly like, "If you don't dance, I kill you." She asked Dany, "What are they singing?", and he prompted her in a low voice, "Hush!" Apparently that was *not* what they were singing. A couple of prosaic dancers carried enameled chamber pots full of beer with a sausage bobbing in it. There were no floats.

"I'd love to go to Ariguanabo Lake", said Ana that evening sipping cognac and ginger ale at the comparatively quiet "Flamingo", leaning against the wall under the picture of the Mediterranean fishing village. She'd settle for it in place of Brazil.

"What's there?", Dany was curious. He stirred his Canadian whiskey with soda.

"It's the biggest lake in Cuba."

"Yes, but with that reasoning, we would just as well go to the Cauto River."

"It must be beautiful."

"Probably, but there's nothing to do there. There may not even be any hotels."

"How do you know? The Textilera is there."

"We wouldn't go visit a textile mill on our honeymoon."

"My grandparents lived in Bauta."

"The house probably doesn't exist any more. You wouldn't find it."

"Maybe not... The 'Cacahual' is nearby, and Baracoa beach."

"We would spend our time driving around." He nibbled a salty deep-fried minute smelt. "And what *is* there? I've never known of anybody who went to Ariguanabo Lake for a honeymoon."

"I don't know what's there, but I don't know either that there isn't anything."

He shook his head, laughing. "Your logic is hopeless."

They went to see "Anna Lucasta" with Eartha Kitt, Sammy Davis, Jr. and an all-black cast, with Spanish subtitles. But something kept harping at the back of their minds throughout the film, as if there were something they were trying to recall and it eluded them.

The lower classes, who had paid little attention to the revolution, turned into its most devout followers.

Countrymen were encouraged to come to Havana for the celebration of the 26th of July. The slogans were "Open your door to a countryman" and "In each Havana home a countryman". The day was declared "National Rebellion Day". Half a million peasants in their *guayaberas* with straw hats and machetes at the waist rained on the capital from all over the countryside, in trucks, buses and trains provided by the government for the "rural concentration", in commemoration of the sixth anniversary of the Moncada attack and the first one celebrated under the new rule.

Ana's name day, Saint Anne's, coincided with the revolutionary festivity. She was hesitant to celebrate it, for fear that it be taken for a sign of adherence. Since it was also Grandmothers' Day, in the Spanish tradition that honored Our Lady's Sainted Mother according to the Protoevangelium of St. James, while they were having lunch a bouquet of yellow gladiola was delivered in the name of Gustavo's children for their grandmother.

The rebel army paraded before the Capitol. Those who had not come down from any hill or had a mane on the 1st of January let it grow. The supporters of the government displayed large cardboard posters along the Malecón, announcing "The color of our revolution is not red, but olive green" and "Our revolution is green like the palms". A few outspoken skeptics commented cynically, "It's like a watermelon, green on the outside, red in the inside". A bombing drill was carried out off-shore.

Shortly after 3:00, having had lunch at her parents', Gustavo and Blanca arrived with the children, bearing gifts for Teresa, and for Ana an unbleached natural linen dress embroidered in cocoa.

"I picked it", said her sister-in-law.

"It's beautiful."

"I asked Teresa your size – eleven, right? – but, if it doesn't fit, let me know and I'll exchange it. I bought it at La Rampa Arcade."

A helicopter flew overhead. Fidel's voice blared from their deaf upstairs neighbor's television set over their own conversation, and from radios and television sets in all the public places and the better part of the homes, as he talked from the podium at the now named Revolution Plaza before a fanatic crowd. And Aguirre, downstairs, was heard saying over his wife's voice, "Let me hear the Horse." His followers had taken to calling him so alluding to the Trojan Horse. The countrymen crossed machetes producing a strange, unpleasant sound. He delivered a four-hour speech, in which he withdrew his resignation and resumed his position as Premier. His ploy had worked.

Carlos and Gustavo played chess. Dany arrived at 7:30 with a bottle of "*Crêpe de Chine*" perfume, a sticker from "La Elegante" on the package, and Ana thought she detected a little disappointment at his gift not being her first one.

Her aunt Esperanza arrived unexpectedly and her cousin Norma with Víctor, his fiancé. And then Rosa Izquierdo, with a tall, thin, blond boy, who had a conceited air and an arrogant smile. There were hugs and kisses, and Rosa and her friend were introduced.

And by 8:30 a party had indeed formed. So Ana displayed her presents arranged, as was customary, on her bed — the perfume, the dress, an ostrich-grain leather handbag from her parents, necklace, wallet, stockings — for the inspection of wandering curious visitors.

Blanca put the children to bed, each wedged between two pillows, on her parents-in-law's double bed, and Esperanza's voice came from the bedroom,

"... *en busca de los civiles, les, civi-... les, les, civiles, les,
que en su casa hay un ladrón,
que en su casa hay un ladrón...*"[(95)]

An unobtrusive trip by Carlos to the corner grocery store provided them with "Pedro Domecq" cognac, "*Matusalén*" rum, Coca-Cola and seltzer water. Teresa prepared finger sandwiches of ham and cream cheese spread. The women took the seats and the men stood about.

In the self-conscious lull before the conversation got underway, came the worn inane questions. To Ana, "When do we eat those sweets?", surprisingly from Norma, twenty, who had been seeing Víctor for six months before he ever mentioned marriage, perhaps getting even with the world for the times she herself had heard the question. Dany, behind Ana, smiled noncommittally, but rested a possessive hand on the back of her chair.

To Norma, "Have you set the date yet?", from Blanca, usually so prudent, perhaps to rescue her sister-in-law. Víctor winced and coughed.

To Blanca, "When is the next one coming?", from Esperanza, who herself had an only daughter. Ana saw her brother, leaning against the refrigerator, stiffen, while Blanca smiled with tolerance at the impertinence.

There was no one present to whom the other two usual questions could be directed, "Have you placed your order with Paris yet?" and "When are you going to stop the factory?"

Teresa sprang to the rescue, "Gustavo, please mix some drinks. You know, for me a lot of Coca-Cola and very little rum."

Blanca seized the tray of sandwiches and passed it around. Carlos offered plantain chips.

"I looked up your name, Anita", said Esperanza, "and it's of Hebrew origin and means 'Grace'. Did you know it?" She had told her the same thing last year.

"No", Ana lied politely.

"They were going to name you Marciana, the saint of your birthday", she said to include Dany.

Ana turned to him and finished, "But they waited six weeks to baptize me, the christening fell on Saint Anne's Day, and they thought that was a better name."

"Saved", said Dany, and Rosa laughed.

Esperanza addressed Dany, "Do you know what yours means?"

"No, but I think he was a Yugoslavian prince of the Eighteenth Century."

There was a flurry of movement, as the aunt, familiar with their bookcase, dashed to get a dictionary. A quick consultation disclosed, "It's a Serbo-Croatian variant and means 'God is my judge'."

"Half a million countrymen were coming today", commented Víctor.

"Like cattle", was Méndez's opinion.

"Poor men!", expressed Norma.

"But they get to see the city", argued the blond boy.

Dany took charge of the record player and selected *boleros, danzones, guarachas,* one *"paso-doble".*

Víctor asked Norma to dance, Ana and Dany followed, then Rosa and the blond, and soon the party picked up and there were four couples whirling around in the cramped space. It seemed, after all, that they were celebrating the 26th of July.

It was hot and, with the exercise in the crowded apartment and the liquor, the dog days' night became unbearable, and during the

Revelation of Communist Take-over

"melopeya"[34] of the *danzón* the dancers spilled out to the tiny balcony. The latecomers stood around the door, ice-filled glasses in hand, the women fanning themselves with makeshift fans and lifting their hair from their napes, the men wiping the perspiration from their foreheads with their handkerchiefs, puffing their cheeks, letting the air slowly out and pulling their shirt collars away from their necks. By 10:30, they started to file out. First Esperanza, followed by Rosa and her vain companion, soon Norma and Víctor, and later Blanca and Gustavo, each carrying down a sleepy bundle. Dany stayed on like a member of the household. He put the records away, Carlos emptied the ashtrays, Ana rounded up the glasses, Teresa made coffee for them, and the conversation took on a comfortable familiarity. It was after 11:30 when Dany left.

Rafael del Pino Siero, who had been living in Florida, flew a propaganda incursion over Havana and tried to land on the Vía Blanca near Guanabo beach, to the east, to pick up two men. He was shot down, wounded and captured by Captain Efigenio Ameijeiras. The two passengers escaped by car to Matanzas.

At the office Carmen Zayas cried silently at her typewriter, while her tears spilled on the keyboard and an occasional drop fell on an order. Raquel Weiss, who sat closest to her, was annoyed. Rosa Izquierdo explained that her boyfriend had broken up with her.

Carmen was 23, wore her black hair short, talked fast and didn't smile often, but occasionally laughed hard and loud. She was self-assured and conceited about that self-assurance, confident about her job, her sufficiency and her intelligence, and yet, when it came to men, she was as insecure as it was possible to be, clinging to them like a vine. Ana had heard her on the phone at lunch time, demanding, all her poise and sufficiency gone, her face stark, starved for their love, even when she herself wasn't even in love with them (there had been another one, a glassware representative, about a year and a half before), prompt to tears, without a shred of dignity or pride. It was an embarrassing picture to watch.

In the lunchroom Ana found herself taken into Carmen's confidence. Still tearful, she told her, "Miguel and I went to see a woman *'notario'* on Street Seventeen – I thought he didn't know her – and, after she'd talked to us professionally, she asks him, 'Have you seen Migdalia lately?' – that's a woman doctor neighbor of his, old enough

[34] a non-danceable interlude

to be his mother, with a son *his* age. I guess she'd recommended her to him — and he answers, 'I went to see her Sunday' — Sunday I'd called him home early and he was still sleeping and when I called again, he'd gone out, and he told me later he'd gone to borrow a history book from a teacher, — and the woman says, 'She told me the girl had been in Varadero — *'the girl'*!, as if I weren't there — and you'd had a quarrel.' — We'd had a quarrel the end of April. — I was so annoyed that he hadn't told me he knew the woman, so hurt that he'd lied to me about going to see the doctor, so humiliated that he'd discussed me with her, so embarrassed that he'd told her about our quarrel, that I cringed. When we walked out of her office — I was upset, — he told me, 'I can't talk to you about another woman, because you turn wild!' Now I was appalled. I protested, 'That's not true!'," Carmen wailed. — "Ana, when we'd been dating about two months, he went out with a woman he picked up at the 'Aloy' bar after work in a co-worker's car and he gave him away in front of me, something about burning rubber,... on purpose I suspect. He admitted he had and, when I asked him why he'd lied, he told me he knew I'd be hurt to know he'd skipped classes to go out with her and he'd never done it to see me. And I just asked him not to lie to me again and never mentioned it again. — I started crying. And he yelled at me, 'Last time I see you!'" Now she started crying anew. She looked so ugly! "I think he wanted to break up with me... The last three months, ever since we had that fight, he'd been acting different." She sobbed.

Ana was sympathetic. They'd been dating for over nine months. Carmen seemed crushed. Ana wondered if he were having an affair with the doctor, and she'd broken them up. "You'll make up", she cheered Carmen.

"No... The day we broke up he went to the Carnival on Infanta Street. You should see how cold he's acted." She sniffled.

"Have you seen him again?"

"No, but he calls me up at lunch time." Miguel worked in a tire factory.

"From Loma de Tierra? Ah, then he cares!"

Rosa joined them.

"But he hasn't talked about seeing me again", complained Carmen.

"He'll get over it, you'll see. He bothers to call you almost every day..."

Rosa put in, "You'll get over him in fifteen days."

Nelia, Palacios' secretary, approached the table.

"Well, I know time heals," Carmen reasoned, "but..."

"But it's those first fifteen days that worry you", interrupted Rosa, nodding in understanding.

Carmen half-smiled through her sobs. Nelia now told her, "I know how you feel. If Emilio broke up with me now, I'd die. Look, make a novena to Saint Anthony. Do it with faith and you'll see he'll help you. When Emilio and I broke up, Berta told me about it. Every Thursday for nine weeks I went to church to pray. Berta used to go with me. I didn't think we'd go back together. And after the ninth week, he called me − I couldn't believe it − and we made up."

Carmen looked up with a spark of hope in her eyes. "Oh!, but, if it doesn't work, I'll..."

Rosa walked away.

"Ah, no!", Nelia interrupted her, "you can't do it thinking that, if it doesn't work, you'll have wasted that time."

Virginia came up to them.

"No, no", Carmen expressed, "I mean, if I let myself hope and it doesn't turn out, I'll feel worse."

"Well, you have to do it with faith."

The three listened to Nelia a little in awe. Here was somebody who'd received a miracle. The back of Nelia's skirt was often rumpled and she gave Ana the impression when she walked of being on her feet only briefly, just on her way to another seat quickly to sit down again.

Virginia waited for Nelia to leave to give Carmen, in a confidential tone, a different bit of advice, "Listen, if you have to beg him to come back to you, don't be too proud to do it."

"But to humiliate myself that way...", objected Carmen.

"Nobody's going to know it but you two. That's going to stay between you and him. And do it while he still misses you, before he gets used to not seeing you and creates an atmosphere for himself."

Ana patted her arm, leaving her to Virginia, and walked out of the lunchroom.

On August 10, Fidel's residence in Cojímar was the target of shooting. There was firing over Havana the night of the 11th.

Fidel turned thirty-three on August 13. Rina, always bold in her opinions, told them, "They say Fidel is just like Jesus Christ: 'His entry in Havana was like Christ's in Jerusalem, he came down from the mountain, he wears a beard, twelve disciples follow him and he's thirty-three like Jesus', so now I'm waiting for him to be crucified." "You're horrible!", Ana reproved her, only partly thinking her horrible. In fact, the only thing that actually made her uneasy was the irreverent reference to Christ's crucifixion.

Early in August a plot was discovered in which José Eleuterio Pedraza was involved, to overthrow Castro with the support of *"Chapita"*[35], nickname that the medals General Trujillo wore had earned him. The Dominican Republic had contacted Major Eloy Gutiérrez Menoyo, commander of the Second Front of Escambray and Major William Morgan, second in command, to lead the movement against Fidel. Gutiérrez and Morgan played along for a while and then terminated the move. An arms-laden plane was captured in Trinidad, Las Villas. Two invaders were killed, one wounded and the other seven arrested, including former Havana mayor's son, Luis Pozo. He was presented by Castro on television on the 14th with three other prisoners, and all were the object of derision. The camera showed Morgan, sitting on the floor of the studio, rocking with laughter.

Camp Columbia in Marianao was turned into a "scholastic city".

A 31-man invasion from Cuba landed in Les Irois in Sud department in Haiti. Over twenty were killed by the army and the rest surrendered. During the spring and summer of 1959 there had been attempted invasions of Panamá, Nicaragua, the Dominican Republic and Haiti.

The gurgled appeal "Save water" started, replacing commercials of products on television.

A conspiratorial meeting was discovered on Gloria Street and six participants taken to prison, one of whom escaped. Men were arrested in Las Villas and Pinar del Río.

A plane dropped eleven rifles in Consolación del Sur, in Pinar del Río, which were seized by the authorities. In Aguacate, the army picked up weapons thrown from a plane in five parachutes.

Two men and a girl forced the captain of a Cubana plane to fly to Miami, where they asked for asylum.

The AJAR (Juvenile Association of Aid to the Revolution) was created by four women.

Miguel gradually stopped calling Carmen at lunch time, and she was devastated. Ana went with her and Rosa once to have lunch sit-

[35] 'little bottle cap'

ting on the low Malecón wall facing the sparkling blue sea. Painting over twelve miles of the curb on the Malecón sidewalk had been the first job of the just created OTV (Volunteer Workers' Organization), which was accomplished in five hours.

"Tuesday the thirteenth, 'neither get married nor take a trip'," announced Leonardo as he entered the office with Nelia.

"'Nor stray away from your home'," finished Guillén, arriving with Rina.

"Are you going to Ramiro's wedding?", asked Ana. The men went on their way.

"That's not on Tuesday, or the thirteenth", inserted Elsa.

"Yes, I'm going to have my shoes covered in the same fabric of the dress", said Nelia, "a print..."

"I had them covered at the shoe store in Guanabacoa", said Rina, proceeding inside. Her clothes always fit perfectly.

The telephone rang. "Good afternoon, Wayne Motors", Elsa answered.

When Ana passed before the Sales Department with Nelia, Rina was talking with Dany at the entrance.

"If you saw her, Danilo, his girl friend treats him with what her mother calls 'left hand', to get her will without his noticing that she's having her way..."

"Yes, I know that because of my sister, but I call it 'cunning'. I couldn't stand a woman like that." He winked at Ana and she smiled. She'd call it 'deceit', she thought.

Gloria was arranging invoices in numerical order. "I like doing this", she commented to her as Ana passed her desk, "because I don't have to concentrate and I can think of something else."

Four men took a yacht and escaped to Key West.

A plane dropped two bombs on the "Niágara" sugar mill, in Consolación del Sur.

The Ministry of the Revolutionary Armed Forces was created on October 16 and Raúl Castro was named Minister. Major Augusto Martínez Sánchez, former Minister of Defense, was named Minister of Labor to succeed moderate Manuel Fernández García, who dropped out of sight.

A rebel soldier committed suicide. Another did so in Santiago de Cuba. As did a military man in Camagüey. So did a rebel military man in his girlfriend's house. And a rebel captain. An army lieutenant hanged himself in the jail in Baracoa, Oriente. A former major commited suicide in his home. A Navy Colonel jumped off a rampart of La Cabaña Fortress. The captain commanding the military post in Florida, Camagüey province, fired a bullet into his head. Such suicides added up to seventeen. It made one realize that they were pushed by terror to escape the wrath that way. A man committed suicide in Río Blanco, Las Villas. As did a landholder in the prison of Boniato, in Oriente. A military man sentenced to death did so in the jail in Santa Clara. Another man sentenced to death hanged himself in the jail in the same city.

On October 17 an international convention of ASTA, the American Society of Travel Agents, was accommodated in the Habana Hilton, Nacional, Capri and Havana Riviera hotels.

It was a little after 5:00 when Nelia got a call from her fiancé, who was himself a travel agent, asking her to gather a few girls to go to the Havana Riviera Hotel together to socialize with the delegates from his company. Ana, Carmen and Berta were the only ones left in the office.

"I can't go", Ana declined.

Carmen was hesitant, wondering. "Do you think", she confided to Berta, "that will be proper?"

"Of course", Berta encouraged her, "if Emilio is taking Nelia."

Carmen took out her compact and started applying lipstick. Leonardo, on his way out, observed, "And you painting like crazy." Carmen herself laughed.

They both joined Nelia. "To tell the truth", she confided, "I'd rather be alone with him necking, but, well... he has to go."

When Ana left, they were waiting in the reception room for Emilio to go pick them up to take them to the hotel. On her way out, she crossed Pablo, the janitor, in the hallway, mumbling to himself.

Salvador was coming out of the "Concierto" with a pack of cigarettes in his hand when Ana came out of the build͟ ͡o.

"Do you want me to drop you off at home?", he asked her. She looked toward Dany, waiting for Salvador on the sidewalk. He would be with them, so it should be all right.

She knew he didn't like her to ride in Salvador's car, though. "No, thank you", she turned him down.

"Your eyes can be read like an open book", Salvador told her. He thought she would like to ride with him. She just wouldn't want to wait for the bus.

As she reached her block that afternoon, Ana looked up and down her street objectively, as an outsider might see it. There were about a dozen houses on each side. Two peepuls, the sidewalk cracked by their roots and scattered with their crushed purple berries; two "woman's-tongues" still laden with papery pods rattling in the breeze and already full of light greenish yellow fluffy flowers; a couple of Indian laurels, the sidewalk dirty under them, and a flaming scarlet poinciana in bloom partially shaded the street, their branches now sheltering the noisily chirping sparrows, starting to gather for the evening, and everywhere there floated the sweet, intense fragrance of night jasmine. Several identical, elegant two-family dwellings, dating from the late thirties stood on the opposite side, starting from the near corner, with wrought iron bars on their ground floor windows, balustrades around their balconies and magenta bougainvillea topiary or gold-splashed bronze crotons by their gates. A uniformed young maid played with a little girl in a garden. There were a couple of old-fashioned houses, about fifty years old, with plain porches supported by tall Tuscan columns running across their full width, rocking chairs on them, not unlike the house where she'd been born; one with two ferns in large cement pots flanking its tall iron gate, another with a sickly crimson turk's cap bush in the flower bed of its cemented garden, yet another boasting an exuberant yellow chalice vine scrambling up to twin finials; a house standing high above the street with a wide stairway leading from its iron gate to its high porch, much like her grandmother María's, where she'd rocked in the evenings; another set back away from the sidewalk behind tall spineless areca palms; the one directly across the street from their building in the mission style locally tagged *"chalet"* with an anonymous cartouche over the porch and red geraniums in its round flower bed. Several modern two- or three-story buildings rose on either side, their balconies either painted in bold, bright shades of cocoa, maroon or indigo, or else encased by wrought iron railings, creepers lining their walks, their own with the cute little lamppost by the sidewalk. There were two two-story houses, one with crenelation, flat red clay roof tiles and a long open porch on the far corner, where a doctor lived, a tall spiked iron fence around its French garden, with waxy white gardenia and flesh pink oleander in it, bordered by a sky blue plumbago hedge, *"Gaditana"* wrought in its iron gate – next to it, in sharp contrast, a dilapidated old brick house, the home of a shoe repairman, with several broken window panes and a rusty discarded old gas stove on the porch, its garden mostly a bare stretch of the Vedado red clay soil, with clumps of pink periwinkles, Spanish needle, orange African marigold, sandspurs and even gold spurges growing wild around the low brick wall and the steps to the porch − and the other one on the nearer corner, with a simulated belfry, green barrel roof tiles, a little banistered porch and a side entrance with double doors, in the ageless style of the thirties, Ana's favorite, where a prosperous *"notario"* lived, with green canvas awnings, and cream colored roses and shaded red carnations in the flower beds of its angular formal garden, surrounded by a balustrade hugged by an Australian pine hedge. Ana knew many of the neighbors from sight and a few, like the architect's family in the *chalet*, by their last names, although she had never been inside their homes. Several other people were just getting home from work. A few cars were parked on the street, two '55 Chevrolets, a '57 and a '58 Ford, a '54 Mercury, an Opel, a '53 Buick, a '56 Plymouth, a '50 Dodge and, at the entrance to the garage of the pretty house, a brand-new white '59 Imperial. These people didn't live badly. And some of them were socialists. They actually wanted to trade this good, free, individual way of life for the grim, regimented, uniform way of communism. She couldn't understand it. A gray kitten came up to the front step and Ana bent down to pet him.

When she walked into the hallway of the building, she met Natalia, the girl in apartment 3 who worked at the hotel, spinning a hula hoop by the stairs. She stepped aside with an embarrassed little grin. On the glass next to the door of her apartment there was a decal with a white cross on light blue background with red letters reading "I believe in God, I believe in Christ". On the stairway, she met the drycleaners driver on his way down, counting some bills, who looked at her absently without recognition.

Major Huber Matos Benítez, the military commander of Camagüey province, bravely challenged the communist infiltration and disavowed communism. On October 20 he resigned together with 38 other military men, and was arrested.

Late in the afternoon of October 21, Pedro Luis Díaz Lanz, residing in Florida, flew a raid over Havana, making several circles, and dropped leaflets over the city. Anti-aircraft guns at La Cabaña, machine guns, batteries on building roofs and battleships opened fire, and two army planes took off from Camp Libertad to shoot him down, unsuccessfully, as he flew out to sea. In the shooting, a man on Carlos III and Infanta was killed. Photocopies of the flyer circulated around the office. It accused Fidel of being a dictator, wanting to introduce communism and destroy the national economy, and it called him a traitor to the Cuban revolution.

On Thursday the 22nd, Major Matos was sent to prison in Morro Castle, built in the 16th Century on the promontory east of the bay and once named Fortress of the Three Kings of El Morro. That day *El Crisol* newspaper printed Matos' letter of resignation to Castro, given to them by his wife. Mrs. de Matos also wrote a letter to Castro and took it to *Diario de La Marina*, which published it, bravely telling him she didn't want to hear that her husband "had committed suicide" while in prison.

What little doubt could have remained in their minds as to the nature of the regime was now gone. They couldn't fool themselves any longer, holding on to a thread of optimism. The truth bored in. Communism had taken over their country. **IT HAD FOUND THEM IGNORANT AND HAD CREPT UP ON THEM.**

CHAPTER 4

APATHY TO THE EVENTS

> *"Y mil necios, que grandes se juzgan,*
> *con honores al peso comprados,*
> *al tirano idolatran, postrados*
> *de su trono sacrílego al pie."*[4]
> *("Himno del Desterrado",*
> José María Heredia, 1825*)*

Camen, dejected, and Ana started visiting the Gymnase Etienne on L Street together twice a week after work. There they exercised for an hour under the watchful eye of Madame Gérard and then showered; they were periodically weighed and measured, and advised on diet.

Two planes dropped subversive leaflets over Havana, Marianao, Guanabacoa and El Cotorro.

A new American film, "Private Property", opened at the "Alcázar" theater, and people flocked to see it. The line reached around the corner for a block up Virtudes Street. Other American movies had not found their way in lately. Afterwards they realized the mediocre film had been shown to point out to the Cuban people the delinquency of the American youth, a plotted rape, an indifferent husband, an unsatisfied wife. It had served its purpose of ridiculing the Americans.

The National Revolutionary Militia were created and a new hymn filled the air.

A bomb was thrown against the door of *"Revolución"* newspaper.

Catholic priests Reverend Eduardo Aguirre and Juan Ramón O'Farrill had criticized the communist infiltration in the labor movement, and they defected.

> [4] And a thousand fools, who judge themselves great,
> bought with honors to the *peso*,
> idolize the tyrant, prostrated
> at the foot of his sacrilegious throne.

Apathy to the Events

The news that Major Camilo Cienfuegos Gorriarán had mysteriously disappeared on October 29 was not disclosed until the next day. Fidel stated on television thirteen days later, on November 11, that Cienfuegos had crashed into the sea, and had pilots of Cubana explain that there had been squalls that day. Méndez wondered, "Why did he consider that necessary?" Suspicion immediately rose that Camilo might have been ordered killed. This was different. He had been an honest man, a tailor, liked by most, one of the best regarded figures. It was rumored that there had been differences between him and Raúl. He had already suffered another air accident four months before, when the helicopter in which he was travelling had fallen in Bayamo, Oriente. Major Cienfuegos had been chief of staff of the army, and Juan Almeida stepped in to replace him. A seven-day official mourning was declared.

On All Souls' Day, Ana and Dany went with Teresa and Carlos to see the traditional *"Don Juan Tenorio"* play. As she watched *Don Juan Tenorio, Don Luis Mejía* and *Doña Inés de Ulloa* on stage, a whiff of a perfume from some long-dormant memory brought to her mind another staging of José Zorrilla's popular drama she had seen eight years before, and she was reminded of Augusto Borges, her unrivaled favorite actor, in the title role, and Armando Bianchi, and the wide sidewalk of Infanta.

American writer Ernest Hemingway arrived in Havana, to his big white house, surrounded by bougainvillea and poinsettia, with its entrance bordered by palms.

Lieutenant Manuel Francisco Artime Buesa resigned from the army on November 7 and his letter to Castro was published in *"Avance"* newspaper. This had become regular procedure with resignations, so as to make the intention public before censorship from the officials could stifle it.

The CTC was purged of all anti-communist leaders in November.

Camilo Cienfuegos' aide, Major Cristino Naranjo Vázquez, had been investigating Camilo's disappearance. At the entrance to Post 3 of Camp Libertad, he was machine-gunned with two buddies by Captain Manuel Beatón, reportedly in a case of mistaken identity.

At the gymnasium, Madame Gérard advised them, "Eat fruit, but not bananas. Eat regularly, don't go hungry for long, because then even little pieces of paper that you ate are absorbed by the body."

The INIT (National Institute of Tourist Industry) was created on November 20.

Representatives of all the universities participated in twelve sessions for the new disposition of the Education Reform.

Manuel Ray Rivero, Minister of Public Works and brother of the official of the Ministry for the Recovery of Misapplied Properties who had committed suicide in police headquarters seven months before, was replaced by Osmani Cienfuegos, Camilo's brother. Suspicious souls said it was to quiet Fidel's conscience, while others more cynical, after sarcastically querying, "What conscience?", claimed it was to quiet Camilo's family.

Dr. Faustino Pérez, Minister of Recovery of Misapplied Properties, was replaced by Navy Captain Rolando Díaz Astaraín. Castro appointed Major Guevara president of the National Bank of Cuba on November 26 to succeed Dr. Felipe Pazos, who left for Europe.

Leaving the office that Thursday afternoon, as they walked down the hall to the elevator, Dany read the headline in the newspaper and commented, "This is one thing I can't see."

Ana seized one of the rare occasions in which he made a comment about the regime to confide, "I think that an Argentinean is not the most appropriate person for president of the National Bank of Cuba."

They had reached the elevator and, when it arrived, Salvador, Elsa and Ramiro got in with them.

"That's not the point, but I never knew 'Che' Guevara to be an economist."

Folgueira, a representative for American paper manufacturers, got in the elevator on the fifth floor. Only Dany and Ana had any familiarity with him, and he exchanged greetings with them. Salvador then said, "What happened was that Fidel asked, 'A good economist raise your hand', Che raised his and was picked and, when Fidel later said to him, 'I didn't know you were an economist', Che said, 'Economist? I thought you said a good communist'."

Elsa gave him a merciless poke in the ribs with her elbow at the same time thrusting out her chin toward the elevator operator. Folgueira, his back to them, didn't look back, and they remained silent the rest of the way down.

On the ground floor, Dany resumed, "This man is a physician."

Ramiro, married some six weeks, introduced his point of view, "Now, if they had made him Minister of Health, that would make sense."

They had reached the door of the building. Folgueira said, "Until tomorrow", Elsa headed west with Ramiro to the stop of her bus to Almendares, and Dany walked with Salvador toward his car. Ana crossed the street to her own bus stop. Guevara soon started disrespectfully signing the bank notes "Che".

Although the day of Our Lady of Charity, Patroness of the country, had been September 8, the statue of the Virgin of Andalusian origin was brought from her shrine in El Cobre in Oriente on November 26 for the National Catholic Congress, which opened with a procession from Prado and Malecón through Reina, Carlos III and Independencia to the Civic Plaza, where a midnight Mass was celebrated, officiated under a persistent rain by Archbishop Monsignor Enrique Pérez Serantes. It remained in Havana until the 29th for the Assembly of the Secular Apostolate at "La Tropical" Stadium.

Dany's father, Ignacio, marched with the Masons from their temple on Carlos III to the Central Park to celebrate the centennial of the A.L. & A.M. Grand Lodge of Cuba.

Captain Antonio Núñez Jiménez, back from Europe, announced on December 4 that INRA had established 485 agricultural cooperatives, and 400 people's stores were functioning on the Island.

Ana had been eligible for her '59 to '60 vacation since the 1st of September and decided now to split it in two halves, take fifteen days in December and leave the other fifteen for the spring. She plotted and schemed with Dany, and left for Isle of Pines on an Aerovías Q plane from Columbia airport with Gloria Serrano, the file clerk, who was in the third week of her own vacation, with all the plans laid out. Gloria's father had a modest flour and cracker meal factory in La Lisa. The air fare was $12. and a half-hour flight over the south of the province and the dark green chain formed by hundreds of keys, the shallow banks and sponge colonies in the Gulf of Batabanó delivered them to the exotic island to the south, famous for its grapefruits and parrots. A ferry, *"El Pinero"*, also made the trip from Batabanó. A few women of humble appearance travelled by themselves on the plane. When they landed at the red dirt airport, they overheard that they were going to visit their husbands in the National Reclusory.

They checked into "La Cubana" hotel in Nueva Gerona, went shopping in the colonial city, and made conversation with the waiters, as it was off season, in the half-empty large dining room, where they had all their meals. One invited Gloria out.

They went dancing, while Ana stayed in the hotel lobby, reading Twain's "Tom Sawyer" in the poor light, serenaded by the crickets.

The absolute quiet was strange to her and she went to bed early. Gloria soon arrived in a state of shock. Ana squinted in the sudden light. Gloria's eyeglasses flashed.
"He got drunk! And he insisted on teaching me how to drive on that deserted road to Santa Fe", she wailed, shaken, her clear skin deathly pale. "I was terrified to have both hands on the steering wheel! To top it all off, the door on the passenger side didn't open, I had to get in and out through the door on the driver's side. And not a single car in sight!"
"Where was he going?"
"How do I know! We got to a town about nine kilometers from here, Santa Rosalía."
"And how did you manage to get away?"
"I don't know. I guess I got so hysterical... he turned back. Since he had to come back to his job here... And he was so drunk!"
"They're used to going out with the tourist women who come here where nobody knows them to have a good time."
She had to sit up long past midnight, on the edge of Gloria's bed, listening to her retell the incident. Afterwards Gloria refused to eat in the dining room again, and had her meals in a restaurant in town. Ana ate by herself. The waiter – he was thin, pale, with curly hair – went up to their room one morning while Ana was having breakfast, Gloria told her, maybe to apologize, and he spoke to her from outside, but Gloria, without opening the door, yelled at him to go away.
They took a dip in the swimming pool and Gloria took a photograph of Ana on the steps, which Dany, when he saw it later, rated as worthy of appearing in *"Trapecio"* magazine.
Ana mailed all her Christmas cards from Nueva Gerona that year. The previous Christmas, Salvador had had them printed for her with her name in Old English type at a discount price, but this year she thought that Dany wouldn't like her to do it.
Gloria left Friday morning, to start work on Monday and Ana lamented the unpleasant incident. And, as they had planned all along, Dany arrived for the week-end and checked into Las Codornices motel nearby.
They rented a car and drove south, between the Caballos and Las Casas ranges. They were amazed to learn that these were formed of marble and that the highways were built of chipped marble, plentiful on the northern part of the island. The countryside was full of Cuban pine, or white, as they were locally called, and dotted with the color

of its parrots and parakeets. The houses had porches that wrapped all around them. They went to Santa Fe and walked around the small park, deserted in the midday haze except for a little boy playing by himself; later under the bridge to drink water from a mineral spring that flowed freely; then over a fence to a terrace, perhaps private, by the Júcaro river; afterwards to the little post office facing the park, and last to a bar on a corner, where they had beer in the sleepy afternoon, while the waiter talked about baseball with the only other customer.

Ana refused to go to Dany's motel room.
"But nobody knows us here", he insisted.
"I'm still embarrassed they'll see me go in."

In a last effort on his part, he persuaded her to go in the rear door, but, when they went around the back, they met the maid cleaning the rooms.

They went into a fenced field and, after the pent-up excitement, they finally fell in ecstasy in each other's arms on the grass under the shade of a locust-berry tree. Peacocks strolled by lazily. A bull wandered peacefully by and Ana was terrified to stir near him, so, despite Dany's encouragement, they stayed in the same spot for over an hour.

That evening they went to a thatched-roof country-style nightclub by the swimming pool of the Rancho del Tesoro motel, in the outskirts. They were pleasantly surprised to see that the local people still did the traditional Pinerian *"sucu-sucu"* on the island, a fusion of the *"son montuno"* and the Caymanian round dance, the couple with their hands on each other's shoulders, so long out of fashion on the mainland.

"¿Quién tiene la culpa?
¡Domingo Pantoja!"[78]

They drank *Cuba-libres*. And they danced until the combo finished off with,

"Se acabó lo que se daba, se acabó,
a las tres de la mañana se acabó."[79]

Saturday they drove past Columbia, founded by Americans and now virtually vanished, and the Presidio Modelo, to Bibijagua Beach on the north coast, claimed to be the only other one with black sand besides Kalapana Beach, in Hawaii.

They sat on the glittering onyx-black sand, under coconut trees.
"What makes it black?", Ana wondered.
"Probably black marble dust from the quarry."

They took a handful of black sand in a glass jar — "To put it on the living room coffee table", Ana said, — and she insisted on taking a tiny dead crab.
"It'll start smelling", Dany warned her.
"It's too tiny."
"It'll smell just the same."
It had. She had placed it on the dresser, and the next morning woke up to a rotten smell in her room and was heartbroken to have to throw the tiny crab away.

Later they sat on a swing on the grounds of the hotel in the autumn evening, until the mosquitoes and gnats drove them into the lobby.

There were many immigrants from Grand Cayman residing on the island. The manager told them that there were about 150 American colonists living there, and many Jamaican charcoalmen and Caymanian fishermen in the south.

That evening they played *"tute"* in the hotel lobby until late. They felt guiltily happy. Having all their meals together for the first time, being together all day long, going wherever they wished, staying up as late as they wanted. With nobody to account to when she got home. Three days! Even if they *were* staying in separate hotels, it was still, well, a little like a honeymoon.

But Dany left Sunday morning. And Ana was left to feel the guilt by herself. As soon as the plane took off, she started to ponder how wrong it was, and to feel remorseful. If anybody found out.... By the time she left that afternoon, she was regretful they had come.

As the plane gained altitude, she could see the four circular edifices of the National Reclusory, fashioned after the Joliet penitentiary, behind the Caballos mountains, near the coast of the Gulf of Batabanó. Many opponents of the government withered away there.

At home, they trimmed the white-sprayed Christmas tree on Purest Conception's Day.

The novelty of the gymnasium had worn off. Carmen Zayas told Ana, "I'm going to the University this afternoon after work to find out about registering for Public Administration." — This career had been receiving encouragement from the government, claiming there would be great demand for it with the new organization, and it would be the only university degree that could be pursued without a previous secondary education. — "Gloria is going along with me."

With Dany at the university in the evenings, her own were empty, and Ana considered the idea. Carmen decided against it after all, preferring decoration, and Gloria, instead, ended up registering for two courses on the open program, and bought two books of bound lectures in the small bookshop by the stairs.

Ana decided to enroll in the Professional School of Publicity, and she registered for the entrance exams. With the irregular schedule followed since the revolution had taken power, these, which would normally have been held in early August, were administered in December. She took them over a period of ten days. They consisted of mathematics, Spanish, geography, civics, beginning publicity and introduction to English. Dany was pleased.

Rafael del Pino, captured four months before, was sentenced to thirty years in prison.

Oil was found in Jatibonico, Ciego de Avila, in Camagüey province.

On December 15 a trial was celebrated against Major Matos at the theater in Camp Libertad. Castro talked for an unbelievable seven hours and ended saying, "If you absolve him, history will condemn you", and Matos was sentenced to twenty years in prison.

Fidel asked workers to denounce anyone who opposed the government. People began to eye each other with suspicion. There was an instance where a woman accidentally found recording equipment in a beauty parlor, and all the women indignantly walked out of the salon.

Official releases claimed the INAV had completed 10,000 housing units in 1959, which lent itself to be misconstrued, but actually meant only 10,000 apartments.

On December 16 Fidel prohibited travelling abroad more than once a year and announced the sugar workers would not receive their Christmas bonuses that year.

Santa Claus was substituted by Don Feliciano, a typical *guajiro* with drooping mustache and beard in two thin strands, who wore a *guayabera*, straw hat turned up in front, baggy trousers and leggings. Christmas trees were banned from import. Santa Claus, like the Christmas trees, had been brought into the country from the States in the thirties. Formerly, the Three Wise Men and Nativity scene had prevailed. Grocery stores put up plaster of Paris Don Felicianos on the counters with a slot in top for the *"aguinaldo"*[36]. Almost every

[36] Christmas tip

house in the suburbs had decorations. It was the "Revolutionary Christmas".

Saturday Dany took Ana and Teresa riding around the Apolo-Marimón and Víbora Park suburbs to the south to see the Christmas ornaments on the lawns of the houses, which were the talk of the city that season. There were Christmas trees, Santa Clauses, reindeer, sleds, chimneys, Nativity scenes, snowmen, poinsettias, lampposts, carolers, fireplaces and stockings lit up or hung with bright color light bulbs.

The last two official executions of the year were carried out in Pinar del Río. The number of executions *officially* reached 708.

On Sunday, they went to Rex Cinema to see the Nativity scene arranged in the windows along the entrance to its lobby with even a flowing river. A Nativity scene was also set up high on the sort of ledge that still remained over the portico on the San Rafael corner of El Encanto department store. Ana remembered how when she was a child that corner of the store had for years remained old as all the rest of it was rebuilt – an inheritance dispute, they said.

The new highway to the port of Mariel at the bay on the north coast of Pinar del Río province had been started by Batista's government and finished by Castro's. The large sizal plantations on the rocky fields along the highway were expropriated by the INRA.

The Regulation on Vacant Lots was approved for the forced sale of unimproved land. What would be the fate of their lot in Santa Catalina?, her father's plans? Would they have to rush construction?

An attempt was made against the life of the Minister of Labor, Major Augusto Martínez Sánchez, on 25th and N Streets in Vedado, and his three bodyguards were wounded.

Ana's classes started at 8:00 in the evening, they had four subjects a day for 45 minutes each, and they ended at 11:00. She was excited to find herself back in school again after four and a half years. She confided to Dany that she experienced a certain sense of satisfaction. She discarded the high heels and stockings she wore to work, and donned flat-soled sandals on her bare feet, and felt like a teenager again. The school had 326 students. She made friends with several classmates, all boys, most of them younger than herself – she had been out of school for so long, – and a closer friendship with Ernesto, a heavy boy of 22 who worked at the electric company and was a very friendly sort. The pertinent questions revealed he didn't know Blanca, they didn't work in the same department. When they arrived early, they went with two other boys to the students' association and had Cokes and talked about their teachers and their jobs, and some braved a few risky comments about the government. And they sat next to each other in several classes.

On December 23 the Ministry of Education passed a law resolving the "Integral Reform of Education".

Reverend Maximiliano Pérez, parson of Managua, fled from Cuba. Fidel called him "Judas", he called Father Eduardo Aguirre "Herod" and Father Juan O'Farrill, "vulture".

The streets were roofed with banners. In many sections streets were roped off.

In the drawing of names at the office for the exchange of Christmas gifts among the employees, Ana drew Guillén's and Dany got Rina's. It was soon known that Mario had drawn Ana's. Ramiro mentioned to Ana that at the card game with the Americans Thursday evening, Palacios had commented that Salvador wanted to trade names with Mario. She hadn't imagined that the Americans discussed such things at their card games. And Salvador made sure Ana heard that he had even offered Mario to buy it. Dany on his part wanted to give Rina's name to Mario and for Ana to swap Guillén's for his, to end giving presents to each other. But the idea appealed to Ana of getting a gift from Mario, who didn't know her tastes, and she thought it a challenge to pick out one for Guillén, who was also a stranger to her. She reserved this feeling and, adducing only that it meant both getting an additional gift, since they were going to exchange presents between themselves anyway, she convinced Dany, and Wednesday before lunch she received a bottle of *"Alma de España"* lotion from Mario and gave Guillén a tie clip. Dany gave Rina a sandalwood fan and got a bottle of "Old Spice" from Elsa. They also had gifts from Mr. Kent and Palacios respectively.

The company gave a party at the Habana Hilton Hotel at noon. Ana wore a navy blue dress with dolman sleeves and white lace collar. Dany drove Elsa to the party. They had a group photograph taken of all the employees standing around a grand piano. There was a generous buffet spread out. Ana joked with Octavio Guillén at the long table. Whiskey was plentiful, but, for lack of cognac, she drank *daiquirís*. When the photographer brought them the pictures, she passed hers around for her co-workers to autograph. When it got back to her, somebody had signed "Richard M. Nixon". She found herself listening to Butler by the piano.

"My mother's husbands", he was unexpectedly confiding in a rare intimacy incited by alcohol, "wiped her fortune. They were literally sons of bitches."

She nodded with a grave expression. Elsa was sitting next to the piano player, singing. Dany was talking with Mr. Palmer. Gloria hadn't attended.

Ana had already had a couple of *daiquiris* and pink ladies when Elvira dared her to drink a glass of straight rum. Unwarily, she swallowed it, hardly breathing, under Dany's disapproving look. Later, there was dancing by the pool. She danced with Mr. Kent, who lost one of his ever-present loafers. Dany told him, "You have to take your shoes off to do the mambo." He took off the other one. And Dany hid them. Ana took her own shoes off so as not to step on his socked feet.

"Give me a raise."

"No."

They walked off the floor out of breath and Dany joined them.

"Are you two going to get married?", Mr. Kent asked them thickly.

"Yes", Dany answered him. It was the first time Ana had heard him say it to somebody other than her. She felt happy.

"Then you're the one who needs a raise", he said, placing a friendly hand on Dany's shoulder.

"Well, then give me one."

"I'll give you one."

"Don't forget", Ana insisted. They all knew he didn't have anything to do with the Accounting Department or Dany's raises.

When they were heading back to the table, Salvador stepped in front of her and asked her to dance. She was still barefoot. He exuded sensuality. She looked down at his feet, he had his shoes on. They danced a five-piece set. He breathed on her cheek. She was vaguely aware that Dany was sitting at the table wearing a straight face to shame her into going back. She knew she was acting wrong and felt he would get mad at her, but the liquor didn't let her reason why she did it. Graciela was also sitting at the long table. And when the music stopped and she went back, Dany pulled her to the lobby and, by the stairs, shook her savagely by the shoulders until her head lolled, while the sight of the bull horns mounted on the wall flashed in and out of her blurred vision, and she saw him so mad, she thought he'd slap her.

"You danced with him and I sat and waited", he accused her furiously. "I could have asked Graciela to dance, or Elvira, but I sat waiting, thinking after each song that, if you saw me sitting, you'd surely come back to the table. And you danced five pieces in a row!" She hoped the others wouldn't notice what was going on, especially Salvador.
"I'm sorry, Dany, but I didn't think you'd mind so much. And I thought it would look better to the others if we both danced with everybody." It was a feeble excuse.
"I don't care about the others!"
A tear trickled down her cheek and landed at the corner of her mouth. She cried partly out of fear, partly out of shame and partly to deter his anger and protect herself from it.
"Besides, I've had too much to drink and nothing is very clear", she said more truthfully.
"I thought so", he said, not so harshly now. "But when I drink, I don't dance with somebody else. And I kept waiting for you to come back to the table."
"Forgive me", she asked him, saddened. She didn't know why she'd liked dancing with Salvador. Maybe because Salvador had made it obvious he liked her, or perhaps because she'd thought she shouldn't; maybe she felt too sure of Dany. She hadn't been really conscious that Dany would get mad at her. She shouldn't drink so much.
"Elvira made a fool of you."
And Salvador? Did he want to annoy Dany? He seemed like that co-worker of Carmen's boyfriend. Every time she drank too much, she did something which she later regretted. She had also had too much to drink that evening in November a year ago. She should make a resolution, she thought foggily, "New year, new life", and drink less.
"Let's leave", he said. She was relieved.
She had her shoes on. He handed her evening bag to her. They left the hotel without saying good-by, across the plant-filled main floor lobby, left his DeSoto on M Street, and walked by Trader Vic's, the Polinesio and Banco Pedroso, down garland-strung 23rd Street, passing the Banco Continental, as Johnnie Walker watched them from a billboard high across the street, down the slope past the Medical Retirement Fund, "La Zorra y el Cuervo", La Rampa building, the Eden Roc, before La Rampa Cinema, the semicircular façade of Pan

American Airways, The Royal Bank of Canada and the large Ambar Motors building, with the Trust Company of Cuba; they waited for the pedestrian signal to cross the star-decorated street to La Rampa Commercial Arcade on the other side, past the Danish House, with its delicate Swedish alabaster figurines, before the Art Déco lamppost at the foot of the street, and left along the Malecón. The white foam of the breaking waves leapt high. The cool breeze from the sea made the effect of the liquor wear off. They walked back past the lone palm in the circle, under the pine trees, around the Shell service station to "Johnny 88" for a while. Due to the holidays, despite the early hour, it was crowded. A combo was playing on the high stage behind the bar. When their Tom Collins were brought, Dany told her, "Don't drink it."

She took out of her handbag the gift she had been carrying all day waiting to be alone with him, and gave him the leather cigarette case with his gold initials. He gave her a square silver compact with silver mirror and her initials engraved in the inside lid. They made up and kissed.

He licked his lips. "It tastes salty." They laughed.

He spent Thursday evening home, as they had agreed they would do every Christmas Eve, and she went with her parents to her brother's for dinner, as they had done for the last four years, ever since Gustavo had gotten married. The natural tree stood in its corner, already shedding needles, the Nativity scene below. And the record player played carols: *"Cascabeles"*, *"Esta Noche Es Noche Buena"*, *"Arbolito"*, *"Adestes Fedeles"*, "Silent Night". Dinner in their dining room, its walls decorated with china plates, consisted, traditionally, of roast suckling pig, baked guinea hens in wine, white rice, black turtle beans, lettuce and radish salad, and yucca with sour *"mojo"* on their party willowware, washed down with red wine, white wine and hard cider.

"Mamá, have more cider", Gustavo prompted.

Ana liked to see her father eat. He enjoyed the meal.

"Carlos, leave room for the nougat", Blanca cautioned.

The fresh aroma of the Canadian fir mingled with the fragrant smell of the guinea hens and the mixture filled the house. For dessert, there were sweet-almond, peanut and yolk nougats, fruit marzipan, quince paste, dates, figs, walnuts, filberts and almonds.

Gustavo went to the dish hutch and came back with a bottle.

"Hey!, Veuve Clicquot Ponsardin champagne!", exclaimed Carlos.

Apathy to the Events

"I was keeping it for a special occasion."
"It has to be chilled", said Blanca.
Dany called Ana after the heavy dinner and they talked most of the evening, while Blanca joked about "the turtledoves".
At a quarter to twelve, they filed out to St. John Lateran's Church, for Midnight Mass, while Teresa stayed with the children. Loud voices and an occasional merry laugh pierced the darkness of the late hour. Several houses were brightly lit. A few families sat on their porches.
Ana and Blanca, groggy from the food and wine, yawned, and their eyes watered with sleep through most of the Mass.
On I Street across from the park two men with unsteady step and glassy eyes wished them with a wide smile, "Merry Chrishtmash".
"The same to you", they answered them.
On Christmas Day, as customary, the streets were deserted until the afternoon.
On Holy Innocents' Day, erroneously celebrated by tradition as a fools' day on Childermas, the date when King Herod had all the two-year-old Bethlehem boys slain, Graciela informed Salvador that her boss wanted to see him. As he reached his door, his co-workers' chant went up, "Fool!" Ramiro was the victim of the same prank when Raquel invoked Mr. Batten's name. And Rosa told Leonardo to pick up the quotation he'd dropped. Rolandito had his laughs asking Gloria, "Is the new fashion now wearing only one earring?"
Guillén told Ana, "This morning our neighbor brought a dessert plate to my wife covered with a napkin and when she lifted it, there was a slip of paper saying, 'Fool'."
The Journalists' Organization started censoring the news by adding a *"coletilla"*[37] or clarifying note below which practically contradicted any anti-communist news printed above. Six newspapers protested this measure.
On December 29 forty persons attempting to leave the country aboard a yacht were arrested.
Elvira asked Carmen's permission to give her address to a boy with whom she wanted to break a date for New Year's to go out with another friend. And Carmen consented.
The Ministry of Labor took over the Comodoro Yacht Club and the Havana Yacht Club on New Year's Eve.

[37] postscript

They hadn't made any reservations for New Year's in time, and went to the Sky Club on the penthouse of the St. John's Hotel, on O Street, Ana in her light blue lace dress and Dany in his black suit with white tie, Norma and Víctor, her official fiancé of three months, again with them, as they would be staying out past midnight. They wanted to go to the *Salón Arcos de Cristal* of Tropicana "under the stars", but there were no tables. Teresa and Carlos were going to dine at Velázquez's home in the fancy condominium building on lower K Street with the balconies that resembled Swiss cheese, and then to the Vedado Tennis Club, of which Velázquez and his wife were members.

From their table they could see the shapes of the Morro Castle and La Cabaña Fortress outlined in electric lights. But there would be no elaborate fireworks as there had been until eight years before. They danced, drank, joked and laughed. At midnight noisemakers, rattles, whistles and horns blared.

When they came out, they found, four or five blocks away, a street roped off to traffic. Feather palm fronds were tied to electric posts, colored light bulbs were strung overhead from one sidewalk to the other. And 3:00 found them dancing in it. They assumed it was proper for them to stay out so late because now they were with a respectable engaged couple.

As the year ended, thousands were in prison. Firing squads wiped out enemies. Terrorism and sabotage flared spasmodically. Peasants were organized into agricultural cooperatives. The PSP (Popular Socialist Party) was the only political organization acting openly. The militia were organizing. Educational institutions were turning into indoctrination centers. And the Ministry for the Recovery of Misapplied Properties had seized goods worth $253,500,000.

CHAPTER 5

THE AGRARIAN REFORM UNDER WAY

*"Menester es ansiar lo que es posible
y asi se endulza lo que amargo sea."*[5]
("Los Deseos", Leonardo da Vinci*)*

For work on Monday Ana put on the white bolero sweater that she had first worn for New Year's Day. Carmen, settled at her desk, kidded Salvador as he went by, a little late, "Did the bedsheets stick to you?"

"And did you fall out of bed?", he riposted.

Somebody placed a newspaper on Ramiro's desk folded to the candid photograph of a girl who looked remarkably like Berta Penabad dancing with somebody, taken in a nightclub on New Year's Eve. Leonardo needled him, "Well, it seems she's not crying over you." Ana felt glad, wanted to cheer for her.

Wayne Motors launched a new advertising campaign to bring out on the foreign market the new Wolverine low sports model with its silhouette of the short-legged stocky glutton on the fender, and at the office they were again weighed down by an increased workload.

A plane dropped incendiary bombs on cane fields at Quemado de Güines and Rancho Veloz in the north of Las Villas and burned 6,000 tons of sugar cane. Sabotage against the sugar crop had begun.

On the Three Kings' Day, Ana got up earlier than usual and, excited in her temporary role of Melchior, Gaspar and Balthasar, walked to her brother's at 7:30, in the vain hope that the children would still be in bed. A boy was riding his scooter on the sidewalk, another spinning a top, and a girl was roller skating. The doctor on the corner and his wife got in their Ford loaded with packages and drove off. A boy reeled a yo-yo and a girl made a doll walk leading it by the hand, a white cat following at her heels. When Blanca, already fully dressed, let Ana in, Gustavito pounced on her with a breadstick in

[5] It is necessary to covet what is feasible and what may be bitter is thus sweetened.

his hand, yelling, "What did the Magi leave for me at your house, Aunt?"

Ana tried to hug him and produced a gift-wrapped package, which he promptly grabbed from her.

"What do you say, Tavito?", Blanca tried to prompt him, but he ignored her, proceeding to tear the poinsettia wrapping paper and reveal a bright red fire engine.

"Is he biting his nails?", Ana observed.

"I've had to dab aloes on his fingers."

The dog was barking. Blanquita was throwing her rubber toys out of her handed-down playpen, calling "Nita!"

Ana María picked her up, gave her her customary kiss on the bridge of her nose and set her down in the playpen again, for fear of spoiling her for Leonor, and she brought forth a stuffed rag black doll with a red kerchief over her head. Blanquita popped her a kiss. She was more affectionate than Gustavito. Now almost two, she was a chubby child with dimples in her elbows and knees, big expressive dark brown eyes and dark brown hair that didn't quite reach over her tiny diamond screw earrings. She squinted her eyes and wrinkled her tiny nose to summon attention or to show her joy. Her features were now a jumble of squints and wrinkles, while she still tried to reach with her lips the jet bead pinned to her shoulder for "evil eye". Gustavo had already left.

"Running away from this din", laughed Blanca.

"Papá was still home when I left", Ana commented.

"Then you crossed Gustavo on the street."

Gustavito asked for a banana.

"After the milk, you don't put in anything", his mother refused him.

"Why?"

"Because it'll give you a stomach ache."

There already were several new toys scattered around the living room *"terra-losa"* floor. Gustavito simulated, "Vroom, vroom!"

"If Leonor doesn't get here soon", complained Blanca, "I'm going to be late for work."

The door bell rang just then, at the same time as the phone, and Ana let Leonor in while the dog barked.

"Did you bring me the cassava?", Gustavito asked.

"Where do you get cassava?", asked Blanca, rushing to the telephone under the reproduction of Eugène Delacroix's "Liberty Lead-

The Agrarian Reform Under Way

ing the People".

"At the market plaza", answered Leonor, picking up toys. "Don't let Gustavito have a banana before nine thirty", Blanca intructed, picking up the receiver. This started another string of "Why's?" from Gustavito, which nobody answered.

Heading for the kitchen, Leonor crooned in her husky voice,
"*La gallina, la jabada,*
puso un huevo en la canal,
puso uno, puso..."[96]

She soon switched to,
"*... traje escotado con su canesú.*
dos y dos son cuatro,
cuatro y dos son...",[97]

while Gustavito followed her around, and
"*A, B, C,*
la cartilla se me fue,
por la calle de la Merced..."[98]

This would be followed by "Little Martina Cockroach", "Little Péez Mouse", "Misifús and Zapirón", "Cucufate and Valentín" and a story about a sea bream, while she went unruffled about her day's chores, then "Little Red Riding Hood" and several counting rhymes which had Gustavito, only three, counting to eleven. Fortunately, nobody had gotten the whim to teach Blanquita "the neighbor's little chicken" or "the little lard cakes". Leonor would make the beds, bathe the children, cook lunch, feed them, clean the apartment, wash the dishes and have dinner ready when Gustavo and Blanca got home from work, before leaving at 7:00, with her own dinner.

The call was from Lorenzo, Blanca's brother. Ana let herself out, calling to Blanca, "Mamá's coming by in the afternoon, after she takes down the Christmas tree. I think she wants to take them to the cartoon show at the 'Cinecito'."

Blanca waved at her with one hand while she held the receiver with the other.

A grandmother loaded with packages waited for a bus.

The traditional yacht races from St. Petersburg to Havana were cancelled.

Juvenile Patrols were organized among children ages seven to fifteen.

Pressure was exerted on everyone to enlist in the militia. And its hymn was heard often. They had sadly seen their Cuban National

Anthem of Bayamo gradually take second place to the 26th of July March, just as the Cuban flag of the lone star had to the red and black banner.

Major Efigenio Ameijeiras got married at the Church of the Angel.

A plane set fire to the cane fields of "Hershey" sugar mill, in Santa Cruz del Norte, in the north of Havana province, causing high losses. Another bombed cane colonies with phosphorus in Bainoa, Caraballo and San Antonio de Río Blanco, in Jaruco, in Havana province.

Channeling operations of the Hanábana river started in the southern Zapata peninsula for the process of draining the Swamp, despite all the advice against it from Japanese, Dutch and other experts.

The government confiscated Gaspar Pumarejo's Channel 4, CMBF *Televisión Nacional*. The employees took over *"Avance"* newspaper on January 18. It was the first newspaper seized. Jorge Zayas, its editor and publisher, went into an embassy with his family.

On January 20 Castro accused the Spanish Embassy in Cuba on television of counter-revolutionary conspiracy. Ambassador Juan Pablo de Lojendio, Marquis of Vellisca, appeared briefly on the television screen behind Fidel in the studio, shouting, "I demand the right to respond! You are a liar!", and the screen went blank. He was heard imprecating, "I have been slandered!" The ambassador was given 24 hours to leave the country.

A plane dropped flammable material over the "Washington" sugar mill in Santo Domingo, Las Villas. The fire burned for over 24 hours.

Castro turned the Moncada Fort in Santiago over to the Ministry of Education to be transformed into a "scholastic city".

The government confiscated the "Reca" Cuban oil enterprise.

The Soviet Industrial Exhibition was put up in the Palace of Fine Arts. On February 4, Soviet Vice-Premier Anastas Mikoyan arrived with 75 functionaries, and he placed a wreath with a hammer and sickle at the statue of José Martí in Central Park the next day. Thirty Villanueva University students carrying placards that read, "Down with Mikoyan and communism" substituted the wreath with another one of flowers in the colors of the Cuban flag. Shooting broke out. Rebel soldiers arrested the students. Mikoyan cut the ribbon inaugurating the exhibit on Sunday the 6th at 2:30, to remain until February 26. A bust acclaimed Alexandr Stepanovich Popov as "inventor of the radio".

The Agrarian Reform Under Way 139

Dr. Guillermo Martínez Márquez, editor of *"El País"* newspaper, resigned after refusing to print a *coletilla* at the foot of an anti-communist article.

The BANFAIC, BANCEC, BANDES and the Cuban National Finance Corporation were dissolved on February 17.

On February 18 at daybreak a plane dropped bombs near Esso Standard Oil's Belot refinery across the bay near Regla. A plane was blown up over "España" sugar mill in Perico, in Matanzas province, and Castro showed the television viewers a passport found in the wreckage bearing the name of an American.

Radio operators formed the FIEL[38] (Independent Front of Free Broadcasting Stations) to broadcast government acts simultaneously.

Twelve ships delivered 75 percent of an order for rifles from Belgium. Shortly after 3:00 in the afternoon of March 4, while waiting for Dalia, in charge of supplies, to order typewriter ribbons, Ana was standing in the Accounting Department looking through the windows at the arc described by the Malecón to the east, where the "Bacardí" and "Philips" signs stood out, and half listening to Mario give instructions to the accounts clerk, while Elvira, the documentation clerk, leaned over Danilo's desk on an elbow, with one of her perennial inane questions. She was always having an excuse to lean over his desk and play stupid. She had an innocent air about her. Her neckline hung carelessly. And she had a very good figure, plus long, thick, shiny black hair, Ana brooded; and she couldn't help simmering. Only Elvira's legs were disproportionate, fat and shapeless with thick ankles – what her grandmother Eva would have called flowerpot legs, – Ana consoled herself. It was a pity her legs weren't visible now. *They* weren't leaning over Dany's desk. Suddenly, there was a deafening noise and out of the east windows they saw a column of black smoke rise into the sky toward the southeast. Ten figures rushed to the windows, while the smoke spread out in a mushroom-shaped cloud. Other employees were coming into the department to look out. They didn't know what had happened.

The freighter *"La Coubre"* from Antwerp, loaded with Belgian weapons, had exploded in Havana's inner harbor, while unloading munitions, against all international regulations, within fifty yards of the shops. Still burning at 6:00 in the afternoon, it slowly sank. Almost one hundred were killed and two hundred injured. Television

[38] "FAITHFUL"

showed the victims. It was a horrible sight. A man, only the upper half of his body left, was being carried, screaming horrendously, on another one's back. It took a moment to take in the scene. There were corpses all among the debris. It was too terrible to watch. "This is too cruel", said Teresa. "It's inhumane", Carlos agreed. The dreadful vision stayed with Ana for a long time. Windows were shattered and old buildings shaken. It was blamed on anti-revolutionary saboteurs at the dock. Warehouses, charred and smashed, collapsed. Gustavo's green 1956 Chevrolet had been parked a few blocks from the dock near the Plaza Vieja, while he worked on the books of an electric appliance importer on Sol, and its hood had been twisted in the explosion. Material damages were calculated at $2,000,000. The government decreed the next day one of national mourning. Fidel initiated the slogan "Fatherland or death".

A campaign was carried to collect money for weapons and fighter planes, belying Castro's remark of a year before of "Weapons, for what?" Television Channel 12 and the radio called for donations.

Two planes dropped incendiary bombs on cane colonies in Matanzas province, where 4,000 tons was burned, and in Pinar del Río province.

The government confiscated Amadeo Barletta's large circulation morning newspaper, *"El Mundo"*, and his radio and television station, Channel 2 *Tele-Mundo*, on March 9. The Italian owner went into an embassy, and then to the States. *"Diario Nacional"* was closed down. *"El País"* newspaper was confiscated and Dr. Guillermo Martínez Márquez, its former director, left for New York.

Juceplan (the Central Planning Board) was created on March 11, bringing under its control all private enterprise. The Minister of Finance, Dr. Rufo López Fresquet, resigned and fled to the States. He was replaced by Navy Captain Rolando Díaz Astaraín. And with him, all the members of the first cabinet appointed by Dr. Urrutia, except for the life-long Minister of Education, had then either fled the country or taken asylum.

The government undertook a campaign it named "the Little Grain of Gold" to collect bullion reserves, and the people were urged to donate their gold. A telemarathon was held, and contributions of jewelry and old coins poured in from all over the country. It was heartbreaking to think of naïve poor people parting with what in many cases were their only treasured sentimental family heirlooms for this

The Agrarian Reform Under Way 141

insensitive cause.

Méndez's office was hardly netting enough money now for two accountants. Many of their clients had left the country or closed down. They had no other choice but to let Alfonso, their clerk of almost five years, go at the beginning of the year, after the holiday expenditures culminating with the Three Wise Men's Day were over. Now, reluctantly, Gustavo applied for a job in a Ministry. He was offered one at $400. a month. The salary wasn't bad, but it would be far from working for himself, as he had for the last five years. In March, though, he took it. And Carlos was left once again alone in the office on Villegas Street to take care of the few accounts they still had left.

The CTC had agreed in November to pay a four percent "voluntary" contribution for industrialization. On March 18 the four percent contribution became compulsory.

Exclusive Biltmore Yacht and Country Club was confiscated and its golf course was dotted with anti-aircraft guns.

Another plane was shot down on the coastal highway in Matanzas, flown by two American pilots, as it landed to try to pick up four persons, all of whom were arrested.

French existentialists Jean-Paul Sartre and Simone de Beauvoir left after a four-week stay in Cuba, to become staunch supporters of the revolution.

Seventy-eight top Soviet political and economic counselors arrived in Cuba in March, among them the head of the Latin-American section of the Narkomindel, to advise Castro on foreign policy. An estimated 5,000 experts from Czechoslovakia, Russia and Red China, including technical advisers and jet pilot instructors, were sent during the early part of the year to help the regime with everything from top-level diplomacy to exploration for minerals.

Commentator Luis Conte Agüero warned of the communist infiltration on March 25 and appealed to Castro on the radio to free himself of the influence. Students gathered in front of CMQ television station to prevent Conte's live speech and they threatened him. He took asylum in an embassy and left Cuba. Abel Mestre, owner of the CMQ network, delivered a tirade against Castro on the "Before the Press" show.

Eight hundred students from the Youth Police Brigades were sent to the indoctrinating schools at Minas de Frío near San Lorenzo, on the Sierra Maestra, to help "educate" the peasants.

"*Diario de La Marina*", "*Avance*" and "*El Crisol*" newspapers published a civic letter signed by the wives of the political prisoners in La Cabaña complaining that their husbands were being mistreated. The Communist Youth Union held its fourth congress at the National Theater, attended by delegates from fifteen countries.

Occasionally in the spring, since Dany had classes, Ana got to hers late and went after work to the Club Marino Estabias, on the gulf coast west of Havana, in Marianao municipality, with Elsa, the receptionist, who now had the use of a car and was also a member of the club, and Rosa, who wasn't. And sometimes Elvira went along with them. Elsa was transformed when she got behind the wheel and became belligerent, yelling insults at other drivers on their way to the club, "Umbrella vendor!", "Cannon shooter!", "Take out the oars!", "Take that coffee pot off the road!", which triggered in them now fear now laughter. Once, sitting in lawn chairs near the water, Ana tried, just out of politeness, to make small talk with Elvira, who pulled her skirt to cover her knees, now, when there were no men around, and she talked about boys.

"I've never had a boyfriend", Elvira told them with a touch of pride. And, astonished, Ana thought of the casual way she leaned over a man's desk with her neckline hanging.

Later Elsa went on home, to Almendares, and Elvira wanted Ana to accompany her to church that afternoon. She went every day, she said. She now disclosed a religious piousness. Posters on the electric poles showed a menacing fly-swatter poised over a fly and urged, "Kill one and count a thousand". They stopped at Jesús de Miramar Church on Fifth Avenue. As they stepped inside and Ana took her sunglasses off, Elvira handed her a little book, which Ana assumed was a prayer book. When she opened it, at the pew, she was surprised to find it was a compilation of Martí's proverbs. She skimmed over it lightly. She and Elvira would never be on the same wavelength.

Four anti-communists escaped in the hijacked yacht "Chelita III".

The regime took away the workers' right to negotiate through their unions. The Ministry of Labor would henceforth settle any grievances. The Ministry ordered a labor census, which began on April 15, and every worker was required to register, including priests and pastors.

When Ernesto Crespo laughed, his small slanted eyes crinkled and all but disappeared behind his chubby cheeks. Ana's fat publicity

The Agrarian Reform Under Way 143

classmate lowered his head when he talked in a low voice and often stood with his legs close together, and he reminded Ana of the "Tody" baby. If he were to put his forefinger in his mouth, she thought, he would be a reasonable replica of the chocolate trade-mark boy, even with his navel covered.

He once commented to Ana about a fat, very fair, blonde girl in their class who got tauntingly close to his desk to ask him questions, "If I married that girl, imagine!, our children couldn't learn to walk, they'd have to learn to roll." The appreciative laugh with which Ana rewarded it, spurred him on. "I heard that, when she came out at fifteen, instead of wearing a long gown, she had to wear a wide one."

His father had been a fireman and had died in a fire nine years before. Ernesto had worked in an advertising agency, so he could help Ana with that subject, while she helped him with Spanish. At exam time, they'd study together.

At the cafe near the school where they sometimes went before class, Ana mentioned she liked the shape of the *crème de menthe* bottles and would like to have one. "Wait", Ernesto said, placing a hand on her forearm, and surprised her asking the waiter, "Would you have an empty *crème de menthe* bottle?"

The man, in white shirt, black bow tie clipped to one side of the open collar, looked at him a little puzzled and then at her, but then pointed to the shelf. "When this one empties, I'll keep it for you."

"Thank you", said Ana, not expecting him to remember.

Russian oil started arriving.

Ana didn't receive her usual $20. annual raise that year. She requested her remaining fifteen days' vacation in April. Blanca also took fifteen days. Saturday, on their way home from the "Riviera" theater in the April shower, after seeing "The Best of Everything" with Hope Lange, Ana told Dany that she wanted to go to Miami with her sister-in-law. He showed his displeasure about a trip.

"You went last year", he told her. He was holding his gray plastic raincoat spread over their heads, as she snuggled against him.

"That was a year ago", she complained.

They passed people hurrying on the street with that frown that rain brings on when it surprises one without protection.

"Not even that", he argued, "only ten months ago."

She wanted to buy some accessories and get a subscription to "The Saturday Evening Post", which wasn't sold at the newsstands any longer. "Why don't you go, too?"

They passed a *"frita"*[39] stand on wheels sheltered from the rain in the portico of the cafe, displaying its array of meat balls, steaks, buns, gritty breaded stuffed potatoes, string-fried potatoes and chopped onions. The lard sizzled in a skillet.

"I can't take my vacation until Mario comes back." Dany was doing the assistant accountant's work while he was away. "How would you like it if I went with my father?"

She wouldn't. "It's different", she contended. "A boy with his father is not the same as a girl with her sister-in-law."

Some children on a porch chanted, "Saint Isidro Tiller,/ take away the rain and bring on the sun". In the next house others on a swing countered, "Let it rain, let it rain,/ the virgin of the cave".

"Why is it different?", he asked skeptically.

They had reached her corner and they stopped under the lamppost in the pouring rain.

"Blanca is married to my brother, so ... she isn't going to ... do anything wrong while she's with her husband's sister, Dany", she reasoned and it sounded absurd, "and, if I'm your girlfriend, I'm not going to do anything wrong while I'm with my brother's wife." It had come out like a tongue-twister.

They were standing on the corner, the raindrops pelting the spread raincoat like pellets. He wasn't at all convinced. And in a certain way Ana felt flattered that he didn't take her for granted. "I'll have to calculate your 'nine-o-nine'[40] Monday", he capitulated. She huddled up to him and urged him on home.

Sunday he arrived, late, to find her reading Calitri's "Strike Heaven in the Face" while she waited for him.

"You only read paperback books", he observed.

"Well, they're cheaper."

"But there aren't any good books in paperback." He was in an argumentative mood. "Those are like Marcial Lafuente Estefanía's cowboy novels."

"What do you mean? These are not like Corín Tellado's romances. The cover doesn't have anything to do... Any book is printed in paperback. In fact, they usually wait until a book proves to sell well in hardcover before they print it in paperback. This is a bestseller."

[39] fried meat patty
[40] 9.09% of 11 months' salary = annual vacation pay

The Agrarian Reform Under Way

"That doesn't mean it's a good book. I'm sure you couldn't find a book like 'Doctor Zhivago' in paperback. Or the classics."

"'Doctor Zhivago'? I'll bring it back to you from Miami."

He kept silent. She realized too late she had brought it up needlessly.

Gustavo couldn't get away from the Ministry yet, but he encouraged Blanca to go to Miami and, even if Ana had wanted to change her mind, she saw herself caught up in Blanca's plans and it was too late to back out. This time they received buff exit validity cards from the DTI (Technical Department of Investigations) – quartered in what had perhaps been one of Rafael Salas Cañizares' houses – in force for indefinite terms. Ana bought $140. in travelers' cheques. Somewhat hesitant before Dany's tacit disapproval, she still left with Blanca by plane for Miami on a Friday, for nine days, while the children stayed with Teresa.

They stayed at the "Colonial" again and Ana was pleased to find that Enrique Carvajal and Estela were still living at the hotel. She introduced her sister-in-law and they gathered in the lobby to chat.

This time Ana only bought five dresses, three pairs of shoes and a belt, all on their first day out shopping, and lost all interest in anything else. They had Southern fried chicken in an open-front restaurant on the Beach, facing the sea, they fed the pigeons on Bayfront Park and took photographs of each other with a pigeon perched on their head. It was hot for April. They walked into the "Hong Kong" restaurant on 2nd Avenue for sodas, and they met Enrique Carvajal at the counter with a boy. As Carvajal made the introductions, the boy cried out, surprised, "Blanca Xiqués!"

"César Villaamil!", reacted Blanca.

They shook hands effusively. They had recognized each other, they explained, as neighbors on Manrique Street until eight years before.

He appeared to be about 24. They brought each other up to date on the news to one side, while, to the other, Ana and Carvajal were excluded. He had been working for Batista's government and had gone to Miami to live when the change of power took place, Ana overheard. He was selling cars. He hadn't gotten married yet. He didn't know Blanca also had a girl now. He asked about Lorenzo, and about Xiqués' drug store.

After the proper preamble, César turned to Ana, next to him, who had been talking with Carvajal, and asked her, "Would you accept an invitation to go out tonight?"

She was taken by surprise, Carvajal smiled indulgently and, without stopping to consider, Ana accepted, before Blanca's somewhat disapproving glance. She told herself later she had done it because he was also a friend of Carvajal's.

She insisted Blanca go along and when César arrived at the hotel that evening to pick her up, he was obviously surprised to find themselves chaperoned in Florida. He drove a convertible, and took them along scenic Venetian Causeway over the bay to the "21 Room" in the Beach, near the ocean. The owner knew him and ordered drinks for them on the house. A buxom blonde sang from the center of the circular bar. César seemed known at the club and Ana felt a vain pride at being out with a popular man. Afterwards he insisted they go to the Capri Club on 8th Street. He carried a thick wad of bills.

Ana soon began to see that Dany had been right. She shouldn't have come. What was she doing here away from Dany? She didn't have any right to accept another man's invitation.

"How come you had to leave the country so soon?", she asked César suspiciously.

"I worked for the government."

"Were you in the army?"

"No."

"Where are you working here?"

"I'm selling cars."

Where had this boy worked that he had needed to leave the country right away? Was so much money made selling cars? Her guilt escalated as the evening wore on, and she withdrew. She wouldn't dance. Blanca discreetly and bravely widened her nostrils, sucked in her cheeks and stretched her upper lip over her teeth to stifle her yawns until her eyes teared. Ana felt guilty for having dragged her to this boredom.

When they pulled up in front of the hotel, Blanca got off ahead of them and César tried to kiss Ana. She didn't actually pull away, but turned so cold and rigid that he just drew back, stared at her and turned the ignition on without even opening the door for her. They didn't see him again.

The next day she found Boris Pasternak's "Doctor Zhivago" in paperback for Dany and bought Grace Metalious' "Return to Peyton Place" for herself in a book shop on 1st Avenue and the spring issue of "Home Furnishing Ideas" at a newsstand on 1st Street, and she

The Agrarian Reform Under Way 147

sent a money order for the subscription to "The Saturday Evening Post". They went back on Sunday. Only Gustavo was waiting at the airport to meet them.

Meanwhile, the new Bank of Foreign Trade was created on April 25 and became the sole exporter and importer in the country. Méndez's work plummeted to almost nothing.

The Goicuría Barracks was turned into a "scholastic city".

Fidel's youngest sister, Emma, married a Colombian engineer on April 30 in the bicentennial Virgin of Mary of the Immaculate Conception Cathedral of St. Christopher of Havana.

David Salvador disappeared from his office as Secretary-General of the CTC. Jesús Soto Díaz replaced him.

On May Day, the International Worker's Day, the militia were exhibited. Nearly 100,000 troops marched for six and a half hours. Signs were displayed with slogans, "Each worker a militiaman", "Fidel is the hope of the world", "We request the independence of Puerto Rico". Castro started talking in the Revolution Plaza at 5:00, and publicly declared that there would be no elections.

Soviet Cinerama came to "Radiocentro" theater. Dany, over his annoyance at her trip — the book having helped soothe him, — went with Ana to see it. They felt that, if they were going to have to live under the system, they might as well learn about the Russians. Frigid Siberia was shown. The drabness of their lives was apparent, even in their film for export. The Chavales de España orchestra was on stage. They sang lively *"Islas Canarias"* and *"Lisboa Antigua"*. Their music was gay and their songs beautiful, and they contrasted sharply with the movie.

That season, Dany and Ana made the rounds of the "Habana 1900" on P Street, with its flocked red wallpaper; unbelievably dark "El Roco" on 17th Street, below the Civil Engineers' Association, where the waiters struck matches for the customers to see their checks; "La Zorra y el Cuervo" on 23rd Street, below the street level, in the Medical Retirement building; "La Red" on 19th Street with its piano; red "Barbaram" on 26th Street. From all the record players, a male singer's voice reached them with the hit *bolero* song of the moment,

*"Volveremos a vernos los dos,
trataremos del tiempo borrar,
no tendremos en cuenta razones
que no sean las de nuestros corazones"*[80]

They went to *jai-alai* games at the *frontón* on Virtudes Street, appropriately dubbed "the Palace of Yells", where they watched the graceful Basque *pelotaris* often throw themselves on their backs on the floor or climb a couple of steps up the side wall to catch a flying ball in their basket and throw it against the purportedly perfect main wall. They enjoyed the lively game. They sometimes took Teresa along. Dany introduced a renown sports commentator to Ana at the refreshment counter. And sometimes they stopped at the Siglo XX restaurant for chocolate, and then walked the long way home.

They went to see an amateur performance of "The Pajama Game" at the Community House, in La Puntilla, staged by non-professionals, half of them American. Occasionally they attended refined recitals – sometimes Norwegian or Finnish – of the Pro-Arte Musical Society at the Auditorium in its Italian Renaissance style, on Calzada.

They once treated themselves to the "Copa Room" of the Havana Riviera Hotel. Ana had never been there before. It seemed very nice to her and the expensive ambiance of the night club was a change from the intimate atmosphere of the small lounges they frequented. She had kept her resolution and was not drinking half as much any longer.

Ana didn't like Elvira, but, when she asked her to accompany her after work to buy some material – she could sew, too, – Ana didn't know why she went along. In the narrow streets of Old Havana, the drivers approached the intersections with their hand on the horn instead of their foot on the brake. Sometimes cars dangerously neared each other as if they were going to smash head on with horns blaring. The smell of diesel fuel was strong. They passed a Chinese laundry. Three Chinamen sat in the back in relaxed conversation. There were never any women. A strong smell of bleach came out. Ana wondered if it were true they smoked opium. They walked down the narrow sidewalk with iron wheel guards in the conf ing quitting time rush, bumping into other women, all along Muralla Street in the direction of the bay, going into all the Poles' open yard goods shops – or were they Jews? – which lined the old narrow street on both sides, to the Plaza Vieja. A few men stepped down into the street to yield the way to them on the sidewalk. The Poles were at the entrances.

"Gome in, whad are you looging for?, jersey? For you..."

"I have some very beautiful fabrigs. Gome in, loog ad this gorduroy. I leave id for you in..."

"Loog, do you lige this bigué? If you wand id, sbecial..."

The Agrarian Reform Under Way

When Elvira had found her fabric, they took their respective buses and went their separate ways. Elvira had all the reserve of Elsa Toledo, with none of her congeniality.

One midday Ana was waiting for Dany by the pool of the Havana Riviera Hotel, five blocks away, to have lunch. They had rented a *cabaña* with Rina, Raquel and Elvira and they took turns, two or three at lunch time and two or three after work. Elvira didn't coincide with them often. She watched her now swim the length of the pool. Ana noticed she swam better than she, better than Dany too. She lifted her arms easily and her feet hardly broke the surface, splashing little water, effortlessly. They didn't talk. When Dany arrived, Elvira was leaving.

After lunch with Dany by the pool, Ana went in the Sales Department to deliver some orders to Leonardo and pick up some quotations, and walked in the middle of a discussion about ethnic origins.

"His parents are *'gaitos'*?", Ramiro asked about Mario.

"Oh, yes, they're 'peninsulars'," said Guillén, his pronounced Adam's apple jiggling.

Leonardo in blue thin striped *guayabera* and navy bow tie, was on the telephone, and Ana leaned against a file cabinet digging her spike heels into the thick carpet, to wait for him to finish talking.

"Raquel is the one who has two disgraces in her life", said Salvador in jest.

"Being Jewish and...?", asked Ramiro.

"... and colored?", ventured Rosa tactlessly, coming in with the afternoon mail for Mr. Butler, Guillén and the assistant export manager for Glass.

"Colored?", Salvador asked, surprised. "She's colored?"

"Yes", Ana answered matter-of-factly, maybe a little defiantly. "Can't you tell?"

"No, I didn't know. I was referring to her being queer." He paused and then wound up, "Then she has three disgraces."

"Yes, when I started working here and they introduced me to her", Ramiro said, "she gave me that strong handshake, and it left no doubt."

"You two have such minds!", said Ana, and Salvador laughed.

Leonardo was again pleading on the phone in a low voice with the girl he had recently met, a salesclerk at "La Fuente de Neptuno", the aquatic equipment store on the ground floor.

"But, Margarita, why? And Saturday? But why not, Margarita?"

Ana discreetly stepped away from his desk.

"How can she be Jewish and mulatto?", Guillén wanted to know.

"Her father was Jewish and her mother is colored", Ana said simply. She had once asked Raquel how her parents had met, and she had told her that her father had come to Havana from Jamaica with a *Jüdisch* vaudeville group to La Comedia Theater in the thirties and had met her mother at the Moishe Pipik restaurant on Acosta Street near the docks. There were some 10,000 Jews in the capital.

"That's strange", said Ramiro, who had Negro blood himself. "Then she's not really Jewish."

"Well, her mother adopted the Jewish religion", Rosa explained, "and Raquel was brought up as Jewish..."

"*Bas mitzvah* at thirteen and all", Ana inserted.

"...but she's not a 'pure' Jewess."

"Well, she wouldn't be considered one if her mother wasn't. The maternal line", Guillén said.

"You know, I feel sorry for her", said Salvador. "She doesn't really belong in either group."

"That doesn't seem to bother her." It somehow annoyed Ana that they should pity Raquel. "She's a very cheerful person."

"We don't know", said Guillén. And they didn't.

Carmen came in with a letter of credit for Butler. She had had her hair cut. Guillén asked her, "Who cut your hair,/ that left your ears?"

Carmen turned to Salvador. "Did you hear what he said?"

"That's older than walking", he answered.

Leonardo had hung up and, now joining the conversation, chanted, "If I loved you before,/ it was because of your hair,/ and now that you're hairless,/ I no longer love you."

Ana moved closer to his desk again.

"A man should never see a woman putting a girdle on", Ramiro was now saying to Rosa, in a counseling tone, "either with it on or without it, but never putting it on." Rosa was nodding.

"There was a shipload of German Jews in the bay for three days twenty years ago, before World War Two", Guillén said.

"Yes, I remember", said Salvador, "the 'Saint Louis'. I was nine years old." Guillén was the same age.

Rosa left, to finish delivering the mail to the rest of the office.

The conversation led to an interpretation by Guillén of the meaning of the two superimposed triangles of the star of David. The talk was in Spanish, the two Americans in the department not a part of it.

The Agrarian Reform Under Way 151

Guillén still had Fidel's picture under the glass on his desk. Carmen walked out. A couple of sailboats on the indigo blue gulf waters seemed to be framed in the north window.

"Well, we got Russian oil", commented Leonardo, "and now we get Russian advisers. Advisers on what?, communism? These ones don't need advice on communism."

"El Che and Raúl may be communists, Leonardo", argued Ramiro, "but I think Fidel isn't."

"Oh, come on, old man!", snapped Salvador, irritated. "The matron in a brothel is never a vi... Oh, I'm sorry, Ana."

Graciela came in with some typed letters for the signature of the assistant manager of her division.

"We're not a colony of the United States any longer", Ramiro contended.

"No, we're not 'Kolonia' any longer, now we're 'Russian Violets'," concluded Leonardo.

As Graciela passed Ramiro's desk on her way out, he said in a stage whisper, "Biplane!"

"Why?", she asked, and every pair of eyes in the department focused on Ramiro, including the Americans'.

"Because every time you go by", he said smugly in a hoarse voice, "you leave my cane on fire." He laughed. Ana was amazed at his obscenity. His marriage less than seven months before – although he had changed his engagement band to his right hand – hadn't restrained his coarse jokes.

The other men in the room grinned very discreetly. Leonardo's close-set eyes glanced briefly at Ana, and, embarrassed, he vigorously attacked his calculator; she pretended she hadn't heard and nearly buried her face in the invoices, orders and quotations on his desk. Graciela tossed her head back pretending offense and walked out of the office proudly, head held high, but suppressing a grin.

Dalia came in and Salvador asked her, "What happened with the pen I asked for?"

"That's what I'm bringing you", she said, holding up a ball point pen. She was suntanned and her skin was oily, her hair was sunstreaked and she had split ends, her nail polish was chipped and her elbows dingy, she wore no stockings, and had razor nicks on her legs and calluses on her heels. Her voice was high, she was missing an upper first molar, she covered her mouth shade-style in an exaggerated display of misinterpreted manners when she used a toothpick, and she crossed her silverware on her plate when she finished eating. Ana again briefly felt mildly surprised that Dalia had gotten a job in Wayne. She took the transfer forms from Leonardo and went back to her desk.

Ana had made fairly close friendships among her co-workers. Carmen sometimes went home with her for lunch. She had lately gone to Ramiro's bachelor party with Dany — she and Graciela the only girls, — to Nelia's wedding at the Church of Corpus Christi, to the bachelorette party of one of the pool typists at the Habana Hilton, to see one of the accounts clerks at the Antonetti Clinic on the birth of her son, to Graciela's birthday party in Santos Suárez, to Virginia's saint day party in Nuevo Vedado, once to the "Rodi" theater with Rina, and another time to the "Atlantic" with Eugenia.

In the spring, rumors started around the office that, because of the increasing restrictions on money export, the company intended to move its offices out of the country. Rolandito, the office boy, who operated the ditto duplicating machine in the mailroom, confided to them, "Meyers gave me a memo to make eleven copies, for the American executives, giving them information on Nassau and Kingston. The memo said they haven't decided yet between the two cities."

"Eleven? There are only eight Americans", Rina noted. "That leaves three copies."

"For Palacios", conjectured Graciela, "maybe Guillén and ...?"

"... and Mario?", Ana ventured wishfully — they did seem the most logical, — hoping that one of them, maybe Guillén or Mario, would share their deliberations with the other employees.

President Achmed Sukarno of Indonesia arrived on May 9 for a five-day stay.

An American pilot was killed when he landed on the North Circuit highway in Mariel to try to smuggle five Cubans out of the country, who were then taken to La Cabaña Fortress.

Diario de La Marina, founded in 1823 and published continuously for over a century and a quarter, was occupied by its employees in the early morning of May 11, and confiscated. José Ignacio Rivero Hernández, its editor and publisher, left for Miami.

Catholic students staged a dramatic symbolic burial of the *Diario*. The funeral candles flickered weirdly in the night, as the lugubrious procession wound through dark Jovellar Street, before its houses in a vaguely Victorian style with their porches hacked out of a corner, to the monumental stairs of the University for the final burial in the

The Agrarian Reform Under Way

knoll at 8:00.

"*Prensa Libre*", the largest afternoon newspaper, was taken over by force. Sergio Carbó Morera, its owner and editor, and Humberto Medrano, its assistant director, took asylum in an embassy and later fled to the United States.

"*Información*" and "*El Crisol*" newspapers published a pastoral letter issued by Monsignor Enrique Pérez Serantes, Archbishop of Santiago, in which he called on Cubans to fight communism.

Propagandist Dr. Carlos Rafael Rodríguez Rodríguez, director of the communist newspaper "*Hoy*" and spokesman for the regime, was appointed professor of Political Economics at the University of Havana.

Dr. Emilio Núñez Portuondo said in the States on May 3 that Fidel had subordinated himself to the Communist Party in 1946 and used the name Fidelio. Rafael Díaz-Balart, the brother of his daughter-in-law Mirta, offered the same information.

Beginning in May, the first anti-communist defectors went into the Escambray mountain range. Since May, broadcasts were heard in the country from the Swan radio transmitter station on the Caribbean island near the coast of Honduras.

By the spring, there was no chicken on Wednesday and dentists lacked gold and porcelain for fillings.

"A pair of scissors will become a prized possession", said Raquel, "to bequeath to relatives in a will. Fabric will be ripped with your teeth." Gloria laughed.

"There won't be any fabric to rip", said Batten soberly, "or wills." Nobody laughed.

Elvira talked Ana into joining a girls' Catholic congregation. "The further away you drift from God", she told her as she gathered together bill of lading, insurance certificate and commercial invoice for a shipment, "the harder it is to go back." Ana, who didn't consider her a friend, wondered that Elvira could influence her. She had such a prim air!

She started attending the congregation Sundays for early Mass in the chapel, which they left singing *Salve Regina*, breakfast in the raised dining room afterwards with the delicious meat pastries, and later the circles. They held conferences about marriage, the Christian Social Doctrine and Papal Encyclicals. One of the lecturers in charge of a circle warned them, "Don't pray too fervently for something that may not be good for you, because you might get it." Another one discussed the rhythm method of birth control and commented on abstinence. The talks seemed indirectly aimed against the socialist government in general, but carefully devoid of any direct reference. It was a sound, healthy atmosphere. But Ana hadn't been to confession in over seven years, she hadn't taken communion since the Lent of 1953, when her cousin Laura had gotten married, and, after what she'd done, she was ashamed to go to confession. The older members, with their pale blue wide ribbons of the Daughters of Mary around their necks, appeared much at ease with each other, seemed to have a comfortable acquaintance to which Ana felt an outsider, and bestowed kisses on one another when they met. Elvira, her good deed of introducing her accomplished, moved in her own circle and left Ana on her own, and she felt an alien.

Dr. José Ignacio Rasco, leader of the Christian Democratic Movement, took asylum in an embassy. So did Aureliano Sánchez Arango. Rasco, Sánchez, Dr. Manuel Antonio de Varona and Lieutenant Manuel Artime Buesa left for Miami in the spring. A new wave fled for Florida, made up of doctors, lawyers, engineers, architects, university professors and teachers.

Herman Marks, the American who it was said had given the *coup de grace* as executioner at La Cabaña to more than seventy death convicts, fled from Isle of Pines with an American girl on a small boat, "Sea Coral", bound for Mexico, alleging that Fidel was a communist.

The government confiscated *"El Crisol"* morning newspaper without a receipt for the properties taken.

Three men hijacked a launch and headed for the United States, where they asked for asylum. The next day others left in another launch from Guajaibón beach, in Mariel, northbound. Three more left from Caibarién, Las Villas and arrived, after twelve days, on the coast of Florida.

By June 8, as many children over five as it was possible lived in the schools, so they would be under the influence of the teachers, instead of their parents'.

The government confiscated the Nacional, Habana Hilton, St. John's and Meyer Lansky's Havana Riviera hotels in Vedado, the Rosita de Hornedo by the sea and Tropicana nightclub in Larrazábal on June 12.

Captain Manuel Beatón Martínez, who had killed Major Cristino

Naranjo in Camp Libertad, expressed himself against communism and was sent to La Cabaña Fortress. In the spring he managed to escape to the Sierra Maestra, with which mountains he was well familiarized, and he killed Major Francisco Tamayo. The rural militia captured him on June 12 in La Bayamesa, near the Sierra, in El Cobre, his shoes torn and his feet bleeding, as well as fourteen others, without food or water. They were taken to Santiago de Cuba. They were tried, Beatón was executed by the firing squad at La Cabaña, as were two other men, and the other twelve were sentenced to prison terms.

Tuesday, as Ana entered the reception room after lunch with Dany at the awning-covered ample terrace full of tables of "El Carmelo", atop its wide entrance stairs, on Calzada, Elsa was disconnecting a line, and she commented, "Do you know that, when answering the phone, they now call the Habana Hilton *'Habana Libre'*?"

"Unbelievable!", reacted Ana, disconcerted.

Elsa shook her head taking the headphone off. After an instant, she said, "Oh, today is your birthday, isn't it? Much happiness. How old are you?"

Mario was coming in just then and inserted, "Happy birthday."

"Thank you. Twenty-three."

"Twenty-three?", Mario said, halting momentarily by the switchboard. "Well, don't tell anybody. You don't look over twenty." He proceeded to his department behind the reception room.

Nelia announced as she came in, "Boza Masvidal warns against communism." Monsignor Eduardo Boza, Auxiliary Bishop of Havana, was rector of St. Thomas de Villanueva University. She headed toward the corridor.

Leonardo gave Ana an orchid corsage that afternoon with the remark, "To think I give you flowers to go out with another...!"

The government put the hotels back in operation on the 17th and announced that wages would be cut. Ex-Senator Alfredo Hornedo Suárez's gigantic Blanquita Theater in Miramar was confiscated.

One evening after work, when Dany was going to classes, Ana went to visit Rosa Izquierdo, in Ensanche de La Habana. One block south was what a decade before had ambitiously started out to be "Film City" and had died in the attempt. The porch gave out directly on the sidewalk. A blue decal of the Diocesan Catechist Council on the window glass asked, "Will this boy be a believer or an atheist?" Rosa was plump and had small hands and feet; she was bulky only around her hips which spread out and surrounded her like a keg, misleading one into thinking she had borne a brood of children. Her light straight hair was wound in a single thick ringlet that hung over one shoulder. There was a copy of Malaparte's "The Flesh" on a little table in the living room. Rosa's mother, a fat, gray-haired woman, insisted that Ana stay for dinner. She thought she'd skip classes. They served lentil soup, pickled kingfish slices, plantain *fufú*, fresh cucumbers and sweet corn flour. Rosa's father, a tall man, and a watchmaker, hardly uttered a word during the dinner.

After supper, Olga, their upstairs neighbor, dropped by, her hair in curlers. She was wearing a frown and seemed sour about something. After the introduction, which she acknowledged absently, she mentioned something vague about her boyfriend having to study, and Ana wondered if that could be the reason for the frown and the sourness. Rosa did Ana's hair in a twist, as the opening music of the "Palmolive Novel" came from a radio nearby. They made small talk, but Olga mostly snapped her answers. After a few futile attempts, Rosa's companion to Ana's name day gathering arrived, wearing his arrogant smile, and Ana decided to hurry and try to make two classes after all, and she rushed off to school.

Manuel Artime's MRR (Revolutionary Recovery Movement) was the most significant opposition group operating in Cuba. Manuel Ray, ex-Minister of Public Works, had organized the opposition MRP (People's Revolutionary Movement) in the first part of the year. The DEUR (Revolutionary University Students' Directorate), formed by university students under the leadership of Alberto Muller Quintana and Juan Manuel Salvat, had been operating since February. Also operating was the 30th of November Movement, made up of followers of ex-Secretary General David Salvador. La Cruz Organization was in Miami.

On June 22, the FRDC (Cuban Democratic Revolutionary Front) was organized in Mexico by Manuel Antonio de Varona Loredo, of the Democratic Rescue Movement; José Ignacio Rasco Bermúdez, leader of the Christian Democratic Movement; Manuel Francisco Artime Buesa, of the Revolutionary Recovery Movement; Justo Carrillo Hernández, representing the Montecristi Revolutionary Group; Ricardo Sardiñas, of the Anti-Communist Organization Bloc, and Aureliano Sánchez Arango, for the Triple A Democratic National Front.

The labor in Cuba was officially headed by Secretary-General Jesús Soto, but the real power was old communist Lázaro Peña. *"La*

The Agrarian Reform Under Way

Calle" afternoon newspaper was run by the Directorate, *"Verde Olivo"* magazine was the organ of the armed forces, "Mella" was intended for the youth, women had *"Unidad Femenina"*, and *"Tierra"* was geared to the countrymen.

The Prime Minister confiscated the "Sabanilla de Birán" latifundium, the property of the Castro family, in Mayarí, its owners being properly compensated. The mother, Lina Ruz González, upset, left for Mexico.

The waiter at the cafe near the school came up to them and addressed Ernesto, but smiled at Ana, "Look", he held the empty *crème de menthe* bottle to him, "it was emptied yesterday and I kept it for you."

"Oh, thank you", said Ana. It had been so nice of the man to remember.

"Wait, I'll wash it for you."

"No, it'll be fine like that", Ana reached for the bottle and ran her palm over the smooth bulgy bottom. "I'm going to put black sand in it that I brought from Isle of Pines."

When Dany was through at the university before Ana was at 11:00, he drove to the school and surprised her waiting for her outside.

Ernesto called Ana home every day at lunch time. Sometimes after classes when Dany didn't come to wait for her outside, he walked her the 16 blocks to her home, out of his way, and sometimes they stopped at a restaurant which advertised turtle soup as its specialty to have hot chocolate with yucca *churros*. He lived near the Medina Park. He had a somewhat cynical attitude toward life and there was a hint of irony in his smile, as if he were mocking the world. When they met, Ernesto would kid Dany. He once called to Ana from across the street, as they were driving away in Dany's DeSoto, just for his benefit, "What time do you get home? I'll call you up at midnight, all right?" Ana knew full well he didn't intend to call her. Dany didn't comment on it, but it was obvious he didn't take the kidding very good-naturedly. It may have been just a coincidence that when he took her home that night, he stayed at the door until 12:15.

She and Ernesto had been studying in Ana's living room over some advertising displays on a Sunday afternoon just before midterm exams and Teresa was about to serve them pound cake and ice cream, when shortly before 7:00 they heard an explosion and the vibration raised the papers from the coffee table a few centimeters in the air. Ernesto ran out to the street. Teresa turned the radio on trying in vain to hear some news. He came back a while later with the news that the San Ambrosio Arsenal had blown up. The pound cake with ice cream was forgotten. They went up on the red-clay tiled roof baked by the setting sun, with Teresa, stepping over the convex wire-covered drains and around the small chimney, and they saw the smoke rising into the sky to the southeast. An explosion had occurred in the Punta Blanca underground munitions depot by the Cayo Cruz refuse dump on the other side of the Atarés inlet near the Vía Blanca, reducing the old quarry-stone building above to dust, destroying the garrison over 300 yards away and causing the better part of the nearby military installations to collapse. There were two dead and 45 wounded. Windows three miles away shattered and the odor of acrid smoke was perceived far away. Damage reached over $1,000,000. People again speculated on the cause. They said it had been the work of counter-revolutionaries. The government claimed it had been an accident. And the truth was not known.

Castro stated, "He who is an anti-communist is a counter-revolutionary."

The Texas Company refinery in Santiago, the most modern plant in Cuba, built at a cost of over 16 million dollars, was intervened on June 29, and the Naviera Vacuba shipping company was confiscated.

Olga came to the office one afternoon to wait for Rosa.

"Why don't you come with us, Ana?", Rosa urged her. "We like to go to the Sugar Bar once in a while. It's really nice there, girl."

"Well, all right, for a while." She had a white waffle *piqué* two-piece dress on with flat gold buttons.

They sat in the top-floor bar of the "Habana Libre" by the glass wall that looked over the west. The lights of the city turning on at dusk, while its night face gradually came to life, made a beautiful view.

Ana asked for a pink lady. Olga Salazar wore a perpetual frown, for a reason Ana couldn't make out. She had green eyes, light colored curly hair which she bleached lighter and wore very short with bangs, and a straight, thin line for a mouth. She was very outspoken and talked in a natural, unaffected way that Ana liked. She had outbursts of laughter and short moments of sullen silence. She didn't work. She said she was dating a well-to-do mamma's boy, owners of a candy factory, who got to see her only on Saturdays or once more during weekdays. The neon ballerina of the Tropicana sign

The Agrarian Reform Under Way

across the street was lit. Twenty-third Street was a moving stream of lights, white streaks approaching, red streaks receding.

The talk turned to personal subjects.

"There's no reason why a girl can't stay a virgin", Olga declared openly. "There are m*a-a-an*y ... things she can do without going all the way."

Ana was embarrassed at the girl's frankness and even afraid she might be overheard — while Rosa only listened, not giving any opinions, — and she hesitantly agreed softly, "That's right".

"Well, I don't do anything", Rosa now stated. "... I went out with Meyers a couple of times."

"Meyers?", asked Ana, surprised. "But he's married."

"Yes", Rosa surprised her even more, "but his wife wasn't here then... The office's really like 'Fabian Publications'," she said referring to the fictitious firm in the movie "The Best of Everything".

"I didn't even suspect it."

"Nobody knows."

In the summer, construction on the INAV housing projects across the bay in East Havana was at a standstill because money was scarce. During 1960, Castro socialized Cuba's economy. By mid-year, 40 percent of the land was controlled by INRA in about 900 cooperatives. The trend was toward Soviet state farms and communes of the Chinese type. The peasant received housing, medical care and education. The *"cooperativista"*'s dwelling was of cement block, with cane **bagasse** roof and tile floor, and had electricity, running water and a toilet. The cooperatives had a school, a small clinic and a people's store.

It was compulsory for medical students to serve for six months in the countryside before being allowed to graduate. Teachers had to serve in the remote rural sections.

They expanded rice cultivation, hog breeding and dairy farming for the population. INRA shipped the best breeding cattle to the slaughterhouses.

By mid-1960, the only political party allowed was the communist one.

CHAPTER 6

GOOD-BY TO TRACES OF THE GOOD LIFE

> *"¿Quién da fuerzas al brazo que, robusto
> hace a Tus leyes firme resistencia
> y que el celo, que más la reverencia,
> gima a los pies del vencedor injusto?"*[6]
> *(Soneto "Dime, Padre Común",*
> Bartolomé Leonardo de Argensola)

On July 1st the government intervened the British-owned Shell Oil Company refinery. When lifting the telephone receiver at any hour during the first few days in July, one had to listen to a woman's voice repeating, "With the fatherland or against the fatherland. Everyone to fulfill his duty to the revolution. On the twenty-sixth everyone to the Sierra with Fidel. Fatherland or death. We shall win."

Since rumors of the company's transfer had started, the employees had drawn much more tightly together and had formed much closer friendships. Sometimes in the summer Ana went to the movies with Graciela, the secretary to the Glass Export Sales Manager, and, after the movie, like Hitchcock's "The Gazebo" with Glenn Ford, to have caramel ice-cream baked Alaska at the "Carmelo" or to the outdoor tables of "El Jardín" restaurant. Graciela lived in Santos Suárez, in one of the high houses on San Julio Street with the garage below, the stairs on the side and the small porch over the garage.

On one such warm evening, after Williams' "Suddenly Last Summer" with Elizabeth Taylor, over sodas at "La Casa Potín" on Línea, they started talking about Dany and a boyfriend that Graciela had had, who had apparently left her.

"When you love somebody, you're not blind to his faults", said Graciela, "you see them, but they somehow don't seem to matter too

---

[6] Who gives strength to the arm which robustly
offers resistance to Thy laws
and makes jealousy, rather than reverence,
moan at the feet of the unjust conqueror?

much."

"It's funny how intensely others can dislike certain faults that don't bother one so much", Ana tried to explain how she saw it. "And they in turn can shrug off other defects that would make you sizzle!" Traffic along Paseo grew. The show at the "Trianón" had ended. "This boy used to have a way of re-living everything he told you about", Graciela recalled with fondness, tapping the ashes off her cigarette with a dreamy smile. "If he was talking to you about hunting, he would get up and aim at his game with an imaginary gun" — Graciela now aimed at a lamppost on Línea — "and simulate the noise of the shot, 'Bang!, bang!'." — Her hand even recoiled. — "If it was fishing, you would see him cast his imaginary line and reel it in..." Her green eyes glinted.

And that, thought Ana, would have made *me* embarrassed. Aloud, she wondered instead, "And what happened?"

"Well, for some reason, he married somebody else..." She paused, reminisced, then added full of wonder, "And do you know that, on his honeymoon, he called me long distance!"

What a cad!, Ana thought. And she imagined Graciela would probably not be one to cry or reproach him over the phone, had no doubt handled it with much dignity and sophistication. Graciela was tall and wore her light hair with a peculiar greenish hue in a bouffant and her green eyes had feline yellow flecks. She walked slightly spinning her heels inward and the tips out, which evidenced she had gone to modeling school. It was obvious the girl was, for some reason unfathomable to Ana, still in love with the man. She wondered if she had still seen him after he got married. They said good night. Rina had mentioned something once about Graciela's dating a married man where she had worked before. Ana climbed the curious stairs on the sidewalk of "A" Street. And, when she had first started working at Wayne, she had briefly dated Palacios, the accountant. Well... She headed on home.

That season saw the hemline hiked up by the arbiters of fashion, and Ana duly raised hers to above the knee.

Dr. José Miró Cardona, former Prime Minister, resigned as professor and sought asylum in an embassy.

On July 5, President Eisenhower refused to buy the remaining 700,000 tons of the 1960 sugar quota. The next day, the law was approved for the nationalization of American property by forcible expropriation. Some 3,000 resident Americans were starting to leave the country.

Twenty pilots and two crew members of the Cubana de Aviación Company asked for asylum when they arrived in Miami in the first week of July.

The "Gravi" factory of toilet articles in Jovellanos was intervened.

Che Guevara stated to Australian journalists on the 13th that any attempt by the Russians to establish a communist satellite in Cuba "would be resisted to the last drop of blood".

The FEU ousted the University governing council and dismissed most of the 650 professors, and the curriculum, the procedures and policies were changed.

Captain Antonio Núñez Jiménez, back from the communist countries, praised them extravagantly on television and won himself the nickname "Little Red Riding Hood".

"Everything is wonderful there according to him", Danilo said sarcastically in the lunchroom in their mid-afternoon coffee break.

Even Ramiro conceded, "He's exaggerating a little."

"Raúl has seen it rose-colored since he was twenty-two", said Rina.

"Listen, my brother-in-law was in the University with Fidel", Salvador remarked, "and he says that he used to skip classes, and only thought of stirring up the students and starting quarrels among them; even back then he was considered an agitator."

"Yes, now it turns out everybody knew him since he was in kindergarten and knew he was a communist", Ana burst out. "But then, why didn't anybody say anything before?"

"And how did you react — all of you! — in January of last year when I tried to tell you that you were going to regret this?", Salvador challenged. "You had been given a brand-new idol and you didn't want anybody to taint him."

"That's true, but you didn't say that he was a communist, or that he'd taken part in the 'Bogotazo', or anything like that, like people are saying now."

"That's because I didn't know it; all I knew was that he was an agitator. And, even if I had known it, you would have told me I was seeing ghosts."

"The truth is nobody knew who Fidel was", said Danilo. "Most of the people are ignorant and they were never interested in finding out where he'd come from."

"We used to content ourselves with telling little jokes", said Elsa,

Good-by to Traces of the Good Life 163

"– started God only knows if by themselves – like that one at the end of the year, and things like that."

"But we had some extremists like Oto Meruelos and Conte Agñero yelling on the radio and calling them 'cattle thieves'," said Guillén, "who drove the people to them even more."

"It was then we should have bothered to find out what kind of a man he was", Danilo reflected.

"I have to confess myself guilty", admitted Ana. "I didn't start reading about him until late July, after Urrutia's resignation."

"The very same is going to happen to the rest of the West Indies and Central America", Guillén predicted.

Rolandito, whom they had asked to cash their paychecks at the nearby Pujol Bank, came in with their envelopes and stuck his right arm out in front, jokingly saying, "Hail Nikita!"

A Mass at the Cathedral of Havana attended by a television actor and a radio announcer was violently interrupted, and thirteen parishioners were arrested. A mob outside the Jesús de Miramar Church shouted insults to the congregation in Mass.

On July 18 the regime confiscated *Bohemia* magazine, with 52 years of publication, *Carteles*, published for 36 years, and *Vanidades* women's magazine. Miguel Angel Quevedo, publisher and editor of *Bohemia*, took asylum in an embassy and was followed by Antonio Ortega, editor of *Carteles*. Enrique de la Osa took over the direction of *Bohemia* magazine. Luis Felipe Gómez Wangüemert, father of the late José Luis, directed *El Mundo* newspaper.

A petard blew up in the door of the office of the Communist Party on Omoa Street.

Castro was absent for nine days – while wishful rumors spread that he had died, – only to reappear on television. Their "greatest leader" had had pleurisy. He publicly shifted his attitude from neutralism toward cooperation with the Soviet bloc. He announced the arrival of automatic rifles from "the sister country" of Czechoslovakia.

People went *en masse* to the "Camilo Cienfuegos" boarding scholastic city near the Sierra Maestra in Manzanillo for the 26th of July celebration that year. The militia yelled, "Fidel!, Fidel!,/ what is it with Fidel,/ that the Americans cannot handle him?" Castro stated that his goal was to "turn the Andes mountains into the Sierra Maestra of the American continent". It made sensible persons shudder.

After classes, Ana and Dany attended a public fair at La Punta

Park by the bay. Ernesto tagged along. The breeze blew in. *"Guapachá"* music blared from the loudspeakers. The rabble shouted.

The First Latin-American Socialist Youth Congress opened at the "Blanquita" theater on July 29.

Raúl Castro visited Prague, Moscow and Egypt in mid-summer.

A pilot of Cubana asked for asylum in Miami, another one and a co-pilot elsewhere in Florida, and two more in New York before the month was over.

Major Raúl Chibás and his wife arrived in a small boat on Key West, where they asked for asylum.

In the summer of 1960, the third wave of exiles arrived in the States induced solely by communist infiltration.

By summer, the rumors going around the office were confirmed: The company was moving its offices.

Gustavo and Blanca were spending fifteen days at Bacuranao Beach when, on August 6, Castro expropriated the so-called Cuban Electric Company — with its Kalisto Kilowatt personification, — a subsidiary of an American company, itself a subsidiary of the Electric Bond and Share Company of New York, also the Cuban Telephone Company, chiefly owned by International Telephone and Telegraph, and 24 other American companies, including Esso Standard Oil Company and Sinclair Company, as well as the 33 American-owned sugar mills.

"Well", Méndez conceded about the sugar, "the truth is that a Cuban industry so intrinsic and basic, should not be in foreign hands."

Blanca returned from vacation to find herself working for the "Antonio Guiteras" electric enterprise. The telephone company would be named "Thirteenth of March".

Sunday a Pastoral signed by Cardinal Arteaga was read in all the churches. At the Cathedral of Havana, the parishioners were besieged and insulted by a mob that attacked them with sticks, stones, pipes and rods. Archbishop of Havana Monsignor Evelio Díaz Cía complained of persecution and asked for freedom of worship.

In Miami Beach the "Liberation Alliance" was founded by Pedro Luis Díaz Lanz, Luis Conte Agüero and nine other Cubans.

Celia Sánchez had all the movement's important documentation in Fidel's residence in Cojímar. Her apartment was on 11th Street # 1007 between 12th and 14th Streets, in Vedado.

Major Juan Almeida got married at the Santo Tomás Church in Santiago.

Good-by to Traces of the Good Life 165

In August the professional associations were taken over by revolutionaries.

Father Manuel Deboya and six members of the Catholic Youth were captured after a gun battle in which two policemen were killed and the priest wounded.

At the Eighth National Assembly of the Popular Socialist Party Blas Roca proposed a fusion of forces.

Five men escaped in a small boat and asked for asylum when they arrived in Florida. Six other persons armed with pistols arrived in Key West on a boat in the early morning hours and asked for asylum.

Alberto Muller, of the Revolutionary Student Directorate, and two other students sought asylum in Miami. Lieutenant Erneido Oliva González resigned as army officer and flew on August 18 to Miami, where he asked for asylum. Ramón Barquín and eight other army officers turned in their resignations because they didn't agree with the communist regime.

Armaments were bought from Italy. By the end of August, Czechoslovakia started sending weapons.

The Federation of Cuban Women was founded, and Vilma Espín elected as president.

In Camagüey masses at La Soledad, Las Mercedes and La Caridad Churches were interrupted by agitators.

Loans to workers in advance of wages paid twice a month were made by chits. The United Fruit Company, the prime target in the attacks on monopolies, operated all year round and paid its workers $3. per day. The cooperative paid the members $2.50.

The Nicaro Nickel oxide condensation plant in Lengua de Pájaro, in Mayarí, Oriente, paid wages from $4.40 a day for common laborers up. The incomplete plant of the Moa Bay Mining Company in Baracoa, Oriente would have been the largest producer of nickel and cobalt in the Western Hemisphere. It had schools for English-speaking and Spanish-speaking youngsters, a Protestant and a Catholic church, a supermarket and a cafeteria. Moa Bay Mining Company was confiscated at the end of August.

José M. Bosch Lamarque, who had contributed almost $1,000,000. to the revolution, left the Island, and all the Bacardí Rum Company property was confiscated.

Ana was walking alone down 23rd Street in front of the Riviera theater in the late summer afternoon toward the "Carmelo" restaurant when she heard a girl's voice call down to her from the stairs of the

theater with its blue sign, "Ana!"
 She turned and looked up to see Olga, Rosa's neighbor, with another girl, looking at the posters outside by the ticket booth. She waved at her.
 "Why don't you call me?", Olga yelled spontaneously, "and we'll get together some time? You have my number, don't you?"
 She didn't, but she could always ask Rosa. "I'll call you up next week", Ana yelled back to her, climbing the stairs to the restaurant next door.
 The government confiscated the three rubber tire companies, U.S. Rubber, Goodyear and Firestone, southeast of the capital, which were valued at over 30 million dollars.
 The General Assembly of the Cuban People took place in the Civic Plaza. Countrymen were brought by trucks and trains from the country. Over half a million people attended. The intoxicated crowd changed their chants to, "Cuba yes, Yankees no!", "Fidel, for sure,/ hit the Yankees hard!" and "Up, down,/ the Americans are turkeys". Castro broke the Rio Treaty, tore up the OAS's "Declaration of San José" and in response, proclaimed on September 2 the "Declaration of Havana", condemning the United States and the Organization of American States. He announced he would establish diplomatic relations with Red China and break off relations with Nationalist China. The peasants' reaction was different from that of the previous year. Later, half of them complained that they had been treated like cattle.
 Castro crushed a conspiracy in the Navy and dismantled the corps.
 The next week, having obtained Olga's phone number from Rosa, Ana called her up on Friday after work.
 "Do you want to go to the movies?", she asked her.
 "I'm cleaning the house now", Olga surprised her by saying. "Mirta, a friend of mine, called me up this morning and she wants to go to the movies too. If you don't mind, she'll be coming along."
 "Why don't you two come over to my house? There are more movies around here to choose from,... uh... six within walking distance."
 "All right", Olga said agreeably. "They're advertising 'Seven Samurai' over the radio, a Japanese one. Is seven fifteen all right with you?"
 "Fine." She gave her the address.
 She had time to shower and have supper. They were punctual. Ana recognized Mirta as the fat girl she had seen with Olga on 23rd

Street the week before. Mirta talked little, in a fictitious way. She wore a lot of makeup and, in general, Ana didn't like her much. She worked as a salesclerk at "Fin de Siglo" department store. After the movies, they went for sodas at Kimbo Cafeteria, on L Street, in the Odontological Retirement building. And Ana later walked them to the bus stop. When it arrived, Mirta gave her a farewell kiss on the cheek and Ana was taken aback by the girl's affected gesture.

Castro confiscated the Portland Cement Company, Owens-Illinois Glass Company in San José de las Lajas and Swift & Company.

On September 4 the Bank of China was seized by the government. Practically all the resident Chinese were Nationalists, and many left the country. The communists took over the three Chinese newspapers, *"Hoy Men Kong Po"*, *"Wah Man Sion Po"* and *"Wan Man Yat Po"*.

Fidel tightened the restrictions for sending money abroad, which sped up Wayne Motors' decision to move their offices out of the country.

Early in September, Mr. Richard Sterling, the president of Wayne Motors International, called the employees to a meeting in the Accounting Department and, standing before the file cabinets, in his blue pin stripe seersucker suit, very solemnly gave them the bad news in English, "The Company is moving to Nassau the end of October. We'll try to take as many employees with us as we can, but the local British government has asked us to take only the more necessary staff and fill the other positions with local residents − which we consider only fair. − Mr. Palmer will talk to you individually." It was the first time they had heard him say so much.

A muffled ripple ran through the room. The meeting was over. They walked out of the Accounting Department somewhat confused and quite subdued. Even though they had been expecting it, it was still a blow nonetheless.

"There is no evil that doesn't turn out for some good", Teresa consoled them that evening.

"Nor good that doesn't bring some evil", alleged Carlos.

The Havana Post English-language newspaper closed down on the 7th. Its owner, Mrs. Clara Park, and her husband had left for Miami.

The Minimax chain of grocery markets, American-owned, was nationalized early in the month.

Castro prohibited the traditional procession of the Virgin of Charity on September 8.

Three Russian ships arrived at the port of Havana.

CMQ radio and television network, Channel 6, was confiscated on September 12 and its owners, Abel and Goar Mestre, left for Miami. Manuel Fernández, owner of Radio Progreso, "the Wave of Merriment", also left for Miami. All television and radio networks were seized and linked in the so-called FIEL, which proclaimed Cuba as "free territory of America" on station identification.

During the following week, they were called into Mr. Palmer's office one by one and asked simply whether they would consider moving to Nassau. Ana had started four days before trying to get another job in Havana and stay, but she wasn't sure she could find one. So she said she would consider it. No offer of a job was made. She wanted to stay in her own country with her family, instead of venturing out into a foreign country to share an apartment with one of her co-workers and be on her own. Her parents would stay behind, at least for the time being. And she was attached to them. She loved them and respected them. And she didn't know whether they would reunite if she left first.

"I have a friend in a ministry", Rina told her when she expressed her wish to stay. "I think you're crazy, but I'm going to talk to her. She's the secretary to the head of a department and has pull because she's having an affair with a big fish in the government."

Lydia Dennis later called Ana in to see Mr. Meyers. He left the office door open.

"Ana, you know we're only taking the more necessary employees with us", he told her and she wondered if he'd had to look up her name. She hadn't been really sure until then that she'd be made the offer to go with the company. "And we've decided to offer you your same job in Nassau. The secretaries to the three Export Sales Managers will be getting a salary of two hundred and forty-five dollars, commensurate with the standard of living there. Will you consider moving with the Company?"

This represented only a $15. a month raise to her, and she'd be starting at the same salary as Graciela and Raquel, whom she had trained, without taking into account her seniority. She was hurt and thought she deserved at least a $30. a month increase, but she swallowed and said, "Yes, I would."

She didn't want to leave. She was satisfied having started college, joined a Catholic organization... When she came out of Mr. Meyers' office, instead of going back to her own desk in front of Mr. Kent's office, she headed toward the Accounting Department. She hadn't seen Dany go into Meyers' office. When he looked up at her from the payroll, she raised her eyebrows in a silent question and Dany nodded − he had already been offered a transfer. − He pointed to the tape from his calculator with his pen. It resembled a roller coaster and it made her think of Coney Island. The east window offered an incredible view of the intense blue gulf. It was almost lunch time. She called her mother to let her know she wasn't going home for lunch. At 12:00, Dany was waiting for her at his desk. He called the "Concierto" restaurant next door to have club sandwiches brought up.

They had the lunchroom, almost always deserted at this hour, to themselves.

"What are you going to do?", he asked her.

"I don't know. I think I'm going to have to accept it. I don't think I'm going to find anything here."

"It's been a very short time. When did you apply?"

"At the Bank of Foreign Trade, on Friday, and they haven't answered me anything. Rina talked on Tuesday to her friend at the ministry who said she could hire me, but she hasn't called me. And my brother hasn't been able to do anything at the Ministry.

"But it's only been six days. It's too soon. I saw you sitting in Meyers' office. What did you say to him?"

"Oh!, I said yes. There's always time to back out. Didn't you?"

"Oh, no!, I told him I'd think it over. I guess I'd better say I will then, hadn't I?"

"I want you to do what you want, Dany, not what I have to," she said only because she felt she must say that.

"What I want is for us to be together, *mi vida*. Here or outside it doesn't matter much." She felt relieved.

Bernardo arrived with their lunch. The factory whistle blew sadly in the distance to the south. They ate their sandwiches, toasted on the grill with the crusts trimmed off, in preoccupied silence.

Teresa had been picking at her food that evening, her hair still damp from rinsing it with rosemary to make it blacker, which Matilde had probably gotten for her from the ambulant herb vendors' pushcarts on the sidewalk of Calzada de Cristina. "I want to go to Miami to take the American money we have out of the country", she announced as she cleared away the rice with squid and brought out the egg custard.

"That's risky, Tera", said Carlos. "They're searching people. Give crackers to Anita."

"They don't search everybody", Teresa argued. "It's more likely they'd search you than me. Look, your father brought lard crackers."

"It's only a hundred dollars. It isn't worth it", her father insisted. "That bakery on Amargura makes good crackers." Since Gustavo had been working at the Ministry, he rode the bus home.

"But it's all we have in American currency", her mother said stubbornly. "Now that Ana María's leaving, it'd be good to have it safe in the United States, and she probably can't take any money out."

"Mamá is right, Papá", agreed Ana. "If I leave first, and you decide to follow afterwards, it'll be good to have a little money outside, and I'll probably be searched. The crackers are good."

"We don't know what's going to happen here", Teresa persisted. Méndez let himself be talked into it.

When Ana mentioned it to Guillén and Leonardo at the office, Guillén asked her, "Do you think your mother will pass a hundred dollars for me into the States?" She noticed that Fidel's picture was no longer under the glass on his desk.

Her mother was willing. She left for Miami Wednesday afternoon, unsearched, to deposit their own hundred dollars and Guillén's hundred in a savings account.

Dany suggested a trip to Soroa that weekend.

"We can't go there by ourselves", protested Ana. "And Mamá's away."

"We've gone out by ourselves before", he said in a great understatement.

"But this is different, it's in another province."

"What about Norma? Or your sister-in-law?"

"Norma's sick and Blanca wouldn't have anybody with whom to leave the children." She was glad he didn't mention Isle of Pines. But they had arrived there separately, and separately they had left.

"Will my sister do?"

She was surprised. "Yes, she'll do." So she was finally going to meet a member of his family!

Ana talked to Sonia for the first time. She had only seen her that one time from a distance in the park and not once had she answered the phone all the times Ana had called in the past almost two years.

She was about 24, with small slanted eyes, suntanned, somewhat overweight, with rather wide shoulders. Dany had told her she worked at the Corporación de Asistencia in Larrazábal. She was pleasant. She smiled broadly and offered her hand, which Ana took briefly. They only said, "Much pleasure" in duo, and didn't talk again during the sixty-mile drive, while Ana sat in the middle and Sonia looked out the window. They drove west on the Central Highway.

Ana had never been in Pinar del Río province before. They passed cloth-covered tobacco fields interspersed with the large gray thatched leaf-drying houses. Just outside Guanajay, a sign to the left of the highway indicated the road to the women's prison. They went through the town, where her grandfather Joaquín had worked as a bookkeeper, and she wondered where the stationery dealer store had been. The peepuls on either side formed a tunnel for the highway. As they approached Artemisa, Dany said, "This is the narrowest point of the island. Do you know it's thirty-five kilometers wide from north to south here?"

"This is where the military blockade was that Maceo evaded, isn't it?", Sonia asked.

"Yes, but across the mouth of the bay", Dany clarified, "on the night of Saint Bárbara's Day."

"You're filled with information", said Ana with genuine admiration.

He laughed. "I just remember odds and ends, from school days."

"But interesting odds and ends." She stopped herself, afraid Sonia would think she was praising him just because she was present. She also refrained from putting a hand on his arm in front of her.

To the left was a large home for the aged. They drove through Artemisa. Her father's grandparents had lived here in the 19th Century. The breeze carried the aroma of roasting coffee to them.

At Candelaria, they turned north off the Central Highway − Cuban pines abounded in the limestone soil − and they soon reached Soroa. The change in temperature they experienced surprised them. They drank coconut water at a thatched-roof restaurant − where Ana decided that Sonia didn't dislike her and her silence wasn't due to any discomfort; she probably only felt a little bored in her role of chaperon, and she had been imposed on to leave her own friends to accompany them, − while a man in an écru-colored *guayabera* and Panama hat sat alone at a nearby table eating a dish of pot *tamal*. The jukebox played,

*"... Domitila,
¿a dónde va?
con mantón de Manila..."*[81]

They started up the winding road that led through the forest vegetation to the top of the hill, 800 feet high. There was a lookout at the top and the view was, without any doubt, the most beautiful Ana had ever seen. The sight of the dark green mountain tops around them was breathtaking. The Manantiales river looked like a silver ribbon and the San Juan de Contreras creek winding below, between the Rosario ridge mountains, a mere silver thread reflecting the sunlight. The whole countryside seemed a scale model. The Guajaibón loaf was somewhere to the west. It was completely quiet, the clear autumn sky seemed barely above them and the whole world within their reach. It made her throat tighten, she felt close to Heaven, and she loved life and the world. It was the most impressive experience she had had. Dany had already been there before and was not so impressed as she. And she was jealous that he was not sharing this wonder with her for the first time.

"One of the most beautiful scenic spots", said Sonia, "is the Viñales lookout on a hill that overlooks the valley. You see the valley stretch away with its varying patches of green to the Organos range, and *'mogotes'*[41] are scattered around at random."

As they started down the mountain, a big family of country people were arriving in a dilapidated old car, five, six, seven people.

"Americans never see this", said Dany.

"They only know the 'Sloppy Joe's', the Prado, Tropicana and Varadero", Ana agreed. "That's because we don't have any tour agencies."

"No, a taxi driver waited for them at the airport or in front of the hotel, nominating himself a guide, asked them, 'Do you want to have a good time?', and whisked them off to a gambling casino, the 'Shanghai' and the prostitutes."

On the way down, they let Sonia walk ahead, and lagged behind, stopping often to kiss.

At the foot, Dany said, "There's a large nursery of rare orchids, a cave with winding steps to the bottom. Do you want to go down?"

"No", said Ana, apprehensively. "I don't want to go down into the earth." Walking up to the mountain top had been a marvelous expe-

[41] hummocks

rience. Going down into the depths of a cave would spoil the feeling, no matter how many orchids awaited her at the bottom to soften the impression. She had never liked even going down into the locker room under the courts of José Martí Park. They drove around the tourist center instead. There was a large swimming pool surrounded by little cottages painted in bright colors. And the new INIT of the government had done this. But it somehow conveyed an air of uniformity, imposition and gloom that made her unconsciously feel depressed.

"The biggest natural cave in Latin America, 'Santo Tomás', is in this province", Dany said pointing to the west, "near Viñales. It's sixteen kilometers long."

The three American banks, First National City Bank of New York, First National Bank of Boston and Chase Manhattan Bank, were nationalized on September 17.

The State Department of the United States advised the American citizens living in Cuba to send their families back to the States.

Berta Penabad, a typist in the pool, jilted by Ramiro now almost a year before, told Ana, "You and I could share an apartment. I hear the rent is higher there. Would you like to?"

"That'd be fine." And she really meant it would be. She knew Berta fairly well and liked her better than other girls in the office. She couldn't stand Elvira for a roommate. Graciela was a little too sophisticated, Rina too intellectual, Eugenia too rich and Virginia had a daughter. And Raquel wouldn't be a wise choice. Gloria and Carmen had not been offered transfers. Neither had Rosa, in spite of going out with Meyers. Yes, if she had to leave the country, she'd prefer to live with her. Berta had attended the University of Villanueva and lived in La Osa.

Nelia, delivering to Lydia some reports from Palacios, called to Ramiro, who, having left some invoices with Gloria, was walking back to the Sales Department, "You're going to become a father soon, aren't you?" Berta's glance shot up and, startled, she fixed her widened eyes on Nelia. She hadn't known.

"Yes", he answered in a low voice and stole a sideways glimpse at Berta, embarrassed, and she hooked her earphone back on and looked down at her work. She still cared.

"When?", Nelia probed, oblivious to having committed any blunder.

"The end of October", he answered over his shoulder and rushed off, his eyes down.

The Oriental Park horse racetrack, the Marianao dog racetrack, La Concha beach house and Coney Island amusement park were confiscated.

A flimsy crop dusting plane took off from Santa Fe beach in Bauta with a former army sergeant tied to the underframe, and landed on the Tortugas islands, in the Gulf of Mexico.

The government called the militia women to active duty.

Ana hadn't been going home for lunch in the last ten days. While Dany went with Mario or Palacios to Le Vendôme, she went to lunch with Berta. And they made plans sipping vermouth before lunch at the "Club 23", with its mahogany bar, below the street level, and took a taxi back to the office.

"Maybe we can get an apartment for eighty-five or ninety dollars there."

"I looked in an atlas. Did you know it has a population of only thirteen thousand?... One sixtieth of that of Havana."

"Imagine what boredom!"

"And what gossip!"

Sometimes Graciela joined them for lunch. On the high sidewalk before the Medical Retirement building, arranged in little piles, Martí's biography by Mañach and communist books were being sold.

In Guiteras park, across from the University, a petard blew up, toppling communist leader Julio Mella's bust.

Ana did all the paperwork to get her residence visa in the Bahamas. She went, with all the other employees being transferred, to the British Embassy on Morro Street. They became familiarized with the men's wives, with their wide hips and hyperactive children. She had lunch with Berta, Graciela and Rina at the Frascati, high above Prado, served by its waiter who looked so much like French movie actor Fernandel. She wrote to the boarding houses around Rawson Square in Nassau and obtained the rates for their first three weeks or so. And she got her visa.

She walked the thirteen blocks to her father's office, past the Ministry of the Interior, the elegant glass-tile domed Presidential Palace, now occupied by Fidel's chinless puppet Dorticós, the Holy Custodian Angel Church, where she had been with Dany last Holy Thursday, and President Zayas Park. An orange vendor peeled the fruit in his pushcart for his customers in a sort of carpenter's bench vise which removed the skins in neat long spirals. She passed the modern gray marble Palace of Fine Arts with its abstract sculpture. On Animas Street a woman on a third floor balcony — board strategically placed across the lower part of the railing — lowered a little basket tied to a rope for the itinerant vegetable vendor to put her purchase in. Then came the Principal de la Comedia theater, the Ministry of Defense, the personable art-déco Bacardí Building, out of a movie of the early forties, and the "Actualidades" theater. A man on a portico called to her, "Mami!", and she rushed on. Past Mayor Fernández Supervielle's tiny park, the Manzana de Gómez, the little Francisco Albear park, "Floridita" restaurant with the crown on its sign, and the luxurious and elaborate Centro Asturiano with its fancy lampposts. The 308-foot high dome of the Capitol came into view to the east just as, before the massive Havana Secondary Education Institute, Ana turned left into the narrow streets of Old Havana with its Sevillian architecture in coral limestone. In front of the vine-covered Holy Christ of the Good Voyage Church, a woman begged for alms.

The tired cage elevator in the old building on Villegas Street rattled laboriously up. Only the clatter of an old typewriter broke the noon silence of the quiet floor. Ana's heels clattered on the worn marble tiles. The transom over the door was perennially tilted, and the pebble glass door — "**Carlos Méndez and Son, Accountants**" now a memory of the past — stood open.. Méndez was on the phone and he waved her in as she hesitated at the door before walking in. She hadn't been in the office in five years, since the day she had been interviewed for the job at the import firm on Monserrate Street. She had come to tell him she had gotten the job. She had felt in high spirits then because in the previous three and a half months she had gone to interviews at a bank, a mattress manufacturer, a lumber yard, a construction firm, an oil company, some decorators, a cosmetic firm, an advertising agency, an automotive sales corporation, a foreign embassy and a nickel and cobalt mining company. One man told her he expected her to "become his shadow" and be willing to work until midnight when necessary, another one warned her he didn't like a girl who cried when he snapped at her, a third one corrected her punctuation, and one with effeminate manners told her he wanted a person whose numbers had "personality" and proceeded to show her how digits should and shouldn't be written. It hadn't been edifying; she had made a mistake spelling "license". She knew the ten best employment agencies in the city from Línea south to Carlos III and from Zulueta west to 12th Street. It was two months after Gustavo had gone to work with their father. They had just hired Alfonso and their office, teeming with activity and the three male voices, had seemed crowded then. Her father had treated them all to lunch of filet medallions at the "Pan American". The office now looked pathetically empty, with its high ceiling, her father facing the door, the one louvered window open behind him and the Banco Núñez blue calendar with raised gold letters on the wall, the other two wooden desks standing around him unoccupied like abandoned bastions. She sat at the one nearest him and waited.

When he hung up she announced, "I was given the visa."

"Good." He smiled, but his light brown eyes belied him. "Let's go down to have lunch." He left the papers spread on the desk, a glass paperweight on them, and the window open, and he locked the door behind them.

He put his arm around her shoulders and proudly introduced her to the pallid, stooped elevator man.

The Lonja del Comercio building peeked among the buildings to the east and its cupola topped by the Mercury rose above them.

"Roque, my daughter", Méndez said to the waiter at the cafe on Lamparilla with its white tiled walls.

"Very pretty girl", said the fat, short-waisted Spaniard. "You must be proud of her, Méndez."

"Very much."

"Thank you", Ana said to Roque.

"When will you be leaving?", her father asked her over the table after Roque had taken their orders.

"In a little over a month. Around October twenty-eighth." He was silent. "Unless I find a job here."

His eyes sparkled for a second, but his sense of duty immediately took over. "You have to think things over well, Anita. You have a future with that company; there won't be much of a future for you here." Their sandwiches in flute bread arrived.

Fidel travelled to New York to attend the General Assembly of the United Nations. He was embraced by editorialist Herbert Matthews. He stayed with the Cuban delegation at the Shelburne Hotel on Lexington Avenue, where he ordered that food be cooked for him in the room and, when reprimanded by management, he moved to the Theresa Hotel in Harlem, in an ostentation of camaraderie. On Monday he spoke before the delegates to the United Nations for four hours and twenty minutes, calling Kennedy an illiterate, ignorant millionaire. Nikita Khrushchev gave him a bear hug. He returned in a Soviet four-engine plane.

Russian weapons and over 600 military technicians arrived at the port of Mariel, in Pinar del Río province.

On September 27 the Democratic Revolutionary Front appointed Antonio Varona coordinator-general.

The company decided to give them all bonuses out of the money they couldn't take out of the country. Each employee received one according to his length of service and his salary. Ana got over $1,000. And Dany's was even larger, since his salary was $50. higher and he had been with the company one month longer than she. The day they received their checks, they went to the Pujol Bank to cash them themselves and then to lunch at the Mandarín Restaurant, high above 23rd Street. There was a lot of domestic money to spend and a very short time in which to spend it if they were to leave the country for good in less than four weeks.

"This was nice of them", Ana commented.

"They couldn't take it", Dany reasoned objectively, then cited the worn American phrase they heard so often, "Maybe it's 'tax-deductible'."

They went up the three wide steps leading from the restaurant to the bar and had a drink before lunch, while their table was set. They talked about so many different subjects — ranging from family to co-workers, from politics to effeminate men, — that Ana would often recall that long, quiet talk. It seemed like a farewell to their way of life. They had their lobster dish looking down at M Street, the Alaska apartment building and the Cattlemen's Association with its varnished wood columns and, despite taking a taxi, they were late getting back to the office.

Packing couldn't be put off any longer, and Tuesday Ana tackled the unpleasant chore sourly. She laid aside the three books she kept in her room, "Cecilia Valdés", "The Hundred Best Cuban Poems" and Heredia's poems, along with her photograph albums. She'd take this with her. And she packed her textbooks, all her other books, including "The Arabian Nights", from the living room bookcase and the records in a large cardboard box, and sealed it with gummed tape. Her parents would dispose of this later. Her brother had left seven books behind in the bookcase when he had married, Burroughs' "Tarzan of the Apes", Defoe's "Robinson Crusoe", Swift's "Gulliver's Travels", Stevenson's "Treasure Island" and d'Amicis'

"Cuore", and two old moth-bored fantastic adventure books by Jules Verne which had belonged to their father. She would take these to Gustavo; maybe Gustavito would read them when he were older. She took four books, "The Labyrinth of Oneself", *"Cresival"*, "Antaeus" and "The Hungry Blood". They were all by the same author. She asked her mother, "Do you want these books by Enrique Labrador Ruiz?"

"No, I haven't opened them in ten years. See if Blanca wants them. They are gasiform novels, that style he created."

She had to return Carpentier's "Lost Steps" to the lending library of the Lyceum and Lawn Tennis Club without having had time to read it. Only "The Treasure of Youth" tomes and the dictionary stood by themselves in the bookcase, and in the record rack, her father's operettas "Cecilia Valdés", *"María la O"* and *"Rosa la China"*.

She cleaned her wardrobe and her dresser of old clothes and packed them neatly for Matilde – they wouldn't fit Azucena. – She held up her fifteenth birthday party formal dress, in very pale yellow lace, covered with plastic, looking at it for a moment. Maybe Blanca would want to keep it for Blanquita. She left only her newer and more becoming clothes hanging in the wardrobe and folded in the dresser drawers, and only her make-up remained in a drawer and her jewelry and perfume on the dresser. She put her typewriter in its case, ready to take with her, and she tore up and threw away several letters already answered. There was one from Alvaro, her old boyfriend from when she had worked at the import company, written from New York, where he'd gone to live three years ago. She set it aside; there was time to throw it away later. She had met him in the little coffee shop on San Juan de Dios Street where she went for a soda on her coffee-breaks. He had worked in his brother's silversmith shop near the Ministry of Defense. For a moment she recalled their first cold, dry kiss on the ferry launch to Casablanca on an autumn evening almost five years ago, and later their inexperienced fumbling on her porch on 24th Street and sitting on the wall around the sinkhole – he hadn't had a car. – She had been his first steady girlfriend too, although he was all of twenty-one. His father had been a motorist on the M-5 streetcar until almost a year before, when he'd been retired as the Havana Electric Railway phased out its 39 lines of streetcars with their wicker seats. She remembered when her parents had made her accompany them to her uncle Guillermo's for dinner and she'd come back looking from the bus at all the wall clocks they passed on their way home, hoping Alvaro would still be around, without daring mention anything to them. Gustavo had been excused from those visits since he was seventeen, free to go see his girl-friend of the moment or get together with his friends at the park. They had sailed through almost two years of bliss, with casual treats to frothy *daiquirís* at the "Floridita" on special occasions, properly chaperoned, until he'd decided to leave for New York. There had only been this letter from him, very warm, but completely uncommitted. She looked at the blue-and-red bordered air-mail envelope with the address in his untidy handwriting. Maybe she would read it again later. But not now. She wondered what had become of him. She found a poem she had written long ago, "Your Memory". It sounded incredibly ridiculous.

"¡*Si supieras cómo anhelo tu mirada,*
cómo aguardo en vano tu regreso,
cómo espero de ti el ansiado beso
que me haga sentir de nuevo amada![69]

She had been eighteen then and didn't even know about what she was talking. Dany would wonder who had inspired her to write it. She put it between the pages of the book of poems.

A five-year old issue of *Vanidades* magazine with her graduation photograph, a few sheets of deckle-edged cream-colored stationery, ink, her fountain pen and a ball point pen stayed in the desk, and the bottle with black sand from Bibijagua beach on it, and in the nightstand, her mass book and her rosary. She'd take the white furry cat to Blanquita. She took Dany's picture in its wooden frame down from the wardrobe and laid it on the dresser, and took down her aunt Beatriz's lithograph of Saint Joseph and the bluebird-and-roses and pansies-and-ladybug prints, and the naked blue walls seemed to stare coldly at her. She took the basket with the black-eyed susan vine down from the window case – their neighbor's living room in the next building was empty – and placed it on the sill. Only the night lamp and the blue radio remained. She felt she had been uprooted. She pushed the box of clothes against the pilaster between the bedroom doors, under the bronze shelf, for Matilde to take Thursday.

On September 28 the Committee for the Defense of the Revolution was created, a neighborhood vigilance committee was organized on almost every block, and informers kept busy watching any move they fancied as shady.

After that first Friday when Ana went to the movies with Olga, it became a regular practice to get together on Friday afternoons. Sometimes they went to the movies and afterwards for ice cream or sodas, sometimes for supper at one of the Chinese cafeterias, others to the small playhouses, "Idal", "Talía", "El Sótano", "Las Máscaras", "Hubert de Blanck", "Las Víboras", "Prometeo", "Arlequín" or "Atelier", which had sprouted in the last six years, as the people became increasingly art conscious, where they saw plays, most by Cuban playwrights, like "Enter a Naked Man" or a soliloquy by Hada Béjar, some by Americans, like "Win a Million". And a couple of times they went to the Sugar Bar to drink cool, tall Tom Collins. But this she didn't tell Dany. She knew he wouldn't approve. He knew that was where Elvira had met her latest "suitor", after *a funeral*. Sometimes Mirta went along, or another one of Olga's friends.

Olga Salazar was an only child. Her father was a lawyer and a lieutenant in the militia. She wasn't too bright, she swore freely and wasn't too proper, but she was a good friend and they got along well. She often asked Ana to lend her the money for her movie ticket and then forgot to pay her back, but, since Ana had a fair salary and Olga had to ask her mother for the money, it hardly seemed kind to remind her of it. They called each other every afternoon and discussed Olga's Saturday boyfriend, her parents and Ana's, Dany, clothes, magazines, Mirta. Ana suspected she was carrying on an affair with the man she dated. But Olga hadn't offered any information and Ana didn't pry.

Saturday after lunch, Ana took her brother's books and the ones by Labrador, her fifteenth birthday formal and the stuffed cat, and she left for Gustavo's house. As she passed the doctor's house on the corner, a shadow in its French garden behind the plumbago hedge startled her. She looked up and saw among the oleanders and gardenias the thin maid in chambray uniform, her skin so waxy pale she looked like a ghost. The *"notario"*'s house on the other corner had been empty for the last four months. The Australian pine hedge was out of shape, its branches growing through the balustrade, and the unattended rose and carnation bushes in its formal garden were showing the signs of neglect. Her footsteps took her out of her way, past the Victor Hugo park with its huge old shade fig trees and its bust of the novelist, and she absently walked around their neighborhood. East on 23rd Street, she passed Margarita de la Cotera's house, porch, columns and banisters painted with ridiculous signs, one reading "Who is who in Cuba?", the Tropicream outdoors restaurant with its red-striped awnings and its Venice-style leaning posts. Down L, before the INIT exhibit, the high, old "Brisas del Carmelo" restaurant, Manolito's beauty salon, a photograph on the window of the owner styling a singer's hair, "La Red" nightclub, the drugstore. Two girls sitting on the front step of a house played slapping their own thighs and each other's palms, while they sang,

> *"Un chino cayó en un pozo,*
> *las tripas se hicieron agua,*
> *arre, pote, pote, pote ..."*[99]

She passed a *"guarapo"* stand on wheels set under a tree on a patch of grass reduced to dirt between sidewalk and curb, with its sugar cane stalks and mound of crushed ice, showing the pretentious sign "Cane juice with *'frappé'* ice" and she smiled to herself, and on before Francisco Frías' monument. She took Línea west, past the tiny grocery store, a beauty parlor, Arturo Montori school, so Cuban it bore the adjective as part of its name, the Hebrew Community Center with its entrance archway, the Havana Business University, and that old low small house that seemed sunk in the lot and all but hidden behind bushes. She turned up G Street, lined with royal palms, passing L'Alliance Française, where Blanca had studied French. Sprinklers were rotating and the smell of freshly mowed lawn floated in the air. A girl of about seventeen passed her on the sidewalk, smelling of soap, shampoo, hair spray and hand lotion, carrying a bulky paper bag, hair rollers sticking out of it, probably on her way to a girl friend's house to set each other's hair for a dance tonight.

The distant sound of hammering could be heard in the drowsy stillness of the balmy early afternoon and it brought her a nostalgic feeling. Old childhood memories rushed at her, memories of long-past walks with the girls of her block around the *"furnia"* in the early afternoon and the sound of construction, bricklayers and carpenters working in the sun; flowers ... They took roses from a garden and pinned them to their hair, and they walked down the middle of the quiet traffic-free street, arms linked, shouting and laughing. A feeling caught in her heart. Ringing doorbells. Sometimes they walked to the Finca Rosa, from where that smell of goats came. Lying on their backs on the patio cement floor at a girl friend's house, making out resemblances in the shapes of the wispy clouds in summer afternoons. Copying poems in a notebook, and songs, an unknown poet with the pseudonym *"El Manquito"*. The impromptu parties in the

neighborhood friends' homes. *"Discoteca Fusté"* radio show through her fifth grade, and through her sixth, "Boogie Time". Radio O'Shea, RHC Blue Chain, *Agapito* and *Timoteo*, lunch to "The Three Villalobos" on the radio, the whistle of the "Spirit", baseball games, the "Habana" lions and "Almendares" scorpions, players "Sagüita" Hernández and Roberto Ortiz. *"Tute"* and *"cargo de tasajo"* card games; her first plaid wool skirt. Bumbling *Rufino*, and *Juanita Calamidad* with her color mottled hairnets; the film *"El Führer Soy Yo"* with Adolfo Otero. The young brother and sister team of tapdancers at the tiny stage of the Colón amusement park singing *"El Pagaré"*. Swiping Spanish limes from the Chinaman's fruit shop, soda with anise, minute *"grageas"* and liqueur-filled sugar bottles, rock candy, poppy seed capsule rattles. *"Vereda Tropical"*, the one-man band on the ferry launch to Regla playing "Isabelita" and *"Chacumbele"*, "Chic" bath soap, the barber shop where her father had his hair cut, with the picture of the Dionne Quintuplets. Stocking up on school supplies at "Cervantes" book store. An unidentified tune persisted,
    "... de las huestes al triunfo final.
    Vocación, tú interpretas el alma..."[(82)]
Some forgotten hymn. The toy living-room sets made from covered empty cigarette boxes, "jingles" in the rhythmic band, *"A la tabla maní, pica'o, cao, cao"*, powdered toasted wheat fights, *"quilete"*, blowing mouthfuls at each other. "Stop it!", she shook herself mentally. "You can't bring back the old times!" She turned left and walked resolutely toward her brother's home.

.

Her first-year final exams had started on Monday and after three subjects on alternative evenings, Ana had the next Monday free before her fourth one. She got together with Olga, however, and they went to "Karabalí" cafeteria on 23rd Street. Having ice cream at the counter, Olga confided, "You know,... I'm not a virgin."

Ana was curious. "Tomás?"

"Yes. It's been going on for a year now", she said in a low voice, twisting her pop-bead pearls between her fingers.

So all that talk about the importance of a girl's virginity, Ana thought, had been only pretense. She hesitated and finally admitted, "Me too,... with Dany."

She had half-expected Olga to say she had suspected it, but Olga didn't seem very interested. She wanted to talk about herself instead.

"I know I don't have much of a chance of getting married this way. Men don't marry girls who go to bed with them." This raised alarm in Ana's mind. "But I'm too weak to say no; I don't have any will power to refuse."

They went to the ladies' room.

"I like creamy lipsticks", Olga commented, applying it, "creamy."

"Maybe Tomás will marry you", Ana said to Olga's reflection in the mirror.

"With that domineering mother he has? Not a chance! Do you know he doesn't see me on Sundays because he has to spend them home with his mother? And he's thirty!" Ana wondered if it were only an excuse. Olga seemed to read her mind. "I call him any time on Sundays and he's home, but he won't go out with me." Ah, the complexities of men!

She passed her last exam on Tuesday. And she had finished her first year. Her sense of satisfaction grew. Although little good a first year of publicity in Spanish would do her in the Bahamas. She was glad Ernesto had passed all the courses too.

Before the indecision, Ana prayed sincerely, "Please, God, if I'm wrong, if I'm not seeing things the way they really are, please, *PLEASE*!, let me see them the right way, let me see the light."

And Friday the break she had been waiting for came. Her brother called her at the office and asked her to go over to see him during her lunch hour. She didn't wait for her lunch hour. At 11:00 she slipped out of the office and, beating the noon rush, took the cream-colored bus with its green stripe around, and an ad of Terry Gold Mesh cognac on its side, to the Plaza Cívica. When, over six years before, these new buses with the eight-cent fare had replaced the old tangerine ones with six-cent fare, they had won themselves the nickname "The Well-Paid's". On the street median between the traffic lanes, an ambulant peddler had ingeniously balanced upright a full assortment of starched blue jeans in all sizes arranged from the tiniest to the largest.

At the Ministry, she took the elevator to Gustavo's floor. She'd never been there before. He had been working all night and hadn't gone home at all, so she waited while he went to wash his face before taking her to the office of a department head.

"Gilberto, this is my sister", he told him. "Ana, this is the Head of the Department."

The man stood up behind his desk and offered her his hand as he introduced himself, "Gilberto Cuéllar. It's a pleasure." She let him shake her hand, smiling. He smiled back and motioned her to a chair, and she sat on the edge, ankles crossed, arms loose over those of the chair, as she had for so many job interviews since she had graduated.

"I'm sure you can use her in the office", Gustavo said, standing. "I told you the experience she has in import." Ana was surprised to hear her brother refer to her like that; she didn't know he had even been aware of where she'd worked. "I have to get back to work." Poor Gustavo! This was so different from his accounting business!

"I'll see you later", Cuéllar said to him and turning to her, "We need somebody to take dictation from the men in the Section. They are four. You take shorthand, don't you?"

"Yes."

"In English too, right? Most of it would be in English. And you'd have to handle the import documents which come from the Accounting Section. Gustavo tells me you're familiar with that." He looked at her for assent and she again confirmed it. "What salary did you have in mind?"

"Well, I've been earning two hundred and thirty. I could start at two hundred and twenty-five."

"I'm not sure we can manage that. Wouldn't you consider starting for less?"

She didn't really like the idea of working for the government, but she wanted badly to stay in Cuba at all costs and that seemed to be about the only way. Private companies were being confiscated daily and the ones that hadn't been weren't taking on any new employees. She didn't want to make a decision. She wished that she could just go to sleep and when she woke up things would be solved. Maybe this would take any decision out of her hands.

"No, I couldn't possibly stay for any less than that", she said firmly and was afraid of what her brother might think of her attitude.

"Well", Cuéllar considered, "I guess we could manage it."

And so, as that time a year and a half before, Ana felt the decision *had* been taken out of her hands. She'd stay on. She'd tell Dany right away. He knew she wanted to stay. And he, too, could get a job in Cuba. He'd be so glad!

But, to her surprise, when she told him, he was disappointed. "I've accepted the offer in Nassau only because you were going."

"Well, then stay."

"I can't back out of it now."

"I don't want us to separate."

"Neither did I, *mi vida*. That's why I accepted the transfer."
"You can tell them you found a job for the same salary here."
"But I haven't."
"But you can find it."
"I sent an application to the Bank of Foreign Trade even before you did, when I didn't know whether they were going to offer me the transfer, and they didn't answer me."
"Try again, *mi cielo*", she pleaded.
"I'm committed with them now."
"So was I."
"No. You were looking for another job from the beginning. In your mind, you always had the reserve that, if you found it, you'd stay and stand them up."
"Then you knew all along that I was trying to stay. You could have done the same, look for another job and quit them if you found it."
"You didn't think you'd find one, you were discouraged. And I too thought that you wouldn't." He paused and Ana waited expectantly. "Well, not in such a short time, *mi vida*. And you wouldn't have if it weren't for your brother."
"That's not true", she argued, all her uncertainty forgotten now. "Rina had talked to her friend. If my brother hadn't found me the job, Rina's friend wanted me."
"She hasn't called", he said realistically.
"I would've called her. The ministries need employees", she ended almost wailing. She was on the verge of tears now.
"This isn't play and I've already given Palmer my word." They were sitting on a bench at the foot of shrubby Paseo with its monuments to the mayors, facing the new, luxurious Havana Riviera with its abstract sculpture in front, the dark hollow carcass of the half-demolished old Convention and Sports Palace to their right, the monument to General Alejandro Rodríguez further south. She placed her hand on his. It was frustrating. She cried, but there was no convincing him. Finally he said, "I'll go for only half a year. I'll be paid in pounds Sterling and can exchange the money into pesos and it'll add up to a sizable amount, and then we won't have to wait any longer. We only have a thousand two hundred ten in the bank now. I spent most of the bonus and gave the rest to the Old Man thinking I was leaving... we were leaving. We have to wait a year, until late October of next year. This way we can get married as soon as I come back,

in early May."

"That's only six months' difference", she said, but in a very low voice now – she knew she couldn't make him change his mind, – "the same time you're going to be away. I'd rather wait a whole year having you near than only half a year having you away."

Dany didn't answer. Their lunch hour was up and they hadn't eaten lunch. On their way back, a solitary street sweeper moved down the empty side street in the early afternoon sun, slowly pushing his large broom ahead in silence, his large waste basket set on wheels resting a few feet behind him in the gutter. A couple of empty garbage cans with the large house numbers painted in black were left overturned on the grass, where the garbagemen had carelessly tossed them after the morning collection.

Back in the office, she went straight into Mr. Meyers' office, bypassing Lydia. "I've found a job here", she told him. "And, considering the expense of moving and the cost of living in a foreign country by myself, I've decided I'll be much better off staying here. I'll be getting the same salary", she lied.

"I don't blame you. I can see what you mean", he said right away. Then he hesitated and added, "But I want to remind you you'll probably be getting a raise in...", he pulled out a chart from under his blotter and consulted it, "... in April." He looked up at her, his lips drawn in a faint smile.

It seemed ludicrous to her. It would probably be a raise for the equivalent of 20 dollars, or maybe 25 at the most. She raised her eyebrows slightly and cocked her head to one side, for want of shrugging. She didn't know what she'd have done if he'd told her they'd give her a $40. increase now.

Berta Penabad was disappointed to hear it. Ana had walked to her desk in the other arm of the angle formed by the office to tell her. Her earphone in her hand, she lamented, "I'm losing my roommate", turning to Leonardo, who had stopped at her desk to give her a red dictation belt. "We were going to share an apartment. Now I'll have to find another roommate."

"That'll be easy for you, Berta. But I am sorry too." It would have been an adventure to keep house.

At 2:30, when she knew Mr. Kent had already been notified of her resignation, she went into his office.

"It's been nice working for you."

"Thank you, Ana. You've been a very good secretary. Good

luck!"

"I'm afraid", she said awkwardly, "you might all think I'm staying because I'm a communist."

"What we think is that you're being a fool." It took Ana an instant to realize that she had heard correctly. "And you'll be sorry you stayed", he predicted harshly. His answer disheartened her.

When she walked into the Sales Department, Octavio Guillén surprised her by standing up and reaching across his desk to shake her hand with a wholehearted smile. "Congratulations! I'm really glad for you. You wanted to stay." His pronounced Adam's apple quivered. "I wish I could do the same! This situation won't last long and, when we all have to come back and be resettling ourselves here, you'll have been here all along."

"Thank you", she said, her spirits lifting a little. "I wonder if I'm doing right", she fished for further reassurance. He had himself once told her that she fished.

"You are, you are." Ana's eyes misted. He didn't mention the hundred dollars her mother had passed for him, and she didn't remember it just then.

Leonardo patted her shoulder, "I'm going to miss you, doll."

Salvador said, "I'm sorry you aren't going."

Her work was up to date. She had taken such pride in her work! She took Dany's picture from under the glass. There was little to take from her desk: hand lotion, a small round hand mirror, a nail file, a box of tissues, a little tin box of "Evanol" tablets and her telephone book. She left a bottle of alcohol and a sardine can opener. It was all neat. She felt a pang of nostalgia.

She said good-by to her co-workers before leaving that afternoon. Fourteen Cuban employees were being transferred: Virginia, Mr. Sterling's secretary; Palacios, the accountant; Octavio Guillén, Assistant Sales Manager for Transmission; Rina, Mr. Palmer's secretary; Mario, the assistant accountant; Leonardo Vidal, the quotations clerk for Parts; Salvador Conde, the Glass quotations clerk; Graciela, the secretary to the Glass Sales Manager; Raquel Weiss, Mr. Batten's secretary; Berta Penabad, pool typist; Elvira, the documentation clerk; Eugenia, the affluent typist. The other quiet typist was also transferring. They were sorry she wasn't going with them. They wished her good luck. Berta, Leonardo and Graciela promised her they'd write to her. Only Salvador was leaving his wife behind, at her sister's, until he sent for her. Elsa Toledo was going to Colombia, her mother's native country. Lydia Dennis was about to get married, but not to Walter Butler. Ramiro, who had married a year before, was staying, his wife about to have a baby. Also staying was Nelia, Palacios' secretary, recently married. Seven others were staying: Gloria Serrano, the file clerk, and Rolandito, the office boy, had not been offered transfers; Dalia, the supplies clerk, the two married women in charge of accounts and another clerk were also staying behind. Rosa Izquierdo, the mail clerk, said she'd call her. Gloria hugged her and said she'd write to her from Arroyo Arenas. Carmen Zayas, the order clerk, didn't have any definite plans, and neither did another clerk. Except for Mr. Meyers and Mr. Kent, the other Americans didn't acknowledge her departure, and neither did Palacios. After three years!

Dany walked her to the corner, waited with her until the pedestrian light went on and gave her arm a squeeze. Ana crossed the street to her bus stop with a heavy heart, while he walked back to Salvador's car. She took the last empty double seat and sat by the window. On the next corner, she saw the man who got off one block ahead of her in the morning get on. There were only single seats left now. She looked out the window, and he walked straight to hers and sat down next to her.

"Good afternoon."

"Good afternoon."

"It's cool this afternoon."

"Yes, it is..."

"I've noticed you take the bus two blocks after I do." She smiled faintly, nodded, and a hint of "Uh-huh" didn't quite make it out of her throat. "I work in the building on the corner, that one", he continued, pointing back with his thumb over his left shoulder. She didn't think she had to offer where *she* worked, ... or had worked. He looked a little like Ramiro, dark complexion, curly hair, trim. He smiled engagingly, "Are you married?", he surprised her by asking.

"No." She thought he'd then say he wasn't either, but, having secured this piece of information, he only smiled again.

They had reached her corner without further conversation and, as he swung his legs toward the aisle to let her pass, they said "Good night". He may have thought he had accomplished the beginning of a friendship and didn't know it was ironically also the end of it. The bus, an ad of H. Upmann cigars on its rear panel, sped away toward Jesús del Monte.

Ana pushed the cardboard box of books toward the corner of her room by the dresser and set Dany's picture back on the wardrobe, and again set her typewriter on the desk. When she remembered Guillén's money that evening, she asked her father to endorse a check for 93 American dollars he had just received through Velázquez over to Guillén, since she wouldn't be going out of the country now to give it back to him. And she gave it to Dany on Saturday to take to Guillén at the office. They still owed him another 7 dollars.

CHAPTER 7

WITNESSES TO THE DESTRUCTION OF THE COUNTRY

> *"La estrella de mi siglo se ha eclipsado*
> *y, en medio del dolor y el desconsuelo,*
> *el lirio de la fe se ha marchitado:*
> *ya no hay escala que conduzca al cielo."*[7]
> *("En Días de Esclavitud",*
> Juan Clemente Zenea)

Fifteen of Major Huber Matos' fellow military prisoners made a sensational escape from La Cabaña and arrived at Key West in boats.

On October 8 the government announced that the revolt in the Escambray mountains had been crushed. Its leaders, Captain Sinesio Walsh Río, Captain Plinio Prieto Ruiz, Porfirio Reemberto Ramírez Ruiz, President of the FEU of Las Villas, and José Palomino Colón, of the MIRR (Revolutionary Recovery Insurrectional Movement), had been surprised in a secret meeting with another man and two women in Mundo Nuevo, Manicaragua, in Santa Clara, Las Villas.

Ana started to work at the Ministry on Tuesday. Getting off the bus at the esplanade of the Plaza Cívica, sun-drenched even in the early autumn morning, gave her such a feeling of apprehension or even desolation, that she was oppressed by regret at having quit her job at Wayne. Paralyzed for an instant, she hesitated; she still had time to get to the office. But she couldn't, she had already resigned. Her stomach gave a lurch. She walked in the glare to the building, walked up the steps and went in. Tucked somewhere in the back of her mind the small comfort remained to which to hold on, that her British residence visa would be valid until January.

Cuéllar took her to the section where she'd be working. There

---

[7] The star of my century has been eclipsed
and, amid the pain and the dejection,
the lily of faith has wilted:
there is no longer a stairway that leads to Heaven.

was a majority of men. The head of the Section, Mestre, seemed a very pleasant man, with very good manners and a polished appearance, and Ana immediately wondered how he could be with the government. She wouldn't have much to do with him, though, or with Cuéllar either. Her work would be with the other four men in the section. Cuéllar's secretary, Aurora, turned out to be Rina's friend. They worked one hour more than at Wayne Motors. They started at 8:30 in the morning, had an hour and a half for lunch and finished at 6:00. It was horrible going home so late. They also had two ten-minute breaks, at 10:15 in the morning and at 3:50 in the afternoon and, since there was no lunchroom on the premises, they were allowed to leave the building, which stretched them actually into twenty minutes. Their trips to the nearby coffee shop were frequent and it was there that the employees got acquainted and carried on most of their conversation.

The name "Year of the Agrarian Reform", which the government had given to 1960, had to be typed under the date in all the letters and documents.

In the Libertad Theater of the Leoncio Vidal Caro Regiment in Santa Clara, 170 prisoners, accused of rising in arms against the state, were tried and sentenced to forced labor.

On October 12 the United States imposed an embargo on exports to Cuba.

The owners of a jewelry store in Havana which advertised itself as "the jewelers of confidence", together with the auditor of the store, arrived in Key West in a small boat, taking with them several hundred thousand dollars' worth of jewelry and precious stones, and they asked for political asylum.

The residence of Julio Lobo, the "Sugar King", was sealed and guarded. He left for Miami the next day, leaving behind the "Hershey" sugar mill and all his vast wealth.

Dany told Ana that an employee of Wayne Motors had supposedly denounced the company to the government that week for "unfair practices" and asked for intervention, which was carried out in two days. And so the company was moving away about ten days before they had planned.

The defectors in the Escambray range swelled to almost a thousand men during October. They and the anti-Castro fighters in Oriente province were all peasants. The American Central Intelligence Agency allowed the Escambray freedom fighters to dry out for lack of food, medicines and weapons. The four leaders and the other male member of the Escambray range rebellion who had been captured were executed by firing squad the night of the 12th at La Campana, in San Fernando de Camarones, Las Villas. The two women were condemned to thirty-year sentences in Guanajay.

Two sailors left with their families from Isabela de Sagua, in Sagua la Grande, on the north coast of Las Villas, in a Navy coast guard launch and arrived in Miami, where they asked for asylum.

Former Prime Minister, Dr. José Miró Cardona, under asylum, left for Argentina.

On October 13, the government seized 404 enterprises. The INRA confiscated all the remaining large industrial, commercial and transportation companies and all forty Cuban banks. The state expropriated 105 of the sugar mills, eight railroad companies, the three largest druggists in the country, two soap and detergent factories, "El Encanto", "Fin de Siglo" and the other eleven best department stores with their provincial branches, 51 chemical plants, 27 paper mills, one printer, 18 distilleries, the breweries, motion-picture theater chains, textile mills and rice mills. Three hundred seventy-six entirely Cuban enterprises were nationalized.

When Ana entered the apartment that Friday afternoon, she was surprised to find her mother sitting in the dim living room in silence with Ernesto Crespo. She felt fear for a moment, as they looked so mournful. She turned the light on and searched their faces anxiously for a sign of what was wrong.

"What happened?", she asked apprehensively.

"Ana María, this is communism", Teresa surprisingly announced sadly, her voice short of breaking.

And, at the unexpected naïve reply, to their surprise, Ana burst out laughing with relief. "But Papá and I had been telling you that for over eleven months now, almost a year. Hello, Ernesto, how are you?" Ernesto hadn't uttered a word. "What made you see that *today*?"

"Well, Ernesto came and told me most of the department stores have been confiscated, 'El Encanto' among them."

"And you needed to have this happen to realize this is communism?" She guessed Ernesto hadn't expected the news to affect her so much and now didn't know how to act.

"But this is... senseless. Why this? There's no reason for it.

Witnesses to the Destruction of the Country 193

These weren't American companies, not even foreign, they were Cuban."
"Why? Because there isn't supposed to be any private enterprise", she said a little impatiently. Her mother had wanted to stay blind to it all. "Because free enterprise goes against a planned economy, and communism has to control the economy to survive."
"I used to look forward to their July sales to buy bed sheets... '*Don Julio*, the month of El Encanto'... and 'Do your August at La Epoca'."
"Enjoying the vacation?", Ana asked Ernesto.
"A little." He spoke for the first time.
She hoped he wouldn't stay long enough for Dany to find him there. But then, he'd probably leave before supper time.
"Is Papá coming home early?", she asked her mother.
"Yes. He stopped off at the Accountants' Association. On Maceo and Cárcel. But he already called to say he was on his way. He was at Velázquez's office today with a jeweler's books... It seems he can only get work through him now."
"Which drug store nearby is on duty this evening?", Ernesto asked. "I have to get methyl salicylate and penicillin ointment for my sister."
"Today is Friday", said Teresa. "... The one on L Street? I don't know. Look in the phone book, Ana María."
"Yes," she said referring to the yellow pages. "That one, and one on Seventeen between F and G. That one's closer and on your way."
She walked Ernesto to the door.

Twenty-eight men and two women had disembarked at Navas bay in Baracoa, on the north coast of Oriente, to join the rebels in the mountains. Their leader, Armando Feria, was killed in Hirán de Nibujón in Baracoa, a man wounded and another taken prisoner. Twenty-two other men and the two women were captured three days later and taken to Santiago de Cuba. And the remaining three were taken prisoner on October 14.

The Ariguanabo textile mill on Cayo La Rosa in the lake in Bauta and the Topes de Collantes tuberculosis sanatorium on the heights outside Trinidad were closed down.

Dr. Teresa Casuso, delegate to the United Nations, announced in New York that she was defecting from the regime.

Four crop dusting planes took off from Colón in Matanzas province with seven passengers and landed in Florida.

On October 15 the Urban Reform law was approved providing that every person occupying rented property was eventually to become its owner, and Castro confiscated private property under the law. Rents had to be paid before the 15th of the month and the new "owners" were to make their own repairs. So they were to be "owners" of the apartment.

Saturday Ana called Berta, who told her, "I'm going to share an apartment with Virginia."

"Did you pack yet?"

"Can you believe not? And I'm leaving Tuesday. I've been going out every night. Last night we went to La Torre Club atop the FOCSA building. And this afternoon I'm going shopping. I need so many things! Mami gave me an ultimatum: I have to pack by Monday *morning*. But, well, I'm only taking my clothes and personal things, because – you know – my parents are staying. So, if they decided to leave later, I'll come back and either take the rest or dispose of it then."

"I thought you might move with Graciela."

"No, Virginia was first going to live with Rina, but then Rina decided to move with Graciela instead. That's why Virginia's going to live with me. Her daughter's staying here with her parents."

"Rina and Graciela?" Graciela, for all her polished sophistication, was very young, not over twenty, and Rina was much older, at least twenty-nine, and so experienced! Besides all her travel in Europe – she had been to France and Germany – and being trilingual, her superior intelligence set her above many other girls.

"Yes. I can't imagine them living together either. Ah!, and Raquel with Eugenia. And that reminds me, I have some gossip. Guess who's getting married... Walter Butler, to a Cuban girl."

"A Cuban girl?"

"A friend of Eugenia's."

"Oh!, then she has money?"

"Yes." Berta had been talking fast and Ana guessed she was rushed, so she said good-by, asked her to write and wished her luck, with just a trifle or envy, or regret. Well...

Castro and Generalissimo Trujillo of the Dominican Republic signed a pact of non-aggression in October.

At the Congregation on Sunday, Ana saw Elvira, who told her, "Dalia was the one who asked for intervention."

"Dalia?"

Elvira nodded, already turning away, and called something over her shoulder, which Ana didn't catch. Well, the supplies clerk living in Luyanó and attending night school would do something like that. She hadn't thought of asking Elvira whether Dalia had been offered a transfer to Nassau. Wayne's employees left during the next week. It made her sad to see them go and to think that the office would now be taken over by the government people. All their modern furniture and equipment. Dany was the last one leaving.

He had lunch with them Sunday and the meal, garlic soup, chicken and rice carefully decorated with red peppers and sweet peas, asparagus salad, fried green plantains and curdled milk pudding, was dispirited. Ana refused to think of it as a farewell meal. After lunch, her father sat down to read the sports section and her mother, the social chronicle. In the next building, the canary was singing.

Ana went up to her brother's office, on a higher floor in the building, on Monday, to tell him about her job. In the small outer office, she asked his secretary, a teenager with acne, her straight hair tied in a ponytail, "Could I see Méndez? I'm his sister."

The girl gave her a broad smile, almost sprang from her chair and went into the inner office.

This was roomier, but plain. There was a bare small window.

"I take dictation from the four men in the section", she told Gustavo. "I don't have anything to do with Mestre, the Head of the Section."

"Do you like the work?"

"Well, yes, but there's not much to do. Sometimes the men explain commercial procedures to me, credit, insurance, formulas, just to talk." She remembered when, in sixth grade, she had been confused between the least common multiple and the greatest common divisor, and he, sixteen then, had explained it to her expertly, and when, at fourteen, she kept forgetting the relative superlative degree of the adjective and he had quizzed her patiently.

"You'll like it. You can learn a lot there."

Ten of the invaders who had landed in Baracoa were executed in the early morning in the San Juan firing range, near Santiago, including the first American to be shot by the firing squad. The other sixteen men and the two women were sentenced to prison terms.

The political affairs editor of The Times of Havana took asylum in the United States.

The labor leader Gerardo Fundora Núñez had taken to the Camarones and La Gloria hills between Madruga and Arcos de Canasí with a small group of men. The camp of the men he commanded was discovered on October 20 and they were taken to the city of Matanzas.

Of the proprietors affected by the confiscations it was said that they had "had their corn stepped on". Homes were confiscated as soon as their owners left.

Tuesday evening, the last time Dany would be seeing her before he left, Ana took his hand and led him out of the apartment. She wanted to be alone with him for a while. They drove up G Street with its monuments to the presidents, crossed 23rd Street heading south, and passed the Palace Hotel and the impressive Aballí Municipal Infantile Hospital, then on to the imposing monument to José Miguel Gómez y Gómez. He parked on 29th Street and they climbed its steps.

"You can see the whole avenue from here, Estrada Palma's statue", said Ana without enthusiasm, pointing to the north toward the sea, "and Calixto García's." They walked around it.

"And the University buildings", said Dany without any more interest, pointing to the east toward the Rectory building, "and the stadium."

They climbed down. They passed in silence before the School of Odontology with those tumbled mammoth stone blocks left over from some construction, and the Orthopedic Hospital, to the little wooded park at the foot of the Aróstegui Hill, the highest point, on the western edge of which, overlooking the city, stood 18th Century El Príncipe Castle jail. It was a clear, moon-less, fall evening, the sky full of stars. Dany pulled her against a tree and looked into her face.

"You thought I was crying", she said to him triumphantly.

"Yes. I'm glad you aren't", he said in a low voice. "I've already explained to you why I can't stay."

"I haven't said anything."

"Not today."

"Because I thought it was too late." She managed a tight smile.

"I'll be back in six months."

"You'll never be back once you realize the difference between the way we've been living lately and independence, and you taste freedom again."

"You'll be here to pull me back, *mi vida*. We'll be writing to each other almost every day, and a call from there must not cost much."

She nodded. She looked around them. There were hardly any cars going by on G or Zapata, only far to the south on Carlos III. Suddenly, Dany pulled her down on the ground under the tree and kissed her between her breasts. She threw her head back and gasped. He pulled her skirt up and caressed her thighs. She arched her back and pulled his face down on hers, and then relaxed and let her legs fall apart on the grass-less dirt, oblivious to the distant traffic, unmindful of their clothes. She looked up at the sky and saw a star twinkle between the branches above them before she closed her eyes. He held her tightly in his arms, enveloping her. He hadn't made love to her with such urgency since the first few months of their relationship.

Later he seemed a little embarrassed at having taken her with such roughness. He kept his arm around her waist as they walked back to his car, and around her shoulders while he drove her home. The Spanish grocery man was rolling down the corrugated metal door for the night.

In the ground floor hallway, they said farewell with a kiss. He asked her, "Say good-by to your parents for me." She stood at the front iron and glass gate with its vaguely Oriental rectangular pattern until his DeSoto turned the corner. When she got upstairs, she went directly into her room, changed her clothes and pushed her dirty cobalt blue dress into a corner of her wardrobe. She'd take it to the dry cleaners herself in a day or two.

When she came out to the living room again, in a housecoat, her parents had settled on the sofas, Méndez in slippers, his pajama top with frogs over some old pants, reading *Información* newspaper, Teresa leafing through *Romances* magazine, the television set tuned to *"Jueves de Partagás"*.

"Is Dany leaving tomorrow?", her mother asked.

"Yes. He asked me to say good-by to you for him."

"Don't be so sad. You said he told you he'll be back in six months."

"Six months is a long time."

"Not for two people who have known each other for two years", said her father.

"What am I going to do for six months?", she asked, momentarily off her guard.

"You have your job and school to occupy your time", Méndez said.

"And the congregation", added Teresa.

She remained silent. A drab job with the government, no incentive, school crowding a whole nine-month school year into five months and a congregation where the senior members had tight little groups not admitting outsiders. People could change a lot in six months, too, especially men, but she didn't want to voice her fears. She sat down with them to watch television.

Major William Morgan was arrested on October 21 as a counter-revolutionary, accused of sending weapons to the rebels in the Escambray range, and taken to La Cabaña Fortress. He had been living on 146th Street in Country Club. They also captured Major Jesús Carreras Zayas.

Dany didn't call Ana the next morning, either at home or at work. She had known he wouldn't. It was almost 2:30 and he was probably well on his way to Nassau by now. Thinking of the growing distance gave her a void in the pit of her stomach. She wondered if his parents had gone to see him off. The telephone on Aurora's desk rang and, after listening briefly, Cuéllar's secretary turned to her with her forced smile, "Ana, it's for you."

Standing by Aurora's desk, she took the receiver and was surprised to hear Dany's voice at the other end. "I'm not leaving."

"What happened?"

"I'll tell you when I see you."

"But what happened?", she insisted, perplexed.

He sounded confused. "I won't be leaving. I'll tell you what happened when we meet. I'll wait for you at the restaurant on Veinte de Mayo Street after work."

Well, when she had already resigned herself to the idea of being separated from him, now he wasn't leaving. She realized she was still holding the receiver, and hung up. She turned away from Aurora's inquisitive smile. It was all she could do to wait for the afternoon to pass, constantly checking her wrist watch against the round clock over the door of Mestre's office.

Dany was waiting at a table when she walked into the restaurant that afternoon. The mezzanine of the cafe projected over the tables on the ground floor. When she sat down, Dany explained, "When I arrived at the airport with my suitcase" − the singular word didn't escape Ana; he *had* intended to return shortly, − "I was told at the ticket counter to report to the British Embassy. There they just told me my residence visa had been cancelled, and wouldn't give me any other

explanation."
"Do you know why?"
"I have no idea."
"Does your family know yet?"
"I called the Old Man from the embassy."

She laughed, her tension easing. She hadn't been aware of how taut she had been. The whole thing suddenly seemed funny. She took his fingers, pulled his hand up to her face and leaned her cool cheek on its back, pressing their palms together. A sound rose, like a purr, from her throat.

Gerardo Fundora was shot in the early morning at the Limonar firing range in Guamacaro, Matanzas province.

On October 24 the government nationalized 166 American-owned companies, including Nicaro Nickel, Woolworth; Sears, Roebuck; General Electric, Westinghouse, International Harvester, Remington Rand and Coca-Cola. Castro seized property without compensation.

Ana typed his résumé and Dany applied for a job on Monday at the Bank of Foreign Trade again, the National Institute of Urban Reform and the Ministry of Labor, all in Vedado and fairly close to her house.

The end of October the youth divisions of the Communist party and the 26th of July Movement merged to form the "Rebel Youth".

Tuesday afternoon Dany arrived at Ana's home in higher spirits. He grabbed her shoulders and, barely above a whisper, gave her the good news, "I got a job."

"Where?"

"At the Corporation of Transport."

"How much is the salary?"

"Two hundred and fifty." It was $30. less than he'd been making at Wayne. "I had no choice", he said, turning his hands palms up – at least it *was* $25. more than she was making, – "and I do like the work."

"What is it?"

"I'll be doing some advanced accounting." He hugged her. They were picking up where they had left off over a month before, when the company had announced they were moving.

A pilot took off from Gibara in Oriente in a crop dusting plane with a mechanic tied to the wing of the plane; the flight lasted three hours and forty minutes and, when they landed on free soil, they asked for asylum. A lieutenant pilot left from the Santa Fe airport, in Bauta, and landed in Miami.

Ana was issued a card with her photograph identifying her as an employee of the Ministry for admission into the building. She was instructed not to abbreviate United States as "U.S." because it could be confused with *"Unión Soviética".* In the course of her work, she had to verify documents and, with more of them coming from Russia, she thought she might as well practice the differences between the Cyrillic alphabet and the Roman one, to make their interpretation easier for her. She started by writing down the five letters that offered the most confusion and their equivalencies:

В = V,   Н = N,   Р = R,   С = S   and   У = U.

She then proceeded to the other 16 characters alien to their language with their approximate interpretations:

Б = b, Г = g, Д = d, З = z, И = i, Л = l, П = p, Ф = f, Э = e, Ж = zh, Х = kh, Ц = ts, Ч = ch, Ш = sh, Щ = shch, Я = ya.

And she could that way decipher the names of government agencies, enterprises, Soviet steamships. She kept the table in the top drawer of her desk for quick reference and, every time she needed to refer to it, despaired at the thought of having to practice the Russian alphabet to perform her job.

Dr. Rufo López Fresquet, former Minister of the Treasury, arrived in Florida by boat. The president of the Court of Accounts escaped aboard a yacht and reached Marathon Key.

On October 28, the eve of the first anniversary of Major Camilo Cienfuegos' disappearance, the division employees were instructed to file out of the building and were led on foot by the side of the Calixto García Hospital of the University, down the skirt of the hill, before the high house with the round clock on its porch wall, the Colina Hotel, 27th Street east, the University Catholic Home, María Teresa Comellas' School, the Mystic Rose Congregation, the little triangular General Eloy Alfaro park, Infanta Avenue north, in front of Radio Progreso station. A thin, young person − it wasn't obvious whether it was a woman − was painting a scene on a canvas, the easel set on a portico. Past the Capablanca Chess Club with the rocking chairs on its porch. In the cafe behind the lattice some men played dominoes. They passed the Architects' Association and the large Ambar Motors building, to come out on the Malecón in front of the lamppost, a walk of over a mile in the sun just before noon. A few employees walked along the wide wall that bordered the gulf, among them a thin, pale militia woman from her department. They threw white flowers to the blue Caribbean Sea, which glittered in the sun, dramatically repeating, "White flowers for Camilo". The performance somehow seemed like a sacrilegious irreverence to the deceased man. She wondered if they might be observing her expression.

Seven sailors deserted the Cuban merchant ship *"Oriente"* when it went through a sluice in the Panamá Canal on its way to North Korea, and they sought asylum.

Ana and Dany went to see more foreign films; Dassin's *"Rififi"* with Jean Servais, German "The Third Sex", Fellini's *"La Strada"* and *"Le Notti di Cabiria"* with Giulietta Masina, *"La Dolce Vita"* with Marcello Mastroianni, Camus' *"Orfeu Negro"*, Brazilian, with Breno Mello.

It became known that there were training camps in Guatemala when the Guatemalan newspaper *"La Hora"* divulged on October 30 that camps were operating in "Helvetia" and "La Suiza" plantations near the town of Retalhuleu, in that southwestern department, to train men for an invasion of Cuba.

A passenger aboard an Aerovías Q plane in flight to Isle of Pines forced the pilot to head for Key West, where the pilot, the wounded co-pilot, a doctor and nine other passengers asked for asylum. A couple left from the Sancti Spíritus airport in Las Villas with their daughter of a few months in a crop dusting plane, landing in Marathon Key.

Five men arrived in Miami on a launch. The secretary-general of the Fishing Syndicate hijacked a refrigerator ship and went to Key West.

A massive landing of weapons and over 600 Russian military technicians caused alarm in Santiago de Cuba.

Indoctrination meetings were held for all the employees in the ministries – Ana's among them, – "corporations", "enterprises", industries and commercial firms, as well as in army posts and schools.

The girl who sold coffee in the office went by twice a day with her huge thermos of steaming black coffee and the large canvas bag of little paper cups slung over her shoulder. The men acted generous then, treating each other and the girls to coffee. The tiny cups cost two cents.

Ana made friends with Mestre's secretary. Yolanda Solís was a tall girl with long, straight, black hair brushed back from her forehead and blue eyes, and the hard pronunciation of the R peculiar to the

Oriente accent. She was from Guantánamo. She wasn't fat, but her lower abdomen protruded incongruously like a lined blown rubber pillow. They started going together on their breaks to a little coffee shop that had just opened near the Ministry. Sometimes Duarte, one of the clerks in the section, joined them. He was a tall, thin young man with a very high forehead, thinning hair and deep-set gray eyes, who seemed to Ana like an unfavorable cross between Wendell Corey and the Duke of Edinburgh. Beautiful straight teeth were his only handsome feature. He shuffled his feet lazily when he walked. He was engaged to a girl in Santiago de las Vegas, his small hometown south of Havana, past the International Airport. He lovingly referred to her as "the Country Girl" and often talked about her admiringly, so Ana came to feel she knew her. The three joked about inconsequential matters over their snack and enjoyed a laugh at the expense of their work, their co-workers, the building or the coffee shop, but cautiously kept away from any political subject.

Dany brought Ana the news that Gloria Serrano had also gotten a job at the Corporation. And Thursday a letter from Gloria arrived from Arroyo Arenas, ten miles to the southwest, where she lived with her parents, confirming the news. She also mentioned Dalia had started working in the same place as Ana, but Ana hadn't run into her. Rolandito had also stayed in Cuba.

Rosa Izquierdo hadn't been offered a transfer to the Bahamas. She had asked Mr. Sterling for a letter of introduction to the American Embassy instead and, a few weeks after the company had left for Nassau, Ana was surprised to receive a letter from Rosa from Miami, where she had gone with her parents on a tourist's visa. She said she was working as a salesclerk in a five-and-ten store and was having trouble with her fallen arches, and her mother sent her regards.

Olga talked about Rosa's departure constantly. Ana gathered that, dispite being her downstairs neighbor, Rosa hadn't said good-by to Olga, for which Ana couldn't blame her. Olga called her a "worm", as Castro had termed the counter-revolutionaries in one of his tirades to reach the populace. Mirta went along with it. Ana kept her opinion to herself and tried to change the subject.

Ana didn't know Yolanda's or Duarte's ideas. Once, in a conversation in the section about the armed militia, she overheard Yolanda, standing, reply to some comment Ana hadn't heard, "My parents taught me firearms are deadly weapons, not something with which to play." She thought it was a good way to justify not joining the militia.

In the movies, between French films, like Resnais' *"Hiroshima, Mon Amour"* with Emmanuele Riva and Clouzot's *"Les Diaboliques"* with Simone Signoret and Vera Clouzot, Olga applauded noisily when Castro appeared on the *"Nacional"* newsreel, Mirta put up a pretense at clapping and Ana managed to go to the ladies' room then.

Once at the "23 y 12" Theater, Olga awaited her with the observation, "You don't applaud him." Ana tilted her head ambiguously, and Olga dropped the subject.

Méndez decided to repaint the apartment and Dany offered to help him over the week-end, and he and Olga had occasion to meet when she dropped by Saturday afternoon.

Their furniture was pulled away from the walls in the dining area, and Dany was on a stepladder steadily painting the upper edge of the wall in the same moss green, while Méndez painted the louvered door to the balcony in a cream color. Teresa was covering the furniture with old sheets and the floor with newspapers, and scraping from the tiles the paint drops that had escaped the newspapers.

A large fly lit on a sheet. "We're getting a visitor", pronounced Teresa.

Soon there was a knock. Ana opened the door, and Olga walked in and stood in the middle of the living room looking on. Dany surveyed her from up on the ladder while Ana mumbled the introduction, and there seemed to be instant dislike.

"I'm going to 'Roseland' to buy a cinch belt", Olga announced, "and then to 'Los Reyes Magos' to get a record. I thought you might come with me."

"You should have called me first", Ana replied.

"But you aren't doing anything."

"I'm helping a little here." – She wasn't going to walk out on Dany and her father to go shopping with Olga, – "at least screwing the switch and outlet plates back on, and wiping the door knobs."

Olga pulled a chair and sat down, offered some unsolicited advice and after a while decided, "Well, then I guess I'll go by myself." And Ana was glad she hadn't given up going. "What a drag! I should've called Mirta."

That evening, after the Irish movie "Pat and Mike", Ana avoided the subject, but Dany brought it up.

"Why are you friends with that girl?"

"Olga? She's very frank."

"It seems to me she's very vulgar."
"Why? She's sincere."
"She uses so much slang...!"
"Ah, that's because she's not very bright. She thinks that's funny. But she's a good person."
"And talking about cinch belts in front of your father, who's an older man, and me, whom she'd seen for the first time."
"That's not so important, *mi cielo*." – If he only knew what else she talked about! – "She's a good friend."
"If you keep hanging around with her, you'll start talking the way she does."
"No, don't worry about that", Ana laughed. "You know I'm not influenced by things like that."

A captain of Cubana de Aviación, when he arrived in Miami on a scheduled flight, asked for asylum.

Former Secretary-general of CTC David Salvador was arrested on November 5 while attempting to sail from the Jaimanitas river in Marianao on a yacht for the States with eight other men and three women, and he was sent to La Cabaña prison. They seized 13,500 dollars on him.

From their conversations, Ana concluded that Yolanda and Duarte were both very religious. One afternoon, when she and Yolanda were having sodas together, Ana gathered enough courage to ask her, "What do you think of the priests' leaving the country?"
"I think it's terrible."
"There aren't going to be enough clergy left", she pressed further.
"It's an atrocious thing."

Yolanda lived in Mendoza. She was attending the university in the evening. Her father owned a coffee roasting mill. A few days later, she talked about the Catholic youth group to which she belonged and how they didn't allow them to participate in any counter-revolutionary activities, but she did seem very well informed about the work and the publications of several underground organizations. Ana talked to her about the Catholic girls' congregation where she attended Mass on Sundays. There was a healthy, clean aura about Yolanda. Dany would approve of her.

Invaders from Cuba attacked the towns of Jinotepe and Diriamba, in Carazo department, in the southwest of Nicaragua.

The Times of Havana newspaper ceased publication on November 11.

"I don't believe all men are created equal", Ana ventured on another occasion, having a *mamey sapote* milk shake with Yolanda.
"They aren't", Yolanda stated emphatically.
"Everybody doesn't have the same intelligence", Ana pointed out.
"Or the same moral values", Yolanda observed sensibly, and made Ana feel ashamed of her more materialistic reasoning. Of course moral values were more important than intelligence, at least more commendable.
"Have you seen Tomás these last few days?", Ana asked Olga one Friday afternoon on the bus on their way to "El Jardín" on Línea.
"Oh, yes!", Olga quickly picked up the topic. "He gave me this handbag", she said, stroking the leather. "Isn't it beautiful?"
"It's very nice."
"At your disposal. It's *'gamucina'*."
"First time I hear of that."
"Well, it was the first time I heard of it too. It's a finer type of suède." She was wearing a black pleated skirt. They had arrived.
"Ah... I saw some *'nonato'*[(42)] handbags on La Rampa Wednesday", said Ana going up the steps of the restaurant. "Beautiful! When did you see Tomás?"
"Saturday." They sat at one of the tables on the covered porch. "We went to a ...", she hesitated, "... a motel", she confided dropping her voice, then picked up, "and listen to this: When you drive in, you go directly into the parking space right behind the vacant room. There's a curtain to conceal the car and the man can draw it before you even get out of the car. Then a few steps lead from the parking space right to the door of the room. So you get in without anybody's seeing you. And that's not all. Listen: Then in the room there's a little low window that opens out into a hallway. I guess a light goes on in the office when you close the door or something, because soon a waiter taps on this window and you can order drinks, ... or cigarettes."

Ana was embarrassed by this confidence. She tried to take it on a light note. "Or magazines", she put in.

Olga laughed. "Oh, come on now!", and dismissed the suggestion with her hand. They asked for sodas, and when the stocky Spanish waiter had walked away, Olga went on, as if wound up now, "And he's paid through the window. Well, the thing is that the whole time

[(42)] "unborn calf"

you don't face anybody."

"And where's that?" Ana's curiosity was finally aroused. It was the first time that anybody who'd been in a motel had described it to her. Not even her cousin Jorge had.

"This one is past the Vento drive-in movie. But Mirta says there are several of them. There are two in back of the old Vedado streetcar depot. But I don't know what those are like. They have high walls and tall hedges around them. And Mirta says there's one near the Canada Dry plant. She goes with that customs inspector at the docks." Ana let her eyes rove over the Flour Retirement Fund building, across the street. "She says once they went to one somewhere in Luyanó, in the factory district, where as they drove in in the car, a man's voice guided them through a loudspeaker to the room. I guess the man saw the car from a lookout or something. And he called out the number of a vacant room and the position. Isn't that something?"

The waiter came with their bottles of soda, and glasses with ice and straws.

"But then the man sees you come in."

"Well, he just sees the car, he doesn't actually see the persons. As long as he doesn't know your car... And you don't see *him* at all. Just hear the voice."

"But so does everybody else."

"And what does it matter? Besides, there probably wouldn't be more than one car driving in at one time, anyway."

She and Dany had been to the Vento drive-in movie. Maybe they had even passed the place.

"And I thought Mirta was a virgin!", said Ana, her thoughts now jumping to another deduction.

"Well, she says they only... pet", said Olga, confused by the directly unrelated comment.

"I wonder what guy would have you alone, undressed, in a room in a motel and then be content to pet." Ana was skeptical.

"... Maybe she goes all the way with the customs inspector."

"Then why all that moralizing about how important *that* is?" Ana found reserve commendable, but hypocrisy was unnecessary. She remembered too late that Olga had done as much.

"And you believed her?" Olga was indifferent. "Look, I hadn't thought about that much, but I've known one thing about Mirta for a long time: She's a liar, anyway. Besides, what about that time she said that a woman had doors open to her where a maiden couldn't go in?"

"Wait, you're telling me all this about Mirta", said Ana, suddenly with a hint of distrust. "Have you told her about Dany and me?"

"Oh, no! I'm telling you this because she'll tell you about the motels herself if you ask her."

"Well, don't tell her. I told you because I'm closer to you, but I don't find anything in common with Mirta at all."

"I won't tell her", Olga assured her, obviously failing to see the importance.

"Well, and what's the room like inside?", Ana was curious.

"Well, the one we went to had ... a bed, of course", she stopped and laughed at her remark, "and a vanity table and, on the wall in front of the bed, a mirror, tilted forward, and a night stand with a coin radio, a big gray metal contraption that runs for a while with a twenty-five cent coin. And a little table with two chairs."

"And what's all that for?"

"The table is in case you want to drink at it", said Olga expertly.

"I guess one would probably drink in bed."

"We did, but...", she shrugged.

"And bathroom?"

"Oh, yes, a shower and everything. A bidet too."

Ana felt a tingle run up her spine. She wondered what it would be like to go with Dany. It'd be safer than lying together in his car parked on the street or on a vacant lot, or worse yet, on the ground in a park like that Thursday three weeks ago. They could be shamefully embarrassed by anyone coming up on them. Or a policeman might arrest them. That would be terrible! But she probably wouldn't feel comfortable in a cold, rented, strange room. Dany had never suggested it, so he probably knew she wouldn't feel relaxed. And that crazy act at the park had been provoked only by the spur of the farewell. She couldn't even mention to him that Olga had told her this, because he would be shocked to know her friend admitted to these things.

She played with the straw among the ice cubes. "Do you think maybe they eavesdrop outside the window?"

"It didn't occur to me." No, it wouldn't to Olga.

"Don't you wonder what kind of people run those places?", Ana mused.

"No, I didn't think of that." Olga wouldn't.

They were both quiet for a while. The multicolored lights of Linea Street were starting to come on, the Rodi theater was two blocks further west. Then Olga looked up from her glass, thoughtful now. "But you know what I *was* terrified of? Running into somebody who knew me. A car was pulling out as we were driving up and I made Tomás drive around the block again before we went in." She burst out in laughter, light again. Ana didn't find it funny. There was something disturbing about it.

"And did it... affect you?"

"What do you mean?"

"Well, did it make you react any differently? You know, did you... turn cold?"

"Well, I did sort of... slow down. You know, it was crazy, but I started thinking about my mother and feeling guilty, thinking how it would disappoint her if she knew. That all she tried to instill in me didn't do any good." Ana knew the feeling well, but she wouldn't have thought Olga had it. "And I couldn't concentrate. I tell her I go have a snack with him. I'd hate to hurt her, she's so good." Her mother, a prematurely gray-haired, thin woman with buck teeth, in her *naïveté* made one feel sorry for her. "But I don't know whether it had anything to do with the place or not. It's sort of...", she hunched her shoulders forward and gazed off toward the inside of the restaurant, "... cold-like."

No, Ana felt that wasn't for her. The sordid idea seemed unclean to her, depressing.

Ana and Dany went to an outdoor cafe on Tacón Street one evening, near the Templete in its Doric Greek style with the silk-cotton tree, the Plaza de Armas and the harbor, and had beer at one of the tables in the moonlight. Dany bought peanuts from an ambulant vendor and they listened to a strolling guitar player, while they made lazy comments induced by the tranquil setting.

Archbishop Enrique Pérez Serantes urged the Catholics to fight communism. A small group of men assaulted CMOX radio station and played a recording urging the people to fight against the communist regime.

Army men took over the Zapaca air base and occupied Puerto Barrios in the Izabal department, in east Guatemala, supported from Cuba.

Olga wanted to try her luck at job hunting and asked Ana for an employment application for the Ministry and, when she took the completed form one afternoon, she stopped by Ana's department to

see her. Ana introduced her to Yolanda. The contrast between the two girls, exchanging a few words in the hallway, was so keen she felt embarrassed for Olga.

Three professors of the Marta Abreu Central University of Santa Clara fled with a merchant in a small boat northbound.

Aurora expressed most confidentially to Ana, "We should be very careful with Duarte. I think he belongs to the G-Two. He's about the only man who hasn't joined the militia. And that olive green suit he has looks suspicious. Have you noticed?" Ana merely assented without giving an opinion. She didn't know what Aurora might have in mind. Aurora hastened to explain, "I'm with the revolution unconditionally, of course, but I think G-Two people aren't to be trusted."

Ana felt apprehensive and that afternoon she told Yolanda, "Aurora told me to be careful with Duarte because she thinks he belongs to the G-Two."

"The G-Two? Ah, I think she's crazy!"

"Why? You don't think so?"

"Well, now you've started me thinking, but no, I don't think so. He doesn't sound like it. There's no way!"

"But he's about the only man left in the department who hasn't joined the militia", she echoed Aurora's words.

"Yes, and I've noticed that olive green suit of his, but", Yolanda shook her head, "no. We've talked and I think he doesn't like this...", she waved her arm about, "...all this."

"Well, just in case, let's be careful around him."

"No, I'm going to tell him what Aurora said instead, and see how he reacts."

"Do you think that's wise?", Ana asked, alarmed.

"Why not?"

"I wouldn't do it."

"I think it's the only way. See how he reacts."

Engineer Manuel Ray, leader of the MRP, arrived in Miami. By November, 60,000 Cubans had left for the United States, mainly for South Florida.

The next morning that the three of them got together at the coffee shop, Yolanda waited until the young waiter, one steaming pot in each hand, poured into her cup the jet of hot milk through a strainer and the trickle of strong coffee while asking "Light or dark?", and she then confronted Duarte point-blank, "Do you know that Aurora told Ana to be careful with you because you belonged to the G-Two?"

Ana winced and pasted a grin on her face while Yolanda poured a stream of sugar into her cup.

"She said that?", Duarte asked, amused. "What a degenerate!" Yolanda added a pinch of salt to her coffee and milk.

Ana thought the label exaggerated. She was looking at his facial expression intently. It didn't tell her anything. He hadn't even been very precise. Maybe he didn't belong after all. Yolanda seemed to be pretty sure. But neither his expression nor his reply gave any definite clue.

From then on Yolanda and Duarte complained freely about the new laws, criticized the weak ones who were joining the militia out of fear, and hoped aloud for a change in regime in front of Ana. She lent an ear, but, still cautious, stayed at the margin of their discussions and didn't venture any opinions when Duarte was present.

He told them he had attended the Enrique José Varona Technical Industrial School and his father was a cigar factory reader, and he showed them a photograph with his girlfriend taken from above as they walked up a hill holding hands. "Uphill on life's road hand in hand", he explained as if it were a phrase with which they had come up together. "The Country Girl" was chubby with dark hair.

Radio and television shows switched their topic to political propaganda. Familiar product commercials with the popular slogans that had become household phrases like "That one that's sturdy, sturdy, set aside"[43], "It does grow, it does become loose"[44], "Soak, rinse and hang"[45], "Are you crazy, Raymundo?"[46], "Tasty to the last little gulp"[47], "Right away, my darling!"[48], "This is Cuba, Chaguito"[49], "I learned it from my father"[50] and "Getting the oil from the olive" gradually disappeared to be replaced by mottoes for revolutionary cooperation and documentaries about Socialist countries. Public places kept their radios continuously turned up full volume with some political speech going on.

[43] "Partagás" cigarettes
[44] "Jon-Chi" rice
[45] "Fab" detergent
[46] "Kolynos" tooth paste
[47] "Pilón" coffee
[48] "Borden" milk
[49] "Hatuey" beer
[50] "Cristal" beer

Three young men hid under the fuselage of a Cubana de Aviación plane by the wings at the Rancho Boyeros airport for nine and a half hours, until they arrived at the Miami airport.

And a bomb blew up by a window of "Los Precios Fijos" store on Reina during the early morning, causing damage in the whole block.

On another occasion, Duarte talked about former President Ramón Grau while he sipped a papaya milk shake. "We attained the best labor laws during his administration", he said. "When the new maximum workday for the buses was being negotiated with Menelao Mora, he said, 'As a doctor I say a man cannot work over eight hours a day'. He's the only ex-president who hasn't had to leave the country. He's still there in his 'hut' on Fifth Avenue. His really was 'the government of Cuban-ity'."

Ex-President Manuel Urrutia took asylum in an embassy with his family.

After a few days, Duarte intimated that he worked with an underground group. Ana thought he shouldn't be talking to them about it at all. If all the members confided in co-workers they had known such a short time as he had them, they'd be very foolish. He didn't mention which group and she was glad. She didn't want to know.

Long lines awaited to get a visa before the aseptic blue architecture of the American Embassy on Calzada – a smaller-scale replica of the United Nations building, – reminiscent of the voters' queues for the last free presidential elections, held in 1948.

Duarte confided another time that he'd run into a problem during the weekend. They'd tried to get a friend out of a sugar cane field who'd gotten burned setting fire to cane scales, and they'd had to take a doctor in to him. He said he had become suspect in his town and he had to report to the authorities when he arrived in Santiago de las Vegas Friday evening.

Ana considered him intelligent, she liked that he was calm, a person of few words, and shared his partiality toward ex-President Grau. In a few days he'd won her confidence.

A few days later, he mentioned that two friends of his needed fake driver's licenses in a hurry to carry something in a car, in case they were stopped. Their usual contact had folded and he didn't know right away how to go about getting them fast. Ana thought of Nelia, Palacios' former secretary, who was now working in the new agency of the drivers' license bureau. She had criticized the government often enough.

When they came out of the coffee shop, she asked Duarte, "Do you want me to see if I can do something?"

He looked at her with a scowl of surprise for a moment, then nodded, "All right", perhaps with a little skepticism.

At noon, skipping lunch, Ana took the bus that sped eastward on San Rafael Street as fast as the heavy noon traffic allowed it. An older man gave her his seat — older men did it more than young ones did, unless they were seeking familiarity. — They passed one of the last few charcoal shops left in the city, the owner of which Ana had fancied to be Canarian, the uniform store, Trillo park, the prosperous construction company, that watch repair shop with the unbelievably dusty window. Two Chinese men, in their straight short jackets and their canvas shoes, spoke animatedly in Chinese on the back seat. They got off on Manrique, two blocks from the edge of Chinatown to the south. Past the antique shop, Singer sewing machines, "Flogar", the ten-cent store, Florsheim shoes, "Fin de Siglo" store, Rex Cinema, J. Vallés tailors, famed for their speed, "Cinecito", to the office on the border of Old Havana. And she risked pulling Nelia out into the hallway to lay the problem out to her in a low voice.

"It can be done", Nelia answered her without any surprise, "but the palm of the clerk who'd do it will have to be greased and he'll need a photograph."

A bomb exploded in the National Capitol, causing extensive damage.

Duarte gave Ana $25. and two photographs the next morning without once questioning her about her means. They showed the serious faces of two dark-haired boys in their twenties in sports shirts. She met Nelia at lunch time at the bus stop in the little park on Monserrate Street with the bust of Mayor Supervielle, amid the deafening blasts of car horns, and she gave her the money and the photographs.

That very afternoon after work she waited for he˙ in Central Park, among the palms, Indian almonds and poincianas. An ambulant photographer yawned in the autumn afternoon near the José Martí statue, his old camera on a tripod next to him, an array of yellowed pictures around it of people posing in the park, the fountain of the lions nearby, the Centro Gallego with its towers tipped by angels and the Louvre Walk at his back. To the east a couple of men came out of the elevator of the Manzana de Gómez with its neoclassical façade and went into the "Salón H" — to eat oysters? — Office workers, shoppers and store clerks were crossing the park in all directions to catch buses home. Nelia appeared soon and discreetly gave her the pink driver's licenses with the names Duarte had instructed. "Careful", she cautioned. To the north, the neon Jantzen girl lit up, poised to dive from the board over the portico of the "Central" cafe. The photographer was packing his gear. Over "El Dorado" cafe came on the signs of the Palacio sheets, Agustín Reyes Russian violets, Cadillac, Buick and Motorola. A digital clock marked 6:35. The portico of the Plaza Hotel got lively. To the south, beyond the Noble Habana fountain of La India Park, high over Monte Street, the RCA Victor white fox terrier tilted his head and perked a black ear before the loudspeaker listening to "His Master's Voice". Did the Cubanacán all-woman band still play in front of El Pasaje hotel in the evening? Further west, the marble bust of Carlos de La Cruz kept vigil at the foot of the Paseo del Prado with its bronze lions, while its baroque iron lampposts turned on.

She took the crowded bus that took her, standing, back westbound on Neptuno Street, passing the Miami restaurant with its display of fruits, the Rialto theater, "Le Chat Noir" night club, its façade the face of a cat and its entrance through his mouth, *Lamela y Torrubia* jewelers, "Los Parados" bar with its varnished screen, "La Casa del Perro" leather store, Roberts tobacco shop, *Baranda y Tosar* hat store, "La Elegante", "El Aguila" soda fountain with its giant scale, Roseland, "Berens Modas", American Photo camera shop, América cafeteria, "La Epoca", "La Filosofia", the Formosa restaurant on the corner, "Lido" shoe store, "Arrinda", "El Palacio de Cristal", the furniture stores, their living room sets displayed one behind the other, sofas artlessly lined up, "El Siglo XX" restaurant, American Grocery store, the Municipal Library, and on to Vedado.

Duarte was visibly grateful and, Ana noticed, just a little surprised. She felt a secret pride. She didn't know with what group he worked, but she trusted his judgment, and she felt proud that he had trusted her and she had been able to do something against the government, however little it might be.

On November 25 Castro promised the people that they'd have grapes and apples from Czechoslovakia for Christmas; however, they wouldn't have the traditional pig, but chickens and 55,000 turkeys would be available.

Another time, Duarte commented, "The underground publication we had been getting out has stopped because the mimeograph was seized. And we were lucky they didn't get any of the boys. Let me knock on wood", so doing on the underside of the table.

"The official national organ?", asked Yolanda, alarmed. Ana realized then that Yolanda knew which organization it was.

"No!, just a mimeographed supplement that the local chapter had been putting out for the last four months", he said sipping his "Jupiña" soda, "mainly for distribution through the ministries."

Ana thought of Folgueira, the Spanish representative for paper manufacturers who had let her use his mimeograph for Wayne when she had first started working for them. He had charged them $1. for a hundred sheets and given them a key to his office, because he met at the Printers' Syndicate and didn't keep regular office hours, so she could get in to use it. Ana believed she still had the key, she didn't recall having returned it. She hadn't used the mimeograph in over two and a half years, for Wayne had since bought an electric one and they had even assigned Dalia to operate it, so Ana hadn't had to use the key again. If he still kept the office, there would be no problem in using his mimeograph.

She didn't want to mention it in front of Yolanda. At her desk, she checked her keyring with the pearl. The key was still on it.

At lunch time, she caught up with Duarte in the hallway and fell in step with him.

"Duarte, there is a man on the fifth floor of the building where I used to work in the automobile company", she told him in a low voice, "who has a mimeograph. I used to operate it for the company and have a key to his office."

"And?"

"If he still has the office", she said with some timidity, "it could be used for the bulletin."

"Do you mean let him *in* on it?", he asked incredulously.

"No!", Ana hastened to appease him. "I meant when he isn't there." Aurora passed them, in a hurry. She was efficiency personified.

"The boys would look suspicious in the building."
She hesitated. "... I wouldn't."
"But, would you have to operate it yourself?"
"Well,... yes, I guess so", she answered him as they walked.
"That's not a job for one person", he shook his head. "There's too much risk involved."

"Yes, I realize you cannot just turn the bulletin over to an outsider." A bearded militia man passed them.

"No, that's not it", he dismissed with a gesture. "It's just a cut stencil and no names are mentioned, so there's not much risk to us, you'd only know me. I mean the risk to you. It'd be too much to be handled by one person. There'd be nobody to... front for you. It was being run by three boys in a shoe repair shop, on a mimeograph they had smuggled out of a printing shop. It was very convenient, because the noise of the sewing machines overrode that of the mimeograph. But Graziani, the shoemaker, just left... went back to Verona — he said he'd rather put up with Fanfani, — and they took over the shop, mimeograph and all." He grinned. "I wonder what they thought when they found it there. Anyway, what I mean is they were three. Men, not one woman."

"Well, I'll tell you what the situation is and you judge. The automobile company was on the sixth floor and this man's office was on the floor below. Before they got the mimeograph, I used to walk down to his office every three weeks or so, to run a hundred form letters. When he started staying out of the office, he gave the accountant a key. I ended up with it and, when the company got its own mimeograph, I never even remembered to return it. I haven't been in his office in over two and a half years, but I did stay on in the building until a little over a month ago. I mean, the elevator men and the janitor are used to seeing me in the building. And the man still had the office five months ago, when the Hilton was confiscated."

"What kind of business does the office do?"

"He's a representative for American paper manufacturers."

"Doesn't he have a secretary?"

"No, he used to have an office boy, but he quit a year and a half or so ago and he never hired another. He has very little business now."

Duarte thought for a moment, biting the inside of his lip. They had reached the front steps.

"Listen", he said somewhat reluctantly, "I'll give you this month's stencil. We'll try it. If there's any risk at all, we'll have to stop getting it out for a while, until we can get a safe way." He gave her his address, on B Street, and said, "There's a large condominium building on the corner."

"That's only four blocks from the office building", she said enthusiastically.

And he surprised her replying, "I know."

That afternoon, on her way back to the office, she called Folguei-

ra's office from the public telephone in a drug store with its mortar and pestle, and nobody answered, which wasn't surprising. She tried the Printers' Union, with the same result. She dialed his home last, expecting to hear a woman's voice. He answered himself; she recognized his voice with the thick Spanish brogue. "Folgueira? It's Ana, from Wayne. Do you remember me?", she asked him leaning on the glass counter, looking absently at the aqua blue cabinets. "How are you?"
"Fine. Sure I remember you, girl. And *Mister* Kent. I guessed you had left with them. And how are you?"
"Fine, thank you. No, I'm working at a ministry now."
"Who else stayed?"
"Danilo, Gloria Serrano..." She paused for the sake of politeness, then plunged into it. "Folgueira, I have some work to mimeograph and wonder if I could use the mimeograph again."
There was a moment of silence. Then, "Sure, you may. The only problem is going to be that I'm not in the office much any more. Some days I don't even go in at all."
"Well..." She had hoped he'd remember. "... you gave Palacios a key a long time ago for me to go in, when I used to run those reply letters for the company. If you authorize me to go in..."
"Oh!, that's right." He drew his breath in audibly, then asked surprised, "You never gave it back to me?", but he didn't wait for a reply. "Well, then there's no problem."
"We'll... *I*'ll pay you for the paper I use. Should I mail the money to you?"
"No, just leave it in the top drawer of the desk. I don't lock it."
"Thanks for letting us... letting *me* use it." Devil!, second time she slipped. "I hope to see you again soon. Until later."
"Until soon, girl."
Well, it had been easy.
That afternoon, after work, she got off the bus at Duarte's corner. She checked the ground-level white concrete nonahedral marker to verify the street. A new Corvette was coming out of the garage of the condominium on the corner, a young man at the wheel. Duarte's building, painted cream, showed the rust stains so peculiar to Vedado buildings running down from the window frames. They said it was due to the iron content from the soil in the water.
She walked up the two flights of stairs and knocked on his door, on which a decal with a cross proclaimed, "With God, all; without

God, nothing". She hoped he had already arrived; he had taken the bus ahead of hers. He opened the door himself, and Ana walked into the sparsely furnished living room and stood just inside the door while he went in and brought the cut stencil to her. She heard another man's voice inside, apparently on the telephone. She put the stencil into a *Vanidades* magazine and rolled it up.

"We'll have to pay him something."

He nodded. "Let me know how much."

She walked to her old De Quesada office building, her hand tight around the rolled magazine, and took the elevator up. The elevator man knew her and nodded. She debated between getting off at the floor where Wayne Motors had been or at Folgueira's. She decided on the former, in case he remembered where she worked.

"Sixth, please."

"It was ten minutes to seven. She felt her knees shaking and, when the elevator stopped, she had a moment's fear that they'd buckle under her. But the elevator boy was used to seeing her in the building after hours and she heard the elevator door close behind her. She hurried to the stairs around the bend of the corridor and ran down the one flight. She rounded the bend of the corridor again. All the lights were out on this floor, except for the one at the south end, a real estate broker's office. She went to Folgueira's office, to the right. She tried the key, half afraid it wouldn't fit the lock, and it turned. She pushed the door cautiously and walked in. She almost expected somebody to come out at her from the darkness. Why had she gotten into this? She turned the light on in the inner office, so there would only be a very dim sliver of light under the door to the hallway, should somebody from the real estate office walk by. She recognized the old wooden furniture.

She pulled the stencil out of the magazine. Its edges had gotten creased and she had to find the blue corrector and apply it to the margins before she put it on the machine. The old mimeograph had to be cranked by hand. She spread the ink on the roller and started spinning the wheel. She didn't dare read the sheets that came out. She absurdly thought that, if she knew what was written, she'd feel more fear. Watching the pages upside down, when she saw they weren't smeared any more, she grabbed the sheets that were already lying in the tray and laid them aside. Duarte hadn't told her how many copies he wanted. She ran 250 and had to ink the roller again. She read the title, *"Guía"*, and the name of the group, Nationalist

Movement, over the month, "November-1960". She had heard of it. Its leader was in the States. She didn't know who the head of the local underground group was. She put the sheets into a large manila envelope. She peeled the stencil off the machine, ripped the cardboard top off and threw it in the wastebasket. She pressed the waxed paper backing and the blackened stencil between the soiled sheets and stuck it all in the envelope. She dropped the magazine into the basket and had her hand on the light switch when she remembered the money. She took $2.50 from her handbag and put it in the top drawer of the wooden desk. She added another *"medio"*[51] for the envelope. She turned off the light and locked the door behind her. The light was still on in the real estate broker's office.

She ran up the stairs to the sixth floor and rang for the elevator. It was 7:30. The elevator operator, the only one on duty at that hour, looked flittingly at her awkward package, but fortunately didn't seem very concerned. Her heart was pounding. She smiled uncertainly at him.

"Hot, isn't it?" The words were barely out of her mouth when she realized it was late November and not hot at all. But she *was* perspiring.

"It always gets warm here after five thirty", the man replied agreeably, "when they turn the air conditioning off."

She wondered if the boy knew in which company she had worked. He covered a yawn and smiled as if apologizing. They had reached the ground floor. She wasn't aware if she had returned his smile. "Good night."

"Until tomorrow", the man answered mechanically.

She walked down the lobby pressing the envelope tightly against her hip and didn't dare look to either side. When she was out on the sidewalk, she felt very much like leaning against the marble slab wall, but she looked for a moment at the window of the "Villalón" office machine dealer, closed now, with its German typewriters, and at the full tops of the trees on Calzada, and she hurried up the block to a little coffee shop on the next corner. She asked for black coffee standing at the small counter with its glass display showing ham croquettes, meat pastries, guava turnovers, milk cream, sweet potato pudding, Morón almond cookies, browned coconut mounds, candied coconut balls and guava jelly layer cakes; and large round jars con-

[51] five-cent coin

taining aluminum foil-wrapped chocolate African wafers, lady fingers, sponge rusks, rings, peanut brittle, San Francisco little buns, Jamaica cupcakes, poundcake and sesame seed cakes, and she drank the coffee in two gulps. A picture on the wall announced "flying saucers". She noticed it was cool outdoors. She passed a neocolonial residence and walked the four blocks back to Duarte's house, the envelope hot in her hand.

She was surprised to see a militia man sitting on the front stoop of the building and hesitated for a moment. Could he be searching the people going in? But they didn't do that in apartment buildings, at least not yet. She stood at the corner, took one shoe off, shook an imaginary pebble out, put it back on, stopped testily on her foot — thinking, if she couldn't get to see Duarte, what would she do with the package — and then she saw a woman with a bag of groceries walk past him undisturbed. Ana rushed past the militia man, smiling in greeting, and into the building. She knocked on Duarte's door again. A handsome boy with closely-cropped hair, about 25, answered and she asked him, "Is Duarte in?"

"Come in."

She walked into the living room.

"Sit down", the boy changed to the *"tú"* pronoun familiar form of address, waving a hand toward the only free armchair. "He's shaving." He cocked his head toward the inside without taking his eyes off hers.

Ana sat on the edge of the chair, holding the envelope on her lap with both hands, her handbag hanging on her forearm. Magazines and comic pages were strewn on the sofa and the other chair. A cheap picture of a seascape hung lopsided over the sofa. There was an end table to either side of it with a lamp on each, and held to one of the lampshades with a paper clip was a newspaper clipping. She focused and made out a cartoon. From a radio inside, turned low, came a *son montuno*. There was an old, large refrigerator. On another wall hung a Sacred Heart of Jesus. The boy stood by a door, and through it Ana saw the small kitchen. She gave him a quick smile, self-conscious.

"Do you work at the Ministry?" She could tell he was being cautious. She didn't know whether he was with Duarte in the movement.

"Yes, that's how I know Duarte." She usually didn't feel awkward with boys.

"Are you... Yolanda?" But something in the tone of his question told her he knew she wasn't.

"No, I'm Ana", more at ease. "Yolanda is the other girl who works wi..." Her voice trailed off. Then Duarte hadn't mentioned that she was coming.

"Oh, yes! Ana." He came forth, smiling, leaned forward, and shook her hand. "He talks about you two often. Alejandro Dávila. Well, excuse me, I have to rush. I have classes at eight. Reynaldo − Duarte, as you call him − will be out soon. Would you like to join me?"

"No, thanks, may it benefit you."

"With your permission." And he retreated into the kitchen, from where noises of dishes and silverware came presently.

She stood up, partly curious and partly restless, and walked over to the lamp. The yellowed cartoon showed the "Black Spy" with a telephone in his hand, looking through a window at a woman in the next house wrapped in a towel and dripping water while picking up her phone. Somebody had printed in blue ink underneath, "El Tico". Ana grinned.

She heard Duarte's voice behind her. "That's an old one. It was Alejandro's idea", and when she turned around, he tilted his head in the direction of the kitchen. "He thought it was hilarious."

Ana laughed. She went to the chair, picked up the bulky envelope and handed it to him, soiled sheets, stencil and all, glad to unload it on someone else.

"How many did you run?", he asked, pulling it out of the envelope.

"Two hundred and fifty. I wanted to run four hundred, but the paper is thick and it was too much to carry out. Even this seemed pretty bulky."

He looked them over, nodding distractedly. "I don't know... Is there any chance we may run into trouble there?"

"I don't think so."

"How much do we pay the man?"

"A *peso* for a hundred sheets."

He nodded, pulled out his billfold and handed her three singles, with José Martí's picture. "We should have at least three hundred and fifty. And that would only give us twenty-five for each ministry."

She took fifty cents from her wallet, which Duarte refused, shaking his head. She wondered how they distributed them, through ministry employees? Duarte hadn't smiled once. Alejandro came out of the kitchen with a little cup of black coffee and handed it to her.

"Do you know how to make coffee?", she asked him trying to be friendly.

"I did learn back at the *'central'*, but the woman who cleans the apartment for us makes this in the morning and leaves it in a thermos."

"The central?"

"The Reforma Sugar Mill, in Caibarién", Alejandro answered as he went back inside.

The coffee was strong, but tepid and too sweet, and it was her second cup in half an hour.

"How do you get home, by bus?", Duarte asked her.

"Yes. It's only ten blocks, but if I walk I'll get home too late."

He put his hand in his pocket. "I don't want to offend you, but I'd like to pay you for a taxi."

"That's not necessary."

"I'd feel better."

"No, thank you", she said firmly.

A large portion of the city of Havana was in darkness, in some neighborhoods for 24 hours, as a result of bombs placed in nine electric registers. Hundreds of electric workers were arrested. It had been the work of the 30th of November Movement.

From the Ministry they heard several explosions that occurred at the Palace of Justice during the day, the most potent one at the entrance to the Examining Court of the Fourth Section. There was considerable damage.

Ana, Yolanda and Duarte passed Sara, a mulatto typist in the section, on the steps of the building Friday afternoon.

"Listen, Aurora came 'pitching over the plate' today."

They generally tried to dodge her, because she often expressed herself against the government, freely and loudly, and her friendship could prove compromising, so they now smiled evasively. Yolanda replied ambiguously, "Well, today is the last day of the week."

"Yes, tomorrow I'm going to Bárbara's house to keep the vigil on the Saint", she announced to them from the door of the building.

"Sure, have fun", Duarte told her from the sidewalk and, turning to Ana and Yolanda, shrugged one shoulder.

Ana met Rolandito, the former Wayne Motors office boy, in the hallway of her own floor at the Ministry. He was wearing the pin of the Rebel Youth on his lapel. Her mouth fell open. He told her he was working at the Treasury Department and was there on an errand.

The Episcopate published an open letter to Castro on December 4 signed by Manuel Cardinal Arteaga and the Archbishops, complaining of the attacks against the Church. **NOBODY WAS LISTENING.**

Another call at work surprised her.

"Ana, it's Rina. How are you?"

"Fine, thank you. What are you doing here?"

"I came for a few days. I was surprised to hear you ended up working in the same department as Aurora after all. Listen, I'd like to see you." Ana was flattered. They hadn't been that close. "Could we meet after work?"

"Sure. Will 'El Carmelo' on Twenty-three be all right?"

"Fine. I'd like to see Danilo too. Can you get together with him?"

Ah!, so it was him Rina wanted to see, she realized then. Only she'd considered it more proper to call her to arrange it. No wonder. Not that she were jealous... although Rina *had* said after they had been to the pool the first time that he "was in fine shape",... but she was at least seven years older than he.

"Yes, I'll call him. I'm sure that a quarter to seven will be all right with him too."

"Until later."

Rina arrived at the restaurant after they did, and there were loud greetings that made three men sitting at the counter by the refrigerator turn their heads. Their reunion was cheerful. They settled with their drinks to a talk about Nassau, their co-workers, Rina's move, the changes in Dany's and Ana's lives, their new jobs. Dany and Ana were anxious to learn details of Rina's new life, she not so much about their dull ones.

"Most of the employees in the office are still Cubans. It hasn't been easy for them to find local help to fill the positions."

They shot questions at her. "How are you all getting along? Have you gotten settled? Do you like it? What is life like? How are the Americans acting?"

"We're getting settled. The company's helping. They paid us for three weeks at the 'British Colonial'. And we've found apartments. The rents are high. Graciela and I are sharing a one-bedroom apartment for thirty-eight pounds a month, about a hundred *pesos*, and it doesn't even have a bathtub, just a shower stall." Ana noticed that she had, surprisingly, picked up Graciela's gestures and mannerisms.

"But you sound so... adventurous", said Ana, "filled with daring."
"We have to do it", she shrugged. "There's no choice." She was quiet for a moment. "There's a lot of work."

Ana asked about Berta, Leonardo, Guillén, Graciela, Virginia, Eugenia and Raquel. Dany asked about Mario and Salvador.

Ana felt uncomfortably self-conscious. She had to talk about it. "I was afraid you might all think I stayed because I'm a leftist", she said smiling hesitantly.

"We all think you were crazy to stay. Kent says you'll regret it."

"Yes, he told me." So he had talked about it again.

"It's hotter than here", said Rina. "The people are good-natured."

Dany brought up the subject to which the conversation would inevitably have to turn.

"What did you all think about the cancellation of my visa?"

Rina turned to Ana and said with a grin, "They think you denounced him."

"Me?" She was appalled. It hadn't occurred to her that anybody would think that. "I was surprised", she protested. She now saw how it *would* make sense to them. − She would have done it to keep him with her. − "It took me as much by surprise as it did him." It bothered her that they should think that.

Dany smiled at the idea. There was a short silence. Then the conversation again spun around their lives in their new surroundings. Ana remained a little subdued.

Before parting, Ana said apropos of nothing, "My residence visa is valid until January." Rina looked at her, her mind already on something else. She did not respond, and neither did Dany.

They said good-by on the stairs with repeated promises to write and keep in touch. And, when Rina walked to the curb to flag a taxi cab, they started down the sidewalk in a let-down mood, their lingering wistful smiles fading slowly from their lips.

They had reached H Street when Ana said, "You don't think I ... I turned you in, do you?"

"No, *mi vida*, I know you didn't."

The professional associations disappeared.

Clodomiro Miranda, a countryman, chief of the Bahía Honda military post in Cabañas, in Pinar del Río province, took to arms on the Organos Range with less than thirty men. Over 10,000 militiamen went looking for him. He was fatally wounded and sent to the city of Pinar del Río.

Nine men arrived in Florida on a boat. The boat on which four electric workers sailed capsized and they were picked up by a sand ship, the captain of which turned them over to the authorities.

The two Canadian banks hadn't yet been appropriated. The government nationalized The Royal Bank of Canada on December 8, but compensated them in cash.

"Do you know Melvin's being transferred to Jamaica?", her mother asked Ana that evening as they trimmed the white-sprayed Christmas tree.

"Who's Melvin?", asked her father, a gold ball in his hand.

"Alicia's son, the one from La Metropolitana building. She called me today." Alicia had been married to an American executive of one of the oil companies. "You know he works in one of the Canadian banks."

"Yes, I know", said Ana. And to her father, "I went to apply for a job there three years ago. Do you remember?"

"That's right. Was that the place where they sent you for a physical examination?"

"Right, but the job was only as vacation substitute. Is she going with him?"

"No, her older son's still working here and she's staying with him."

"I thought she was more attached to the younger one", said Carlos.

"Oh, no!", said Teresa. "She's always said Marvin, the older one, is more like her and Melvin like their father. But anyway, even if she weren't more attached to him, she still wasn't going to leave him behind, without knowing whether he can get out later."

Recently arguments had been springing up between Ana and Dany. Since his residence visa in the Bahamas had been cancelled, he seemed – perhaps out of spite – to have turned toward the revolution. He had read in the last two months Marx's *"Das Kapital"*, his and Engels' The Communist Manifesto and several books on economics and socialism, and he tried to convince her that the government was doing a very good job. Sometimes they sat at a white marble table with iron legs in an old-fashioned cafe on Hospital Street across from Vaillant Motors for over an hour with a watery soda before them, the blades of the old ceiling fans whirring overhead, discussing this until she felt weary. He always asked her why she didn't agree with any of it. And she always held that she was in favor of free enterprise and thought that planned economy killed incentive and ambition. She insisted that most normal people would rather be poor, but have hope and know they were free to do as they pleased, than have a more adequate situation, but be told how to live and not look forward to any change. They went over this many times, until it became tiresome.

She tried to avoid conversation about politics, but Dany somehow always managed to lead them up to it.

"Please, *mi cielo*, let's just forget about politics while we're together."

"It's just that you don't know about economics."

"I may not know about economics, but I know how I want to *live*."

"You sound like a scratched record, Ana."

"So do you. Why are people fleeing by boat, Dany?"

"Those are melodramatic."

"Because of melodrama they'd leave a life that was good for them to go live one they don't know?"

"To try the adventure. If you at least backed your stubborn answers with some sensible reasons..."

"I don't want to talk about it", she insisted. She didn't want to admit that she didn't actually know how to offer a sensible reason. She was completely sure of the way she felt about it − under another system Gutiérrez wouldn't have been able to achieve what he had reached, − but she didn't know about economics or politics and she felt frustrated not being able to explain her ideas to him sensibly, so she avoided the discussions. She envied Rina then, confident with her knowledge. At times like that she made up her mind that she'd read about economics and she'd verse herself in the characteristics of communism and those of capitalism and their distinguishing features, beyond the obvious ones of repression and individualism. But she somehow never quite got around to carrying it out. It was so boring!

On December 9 two thousand workers of the Electric Company left from their syndicate's office on Prado and marched in protest to the Presidential Palace on Refugios shouting, "Cuba, yes!, Russia, no!" and they hoisted the secretary general of the electric workers up on their shoulders. He was ultimately admitted to see Dorticós.

Ana was concerned by the briefing on it that Ernesto had given her that afternoon over the telephone. While Blanca addressed their Christmas cards at the dining table that evening, after the children were in bed, Ana asked her sister-in-law whether she had been among them. Blanca just pressed her lips tightly and turned her head toward Gustavo, who was solving a crossword puzzle in a chair in the living room. And Ana knew she wouldn't talk about it within his earshot. Maybe not out of it either. Perhaps she had been.

Seven Navy sailors left from Bahía Honda, in Cabañas, in a small boat. They were picked up by an oil ship near the American coast and taken to Miami.

New employees were being hired at the Ministry and they were being constantly moved to other, bigger offices. They sometimes arrived in the morning to find the first employees who had arrived busily moving the desks under the watchful eye of Aurora or Mestre. They had no voice as to where their desks were placed. Signs affixed to the walls hammered revolution slogans at them.

Arguments continued between Ana and Dany.

"Why do you keep denying this is communism?", she asked him, puzzled.

"And why do you say it is?", he countered. "The Cuban government doesn't answer to Russia", he reasoned.

"To be a communist one doesn't necessarily have to be an agent of Moscow. Albania isn't, or Yugoslavia. Nor for that matter is China", Ana sustained with logic. "Russia isn't the cradle of communism, it was only the first country to adopt it. Karl Marx and Friedrich Engels weren't Russian, they were German; even Georg Hegel before them." That much she did know – ... but even that she had learned only in the last two months!

He shook his head slowly, as one would at a backward student. But he didn't answer. Maybe she'd held up her end.

With her Christmas cards, Ana wrote letters to Leonardo Vidal and to Octavio Guillén in Nassau. They answered her with their Christmas greetings. They had gotten established with the help of the company and found apartments. They complained a lot about the amount of work and the high cost of living, but their letters spelled excitement and seemed to Ana filled with adventure. And she wondered if she shouldn't have gone. The atmosphere at the Ministry was constrained. And the people were different, tasteless. She wasn't dressing as well herself. She reminded herself again that her visa was still valid until January, but she knew she wouldn't leave Dany. She also wrote to Graciela, sending her regards to Berta Penabad, with whom she was to have shared an apartment, but she didn't receive an answer from Graciela.

Ana talked to Yolanda about Dany on their break. "He's changed

Witnesses to the Destruction of the Country

so much! I remember the day Che Guevara was named president of the National Bank – and that was ... how long?, a year ago? – he reacted so differently! He said he hadn't known him to be an economist. And even five months ago, when Núñez Jiménez came back from Eastern Europe, he still criticized his praise of the socialist countries. But in these last two months he seems to have changed so much... You know,... it might be crazy, but I feel almost a- afraid of him."

"It's strange that he should have changed in *that* direction", Yolanda observed, sipping her chocolate milk shake with a little frown.

Ana nodded. She had her back to the street. "He's read a couple of books on socialism and keeps trying to convince me of how beneficial it is for the country. I have to admit to you that I don't know one word about economics, all I know is I want to feel free to live and work where I want and I think, if anyone wants to go into a private business, he should be free to do so."

"And that's not enough for him?" Yolanda raised her eyes over Ana.

Ana shook her head with a grimace.

"Who's that?" Duarte had reached their table against the wall.

"Her boyfriend", Yolanda answered. And to Ana, "Economics and politics are not so boring once you start reading. If you get a good book, you find it interesting", she said almost cautiously, maybe afraid of offending her. "I did in college. You could acquaint yourself with it a little, enough to refute his arguments."

"Has he turned socialist?", Duarte asked, pulling out a chair to join them.

Yolanda briefed him on the highlights of the matter.

"He's brainwashed himself", he said somberly, a little amazement in his gray eyes. "Is he trying to brainwash you?" He had asked it suddenly.

"No", answered Ana, at the same time Yolanda answered, "Yes". They looked at each other. Ana smiled sheepishly, as if apologizing. She knew what was crossing Duarte's mind.

"I'm going to lend you a couple of books on economics", Yolanda offered.

Sara approached the table, starting to talk before she reached it, "Ana, Saturday Bárbara and I met a boy in Guanabo beach who says he's a classmate of yours. Fat, with a hairless chest and slanted eyes."

"Ah!, that must be Ernesto."

"Uh-huh!, Ernesto, that's it."

"Yes, we've been together in school for about a year", Ana explained, getting up.

Leaflets were dropped from a plane by the Democratic Revolutionary Front on December 12 urging the people to turn against the government and instructing them to engage in sabotage.

In December, after two months' vacation, school reopened and Ana started her second year of Publicity. Studying now seemed easier to her, and she was glad and felt proud of having gone back to school. She was filled with what Ernesto termed a sense of accomplishment.

Danilo's own fifth year consisted of Intervention and Prosecution Practice, Fiscal Law, Commercial Law and Business Administration.

There was a fire in CMQ television station, started in the air conditioning, where phosphorus had been thrown, and it completely destroyed two floors of the Radiocentro building.

Dany was picking Ana up after school almost every night now. He had taken to skipping his own last class to meet her in time. And she was glad they had more time together. They met at a coffee shop near the school and they had black coffee, or banana shakes or, if it was cold, hot chocolate. And afterwards they made love harmoniously in his car, parked on 6th Street or on 3rd. They knew all the darkest spots, the stretches with fewer lampposts, the blocks with fewer houses.

In December the militia and the Rebel Youth broke up religious services. The news brought Rolandito to Ana's mind.

One afternoon Ana and Dany were sitting over Coca-Colas at the counter of a little coffee shop low on O Street, near the Hotel Nacional, and Dany had been praising the wonders of the revolution for a while, when Ana, unable to contain herself any longer, snapped at him, "If you're with the revolution so much, how come you don't join the militia? It's easy to swim out of the water, talk about it, but you wouldn't want the discipline that goes with it, not that."

He didn't answer and she thought she had won the point. He, who was late to every place!

A national indoctrination school was established in the old Belén School, classes were held in the afternoon and the textbook was by Blas Roca. Fidel had dealt the ultimate revenge on his old school.

The next evening, in a coffee shop on Infanta Street near the "Astral" theater, Dany told Ana as soon as he sat at the counter, "I registered."

"In what?"

"In the militia." At first she didn't know whether he might be joking. But, to her dismay, he added, "I got to thinking about what you said to me yesterday and I realized you were right. If I support the revolution, the best way to show it is by doing something constructive. Joining the militia is one way."

She was astonished. She regretted having said that to him. From then on, they had less time together. He went marching evenings. He had to take the initial regulation 39-mile hike.

About the militia, there were some who mockingly chanted, "One, two, three, four,/ filling up on baloney and wearing out shoes."

Sometimes Dany skipped classes to go to practice. And Ana felt hurt that he didn't do it to see her. Their relationship seemed to deteriorate somewhat.

For the first time in 53 years, since 1907, the Cuban Winter Baseball League teams had no American ball players. And Castro banned cockfighting, the humble pastime of the hopeful poor.

A decree eliminated the President of the Supreme Court, Dr. Angel Fernández Rodríguez.

One evening after classes, Ana and Dany were sitting on a marble bench on lower G Street, talking, surrounded by the red cannas, their wide coarse leaves a gleaming bronze in the scant light, and the trimmed bushes, with the double row of graceful royal palms lining each sidewalk, across from an old large house on the east with a peak roof and exposed braces that seemed to Ana out of place, straight out of a Basque mountain scene. The red brick Presidente Hotel towered behind them nearby to the south, President Estrada Palma's statue rose close by to their right, and a fountain stood not far, the Maternity Hospital further away. Beautiful residences lined the street, and at the north end on the Recodo the black equestrian statue of Calixto García faced the gulf, with the José Martí Park to one side and the "Recodo" drive-in restaurant to the other. They had been talking about their work and their classes for a while in the mild evening when Dany steered the conversation to politics. He seemed obsessed with it.

"Please, Dany", Ana pleaded with apprehension, "you know as soon as we start talking about politics, we start arguing."

"But I wish I could convince you", he said in frustration.

"Well, so do *I* wish I could convince *you*", she said helplessly, "but I can't, so let's just give up trying to convince each other and enjoy our time together."

"Stupid." At first she couldn't believe it. It had come out, muffled, through clenched teeth. She looked at him with wide eyes, stunned. She felt a surging urge to cry, but was so cruelly hurt, she held her tears back and went away in a rage, walked the eight blocks to her house. On the way, the desire to cry dissipated and gave way to a rising bitter anger. It seemed impossible this could be the same boy to whom she had felt so wonderfully close, such a considerate, kind man, on whose shoulder she had cried her regret, who had shared with her his dream of racing cars and had driven around on a Sunday looking for an open jewelry store to buy her a locket. She wondered for the first time if his thoughts had been known to the British Embassy when they cancelled his visa. When she got home, she closed her bedroom door and lay in the dark.

On December 16 President Eisenhower cancelled the Cuban sugar quota for the first quarter of the coming year.

Sara, the typist, approached Duarte, Yolanda and Ana where they sat in the coffee shop, stood by their table by the railing and vented her gripes loudly enough for the whole restaurant to hear, "Did you hear what Aurora said to me this morning? That she thought I should join the sugar-cane cutting. I asked her, 'Why don't you?' and now she's having a fit about me, but she kept quiet. What gall!" Duarte looked at her with amusement, Yolanda laughed in embarrassment, Ana looked around at the other tables. Lack of response didn't daunt Sara. "I'm telling you, if these bums think I'm going to cut cane or work at the paper mill or join the militia", she jabbed her chest with her thumb for emphasis, "they don't know how wrong they are. Let them sit down to wait! Me they don't take advantage of."

"Shut up, Sara", Yolanda finally said mildly, "everybody's looking at you."

With a shake of her dry, long, black, curly mane, she swept away from their table vigorously swinging her ample behind, to join another girl, Bárbara, a bleached blonde from another section.

"She's going to get into trouble", Yolanda predicted, following her with her eyes.

Duarte shook his head, smiling and concentrated his attention on his wheat milk shake for a moment. After an instant, he said, "The Country Girl wants to go to the Rincón tomorrow."

That afternoon Dany called Ana at work. He didn't apologize for his outburst and no mention was made, then or ever, of the argument of the night before. But that evening she waited for him watching television alone, as her sadness grew, and he didn't come. In her lonely need of him, she forgave him, and only wished to be next to him again. But she didn't call him. She stood on the balcony and heard music. It was a rite beat. It came from the shoe repairman's house, on the opposite side near the corner. She could see several people standing on the porch, all very still. − *"Babalú Ayé".* − She remembered then that it was Saint Lazarus' Eve. She looked at the time. It was five minutes before midnight. She got absorbed in watching the people disappear briefly one by one and then reappear to occupy the same spot. They were apparently approaching the image of the Saint to light candles. At five after twelve they spread and the dance music resumed, at a much lower volume. Ana went to bed.

The electric workers' leader took asylum in an embassy.

The Bank of Nova Scotia transferred its holdings to the National Bank of Cuba. It had eight branches in the country and its funds were estimated at 57,000,000. dollars.

Gustavo and Blanca came with the children on Sunday to take them all to "El Congo" country restaurant in Catalina de Güines. They piled into the blue '57 Chevrolet − successor to the Chevrolet that had been twisted in the explosion of *"La Coubre"*, − the children on Teresa's and Carlos' laps, and travelled the 32 miles southeast, through Jamaica, San José de las Lajas − "El Aljibe" restaurant by the junction with the highway to Güines − and Zaragoza. They gorged on pork sausages and turnovers in the rustic setting, while the record player blared,

> *"...Amalia Mayombe,*
> *¿Qué tiene esa negra,*
> *que amarra a los hombres?"*[(83)]

In school, Ana ran into Ramiro and Rolandito, who announced to her, "Danilo was promoted to assistant accountant."

It annoyed her that they knew she hadn't heard the news. Outside, a piercing, thin, cold drizzle fell.

Paraguay announced having confirmation from prisoners captured in Itá Enramada, south of the capital, in the Central Department, that their expedition had been inspired and financed by Castro.

Thursday several employees stayed late at the Ministry to hang Christmas ornaments for the parties they were to hold in the different departments. Ana didn't want to stand out by not staying.

They were standing on the desks to hang the garlands and red paper balls up on the wall when Aurora, watching them thoughtfully, suddenly observed, pleased, "I know we here are all chemically pure."

Ana considered the expression, another of those recently adopted by the revolution, so ridiculous, that she had to refrain from giggling. Sara heard it and Ana saw her shoot a look at Yolanda with a grin, but the latter just turned away pretending not to notice.

On December 23 what remained of the Cuban press was taken over. The government confiscated *Información* newspaper. Nineteen daily newspapers had thus been either silenced altogether or else subordinated to the system. And their place had been taken by instruments of the government such as *Revolución, Combate, La Calle* and *Hoy*.

Friday at the Ministry the employees exchanged Christmas presents. Ana gave Abreu, the older man whose name she had drawn, after-shave lotion and Morejón, the colored man who drew her name, gave her a green silk scarf and Aurora, a pin with a black enameled horsewhip. Duarte had left early with the excuse that he had to travel 24 kilometers. How different the party from the ones at Wayne! That last one at the Habana Hilton, thought Ana with nostalgia... Somebody, perhaps Sara, brought a portable record player, which they turned on with the department door closed, because, she learned, it was actually not allowed. Sara had too much to drink, from liquor somebody smuggled in. "For that streak you have, my child", she advised, baffling Ana, "you should exorcise yourself with sweet basil." After a prudent while, Ana snuck away. Yolanda had already left unnoticed.

Dany hadn't come by, met her or called her for a week, since the Friday before. And Ana felt empty.

She repeated José Heredia's *"Soneto al Niágara"* to herself over and over, listening in her mind to the roll of the R's, resembling the roar of the water rushing over the rocks to its fall. She read Villaverde's *Cecilia Valdés* again, but Leonardo's murder depressed her and, strangely, for the loyal Pimienta. She hadn't unpacked her records and books. She listened to the "With You at Midnight" poetry radio program.

> *"...porque me causa la muerte*
> *con la tristeza de amarte*

> *el dolor de comprenderte.*
> *Mientras pueda contemplarte,*
> *me ha de deparar la suerte...*"(70)

There were six television channels, but, while her mother watched *"Casino de la Alegría"*, *"Escuela de Televisión"* and other variety shows, the only program Ána watched regularly was the nightly serial *"Mamá"*. The characters were so real, their dialogue so commonplace, their gestures so natural! It seemed the modern trend. And there was still no reference to the revolution in it. Political propaganda had invaded television and this remained one of the few shows not yet permeated by revolutionary allusions. She enjoyed watching it, and it became her only recreation.

And she waited. For the phone, the door knocker, his car. But none came.

She took great pleasure that year in buying everybody in the family something for Christmas. They were all going to Gustavo's for Christmas Eve dinner. This year, besides her parents and her, also coming were her aunt Cristina with her husband Marcos, their daughter, her cousin Norma; her uncle Guillermo with his wife Beatriz and their son, her cousin Jorge, about thirty. She rushed around the business district all Saturday afternoon, buying at the last moment scarves, tie tacks, necklaces, handkerchiefs and socks. She was running so late she had to take a taxi, and wasn't even careful to "adjust the run" in advance. She asked the driver to wait for her while she went into "El Nogal" bakery on 12th Street, for the last gift missing, meringues, for her aunt Beatriz.

It was the "Free Christmas", the government proclaimed. The Nativity scene was hardly seen. There were no American Christmas decorations. Her parents were waiting for her at her brother's. They probably thought she was with Dany.

"Merry Christmas", she said to the chauffeur, almost springing out of the taxi in front of the building.

"The same to you, miss", he answered, a little surprised at the generous tip.

Her aunt Beatriz opened the door for her and, after the greeting kisses, she followed her, giving her a pat on the back. "This girl is skinny as an American", she announced. "Look at that small waist!" Her aunt, of the old school, equated chubbiness with good health, and, given a chance, would probably warn her about anemia. Ana was the last one to arrive. The family were gathered in the dining room.

They had the usual big dinner. Gustavo had, a little skeptically, ordered the roast suckling pig from the Spanish corner grocer, and they were all surprised when it was delivered. Her aunt Beatriz had baked guinea hens in dry wine "just in case". They had red wine with the dinner and white wine with the desserts. Gustavo lamented, "I wish we had film in the camera. Nobody thought of it. We're all gathered. It might be the last year we're all together."

"*Ay*, Gustavo!, don't talk like that", said his mother.

"Don't be pessimistic, my love", Blanca responded, knowing her husband feared a separation.

"Don't be an owl", Marcos reacted, thinking Gustavo foreboded a death.

After dinner, Ana gave out her presents. Méndez had bought toys for the children at "Sección X". Dany didn't call her that evening. She felt disappointed, but not surprised. She had expected it. She tried to convince herself that he could have tried to call her at home, not knowing she was at her brother's. After all, there had been only two Christmas Eves since they were together and they hardly had an established pattern. She helped her sister-in-law put the children to bed. Teresa helped Blanca clear the table. Comatose with food, Ana was bored. She gave Olga's phone number to her cousin Jorge to play a joke on her and, while he called her from the extension in Gustavo and Blanca's room, she listened on the living room telephone. Jorge, cheered by the liquor, pretended to be a secret admirer, and Ana was surprised at how gullible Olga was.

When she hung up, leaving Jorge to play his role of Don Juan, she joined the conversation in the living room. The children had fallen asleep and the dog was shut away. Gustavo and Blanca were telling the others about a Russian couple they had met in the course of Gustavo's work at the Ministry.

"The woman was a teacher", Blanca was saying, "but she decided to quit teaching and go to work as a maid." She sounded amused. To Ana she specified, "Vladimir Vasiliyev and Ludmila Sergeyova." Ana had heard her mention them.

"They are free of prejudice", Gustavo stated.

"But imagine that!", said Guillermo. "Leaving a job teaching to take one cleaning!"

"Yes, really...", said her aunt Cristina.

"They're from Gor'kiy", offered Blanca.

"How cold it must be there!", remarked Norma. Marcos nodded, with pretended knowledge; Beatriz raised her eyebrows in open ignorance.

Gustavo surprised them a little reflecting, "Maybe that's the right attitude. To them there's no difference between being a teacher and being a maid. They see either one as a service."

"Yes, but you don't need the same education for one as for the other", Carlos voiced his opinion perhaps a little cautiously. "It takes much more effort to prepare yourself to be a teacher."

"And cleaning tires you more physically", said Teresa.

Blanca didn't seem to accept it with the same ease as Gustavo. The conversation was changed when Jorge came out of the bedroom laughing and asked Ana to dance.

"What a fool your friend is, that Olga!"

"Hey, don't squeeze", she complained.

"Oh, Ana!, haven't you heard that 'cousins squeeze'?"

Jorge, now a sugar chemist, hadn't worked until he was 24. Ana had been a little surprised he attended the family gathering.

Guillermo and Marcos drank "Spain in flames"[52]. Their parents danced. Ana suspected her father and her brother had had too much to drink. Norma was talking with Beatriz, Guillermo with Marcos, Cristina with Blanca.

Suddenly, Jorge stopped, put on a serious expression, widened his eyes and made straight for the bathroom.

"Have you set the date yet?", Blanca asked Norma.

"No, not yet. It'll be in early September."

"Where are you getting married?"

"At Saint Anthony of Padua's Church."

"Isn't the ring beautiful?", prompted Cristina. "Eh, Tera?"

Teresa inspected it and agreed, "Very pretty."

"You know", Norma said addressing Blanca, "that I lost it eight days ago and I had Saint Dimas tied with a handkerchief all of Friday?, and I found it less than five minutes before Víctor arrived. What a scare I had!"

"Where was it?", Teresa asked.

"She'd dropped it in the manger setting up the *crèche*", Cristina answered. "It's that it's too big on her, because she's lost weight."

The four men were talking aside, laughing.

[52] cider and cognac

"Where are you going to register your bridal gift list?", asked Ana.
"At 'Fin de Siglo'. But it's still a long way off, not until the end of June."
"Are you making yourself a *'trousseau'*?"
"Yes, but only six sets of sheets − a lady on Forty-seven is making fagoting and embroidering the initials on two of them for me, − twelve towels and three tablecloths. That's enough."
"I can embroider a couple of towels, if you want", offered Teresa.
"Oh, good, Aunt! Thank you."
The men's voices intoned,

> *"...no me martirices más,*
> *que mi corazón está*
> *que se devora*
> *de quererte tanto, mora..."*[84]

"Do you want children right away?", asked Beatriz.
"No, I'm going to have a contraceptive ring fitted. I want to finish Pedagogy."
Jorge reappeared in the living room, a little pale. And Víctor arrived. They both joined the men's chorus.

> *"Yo te daré,*
> *te daré, niña hermosa,*
> *te daré una cosa,*
> *una cosa que yo solo sé..."*[85]

There had been a few pigs after all, and chickens, turkeys, rice, black beans, apples and nougats for the traditional dinner. But figs, dates and nuts were conspicuously absent.

They went to Midnight Mass, to fight back yawns and narrowly escape falling asleep in church. There were few worshippers. A drunk walked in who reminded Ana of the joke about the hat. The streets were quiet. The relatives parted after Mass, some outside the church, others in front of Gustavo's house.

A potent bomb exploded in the basement of the building of the main offices of the Electric Company on Carlos III, which gave the family a horrible scare for Blanca. Ana called Ernesto on the phone that afternoon, without mentioning the incident. He was all right.

A bomb exploded in the Flogar store cafeteria at noon, and another at a motion-picture theater in Marianao.

Audio of an anti-Castro broadcast by the Revolutionary Student Directorate came through on Channel 2 *Telemundo*, which had been closed for weeks, but there was no video.

Major Ernesto Guevara returned from the Soviet Union and announced that Russia would build a hundred plants in Cuba.

The government already having control of the 161 sugar mills, the four oil refineries and the mines, Guevara then consolidated 22 vehicle and motor companies, 34 steel and metal works, 82 shoe manufacturing plants, 13 soft-drink companies, 26 plow mills, 72 cigarette factories, nine match factories, eight salt manufacturers, ten dry cleaners and eight communications firms. The government nationalized and controlled the industry, 43 banks, all the apartments, the transportation system, thirty insurance companies, fisheries and 95 percent of the agriculture.

The chain markets were nationalized. The government opened people's stores. Privately-owned grocery stores in the countryside went bankrupt.

Revolución newspaper headlines announced that 170,000 pounds of grapes were received in port.

Thursday Ana carried out the mimeographing of the December bulletin without difficulty. She ran the 350 copies Duarte had requested this time, and took them up to his apartment.

Prisoners were tortured at G-2 headquarters, headed by Ramiro Valdés Menéndez, on 5th Avenue in Miramar. At La Cabaña Fortress and the Isle of Pines reclusory, prisoners were placed against the execution wall, in a favorite diabolical form of mental torture, and the firing squad shot at them with blank bullets, repeating the procedure as many as three times. Guards sold the scarce water to the prisoners at El Príncipe Castle on the plateau at Zapata Street in Vedado.

Cuba had established diplomatic relations with the Soviet Union and "sister countries" North Vietnam, Albania, Outer Mongolia and Hungary.

For Ana it was a sad, lonely week.

On New Year's Eve, a fire broke out at expropriated "La Epoca" four-story department store, which burned for four hours and was completely destroyed. The loss of the building was calculated at $2,000,000. and they had stock valued at three million. The fire started on the second floor. The manager, the cashier and the head of personnel were in the building. Twelve warehouse employees were arrested.

After dinner, there was a knock on the door. Ana was eating a sapodilla and her heart skipped a beat. But she was disappointed when her mother opened the door to Ernesto. He had brought an issue of "Look". Ana offered him a sapodilla and they sat in the living room to comment on an article in the magazine, which led to a discussion about the permanence of the Catholic Church.

"It worries me to think that communism may threaten religion", Ana expressed, her lips sticky from the fruit.

"There's no danger of that. The Church has survived bigger threats for twenty centuries and a doctrine barely over a hundred years old isn't going to shake it."

"But communism undermines the faith,... fights religion."

"Look at it this way: Saint Linus was a Pope in the year sixty-seven and there were popes for almost eighteen hundred years before this system was even conceived. And the Pope's going to be there long after it dis-..."

The telephone rang, interrupting him. Ana answered and again held her breath. But she was again disappointed to hear Olga's voice.

"Come over to my house. We've just gathered here and are dancing. Don't sit home and brood about Dany."

"No, Ernesto's here and I wasn't planning to go out", she said. "I thought I'd just walk over to Gustavo's before midnight to be with the family and then come back home."

"Well, ask Ernesto to come too. And, if you want to greet the New Year at your brother's, come afterwards. This is going to last until late."

"No, I'm not sure." She lowered her voice. "I can't go alone with Ernesto."

"Bring your mother along."

"I'll see."

"I'll wait for you."

"I don't feel like dressing up", Ernesto said. "I'd have to go home and at least put a jacket on. And I'm not in a cheerful mood. But I'll leave, so you can go. I may go to the 'Gris' theater."

"No, no, that's all right, I'm not interested. But you will go over to my brother's with us, won't you?"

"Well, yes, that I'd do."

Shortly before midnight, they walked over to Gustavo's with her parents. There was no dancing on the streets as in the first year. At midnight, to the chords of the National Anthem coming from the radio, they all ate the twelve fortune grapes for good luck in each month of the coming year. And they toasted with cider. Gustavo tried to call their aunt Cristina on the phone to have her and Marcos join them, but there was no answer. They were probably out with Norma and Víctor. Méndez and Gustavo settled to a game of chess.

Later Ana went into the kitchen to leave some goblets and saucers in the sink, and she found her brother rinsing a glass. He looked pensive. He let the glass drip and leaned against the sink.

"Sometimes one worries, fearing one may lose the old folks", he confided, "eh, *Basurilla*?, but then I see they're still strong and feel relief."

Ana felt those icy fingers she knew on her heart and nodded with a sigh. She knew her brother capable of feeling it, but was surprised he'd reveal it. She remembered how he'd cried when their grandmother had died. They both shook their hands off over the sink and walked out to the living room.

She intended to go have coffee with Ernesto nearby and go to sleep. She called Olga to tell her they weren't going. Olga must have been bored. "Put Ernesto on", she asked her.

Ana heard Ernesto ask her how she was and then remark, "That far?" Ernesto, who had only seen Olga once, let himself easily be talked into it. When he hung up, he commented, "Olga says the circles under her eyes reach her chin."

"Yes, she exaggerates a little", Teresa understated.

It took more persuasion, and a lot of encouragement from Blanca, to convince her mother to accompany them.

"Teresa, go with them. Carlos can stay with us. Mamá and Papá are coming and we're going to bed late. We'll still be up when you get back."

"Yes, Mateo and Elena are coming", said Carlos. "And we'll roll a few hands of dice."

A little after 12:00, they walked to get the bus to Ensanche, Ernesto without a jacket after all. It wasn't cold. A few buckets of water were emptied out front doors promptly after midnight to "wash away the bad of the old year", occasionally soaking an unwary pedestrian.

They passed the School of Veterinary. When they got off, they walked past the "Maxim" theater and saw Olga come down to the sidewalk to meet them in front of her house. It was obvious she had had quite a bit to drink. There were half a dozen couples dancing on the terrace. Ana was introduced to a few neighbors at random, and Teresa and Ernesto to Olga's mother. Ernesto headed for the kitchen, while Teresa took a seat by Olga's mother, who smiled naïvely, showing her long teeth. Ana had seen one of the girls once at Rosa's house downstairs. Olga's father was nowhere in sight. A boy — Mirta's cousin, Olga told her — asked her to dance. None of the others — most of them younger — did, but Mirta's cousin, Wilfredo, kept coming back often and later fixed her a drink. He was a good dancer. Ana didn't notice his looks, except to register dark hair and eyes. She listened for the first time, although she had probably heard it before, to "Summer Place", which she'd remember long afterwards. She noticed Olga danced better than she would have guessed.

She held a half-empty glass in her hand most of the night, which, it turned out later, made her mother think she had been drinking all night. She made her way to the kitchen to empty the melting ice cubes and found Ernesto leaning on an outstretched arm against the refrigerator, his palm flat against the door, all but blocking a giggling Olga from view behind his ample anatomy, both oblivious to Ana's presence, so she dropped the melted ice in the sink and discreetly exited to the living room.

She had to admit to herself that she felt better than if she had stayed at home. Olga had developed a sudden infatuation with Ernesto and he, too, seemed glad they had gone. She had seen her mother laugh with Olga's.

On their way back on the bus, after 2:30, Ernesto parodied Laura Reynolds of Anderson's "Tea and Sympathy", in English, "'Years from now, when you talk about this... and you will,' ...don't mention my name." They thought it was hilarious. Giddy from their laughter, he overdid it by trying to raise himself up on the handles of the seats in the aisle of the empty bus as they were approaching their stop, and the bus almost drove off with him before he realized they had gotten off.

"Volunteer work" was becoming compulsory. Employees were pressured to cut sugar cane on weekends — women also. — Some worked at the National Printing Press. *INRA* magazine was pushed on them at work and it was difficult to get out of buying it. Ana somehow managed to elude it.

Peasants were incorporated into monolithic organizations which dominated their lives. Countrymen were forced to work in cooperatives. The laborer had to work for INRA where he was required. Under the Agrarian Reform, the peasants grew the crops ordered by INRA. Half their salary was paid in chits good only to buy in the people's store. Labor standards were cut in half.

Wages in the sugar industry were 40 percent lower than before, and workers didn't have the right to strike, complain or change jobs.

Wage earners contributed 5% for group security, 4% for industrialization, 3% for weapons and planes and 1% for the Confederation of Cuban Workers, which represented deductions of thirteen percent. There were those bent on finding a lighter side who made up phallic-slanted dirty jokes about what was left after the deductions.

Very few people knew that, as President of the National Bank, inexperienced Guevara received daily lessons on Marxist economy from the Mexican Juan F. Noyola Vázquez.

During the second half of 1960, 194 boats arrived in the United States with 1,801 Cubans.

CHAPTER 8

THE EDUCATION CAMPAIGN

"¡No lamas como un perro la mano que te ata!
Haz pedazos los grillos y, si te asedian, ¡mata!
No temas nada y hiere, porque Dios es tu amigo
y por tu brazo a veces desciende Su castigo."[8]
("Manelic", Antonio Médiz Bolio)

The starting year, 1961, was named the "Year of Education".

In Sancti Spíritus, a 24-year old office worker, the daughter of an ironsmith and member of a Catholic parish students' group, terrorized by the chief of G-2 in the city, doused alcohol and set fire to herself in her bedroom.

Six women and a man, fleeing from the Cuban coast, were picked up in the Straits of Florida by an Italian ship, after over 24 hours at sea, and taken to Key West.

On January 2 Castro paraded the armed forces through Havana and displayed his military strength from 11:00 in the morning until nightfall. He boasted 54 tanks as well as Soviet and Czech weapons. There were thousands of men and women. Most were pressured to parade for fear of losing their jobs. Ana defied the possibility staying home and came through safely.

The United States broke diplomatic relations with Cuba on January 3. President Eisenhower stated that the final reason for the break was Castro's order to reduce the personnel of the American Embassy in Havana to eleven employees. It was the seventh nation to break diplomatic relations with Cuba. The Embassy closed on the 4th. Switzerland was designated to take care of the consular affairs of the United States in Cuba.

Although Ana's and Teresa's American tourist visas, obtained only in February of the previous year, would still be valid for another

[8] Don't lick like a dog the hand that ties you!
Break the shackles to pieces and, if you are besieged, kill!
Do not fear anything and wound, because God is your friend
and His punishment sometimes descends through your arm.

year and a month, Méndez's, on the other hand, had expired ten months before, and he was uneasy about the severed relations, in the unlikely event they should want to leave the country.

"It makes one feel abandoned, marooned", he confided at the dinner table that evening.

Police arrested the Treasurer of the American Embassy when he tried to leave the country.

♪

Ana was having lunch at home that Wednesday, snapper-and-potato salad, when she was surprised by a telephone call from Dany. She was aware that her voice was very low, but she wasn't able to talk any louder and the pounding of her heart seemed to her audible. He came after dinner.

Their reunion was sweet, all differences momentarily forgotten. They treated each other tenderly, almost cautiously. The relaxation of their tension seemed to dull their physical desire somewhat, to give way to a more spiritual need, and they chose to stay at her home and talk on the balcony, in low voices, with few words, leaning on the railing, the smell of Spanish jasmine strong, that of sweet basil softly drifting toward them in the crisp air, which brought an occasional penetrating, sweet whiff of night jasmine.

"I had to get eyeglasses", he told her. "I went to the League Against Blindness", he said, pulling them out of his pocket to show them to her.

Their relationship seemed to pick up greatly in the next few days, and Ana felt hopeful that they might, after all, have a future together to which to look forward.

The militia made preparations to receive an attack from the United States before January 20, when the new President-elect would be inaugurated. Kennedy made statements in his electoral campaign which had fed the hope of the counter-revolutionaries. Troops and guns were stationed at strategic points. Anti-aircraft machine guns were placed on roofs. The guns were surrounded by sandbag barriers. The beautifully manicured lawn of the Hotel Nacional was wrecked in the process.

Barricades were built with wet sand bags in front of the entrance to all important buildings. Armed militia guarded the entrance to office buildings, factories, stores, theaters and other public places. They searched those going in thoroughly — wallets, compacts, lipsticks, lip and eyebrow brushes and pencils, pens, cigarette cases and match boxes included. – Militia women searched the females, and militia men the males. Militiamen rode elevators. And, when one got off the elevator on his floor, he was searched again. These somber people in drab uniforms wearing angry expressions were Cubans, the same easygoing, merry, fun-loving, warm people who a short three years before had enjoyed dancing, singing, laughing, telling jokes, going to the beach, playing the lottery, worshipping the saints, betting on cockfights. Where had their gaiety gone? How could they have changed so!

In the course of one of those searches at the entrance to the Ministry, one American copper penny and a little silver colored medal of St. Joseph were surreptitiously removed from Ana's wallet and went undetected by her for a while.

Posters bore the excerpt from a speech, "We shall defend every house from the roof to the basement and, when there isn't a single floor left, we'll defend the ruins. Fatherland or death. We shall win."

The highways and bridges throughout the island were mined.

A desolate atmosphere of impending doom prevailed in the city, and the threat hung menacingly over it. This gray, austere, punished city was Havana, the same noisy, cheerful, sunny, friendly city where she had grown up and dreamed, which she loved and tourists had visited in search of fun. Where had its gaiety gone? How could it have changed so!

It was rumored that buildings were mined. Almost two years before Castro had declared that, if the United States tried "to take Cuba, they'd only pick up the dirt of its ground soaked in blood". It was alarming!

As she glanced out the window from her desk at work, Ana noticed the side street by the Ministry being pick-axed open in the middle of the day, and boxes or blocks placed in the rectangular hole, which was then paved over. She commented on this to Duarte, whose desk was also by a window.

"Yes, I noticed that the other afternoon. And I wondered if they could possibly be mining the street."

The people were kept in constant nervous excitement, their passion ignited. Employees parroted new slogans, "On your knees, for what?", "A step backwards, not even to gather impetus", and "Fidel, shake the tree".

The University Catholic Youth headquarters and three seminaries were seized by the militia.

The Education Campaign

On January 6 the government suspended the issuance of military exit permits. This, added to the closing of the American Embassy, brought panic to the people who wanted to leave the country.

The Consul General of Cuba in Tampa resigned his post. So did the military attaché of the Embassy in Washington.

The Swiss Ambassador who was to take care of the consular affairs of the United States in Cuba arrived in Havana.

The Cuban-American Cultural Institute was confiscated and renamed Abraham Lincoln Academy, intended for the teaching of all languages except, ironically, English.

Castro went to Las Villas, and sent word to Army Captain Osvaldo Ramírez, who had risen in arms against the regime, to come down from the Escambray mountains, to convince him that "*that*" wasn't communism. Ramírez sent word back to Fidel for him to go up.

Saturday afternoon, while Dany did the bookkeeping and filing for his father's hardware store – which, because of its modest size, had so far escaped confiscation, – Ana went shopping with Olga. On San Rafael Street, vendors had displayed their wares on the sidewalk. There were small busts of Fidel with a dove perched on his shoulder, even one with his finger in his nose. It resembled an Eastern marketplace. They bought roasted cashew nuts at the "ten-cent" store, and went to "El Encanto" department store, now confiscated, to the fabric and gift item department. Strolling through the aisles between the tables of fabric bolts, fingering the material, before the shelves of fine ornaments, handling the china, Ana noticed how Olga picked the figurines up carefully to examine them, admired them, then put them gingerly down again.

"You love things for the house, don't you?", she asked her.

"I do. That's why I'd rather stay home and clean house than go out to work", Olga answered. "I'd love to have my own house and fix it up. And I suppose I never will."

"Of course you will."

"Who's going to marry me now, Ana?", she asked, smacking her tongue against the roof of her mouth.

"A boy who may fall in love with you and not mind."

"Do you think so?" She sounded so unsure, so anxious to believe.

"Of course", Ana reassured her.

"Yes", Olga said, again pessimistic, "and, as soon as he tries to go over the limit and I let him, I lose him."

"Then don't let him."

"Oh, Ana! You're the only friend I can talk to", Olga said, turning to her with sudden vehemence. "I can't talk to Mirta. I trust you. I know you give me good advice. I don't have any will power. Look, I need somebody to admonish me. I'm going to behave and tell you everything I do and when you see I'm not acting properly, you scold me."

"Eh! I can't do that, Olga!", Ana reacted, grinning in alarm. "You have to do it because you *want* to, not because *I* tell you."

"But I want to! Please, Ana, help me!"

"I don't know. Well, all right...", she said reluctantly before the responsibility, "but I don't think it'll work. When you're tempted, you'll just lie to me. And, besides", she asked jokingly, "who's going to admonish *me*?"

"You're different. You have will power."

Ha!, she thought, but she didn't want to shatter her friend's ungrounded faith in her. She had noticed that people got that impression of her. Besides, Olga'd probably soon feel she didn't *want* to behave. Ernesto had evidently not called her again in the last two weeks. If Dany left me, Ana thought, I'd find myself in the same predicament. The sobering thought chilled her. She shifted her attention to a beautifully finished spinning-wheel planter set on the floor by a column. "I love this", she said lightly. She turned the price tag over in her hand, $35.

They went to have sodas at "Kimbo" cafeteria on Galiano.

"They say there's a woman doctor who helps girls who've 'taken a false step' to... 'start their lives over'," said Olga. "She gives them a stitch."

"That doesn't sound possible, Olga."

"I've heard it's called the 'French stitch'."

"There's even a name for it?"

"She stitches the membrane. And nobody can tell. They told me she's on San Lázaro. She used to perform it on society girls, like the daughters of Batista's government officials."

"She's probably left then", Ana ventured. "It must be expensive."

"I guess. I think her last name is Herrera."

"But you couldn't go through with it if you're going to do that again."

Two men arrived in Kingston, Jamaica, from Santiago de Cuba in a single-engine plane.

The government established "people's farms" that bore a resem-

The Education Campaign

blance to the Russian *"Sovkhozy"*. They were heavily militarized and indoctrinated. In each people's farm was located a 167-acre youth farm, where children ten years and older were housed, fed, taught agriculture and indoctrinated under communist discipline. The regime's slogan for youth was "Study, work, rifle".

Four men and three women were arrested by the G-2 in Varadero when they tried to flee the country in a boat, and were taken to jail.

Six hundred terminations were handed out at the electric company early Monday morning. Tuesday evening as she cleared the dinner table, Blanca confided to Ana, "This afternoon a group of workers from the company met on Belascoaín after five to go to the statue of Martí to place flowers and protest the dismissals. Well", she sighed, "the police arrived and dealt clubbings, and there were three women wounded, one of them a co-worker of mine, and eighteen men arrested."

Gustavito was piecing a block puzzle on the floor.

"Do you know if my friend Ernesto was there?"

Blanquita was taking the blocks away from her brother.

"I don't know if he went, but there wasn't any Ernesto among those arrested."

Gustavo was filing his nails in front of the television set.

Three electric workers were shot at La Cabaña in the early morning.

When Ana reached her bus stop Wednesday, she suddenly felt impelled to look back, as if pulled by a magnetic force. She looked down the street she had just walked and, about 50 yards behind, saw an employee of her section, Valdés, a militiaman who limped, cross the street to the north side. She was surprised. Could he be following her? He looked at her, but didn't greet her.

The militia occupied former President Prío's "La Chata", north of Rancho Boyeros.

Thursday as she was putting her work away to go to lunch, Ana heard Morejón, the colored man from Yateras who had given her the silk scarf for Christmas, talking with Sara.

"A Negro can get a good job now", Morejón was saying.

"A Negro could always get a job working for the government", she responded. "Whether you were lily white or pitch black, you could always get a job in a ministry before."

"You had to have pull, *chica*."

"And who didn't know a councilman, Morejón?"

Abreu, the older man with acne scars to whom Ana had given the after-shave lotion for Christmas, walked over to them, to listen to their conversation. Sara thrust her chin out and went on, now to include Abreu, "I've always been proud of being mulatto. I went to school at the Oblate Sisters and belonged to the *Jóvenes del Vals* and the *Ateneo Cubano*, where I always went to the dances. I've always stuck to my own race and never wanted to promenade among the white people."

"Ah, I'm also proud of being black; that's not it. But you've always been well off, Sara", protested Morejón, less emphatically now that a white man was a witness to his black man grievances. "I've seen that house where you live in La Víbora... 'with the whole works'. And you're not the average colored in a *'solar'*[53]."

"But, *viejo*, only because my parents wanted to make an effort to make something of themselves", Sara said flaring her wide nostrils. "And they took the trouble to go to school – and to public school at that, because my mother became a stenographer at the Night Secretarial School on Monte and my father's an electrical technician from the Arts and Crafts School on Belascoaín and my aunt a midwife graduated from Mazorra Hospital."

"Well, don't get off to the mount, girl."

"Me, get off? You're the one who can't take it."

Abreu hadn't offered an opinion.

"This government is giving blacks more opportunity to better themselves", Morejón insisted.

As Ana passed them on her way out, she overheard Sara say with a snicker, "Go on sleeping on that side."

Waiting for the elevator, Ana heard Abreu, coming down the hallway, comment to Aurora, "Well, Morejón is from Yateras and, since they say that 'in Oriente he who isn't part Congolese is part *Carabalí*', he must know the conditions well."

"Yolanda's from Guantánamo and she's white", Aurora debated now with her strange smile.

"With blue eyes", Ana put in. "Her maternal grandfather was an American Navy ensign."

"You'd still have to 'look for the grandmother'," replied Abreu with cynicism. "Look, on Valdés you can tell by the beauty marks."

"That's true", agreed Aurora after considering it for a moment,

[53] rooming house (from manorial paved lot)

The Education Campaign

"even on his temples."

"And what do beauty marks have to do with it?", asked Ana.

"Ah, that in some *'cuarterones'*[54] the excess pigmentation is concentrated in beauty marks", Abreu explained.

"Yes, my father used to say that", confirmed Aurora, as the elevator arrived. "And the dark gums, purplish."

President John Kennedy was inaugurated on January 20 and there had been no attack, so the militia on duty, the novelty having worn off, slackened their guard.

On January 21 a thousand children of Cuban workers left to study in the Soviet Union.

Castro ordered a quart of blood to be extracted from prisoners sentenced to death by firing squad, to be sold to the government of North Vietnam.

On a Sunday in late January, as Ana and Dany passed Duarte's building on their way back from the "Rodi" theater in the cool evening, his arm around her waist, Ana noticed in silence a militia man and a militia woman on the steps, searching the people going in.

Three men were shot by the firing squad at La Cabaña Fortress.

Monday at work, Ana asked Duarte about the searches.

"I was going to warn you precisely today to be careful", he said in a low voice. "It seems they got somebody with weapons on Saturday in an apartment downstairs, a dentist's. Don't take the bulletin up to me there any more. I'll arrange some way to pick them up. And, if you have to go, should they ask you who you are, tell them you're my sister. It may seem strange for a girl to be going to the apartment of two men."

"But, if they search my wallet, they'll see my identification."

"Well,... leave the Ministry identification card in your desk drawer here whenever you're going to go up and leave all the others at home altogether. If they stopped you at the entrance here because you don't have the Ministry card, you can always have them call Aurora from downstairs or something and she can get the card from your desk. Of course, if you could... No, it isn't necessary."

"What?"

"... Get an identification card of some kind with my last name, that would help more,... but it's not indispensable."

When she went home for lunch, Ana took her retirement fund,

---

[54] quadroons, *'moriscos'*

professional association, school and beach club identification cards out of her wallet. She remembered the silver compact Dany had given her with her initials for Christmas and took that out also, and put it all together in her dresser drawer.

Then she debated about calling Nelia again. She had already bothered her for something more important, and this wasn't so necessary. She also worried about Nelia's discretion; sometimes she talked without thinking. And this time the identification would be for her. She finally called her that afternoon and talking in a jargon she wasn't sure Nelia had understood, asked her to get an identification card with the name Julia Duarte. Julia was the name of her maternal great-grandmother from Matanzas and her first-grade teacher.

Eloy Gutiérrez Menoyo arrived in the United States on a launch with the other fifteen highest members of the Second Front of the Escambray.

Twenty-three Cubans landed in Nicaragua on an expedition sponsored by Castro.

With the longer working hours at the Ministry, it took Ana excessive rushing and many gulped dinners to arrive at school on time, but it fed her sense of accomplishment. Ernesto had hit upon the right term.

"You'll get nervous dyspepsia", Méndez predicted disapprovingly.

She and Ernesto sat next to each other in most of the classes, lent each other notes and some of the students, the fat girl informed her, thought there was something between them. Since the girl obviously wanted to assure herself the field was clear, Ana promptly set her straight.

Ana sat at the counter of the coffee shop after classes and ordered a "Materva". She looked in the mirror on the wall behind the counter. She had the feeling that this situation was temporary. It was a good moment. She wanted to enjoy it fully, assimilate it, soak in it, live it, because she suspected it would not last. It would be gone soon. She looked around. She wanted to remember every detail, engrave it in her memory, feel it, breathe it in and let it pervade her, so as not to lose it. There was a "Cristal" beer ad over the mirror and on the large-hinged white enameled refrigerator, a lattice-topped apple pie and a juicer. The "Salutaris" soda thermometer on the wall read just under 23 degrees Centigrade. A girl was dialing a number on the public wall phone. There was a man at the counter eating a *"media noche"*, a couple at a table. Dany touched her shoulder, startling her.

The Education Campaign

He had come wearing his militia uniform.

After he'd been sitting beside her for a while, she said a little fearfully, "I'd like to ask you a favor. Don't get mad, *mi cielo*", and finished in a low voice, "but, please, don't come... in uniform,."

"You don't want to be embarrassed in front of your schoolmates?", he asked her, a sarcastic half sneer playing on his lips.

She only smiled back meekly. That was only the half of it. The other half was that she was afraid she might be checked by the movement and it might be misinterpreted.

Only six days after his *Finca* "La Chata" had been confiscated, Dr. Carlos Prío Socarrás returned to Miami, seeking asylum in the United States and, after defending the socialist government for over two years, he made statements against "Castro's tyrannical regime".

In two days, the fat girl in their class had gotten herself invited by Ernesto to "Los Violines" on Paseo for a drink after school.

The next time she sat at a table in the cafe after classes to wait for Dany, Ana saw between the columns a man approaching with his olive green pants pulled down over his black boots and wearing a leather jacket over his denim blue shirt. The canvas awnings with the Cinzano ads obstructed a view of his face. It wasn't until the man reached the entrance of the cafe that Ana saw it was Dany. He had even folded his black fuzzy beret and stuck it under the epaulet of his jacket. It took a close look to notice he was a militiaman. She was grateful and her heart went out to him. He might not agree with her, but he cared how she felt.

He smiled, knowing he had surprised her, and apparently proud of it, but they tactfully kept from mentioning it.

Ana's British residence visa expired, and she felt she had burned her sails behind her.

In three days she had a Ministry of the Interior identification card along with Nelia's concerned advice, "Be careful, Ana, for God's sake."

Thursday Duarte asked her to meet him at the coffee shop near the Ministry the next afternoon to give her the cut stencil, and instructed her to deliver that month's mimeographed bulletin to Alejandro at a cafe near their house when she had it.

Two Cuban pilots sought political asylum in Madrid, Spain.

Duarte was waiting for her in the coffee shop on Friday, his slender frame leaning on the counter, and he invited her to join him for a cup of black coffee. He appeared to throw the contents of the thimble-sized cup into his mouth, while she sipped hers. He asked her what she was reading and she pushed the *Vanidades* magazine she was carrying toward him. He leafed through it, looked at the ads of the "Hatuey" beer's "little piece of Sunday that you deserve" and "Edén" cigarettes' "pocket vacations", and he slipped the stencil between its pages so inconspicuously even she was not sure he had, when he slid the magazine back to her.

Ana didn't see Folgueira again. When she put the $3.50 in the desk drawer at the office, the money she had left there the month before was always gone. Also gone from the wastebasket was the *Vanidades* magazine in which she had brought the previous stencil.

As she came into the cafe late that winter afternoon with the mimeographed bulletin, she saw a man get up from the table where Alejandro remained seated, lean forward for an instant to tap him on the shoulder and then walk away. As she neared the table, the man passed her looking straight ahead. He was a heavy man in his middle thirties, wearing a tan suit and light brown felt hat; dark brown curly hair showed at his temples under the hat and he had a broad chin and a round nose like a knob. Ana knew instinctively this was the head of the local underground group. What did they call them?, coordinators? She had never seen him before, and probably never would again. She thought the hat made him conspicuous, easy to pick out. Not many men − not many people − wore hats any more in Havana. But then, she reflected, the hat did hide his face some-what, and he could be covering a scar or a bald spot that would make him easier to identify.

Three men were noisily playing dice at the slippery counter, worn smooth by use, the waiter looking on, a damp napkin draped over his left arm. A sign over the cash register read, "I don't grant credit today, tomorrow I will."

She realized the boys weren't taking much risk with her. If she should get caught with the bulletin or the stencil, there was nothing she knew to tell. She didn't know who their local leader was, she only knew two of the members. And their names weren't mentioned in the bulletin − no one's was, of course. − She didn't even know where Alejandro worked. Perhaps he hadn't even given her his real name. She didn't know their families. They weren't running much risk that she'd give them away.

Alejandro was having an "Hatuey" beer. She set the manila envelope on the white marble table and ordered an "Ironbeer" soda.

The Education Campaign

"You're frowning", he observed.
"Oh!, was I?" She smiled.
They talked while she drank her soda, he his beer, she awkward at first, he friendly, drawing her out until she opened up.
"You go to school, don't you?"
"Yes."
He peeled the label carefully, rolled it up and dropped it into the empty bottle.
"What are you studying?"
"Publicity."
The label stuck to the inside of the bottle and he rolled the bottle slowly as the label unrolled until it showed the golden face of the Indian through the amber glass.
"Where?"
"At the School of Publicity, on Two."
It was late. She'd have to hurry even more than usual to get to school. She finished her soda and said good-by, leaving the manila envelope on the table.

Her parents had invited Velázquez and his wife for seafood at the "Castillo de Jagua", but Ana wouldn't join them. She wasn't included in their plans on school nights.

There was a fire at the José Martí International Airport in Rancho Boyeros.

Eight Cubans took asylum in Venezuela.

There were barter agreements with the Soviet Union, Red China, Czechoslovakia, East Germany, Poland and Hungary, and also with Indonesia, Egypt, England, Japan and African nations.

In the mid-morning break, Ana found the opportunity to comment to Yolanda, "About two weeks ago, coming to work in the morning, I saw Valdés on the corner of my house. Do you know where he lives? I get the impression he's following me."

"I don't know. But be careful with him, he's the 'fatherland or death' type."

Sara joined them. "Well, Ana, so Aurora wants to have lunch with us."

"Yes." She added thoughtfully, "I don't like her."

Duarte arrived at their table and pulled out a fourth chair.

"You don't like her?" Sara was surprised. "I thought you did."

"With the way she orders me around! How could I like her? Did you see how she lent my typewriter to Bárbara before I got in and then wanted me to go get it back?"

"Well, I thought you didn't mind. I thought, 'This girl is so good-natured, she doesn't even notice the way Aurora orders her'." She turned for confirmation to Yolanda, who widened her blue eyes and nodded, and to Duarte, who nodded a couple of times, smiling.

"I notice", Ana said simply.

"But you don't react. You don't even change your expression."

Ana shrugged. She didn't have much choice.

"The bitch!", said Sara.

"Sara, you 'shoot at her with lightning'," observed Yolanda.

"It's because she's 'lodged in my skin'."

"I disliked her almost from the beginning", Duarte said. "That way she smiles."

"Yes", said Ana, surprised that he'd have noticed the same detail. "She draws her upper lip down over her teeth and holds it there."

"That's it! Have you noticed? I'd never seen anybody smile like that." They were all warming up to the confidential criticism.

Sara pointed out, "Well, you're now 'tearing off the strips of her skin' too."

Duarte reflected, "When I like somebody, he may do a hundred wrongs to me and it takes the one hundred and first to turn me against him, but, when I don't like somebody, I turn against him from the very first wrong he does to me." He paused. "And I don't forgive."

"I do forgive", Ana said, "but I don't forget."

"I don't know what may be worse", considered Yolanda.

"It's all the same in the end", was Sara's opinion.

"I forgive because I ask myself if, in similar circumstances, I might be capable of acting the same way", Ana explained, "but I don't forgive because the distrust always remains in me that they may do the same to me again."

Duarte cocked his head considering the logic.

"Well, we 'got wood borers'. We're going to have a pleasant lunch", said Sara sarcastically, patting Ana's shoulder as she got up, without having ordered. The new knowledge of Ana's dislike of Aurora seemed to draw Sara closer.

"I'm very nervous...", Ana started when Sara had left.

"She says she's nervous", Yolanda interrupted her, looking to Duarte with raised eyebrows.

"I never saw anybody calmer", said Duarte.

Yes, you, thought Ana, and went on, "... and Aurora's taut irony and Sara's acid criticism upset me."

Back in the hallway, a militia man passed them whistling the catchy Paraguayan tune *"Chogüi"*. When they entered the section, Sara was standing by the desk of a short girl, a former militiawoman. As she passed them, Ana heard Sara ask her, "And how could you leave the militia?"

Ana herself had felt curious and she now paused to listen to the reply of the girl, who answered with a slight lisp, without fear at Ana's presence, "When I did it, it was easier. When the 'revolutionaries' here ask me why, I say very enigmatically that maybe I have a more important mission to fulfill outside, and they swallow it. They are actually 'yams with neckties'."

"When did you leave it?", Ana asked her.

"When the Episcopate issued the open letter in December complaining about the attacks against the Church", she told them in a low voice, "and the two Canadian banks were nationalized, and I realized this was communism."

Somebody *had* been listening.

"I realized this was communism on January first", said Sara, in a not too low voice.

"Ah!, you were premature then", the short girl said, laughing.

Ana grinned and went on to her desk.

Lunch with Aurora and Sara at the "Eden Roc", on O Street, below the street level, was a dull, but relaxed meal. Over the roast leg of lamb, Aurora dominated the conversation, Sara for once a quiet listener.

"When I was young", boasted Aurora, who looked around 34, with her eyes fixed on the nape of a man at the next table, "when I liked a man, I cast my eye on him and used my wiles to make him notice me, and", she ended with a hoarse laugh, "I even had my ways to make him think that *he* had chased me."

Ana wondered why she sounded as if love were over for her.

She reached their table in their mid-afternoon break as Duarte was asking Yolanda, "What ever became of Ernest Hemingway?"

She joined them.

"I never heard of him again. Isn't he still living in San Francisco de Paula?"

"I don't know. I doubt that the *Finca* 'Vigía' would still be his."

Sara arrived in the coffee shop seeking Ana out.

"Did you hear how Aurora brags about her 'wiles' to get a man to notice her?"

"She's conceited", Ana agreed.

"She 'doesn't have a grandmother'," pronounced Sara. "I never made an advance on a man, in spite of what a flirt I appear to be. I wait for him to take the initiative."

"I'm not coquettish at all", said Ana. "I don't know how to be."

"There are different ways of being coquettish", Duarte stated matter-of-factly. Ana looked at him thinking he was going to add something, but he returned his attention to his malted milk. She didn't know whether he had meant it as a compliment or not. She accepted it without comment, and it seemed to her Yolanda didn't like the remark.

"Is she with the government?", she asked Sara, voicing a curiosity she had felt from the beginning.

"Half-way. You know she's having an affair with a high government official, don't you? — Serafín Monteverde, — and that's the reason she got the job as secretary to the department head."

"Girl, if you were mute, you'd have burst!", Duarte laughed.

Ana remembered Rina's briefing. "Yes, a friend of hers told me something about it." Aurora's attitude now seemed to fall into place.

"Well, her allegiance to the government seems to increase or decrease with the frequency with which she sees the guy." She paused and changed the subject. "I'm going to play miniature golf on Twenty-three this afternoon with Bárbara and some friends. Do you want to come?"

"I can't", said Ana. "I go to school evenings."

"I don't have time", Duarte said.

"I live too far", said Yolanda. "I'm going to the bowling lanes on Juan Bruno Zayas."

Ana talked about the lunch with Aurora to her parents over dinner. And the conversation gradually led to Duarte and Yolanda.

"I think that Yolanda..." She stopped, uncertainly.

"Is in love with Duarte", Teresa finished confidently for her.

"Yes! And what made *you* think of that?"

"From what you tell me she says."

"Intuition, Anita", her father explained, snapping the tail off a shrimp.

"But he's engaged and seems very much in love with his girlfriend."

"Yes, that's him, but she likes him anyway."
"She's very decent." Ana used the elusive term that for Cubans encompassed being moral, honest, polite, good-mannered, well-bred.
"Platonic love", said Teresa bringing out the rice pudding.
Ana grinned. Yes, her mother had that sixth sense.
"The devil knows more because he's old than because he's the devil", Méndez said, repeating a favorite proverb of his wife's.
Teresa protested now, however. "I'm not that old, *Okay*?" And her husband laughed.

The government soon confiscated the "Eden Roc", turned it into a Russian restaurant and renamed it "Balalaika", spelled on the entrance sign in Russian letters, Балалаіка, which made it look to the unaccustomed eye like four A's lost among five strange symbols traced backwards.

Seventy-five Cubans travelling aboard the Spanish vessel *"Covadonga"* asked for political asylum when the ship arrived in the port of New York.

Six Americans were sentenced to thirty years' prison terms. Thirty-one Cubans were condemned in two trials to thirty-year terms.

The government confiscated the Vedado Tennis Club. The Havana Country Club was nationalized and used as a school.

Fidel Castro himself stated that they extracted most of the blood from the counter-revolutionaries sentenced to death by firing squad minutes before their execution, to save the lives of militiamen.

The regime seized the Caimanera aqueduct, which supplied water to the Guantánamo Navy Base, but the water wasn't cut off.

Eight men were sentenced to thirty-year prison terms. A bomb exploded on Muralla Street and two militiamen died. The Cubana de Aviación Company suspended its flights to Miami. When they arrived in New York, two Cubana pilots asked for political asylum. Three men fled in a ship of Panamanian registry.

It was announced that the Premier of the Democratic Republic of the Congo, Patrice Lumumba, had been assassinated in the Southeast province of Katanga on February 12. He became a martyr and the government declared three days of official mourning. The irreverent soon composed an octameter verse about it.

"...Lumumba muere en Kat anga
y le zumba la mal anga
que formen tremenda pach anga
por un negro comuñ anga."

Two bombs exploded near the University while professor Carlos Rafael Rodríguez spoke. A big fire destroyed the Rothschild, Samuels & Dulgman tobacco warehouse on Dragones and the losses were calculated at several millions.

Belén Electromechanical School in Alturas was taken over by the government. The Daughters of Galicia sanatorium was confiscated.

A questionnaire was distributed at work to be completed, declaring the members of the family, size of living quarters, all electrical appliances, jewelry, mechanical devices, automobiles. They kept digging deeper into the people's private lives.

Workers at industries and offices were pressured to volunteer to cut cane on week-ends. Aurora went once. She brought back stories about Morejón and Valdés, who went regularly.

The editor of the Havana Post newspaper, George Wehby, arrived in Miami. Geographer and economist Leví Marrero Artiles took asylum in an embassy. Just four months before, he, writer Enrique Labrador Ruiz and 38 other intellectuals had offered their support to Castro's regime. The cartoonist creator of "Black Spy" was arrested by the G-2. Ana thought of Alejandro and the clipping on Duarte's lamp.

On Monday, Duarte brought Ana and Yolanda croquettes from "La Dominica" in his home town, which they ate on their mid-morning break.

A girl came to Ana's home to tell her of Carmen Zayas' "farewell to singlehood" or bridal shower at the "1830". It was the first she had heard from Carmen since Wayne Motors had moved away. So she had finally caught Miguel! Or was it perhaps another boy? Gloria Serrano called Ana on the phone and came to her house, so they could attend the shower together. She carried in her hand Lin Yutang's "A Leaf in the Storm" that she had been reading on the long bus trip from Arroyo Arenas. At the Calzada restaurant they met Carmen's mother, a heavy lady with straight hair pulled up in a bun, who took the precaution of covering her mouth when she laughed to hide a couple of missing teeth, probably a recent extraction, judging from her preoccupation. It *was* Miguel that Carmen was marrying after all. The organizers hinted that her gift list had been registered at "El Encanto", which they conveniently chose to ignore.

Major Guevara, head of the National Bank until then, was named Minister of Industries. Raúl Cepero Bonilla replaced him. The Ministry of Foreign Trade having charge of the imports and exports, the

Ministry of Domestic Commerce was created for the distribution of goods. The Institute of Sports, Physical Education and Recreation was established, headed by Commissioner José Llanusa Gobels.

Militia men took over the direction of La Luz School on 25th Street. Teachers of Edison Institute, whose principal had left the country, asked that the school be turned over to them. LaSalle School was confiscated. A teacher requested the intervention of the Marist School in La Víbora.

When Ana entered Folgueira's office Friday afternoon to mimeograph the February bulletin, the money she had left in January had been taken from the drawer, but she noticed the wastebasket hadn't been emptied and the old *Vanidades* was still in it with the "Gravi" toothpaste ad on its back cover in view. She felt a flicker of alarm, but she added the current issue to it and went cautiously ahead with the mimeographing.

When she met Alejandro at the cafe later, with the bulletin, there was a small brown paper bag set upright on the table. She laid the envelope next to it and, when the waiter swiped at the table with his damp napkin, Alejandro ordered a soda for her and a "Tres Cepas" cognac for himself.

He held the bag out to her. "I went home last week-end and brought this for you."

She opened it. It was a slender truncate pyramid of pan sugar wrapped in yellow cellophane. "Pan sugar!"

"Santa Clara pan sugar", he specified.

"Thank you very much. I haven't had any since I was a child. It was nice of you to remember me."

"It's easy to remember you", he said gently. She looked in his eyes and lowered hers. She couldn't remember now whether she had noticed before that they were hazel.

"Thank you", she repeated. She fingered the cellophane. "I've never been in a sugar mill. What is it like?"

"Well, friendly, I don't know... comfortable. You know everybody."

"My uncle used to work in the 'Toledo'. Is yours — 'Reforma', no? — big?"

"It's medium-sized — I think the 'Toledo' is bigger, — it utilizes over three hundred *'caballerías'*[55] and employs almost twenty-two

[55] 10,000 acres

hundred laborers during the season." She had no idea how that compared with others, but he explained. "It doesn't even come close to the 'Jaronú', for example, which can grind twelve thousand five hundred tons a day."

"What's the *'batey'*?" She felt embarrassed at her ignorance. "The Dominican *merengue 'El Negrito del Batey'* comes to my mind."

"The tight little settlement of the laborers' houses huddled around the plaza where the trucks park, with the general store, the restaurant, the bar, the butcher shop, the school and a boarding house. It's a word that survived from the 'Taíno' language, like *'bohío'* from *'bojío'*. The cane scale is near, the sugar warehouse, the railroad and the boiler house."

"How many people live there all year around?"

"I don't know exactly, they may be over twelve hundred, I guess; I don't really know."

"Is it old, the mill?" They were trying to live up to the unspoken need to appear like any couple meeting leisurely for refreshments after work.

"It was founded about seventy years ago, in the last decade of the Nineteenth Century. I guess for somebody not used to it, during the grinding season the sweet smell prevalent everywhere may be nauseating." He looked at his watch. "What time do your classes start?"

"At eight."

"It's five to eight now."

"I know. I'll skip the first class."

"The sugar industry is basic to that region", he explained. "There are twenty-four mills in the area." He paused and then said proudly, "I like it. I feel I've had a taste of several ways of life there: I grew up in a sugar mill, I know country life and was very close to a fairly big city, Caibarién, with almost twenty-three thousand people; I was close to the coast and the beach, I lived on the Coastal Plain and near the Bamburanao range", he had been punctuating his relation hitting each fingertip on the table top as he talked and now stopped, his thumb poised, "I was used to the roast pork meat of the inland countryman and to the seafood of the fisherman..." He smiled with a hint of what seemed like satisfaction. "Did you grow up in Havana?"

"Yes, I was born and have always lived here." She suddenly felt fate had cheated her out of a whole facet of life. But another thought was starting to push forward in her mind.

"I'd like to take you to the 'Hershey' sugar mill", Alejandro told her, partly promising, partly wistful. "There's a train with little wooden cars from Casablanca to the mill. It has a nice cafeteria that serves good ham steaks with pineapple slices and prunes."

They could run the risk of overstaying a safe while. "One of these days", she answered vaguely.

"My father used to work in the mill, as my grandfather Juan had. He was *'abulense'*,... from Arévalo. I remember the suckling pig roasted in a skewer over guava leaves in the mill and the rum *'mojito'* with mint sprigs", he said now with nostalgia, "the *'parrandas'* in Caibarién around Christmas and the Saint John celebrations in Remedios in June. We used to take excursions to the Guajabana Cave."

Ana enjoyed listening to him talk and now risked the time for another question. "What made you move to Havana,... if it isn't prying?"

"No, when I graduated from secondary school in Remedios, I wanted to work in the capital", he answered simply, and didn't offer where he worked, or what he was studying now, but asked instead, "Why don't you skip school altogether, and we can talk a while longer, Anita? I've been talking about myself and would like to know about you."

"I can't, I'm sorry. Another day." She had been dimly aware of the advancing hour and he had now unintentionally forced her consciously to acknowledge it. Didn't he feel at least a little uncomfortable, sitting here with those bulletins lying there between them? She felt compelled to apologize, "I'm afraid I won't have the required eighty percent attendance."

"And somebody's waiting for you?" It was only partly a question, but with a positive tone as if accepting no denial.

She nodded. She drank the rest of the soda, watery now, stood up taking the paper bag, and left the envelope on the table. "Thank you for the pan sugar. I'll see you."

Alejandro half rose. "Until soon."

She felt his eyes on her as she walked self-consciously away, her hips held in check. She was wearing a short-sleeved red dress with printed white chess pieces.

That night as she came out of school, she thought she caught a glimpse of him in a beige car. Her imagination must have played a trick on her, she reasoned.

Castro ordered 25 million dollars transferred to Soviet banks through the Bank of Nova Scotia in Toronto.

The Dominican Republic, Haiti, Nicaragua, Guatemala, Paraguay and Perú had broken diplomatic relations with Cuba by February 28.

Ramón Ruiz Sánchez was smuggled into the Escambray range to establish a drop zone and communications with the rebels.

A twin-engine plane dropped anti-government leaflets over the park of Manicaragua in Santa Clara. A bomb exploded in the "Nobel" Academy in La Víbora. The resistance burned 750 tons of cane in the "Castellana" colony in Jagüeyal, in Ciego de Avila. In Montes de Píbalo resistance men killed two militia men and wounded seven. The militia captured five patriots in "La Pujanza" hill in Oriente.

Ernesto accompanied Ana home from school whenever Dany didn't meet her because he stayed for his last class or had militia practice. Sometimes they took the bus on Línea when it rained or was cold, but they often preferred to walk because it gave them a chance to talk without fear of being overheard. Ernesto was decidedly opposed to the government and complained bitterly about the repression of opinion.

"I have a neighbor, a woman stupid as a plow, with a daughter who has no education, has never worked and spends the whole day lying around reading cheap novels", he commented, visibly distressed, his fat fingers gathered together for emphasis, "and they call anybody 'myrmidon' who says anything against the government. They say they're poor because they've never had a fair opportunity, that the revolution is going to give the people a chance and help them up. They won't admit that they've never taken advantage of an opportunity because they're lazy. They think the revolution is going to change their lives."

He carried with him a pack of little gummed stickers bearing an *ichthus*, the simple shape of a fish, symbolic of the fishermen of Galilee and of Christianity, drawn in blue strokes, and he stuck them on public phones, electric posts, billboards, public restrooms, store windows, edges of counters. Ana briefly considered once telling him she had gotten involved in the counter-revolution, but immediately decided against it. She wanted to feel certain that nothing were known through her.

The revolutionaries had composed a song directed against the priests, to the tune of *"Mi mamá no quiere que yo vaya a la pelota"*, which went,

*"My mother doesn't want me
to go to church,*

*because the Falangist priest"
turns me into a terrorist."*

Sometimes, when they rode the bus home at night, a few braver students, the fat girl among them, sat in the rear seats and daringly sang the lyrics with which the counter-revolutionaries had parodied it, attacking the few priests who supported the government,

*"My mother doesn't want me
to go to church,
because the Fidelist priest
turns me into a communist."*

Ernesto and Ana kept to the front seats. And she curiously watched in the rear-view mirror the expressionless face of the driver, who stared straight ahead.

Revolución newspaper published photographs of the Cubans' military training camps in Guatemala, reproduced from American publications.

A C-54 plane dropped weapons and munitions in La Vela range in Guantánamo, Oriente, at 1:00 in the morning.

A fire in the "Desembarco del Granma" cooperative produced losses of almost 1,200 tons of cane and another one caused the loss of 200 tons at "Godofredo Verdecia" in Belic, in Niquero.

Four men arrived in the United States in a small boat named *"Blanca Estela"*. A plane with nine Cubans landed in Jamaica, leaking gasoline, with bullet holes in the fuselage.

Two Telephone Company employees were sentenced to death.

The government mobilized 60,000 militia men to prepare the "Cleaning of the Escambray"; all peasants were removed from the 82 square-mile area, and they surrounded the mountain region with militia. The regime reported 28 losses. Three hundred eighty-one rebels were captured after they had run out of food, medicine and other supplies. Ten of the forty patriots who died couldn't be identified. There were many wounded and the resistance collapsed.

A bomb exploded in the office of the Communist Party on 12th Street, which shattered the glass panes, the door and window frames, and damaged the ceiling. Bombs exploded in the Esso and Shell refineries, causing extensive losses.

The coordinator of the 30th of November Movement arrived in Miami in a small boat with three other men.

Four men were shot against the execution wall.

On March 9 Major William A. Morgan Ruderth was tried by a

kangaroo court and sentenced to death by firing squad, as was Jesús Carreras, and eight other men were sentenced to thirty-year prison terms. He was executed in Los Laureles dry moat of La Cabaña Fortress at 10:00 on the night of March 11. His widow, a Cuban, was again arrested four days later in Santa Clara.

It was rumored that through underground channels a political testament had been smuggled out of death row in which Morgan swore he was innocent of the charges of which he was accused and that his crime consisted of being the last anti-communist with the rank of major left in the rebel army.

On Monday, Duarte commented to Ana and Yolanda about his own leader in Miami, "They say he's an atheist and that has me worried. Some people say he only wants 'Fidelism without Fidel'."

"I've heard it too", said Yolanda.

"I haven't met him in person." He pressed the tips of his thin fingers against each other over the table. "I don't trust an atheist."

Ana only listened, feeling uneasy. What if their efforts should be directed toward the wrong goal? She couldn't dismiss the remark.

"Now the government wants to make us believe José Antonio Echeverría was a communist", said Duarte. "And he wasn't. 'Little Apple' was religious."

"A boy of daily communion", Yolanda confirmed. Four years had passed since Echeverría had been killed.

Ana was filing away in her desk drawer one of the many memos requesting their attendance at a "demonstration" in support of something when Valdés came up to her and pronounced, "I've noticed how you keep everything about the revolution and I can tell you're unconditionally devoted to it." Because she kept the memos, he had drawn that conclusion? She punched holes in them and held them with a fastener. – She never attended the demonstrations. – Had he gone through her desk? It was kept unlocked. She also had the table of the Russian alphabet in the top drawer. Well, she'd passed the test without even being aware of it.

Fire was set by the counter-revolution to two Woolworth ten-cent stores, on Obispo and on Monte Streets.

Radio commentator José Pardo Llada, editor of *"La Palabra"* newspaper, defected and fled to Mexico; his wife and daughter stayed behind.

The leader of the electric workers, in asylum, arrived in Miami.

Eighteen Cubans, two women among them, arrived in Miami in

The Education Campaign

two small boats, *"Lor Maria"* and *"Cuquito I"*, which had sailed off Cojímar.

The last twelve surviving warriors in the Escambray were rescued and taken to the United States.

Dr. Manuel Antonio de Varona Loredo, of the Frente; Eng. Manuel Ray Rivero, of the MRP; Manuel Artime Buesa, of the MRR; Dr. Justo Carrillo Hernández, of the Montecristi; Aureliano Sánchez Arango, of the AAA, and several other revolutionary groups formed the Cuban Revolutionary Council for the National Liberation in Miami, and they agreed on a program. A provisional government was proclaimed in New York, with Dr. José Miró Cardona as President.

The Industrial Exposition of Red China was opened at the Palace of Fine Arts, and Ana and Yolanda headed up its ramps to visit it. When they were leaving, they had to push their way with their elbows through the crowds that surrounded the booths set up on the grounds before the relief-treated façade to reach the counter, and they bought hand embroidered silk blouses for $7.50.

A local Chinese resident, who, perhaps not daring shove his way among the women, hadn't ventured to reach a booth, now timidly asked them in Spanish, holding a $10. bill out to them, "You do favol to me to buy one fol me?"

He was so grateful to them when they did, that he effusively invited them to have lunch on him at his restaurant on Zulueta Street. "Boneless chicken almondine vely good", he encouraged them showing his large teeth and widening his slanted eyes.

They debated whether to take him up on the invitation or not, but Yolanda was reluctant, and they finally decided to pass up on it. They crossed the Prado Mall shaded by the canopy formed by the Indian laurels, with its urns and marble benches, and headed south. They passed before the once exclusive Casino Español, its rocking chairs on the porch now empty, the elegant mansions of the nobility of yore, the "Sloppy Joe's", the "Nobel" Academy, which Gustavo had attended, and the Miami restaurant with its honeycombs, and on Neptuno they took their respective buses home.

The afternoon was falling when Dany came to get Ana on Saturday.

"They say that at Our Lady of Lourdes School on Santa Catalina the Mother Superior who died recently appears at a window at night", she told him, "and the people gather across the street to see her."

"Who told you that?"
"Yolanda. She lives on Vista Alegre."
"Has she seen her?"
"No, but a girl in her Catholic organization did."
"Do you believe it?" He wasn't being facetious. He seemed interested.
"I don't know. Should we go tonight and see?"

They took Infanta south. They passed the furniture store standing away from the avenue, which advertised itself "From the factory to your home", and the Normal School for Teachers across the park. A crowd headed down Estévez Street for the stadium, to the west; there was a baseball game that evening. The match factory with its tall iron fence, the old cockfight ring and the ancient movie theater standing high with its royal palm. From the bakery came the smell of freshly baked bread and just brewed coffee. The Esquina de Tejas, narrow, old, where Monte, the realm taken over by the countrymen just arrived on the rural buses, ended, and Calzada del Cerro started, which led to the neighborhood where her maternal great-grandmother had been born. The umbrella repair shop, a dentist's office with the vertical sign on the column of the porch, the sprawling Purísima Concepción sanatorium for Spanish shop clerks, and the large Agua Dulce plaza. In the high window of "El Zorro" uniform store, to the left, a man and a boy mannequins showed off their gala. Two movie theaters, the police station, that canvas awning with the odalisk in the Troya bedsheet ad with her bare breasts pointing weirdly outward, the delicatessen-restaurant with its vertical neon sign: "Toyo - bread, coffee, pastries, crackers", the ten-cent store, another movie theater.

They stood on the other side of Saco Street in front of an ice cream shop, across from the side of the once-religious school formerly run by the Philippian nuns — now turned into a secular child day-care center, all its images removed — facing the dormitory windows. Night had fallen and people started gathering on the sidewalk. Soon what could be termed a sizable crowd had formed. They all stared up at a window with a sheer curtain. There were two cleancut boys of about fifteen in front of them to one side. A tall blackhaired woman of just over thirty, wearing a white uniform, stood to the side just behind the boys with an older lady. Yolanda had told Ana that the deceased nun had appeared to a militia woman, who had screamed in fear and fainted and, as soon as word had gotten out, people had started gathering before the school hoping to see her.

The Education Campaign

One of the boys commented they attended the Marist Brothers' School. The older lady kept up a constant patter in a voice too low for them to make out. The breeze blew the curtain softly. A woman said, "I see something."

The woman in the white uniform agreed, "There's a shadow."

One of the Marist boys said, "The curtain moved."

Ana's breath caught in her throat. Dany was holding her hand.

Another woman said, "It was the wind."

They were all intent now, their eyes fixed on the window, waiting. Suddenly, a patrol car pulled to a stop by the curb near the crowd and three militiamen got off slamming the car doors.

"Get moving", they said as they picked their way among the people on the sidewalk. "There's nothing to see here, comrades. Break it up." A few persons moved reluctantly away.

"Break it up. Get moving, comrades", they repeated.

One militiaman addressed one of the students, "Go away, boy."

The boy refused to move. "I'm not doing anything wrong", he replied calmly. "A schoolmate of ours says he saw the nun and I want to stay to see her."

Dany moved backwards, one arm extended sideways, pushing Ana behind him. They retreated up the steps into the ice cream shop.

The militiaman, short and thin, in his middle thirties, ugly, with thick eyeglasses, said, impatiently now, "I said move."

The boy didn't budge. They could hear his voice plainly. "I'm not doing anything wrong", he repeated. "I'm only standing on a sidewalk, looking." Maybe he was forced by the pride of adolescence.

But he had dared too far. The frustrated militiaman, enraged, brought his hand up clenched in a fist and hit the boy in the right eye. The boy, taken by surprise, reeled and, holding his hand up to his eye, fell back, startled, against the woman in white uniform, who hadn't moved. A few women screamed and scattered, pushing each other as they made a clearing around them. By the time the uniformed woman had steadied the boy back on his feet, his eye had swollen shut alarmingly fast. Suddenly the woman seemed to pounce on the militiaman, throwing him momentarily off balance. She yelled at him, "Coward! Can't you see he's only a boy?" She scratched his face and pushed him. "Why don't you pick on a big, heavy man?" She pounded him wildly on the chest with her fists, as the man tried to fend her off with his arms. His eyeglasses had cracked. "You're garbage!", she screamed, almost hysterical now, apparently unable to control herself, while the older lady kept vainly tugging at her sleeve, pleading.

"She's crazy", a man said, moving away.

The other two militiamen went about arresting the three persons who remained nearby, pushing them ahead into the patrol car, but they prudently walked around the woman in uniform, who pulled the dumbfounded boy along by the hand. "You have to get to the house of succor", she stated firmly, as the older woman and the boy's buddy followed them down Santa Catalina to the first aid station two blocks east.

The militiamen gone, a new crowd started gathering in the ice cream shop to comment on the incident. The newcomers inquired curiously, those who had witnessed it enlightening them. Everybody seemed to be talking at once.

Ana and Dany hadn't uttered a word. It would have been superfluous for her to condemn the militiaman's conduct. It would have been absurd for him to justify it. They walked in silence to Luz Caballero, where he had parked the car, she shaken, he evidently subdued.

Four men had to stop off at Elbow Cay, on Great Abaco, in the Bahamas, due to a malfunction of the engine of the launch "Carmen", in which they had left from the north coast of Cuba.

Ana met a friend of Duarte's and Alejandro's whom they called "El Tico", a rosy-cheeked Costa Rican boy with brown curly hair who was studying medicine at the University of Havana. He'd be the one to whom the cartoon on the lampshade referred. He had met their leader in Cartago during his visit to his family in Guaria in August for the festivity of their patroness, the Virgin of the Angels, when the revolutionary had been soliciting contributions from Heredia coffee plantation owners sympathetic to the cause. Carrillo, his father, was mayor of San Juan de Irazú.

The teachers trained in Minas de Frío, in Manzanillo, in the Sierra Maestra, received the title of "Revolutionary Vanguard". The first "alphabetization brigade" was organized on March 8. Hundreds of children from the sixth grade through secondary education were taken away from their parents' influence and joined the "Army of Education" to carry out indoctrination under the respectable label of "alphabetization". Secondary schools were ordered closed on April 15 so that youngsters from age twelve to twenty, numbering 100,000, could go, duly indoctrinated, into the interior, to teach the peasants their letters and thus pass on to the countrymen they taught the indoctrination they had received.

Late on a Tuesday afternoon at the end of March, Ana went to Folgueira's office as usual, the stencil for the March bulletin in a *Vanidades* magazine. She walked down the flight of stairs from the sixth floor, and as she reached the corner of the hallway, before she rounded the angle, she saw the light reflected on the terrazzo floor of the hall through the open door of the paper representative's office. She considered going back up the stairs, but the elevator had stopped on the fifth floor on its way down and the elevator operator was leaning out looking at her mildly curious, and she had no choice but to walk around the bend to the office with slow, heavy steps. She stopped at the door and saw a heavy man in a militia uniform and one in plain clothes just inside the door. She thought of going on to the ladies' room, but at the click of her heels, the two near the door turned – it was too late, – while another militiaman with a beard went through the desk drawers. He pulled one out and scattered the contents on top. She stammered, "Is Fo- Folgueira in?"

At the sound of her voice, the bearded militiaman at the desk looked up at her. She recognized him from the Ministry; she had seen him searching the men at the entrance.

They didn't answer her. The sweaty, fat militiaman near the door asked her, "Who are you? What are you doing here?"

"I come to use the typewriter for translations sometimes. School translations."

"What's your name?", the bald man in plain clothes asked in turn.

She thought the bearded militiaman might know her name. "Ana Méndez." She didn't have any identification on her.

"Are you related to this Folgueira? Do you work for him?", the fat militiaman asked her. He smelled of sweat.

"No." She had the key to the office with her.

"To what school do you go?", asked the bald man.

"To Publicity."

The sweaty fat militiaman started to ask her something, but the man in civilian clothes silenced him with a gesture of his hand. "When were you here last, comrade?"

"A month ago", she replied truthfully. "Is something wrong?" She was starting to feel more confident. The men didn't look so frightening.

"This man left the country three days ago and a houseful of incriminating evidence was found", the bald man answered.

"Oh!, I didn't know." And it was true. She hadn't had the slightest inkling that Folgueira might be involved in anything.

"I'm sorry, but we'll have to take you to the DIER", said the fat militiaman.

Her heart seemed to sink. She tightened her hand around the rolled magazine until her knuckles turned white. The bearded man said apathetically from the desk, "I know her. She doesn't work for him. She works at the Ministry."

"You know her? Well, maybe somebody in the building can vouch for you", suggested the man in plain clothes. "Can say what you do here. Do you know anybody here?" She thought of the elevator boy, but wondered what he'd say after leaving her off at the sixth floor and seeing her now on the fifth.

"No, I can't think of anybody." Then she thought of Bernardo, the waiter in the restaurant next door. "I used to work in the building. The boys in the restaurant probably remember me", she said hopefully.

"Let's go down", the bald man said not unkindly. The bearded man had walked to the door and stood looking after them with the sweaty fat man as they walked down the hall. The man rang for the elevator. When it arrived he followed her in. The elevator man looked at them sideways and then stared unblinkingly at the door. When they reached the ground floor and were about to get off, the man suddenly turned to the elevator boy, "Do you know this young lady?"

Ana held her breath expectantly.

"Sure! She worked in this building for quite a while, up until about five or six months ago."

"With Folgueira?" The bald man thought he had caught her in a lie.

"No, not with him, with... other people. And she's been coming here once in a while ever since. She's clear, comrade."

Ana breathed again. She was thankful, but didn't dare to smile at him. She wondered if the man had omitted the fact that she hadn't been down to the fifth floor in over two and a half years on purpose.

"She says the boys in the restaurant know her", the man pursued.

"They probably remember her. These girls used to go there often for lunch."

Surprisingly, the bald man said, turning to her, "You didn't actually do anything. Just came up to the door. It wasn't as if we'd found you inside. Or you were a relative of the man." She nodded. He shrugged.

They walked to the "Concierto" restaurant next door. The glass door stood propped open. It was almost empty at this hour, after the offices had closed and before dinner time had started. The air conditioning wasn't working. As she went in with the man, Ana looked around for Bernardo. He was behind the counter and she called confidently to him, "Hello, Bernardo. How are you?"

"Fine, fine. And you?"

They walked to the counter, the man holding on to her elbow lightly. The place was stuffy.

"It seems as if I need some identification. Can you vouch for me?", she asked him smiling.

"Vouch for you?" And to the man, "What did she do?, borrow from you?", he asked kiddingly. "We here have known her from the building for almost four years." And he looked to the other waiters for agreement. She smiled at them. The thin one agreed.

The older one contributed, "Oh, yes, she's clear, sir." They didn't mention either that they hadn't seen her in over six months.

The bald man turned to her. "Where do you work, comrade?" He remembered, "Ah, yes, with Capote." He was obviously referring to the bearded militiaman upstairs.

Bernardo repeated, "We know there's no trouble with her, comrade."

"Well, I guess it's all right", the man said to nobody in particular. "If she'd been involved with the guy, she'd have known and wouldn't have shown up by his office." And to her, "Drop friends like Folgueira. They could incriminate you." He then turned to Bernardo and the other two in friendly conversation, the incident obviously concluded, apparently half dismissed. "Do you know that Spanish guy, a paper agent on the fifth floor? Well, he took off three days ago, and we've found a lot of messy propaganda in his place."

"Really?", Bernardo asked, shaking his head in amazement.

"You don't say!", inserted the thin one.

"Certainly!", the bald man answered. "Give me a little coffee."

Ana took the opportunity to call to them, "So long, Bernardo. Good night, sir." The man was waiting for his coffee attentively, an absorbed look on his face, and didn't pay much attention to her. She couldn't help thinking that the two militiamen upstairs would be waiting for him to return.

"We've had so much trouble with these foreigners...!", the bald man was saying. She left the restaurant, the rolled magazine burning in her hand. This had been a close one. Luckily, the man wasn't too zealous in his duties.

Well, that was the end of the mimeograph. She had to tell Duarte and leave the stencil with him. It was only 6:35. Alejandro wouldn't be at the restaurant yet. She'd have to go to their house. She asked herself how she'd ever gotten involved in all this. She was definitely a coward. She walked the four blocks to Duarte's house. She read about women who had fought in the Spanish and the Mexican Civil Wars, and knew of women among her own ancestors involved in the War of Independence in 1895, and she admired them, but had never felt akin to them. There had been women like Mariana Grajales de Maceo, Adela "*La Capitana*" Azcuy Labrador, Marta Abreu de Estévez, América Arias de Gómez, Emilia Casanova de Villaverde, Emilia Tolón de Teurbe, Emilia de Córdova, "*La Mambisa*", "*La Patriota*", "*La Cubanita*", "*La Solitaria*", the other Mariana they had caught embroidering the flag, and she could recall six more by name. She didn't share their courage. She took the key to Folgueira's office from her ring with the pearl and bent to drop it down the grilled storm sewer on the corner. And she thought back to the day Yolanda had told Duarte that Aurora said he belonged to the G-2. What if he had?

There were no militia at the building entrance. She didn't have the Ministry of the Interior identification card with the name Julia Duarte on her. She half ran up the two flights of stairs to the door with the decal. Alejandro answered the door. She walked past him into the living room and dropped in a chair. Only then did her nerves give way — because of the militia in Folgueira's office, the stencil in her magazine, the bald man's hand on her elbow — and she started shaking.

"They searched the office where I'd been using the mimeograph, so that's out now."

Alejandro came near and dropped on one knee by her chair. "When?"

"I've just come from there. It seems the man had been involved in some activity also. I didn't even imagine it."

El Tico appeared and nodded slightly. "Miss." She acknowledged his greeting with another nod and he disappeared.

The Education Campaign

"Did they get him?", Alejandro asked.

"No, he left the country, I don't know if for Spain or where. I think he was from Betanzos. They found propaganda in his house. The militia were in the office and a man took me down to the restaurant next door to have a waiter state that he knew me... and I guess that that I hadn't been involved with Folgueira, wasn't related or worked with him... I don't know." She had been talking fast and stopped to catch her breath. A voice came from a radio inside, it sounded like a newscast. An *Urbe* city street directory was on the coffee table open to Lealtad Street. "Where's Duarte?"

"Reynaldo must have stopped at the Dominicans' school to pick up a tape recorder they were going to lend us. Wait for him. He won't take long." He was very close. He asked her sympathetically, "Do you want some water?"

"Well, please." He got up, poured water into a glass from on top of the refrigerator and brought it to her. No ridiculous saucer, fortunately. When she took the glass, Ana realized she was still holding the stencil. She handed him the magazine. She leaned back, rested the glass on the arm of the chair and closed her eyes.

After a while, she had stopped shaking and felt very tired. "I'm not going to wait for Duarte. I'm exhausted. Tell him what happened."

Ana got home feeling unreasonably guilty because Alejandro had complimented her light brown hair when she was leaving – "like polished filberts", he'd said, probably just to lift her spirits after the scare she'd had. – And she was surprised to find Dany waiting for her on a sofa. It was only twenty to eight.

"Where were you?", he asked her, getting up and putting his cigarette out in the blue ashtray.

"Well, you know I now work until six", she started hedging. "Then I went with Yolanda to her Catholic organization. I didn't worry because, even when you don't go to the university, you get here close to nine." She hated to have to lie to him.

"I'm not going to the university tonight. I had to stay working three quarters of an hour late and wouldn't have had time to go home, shower, eat and get to the university, so I ate at 'Kimbo' – I was going to call you, but figured you'd have already left work, – and came to take you to school and then go on home to shower. I got here at seven thirty", he added accusingly.

"I'm sorry."

"You haven't eaten?"

"No." The water seemed to slosh in her stomach.

"You've missed the first class. Weren't you planning to go to school tonight?" He seemed to pierce her with his eyes; he doubted her.

"Of course I did. I thought you'd go meet me after school. Only I thought I'd arrive in time for the second class at a quarter to nine." She felt flustered.

"You won't have the required attendance", he admonished.

"I'm hardly ever absent, *mi cielo*", she placated him, trying to smile engagingly. "You often skip the last class, and tonight you're not even going at all."

"I was attending the university three years before you even started Publicity, am organized and only have four more months to go", he said sternly. It was not like him to be patronizing.

Ana excused herself to gulp down her dinner, pot steak, faster even than usual, while Dany waited in the living room smoking impatiently. He turned down the black coffee Teresa offered him. Méndez obviously approved of Dany's attitude and, apparently thinking she was already getting enough reproach from him, didn't add his own to it.

Teresa made a feeble attempt at conversation. "Aguirre's wife, the teacher, told me today that the duplicating-machine repairman's daughter in three who works at the hotel, Natalia, got engaged to the electrical technician in seven." Nobody answered her.

Ana made the second class. The fat girl had been transferred by her enterprise to Quivicán, 24 miles south, and Ernesto moaned, "She deserted me."

Nine men arrived in the United States on the launch *"La Bayamesa"* from the Canímar River, in Matanzas, after 16 hours at sea. Two young men arrived at the Florida coast in a flimsy boat. A 23-year old man was eaten by sharks at high sea. The Straits of Florida had earned itself the name "**the Corridor of Death**".

Six men were sentenced to thirty years' prison. The army captured four men in "San Ignacio", in the Imías district in Baracoa, and took them to Santiago de Cuba. The rebel army surprised a countrymen's clandestine meeting on the hills in Manguito, between the "Araújo" Sugar Mill and Jagüey Grande, in Matanzas province, and attacked them with machine guns, killing three men and arresting eleven other men and one woman.

The Education Campaign

Two men arrived in Kingston, Jamaica on a Tri-Pacer plane two and a quarter hours after taking off from the Santiago de Cuba airport. Grocery stores were empty and markets were closing. There was mail censorship in the country, but not every single letter was opened, mostly conspicuous-looking ones going out addressed to publications, foreign government offices or exiles abroad, or those coming in from them. Ana was still receiving by mail the Saturday Evening Post, to which she had taken a one-year subscription when she had been in Miami in April of the previous year, but that would expire soon, and no money could be sent out of the country. No American magazines were sold any longer at the newsstands in La Rampa Commercial Arcade or the lobby of La Rampa Cinema, or at the book shops she had patronized on Galiano Street and Concordia, O'Reilly, Animas or Infanta Street and San Rafael. Their place had been taken by the magazines published by the government, *"U.R.S.S."* and "China", published in Spanish, Czechoslovakian magazines, *et cetera*, and books about communism, The Communist Manifesto, *Das Kapital*, Fundamentals of Marxist Philosophy, biographies of renowned communists, anti-American books like Asturias' "Week-end in Guatemala" and Arévalo's "The Shark and the Sardines" books by Juan Marinello, and so on. Dany read some of these. Books like Ravines' "The Great Swindle" and Orwell's "1984" and "Animal Farm" were taken out of circulation. The precious few owned, dog-eared from handling, were lent and re-lent among close friends with words of entrustment. There was word that a book titled "Red Star Over Cuba" had been published by Nathaniel Weyl, which, of course, hadn't reached the Cuban people. – ***The Bagasse Curtain*** had dropped.

A professor lent Ana "The Ugly American" by Lederer and Burdick, from the library of a former American private school where he worked during the day. She went to her beach club, the Club Marino Estabias, on three consecutive Saturday afternoons to read it – while Dany tended to his father's bookkeeping and filing, – not taking her bathing suit along, because Dany wouldn't have approved of her bathing in the beach without him and she had no desire to upset him.

"Bridge!", the conductor cried as the Route 32 bus approached the 23rd Street bridge over the Almendares River toward the marble fountain and beautiful, expensive Fifth Avenue, lined with pines, with its clock tower, the "Goblet" and the neatly trimmed cylinder-shaped trees, bringing Ana out of her absorption in her reading long enough to get the two cents out for the bridge toll. Elegant houses beautified the street. The spreading ancient fig trees shaded the shadowy paths of the twin parks to either side of the avenue and St. Rita's Church followed. She got off just before Coney Island park and walked north up the drive lined with hibiscus and thorny bougainvillea to the sea. And she sat by herself on the light, fine sand of the beach in slacks, away from the young members early for the afternoon tea dance, and read for an hour and a half or two, occasionally looking up from her book and adjusting her eyes to focus on the early season bathers away in the deep blue water. A boy was swimming toward the dock with a girl hanging on to his neck on his back. The book impressed her greatly.

She once sat by the edge of the pool until a young man came around from the far end to make conversation. Ana got up then and went toward the lockers. As she passed the soda fountain, she saw Valdés step away from the counter and come limping to the door. She didn't know he was a member of the club. He said, "Hello". "Hello", Ana answered and went on her way.

And she went home before the sun set over the gulf in an ostentatious splash of tangerine light, to tuck away the book, take a shower and get ready for Dany's visit.

A freight ship picked up five Cubans in the Gulf of Mexico and landed them in New Orleans.

The government founded the Union of Young Pioneers, made up of children aged seven to thirteen, to keep vigilance in the primary schools.

At work, Ana's inquiry as to whether there were any new typewriter ribbons had been met from the clerk in charge with the answer in fashion, "Negative, comrade."

When they finally arrived Tuesday morning, she was already typing practically in stencil, and Valdés gallantly offered to dirty his fingers for her – euphemistically declaring, "Don't you do without anything", – which Ana accepted graciously. He always wore the same tie. Aurora had once told her that his father was "a son of the Cradle House". While he removed the hole-studded, ravelled, dry strip, sitting in her chair, he remarked, "This ribbon is like the Yankee imperialism."

Standing beside him, her eyes on his receding hairline, feeling pampered and a little heady, Ana didn't think the remark merited an

The Education Campaign

answer and didn't intend to reply anything, but his eyes went up to her expectantly and she realized Abreu and Morejón were looking – What was expected from her?, – and so she prompted, "How, decadent?"

Valdés smiled appreciatively, satisfied, as he turned back to his self-appointed chore, and Ana saw Duarte look at her, faint amusement pictured in his deep-set gray eyes, and she felt a trace of shame. Abreu commented, a grin on his pocked face, "That's a very revolutionary observation." She inhaled and swallowed.

When Valdés stood up, he surprised her sighing, "Those hips!, ah!", while rolling up his eyes, as he limped away. She recalled then the beach club.

Glass tumblers were becoming increasingly scarce. At the coffee shop that afternoon their water was served in the bottom halves of sawed-off clear bottles.

Yolanda had been talking about Eladio, a boy she'd met at the university. Half her own break already spent, she now leaned forward over the table, "Did you hear that the other day at the 'Foxa' when Fidel came on in the newsreel, a woman flung her shoe at the screen and it landed on the stage?!"

"Really? Did they get her?"

"No. They turned the lights on, but they didn't know who had done it." Yolanda sounded admiring. "So, when the show was over, there were two militia women posted at the exit watching for a woman with one shoe. But nobody limped by", she finished with satisfaction, leaning back in her chair.

"Maybe somebody had taken along an extra shoe. It could've even not been a woman", Ana speculated.

Yolanda had left to go back to work and Ana was alone, still musing about the incident over her soda, when Duarte arrived at her table.

"Who's the militiaman who meets you after school?", he asked her as soon as the young waiter was out of earshot, and she could tell he had been waiting to find her alone.

"Danilo, my boyfriend of two and a half years. Why?" She knew why. He didn't answer her, but seemed to look through her at some distant point. Had his look in the office held distrust? "Who saw me?"

"One of the boys", he said with something like irony, "it doesn't matter which. Is he the one about whom you were telling Yolanda here that time a couple of months ago?"

"The only one." It seemed important to convey to him that their relationship had begun long before she had started mimeographing the bulletin for them.

"What does he know about what you do?"

"Nothing."

"And what do you tell him when you're late?"

"He only found out once, and I told him I was out with Yolanda."

"Does Yolanda know?", he shot at her.

"No, and Yolanda doesn't know what I do either − unless you've told her, − but he doesn't know her. He'd break up with me if he knew", she tried to explain.

"It's likely he'd give you away first", he said unkindly.

"No, he wouldn't. I know him well. We're very close."

"But he'd be hurt that you'd kept this from him."

"I know. I've thought about it", Ana said truthfully, and looked down at the table. "And he'd also be afraid I'd involve him and destroy the confidence he may have built for himself."

"I trust you", Duarte said firmly, tapping his cigarette on the edge of the plastic ashtray. "Watch yourself with him."

Now approaching age 54 and with nineteen years of contributions to the accountants' retirement fund behind him, Méndez applied for his retirement pension. His office had been doing very little business in the last year − mostly from loyal old friends not much better off than he − and his income had dropped gravely, to the point where it had become difficult to cover essentials, let alone continuing to contribute to the retirement fund. The government wouldn't hire a man over fifty without contacts. There wasn't a large selection of luxuries offered, however, so his income plus Ana's semi-monthly contribution of $55. therefore proved enough to live on. He had refused to touch their savings in solid Banco Gelats − "the only Cuban bank which didn't go bankrupt in the bank crash", he had remarked when he had started adding to it a decade before, − in the event of an emergency.

After over a year in his job at the Ministry, Gustavo had fairly adapted. His salary was still the same, of course; there had been no raises; the revolutionary government called for "sacrifice" from their workers. Blanca continued in her job at the Antonio Guiteras Enterprise, as the electric company had been named, with little significant change. Gustavito, who'd turn five years old in another four months,

The Education Campaign

would be starting school in the new academic year beginning in September. Blanca had mentioned LaSalle, because, although reputed Arturo Montori was closer to home, the former one was the nearest Catholic boys' school – even though now confiscated, – and he could also stay in the same school from pre-primary through university in Ensanche del Vedado. And Blanquita, just two, was still a darling, happy, chubby child venturing out to increase her vocabulary, and giving little trouble to loyal Leonor, who, now well into her third year, had been with them a record time.

Ana and Dany now saw their goal within probable reach. Their joint savings account in the Bank of Nova Scotia had been increasing steadily. They enjoyed talking about their future, now foreseeable. Sitting in his old DeSoto Tuesday night after classes, they went over their plans again.

"How much do we have in the account now?", he asked her, as he did twice a month after he gave her his share.

"A thousand five hundred ninety-eight", she informed him proudly on their progress, having added her own $10. and deposited the day before.

"We're only four hundred two *pesos* away from our goal, *mi vida*."

"How long will that take us?"

"Five months and... and a half."

"It seems incredible. We timed it perfectly! It'll just give you time to finish your career."

"I only have the final exams left to pass. Four more months."

"Will we get married on a Saturday?", she asked him unnecessarily, only because she liked to hear him repeat it, nestling against him.

He nodded. "That we already established. Decide on the date."

She added mentally, ticking off her fingers. "Between the fifteenth and the twenty-seventh."

It was his turn to count in sevens. "The twenty-first falls on a Saturday."

"The twenty-first then."

"In the afternoon, right? Because it'll be informal."

"Yes, at six. I'd like to get married in the Church of the Sacred Heart of Jesus."

"Where's that?"

"The Parochial Church of Vedado, on D. It's only nine blocks from my house. And it's my parish."

"And we have to get married in your parish, don't we?", he said uncertainly. "All right. I've never been in it. Is it nice?"

"Yes, I like it, I think it's very nice, warm. It's of the order of the Dominican fathers."

"Is that where you were baptized?"

"No, I was baptized at the old El Carmelo church. And you?"

"In the Baptist Church, on Zulueta."

"We have to notify the church in time", said Ana, "so they can start publishing the banns. Will your parents go to the wedding?"

"Sure they will, *mi vida.*"

"Have you told them yet?"

"Not yet."

"Do you think your mother will want to be the *'madrina'* of the wedding, *mi cielo*?" She had been afraid to ask him.

"I think so." He didn't sound very convinced.

"But, since your father is a mason..."

"I don't think it'll make any difference to them. Will your father be the *'padrino'*?"

"Of course."

"Have you asked him yet?"

"No, I don't have to ask him. I've talked about our plans. It's understood."

"And what has he said?"

"He likes you. I can tell."

"And your mother doesn't?", he surprised her by asking.

"Oh, yes, she does too." She wasn't so sure as she wanted to sound.

"I respect your father a lot... It's strange. You know how the father's supposed to be jealous of the son-in-law and the girl is supposed not to get along with the mother-in-law. And with us it's not that way at all."

"No, that's true, it's the other way around. It's your father who can't accept me."

"Don't say that." He was quiet for a while, then said, "I was thinking today. Do you know where I'd like to buy your engagement ring?"

"Where? Not from the 'Casa Quintana' or 'El Cairo'?"

"No. In that same jewelry store on Calzada de Columbia where I bought you the locket for your birthday the year before last."

She smiled at his sentimental thought. "That would have meaning. I'd like a plain ring. Just three little diamonds the same size, maybe in florentine gold." She paused and then switched the subject. "Are you going to have a party when you graduate?" Would she, at this late stage of the game, still be excluded from their family celebration?

"I don't know. I don't think so. The Old Man and my uncle will probably want to take me out, you know." He changed the subject now. "It's going to be hard to find an apartment."

Apartments *were* very difficult to find now. But Ana didn't want to worry. "There are offers for exchanges in the classified ads", she said; "we'll find something." Now she wanted to make other plans. "Where are we going on our honeymoon?"

"Where would you like to go?"

"To the Ariguanabo Lake", she answered only half jokingly.

He laughed. "You haven't forgotten about that?"

She wrinkled her nose to make a face and punched his right shoulder with her right fist. "Well, where do *you* want to go?"

"We could go to the San José del Lago resort in Mayajigua and stay at a *'jiquí*[56]. There's an airport there. We can go by plane. I think that's the only way to get there."

"Where is it?"

"In Yaguajay. Or we may go to Varadero beach and visit the Bellamar Caves and the Yumurí Valley."

"Wherever you want, *mi cielo*. We went to Varadero on that excursion with Wayne in fifty-eight. Where I *would* love to go is Rio de Janeiro, but that's just an impossible dream; there's no money for that. So Mayajigua's a good idea, or wherever you want to go. I *would* prefer a place where you haven't been before, though", she added, remembering how the thought of his having been in Soroa before had robbed her of some of the wonder of its impact.

"I haven't been to Mayajigua."

"Then let's go there."

"Fine, it's settled then, that's where we're going. Ah!, you know, Sonia was talking about her boyfriend today at dinner. It seems he's serious."

"Oh, I'm so glad! Where did she meet him?"

"At the Corporación de Asistencia, where she works. In Larrazábal." He was again quiet for a while and then said, "You'll want to

---

[56] pillared loft

finish school, won't you?"

"Yes, I'd like to, before children come." Her voice caught in her throat. Guilt rose anew. She blinked it away and swallowed. "But now that you'll have finished and we could have more time together, I don't know whether I'll want to. I already have the three-year commercial course, in any case. And publicity won't be very useful here now." She didn't like to think of him alone, newly-wed, while she went off to school by herself in the evenings. There was a pregnant young girl in her school, but her husband was attending too.

"It'd always be good. We'll see about that later."

Ana experienced such a secure feeling, snug in his arms, planning their future. It was near after all. They had stayed together two and a half years. They'd have other children to vindicate themselves, if such a thing was possible. She had been leaning back against his chest, her left hand on his right thigh, his right hand resting lightly on her right breast.

He now turned her with his left hand to face him. "I love you", he said looking her in the eyes out of his deep dark ones.

"And I do too."

He encircled her in his arms and she slipped her left arm around his waist.

•

In the last two years they had grown used to seeing rebel soldiers and an ever-increasing number of militia men and women all around the city, and to being occasionally searched when going into movie theaters, department stores, office buildings, restaurants and other public places. There were no apples, evaporated or condensed milk, bacon or detergent to be found in the markets; and hardly any bread, soap, deodorant or thread. Homogenized milk seemed to grow more watery by the day and its thickening corn starch content increased blatantly.

With the bleak prospect of two extra hours of work ahead of her that evening, Ana rushed home earlier Wednesday afternoon for dinner. The Minister wanted some lengthy reports and the whole department was working on them. The girls who could type had been rushed home for dinner earlier to return for another two hours of typing, while the accounting clerks stayed behind working on the figures, to leave when the typists got back. She'd leave a message for Dany now to call her as soon as he got home from work.

A dog in a garden barked at her as she went by. Some children

were playing on a porch.
> *"Pues daremos la media vuelta*
> *y la tiraremos del balcón.*
> *En el medio del salón..."*[(100)]

When she crossed the street, Natalia, the girl in apartment 3, the daughter of the repairman, caught up with her at the curb. "Hello."

"Ah, hello! I hadn't seen you in weeks."

"I'm working at the INIT now, nearby", she waved over her left shoulder, "and get home earlier." She had lost much weight and seemed ill, but her face was paradoxically somehow radiant and managed to make her look healthy.

"And I've been getting home later. Mamá said she heard you were getting married." Although Ana knew it was to be to the electrical technician in apartment 7 upstairs, she didn't know his name, so she left it at that.

"Well, yes, but not for a while yet. The electric contractors for whom my 'future one' worked closed down. He was working in Channel Eleven, *Televisión del Caribe*. And his brother in the United States claimed him. My uncle in 'the North' claimed *me* and, as soon as either one gets the visa waiver, we'll get married then, so that the first one can claim the one who stays behind."

"And be separated right after getting married?", Ana asked in a slip of tactlessness.

"Well, it's the only way one can claim the other", Natalia replied defensively and added, laughing in a conspiratorial tone, "I'm not going to let us separate without marrying and then trust him to marry me by proxy!"

"You're right", Ana amended, "don't! Where's Channel Eleven?"

"On Avenida del Río, by the Almendares River."

They had reached the building hallway – Felipe was watering the lawn and the purple queen, – and they said good-by, Natalia going into the rear apartment and Ana starting up the stairs. The thought stayed in her mind of a newly-wed young girl away from her groom and, if she should be the first to leave, venturing alone into a strange country, leaving her parents behind, to stay with an uncle and claim her brand-new husband. Sad.

As she reached her landing, she was surprised to meet Matilde coming out of their apartment.

"How are you, miss?"

"Fine, Matilde, and how are things going with you?"

"Ah!, the same, miss. How could things ever change with me, unless it were to get worse?"

"Don't sound so tragic. You're here a day early, aren't you?"

"Tomorrow I have to take my daughter Luz to the hospital to get a shot, she has a bad cold. Well, you already know my husband was fired, don't you?"

"No, I didn't know. Why?"

"Didn't you know that, when the Urban Reform took over the building where your brother lives, they said they didn't need a janitor? You know we had a room, at the rear in the basement... and they told us to move."

"No, Blanca hadn't mentioned it. I'm sorry. Is he working?"

"Yes, he found a job as janitor in a ministry, but it's not the same. He has to clean the toilets. But that's the least of it, the worst is that the salary's lower and now we both have to pay bus fares on that route ten."

"Where are you living?"

"We moved in with my mother in Jacomino. We're eight in two rooms. Imagine!" Her prominent cheekbones protruded even more above her sucked-in cheeks and her light cinnamon skin, drawn taut across them, now looked sickly waxy and yellowish. Her back was hunched and her shoulder blades were sharp under her blouse. She shook her bony head and Ana did likewise in sympathy. She felt ashamed of having accused her of sounding tragic when she'd said things were the same; they were actually worse. She wondered how old Matilde was. "I don't know how far these people are going to take the country", Matilde said, still shaking her head slowly. "Everything's worse now."

"You shouldn't talk like that to just anybody, Matilde. You don't know who anybody might be."

"You're not just anybody, miss. With you I know I don't need to be careful. How could you like this? The lady told me today that the master has to retire."

"But somebody might overhear you", Ana insisted, concerned.

Matilde didn't reply. She started down the stairs, the small bundle of work clothes under her thin arm, and then looked back over her bony shoulder to call as an afterthought, "Until next week, miss."

Felipe was coming up the stairs. They nodded to each other in passing. Ana watched her descend, shoulders hunched, head bowed. Poor woman! Felipe stopped at the landing to look after Matilde with Ana.

"She'd better be careful of Aguirre, in two, who's for 'fatherland or death'." He had apparently overheard her. He went on upstairs.

Ana went into the apartment to call Dany's home. Her mother served her first as an exception because she had to go back to the Ministry. Dinner consisted of roast meat, golden potato halves, watercress, corn fritters and egg pudding.

"Felicia brought the skirts she lined for you", Teresa told her.

"Which?"

"The gray woolen one and the plaid one", her mother said, sitting down to keep her company while Ana ate.

"Ah!, that's right. Fine time, when winter's over. I had even forgotten about them."

"Yes, it's been about two months since she took them. She says she couldn't find thread." She traced a wavy line on the tablecloth with her fingernail. "Her husband had a mad fit and she's had to commit him. She's now living in a mezzanine on Reina."

Ana was half-way through dinner when her father arrived, newspaper folded under one arm, briefcase in his hand, reading glasses in his pocket. Teresa started to set the table for them and Méndez announced, "I was notified today my retirement was approved."

"Oh, that's good, Papá!", said Ana with pretended enthusiasm. "Have you told Gustavo yet?"

"No. I'll call him after dinner."

"Let's go over", suggested Teresa.

"Do you have to leave soon?", Méndez asked Ana, when he noticed she was almost finished with dinner.

"Yes, I have to go back to work."

Her father frowned. "Aren't you going to school?"

"No, I won't have time."

"You don't look happy", Teresa said to Carlos.

"After eleven years, I'm going to miss the office." He went in to shower.

Dany called then. "Aren't you going to school tonight?", he asked her. She explained. "Then I'll go over to see you for a while after classes and we'll go for a ride", said he. "I'm only going to the first two. Since we've just started the second semester this week, it hasn't taken its course yet. Well, I have to rush now. I'm running late because I've found that Sonia's boyfriend's coming tonight to ask for her hand, the Old Lady's late with dinner, the Old Man's mad and Sonia's talking non-stop."

"Congratulate her for me."

"I'd better congratulate her after the guy's talked." He threw her a kiss before he hung up.

"Azucena called me this afternoon", her mother told Ana. "She says she couldn't bring the clean wash this morning because her little boy has tonsillitis and she couldn't leave him with her husband because he has bronchitis, or asthma, or something, I don't know. And she can't come before Saturday. And I only have one clean sheet left and not a single towel. I was going to go to her house while you were in school, but I don't want to leave your father alone tonight, as depressed as he's feeling."

"I know."

"Since you're not going to school, will you do me a favor and go get it when you're through at work?"

"Sure, I'll go."

Teresa produced a slip of paper with the address. "It's near Santo Tomás Street, somewhere around El Pontón."

Ana went in to put on the gold heart-shaped locket Dany had given her. Méndez came back to the table in his slippers, his pajama top over a pair of old pants, evidently with no intention of going out again. There was an uncomfortable silence as Teresa served their food.

"I had planned to work at least another eight years, or even longer", he grumbled.

"Well, now you can take things easy."

"I'll grow moldy."

"We can go visit my family in Guanabacoa — we haven't seen them since Gustavito was born — and yours in Bauta — them we haven't seen since Gustavo got married, — and spend some time in the country." Teresa tried to cheer him up. "We could go to Trinidad, where we went on our honeymoon."

"We'll have a second honeymoon", he said, trying to sound cheerful for her benefit.

When Ana left the building, subdued, she noticed that the *notario's* house on the corner, her old favorite, was occupied. The porch had been divided with a hardboard partition, a couple of windows had been boarded up, the green canvas awnings were shredded, the double doors at the side entrance stood open and bare partitions could be seen inside. Several men and women, mostly black, were sitting on the porch banister and the steps, a few dirty children ran in the garden among the dying rose and carnation bushes. It must have been occupied for a few weeks; she didn't know how she hadn't noticed before.

On 23rd Street she saw the man who used to travel with her on the bus with a boy of about seven by the hand. She felt disappointed.

The reports typed, Ana left the Ministry at 8:10, to Aurora's words, "You'll all be expected here tomorrow at eight thirty in the morning, as always". She met the short former militia girl in the hallway, who said, "A bummer, eh?"

She had to transfer on Belascoaín. The globe atop the Great Masonic Temple and University on Carlos III which Dany attended, was lit against the night sky; the ornate Church of the Society of Jesus on Reina rose in gothic splendor further east. She took the wrong bus; route V-6, after passing the Ministry of Health, the monument to Carlos Finlay in the park in front, the Fernando Aguado School of Arts and Trades, the Habana-Madrid Jai-Alai Frontón, the Félix Alpízar Municipal Music Conservatory, the Fifth Police Station and the old Ministry of Justice, continued southeast on Belascoaín toward Cuatro Caminos. She had to get off just before the fork and walk down Nueva del Pilar Street south for two or three blocks.

People were sitting in straight chairs and rocking chairs on the wide sidewalk before the open doors of their porch-less houses, in the balmy spring evening. A few had to move their chairs out of the way to let her go by. There were few pedestrians. Radios could be heard and television screens seen through the tall, wrought-iron barred windows opening directly on the sidewalk. "The vibrant pages of the Novel of the Air open to make you live the excitement and romance of a new chapter." A boy was climbing the iron bars on a window. A woman in a rocking chair yelled at him, "Get down from there, Chaguito, because, if you fall, on top of the fall I'm going to give you a spanking!"

Ana turned west on a side street looking for the address and came to a rooming house. The front wrought iron gate, crowned by spiked iron bars fanning out like lances in a semicircle, opened to a large square courtyard surrounded on three sides by rooms arranged in a U shape, their doors high above the yard floor, a typical *solar*. Several children, black and white, were playing in the yard. A few charcoal stoves and washtubs with scrub boards sticking out of the soapy water stood by the solid doors painted turquoise, and a board was placed across the lower part of a door, probably to keep a crawling infant or a puppy from getting out. Clotheslines, now bare, crisscrossed the yard. Radios blared and a woman's voice rose to intone one of the songs along with the singer,

> *"Santa Bárbara bendita,*
> *virgen venerada y pura,*
> *nuestra oración infinita,*
> *llévanos hasta su altura"*[86]

Slippery grooves worn in the cement floor ran from several points around the courtyard to a grilled drain in the center. There was a sink in the far wall and to one side of it a shuttered narrow door stood ajar. A smell pervaded the air, a curious mixture where bleach, starch, hot iron and hot comb, hair straightener and balsam-apple alternately stood out. A boy sitting on a door step, his head shaved except for a tuft at the top, was eating a mango. Two men sat by their open doors. Ana walked to the one nearer the entrance, a thin mulatto in his undershirt, toothpick pressed between his lips, huge gold medal of Saint Lázaro on his chest, chair tilted back against the wall, precariously balanced on its rear legs, and she asked him for Azucena. He directed her to a room across the yard. A woman came to stand at a door, arms akimbo, and yelled to her son, "Cheíto!"

The door stood wide open. Azucena was standing before the ironing board resting on sawhorses, wearing wooden-soled slippers with rubber straps, her six tight little braids standing out untied, smelling of massicot, a charcoal iron poised in her hand.

"*Ay*, miss!, I'm so sorry you've had to come all the way here!", she apologized, "but Lazarito is sick to his tonsils and I couldn't leave him with Isidro, because *he*'s sick again." She put the iron down on its trivet, the pouch of starch next to it.

There was a smell of Florida water in the room. A man snored on the double bed, in pants, shirtless, on a clean white sheet. Several large pieces of furniture filled the room. A three-section wardrobe with a full-length mirror on the center door was angled in the corner to serve as a screen providing privacy for dressing. A little boy about five, in a clean blue shirt, was sitting on a chipped enamel chamber pot near the bed. A cretonne curtain hanging from a string covered the tall barred window that looked out over the yard.

"I told the mistress, if she could wait until Saturday, I could take it to her." She tucked the end of one little braid under another, em-

barrassed at being surprised in her domestic privacy.
"It's all right, Azucena. Don't worry."
"Sit down."
Dropping in a woven cane seat straight chair, Ana talked in a low voice, "I had to walk five blocks."
"Oh!, you can talk aloud, he won't wake up. You came up Belascoaín? Going back, you'd better walk to Infanta and take the M-seven there, or route two. The other way it's further and it's dark as a wolf's mouth. Will you have a little coffee?"
"All right. Is he better?"
"I gave him a lemon decoction with honey." She brought out the clean wash wrapped in brown paper and tied with twine, and set it on the oilcloth-covered leaf table next to Ana. The man coughed in his sleep.

On a corner shelf was a small plaster statue of the Virgin of Mercies, the Catholic syncretization that Azucena's stalwart *Lucumí* ancestors, brought to Cuba from Nigeria across the Atlantic in the 18th Century, had given to their Yoruba god *Obatalá*, the representative of bisexual virginity and creation. It was dressed in his color, white, and surrounded by white gladiola, and a small votive candle burned in a milky glass holder.

Azucena had once told Ana that her slave great-grandfather had come from Oyó in the early 1860's, almost two decades after the official cessation of the trade. Prevented from worshipping the wooden figures of their gods in their traditional manner, they had substituted them with the Catholic images embraced by the Spaniards. She had also told her *"Lucumí"* was actually a Yoruba greeting meaning "my friend". Six prayer cards were arranged symmetrically around the shelf, three on either side of it, Bithynian Saint Bárbara of Nicomedia, the Black Virgin of Regla, the Virgin of Charity, Saint Peter, Saint Francis of Assisi and the Holy Infant of the Basilica of Atocha. These were the respective equivalents of the Yoruba animist gods which, with *Obatalá*, constituted the "Seven African Powers": *Shangó*, *Obatalá's* grandson, the god of war, thunder and virility, whose color was red; *Yemayá*, *Shangó's* mother, of the seas and maternity, whose colors were blue and white; *Oshún*, *Yemayá's* sister, of love, gold and amber, whose color was yellow; *Oggún*, *Yemayá's* son, of iron, whose colors were green and black; *Orunla*, of destiny, wisdom and oracles, whose colors were green and yellow; and *Elegguá*, the path opener, whose colors were red and black. A faint smell of incense lingered about. Ana wondered if Azucena carried it so far as to serve *Obatalá* his favorite food according to the Rule of Orisha, *"ecrú"* of black-eyed peas, on her day in late September. The other four most worshipped *orisha* of the *Santería* seemed to be *Babalú-Ayé*, the god of illnesses, *Orishaoko*, of crops and the farm — the Catholic equivalents of which were revered in the names of Azucena's son and husband — and the *Ibeji*, the divine twin sons of *Shangó* and *Oshún*, his aunt.

"Have you gotten the scholarship for him in a municipal boarding school?" Ana paid her.

"It's hard..."

A woman came up to the door and informed, "Listen, Azu, Mongo wanted me to give him the five *'baros'* I got Saturday and I told him not even to dream of it and he threw a tantrum." She was apparently referring to her husband. "Will you lend me your grater?" She looked into the room. "Oh, forgive me, I didn't know you had a visitor. I'll come back later." She backed away.

Azucena went on, "I may have to go into the militia to get it." She handed Ana the little cup of black coffee.

"Don't do that!", Ana blurted spontaneously, and then added more ambiguously, "They make you dedicate so much time to it!", safely, while she sipped her coffee.

"But, miss, it seems like the only way to get it. He's going to be six in July." She leaned forward and lowered her voice to barely above a whisper. "And, no matter how much I hate Fidel, I care to get my son into a good school. You know, this man was going to better life so much. Well, all my nephews and nieces went to municipal schools, Valdés Rodríguez, Alfredo María Aguayo, Romualdo *'e* la Cuesta, José Miguel Gómez, good schools. You just went to a councilman then and he could give you a scholarship. Now everything's harder."

Ana was surprised at Azucena's outburst. "I thought you were with the government", she said testing her.

"Me? Are you crazy?" She waved an arm outward. "Batista was bad, but this guy's worse. I'm still living in the same room in the same house where I've lived for eight years. And before, you could go to the owner when you paid the rent and complain that the toilet was stopped up and he even used to give us light bulbs. Now you can't go to anybody, because the man doesn't own the house any more and the rent is paid to the Urban Reform, and *they* don't care if the toilet is stopped up or your light bulb burned out."

Ana nodded understandingly. "They say they're going to tear these houses down."

Azucena shrugged. "That's what they say... They wash their heads." – Did she mean their *brains*?

The little boy got up and pulled on a pair of blue pants.

"Say hello to the miss, Lazarito", Azucena prompted him.

Lazarito mumbled hello with a frown. Ana smiled at him. He reached to the table and grabbed a cracker with a slice of guava paste that had been lying on a corner, and got on a narrow bed by the rear wall.

"And I think we have 'fidelism' for a while", Azucena went on. "A man on Clavel who 'tosses the coconut' sa-..., well, I know you don't believe in that, but there's something stronger, ...and he says there's no change in sight." She picked up the chamber pot and excused herself.

Ana picked up the bundle of clean wash and got up to leave. "It's late and I have to go. Thank you for the coffee."

"It's nothing. I'm sorry you had to come."

"May he get better. Until next week."

"Thank you. Saturday I'll go pick up the dirty laundry."

Ana nodded. As she crossed the courtyard to the front gate, she saw Azucena go across to the shuttered narrow door on the far side with the pot in her hand.

The woman's voice was now singing along with the singer on the radio,

> *"Esa mata nace en el monte,*
> *su tronco tiene poder,*
> *esa mata es ... siguaraya"*[(87)]

A new smell was present in the mixture now, a strong cheap perfume, which Ana guessed was probably one of those she had at one time or another heard mentioned, *"Amansa guapo", "Abre caminos", "Rompe zaragüey", "Siete potencias".* A darker man approached the one who had directed Ana to Azucena's room.

"What can you tell me, *'asere'*?"

"Here, Ñico, what's new?"

"Should we get a shot on the corner, *compadre*, and roll a few hands?" They were talking in their Cuban unconscious variation of the gypsy *"caló".*

"No way, *negro*! It's hot, it's late and I'm 'skinned'."

The voices of a man and a woman rose in a domestic squabble. "May lightning split you!"

The other man sitting by his door further away commented, "Ah!, the worm pit stirred. And even though they want to pass themselves off as *'macri'*[57]."

"Yes, that's turned into a pot of crickets", the mulatto in undershirt answered him.

"What, Chucho, are you afraid of your black woman?", the dark man needled the lighter one. "And then you say you eat sugar raw and swallow water without chewing."

"Will you lend me two *'pesetas'*[58], partner?", the thin mulatto asked him, his pride peaked, and when the dark one agreed, responded, "Let me go put a shirt on."

Ana crossed over a railroad track. Would this be the one that went right to the very market on Carlos III? It was dark. She walked to Infanta. The bundle was too big to carry comfortably. She waited near Las Animas contagious disease hospital. When the route 2 bus arrived, several students of the Normal School for Teachers, a few blocks south, were on it, joking and giggling. There was an empty seat next to a man wearing a coarse blue chambray work shirt. Strangely, he reminded her of the laborer who had usually sat on the seat in front of her on the bus on her way to Wayne Motors in the morning for three years. She sat next to the man and had paid the conductor her fare before she noticed him looking at her. She then recognized him as Ovidio Medina, the countryman who sold fruit, to whose house near Managua Dany had taken her two years before.

"How are you?", he asked her timidly, when he saw she had recognized him. "Do you remember me?" They were passing the Arena Cristal stadium.

"Yes. Fine, and you?" They passed the Canada Dry plant.

"Fine, thank you. How's Gutierrito?"

"He's fine. Don't you see him?" They were passing La Campana night club.

"Well, I saw them about five months ago. But I don't sell to his uncle any more. Well, I don't sell fruit at all any longer." He laughed, showing the gap between his front teeth.

"I'll tell him I saw you. He'll be glad." They passed *Carteles* and

---

[57] white, slang, perhaps < African
[58] twenty-cent coins

The Education Campaign

Vanidades magazines. "How's your wife? And the children?"

"They're all fine, thank you. Now we have another one – it turned out a girl, – over a year and a half old now."

"Ah, congratulations!"

"And the older two growing like purslane."

"Many students, eh?" To the right, a movie theater.

"Yes, many. Youth."

"I came to pick up the clean wash from the laundress." Ana jabbed the brown wrapping paper with her index.

"I'm going to my *compadre's* house, near the depot."

There was a long silence. Another two theaters; in one they were showing "Forbidden Games", in the other, a Japanese movie – she crossed herself in front of the Church of the Virgin of Carmen, the tallest in the city, with its bronze statue, – and, before turning west on San Lázaro Street, the lamp store.

"Are you still... planting?", Ana finally asked him.

"I had to go into a people's farm", Ovidio answered ambiguously.

To the left, the little Guiteras park, Mella's bust now gone and, before the bus turned north again, from her throne high above, Korber's the Austrian's Alma Mater, inspired on Minerva, opened her motherly arms over the majestic stairs of the University to embrace the students, as she had for a third of a century.

"Ah, did you?" Should she appear glad?, sorry? He *had* said "had". Radiocentro to the right. What had happened to his station wagon? But they had reached her stop. "Say hello to your family for me. I'll tell Danilo I saw you."

"Give him my regards."

She got home as Dany was knocking on the apartment door. It was 9:40. He wanted to go to the "Peking" restaurant for a soda. In the car, Ana asked him, "What's your sister's boyfriend's name?"

"Lino Soler."

"Where does he work?"

"In his father's business near 'Tropicana'. His old man trucks in fruit from the country."

"Ah!, do you know whom I met tonight on the bus? Ovidio, that man in Managua to whose house you took me that day." They passed the Medina park, with the statue of Mariana Grajales and its fountain always empty.

"How is he?"

"All right. You know he doesn't say much. He says he had to go into a people's farm."

"Oh, yes. He came by the hardware store once about four months ago. He's better off now. But he wasn't happy."

"Well, maybe he felt more independent before."

"Yes, independent, so what? He was living in misery." They passed before her old school, on the southwest corner, symmetrical, with its twin little towers and its green clay barrel roof tiles.

"But he was free."

"Free! What's freedom if you have poverty?"

"You don't know how he's living now, *mi cielo*."

"I'm sure it couldn't be worse."

"Maybe not as far as the dwelling is concerned, but his way of life may be worse. He must not have the station wagon if he was riding the bus."

"Oh, Ana! Again?"

"You're right." She held up a conciliatory hand. "I'm sorry. I don't even know the man well after all. Let's talk about something else. Have Sonia and her boyfriend decided yet when they're getting married?"

"She's been talking about late September, but I don't know if it's definite." He parked the car on 12th Street, facing north, with the driver's side to the left-hand side curb, in front of a bakery. She waited for him to finish parking; she had learned he didn't listen while he was parking.

"So soon?", she asked at last.

"Well, she's twenty-five and he's twenty-eight. Why would they wait?"

And I'm twenty-three, Ana thought. She wondered if she'd be invited to the wedding. The roots of a tree in a garden grew over the high rock wall.

"Papá's retirement was approved today."

"Is he glad?"

"No. He feels depressed." They walked south, holding hands.

"I can understand it. If they took my old man's hardware store away from him, he'd wilt away."

They'd been spending so much time in restaurants lately! Sitting at the next table, was Nelia, Palacios' former secretary, now very pregnant, with her husband, Emilio. She looked about four or five months along.

"Hello, people!", she called to them.

The Education Campaign

They exchanged greetings in loud voices, with wide smiles, while a couple at another table looked on curiously.

"I hadn't seen you in about six months, Danilo", said Nelia, "well, since the company left."

"That's right. How have you been?"

"I didn't know you were pregnant", said Ana. "Congratulations!"

"I already was the last time you saw me", Nelia laughed. "When was that?, in January, wasn't it?"

Dany looked at Ana questioningly, and she tried to think up something to tell him when they were alone again.

"When are you two getting married?", asked Nelia.

"She wants to see everybody hooked", Emilio said laughing.

"Look, you can't complain", she said to her husband, and to Dany she asked, "What, are you afraid?"

"Hey!, don't meddle", said Emilio, embarrassed.

"Don't think, sign", she advised.

"Soon, soon", Dany answered, laughing. Ana would have preferred to hear him answer "In October".

"Order me a pie *à la mode*", Nelia asked her husband.

"You know the doctor told you to be careful with your weight. She's gained seven pounds in a week", he said addressing Dany, who oh'ed dutifully.

"Watch it, you'll get a sty."

"You've been taking advantage of your pregnancy to get away with anything", they heard Emilio say, turning back to his wife, "blaming it on the cravings."

They talked about their classes. When Nelia and her husband got up and turned away, Dany didn't waste any time in asking, "Where did you see her in January?"

"Oh, I ran into her at lunch time", Ana tried to dismiss it as inconsequential.

But, when her husband went ahead to pay the check, Nelia stayed behind and came to stand close between the two, a hand on Ana's shoulder. "Ana, be careful. Danilo, make her be careful with what she's doing", she whispered. "It's dangerous to get involved in anything."

Dany's eyes darted to Ana's. Nelia didn't know Dany was in the militia. Gone was any possibility Ana might have had of making up something. She felt a void in her stomach. Nelia slapped her on the back and Emilio waved at them from the register.

"What did she mean?", Dany asked her as soon as they'd left, pushing his soda away.

"Nothing. You saw she was kidding."

"No, because she didn't even talk in front of her husband. She waited until he walked away."

"Still, it's nothing. You know how she is, she gets alarmed over nothing."

"Ana, don't lie. I think you had never lied to me before."

Yes, eight days ago, she thought. Her name on his lips had sounded so harsh. She kept quiet, sipping her soda. She was afraid.

"You've gotten involved with the counter-revolution, haven't you?" She still didn't answer. "How could you? I'm with the government and in the militia, and you don't care that you could get me in trouble."

"Is that all you care about? That I could get you in trouble? You know how I think. You do what *you* think is right, and I do what *I* think is right." Even as she was still talking, she was already regretting admitting this much to him. "I can get in as much trouble with the people with whom I'm involved for going around with you as you can with the government for going around with me, and I haven't cared." She had been talking without catching her breath and now gasped. "I've risked it because I love you and wouldn't leave you, and all you can think about is the trouble I could get you in!" She bit her lower lip hard.

"But we've been talking about marriage in six months. Do you actually think we can get married and each go in so opposite a way?"

"I don't know", she said hopelessly. "For eleven months now, I've been thinking all this is going to end soon."

"Haven't you thought, if it ended, we'd have to separate?" He stood up and walked to the register to pay the check.

"What can I do?", she asked under her breath. "I'd feel guilty if I crossed my arms and didn't do anything against what I think is so wrong!"

As soon as they were out of the restaurant, he said illogically, "I can't talk to you about anything because you turn wild."

"That's not true", she protested, surprised and hurt, but discouraged. Her eyes welled up and tears spilled out. They were on the sidewalk. She tried to keep her face turned away from him as they passed in front of the florist and the corner restaurant. They crossed the busy intersection a block north from the Colón Cemetery and she walked just a pace ahead of him before the other corner restaurant to the car, past 21st Street. A shoeshine man stared curiously at her. She tasted blood on her lip.

When he opened the car door for her, Dany noticed her tears. He walked around and from the sidewalk, as he opened the door on his side, snapped, annoyed, "Don't start crying!"

She couldn't stop. She got back out of the car on her side, into the oncoming traffic of 12th Street, as he, getting in on the driver's side, yelled at her, "Last time I see you!"

Ana slammed the car door and walked back south, still crying. Dany started the car and drove away, tires screeching, headed north. She thought he'd cool down, turn left, drive counter-clockwise around the block and catch up with her on 23rd Street, but he didn't. She crossed the street again and on the south side caught a bus bound for downtown. She seemed to recall something very familiar, from Carmen's break-up, in his words. After the curve at narrow Rayo Street, she got off on Galiano and San Rafael, in front of Flogar's. Along the way the tears had stopped. She narrowly missed bumping into a telephone booth and crossed San Rafael Street — the intersection which had gained the hyperbolic nickname "the corner of sin" for no reason other than because the men stood on the portico to watch the girls go by and call out compliments to them — toward Woolworth's ten-cent store, closed at this hour, and passed the elegant Casa Quintana jewelers with the lamps in its high window. From the portico of the "Bazar Inglés" with the fabrics displayed in its window, she crossed San Miguel Street, after looking toward La Opera to the north, and Galiano, after looking toward El Encanto store to the east — already gone from the sidewalk was the chestnut vendor — to the portico of El Encanto cafe — of the "old rakes". — She passed Los Reyes Magos toy store, El Louvre ladies' store and La Isla men's shop. She went down the steep steps from the portico of El Llavín hardware store, devoid at this hour of its usual ambulant vendor with his case of rings and costume jewelry, to the narrow sloping sidewalk, she crossed Neptuno Street, and found herself sitting at the counter of América cafeteria. She tried to organize her thoughts. She ordered a soda and didn't drink it, she played with the paper napkin. They'd make up the next evening. This couldn't be different from any other fight, Ana told herself. She left before the night-show crowds from the América and Radio Cine theaters came out. On Galiano and Neptuno, in front of the coffee stand, she took another bus back home.

She arrived at 11:35. Her aunt Cristina was visiting, and Ana greeted her briefly, but she couldn't stop to talk. She went straight to her room and turned Dany's picture face down on her wardrobe because she knew well she couldn't bear to look at it later. She left her door ajar and lay on her bed face down. She felt a pressure on her chest, and had a sensation in the pit of her stomach that at times seemed to be a void pulling in from its center and at others a lump pushing out all around it, and she couldn't cry, not then. The wind slammed the door shut.

The next day Ana went to the Bank of Nova Scotia on L Street in her lunch hour, withdrew from their savings account the amount she figured Dany had contributed, $1,060., and left in it what she herself had contributed, $470., plus the interest earned, $68. She bought a postal money order at the main post office on Independencia and mailed it to him with a note asking him to bring her photographs and the letters and postcards she'd written him from Miami, and pick up his graduation ring. It was childish. She was spurred by pride, not once really believing that it was all over between them. But he had, after all, yelled at her that it was the last time he'd see her. He'd probably come tonight after class, even before he received the money order, with the excuse of bringing her photographs to her. He'd meet her and they'd make up. When they saw each other tonight, everything would be all right again. The certainty sustained her. The money order didn't mean anything. He'd never even cash it. They would deposit it again.

She came down with a cold that day, which she blamed on the recent dusty Lent wind, but a psychologist would probably have termed it as psychosomatic. But Dany *didn't* come after classes.

The warehouse of Julio Lobo's "Hershey" Sugar Mill, in Santa Cruz del Norte, was set afire. Ana remembered Alejandro's intention to take her there. Four men were shot by the firing squad.

By Friday, Ana's cold had gotten so much worse that, even though she knew absenteeism was being punished, she just couldn't force herself to make the effort to go to work. Dany called her in his lunch hour.

"I can't bring myself to see you again just yet. There'll be a scene. I have to take a gun to Sonia's boyfriend. I'll see you Monday afternoon after work."

She felt let down. That he'd choose not to see her for four days hadn't occurred to her. She hadn't imagined that he'd take this as final. He didn't ask her why she was home; he didn't even mention whether he'd called her at work. Ana mumbled indistinctly, "I sent you a money order yesterday... for... the..." She didn't finish. She expected him to say it hadn't been necessary. He didn't. He just said good-by.

She cried then. She lay in bed and cried constantly, without provocation. Nobody asked her what was wrong. The telephone lay silent. Only three days before, they'd been planning their wedding and their honeymoon. How could he discard their plans, throw away their future together? Her father was so concerned about her state, he moved the television set into her bedroom, and Ana stared fixedly at it through her tears for a day and a half. The window of the apartment in the next building was closed. She prayed the rosary often, not asking for anything, just taking refuge in prayer. Some women prayed to Saint Anthony for their man. Maybe she would do that, pray, perhaps, soon, when she could bear the strain. The canary was singing in the next building.

Saturday Ana heard the mailman's whistle blow outside their door. Her mother brought her a letter from Gloria Serrano in Arroyo Arenas. She wrote that she'd been transferred to the department where Dany worked. Great.

She asked her father to move the television set back to the living room. She was depriving them of their shows and not enjoying any herself.

When she came out of her room late Sunday morning, the girl's voice in English with the fake heavy French accent was calling out, "Cigars, cigarettes!" They were showing the same old movie on television again. She came into the living room as a man came out of a door to a hallway and grabbed the girl who was carrying a cigarette tray, by the arm. Ana had this vague idea that the picture, American with subtitles, dating back to the forties, was about a girl who followed her boyfriend on a reporting assignment. Channel 12 had been running it every Sunday for weeks now, or months, but she'd never sat through the whole movie. She now switched to the "Silent Comedy", with its narrator's peculiar vocal version of horse galloping sound effect, and sank into a love seat, her eyes swollen.

Her first time out after the cold, Monday morning, Ana threw a sweater over her shoulders and moved slowly down the street. It was windy, and when she stepped down from the bus, she felt so weak, it was hard for her to walk against the wind that blew in the Plaza. Her second-year final exams were starting that evening and she'd have to make it.

Dany was waiting for her after work to take her home. They drove up G Street in silence, Ana with a lump in her throat, he gripping the wheel with both hands. He parked on I Street near 19th.

"I feel empty", he said.

"Empty?" She looked at him, anguish in her eyes.

"I don't have any feeling." She wanted to cry, plead, beg. She sneezed. "May Jesus guard you."

"Thank you."

"The Old Lady is sick", he said then.

"What?"

"Her gall bladder."

Ana couldn't remember later what else had been said.

"I'll come to your house tonight", he finally said, "to bring you the photographs."

Ana got out of the car and walked home, depleted. When she went into the apartment, her mother was waiting for her at the dining table to talk to her, her face moist with orange blossom water to tighten her pores. "Look, Ana María", she started as soon as she sat down, "Dany's a good boy, but he's too young. He doesn't have any firm ideas. You know you've gotten him to do what you want often all this time. But, just as easily as you can sway him, so is he susceptible to others." She could see it was difficult for her mother to say this. "His father doesn't like you much. Maybe because you're a little older than he, possibly because he hasn't met you or us, perhaps because we're Catholics, or only because Dany hasn't finished his career. And he's probably been chipping away all this time. And a drop of water can bore through marble." Ana patiently listened in silence. "From what I've seen in these last three months, I think he's acting... strange. Besides, that adherence of his to the government is much too unconditional."

Ana raised her eyebrows, rolling up her eyes, and puffed her cheeks. She didn't want anybody to tell her this. Her mother was only partly right. She didn't know the direct cause of their fight, Nelia, the identification card, the movement, the bulletin; but one indirect factor *was* indeed his father's steady undermining. But she didn't want to hear this. She felt more confident. He was coming tonight and they'd make up. If not, why hadn't he just brought her photographs this afternoon?

She got up, went into her room, ashamed of her display of disrespect, and showered. After dinner, she put on her rust color dress with the high neckline and round collar which flattered her figure so much, combed her shiny light brown hair carefully, dabbed "Sentiment" perfume – undiluted now in the evening – and, when Dany arrived, intentionally had her single strand of pearls in her hand. His photographs and a letter he had once written her on a paper napkin at the "Flamingo" were tied together with cord, and she had taken his graduation ring off. She intended to keep his framed photograph, which remained face down on her wardrobe.

She received him casually, with an impersonal smile. Her parents were in their room. He sat on the edge of the chair, her photographs and letters in an envelope on his knee. He hadn't brought her framed enlargement either. Ana brought out his photographs and the ring, laid them on the center coffee table and remained standing. She fumbled with the clasp of her strand of pearls and, as she had expected he'd do, Dany got up to help her with it. She turned and raised her hair away from the nape of her neck. Her skin tingled with the anticipation of his touch. When he touched her, he'd long to kiss her and he'd turn her to him. Her flesh throbbed with the yearning to be in his arms. He clasped the necklace and the feeling of his fingertips brushing her neck sent a shudder down her spine. His hands lingered for an instant and she craved to turn around and nestle in his arms. But he took his hands away and the precious moment was gone. She let her hair fall back on her neck and slowly turned to face him, still hoping.

"Thank you."

There was a longing look in his dark brown eyes. Or did she just imagine it? Ana took the pack of photographs and the ring from the table, handed them to him and remained standing.

"Are you going out?", he asked.

"Yes, my final exams start tonight."

"Do you want me to drop you off?"

"No, thank you. I'm going to walk."

"Are you leaving now?"

"Yes, it's twenty to eight." She couldn't bear to stay behind when he left.

They walked down the stairs together, without talking. It took all the will power she could muster to keep her composure. When they reached the sidewalk, he insisted, "Don't you want me to leave you there? It's eleven blocks."

"No, thank you. I want to walk."

She started up the street before he started the car. She saw him drive by out of the corner of her eye, but didn't look. She didn't want him to wave at her. He hadn't wished her good luck.

She waded through the exam somehow, as if in a daze. Ernesto asked her to study with him the next evening, and she wasn't aware she had agreed until he asked her, "Do you think the lobby of the Hotel Nacional would be all right?"

By April 10, El Salvador and Honduras had broken relations with Cuba, adding up to fifteen countries.

At work the next day, Ana's eyes misted over the page she was typing, and she remembered Carmen when Miguel had broken up with her. Raquel then had been annoyed at her tears. Would somebody here notice hers?

Her aunt Cristina came to get her in the afternoon to go to the Club Estabias with her. Sitting on the rocking chairs in the clubhouse, Ana told her that Dany had broken up with her, and she was touched to hear her aunt and godmother try to instill hope in her. "You'll make up. Marcos and I used to have fights before we got married. But Mamá — your grandmother — gave me some advice: 'Never say good night mad. Always make up before the day is over.' If you let the disagreement nourish overnight, by the next day it'll have grown and it'll be that much more difficult to overcome."

Everybody was trying so hard to console her! They all meant well, but advised her wrong. Nobody knew the truth. Nobody knew she'd been his, or that he was so deeply indoctrinated, or that she was involved with the counter-revolution. But it felt so good to have them care about her!

"I didn't want to let it go on this long, Aunt. I wanted to see him, make up, the very next day. But he chose to let four days go by before he saw me and, when he came, he was so distant..."

"Probably so were you, Ana María." Her godmother had cut paper dolls out for her when Ana was little.

"What could I do?"

"It'll pass. He's a good boy. You'll make up."

They stared over the few bathers on the shore at the cobalt blue water. The sun was tinting the clouds pink as it slid behind the horizon. Who would marry her now? She was, after all, in the same pre-

The Education Campaign

dicament as Olga. Cristina later told Teresa that men looked at Ana on the street, and she walked looking down and didn't notice.

She and Ernesto walked up the sweeping palm-lined driveway through the lush gardens of the Nacional, and tried to study in the main lobby, with its tiled border and its Moorish high ceilings overhead. Ernesto mentioned something about wanting to leave the country. Fidel's voice blared from the amplifiers. People milled about. It was difficult to study.

"Let's go to the pool of the Habana Hilton", Ernesto suggested.

"What for?"

"To study there."

They lugged their books the four blocks to the Habana Libre, across the lobby with its bubble top dome, up its wide spiral staircase, past the bar, and they settled at a table by the pool. A few alphabetizers — several boys and a couple of girls — were diving into the pool, seed or conch shell necklaces around their necks, yelling, splashing each other. The water was murky. The wind blew their papers off the table. It was impossible to study. They watched the alphabetizers rough each other up. Ernesto again said something about leaving for the States; he mentioned a co-worker, an Adelaida. Ana wasn't paying attention.

She looked up from her book and into his eyes, he patted the back of her hand compassionately over the table, nodding understandingly.

"I want to die", she blurted.

CHAPTER 9

THE FREEDOM FIGHTERS

> *"Despierta, ¡oh,Cuba! Tras tormenta fiera*
> *asoma el sol radiante.*
> *¡Esperanza y valor! Oprobio fuera*
> *no llevar por divisa en tu bandera,*
> *¡Adelante!, ¡adelante!*[9]
> *("¡Adelante!",*
> José Agustín Quintero*)*

The atmosphere changed. Tension mounted.

Ana got a passing grade on her first exam and, after the second subject on Wednesday, had Thursday off to study for her third exam. She studied with Ernesto again in the evening, but this time they went to the José Martí National Library at the Plaza Cívica and enjoyed the cool quiet of the imposing building.

The Club Marino Estabias was intervened on Friday. Castro's secretary, Dr. Juan Orta, took asylum in an embassy. Two men were sentenced to thirty-year terms, and two were shot in La Cabaña Fortress.

In the evening, fire was set to Cuba's largest department store, the five-story "El Encanto". The fire started at 7:00, and three quarters of an hour later the highest wall tumbled to the street. The luxurious, elegant store on Galiano Street, loved and admired, burned down to its foundation — Ana had a frivolous thought for the spinning wheel planter in the gift department. — The losses exceeded $6,000,000. A militia woman died in the fire. That marked the start of a period of fright. Fires had been set before and "La Epoca", almost across the street, had been practically burned down three and a half months before, and many bombs had exploded throughout the country, but

---

[9] Awake, oh, Cuba! After a fierce storm
the radiant sun appears.
Hope and bravery! It would be an infamy
not to have, Forward!, forward!
on your flag as a motto.

The Freedom Fighters

the people sensed this somehow signaled the beginning of a more violent phase.

"La Comercial" and "El Ancla" stores in Santiago de Cuba burned, with total loss of their stock.

Ana's third exam was held that evening, nonetheless. She had maintained an 86 percent grade average, but publicity no longer served any practical purpose, there were no products, services or private enterprises any longer which advertised, publicity wasn't needed any more, and she feared the school might be closed at any moment.

Saturday at daybreak, her parents' voices woke Ana up. "Is that thundering?", she heard through her drowsiness her mother ask her father in a frightened voice.

"It's not thundering", she mumbled to herself into her pillow, still half asleep, and then she realized *what* it was and sat bolt upright on her bed. It was an air raid! She heard the explosions and the answering anti-aircraft fire. She threw a housecoat on and went out to the living room. Her parents were standing at the half-open dining room door to the balcony, looking at the sky toward the south-west, where an intermittent brightness, like lightning, could be seen.

"What is it?", she asked them, afraid of the answer.

"I don't know. It seems like bombing", her father confirmed. On hearing the admission, Teresa's hand went up to her husband's back and Méndez put his arm around her shoulders.

Ana went into her room and turned the bedside radio on. There was no news yet about what was happening. Her wristwatch said 6:00. She sat on the edge of her bed, while the distant noise continued. It seemed to be in Marianao. She was frightened. Was it getting closer?, maybe into Havana? Gustavo called, wanting to know how they were. He didn't know what was going on either. Teresa called Cristina in Kohly and Marcos could only tell her, "It's further west."

The anti-aircraft gun noise lasted about 45 minutes. Her uncle Guillermo called later from Lawton and Carlos then called Esperanza. Nobody knew what was happening.

Later in the day the radio said three planes had attacked the Camp Libertad headquarters, hitting a munitions dump and crates of ammunition had exploded, causing a great fire. Dany lived close to the airfield and Ana wondered how he was. Twice she lifted the receiver to call him and again put it down. If pride would only let her call him! She thought of his father answering the phone and desisted.

One of the attacking planes had been hit by the answering shots. Two other air bases were attacked that day, the San Antonio de los Baños main airfield by three planes, where five planes on the ground were destroyed, and the Antonio Maceo military airfield in Santiago de Cuba by two planes, where five more planes were destroyed. Castro termed the attack an act of cowardice and said that every Cuban must take his post at his center of work.

In the afternoon the phone rang. Aurora, Cuéllar's secretary, told Ana in an unusually brisk way, "In case of an attack, all the personnel will be expected to report to the Ministry." Ana was surprised that she had her phone number. She had not given it in the department. Aurora would have had to go to her employment application in the personnel department to get it. She regretted having answered. But the rest of the day and Sunday passed uneventfully.

☼

Monday morning, when Ana walked into the office, Mestre, the head of the section, had the radio on in his office and Betancourt, the director of the division, was standing in the small office, filling it, his back to the open door. Some of the clerks were gathered around it, Morejón and Valdés among them. Ana couldn't hear the radio. She didn't know what was happening, but she hoped it weren't as bad as she feared.

Betancourt suddenly raised one arm in the air, "Fatherland or death!", he shouted in his thunderous voice, the nape of his neck scarlet, and he stomped dramatically out of Mestre's office through the section, to his own spacious office across the hallway from Cuéllar's.

A few sycophants fawningly chorused, as "amen" to a prayer, "We shall win!" It seemed like a battle cry and it raised goose pimples on Ana's arms.

The murmur grew louder as the knot by the door dispersed, and the broadcast from Mestre's radio reached her. Disembarkings had taken place at several points on the island and the rebel army and the militia were fighting the invaders back. A tiny seed of hope sprouted to life inside her. Maybe.

She sat down and looked furtively, first at Yolanda, who seemed absorbed in typing by Mestre's door, and then at Duarte by the window, who looked away and busied himself with papers. Without looking straight at her, Ana could see Sara standing by her desk facing

Mestre's office, a sheet of paper hanging limply from her hand. Abreu was standing behind his desk. When Morejón and Valdés walked away from Mestre's office, they went to join him. Aurora was with Cuéllar in his office.

As Ana, sitting at her desk, started to uncover her typewriter pretending a calm confidence in the revolution, a girl and a tall man wearing militia uniforms entered the department and stopped just inside the door. The man talked to the girl in a low voice, he pointed out something on a sheet of paper in his hand with his index and to the other section with his thumb. He went with the paper into Cuéllar's office, to one side of Mestre's, and the woman came into their section, passed Aurora's desk and looked over the others.

"Ana Méndez!", she called and her voice sounded loud in the silence that had followed their entrance.

Ana felt a violent jump in her stomach. She got up, her eyes widening involuntarily. She heard a faint gasp behind her. The militia woman passed Yolanda's desk, but didn't quite reach Ana's by the window. She was wearing the olive green blouse and flared black skirt of the militia; her hair was frizzy. Ana tried to smile, but the girl didn't return the smile.

"Ana?", she asked from a distance and, at her answering nod, she said with an air of importance, "Come with us."

Ana took her handbag from the drawer. Cuéllar emerged from his office, slip in hand, looked fleetingly her way and went with the militia man toward the other section of the department on the other side of his office. Mestre hadn't left his small office.

Ana followed the militia girl to the door of the department, feeling all eyes on her. With the tall militia man came two men, one of them Chinese, no expression on their faces. The five walked out into the hallway leaving a hushed murmur behind. A bearded militia man joined them with a typist who wore strange eyeglasses that made her look cross-eyed and an exceptionally handsome boy Ana had first noticed a couple of months before, from another department. The bearded militia man led them to the elevator and the tall one followed them down the hall, while the militia girl walked alongside. They rode down in silence and, on the main floor, the bearded militia man again walked ahead of them and stood at the door, as the five arrested employees filed out of the building, the militia woman unnecessarily propelling the two girls on with a little shove on their shoulder, and the tall man following them. They were herded to the driveway by the side of the building leading to the parking area. It was dim. There were over a dozen employees from all over the Ministry, mostly men, sitting on stools and standing around. At first glance, Ana saw a thin woman from another division whom she didn't know by name and two men she knew only from sight. The woman looked her in the eyes, but they didn't talk. They all stood quietly. Only the militia talked.

After what seemed like ages, but must have actually been only about half an hour, a station wagon pulled into the driveway. Several men's loud voices rose at the same time, giving instructions. Ana was shoved into the station wagon with five other women by the militia girl with frizzy hair. She sat by the window. A gray-haired woman, next to her, nervously chipped the polish off her nails. The typist with the strange glasses, sitting in front, stared silently ahead. To the other side of the gray-haired woman sat the thin woman. In the back were a mulatto girl and an older woman. They didn't talk. The militia girl got in the front seat, pushing the typist, and the tall militia man in the back seat. With the bearded driver, they were nine. A truck pulled up behind them, a cry of "Fatherland or death!" went up, answered by a chorus of "We shall win!" and, as the men were being shoved aboard the truck, the station wagon drove off.

They passed Hidalgo and Ensanche del Vedado; the wagon took them along Calzada del Cerro before the Luminous Fountain, down Calzada de Puentes Grandes in Aldecoa, 44th Street in La Ceiba and 51st Avenue in Alturas del Bosque to the Railroad Line and, from that point on, Ana didn't recognize the way. She had a void in her stomach.

It had to be a mistake. She hadn't been doing anything for twenty days. And who knew of it? Duarte, Alejandro, El Tico. Who could have possibly denounced her? El Tico wasn't Cuban. Valdés? He hadn't even seen her do anything. Olga? Because `e didn't applaud Fidel on the newsreels? Yolanda? But she didn't know anything other than that she didn't like the government. Ernesto? She hadn't confided anything to him. Nelia? For the drivers' licenses and the Ministry of the Interior identification card! But she had committed a worse offense. Dany? No!, Dany wouldn't do it. Duarte had warned her. But Dany didn't know what she did. Dany couldn't do that. It had to be a mistake.

The wagon sped for over half an hour along the streets of Marianao and stopped at a large gravel lot where several vehicles were parked, by a bare, new, low structure with the smell of fresh plaster about it. As they got off the station wagon, their shoes raising a little dust from the gravel, the militia girl pushed them ahead by a side door into the building and the tall militia man followed them. Where were they? Was it a police station?, an army garrison?, some agency of Camp Libertad?

There was a large office, sparsely furnished with three wooden desks painted a Public Works Ministry gray and a few steel cabinets, where several militia men and a couple of civilians moved around in confusion. A civilian tried to call the attention of a militiaman by pulling at his shirt sleeve. A fat, young mulatto militia woman, rings of perspiration under her arms, stood before one of the desks with fingerprint cards scattered on it, looking somewhat confused. Black ink pad and ink-soaked roller sat on a table at her back. A man waited in the chair by the side of each desk. A photograph of Fidel dominated a wall. The tall militia man rushed ahead across the room and opened a door on the far side.

Three women waited in the smaller room, a woman in a nurse's uniform, a pretty girl wringing a hand-kerchief and a fat girl with a bored expression. There was one empty chair. To one side was a closed door with a scrawny militiaman leaning against the wall next to it and before the opposite wall, a bare gray table. The gray-haired woman with the chipped nail polish headed for the empty chair, but the militia girl stopped her, "Against the wall", and she pointed to one side.

The six stood with their backs to the wall and the girl's voice again rose, "Face the wall and raise your hands." She came behind them now and felt their clothes.

Ana was the first one on the line and, after she'd been searched, she dropped her hands. The militia woman touched her elbow. "Keep your hands up."

Ana raised her arms again and placed the palms of her hands flat against the wall. They had been standing for about a quarter of an hour when the older woman who had ridden in the back seat of the wagon leaned forward on her forearms. The militia girl quickly slid her hand between the woman's forearms and the wall without saying a word, and the older woman momentarily lost her balance, fell forward against the wall and instantly stood back, while the other five women looked on sideways.

They stood in that position for about an hour and a quarter. The

muscles in Ana's upper arms hurt and her elbows felt heavy. Her hands were numb from lack of circulation and the pain was starting to shoot up her neck. The door to one side opened several times and the voices in the outer office multiplied and grew louder each time. Then a man in civilian clothes with glasses who had been sitting at one of the desks in the front office walked in with the tall militia man who had come with them. Ana felt the inside of her stomach twist. He stood behind the gray table, placed a couple of sheets of paper on it and, while the militia man looked over his shoulder, he called, "Dulce Ramírez, Concepción Gómez, Dolores Sánchez and Caridad Vásquez." He paused, not looking up. The pretty girl with the handkerchief stood up and the gray-haired woman, the thin woman and the mulatto girl who had come in the back seat turned around from the wall, fear in their faces. The tall militia man motioned them toward the door to the side which had remained closed, and the scrawny militia man who'd been leaning against the wall opened it now. The tall man led them into the inner room and, as they disappeared into it, closed the door behind them.
"Mercedes Suárez", the civilian went on. The older woman turned. "Ana Menéndez... Menén... Méndez", the man looked up from the list for the first time, hesitated a moment, scribbled something on it with a red pencil and then ended, "and Regla Jiménez." The fat girl got up nonchalantly and he nodded toward the outer office. The militia woman opened the door for them and followed them out. Two women were left behind, the typist with eyeglasses from Ana's division, still standing by the wall and the nurse, sitting on the edge of her chair and, as Ana walked out, she heard the man's voice behind her, "You two stay here until we contact your place of work. You sit down." His footsteps receded further into the room, as the militia girl closed the door behind them.
The outer room was now crowded and the noise was bewildering. Ana elbowed her way between the sweaty backs of several militia men. The older woman, Mercedes, was already sitting by a desk, occupied by a militia girl with her hair in a thick long braid, a typewriter sitting on it, too high to type comfortably. Ana heard the militia girl ask her for identification. The girl with frizzy hair who had brought them placed a piece of paper on the desk.
When the older woman got up after a time, the militia girl behind the desk shook her braid back and nodded to Ana to come close. Ana bumped into Mercedes, leaving, and, as she got near the desk,

she noticed something scribbled in red next to her name.

"Are you Méndez or Menéndez?", the girl asked her.

"Méndez." Ana pulled her Ministry identification card out without being asked and held it to the militia woman, who looked at the photograph on the card and up at her face verifying the likeness. "Do you live on Unión y Ahorro?"

"No", Ana replied, puzzled — She hadn't even known there was such a street. — A man bumped against her chair.

"In El Cerro?" The girl signaled to somebody.

"No, in Vedado."

The civilian who had read their names emerged from the crowd, approached the desk and placed a hand on the back of the militia girl's chair. "Did you ever live there, comrade?"

"I've been living at the same address for five years now."

A militiaman smoking a cigar pushed the door open. A truck full of men had arrived on the lot. The man with glasses straightened up and yelled, "No more!"

"What do we do with them?", the militiaman asked.

"Take them to the Blanquita."

"The Blanquita's full."

"Full?", he echoed, surprised. "Well, no more here."

"Comrade", the one with the cigar started to insist.

"There's no room", the civilian held firmly.

The militiaman slammed the door behind him. The man with glasses again leaned over the militia girl's shoulder, who prodded further, "Do you have a brother named Armando who was in the army and is now in Miami?"

"No", Ana answered. She didn't know about what they were talking. The militia girl looked questioningly at the man and he shrugged.

"Then there's a mix-up." She handed the card back to Ana. "We want... are looking for an Ana Menéndez. When they asked for her in Personnel in your place of work, they were referred to you."

"Ah!" Ana tried to breathe deeply, but her breath came out like a jagged sigh in little gasps instead, and she ventured, "Then may I go?"

"Yes", the man answered, and added in a defensive tone, "You realize how careful we have to be now, comrade."

"Yes, of course, I know", Ana agreed readily. She turned her back and rushed out of the crowded office, while Regla's, the fat girl's eyes followed her with boredom. Outside, the sunlight made her blink. She breathed with relief. The truck was still in the parking lot. She stopped and hesitated. Could she just walk away? She looked at her wristwatch. Only a quarter to twelve. It had seemed to her she had been there four hours. Out of the corner of her eye she noticed a movement in the parking lot. A man had jumped from the truck and tried to run away. A militiaman pounced on him and they struggled. Ana rushed away from the place.

She walked three blocks to a wide street. She didn't know the neighborhood. She looked up at the numbers of the streets at the intersection. A man in a barber's white smock was approaching, scissors and comb sticking out of his pocket, a newspaper in his hand. She had to ask him, "Excuse me, how can I get to Vedado from here?"

"Take the I-two", he answered her shortening his step slightly, then looked back over his shoulder and added, "that way", pointing east.

She crossed the street to the south side. After considering for a moment, she realized she must be fairly close to Dany's house. There were a couple of eggfruit seeds on the sidewalk. She waited for the bus and, when she got on board, she sat by a window in a rear seat on the right side and looked at the street numbers rushing by. She didn't know whether the bus passed in front of Dany's house. She imagined it would be a bare, tasteless, modern, square concrete house with a low, flat roof and large aluminum windows, the hardware store next to it not more than a box with a wide door, perhaps rolling, of corrugated iron.

Soon, when she figured by the house numbers that she must be near, she held her breath. There were several similar houses that looked about eight or nine years old, nothing like what she had imagined, with low brick walls and small iron gates, narrow gardens in front, little porches and a rough concrete texture. She saw a young man open a gate and walk into the garden of one of them. He looked like Dany. But she couldn't be sure. There was no hardware store. But Dany would be working. At the Corporation of Transport, in Vedado, far from here. And near her home. The boy reached the porch. And the bus sped away. When she could no longer see the man or the house, she remembered she hadn't had lunch yet. She got off near her home.

Her mother wasn't home. There was a cold tuna-and-noodle salad

The Freedom Fighters

in the refrigerator, but she wasn't hungry. She collapsed in the chair and closed her eyes. She felt warm. The phone rang. − It'd probably be Ernesto to comment on the events. − She didn't answer it. She got up, opened the balcony instead, stood with her hands on the doors and breathed deeply. Just before 1:00, she took the bus to work, got off and stood across the street to wait for Duarte. In a few minutes she saw him get off the bus, she waited for him to reach her and fell in step beside him to cross the street. Ana saw him smile relieved.

"I just came out", she told him.
"It was soon. You were lucky."
"It turned out it wasn't me for whom they were looking after all. They gave them the wrong name."
She had to strain to hear what he mumbled. "Their inefficiency is our advantage. Where did they take you?"
"To a place in Marianao."
"It must have been the Police identification bureau."
"I don't know... What happened, Duarte?"
"All we know is there's been an invasion, but we don't know yet where, or its scope."
"They kept a typist of the division who wears strange glasses."
"One who looks cross-eyed?"
"Uh-huh. And I didn't see the three men again."

Barricades were again being built with sacks of sand in front of the entrance to their building and all important ones. Wooden planks were placed on the streets to force vehicles to slow down.

When they walked into the section, Yolanda was already at her desk and looked at her, but didn't talk, and Ana didn't stop. There was a hushed rustle at the back of the office as she sat at her desk.

Radio broadcasts announced that the landing had taken place at Cochinos Bay on the southern coast of the island. Cienfuegos, on the bay in Las Villas, had been bombed.

At the Ministry an order was passed prohibiting the employees from leaving the immediate area of the building when going out to lunch, and then they would have to secure passes even to leave the very premises. Employees enrolled in the militia who had not yet been mobilized were requested to stay in the building evenings, and civilians − women as well as men − were exhorted to take turns in keeping post at their offices overnight.

Betancourt, the director, called the employees of the division out to the hallway and in his thunderous voice told them in no uncertain terms, "Anyone being absent from work for *any* reason whatsoever will be considered a counter-revolutionary, treated as one, and as such made to feel the full force of the law."

Militia searched many houses in the better neighborhoods. Valdés was among those who conducted the searches. Morejón volunteered to help. Many people were arrested for having in their homes what was deemed as "subversive propaganda". Suspected employees were taken away from their jobs and sent to jail. Auxiliary Bishop of Havana Eduardo Boza Masvidal was arrested at the Church of Our Lady of Charity.

Wild newscasts were transmitted by radio and television throughout the day. When she got home that afternoon, Ana found her father there in a sports shirt. "How did it go?", he asked her. "I wanted to call you, but was afraid it might look bad on a day like this."

"It was all right. I was afraid, like most." Her mother came out to listen. She didn't tell them she had been arrested. They'd worry. Would Cuéllar tell Gustavo? "Will the invasion stand a chance?", she asked hopefully.

"It might. Many people are going to join the invaders and turn against the army."

"May God permit it!", Teresa expressed.

"It might be bigger than the government is letting on", said Ana wishfully.

"They might also be exaggerating. Don't get your hopes up", cautioned Méndez. "Ah!, I saw the comedian who plays *'the tobacco planter from Remates'* on television keeping post at the entrance to Channel Two Telemundo..." He paused and then said, "I started to dismantle the office today. I gave the machines to Gálvez, the insurance agent next door, I brought the books home, I'm going to give the fan and the lamp to Gustavo and the office supplies to Velázquez, and I'm going to have to close the door on the furniture."

In a eulogy speech in the Colón Cemetery at the burial of the seven casualties of Saturday's air raid, Castro yelled, "Hail our socialist revolution!" It was the first time he had used the term in public and it made headlines.

Nine men were shot against the execution wall in La Cabaña Fortress on Tuesday morning. Several priests were imprisoned, accused of helping the conspiracy, nine in Manzanillo alone. Churches were watched.

The Freedom Fighters

One of the men in the division who had been arrested the day before, a tall man in his late forties, with a straight, deliberate carriage, walked into the section to the water cooler.

"What happened?", Morejón asked him.

"Oh!, it was just an error", he said drinking water. "I'm clear." He tossed the empty paper cup into the basket and strode out of the office. He seemed to have come in only to show them that he was free.

At lunch time they were issued passes to leave the building and they had to go out in pairs. Ana went with Yolanda to the restaurant on 20 de Mayo and a militiaman with a mustache from the division accompanied them.

The air conditioning didn't seem to be working and the door was propped open. When they walked into the restaurant, Ana saw her father. He came near, but the militiaman intercepted him, "You may not talk to her, comrade."

"I'm her father."

"You still may not talk to her."

Méndez stepped aside frustrated and looked at her from a distance, perplexed, while they had lunch. They waved at each other as Ana went back to work with Yolanda and the militiaman.

In the elevator, Valdés commented lightly, "We can take anything. We'll get so used to it, you'll see they'll be dropping bombs and we'll be working."

The *"Internationale"* was broadcast. In the afternoon the employees in the division were instructed to stay after work for an indoctrination lecture by Betancourt with obvious brain-washing purposes. Ana's exam that evening had been postponed until Thursday due to the state of alarm. She called home to say she'd be late.

Betancourt started his involved dissertation about dialectics, materialism, Marx and Engels, with the help of a blackboard and a pointer. He punctuated his talk several times with "I want to plant a restlessness in you."

Then they heard the gunfire. The employees were instructed to move away from the windows and led into the inner halls, and the lights were turned off. There were no underground raid shelters in the country, as war had always seemed something remote and foreign, European. They were ordered to remain there in the dark until the alarm was over. Ana was surprised, and glad, that they didn't make them stay. The elevator having stopped running with the blackout, Abreu walked with her down the stairs. Going down, lighting their way with matches, a few joked, "He did plant a restlessness all right."

When they came out on the street, all the lampposts were out and the streets were dark. "I'll walk you to your bus stop", Abreu offered. They made no comment about the attack as they walked to the stop, where Ana thanked him. He lived in San Miguel del Padrón, some seven and a half miles east and the trip on route 12 bus would take him over half an hour. It was soon learned that a plane had tried to shoot at La Cabaña Fortress. The lecture was never resumed. When Ana got home, her mother was waiting for her with the apartment door open.

A honeymooning employee of the electric company and her bridegroom were murdered in their apartment by the militia.

Religious organizations closed, among them the Catholic Youth group to which Yolanda belonged. The Daughters of Mary congregation where Ana had been attending Sunday Mass was converted into a militia barracks.

Claribel, a militia woman in the department, pale, skinny, with a long nose and straight hair, who smelled of *"Pompeia"*, discoursed, "We'd been made to believe that Communism was a cussword to be whispered, but now we know what socialism is and it's good." − They still didn't say communism was good. − It sounded like a play on words.

Wednesday it was broadcast on television that nine planes had been shot down and one of them was piloted by an American, who was identified after death, from documents found in his clothes, as a resident of Boston. A Navy ship anchored at Isle of Pines had been bombed. Unconfirmed rumors spread that the island had been taken by the counter-revolution. They didn't know whether this was true. The bridges and some buildings were mined by the government.

The Confederation of Workers asked for solidarity from the laborers. Nine men were executed in Pinar del Río early in the morning. In Santa María del Rosario the militia arrested three priests, a sexton and the cook, accused of being counter-revolutionaries. Nine men and eight women were sentenced to thirty years in prison. Dr. Humberto Sorí Marín, former Minister of Agriculture, and five other men were sentenced to death by firing squad and executed in La Cabaña Fortress the next morning. Two men were executed in the province of Camagüey.

Thursday many invaders were captured. Newspapers bore the

headline, "INVASION ANNIHILATED". Ana didn't want to believe it. In the afternoon, Castro stated the invasion had been wiped out.

A man who had landed with the invasion was rescued about 330 yards from the coast of Cuba, holding on to a trunk of wood, nude and in a state of complete exhaustion.

That evening, Ana passed her last exam and she had finished her second year. And that was to be the last she would study in Cuba.

When she came out of the school, a car was approaching very slowly headed north. She guessed it might be Alejandro, but wasn't sure. It was a beige '57 Ford. She stopped on the sidewalk, but couldn't see the driver's face from where she stood, and didn't want to risk bending down to look, lest she be embarrassed if it weren't him. After an instant, the driver reached across the passenger's seat and opened the door for her.

"Get in? It *was* Alejandro. She got in, surprised and pleased. He was wearing a tan thin striped *guayabera*, smelled of "Yardley" lotion and looked very handsome. "Isn't anybody meeting you tonight?"

"No." It crossed her mind to answer him kidding, "Yes, you", but she was afraid he'd take it as forward. He started the car.

"Last exam?"

"Yes. How did you know?"

"I guessed. Do you think you passed it?" He turned east on 5th Street.

"I think so."

"Did I surprise you?" On H Street he turned south to follow curving Calzada.

"Yes", she answered demurely. "What are you studying?"

"*Was*. Commerce, in the big school on Ayestarán, but I left it in January, when they transferred me to the new small one on G, where the old Márquez Sterling Journalism school used to be." They passed the Chibás apartment building. "Reynaldo told me they detained you Monday."

"They only held me for a couple of hours. They had mistaken me for somebody else, an Ana Menéndez."

He parked in front of the ice cream truck in the clearing in the pine trees in the little park on 19th Street at the foot of the Hotel Nacional.

"What flavor do you want?"

"*Mamey sapote.*"

It was a beautiful clear evening. It was difficult to imagine that somewhere men were fighting and being killed or imprisoned. He walked to the truck and came back with two cups, coconut for himself. When he'd again settled behind the wheel, he asked her, "Were you afraid?"

"Yes. What's happening?"

"The underground in Havana is hardly aware. We knew nothing of the invasion."

"What have you heard?" She started to eat her ice cream.

He informed her. Monday at 2:00 in the morning the invasion had landed on Girón Beach and Larga Beach in the Cochinos Bay, in the Zapata Swamp, in Aguada de Pasajeros on the south coast of Las Villas province. The combatants had been transported in seven ships. Transport planes had dropped thirty paratroopers in San Blas, at La Horquita outside of Yaguaramas, in Jócuma and in Pálpite. The villages of Girón and San Blas in Aguada de Pasajeros were taken by the invaders. Manuel Francisco Artime Buesa was the commander in chief of Assault Brigade 2506; José Alfredo Pérez San Román was the military commander of the liberation army; Erneido Andrés Oliva González, a black man, was second in command. There were five principal transport ships, the flagship Blagar, the Houston and the *Río Escondido*, the Atlantic and the *Caribe*, which were merchant, and two escort vessels, the Barbara J and the Lake Charles. There were six battalions. A drive began toward the Jagüey Grande air strip in Matanzas province.

Castro learned of the landing at 3:15 in the morning. The steamship Houston, commanded by Luis Morse Delgado, was hit by a rocket from a T-33 jet in front of Larga Beach at 8:00, with the Fifth Infantry Battalion, medicines, food, oil and reserve ammunition aboard, it ran aground and about thirty men drowned. A C-54 plane dropped supplies on Larga Beach. Many militiamen defected. A militia regiment deserted. Over fifty men, including peasants, joined the freedom fighters. Five hundred sugar workers prepared to join the invaders. The steamship *Río Escondido*, commanded by Agustín Tirado Salvidegoitia, was sunk, burning, by a Sea Fury pursuit plane before 10:00, with all the communications equipment, medical supplies, food, fuel and stores of weapons aboard. The supply ship did not unload. The vessel Lake Charles did not arrive on time. U.S. B-54's dropped supplies on Girón Beach, but the wind blew these into the sea. Seven of the invaders' seventeen B-26 bombers were lost. Castro's air force consisted of seven planes: three British Sea Furies, two American T-33 pursuit jet planes and two B-26's. Fidel's 25 battalions were supported by Soviet T-34 tanks. More troops and plenty of artillery were being sent to the scene. By mid-morning the invasion was doomed. A C-46 plane landed before 6:00 with supplies and picked up a wounded man. Nineteen freedom paratroopers held up Castro's battalions for 24 hours in Yaguaramas and Central "Covadonga", and they had to rereat to San Blas. Fidel's troops attacked by the road from Soplillar and El Jiquí. The invasion force fought for 30 hours without rest or food. At 1:00 in the afternoon of Tuesday, San Román sent an appeal to Washington for air support. This morning before dawn three planes tried to ferry in fresh supplies. Ex-navy colonel Vicente León had been killed in the morning by the tanks.

The commander of the First Battalion of Paratroopers was Alejandro del Valle Martí, the one of the Second of Infantry was Hugo Sueiro Ríos and that of the Third Armored Battalion, Valentín Bacallao Fonte. The commander of the Fourth Heavy Gun Battalion was Roberto Pérez San Román, that of the Fifth Battalion of Infantry, Ricardo Montero Duque and the one of the Sixth of Infantry was Francisco Montiel Rivera. Manuel Villafaña Martínez was commander of the air force, Ramón Ferrer Mena was chief of staff and Rodolfo Díaz Hernández, commander of the tanks.

"Tanks?", Ana asked.

"Yes." Alejandro finished his ice cream. "The invasion was expertly planned, but poorly coordinated", he concluded. "We're busy, but I'm discouraged."

"Oh, by God!, don't tell me that", she reacted, and they were silent for a moment.

"Anita, I have something to do. I'll let you off at home. Where do you live?"

She gave him the address. They rode in silence. When he stopped in front of her building, she told him, as he reached across to open the door for her, "Let's have faith." She got out.

"Hope is the last thing to lose", he answered her, as he started off heading west.

✯

Television broadcasts showed lines of captured invaders filing through the thicket, in camouflage uniforms, with their hands over their heads.

The captured men were presented on television. Ana felt her last flame of hope quenched. The invasion *had* been annihilated. She felt desperation, anguish, desolation, more acute now that she recognized the reality of the situation. José Antonio, José Miró Cardona's son, and Jorge, former Vice-President Guillermo Alonso Pujol's, were taken prisoner. Ulises Carbó Yániz, journalist Sergio's son, and television actor Carlos Alberto Badías Díaz were captured. Forty-five prisoners were interviewed by the press on television in the Workers' Palace on Thursday. They had patches on the shoulders of their camouflage uniforms with a Latin cross. Several, in a state of exhaustion, said they had been deceived by the CIA and realized most of the people supported the regime.

"They've probably made them promises of leniency for statements favorable to the government", Méndez conjectured.

"You can see their statements are influenced", thought Teresa.

Fabio Freyre Aguilera, a cattleman from Holguín, sugar landholder Delio Núñez Mesa's son-in-law, and Felipe Rivero Díaz, editor José Ignacio's nephew, however, said that there was no democracy in Cuba and they were fighting for liberty. Carlos Manuel, Manuel Antonio de Varona's son, asked, "If there are so many people with you, why don't you hold elections?"

"I liked best how the cattlemen talked", said Ana.

Piarist Father Segundo de las Heras Cabo, who had gained the nickname "the parachuting priest", and Father Ismael Lugo, a Capuchin, were interrogated. Jesuit Father Tomás Macho Castillo was the third Spanish priest in the Brigade.

Three men considered genuine Batista war criminals, Ramón Calviño Insua, Rafael E. Soler Puig and Jorge King Yun, were put before the cameras to inflame the people.

Sara brought some documents to Ana's desk on Friday. "They arrested Bárbara", she told her under her breath, and Ana supposed she must be referring to her dyed blonde friend from another section.

Aurora passed a list with the names of all the employees in the department for the purpose of assigning post duty, and those who had any objection to keeping post were to write the reason beside their names. Ana was one of the few who dared write any, that she didn't know how to use a firearm and would prove a hindrance rather than help to them.

Aurora confided mysteriously to her that it was Claribel, the skinny militia woman in the department, who had turned Bárbara in.

Ana later heard that same long-nosed militia woman comment about the Chinese man from the other section who hadn't come back, "I knew he was a worm. Once a short while ago we were having lunch at the same table in that little restaurant and I said, 'Everybody who doesn't cooperate with the revolution should be shot' and he didn't answer anything." The woman seemed to be wound up today. "The last time I went into a church", she boasted, "was the day I got married." To Valdés' curious question, she answered that her husband had been away in Santa Clara for six months.

"How *'chusma'*[59]!", Abreu commented in a low voice. "She ran back to the *'solar'*."

"It's a matter as to 'turn out the light and go'," inserted the short former militia girl with the lisp.

Twenty-five Americans working for the Cuban government had organized the Committee for Friendship.

More than 150,000 people were arrested in Havana and about 275,000 throughout the island. They were no longer bothering to identify them. Five thousand prisoners were crowded into Hornedo's former Blanquita Theater — now "Chaplin" — on 1st Avenue in Miramar, where one person died of a myocardial infarct and a woman aborted. The Sports City stadium on Rancho Boyeros Avenue in Palatino held over 6,000 prisoners. The Matanzas baseball stadium, schools and churches were used as prisons. Several hundred men were thrown into the moat around El Morro Castle, exposed to sun and rain. La Cabaña Fortress was overcrowded. Hundreds of priests were held prisoner there.

Political prisoners in the Isle of Pines reclusory were ordered to undress and kneel in the courtyard, and one prisoner was shot for praying. The circular buildings were mined with plastic explosive.

In Jatibonico, in Camagüey province, a priest was made to dig his grave and kneel in it.

Churches were searched, money and jewels were seized. In the St. Francis convent in Camagüey, militiamen smashed the altar searching for money and arms. Manuel Cardinal Arteaga Betancourt took asylum in an embassy. In the town of Soledad in Florida, Camagüey province, they dug up graves looking for gold. Hundreds of homes were looted.

[59] rabble, trash, low

After the first few scares, life went on as usual and things took on their normal pace, and people went on going to work and to school and, when there was no shooting, traffic went on and they walked on the streets − continuously conscious, or afraid, or plain scared, but they walked on just the same − and they slept − an exhausted sleep, and they woke up and sat up in bed with a start at the slightest noise, but nevertheless, they slept, − and they went on living, waiting, hoping.

Saturday Olga called Ana and asked her about the activities at the Ministry. Ana was always careful how she talked to her. She now made the mistake of telling her a list had been passed for post duty purposes.

"And what is your shift?", Olga immediately asked her.

"Well, I don't know how to use a firearm", she hesitated, regretting having touched the subject, "and I think I'd be a hindrance rather than help to them."

"What do you mean?", Olga demanded, indignant. "You can always help your country in some way", she almost yelled. She was furious. "Now is the time for us to sit up and see how we can be useful...", she went on without respite. It was more than Ana could take. Help the country by keeping it captive? Be useful to communism? With her depression at the failure of the invasion and her feeling of frustration, she was so angry she just hung up on her and went to sit by the dining table near the balcony. After a few minutes the phone rang again − she had to answer, − and Olga asked her surprised, "What happened?"

"Oh!, we must have been disconnected", Ana answered impassively. "I tried to call you back", she lied, "but your line was busy."

"I went on talking. I didn't know we had been disconnected." Unbelievable.

Ana quickly changed the subject, "Are we getting together tomorrow?" It was a lucky thing Olga was rather stupid.

The steamship *"El Luisse"* rescued six brigade members who had fled Girón Beach on a small rubber raft, and it took them to Texas.

Three men were shot in the garrison of the Juan Rius Rivera Regiment in Pinar del Río on Saturday. On Monday two others were executed in the city of Matanzas. No priest was killed, though. Most were released, including Auxiliary Bishop Eduardo Boza Masvidal.

Monday, in the mid-morning break, at a little table against the rear wall of the restaurant and in hushed tones, Duarte filled Ana in on

The Freedom Fighters

details.

A big recruiting drive had begun in January of 1960. The CIA had refused to allow Manuel Ray's MRP to take part in the attempt. The training and equipping of Cuban refugees had started on March 17, 1960. It had been learned that exiles were being trained in Guatemala for an invasion and two "Times" correspondents wrote about it. The CIA chose Manuel Artime as commander-in-chief. Puerto Cabezas, in Zelaya, on the Mosquitos coast, in Nicaragua, was the port of embarkation. They set off on April 14 by sea, seen off by Anastasio Somoza Debayle, brother of the Nicaraguan president. The invasion had been originally scheduled to take place in November of 1960. The CIA did not tell the head of the underground that the date of the invasion had been set. It never gave them word to carry out sabotage to power plants, highways and railroad hubs to coincide with the landings. They ignored the underground. The San Julián, Managua and Baracoa air bases were also scheduled to be attacked on Monday by bombers from Guatemala. The scheduled attack on the San Julián base in Guane, in Pinar del Río province, was cancelled by President Kennedy. Kennedy decided not to give the invaders air support. The CIA notified José Miró Cardona that Kennedy approved the invasion, but did not inform him that the original plans had been modified. The Revolutionary Council were held incommunicado at the abandoned Opa Locka airfield for three days. Thirty-eight telegraph operators were in contact with CIA agents. The bombers took off from Puerto Cabezas. Transport planes came from Guatemala and Nicaragua. The disembarking on Caleta Verde, south of Guasimal in Sancti Spíritus, between Punta Aristizabal and Ojo de Javier did not take place. The steamship *"Santa Ana"*, commanded by Higinio Díaz Ané, which should have landed 168 men on Mocambo Beach, in Imías, on the south coast of Baracoa, Oriente, could not carry it out. Four platoons with 140 men quartered in a farm in Homestead, Florida, ready to embark, were prevented by later orders from doing so. Of the original force of 1,443, 1,297 men had landed.

President Kennedy was urged to make an air strike from the aircraft carrier Essex, lying off the coast of Cuba. Premier Khrushchev threatened Soviet intervention in Cuba. Kennedy replied to him that they intended no military intervention. Admiral Arleigh Burke asked that a detachment of marines be permitted to enter action. Girón Beach fell at 5:30 in the afternoon. On Thursday the 19th, Miró Cardona met with President Kennedy and asked for an intervention, but Kennedy refused it. Alejandro del Valle and 21 other brigade members fled on a launch without course. A boat was picked up by the American steamship "Eaton". The underground leader, known by the name of "Francisco", had been shot in La Cabaña Fortress on Thursday together with Sorí Marín. A hundred forty-nine prisoners had been packed on orders from Osmani Cienfuegos into a trailer truck which travelled from 1:00 hermetically shut for eight hours. When it was opened in Havana, nine men had suffocated to death on the way. One thousand one hundred sixty-six prisoners remained. The average invader was thirty years old and from the middle or upper class; there were about a hundred from the working class, some fifty Negroes, 240 students, 135 military men, some Hebrews.

The prisoners were referred to as "mercenaries". Castro interrogated a small group of them at the Sports City stadium on television Monday night starting at 11:15.

Carlos Onetti Auñón, a paratrooper, asked him, "Doctor Castro, are you a communist?" Fidel ignored him.

He asked Tomás Cruz Cruz, who had belonged to the army, "*Negro*, what are you doing here now that blacks are enjoying the new life?", and he told him blacks could now swim in the beaches the same as whites. Cruz answered him that he hadn't gone there to go swimming. Wanting to ridicule him, Castro said, "But you got wet in the landing at Girón."

Cruz squelched him, "I didn't get wet in the landing, I dropped by parachute."

A Negro said he had never noticed any discrimination by the upper class and he had never thought of going to the Officers' Club. Jorge Suárez-Rivas López-Bosques, Senator Eduardo's son, was interviewed.

Néstor G. Pino Marina asked Fidel, "Major Castro, are you a communist?"

Fidel answered him furiously, "Well, and what does it matter if I am or am not a communist?"

Pedro Arozarena Castellanos was a dark, strong Negro; Ramón Quintana Barbón was a small, dark Negro; there was another Negro named Sergio Carrillo Abreu.

Duarte asked Ana to stop by his home at lunch time, where Alejandro would give her the address of a doctor she should contact about penicillin; he hadn't been very explicit. After having lunch, she left home early and got off the bus near Duarte's. She had been careful to leave her Ministry identification card in her desk and the others in her dresser. She hadn't been in the building since the end of March, almost four weeks before. The militia girl at the front steps searched her handbag, wallet, pen, lipstick, lip and eyebrow brushes and eyebrow pencil. Ana repeated her customary explanation, "My brother lives on the third floor."

The militia girl returned her handbag to her. "Go on up, comrade."

A woman let her in the apartment, whom Ana assumed to be the cleaning lady.

"Is Alejandro in?"

"He hasn't come. Come in." She was fat, her hair pulled back into a careless bun and her face gistening with perspiration, a broom in her hand. Ana stayed standing. "Ah!, three now", the woman lamented. "Alejandro's cousin is now staying here from Tuesday to Thursday. They're all good boys, but you can't imagine how they mess up the place. Look at these magazines. I pick up..."

An authoritative knock on the door interrupted her. Alejandro would have a key. Ana grabbed a magazine from the sofa on her way into the bedroom. It was the first time she went into it. There were two twin beds and she threw herself face down across the one nearest the door, opened the magazine on it — it was an old *"Gente"*, — and propped herself up on one elbow. She could see the front door from there. The cleaning woman opened it to two militia men. Ana wasn't surprised. One came into the bedroom and she sat up with studied surprise. The man looked at her briefly and turned to the cleaning woman, still by the door. He had a mole next to his nose.

"Alejandro Dávila."

"He... is at work", the woman said and Ana realized she knew more than she'd have thought at first.

The man went to the small closet and flung the door open, revealing, besides the hanging shirts, pants, belts and ties, pillowcases filled with dirty laundry and a shopping bag on the floor. He looked under the beds and moved the night stand. He pulled the chest drawers, felt the clothes and closed them again. He ran a hand over the backs of the books in the two cases. He went into the bathroom and Ana heard him shove the shower curtain aside. The other militia man, a mulatto, appeared at the door, a cigarette in his mouth.

"Living room and kitchen clear", he announced, almost disappointed.

The cleaning woman was leaning against the bedroom door frame. She wore no expression on her face, but Ana could detect the fabric of her blouse rising rapidly from her accelerated heartbeat. The irritating buzzing of a fly annoyed her.

The militiaman with the mole came out of the bathroom and suddenly asked, "Who are you, his mother?"

"No, Asunción Ramos", the woman answered. "I clean the apartment for them three times a week." The man then looked at Ana. "She's visiting", Asunción hastened to inform him.

"Who else lives here?"

"Reynaldo Duarte."

The one with the mole looked at the mulatto questioningly. The latter shook his head, flicking his cigarette ashes on the floor. They left the apartment slamming the door behind them.

Ana got up and walked out to the living room. "It's one twenty", she said. "I have to go back to work. Tell Alejandro I waited for him." She made no comment on the search. He'd probably never get the message — if he was lucky enough to be warned before he got home. — As Ana let herself out of the apartment, Asunción dropped in a chair, without answering her. She was still holding the broom. The militia girl remained at the front entrance.

Ana hoped to see Duarte before they went up, but she was late and didn't meet him. She didn't dare go near his desk in the afternoon. She anxiously counted the hours. At quitting time, she waited for him at the elevator and, as they walked out on the sidewalk, she let it out in one breath, "They're looking for Alejandro. I was waiting for him at your house, but he didn't show up, and two militia men came looking for him. Do you have a way to warn him?"

"Alejandro's already gone. His cousin told me at lunch time that, when he got to work this morning, they were waiting for him at the Trust Company on the corner of P to warn him and he didn't go in." Duarte was frowning. "Did they search the apartment?"

Ana nodded and he raised his eyebrows.

"The cleaning lady was there. Asunción? They found it clear. What were they looking for?"

"I guess weapons." He let out a sign. "Where were you, in the living room?"

"No, sitting on a bed", she answered him a little embarrassed.

"Well, brace yourself", he told her grinning. "You were sitting over an arsenal." And, as Ana looked at him blankly, he explained, "There were seven rifles in the box spring of each bed. We're getting them to the hills."

"Oh!, I'm glad I didn't know it then. I'd have fainted." Even now it frightened her.

"No, you wouldn't have. But I too am glad you didn't know it. They might have noticed something in your expression."

On an impulse, Ana asked him, "Was it Alejandro who told you he saw me with Danilo?"

"Yes." He looked at her sideways with a grin. "I think he's fallen in love with you."

"Don't say that."

"You should have heard him the evening he saw you with the militiaman. He saw you meet him in a cafe after classes. And he came home in the worst mood. Punching things."

"He must have been watching me only out of distrust. But didn't he know I had a boyfriend?"

"Yes, I had told him, but he hadn't actually seen you with him. I guess it wasn't the same."

"He himself had asked me once if somebody was waiting for me."

"Well, it seems when he saw him, the 'phantom' took on a body. Besides, we didn't know he was in the militia..."

"That's it, it was mistrust."

"...He called him a cretin."

She shook her head. "I don't think so." Bur she *had* thought so. "Doesn't he have a girlfriend at the *central*?" Her bus came into sight.

"Nearby, in El Crucero. *Had*. She broke up with him when he came to Havana. The very day she went to see him off." Ana said good-by now and got on the bus.

Diphtheria broke out in the moat of El Morro Castle. In La Cabaña Fortress several men died of rat bites.

Yolanda wondered about Bárbara. She hadn't come back to the office. They didn't know whether she had been fired or had quit. Aurora had seen her downtown, so they knew she wasn't in jail.

When the list with the assigned post duty was distributed − to Ana's great surprise, by Aguirre, her downstairs neighbor, − her name appeared on it, despite her excuse. Her defiance had been to no avail. And she didn't dare object again.

That night Ana remembered that time seven months before when she had prayed asking to see the light, and she now kneeled by her bed, closed her eyes tightly and prayed again with the same fervor, "Please, let me know if I'm wrong, let me see things the right way, please."

Friday afternoon as she was going down the stairs of the Ministry, El Tico approached her.

"Good afternoon. Did Reynaldo leave yet?", he asked her going up a few steps.

"He just left."

He shook her hand. Ana felt he had left a piece of paper in her palm. She closed her fist. He said good-by with a nod and went back down the stairs.

Ana guessed she was to give the paper to Duarte. She'd go by his house. He should have arrived. She didn't have either her own identification card nor the one of the Ministry of the Interior with her. When she was sitting on the bus, she couldn't control the curiosity of looking at the piece of paper in her hand. She saw that it listed thirty-five cities and towns in the province of Havana with figures next to them. She swept her eyes over it and seven at random stood out: Havana 785, Bauta 12, San Miguel del Padrón 61, Aguacate 4, Santiago de las Vegas 11, Melena del Sur 4, Güira de Melena 14. She didn't know what it meant.

There was no militia searching at the building entrance. Her ring was answered by Alejandro. She was aghast. What was he doing in the building? A neighbor could give him away! She felt afraid for him. She walked in and when he had closed the door, she expressed it. "What are you doing back here? I thought you were in Las Villas."

"There's work to be done here tonight", he answered her simply, and Ana remembered the rifles Duarte had mentioned.

"Is Duarte home?"

"Reynaldo went to get a haircut. He's going to Santiago tonight to see the 'Country Girl'... Zoraida. It's Friday. He'll come by before, though, to shower. Wait for him. How glad I am to see you! I didn't expect it."

"Thank you", she smiled and sat down, a little uneasy.

"Will you have a little wine?"

"No, thanks."

"Come on, Anita, don't slight me."

"All right."

"White?"

"Fine."

He took two stem glasses from a bar-cart and brought her one and another for himself.

"Monday was your name day, wasn't it?", Ana asked him.

"Yes. How did you know?"

"I saw it in the calendar. Happiness."

"Thank you. It's what I say..." He didn't finish.

"What's your impression now?", Ana asked him, sipping the wine.

"Well, it's...", he sat down, "almost as if they had intended it to fail."

"How can that be?", she asked, surprised.

"Yes, think, Anita. The Cubans in the United States who wanted to fight, overthrow this government, presented a problem for them there. Well, they rounded them all up enlisting them to have them under their control, they sent them on a suicide mission and that way they've gotten rid of the men who represented a nuisance in their country, all together."

"How could they do that!", she repeated, appalled.

"Why wouldn't they give air cover? Why didn't they notify the underground here?"

Ana didn't answer. She didn't know. The possibility seemed so horrible, it was difficult to comprehend at once. Alejandro seemed disillusioned, but as if driven by some last force.

The telephone rang, he gulped the rest of his wine and went to answer it. He talked in a very low voice into the receiver, but she was sitting nearby, the radio was not on and she could, while she sipped her wine, partly hear what he said.

"Yes, Alejandro ... That's right, I do ... I have it. Look, if I'm not back by ten thirty, report it as missing, so you won't be implicated ... No, you won't hurt me. Say that your car disappeared. You don't know where it is. Did you leave the key in? No, you didn't. Do you suspect anyone? No, you don't. Do you understand? ... With a little luck, by the time they get around to suspecting I may have taken it, I'll be where they won't be able to find me ... I'm going to pick up Juanillo, Panchito, Manoliño, Pepucho and Toñín ... That's agreed ... Thank you ... No, that's your end ... Yes ... So long." He hung up. The five had been nicknames and diminutives. But, still, wasn't he afraid the phone might be tapped?

Ana gave him the slip of paper. "El Tico gave it to me, for Duarte

I think." Could it be a list of members of the movement who had been arrested? No, it seemed like too many. The ones left free? Too few. Codes? He looked at it and put it in his shirt pocket. "Well, I'm going to the movies or something", she said.

He took her hand to shake it. "In case we don't see each other again."

"We may not?" She felt her heart plunge into her stomach.

"We may not. So long and good luck."

"Good luck to you, Alejandro. You men are doing it all. There's little we women can do."

"There are many women active, but mostly outside of Havana." He paused. "You're nice, I like you and I'm sorry I won't be seeing you." She thought of what Duarte had told her four days before. She tried to retrieve her hand, but he held it up to his face and ran the back of it lingeringly down his cheek. He closed his eyes and drew his breath in. There was tenderness in the gesture and more, there was patent desire. A strange current seemed to flow from his touch up her arm. They were alone in the apartment and Ana briefly felt fearful. But he opened his hazel eyes, let his breath out in a jagged sigh and let go of her hand, which stayed poised in the air for a moment, before she brought it again down to her side.

She looked back at him from the door before she went out of the apartment. He looked taller and heavier standing straight there in the middle of the small living room, but so alone.

She felt too tired to walk home, so she took the bus. When she arrived, her mother was embroidering the initials $\mathcal{N}$ and $\mathcal{D}$ in navy blue on light blue towels, for Norma.

"Where's Papá?"

"He went to Velázquez's, who's leaving for Puerto Rico tomorrow."

"Do you want to go to the movies? There's a West German picture in color playing at the 'Foxa'."

As she lay in bed that night, Alejandro's face came into her mind. She missed Dany more than ever. Would he be in bed now? How long had it been since he had broken up with her? Twenty-three days. Did he think of her? So many things had happened in little more than three weeks! Ana fell asleep with her arms open wide in cross and dreamt about Dany.

Guevara outlined Juceplan's goal and announced a four-year plan.

Ana was getting dressed Saturday morning when she heard her

The Freedom Fighters

parents talking. It seemed from her room she had heard her father say it, but she couldn't be sure. She finished dressing and went out to the dinette area. Her mother had set the table for breakfast and her father was sitting at his place, his back to the balcony. He motioned Ana to sit.

"Anita, I think we should leave." She had heard right. From the way her mother received it, Ana knew they had already discussed it before, perhaps since last Saturday, when the invaders had been taken prisoner. "I'm lost without the office to which to go, I feel useless without work to do. You lost a good job with a good company. After the failure of the invasion, I've lost hope for a change. There's no chance for you to advance and have a future here. As far as the household goes, things are scarcer, food worse. And that would be the least of it if there were an objective, but there is no incentive, we have lost our individuality. We feel oppressed, afraid; we catch ourselves whispering. At your job they hold indoctrination talks, outside they hold 'demonstrations' — the day after tomorrow is May First, you'll have to go to the parade, — in the schools they've altered the subjects to conform to the doctrine. You must have thought what it'd be like to raise children under this system, without knowing another way of life. If you go back with Dany" — she tried to shake her head, but he went on preventing her from interrupting, — "you'll have to adapt yourself to his militia duties. I can well work for another eight years, or even longer if it were necessary."

To leave Cuba... "Where would we go, to the United States?"

"I think the United States is the *only* place we can go. We'll try Jamaica also, but I doubt we can."

"But you can't speak English. It'd be hard."

"But life here is becoming unbearable", he explained, a little impatiently before her resistance.

"I hadn't thought it would. I quit my job with Wayne to stay."

"I know, but you can't deny things have taken a turn in the last six months. Even more so in the twelve days since the invasion. Look how they're treating the people. There are no rights."

"Perhaps Costa Rica...", Ana said distraughtly. "They speak Spanish." El Tico made it sound pleasant.

"Maybe, but it rains too much, there are nine volcanoes and they have earthquakes. And I guess there'd be no jobs."

Teresa hadn't said anything, and Ana looked at her mother. Could she leave her son and grandchildren behind?

"Now we're not only afraid of the government", her mother said now, "but also of an attack from the States. But you two are the ones who earn a living and it has to be up to you to decide."

CHAPTER 10

ON LEAVING THE HOMELAND BEHIND

"Hoy que la vida me parece hermosa,
de tu amor con el bello colorido,
te diré muy en breve, pesarosa,
¡Adiós, adiós, la suerte lo ha querido!"[10]
("A Un Retrato",
    Concepción Trillanes y Arrillaga)

On May First, the big Worker's Day parade would take place, this year considerably longer and more expansive, followed by a speech by Castro. It was compulsory for government employees. Ana considered it humiliating to be made to attend. Monday she got up before dawn and went to the front of the Ministry, where they were to meet at 6:00 in the morning. She greeted noisily the employees already gathered on the sidewalk, shook hands with a few, congratulated some, waved at others and made herself noticed. Yolanda arrived a little later and they wondered aloud what could have delayed Duarte. He had already told them he wasn't going.

"He usually has breakfast at the little coffee shop across the street", Ana commented loudly. "Let's walk there." It'd seem natural, the three were almost always together.

They crossed the street, greeting those they met on their way, and pretended to look into the coffee shop. It hadn't been planned, but now they both seemed to see the possibility at the same time.

"He isn't here yet", said Yolanda. "He gets off the bus over there. Let's walk to the corner."

They walked to the next corner. They didn't meet any co-workers on that block. They stood at the corner for a moment and looked back toward the entrance of the Ministry. Nobody seemed to be looking their way. Employees of another government agency were

[10] Today when life seems lovely to me
with the beautiful coloring of your love,
I will very shortly, sorrowfully say to you,
Good-by, good-by, fate has wanted it so!

walking in another direction and gathering at a distance. Without talking it over, Ana rounded the corner and Yolanda followed her. They rushed down the street to the next bus stop and caught the first one that came by. They got off on Carlos III.

By the side of Freyre Andrade Emergency Hospital they saw a group of members of the Rebel Youth. It was the first time Ana had seen them. The sight was hideous. The boys, tangled, dirty manes down to their shoulders, were filthy, and they carried, hanging on string around their necks, tin cups and forks which jangled as they ran down Espada Street headed north. They looked subhuman. She gaped at them.

"Don't stare at them like that", Yolanda hastened her.

On Neptuno, between Channel 4 Televisión Nacional and the little Guiteras Park, they came upon a group of people walking down the middle of the street, chanting,

"We are socialists, forward and forward,
and he who doesn't like it may take a purgative."

They hugged the walls of the buildings to let them by. Mirta, Olga's friend, had told her that the counter-revolutionaries replied to this with another chant,

"We are the worms, how good, how good!,
and he who doesn't like it may take poison."

She kept Yolanda company on 23rd Street until her bus arrived, and then walked home. The parade started after 10:00. The five channels were telecasting it in joint transmission — it droned on, — there was nothing else to watch and Ana didn't dare go out, so she took Olof Ekström's *"Hon dansade en sommar"* to read in bed.

The army paraded with its ugly tanks and weapons. The navy marched, as did the air force, the police, the militia, the firemen and the Rebel Youth. There were some nice floats. The alphabetizers took part, as well as the vigilance committees, the students, the Federation of Women, the laborers, the countrymen, the professionals and also the shoeshine men. The demonstrators carried signs that read, "Firing squad for the invaders", "We will dig the graves of the Marines", "Russia gives us, Yankees take from us,/ that's why we're with Nikita", "If Fidel's doings/ are communist doings,/ put me down on the list/ because I agree with him." They released pigeons and balloons.

In his speech at the Plaza Cívica, Castro proclaimed that he was making Cuba a socialist-type republic and there would be **no** elections. He ordered all foreign-born priests — who constituted over 75% of the mere seven hundred — to leave the country. He resolved that Public Works employees remove the crowning bronze spread-winged eagle atop the tall twin white marble pillars of the Monument to the battleship "Maine" on the Malecón Drive; the inscription at the pedestal was changed and the brass cannons displaced, the eagle supposedly to be replaced by a "dove of peace". The busts of two American presidents and a general in the Plaza were also removed.

A passenger on a National Airlines plane in flight to Key West forced the pilot to fly on to Havana and, when it landed, he got off and disappeared in the crowd. It was the first such hijacking.

Afraid the next morning that she might be asked where she'd been, Ana decided, since she had carried the lie this far, to carry it all the way. She rubbed lipstick with her fingertip heavily on her cheeks and her nose and more lightly on her forehead, chin and low neck where she would have supposedly been exposed to the sun, and set out for work.

When she walked into the section, Morejón asked her, "How late did you stay?"

"Until seven thirty", she ventured. It went without saying that she meant in the evening.

"Then you just saw the tanks starting to roll", said Valdés.

She had no idea, and it occurred to her that he might be trying to catch her in a lie, but she nodded. Some fussed over her sunburn and Aurora told her, "Put some ointment on, it could be second degree burns."

She wondered if anybody could notice it was make-up. The fluorescent tube light in the office was different from the incandescent bulb light she had had in her bedroom. She was afraid somebody might touch her.

On their break, Yolanda said, "I think you carried it too far."

"How barefaced you are!", Duarte kidded her. He had dared simply not to attend.

"This was actually Yolanda's idea. She had said she was going to do it too." She looked at her exaggerating her reproach. "But she left me stranded."

Méndez was smoking heavily and drinking a lot of black coffee. Teresa hardly ate and she complained of insomnia. Ana had been having tachycardia. She went to the heart specialist of their clinic, who took an electrocardiogram and diagnosed extrasystole caused by a nervous condition.

It hurt to see families split apart by different political tendencies. Parents and children had disagreements, brothers broke up, marriages teetered over the cliff.

Wednesday Méndez took the first step to leave the country: He wrote to Velázquez, now in San Juan, asking him for a visa waiver for himself. With the American Embassy closed, tourist visas couldn't be obtained.

Manuel Artime and 32 other patriots were captured in the Zapata Swamp, three of them wounded.

The oil tanker "The Atlantic Sea Man", bound for New Orleans, 182 miles off the Mississippi delta, rescued twelve survivors on the launch "Celia", which had left the Cuban coast on the 19th, among them Roberto Pérez San Román, commander of the Fourth Heavy Gun Battalion. Ten men had died in the fifteen days on the Gulf without food or water, among them paratrooper commander Alejandro del Valle Martí and Raúl García Fowler, son of the former mayor of Havana.

Castro commented to some militiamen that he had "respected ex-president Grau because he was old and hadn't left the country". Grau, the only one of the three living Cuban ex-presidents who lived in Cuba, replied days later, "I'm sorry he won't be able to grow old, or leave Cuba."

The President of the National Bank prohibited the citizens from having foreign coins, and ordered being informed of gold coins used in making jewelry.

Monday Ana went to the British Embassy at lunch time to find out the requirements for tourist visas to Jamaica. She was informed they needed a reimbursable 200 American-dollar deposit each for their stay while they got their residence visas in the United States.

Four recreational associations in Santiago de Cuba were confiscated by the government.

A War Navy launch with seventeen men disappeared from in front of the port of Mariel on the north coast of Pinar del Río province.

Tuesday Méndez made flight reservations to Miami for the three of them at the Pan American airlines office on 23rd Street, and the earliest date he could obtain was August 3.

Thursday they got up at 6:10 in the morning, arrived at the nearest first aid station, on 10th Street, with its globe lamps, at 6:40 and received turns in the forties. Ana called Mestre from a restaurant on 14th Street and told him she didn't feel well and was going to be late. They were vaccinated against smallpox, obtained their Public Health Ministry immunization certificates and were back home at 12:20. Ana had heard that if one put lemon juice in the vaccination, it wouldn't "take". She didn't want to have a reaction, and besides she had been vaccinated when she was eleven, so she now squeezed lemon juice in the needle mark. After a meat-free lunch, she went to work in the afternoon.

Five men fled on the launch "Alexis" bound for the United States.

Saturday parents and daughter went to have their visa-size photographs taken at a studio on 12th Street.

By May 13 commercial relations had been established with Yugoslavia.

On Mother's Day the government brought 10,000 peasant mothers to Havana. The Mass at the Plaza Cívica was officiated by Father Guillermo Sardiñas, a priest who had joined Fidel in the mountains early in 1957 and fought in the rebel army; he had received the rank of major and wore an olive green cassock with his army rank insignia on his shoulder.

Father Germán Lence was also a supporter of the revolution and attended the meetings. The JOC (Catholic Labor Youth) were officially with Castro.

When Ana went to the studio with her father to pick up their visa photographs, the photographer, a tall, thin, dark man with a cowlick on the crown of his head, pulled Méndez aside by the arm and told him in great secrecy, "I noticed the photographs you had taken. Are you leaving? Where are you going?... I'd like to leave too. What are the requirements?" Méndez supplied what information he could.

Twenty-seven nuns, headed by the Mother Superior of the Sacred Heart, arrived at West Palm Beach from Havana on the ferry "City of New Orleans". Nine men arrived in Venezuela aboard the Spanish steamship *"Satrústegui"* and sought political asylum. Lines were forming before the Spanish and Mexican consulates.

Ana went to see Alicia, her mother's friend, in La Sierra to ask her about the possibility that her son Melvin put up the reimbursable deposit for her in Jamaica for her visa. She had known Alicia all her life. In the low wall that bordered the garden of their house there were jagged bottle bottoms embedded in cement. Alicia, who still worked as secretary in a lawyers' firm, received her with Marvin, her older son, talked about tearing up incriminating information, and gave her the address of the Canadian bank, a post office box in Montego Bay, but she told Ana she didn't think Melvin had 200 dollars. Ana didn't believe her and left disappointed in such an answer. She wondered if her mother would have obtained a better response.

The Havana Yacht Club, Miramar Yacht Club, Casino Español, Club Náutico de Marianao, Bankers' Club, Casino Deportivo and Daughters of Galicia were turned into workers' social circles.

President Kennedy stated in Palm Beach, Florida, that the North American people would never forget the Cuban people, would always identify with their fight for freedom and that this would arrive. Alejandro would probably consider it ironic.

Just then, Betancourt, the division director, called Ana into his office to interview her and offered her the position as his secretary. His previous girl, a quiet brunette Ana had seen silently dashing in and out of her department, had resigned for "health reasons".

"You don't have to accept it if you don't want to. I know many people wouldn't want to work with me and I'd understand", he told her candidly and Ana suppressed a smile, but she felt it had reflected in her eyes, and they exchanged a look that turned out almost conspiratorial. "Think it over and let me know when you decide."

There was no mention of a raise. The revolution was simply not giving raises. The position, however, would be above Aurora's.

On the one hand, Ana didn't think she could get along well with that man of whom everybody in the division was afraid and whom she had seen red with rage several times when he seemed on the verge of suffering apoplexy, so she didn't want to work for him, but she didn't dare refuse. On the other hand, she did think that, since nobody could bear him, once their departure were ready, it'd be easy for her to start an argument and have everybody in the department believe her if she said she resigned because she just didn't get along well with him.

On Wednesday Ana wrote to Alicia's son Melvin at the Canadian bank in Montego Bay, asking him to put up the reimbursable 200-dollar deposit for her in Jamaica.

Five prisoners from the invasion were sentenced to death, and nine to thirty years' terms. At the closing of the National Association of Small Farmers in Rancho Boyeros on May 17, Castro proposed to trade 1,214 prisoners for 500 bulldozers. He was going to negotiate with their lives!

Ana had told Duarte she had intentions of leaving the country, but hadn't mentioned it again. He had joked, "In the Consulate of El Salvador, if you go to apply for a visa, they pull out a chair for you, they give you the newspaper and a cigar."

Yolanda had told Ana she was leaving and she had already been vaccinated at the dock, but they hadn't confided in each other as to how their plans were progressing.

Yolanda leaned toward her over the table on their break with a smile, "I have some news." She paused for effect. "I got engaged. Can you guess to whom?"

"To Eladio."

"Yes!" She was surprised. "How did you know?"

"By the way you talk about him." Lately Yolanda had been talking about the boy she'd met at the university in a different way. "Congratulations." She was really glad for Yolanda, but her mind was on something else.

Abreu warned Ana about Betancourt, "That man is impossible to get along with."

Morejón confirmed it, confiding to her, "That's the reason Ana had to quit. She couldn't stand him."

She thought he had confused the names. "Ana?", Ana Méndez asked him.

"Yes, his former secretary", Valdés clarified.

So she walked into his office and informed him she accepted the position. And Betancourt must have instantly liked that, despite his warning, she still chose to work for him.

Thursday the reaction to Ana's vaccination started, in spite of the lemon juice. Teresa called Mestre to tell him Ana had tonsillitis. She spent three days in bed with a fever of 102°.

Sixty-three nuns and priests arrived in Montréal, Québec, Canada, from Cuba.

Castro visited the commanders of the Assault Brigade at the Naval Hospital, still unfinished, in East Havana.

The Swiss Embassy offered the evacuation of American citizens and registered the repatriates. Only 66 pounds of luggage could be taken. The first plane left Friday at 5:00 in the afternoon with 54 evacuated Americans, among whom were four journalists. It was surprising there were still so many Americans in the country.

In an odd deal, a commission of ten Brigade prisoners, including Hugo Sueiro, Ulises Carbó and Luis Morse, arrived in Miami by plane on May 20, to negotiate obtaining 25 million dollars for the proposed trade.

"If Castro considers them mercenaries and assassins", Méndez said, "how come he knows they have the honor not to run out on their fellow soldiers?"

A small plane landed at the Key West airport with seven men aboard, who had hijacked it.

Ana went back to work on Monday, careful to wear a dress with sleeves long enough to cover the vaccination blister on her arm, and to Aurora's question, she repeated, "Tonsillitis."

She moved to the division director's office across the hallway, and braced herself for Betancourt's first outburst. The secretary to the director of the other division came to her desk on the first day.

"What's your name? Mine's Ofelia Barquet." She seemed very friendly and helpful. She also didn't look like a revolutionary. "If you have trouble with the Executive typewriter, I can teach you the spaces and backspacing. I've been using one like that for five months."

Wednesday Ana wrote to Octavio Guillén in Nassau, asking him to send her a money order for 45 dollars for her air fare, but not to say anything about it at Wayne Motors until she let him know. She walked past the veterinarian's dispensary with its two black wooden dogs standing guard at the sides of the bench by the door on the side porch, to the post office branch to drop the letter in the blue and red air mail box. Some jester shouted at her from somewhere, "Yell where it's going!"

A hundred LaSalle brothers arrived in the United States, 84 of them Cuban.

Méndez wrote to Velázquez in Puerto Rico and to Peláez, a chemist friend of his now in New York, for the other two money orders for Teresa's and his plane fares.

Saturday Méndez found out at Mediterranean Tours, the travel agency on the ground floor of the "De Quesada" building where Wayne had been, about the purchase of the plane tickets. They bought two cardboard suitcases on San Nicolás Street which cost them $26. each and weren't worth more than $9.

Ernesto had called Ana up at lunch time one day and told her he still had an American tourist visa and had decided to leave on his vacation. So she had then confided that they had decided to leave too. And he was the only person she had actually told they *were* leaving.

They always ended up talking about politics. They complained about the drastic laws, and about the informers. But she had never confided to him that she had done any work for the counter-revolution.

Sometimes on Sundays Ana still went to the Club Marino Estabias by herself and she once agreed to meet Ernesto there. He suggested going for a ride in a row boat. When they were far from the shore, he told her as he rowed, "I've met the usual remarks from friends, 'Why leave now?', 'This can hardly have any time to go', 'There can't be much longer to wait now.' But I've already made up my mind." He had considered it necessary to move away like this to tell her this.

"We've been thinking we didn't have much longer to wait for seven or eight months now."

"I'm taking my vacation on the fourteenth of July."

Sometimes her cousin Norma or Jorge was at the club.

Méndez went to pick up the suitcases on Monday.

Since she was now on the other side of the hallway, Ana didn't go out with Yolanda and Duarte on their breaks so much any more. Sometimes she went to the coffee shop with Ofelia. Ofelia was a tall, thin brunette with dimples and straight black hair which she wore up. She wore a medal of Our Lady of Harissa around her neck and talked about religion often — she was a Maronite, — she didn't buy *INRA* magazine or call anybody "comrade", and Ana suspected she wasn't a sympathizer of the system.

A militia girl in the division who often took up collections for "operations" came into their office and, at her manly manners, Ana risked wrinkling her nose at Ofelia behind the militia girl's back. When she'd left, Ofelia came to her desk.

"I can't stand militia women either. They've become so masculine with those uniforms. But be careful", she warned her in a whisper, "with the other two secretaries, they're 'fatherland or death' types. Betancourt's former secretary was different. That's why she quit. Coincidentally, she was your namesake."

From memoranda in the files, Ana learned the girl's whole name, Ana Gloria Menéndez. Ana Menéndez! Of course! She was the one with whom they had gotten her mixed-up.

A grenade placed in a militiaman's car on Estrada Palma Street in Santos Suárez exploded, wrecking the car. A bomb exploded in the "Riesgo" theater in Pinar del Río.

Early Wednesday, Ana heard a racket in the street. She went out on the balcony to look. Near the east corner, by an electric post, a black man was beating a tune on the bottom of an upturned pail with a stick. Méndez came up behind her to look out. Generalissimo Rafael L. Trujillo Molina, president of the Dominican Republic, had been machine-gunned the day before in a blue '57 Chevrolet sedan on the way to his Hacienda *"Fundación"* in San Cristóbal. The rabble celebrated.

Alicia called Ana to tell her that her son Melvin had written to her telling her that he couldn't put up the 200-dollar deposit in Jamaica. He hadn't even taken the trouble to answer her directly. What if her father didn't get his visa waiver?

A young man who had disembarked on Girón Beach managed to evade the vigilance of the militia with the help of some countrymen and reach Havana, where he got political asylum in an embassy and, after 35 days, he arrived at the Miami airport.

Sarrá Druggists, the largest one in the country, where Ana's uncle Marcos worked, was nationalized.

Two men were sentenced to thirty years in prison.

Betancourt's outburst didn't come. He was very pleasant to Ana. He liked her work, complimented her on her aptitude and treated her with deference. He even praised her to the other men in the division. He once asked her to go buy a flower arrangement for his office for about $6. and gave her a $10 bill. Ana found one with yellow chrysanthemums and brown cattails that she liked in "Los Reyes Magos" and risked spending $7.50 on it. Betancourt loved it, placed it on the credenza at his back and showed it to everybody who went into his office. Sara's cynical advise was, "Take advantage; new broom sweeps well." He once showed her photographs of his son, in cap and gown. About an assertive secretary in the division, Betancourt once commented, "She's... Are you familiar", he asked her in English, "with the term *'eager-beaver'*?" He said he'd found Ana was a decent person. And Ana found he was intelligent. He had a perfect command of English.

Friday Teresa called Ana at work and told her, "The seamstress already finished your dress." In the code they had agreed, it meant the Swiss Embassy had called the house and notified them that Carlos' visa waiver had arrived. Ana felt an enormous relief.

The new electric plant of Casablanca, in the province of Havana, built by the French, was turned over to Che Guevara.

Saturday Méndez inquired at Mediterranean Tours about their exit permits.

On Leaving the Homeland Behind

La Concha beach house in Marianao, always open to the public, was now turned into a workers' social circle.

Monday morning Ana went up to her brother's office. His secretary greeted her politely, asked her how she was and announced to Gustavo from the door, "Méndez, your sister to see you."

Ana heard him reply, "Ah!, have her come in."

"Could I talk to you, Gustavo?", she asked him from the door.

"Sure, come on in."

She closed the door behind her and stood before his desk. "Gustavo, since you got me the job here", she said nervously in a low voice, "I don't want to involve you in anything. I wanted you to know I'm quitting." By the way he looked at her, she knew he had been expecting her. Papá had talked to him three weeks before about their leaving. They both sat down. "I don't dare resign. I've tried to keep from everybody that you're my brother as much as I've been able to, so as not jeopardize you. But, if they asked you, just say you had no idea I was quitting."

"But why are you quitting?", he asked her now, perhaps in a last effort to comprehend a reason strong enough to force them to leave their own country, break up their family.

"I can't stand this, my brother." She looked around at the walls. Yolanda had told her there were hidden microphones. She didn't know whether to believe it.

She imagined he divined her fear and considered it ridiculous. "You can't stand *what*, Ana María?" He sounded irritated and had used her full name. His attitude intimidated her.

"The pressure", she answered him, impatient at his recalcitrance. "My time's not my own. Not even after I've put in a whole day's work." — He more than anybody should understand it, sometimes having to work overnight. — "There's 'voluntary' work on week-ends. And guard duty. And I'm being pressed more everyday to join the militia. I've lost my individuality. There's no incentive. And I'm afraid to talk. I'm a nervous wreck", she continued in what she was afraid he might take as melodrama. "I have extrasystole and my hair's even falling out."

He gave up trying to reason. "You should hand in a letter of resignation", he said a little abruptly.

"What if they don't accept it?" She didn't want to refer directly to their departure.

"They will."

"I don't know." She saw his face cloud. She sounded pleading and he was silent. It hurt so much to do this to him! And then she choked on her words, her chin quivered and a sob came out. He stood up then, came around his desk and put his arm around her shoulders. He seemed close to tears himself.

"I know this isn't the type of government of which we'd dreamed, *Basurilla*. But it isn't so bad either. It's the first truly Cuban one we've ever had. And this *is* our country. We have to sacrifice ourselves."

He usually wasn't so eloquent. Could he be right? How could she know? — Truly Cuban? — But she did know she couldn't stand the lack of freedom any longer. That was the worst part. The work and the scarcity she could take. But not the pressure and the fear. — Sacrifice themselves toward what goal? — If he would only leave too! To bring up his children free. She grabbed his hand and bowed her head. She realized that was impossible. She wanted everybody to leave with them. They all had a way of life and weren't willing to be uprooted.

Ana received the money order from Guillén on Monday. He had acted promptly. She cashed it the next day following procedures at Pujol Bank on Línea, where she still had her individual savings account.

A bomb exploded in the hotel "Casa Grande" in Santiago de Cuba, causing considerable damage.

The law was approved for the nationalization of private education, and all privately-operated schools and universities, and the properties that made up their patrimonies were adjudged in favor of the state. The government seized the Catholic schools, hospitals, convents, homes for the aged, land and the University of Villanueva, worth over three million.

Betancourt observed, "I'm surprised that a girl integrated to the revolution like you should not attend the talks after work."

She smiled evasively. "I have so much to do in the evenings..."

"You should make an effort."

Gustavo came to the office with another man on Friday to see Betancourt. He stopped at Ana's desk to talk to her for a moment. After talking in Betancourt's office, he waved at her as they were leaving, and Betancourt, standing at his door, saw him.

"Gustavo Méndez", he seemed to mull to himself. Then he asked Ana, "Are you two related?"

On Leaving the Homeland Behind

Away from Cuéllar's department, Ana had thought she could now keep their kinship quiet and spare Gustavo any harm, but before the direct question she could do nothing but admit tersely, "Yes."

"What's the relationship?", Betancourt probed.

"I'm his sister", she said in a low voice.

"Fine boy", he said.

Olga was working as a volunteer at the Ministry of Agriculture without drawing a salary, to cooperate with the revolution, she said. They still went to playhouses and the movies together, mainly because, since Wayne Motors had moved, Ana didn't have many friends left. But their talk was now restrained by Ana's fear. Mirta no longer went out with them.

When Ana voiced her concern over her unchaste condition and her loss of Dany, Olga advised her, "Use alum. You douche with alum diluted in water and it tightens you. It's an astringent. No man can tell." She was suddenly an authority. If that was so easy, then why had she been considering the "French stitch"?

A thousand country youngsters left aboard the ship *"Gruzia"* for the Soviet Union.

Velázquez sent a money order from San Juan, but they were still missing one. The money order from Peláez, Méndez's friend in New York, for the other fare finally arrived the following Monday. Carlos cashed them on Tuesday at the Banco Continental on M Street.

For her birthday, Ana received a telegram from Gloria Serrano. Ernesto called her at lunch time and it made her late. When she went back to work, Aurora was waiting for her in front of the elevator and asked her to come into the department to take some papers back to Betancourt. When she walked into the department, a surprise awaited. Her co-workers sang "Happy birthday". They had a cake. Aurora gave her a pair of brown mink puff earrings and the other employees had chipped in to buy her a bottle of French perfume.

Suddenly, Cuéllar told them abruptly to break up the party and get back to work. Aurora was visibly surprised at the outburst.

Thursday they bought their round-trip plane tickets to Miami at the agency on D Street, at $58.30 each. They had heard that they had to buy round-trip tickets.

Since they were only allowed to take 66 pounds of luggage each with them, Carlos and Teresa went looking all over the city for a bathroom scale to weigh their suitcases and use up every last ounce. Excess baggage was simply not permitted. There weren't any scales in any of the department or ten-cent stores. They finally found one on Friday in a hardware store on Aguila Street and were charged $24. for it.

Fourteen clubs in Havana had their names changed to those of communist personalities.

That evening they learned that a nephew of Marcos', her aunt Cristina's husband, had been arrested, accused of clandestine activities. They knew that her aunt's house would now be watched closely.

Ana called Olga Saturday afternoon. Her father was quartered, Olga told her, and she felt bad about leaving her mother alone. Ana wondered if her father's duties were legitimate. Rosa claimed he ran around with a woman. They didn't go out.

Four men travelling as stowaways on an American freighter were admitted to the United States under political asylum.

After dinner that evening, Ana stayed at the dining table, a *Romances* magazine open in front of her. She couldn't concentrate on the article. Her mind kept wandering to her brother, their departure, Marcos' nephew, Olga's volunteer work. On the radio in her parents' room the "Karachi" nightclub was advertised. A nice breeze blew in from the balcony. Ernesto and Yolanda were leaving. A documentary on television about Communist China was showing their incredibly immense May Day parades. The telephone rang. It would be Blanca. Teresa was in the bedroom sewing. Ana answered.

"Hello", said Dany's voice. Ana felt her legs wobble. "How are you?"

"Fine." She hoped her voice wasn't shaky. "And you?"

"Fine... I've written a letter to Mr. Palmer in Nassau, but I'd like you to correct my grammar before I send it out."

It seemed a weak excuse to her. Surely he knew other people who spoke English well. But she was so happy to hear his dear voice again, she could only croak, "Sure."

"May I come to your house?"

"Of course."

"Tonight?"

"All right."

"At what time? In half... at eight fifteen?"

"That'll be fine."

"I'll see you in a while."

"Until later."

She put on the blue and white striped dress with full skirt she knew he liked. Her vaccination scab had fallen off. She thought of putting on the filigree bracelet he had given her for Saint Valentine's Day, but then considered it out of place.

When Dany arrived, she asked him very casually to come in and she sat at the dinette table, her portable typewriter before her, all business. "Let me see what you wrote."

"I'm sure it's full of mistakes", he said modestly, pulling the folded sheet out of the back pocket of his pants and handing it to her.

The language was too elaborate, but it had few actual mistakes, she noticed as she ran over his large handwriting, and she corrected only the grammatical errors, not altering his style.

"Do you want me to type it for you?"

"No, that'd be giving you too much trouble. If you'll just let me use the typewriter, I'll type it myself."

She didn't insist. She provided paper and he started typing slowly. He would finish at the university in two months, Ana thought as she watched him, and he would be a public accountant. When he had finished typing, he said timidly, "I'm very grateful. Would you let me invite you for a drink?"

"Well,... it's after nine now..." Maybe he was doing it just to show his appreciation.

"But tomorrow is Sunday", he started to insist. "I bought a car. Well,....."

"All right. Let me go get my handbag." Did he really mean he himself had bought it, or his father? She went into her room – fixed her hair, touched up her lipstick, – across the bathroom and into her parents' room. Teresa was sitting on the bedside mahogany rocking chair mending socks over a marble darning egg as she listened to the poetry show on Radio García-Serra, the station that urged, "Live happily, forget the time." She whispered to her mother that she was going out with Danilo and kissed her. She went back through the bathroom into her room and took her handbag. Could he have possibly spent their money so soon?, in only ten weeks? What would they have now?

"The car isn't new", he said as they went down the stairs, "but it's eight years newer than the other one."

It was parked in front of the building. It was a light green '59 Chevrolet, the last year that American cars had been imported.

"It's very nice." She couldn't work any enthusiasm into her voice.

He opened the door for her. It was comfortable. She wondered if he had gone out with the nurse neighbor of his. He drove to La Red, on 19th Street.

They danced in the dimness and she leaned her face against his shoulder. She rubbed her cheek against his shirt and said, "It's been a long time since we'd been here."

"It's been a long time since we'd danced." He lifted her chin with his left hand and pressed his cheek against hers. He kissed her hair. "Your hair has the same familiar smell of lemon. I've missed you, *mi vida*", he whispered. "If I'm to be honest, at first I thought I'd get over it soon. With all the differences we had... But I can't forget. I guess two and a half years cannot be forgotten so soon." She knew, oh, how she knew! Her eyes moistened.

They had, before, planned to get married in October, in four months. Now they never would. She'd be leaving in just a little over a month and a half. What did the money matter! She felt like crying out of frustration. And getting drunk. She couldn't cry, so she held her voice steady and said, "Should we have another drink?"

"Have you missed me these last two months?", he asked her as they sat back in the booth.

Two months and twelve days, she thought, but answered only, "Very much." She didn't want to say 'longed'. "I've had to turn your picture down on my wardrobe, it hurt so much to look at it", she said honestly.

"I can't hear Fernando Alvarez sing without thinking of you, of us. Why didn't you call me?"

"*CALL* you? *You* broke up, Dany. You were final. Why didn't *you*?"

"We argued so much... And you always looked so hurt. You made me feel guilty. I thought I was doing you more harm than good."

"I was going to... I started to call you once, when the Camp Columbia airfield was bombed, but I stopped myself."

"Why?"

"Pride,... your father..."

"I'd have come back to you that much sooner."

"No, you wouldn't have. That was only ten days after you told me it was the last time we'd see each other." She thought, I'd only have made a fool of myself.

"I felt empty after I said that to you. In ten days I'd gotten over my anger. I left the militia."

"How could you, *mi ci*...?"

"I alleged that I felt I could better serve the revolution outside the militia, from my work 'trench', than in it."

"What made you leave it?"

"I didn't like the way they acted during the invasion. I feel the invaders were a group of mercenaries who had no right to interfere in our way of government and affected men who wanted to recover their property — that's beside the point, — but I think the militia and the army got carried away arresting people, and I feel the prisoners were treated unnecessarily roughly." He squeezed her right hand over the table. "I was afraid you might have gotten arrested."

"Why didn't you try to find out?"

"We don't have any friends in common I could ask. I was embarrassed at the way I had acted. I thought you weren't likely to forgive me. You acted so cold the day I brought you your photographs!... After having acted mellow in the afternoon... You wouldn't even ride in my car. I worried. I wanted to ask Gloria if she'd heard from you, but it was a touchy situation. If they had arrested you, it'd have seemed ironic of me to ask. I couldn't call your office to hear your voice, because you don't answer the phone. And at the house, I was embarrassed your mother might answer."

"When did you leave?"

"The Wednesday after Fidel interrogated the prisoners at the Sports City. When I saw those black men there, I thought I might have my ideals, but they, even if they were deceived, were sincere about theirs too. But I do wish you'd share mine."

"Suppose you were wrong and I were right."

He thought for an instant. "Well, even if I were. Then so are three million people. And you know how I feel for the country."

"I know, Dany, I know."

"I'm with the revolution because I think that's what's best for it. For us. I like the way things are going so far."

Here we go again!, she thought. She stopped him. "All right. So you like this. And I respect your ideals. Haven't I always? I don't even talk about it to you. But I don't share them. *I* don't like it. I want to be an individual. So why can't you respect *my* ideals? Why can't we, like I wanted, avoid all reference to political issues and enjoy our time together?" She didn't know if she was risking it all, but she couldn't bear for it to be the same all over again.

"You still sound the same." This time he said it smiling and pulled her to him. "I guess you're right at that. But at times like these through which the country is going, politics creeps into the conversation."

"Not into mine it doesn't."

"Do you want to try?"

"Yes." What was she doing saying yes?

He kissed her. And then everything seemed to be all right. Her mind spun wildly. They could enjoy this month and a half they had together. Maybe he'd even change his mind in that time. After all, he *had* become disillusioned with the militia. They played "*Place Pigalle*" on the record player.

"Do you remember", Dany asked her laughing, "the day we sat on the Malecón wall near Two and saw the flames from the top of the Riviera and were thinking of going in to tell the desk clerk the hotel was on fire?"

"Imagine!", she laughed. "And the day we went to the 'Sixty-six of Barlovento' and you saw a mouse on the railing?"

"And you found a spider in the ladies' room."

"And the night your car stalled coming back from the Vento drive-in movie", she recalled, "and you went in to show Papá your greasy hands?"

"And the day we went to see Berta at the clinic when she had her tonsils out?"

"And Salvador's wife at the *'quinta'* when she had their son."

"And the Sunday afternoon we came back from Salvador's daughter's birthday party and you found the apartment had been burglarized and you were scared and called me back, and I stayed with you until your parents got home?"

"And the night my parents had gone to the 'Puerto de Sagua' with Alfonso, and Nelia and her husband came and you hid in the bathroom and, when they left, I found you asleep sitting in the tub?" They both laughed remembering it.

"Can you imagine if your parents had come home early, before they left, and found me in the bathtub?" The laugher turned to roars.

"I would've gone in to warn you before they came in", she tried to tell him through her laughter, tears running down her cheeks.

"But I couldn't just come out then in front of Nelia and her husband." They both burst out laughing again. The couple in the next booth shushed them. This was not the place to come to laugh loudly.

"And the night the policeman shined the flashlight in our faces at La Puntilla?"

"Let's not remember *any* bad moment. And the night after Graciela's birthday party, when you kept admiring my rib cage?" She remembered he'd acted enraptured that evening.

"And the day the boxspring fell?" She remembered, but that embarrassed her and she didn't answer. He noticed it and changed his tone. "And the night at the Autopista Club when we kept looking at the redheaded transvestite singer's feet to see whether it was a man or a woman?" He hugged her and kissed her again, now more ardently.

"That was the night of the Christmas 'fifty-eight office party with Kent and his wife, when you got drunk and I kept trying to make you drink black coffee."

"And the night of the farewell party for Sterling's secretary, when *you* got drunk?" He stopped, maybe shy. That was the first time they had made love. Ana had never gotten over her feeling that they were doing wrong, and that hung between them like a fog for a moment. She lifted her glass and the ice rattled in the empty bottom. She leaned her head against his left shoulder. He pecked her cheek. "Let's dance."

"Gloria wrote me that she was transferred to the department where you work", she told him while he held her close.

"Ah, yes! That was two months ago. She replaced a girl who went to work at the Ministry of Foreign Trade."

"I got a telegram from her Wednesday."

"I remembered your birthday too. I owe you the present."

"No."

"Too late?"

"Uh-huh."

"I haven't turned your picture face down", he said with some reproach.

"Maybe it hurt you less than me to look at it."

"I need you", Dany said, pressing her against his chest.

"I need you too", Ana answered, snuggling against him.

Monday morning, Duarte came to get her on their break.

"Alejandro left for Yaguajay on Saturday", he told her in the coffee shop.

"Why?" Mayajigua illogically came to her mind.

"To join the rebels in the mountains."

"There are rebels on the mountains? Now?"

"Yes... And he asked me to say good-by to you for him."

"I haven't seen him in over a month and a half. He's very nice."

"He thinks the same about you. When Yolanda told me you'd broken up with your boyfriend, I told him, but he was already planning to leave in seven weeks."

Then, Ana reasoned, he'd known they'd broken up the last time they'd seen each other.

"Did he already know it, that we'd broken up, the Thursday after the invasion?"

"Uh...", Duarte had to think for an instant. "No, *I* didn't know it then."

"No, that's right, I hadn't told Yolanda yet. He went to meet me after classes. Did you know it?"

"No, he didn't tell me, but I'm not surprised. When did you break up, if you don't mind my prying?"

"No", she smiled, feeling guilty about baiting him. "A little over a week before El Encanto was burned... The very day after you asked me who the militiaman was."

"I'm sorry, but..." He didn't finish. "If Alejandro had known it then – he wasn't planning yet to go up into the mountains, – he'd have talked to you."

"I was still very depressed then. That was two weeks after we'd broken up. I felt very vulnerable. If he'd said anything, I'd have probably listened." She remembered the evening well, Alejandro's smell of "Yardley", the ice cream in the car and his recounting of the invasion, and a week later, having thought of him before she fell asleep.

"I hope you won't be offended, but... you did the right thing, you're better off without him. Your goals are different."

"Duarte", she stopped him, and there was a touch of mischief in her tone, "I'm back with him again now. Since Saturday."

"You are?" He was surprised and shook his head, then raised his eyebrows. "I guess you must know what you're doing." He could as well have said he washed his hands. She felt the same as when Kent had told her they thought she was being a fool.

"How did you get the rifles out of the apartment?"

"We slid them down the dumbwaiter, tied with a rope, at night. One eases them from upstairs, another one grabs them in the basement, takes them out to the alley in a couple of trips and passes them over the wall to the other one in the vacant lot in back, and a car waits on the back street."

The dumbwaiter! But of course! Why hadn't she thought about it? Because she didn't know the building had one — hers didn't. — It was the easiest way, the only way.

"But don't they bang against the walls of the dumbwaiter going down?"

"We wrap them in quilting", he said reluctantly. He suddenly frowned. He obviously didn't think he should be telling her all this, maybe especially now that she had gone back with Dany. Ana understood.

"You won't be using that way any more", she said. "I wouldn't have thought of asking if you still had more weapons in the house to smuggle out."

He smiled. The question hung in the air. She *didn't* know whether they had more.

"They changed the name of Alejandro's central, the 'Reforma'," he said, "to 'Marcelo Salado'."

They went back to work.

A powerful bomb exploded in the bar on the tenth floor of the hotel Santa Clara Libre.

The Ministry of Health nationalized fifteen drug stores.

The mayor of Matanzas arrived in Florida with three other men.

In late June, Antonio Varona stated that the Council had not been informed at any time that Kennedy refused to allow American planes to cover the landing at Cochinos Bay.

Ana stopped going out with Olga. Since Gutiérrez's hardware store wasn't doing any business now and he could no longer use statements to mail or invoices to file as a pretext, on Saturday, she went instead with Dany to the "Brisas del Carmelo", the old, pleasant, cool restaurant that had survived high on the corner of 21st and L Streets as a relic of other times. Later they went to the exhibition that the INIT kept across the street.

Castro stated he'd end by execution any attempt to overthrow him.

The transatlantic liner *"Marqués de Comillas"* arrived at La Coruña, in Galicia, Spain, with 450 priests and nuns who had been expelled from Cuba.

A small sailboat arrived in Nassau, Bahamas, with 23 Cubans. Another small boat arrived in Port Everglades, Florida, with two men on board, who had been at sea six days, and whose hands were blistered from rowing.

The United States government prohibited its citizens from travelling to Cuba. In order to visit it, they'd have to request a permit from the State Department.

Ana and Dany were lying on the grass in the park that had just been made on the east bank of the Almendares River, by the 23rd Street stone bridge, where La Chorrera settlement had once been. They were side by side under the shade of a tree, Ana on her stomach leaning on her elbows, splitting a blade of grass with her thumb nail, Dany on his back, his arms under his head serving as a pillow, squinting up at the blue sky.

"You know", he said, "I've never felt so close to a woman before. I didn't think one could. I don't mean physically, but..." He searched for a word.

"I know what you mean", she said tenderly.

She wondered if she should tell him now that she was leaving. It was deceitful to let him feel so close. There was no fear that he would give her away; that was out of the question. He wouldn't even censure her, she was sure. A yellow butterfly fluttered by. Maybe he'd even understand, she dreamed. She turned to look at the Bosque de La Habana across the river on the west bank. She thought of Natalia's electric technician boyfriend in apartment 7. She could ask him to leave too, so they could be together. And perhaps, just perhaps, he might, even if only for the sake of being with her. She knew he loved her. But, even as she thought about it, she knew it was wild. No, he wouldn't censure her, but he wouldn't understand either. He'd attempt to talk her out of leaving. He'd try once again to make her see things his way. It'd be cruel to break his mood. It was hot. The sun was high over Miramar. Why had he waited so long? If he'd come back eight weeks before, even only seven... She rubbed her eyes and behind her closed lids a kaleidoscope of lights spun fast for a moment like a disk on a tight string pulled hard before her eyes. And she kept it to herself. She had kept so much to herself in the last seven months, that her chest ached.

"What are you thinking?", Dany asked her.

"I was thinking how close we feel whenever we sit on the grass near the water in the afternoon, far from the people and..." she answered him remembering that Glory Saturday at the Christ of Havana, "... and we don't even need to talk."

He reached out and stroked her chin. She touched the back of his hand and smiled. "Where's Channel Eleven?"

"I don't know", he answered. "In Kohly?"

Monday morning, going down the front stairs of the building on their break, Duarte told her, "Eladio, Yolanda's fiancé, called me last night to tell me he'd received a cable from her from Caracas, that she'd arrived safely. He said he'd been calling you at home all afternoon to tell you, but nobody answered, and he asked me to let you know."

"I was out with Danilo."

They sat before their sodas, a little subdued. Ana said, "Yolanda's a very nice person, very decent."

"I'm going to miss her. There's nobody left with whom I can talk." Ana recalled when she had thought Yolanda was in love with him.

"Hey!, I'm left."

"You're leaving too, Ana", Duarte dismissed her remark. "I'm not. And I'm not getting married until that guy falls. I've told the Country Girl, we're not getting married while those people are there, and we agree."

Poor girl! There was a silence, which Ana broke, "Did you hear that Ernest Hemingway died in Idaho?"

"Yes, I heard it this morning. A twelve-gauge shotgun he was cleaning went off in his head, in Ketchum. I wonder if it was suicide?"

"Do you think so? Remember you were talking about him a few months ago?"

Two crop dusting planes which had fled from Cuba, each one with a man at the controls, landed in Key West, and a third, with one man as pilot and another hidden in the fumigation tank, landed in Marathon Key, in Florida. The four men asked for political asylum.

Five men, a woman and two children arrived in Jacksonville, Florida, in a Venezuelan Navy ship which had picked them up from a 33-foot boat in the Gulf of Mexico. The steamship "Constance" of German registry rescued 13 men a few miles off the Cuban coast when the engine of the boat in which they had left Las Villas broke down. Four young men who had left on a boat from Cojímar Beach, in Havana province, arrived in Key West in an American coast-guard ship. The yacht "Sea Pal", which had left from Santa Lucía Beach, Nuevitas, on the north coast of Camagüey province, arrived in Miami with four men, five women and fourteen children on board, who sought asylum.

A man was arrested at his home in El Cotorro, Santa María del Rosario, and the next morning his wife was notified that he had been found dead in the old limekiln in Regla, his body bullet-ridden.

Saturday afternoon, Ana went to Nelia's baby shower in Nueva Habana near the Vento Highway. They lived with her parents, in a newly-built upstairs apartment. Nelia's shoes were covered in the same pale airy fabric of her maternity dress. Carmen Zayas was there. Kisses were exchanged. The gifts of layette in pastel colors were opened. They ate the finger sandwiches and the cake decorated with a stork from the table covered with a cloth trimmed with little umbrellas. The party had an Americanized flavor. Emilio was nowhere in sight. Gloria hadn't attended because it was too far for her. Nelia said that Berta had written to her. And Ana left feeling a little alien to friends with whom she no longer had much in common.

When she got home, Gustavo was talking with their parents in the dinette.

"Listen, Tony Varona says here", Méndez was commenting, quoting from an article that Peláez had sent him from New York, "that free enterprise placed Cuba among the countries with the highest standard of living in the Americas. 'In nineteen fifty-two Cuba was: Third in per capita income in Latin America, second in meat consumption, second in ratio of doctors to population, second in kilometers of paved roads per thousand square kilometers and third in standard of wages paid to sugar workers'."

"In nineteen fifty-seven, when I started working in Wayne", said Ana, joining the conversation at the table, "Cuba was first in automobile owners among the Latin American countries. And it had more kilometers of railways per area than any other."

"In nineteen fifty-nine, during Prío's term", Teresa contributed, "Cuban workers' living standards were higher than in all tropical countries and than nearly all Latin American countries. According to the statistics, the national per capita income was nearly thirty percent above the average of neighboring countries." Ana had been fourteen then.

"These people now talk of mono-crop", said Méndez. "That's nonsense. This country has produced sugar cane, tobacco, coffee, pineapple, grapefruit, sisal, tubers. Those are the most appropriate crops for this climate."

"We depend on sugar cane entirely too much", Gustavo argued.

"We are situated between latitude nineteen and twenty-four degrees north. How much variation in conditions can you have within five degrees of latitude? We're limited. You have to adapt to the climate, not go against it. Diversifying? It'd be a loss of money, time and effort to try to plant crops here that aren't suited to these conditions. Like the instance of the Zapata Swamp, that the notion struck them to drain it against the advice of all experts, so as to plant rice — oh, we weren't going to import any more rice, — and then they found the terrain was brackish and it wasn't adequate."

"But we're still a chiefly agricultural country", Gustavo debated.

"Thirty-five percent of the population lived in cities with a hundred thousand or more inhabitants, over sixteen percent in the capital alone, and twenty-two percent in places with fewer than five thousand people. Only a small part of the population lived in rural areas."

"We need to promote tourism", said Gustavo.

"Dany and I were talking about that", Ana said, agreeing.

"And what about industrialization?", Gustavo asked.

"Industrialization is essential. But you have to proceed sensibly", said Carlos. "We have manganese and asphalt; let's produce that. And let's increase the production of nickel, cobalt, chrome, copper, iron and salt."

"That's only mining. And it was exploited by American capital."

"And now it isn't exploited by *ANY*body."

"I'm referring to basic-need products. Here we import everything."

"At the beginning you can't import machinery to make products which are not indispensable. You have to tread with caution. There's enough cattle and milk, and poultry. The Textilera and the Rayonera are there. We have shoes."

"It's not enough to be self-sufficient, Papá", Gustavo contended. He was an idealist. He was trusting. He was still dreaming.

"There are distilleries and cigarettes. And cement, soap, paper, chocolate. We could go on from there. We'd do well if this government wanted. Around Rancho Boyeros and San José de las Lajas..." There was a knock on the door. It was Danilo. Méndez hastened to finish, "... there have been many factories for six years." But the conversation changed and Ana went to sit with Dany aside in the living room.

Arnoldo Martínez Anorades rose against the regime in the province of Camagüey with two men. In time he had 56 patriots under his command.

A Cubana de Aviación DC-3 was hijacked and, when it arrived in Miami, thirteen of its sixteen passengers and the steward sought asylum. The plane returned to Cuba with the remaining three passengers and the flight crew.

An INRA rice-field fumigating plane landed on Marathon Key, in Florida, with two men, who sought political asylum.

Ana received a short letter from Yolanda Solís from Caracas on Tuesday. She said she was well and Eladio would be joining her soon to get married.

Four men arrived in Guatemala, and asked for asylum.

During 1959, '60 and the first half of '61, fleeing Cubans were from the upper and middle classes, professionals, but in the second half of 1961 peasants and fishermen began to arrive in Florida.

The boats *"Hilda María"* and *"Arroyo"* of the INRA fishermen's cooperative in La Coloma, San Luis, left the Cuban coast with 53 persons on board; countrymen, fishermen, laborers, office clerks, engineers, students, one seriously ill teacher and several children, all residents of San Juan y Martínez, in Pinar del Río province, and after sailing for forty hours, they arrived in Key West, where they sought political asylum.

Ana and Dany went dancing, or to the movies, to see Russian films, like Samsonov's "As Old as the Century" and Kheyfits' "The Lady with the Little Dog" with Iya Savvina, Chinese, like "The Man of the Little Cart", or Japanese, Yugoslavian or Czechoslovakian, and the five-year-old American "Written on the Wind" with Robert Stack. And politics wasn't discussed.

In Balboa, in the Panamá Canal Zone, a Cuban sailor left the Swedish freighter *"Scottern"*, which had left from Santiago de Cuba with 9,000 tons of sugar bound for Nakhodka in eastern Siberia, and the immigration authorities granted him asylum.

Ernesto called Ana on the phone Friday at lunch time to say goodby and on Saturday left for Miami on vacation, from which he had no intention of returning.

Fourteen Hebrew families residing in the country for many years left on the German ship "Adolph Vinnen" bound for Haifa, Israel, perhaps much as they had arrived from Europe. Twenty-one large crates contained their furniture.

It was Wednesday afternoon when Méndez told Gustavo the definite date of their departure, in fifteen days.

Two young bank employees, on their vacation, fled on an eighteen-foot launch. When she arrived in Islamorada, Florida, a young INRA employee who had fled on the launch *"Alborada"* asked for asylum.

Friday Ana packed the dresses she liked best, her shoes, underwear, stockings, nightgown, slippers, handbags, bathing suit, pants, housecoat, stoles, beach robe and raincoat, also her photograph albums, the grades from the examinations of her eight courses, costume jewelry, perfume (they said you were allowed to take only two already opened bottles), her prayer lace veil, her rosary beads, her camera, two towels (each one was taking two), Villaverde's "Cecilia Valdés", The Hundred Best Cuban Poems, Heredia's tome of poems and a page from a newspaper. The only book Teresa packed in her suitcase was Vicente Blasco Ibáñez's "Around the World of a Novelist", and Carlos didn't take any book other than the Illustrated Petit Larousse dictionary. Sixty-six pounds of possessions was very little when you were moving away permanently.

They packed their bedsheets, pillowcases, bedspreads, tablecloths, napkins, mats, china, glassware, the three glass tumblers in which they had had their names etched on the sidewalk before "La República" hardware store, silverware, pots, flower vases, pictures, mirrors, ashtrays, the bottle of black sand from Bibijagua Beach, all the china ornaments and two table lamps in two large cardboard boxes and a steamship trunk. They took The Treasure of Youth to Gustavito and the operetta albums to Gustavo.

Ana withdrew all her money from the banks, $830. from her individual savings account at Banco Pujol near her old office building, in which she left a balance of $3., and $611. from the joint savings account she had had with Dany in the Bank of Nova Scotia, where she left another $3., and she put the $1,441. in an empty chocolate tin box together with the little money left from the joint savings account she had with her mother at Banco Continental, her father's savings from Banco Gelats on O'Reilly, the funds from his checking account in The Royal Bank of Canada on Muralla, and an envelope with two hundred American dollars.

Ana finally confided to Duarte on Friday that they were leaving soon. He showed an interest in buying their refrigerator, television set and toaster for his wedding to Zoraida. He came to the house with her Saturday morning to see them. Ana finally met "the Country Girl". A shy, chubby girl with black hair, she hardly talked. He too acted bashful in front of her. And he told them, "I'll let you know."

In an attempt to be checked over as they wouldn't be able to once they left, Ana went to the dentist on Amistad, to have her teeth cleaned and one filled. The dentist, a young man, confided to her that he was leaving soon. And he explained how he intended to smuggle bills out of the country in the lining of his jacket.

Ana bought a lime color striped shirtdress with a full skirt for the trip at the little shop on San Rafael Street, and Sandra, its owner with her deep-set eyes, took it in for her. She went to the little beauty salon on Línea Street on Saturday to have her hair trimmed and her nails done for the last time before leaving. And Claudia, the beautician who resembled a physical training instructor, said she was interested in buying her parents' bedroom suite. They went to see it in the afternoon, and they also said, "We'll let you know."

In Circular One of the Presidio Modelo on Isle of Pines a group of political prisoners were gunned down to silence their protests of mistreatment, and sixteen convicts were wounded.

Méndez placed a classified ad in the Sunday newspaper offering their furniture for sale.

Starting Monday, Ana had to alternate a maroon open-worked cotton dress and an embroidered light blue blouse for work, which were the only clothes with sleeves that would cover the vaccination mark on her arm that she hadn't packed.

She received a short letter from Ernesto sending her his address and telephone number in Miami.

An Eastern Airlines plane in flight from Miami to Tampa with 33 passengers and five crew members was hijacked to Havana at gunpoint.

Méndez called a furniture warehouse on Monday to store the two cardboard boxes and the steamship trunk, with Ana's desk, the cane **bagasse** bookcase, the telephone shelf, a ceiling lamp, a hat rack, two stands, and a children's little chair and rocking chair. The storage moving men picked them up on Tuesday. They had to place the telephone on the floor.

They sold their furniture to a buyer-reseller on Concordia Street; two bedroom suites, the living room and dinette sets, the refrigerator, recordplayer table, two mattresses and three ceiling lamps, all for $950.

When the furniture had been taken out, Ana stood at the door and looked around her empty bedroom, and she remembered sadly the day five and a half years before when they had rented the apartment.

She had stood at this bedroom door as she did now and the room had looked much the same. Except that the walls had been a neutral cream color. The apartment in the next building was empty.

They told Georgina, the drug store clerk in apartment 4, Villar's wife in 6, Aguirre's in apartment 2, and Irene, the salesclerk in 9, that they were moving to Matanzas, where Teresa's paternal second cousins and her aged godfather lived. They all seemed to believe it. The only one who showed skepticism was Felipe, the janitor.

With all their furniture gone, they went to stay at the "Santa Elena" Hotel on 19th Street every night, and went back home during the day. Méndez and Teresa spent part of the day there, biding their time, and part in the street, window shopping, riding the bus, walking in the streets and strolling in the parks, drinking sodas and coffee. When Ana arrived from work, they went to the hotel and out to dinner.

Teresa took on the task of snapping photographs of the more important buildings on the main streets around their neighborhood, 23rd, L, Línea and G, and she and Méndez later took photographs of each other under the fig trees in the park.

Russian cosmonaut Yuri Gagarin was a guest for the 26th of July celebration. Three Brazilian communists and two Czechoslovakian public officials also arrived in Havana to attend the festivities. The act started after 3:00 in the afternoon. There were signs on the buildings surrounding the Revolution Plaza remembering Girón. The anthem of the Soviet Union was played. President Dorticós decorated Major Gagarin with the national order of Girón Beach. Fidel proclaimed Cuba a socialist state. He repeatedly called the Cubans who left the country "parasites". A merger of the 26th of July Movement and the Communist Party was announced.

Ana and her parents went to dinner at excellent "La Roca" on 21st Street for filet *mignon* with bacon, where French and Italian dishes were served, the waiters wore white gloves and violinists played strolling among the tables; to the "Monseigneur", on Calzada near the Swiss Embassy, of classic French elegance, to have onion soup; to the "Mandarín", Chinese, overlooking 23rd Street, to eat sweet and sour pork; to "La Carreta", country style, on K Street, for roast suckling pig; to "Club 23", low on 23rd Street, to have shrimp *scampi* and *shish ke-bab*; to the "Ember's", Italian, on L Street, to eat pizza *napoletana*; to Willy's, high over 21st Street across from the Capri Hotel, with its piano, to have Continental food; to Trader Vic's, marine style, on 23rd Street below the Hilton Hotel, for sea fare; "El Jardín", Spanish, on Línea Street, to eat steak; the "Casa Potín", on Línea, and "El Carmelo", on Calzada. And they savored different cuisines, different dishes, different seasonings. Now that they suddenly had money to spend, they had little time left in which to spend it. They just didn't remember traditional La Zaragozana or superior Frascati until it was too late.

Ana found an excuse to meet Dany outside every time they saw each other, so he wouldn't see the empty apartment, but, since he was already only one month away from the end of his career, he was busy with exams in the university and didn't have much free time. He called her on the phone at work during the day and in the evening at home, and Ana talked to him sitting on the floor.

Olga didn't know anything.

On Thursday the three set out to visit her aunt Esperanza in her home on San Miguel with its elevator and the flower garlands on the ceiling. They mentioned vaguely the possibility of leaving the country. Laura and Adrián took it enthusiastically − they said they might leave also, − and her uncle Augusto took it trivially. Ana left her $10. and Esperanza said she was going to buy herself a silver neckchain with it.

On Friday they took her aunt Cristina to dinner at the "Mandarín". Since her daughter Norma had become engaged to Víctor, Cristina didn't go out much, as Marcos went out a lot by himself or with his friends and left her home alone. Ana had sweet and sour chicken, while Aurora del Mar González sang. They then went to elegant "La Roca", in a Swiss chalet style, with its enormous rock set in a fountain in front and its doorman at the entrance, where Ana had a pink lady and her godmother, cider. They later went to a playhouse to see Inge's "The Dark at the Top of the Stairs" and they took her back to Kohly in a taxi. Cristina was ecstatic. Ana gave her $15. They left her at her green-tinted glassed-in porch and went home in the taxi.

Saturday they went to see her uncle Guillermo in Lawton. In his Streamline style house leaving the country was discussed more as a probability. Her godfather took the news somberly and Beatriz echoed her husband. Jorge was out. They hadn't seen him in seven months, since the Christmas Eve dinner. Ana left her aunt Beatriz $20.

Ana bought medicine for Carolina, their former next-door neighbor and mother of Idalia, a girl who had grown up with her on 24th Street, and for Blanquita a navy blue taffeta dress with cream color

On Leaving the Homeland Behind

crochet lace collar and a red *moiré* ribbon.

A waiter from Kimbo restaurant on L Street came to see the apartment and Felipe, the janitor, brought a man. They repeated that they were moving to Matanzas. A man from the Urban Reform came to knock on their door, tipped off by a neighbor, perhaps Aguirre, about the empty apartment. Méndez talked to him through the peephole and refused to open the door. When the man insisted, Carlos, annoyed at his lack of respect, told him, "When we move out, you come in, but we're still paying rent here."

Teresa tugged at his shirt sleeve, "Carlos, for God's sake, don't talk to him like that. You're going to spoil the departure for us yet."

The man tried to look through the peephole. Méndez closed it in his nose. Ana secretly felt a little proud of her father.

A militiaman and a policeman came, but they didn't open the door.

Two members of the prisoners' commission in Miami deserted before the established return date of July 31.

Each one wrote down the number of the savings account in Miami in his address book, and Méndez tore up and burned the bank passbook. Ana destroyed both her own Ministry identification card and the Ministry of the Interior card in the name of Julia Duarte.

They took Ana's blue table radio, her blue lace night lamp, her portable typewriter in its case, her fifteenth birthday picture in its amber frame, her framed commercial course diploma, the two graduation photographs in their frames, the bathroom scale they had just bought, the iron, toaster, television set, record player, a portable radio, clock, the box of books and records that had remained sealed for ten months, Ana's black-eyed susan vine in its yellow pot, Teresa's jasmine, the dining room philodendron and the *Vanidades* magazine with Ana's graduation photograph to Gustavo's house Sunday morning, along with the chocolate tin box with the Cuban money, an envelope with the 200 American dollars, the four savings account passbooks, Carlos' checkbook, the furniture storage contract and all the keys. Teresa left her diamond earrings with Gustavo, for Blanquita.

"Papá, where are you going to work?", Gustavo asked with concern, while they were all gathered in the living room.

"As bus boy in a restaurant or a hotel; I don't know... whatever I can find."

"And you, Ana?", asked Blanca in a practical attitude.

"As stenographer in an export company or an insurance agency."

I'll go to the State Employment Service."

Ana picked up Blanquita, now three and chubby, gave her a kiss, she played "Old Maid" with her, taught her how to say *"Madrina"* and admired her dolls.

"We'll rent a small apartment close in", said Carlos.

Ana tickled Gustavito, now almost five, in the stomach, played pick-up sticks with him sitting on the floor, while the Pomeranian dog tried to take them in his mouth, she tried to teach him how to play cat's cradle and admired his toy soldiers.

"We know a couple there", Teresa started, "the Carvajals."

"Oh, yes! I met them when we were there", Blanca inserted, "in April of last year."

"And they can direct us", Teresa finished.

"I have the addresses of Ernesto Crespo and Rosa Izquierdo", said Ana.

They had lunch with them. Blanca served breaded steak, rice with corn, green tomatoes, slices of Chinese yam and pumpkin pudding.

"The last time I was there", Ana said during lunch, "I was looking at the classified ads and an oil company street map of the city. A job as bilingual secretary pays about sixty dollars a week. You can live up to about Thirty-fifth Street and up to the Twenty-fifth Avenue. And I think a small one-bedroom apartment would be about sixty-five dollars a month rent."

"Why do you say 'the Twenty-fifth Avenue'?", Gustavo asked. "Here we say 'Avenue Twenty-five'."

"That's the way the people who live there say it", Blanca explained to him, "translating it literally from English."

"There are furnished ones", said Teresa.

"Where are you going, Grandma?", Gustavito asked over his pudding, his eyes very wide.

"To Miami, love."

"We're going to miss you", Blanca said.

"*Ay!*, don't talk about that", Teresa stopped her.

Blanquita started crying and tipped over her glass of milk.

Méndez gave Gustavo $35. for the children, $30. for Guillermo, $25. for Cristina and $20. for Esperanza.

"If you need money", he offered, "take it."

By July 31, according to their official statement, 897 persons had been shot since the beginning of the revolutionary government. Objective sources, however, figured that actually 4,619 Cubans had been shot by that date.

Tuesday was the last day Ana worked. Betancourt gave her a sample can of white sturgeon caviar they were beginning to import from Russia, for her to taste. She'd never been able to pick a fight with him in the month and a half she had worked with him. She admired him. She stayed half an hour late working on the translation of some studies on silk for import, to leave all her work up to date. Ofelia Barquet left while she was still working. Ana wished she had been able to say good-by to her, she'd been a good friend, but she didn't know how to tell her − or anybody, − that she was leaving. She tore out some little maps from her pocket calendar book which she knew Ofelia liked and left them on her desk for her to find the next morning. She'd know then. She looked into Duarte's section as she was leaving, but he was already gone. She'd also have liked to say good-by to him.

Ana had written a letter of resignation which she was going to leave with her cousin Norma to deliver to Betancourt when Gustavo received a cable from their father from Miami saying they had already arrived.

II

When she got home from work, before dinner, Ana walked to the Victor Hugo park by herself. She needed some time alone, away from the empty apartment or the crowded hotel room. There was a smell of croton, fern and plantain weed. She stepped on a brittle papery woman's-tongue pod, which snapped under her foot. It took her back many years to her early childhood on 24th Street, when her mother took them to the neighborhood park. Childhood memories, long forgotten, rushed at her: the walk to the park along tree-lined streets, their shade, the lacy heart-shaped peepul leaves on the sidewalk, the rotten crushed purple berries with an acrid smell, a chauffeur at a gate ... She played on the grass ... There was the tall, retarded girl who ran and lived near the park − was her name Inés? − The grown-ups talked to her, but the children taunted her and shouted ... The chubby little boys with hair clipped short who played with her brother ... Her shyness; she'd been afraid of the boys and bashful with the girls ... The two fat little girls with pastel dresses who'd given her the whooping cough, who seemed better off than she, Vitalia, the triplets in their stroller, the big boy, Gerardo, across the street ... The governesses, sturdy Spanish women with thick ankles and curly black hair sprinkled with gray pulled back behind their ears under nets, no lipstick, white face powder, their thick brogue ... "He didn't mean it", a voice drifted to her from a bench long ago ... "Like he who says, nothing." Who was "*Hewho*"? ... "I was as tall at fourteen as I am today", while rain poured. They were in a doorway waiting for it to slacken. The woman was Spanish too, but she wasn't a nursemaid, she was talking about her daughter, older than Ana – twelve?, – Violeta, a tall, thin girl with a very pretty face, white, round, sort of flat, and black curly hair. Who were they? ... The florist's little blue wooden house ... "How's the girl?" A black face at the door from the dining room over a fat shape. She must have been three ... The little chicken on the leg of the up-turned table on the double bed, house cleaning. The landlord was coming. "Don't wet the chicken, Baby, chickens don't take baths." But there was house cleaning ... The round table, the rear window, the nursery in the back alley. A wasp stung her stomach ... The kitchen sink ... The children next door. "Menocal has a flivver in his belly", they sang, their voices floating over the wall of the side yard ... Her occasional baby-sitter when she was three and four, Delfina, who picked her nose ... The jump rope, the porch, the rough finish of the façade ... Her father with the 'connect-the-dots' puzzle in the Sunday *"El País Gráfico"* supplement ... Plums, Rodolfo the Chinaman's fruit stand ... Shoe-string fried potatoes in a paper cone, the *frita* stand before the restaurant across the street ... Seltzer water, Spanish Don Pancho's grocery store on the corner ... The carmine four-o'clocks in their garden, the two boys next door, Norberto and Genaro, who had built a wooden dollhouse for her on the porch and their mother, Lucinda, a seamstress ... The boy on the other side, Aurelio, and Carolina, his mother, wringing her hands – "*Ay*, Teresita!" – talking over the banister to her mother on the porch about the *"bolita"* numbers ... The old lady, Delia, with her peculiar old smell, her colics and palpitations ... The Spanish woman, Amalia, who was forever scrubbing the living room floor on her knees and smelled of sweat, with her three children, Marcia, who went in and out of the house running, Alfredito, with an up-turned mop handle under his arm pretending it was a crutch, and Juanito, who worked in the Spaniard's grocery store ... The mulatto woman, Olimpia, with all her potted plants hanging from wires in the porch ... The French woman, *Mademoiselle* Beaulieu, to whom nobody wanted to talk because she had a lover, a radio announcer, Durán ... The tall road footman ... Idalia, Carolina's daughter, who knew how to tie her shoelace, and had cut herself on a broken toilet in the vacant lot across the street ... The traveling circus on the corner ... The colored woman, Herminia, who sold *"boletos"* and lived in the rooming house at the end of the block ... The laundress', Marina's sons ... *"Cuscurrones"*[59] ... "The Beer Barrel Polka", Tito Guízar, *"La Tremenda Corte"*. What was the mouth like inside the radio? ... The first time she'd gone to the beach, the tall hedges along the way. Her bathing suit had no top ... Strawberry ice cream at "El Aguila" soda fountain, the huge scale and the filthy restroom ... She'd been five then. The memories spun around like a whirlpool. When they ebbed away, they left her weak, afraid. She'd thought she'd feel cleansed, she didn't. Drained, she went back home.

...

That evening, she went with Dany to the little coffee shop low on O Street across from the Hotel Nacional near the old Esso building, where she'd dared him to join the militia, and afterwards they sat on the Malecón wall, facing the Maine plaza, in the same spot where he'd first talked to her about marriage.

"It was my father who denounced me as a leftist to the Embassy", he told her unexpectedly.

"Why?" She looked at the monument before them with the chain and anchor from the battleship at the base.

"So I wouldn't leave with you."

"How did you find out?"

"Sonia told me."

"It's ironic that I didn't leave." She looked toward the lone royal palm at a distance to their left.

"Come with me to the house Saturday", he said to her now, "with your mother."

"Saturday?", Ana asked, confused by the surprise.

"So they'll meet you."

Why now? He was reacting to the revelation with the decision to assert himself. Saturday they wouldn't even be here. She didn't answer. After having waited for it so long! He interpreted her silence as agreement. Ana turned to face the water of the Gulf, dark in the moon-less night. Her heart was beating hard. The soft waves broke below with a warbling murmur. The air smelled of salt, iodine.

"The rocks look black", she observed. Dany turned to look down at them with her. The breeze blew their hair over their forehead and

[59] well baked small bread crust balls

their eyes. Muffled voices reached them in the distance, from outside, below. There was somebody on the reef. Fishing? Cars sped by west-bound. They didn't talk much.

When they parted that evening, she pressed against his chest with anxiety. He showed a little surprise at her apparent desperation, but he circled her in his arms and kissed her.

The ORI (Integrated Revolutionary Organizations) was founded, established by Aníbal Escalante, an old-guard communist, to form a one-party system and Blas Roca was appointed secretary-general.

By the summer of 1961, the process of socialization had been completed, the upper class had been destroyed and the middle class had been uprooted.

Wednesday Teresa called the Ministry and left the message for Betancourt that Ana was ill. They went to the Swiss Embassy to pick up their travel documents, and wasted most of the morning there.

On the corner of K and 17th, they ran into Felipe, who looked at Ana somewhat curiously, apparently surprised that she weren't working.

"We're on our way there now", her father said, pointing toward the house, who knew why.

In the evening, Ana waited for Dany at the front steps of the building and he picked her up in his car a few minutes before 9:00. He took 23rd Street west. They passed "Le Printemps" florists. At the corner of 26th Street, he waited before the "Hong Kong" restaurant for the simultaneous green and yellow lights to turn left. They passed before the Acapulco theater, the Chinese cemetery, the "Barbaram" with its porch trimmed with white wrought iron, the old Minimax supermarket, the sculpture of the deer in front of the zoo entrance, Pozos Dulces Forestal School and the Clínico-Quirúrgico Mercedes del Puerto Hospital, and they went to Ward's on Santa Catalina Avenue. They had ice cream sodas. They talked about Dany's exams, his work, and about inconsequential subjects. And later they leafed through the magazines on the rack at their backs.

On their way back, they passed the Coca-Cola plant. Ana looked to the south toward the peak roofed houses, trying to guess where her parents' lot had been located. On Rancho Boyeros Avenue in front of the Sports City, Dany turned right toward the colorful Luminous Fountain. On the rotunda a snapping neon split bun chased a fleeing hot dog over the entrance of a restaurant. He parked on Genios Street, by the side of the zoo. He kissed her and she held on to him tightly, with urgency. It would be the last time they'd see each other. She felt an uncontrollable desire, but at the same time, the restlessness she suffered didn't let her overcome the tension that gripped her.

"What's the matter?", he asked her immediately, pushing her away from him a little so he could look in her eyes.

"Nothing. Why?"

"I sense something in you, *mi vida*, but don't know what. You're tense. You've been too quiet, since yesterday, like subdued. Is there something wrong?", he insisted.

"No, nothing, *mi cielo*", Ana maintained.

"At home?", Dany ventured. "With your parents? About me? At work? Do you feel sick?"

This was the moment, if she was going to tell him at all. They had been closer in this last month and a half than they had ever been in the other two and a half years. They were now so much more conscious of each other's moods and changes, so much more careful of holding on to each other. Now she was sure that he'd understand their reasons for leaving. But what could she tell him now? That she was leaving tomorrow? That held more deceit in itself than she'd be able to explain. She had been positive all along that there was no danger of his reporting them. So how could she explain to him now why she hadn't told him? Because she wouldn't have been able to make him leave with her? "I didn't tell you before", she imagined herself saying to him, "because I wanted to beg you to go with me and I knew you'd try to talk me out of leaving, so it was better not to tell you at all." It sounded senseless even in her own mind. The truth was that she knew he wouldn't understand how she could leave if she loved him — she couldn't understand it herself, — and he wouldn't have seen any sense in being with her for a month and a half if they were to separate. So she kept quiet.

"No, there's nothing", she persisted, and buried her face in the hollow of his neck. The wedding date, now just over two and a half months away, would never be kept. If they hadn't broken up four months ago; if, three months ago, they hadn't been apart, she wouldn't be leaving. They would have been planning their wedding when her father had decided to leave. Nobody would have expected her to go. They would probably have postponed their trip until after her wedding. If she wasn't leaving, maybe her parents, by themselves, wouldn't have decided to go, leaving their two children behind. He would finish at the university, become an accountant in a month, and she wouldn't share it with him. How she was going to miss him! She wouldn't be here Saturday to go meet his parents. She didn't think she wanted life without him. Now that everything was perfect. Restlessness pervaded her, but desire finally overcame the tension and she abandoned herself to her senses. She closed her eyes and kissed him. He placed his palms on her back and brought her to him, pressing her against his chest.

"I don't know what", Dany told her afterwards, "but I know something's wrong with you, but few times have I felt you give yourself to me so completely."

She only kissed him again by way of reply.

... And the day arrived. Thursday they left the hotel where they had slept for the last time, with the clothes they had worn the day before and the sleepwear of the previous night folded in a paper bag. They were wearing the new clothes they had bought for their trip, to start their new lives. They walked the three blocks to the apartment, where their three suitcases stood packed and ready to lock.

Ana picked up the telephone from the floor and called Dany at work, letting him think she was on her break. Her father was closing windows, her mother checking the kitchen cabinets. There was nothing left. Dany was busy; they were waiting for the work he was doing, he told her.

"I love you", she blurted into the phone past her tight throat.

"I do too, *mi vida*." He threw her a kiss and she returned it.

"*Mi cielo*,... I'm leaving."

"All right." There was a click, the connection was cut, the dial tone buzzed and Ana stood holding the phone in her hand for a moment.

"Did you tell him?", her mother asked her.

"Yes, but he didn't understand me."

Teresa gave her a compassionate pat on the shoulder and rushed out of the apartment without a backward glance, a tear, Ana saw, trailing down her cheek. Carlos stood at the door and surveyed the empty apartment slowly for the last time, Ana at his side. The bare moss green walls seemed to confront them indolently.

"What do I do, lock it?"

"Yes, lock it, Papá."

And he locked the door on five and a half years of their lives. They took their three suitcases and sought Felipe out to say good-by. They found him in the front hall with a long dustmop in his hand.

"Where is it you're moving?", he asked with a touch of skepticism.
"To Matanzas", Teresa held, "to my aunt's." She seemed to have possessed herself of it.
Méndez shook his hand. "Thank you."
Gustavo came with Blanca to take them to the airport in the car. They had left the children with Leonor.
"They wouldn't understand", said Blanca. They could see Teresa was very disappointed.
The ride to the airport was quiet and tense. It was hot in the full car. They had the last issues of several magazines and Gustavo bought the day's newspaper for his father. Their luggage was checked in, each bag weighing six ounces under the limit, and they sat in the waiting room chairs. Ana entrusted her resignation letter to Blanca. Nobody had called Betancourt today, she thought. Carlos ordered bottles of rum and cream of cocoa in the duty-free store that they could resell when they got to Miami. They joked nervously.
When the passengers of the "freedom flight" were called, they all hugged emotionally, and father and son slapped each other on the back. There were some kisses exchanged with serious faces and the three women's eyes misted. And the three were swallowed by the glass-enclosed section, the "fish tank". When they had been sitting inside for a while, they saw through the glass her uncle Guillermo and his wife Beatriz arrive with her aunt Cristina and her husband Marcos to see them off. Apparently Gustavo had called them. Guillermo, retired from "Toledo" sugar mill, would have been at home, but Marcos, still employed at Sarrá druggists, should have been at work. They hadn't been able to embrace them.
Ana wanted very much to see Dany for a last time. She approached the militiaman who was guarding the door and asked him, "Could I make a phone call?"
"Too late, comrade. You should have thought of that before. You had plenty of time."
"Could I ask somebody outside to make it for me?"
"Well...", he hesitated, "but only if he knows the number. You can't go passing a piece of paper to anybody."
Ana nodded, she signaled to Blanca to get close to the door and asked the militiaman to let her talk to her. The man opened it only a few inches and she called out to Blanca over the people crowded before the door, "Please call Dany at work for me. Ask him to come to the airport after work. The number is F, three one, sixty-four, fi..."

The people outside, at the sight of a crack in the door, started shouting to their departing relatives inside.

"Three four, sixty-one...?", Blanca yelled over the confusion.

"No!, three one, sixty-four,...!", Ana screamed frantically.

Just then they were called to the table. And the guard impatiently closed the door again. They stood in line to have their blue passports with the silver coat of arms inspected and their departure stamped. That done, they moved down the table to where a militiaman took their exit permit cards.

"Where do you work?", he asked Méndez.

"I had to close my accounting office for lack of business."

"Income?"

"I'm retired. The pension is a hundred and ninety-three a month."

Teresa was next and she told him, "Housewife, as the card says. No income."

"Where do you work?", he asked Ana, who followed, "and what's your income?"

She thought for a second and remembered her card showed "Wayne Motors", so she answered, "I used to work at Wayne Motors International, but the company left last October and I've been out of work since."

He wrote "Null" in pencil across the buff color card and returned it to her.

They sat down to wait. There were about thirty people in the room. Ana felt unquiet at not being able to have Dany called. Suddenly a woman crying at the table caught their attention.

"What happened?", somebody asked.

"The stamp on the passport doesn't cover the photograph", somebody else answered.

"I'm sorry, but you can't leave", said the man behind the table. "This isn't valid."

"Please!", the woman wailed.

The clerk shook his head adamantly and said something they couldn't hear. A man was standing by the woman with a boy of about two in his arms. The little boy's eyes were wide.

The woman's plea was repeated and met with the same head shaking. She was sobbing loudly, with desperation. They were watching her with interest. Ana felt compassion at her anguish. The man, apparently her husband, said something to her softly.

"No, you go", she answered, crying. "You take him! Take him!"

She pushed the arms that held the boy. She didn't move away. Another clerk approached them and moved them aside.

The line moved on. The woman was led down a corridor, while the man stood aside holding the boy, who was now crying in fear and held his arms out to his mother.

They were handed Cuban National Bank forms on which to declare all the jewelry and valuables they were taking. Ana listed her gold wristwatch, her pair of earrings with unfaceted sapphire chips, her ring with a natural pearl — her birthstone — and her neckchain with a medal of Saint Anne. She hid her gold bracelet in the breast pocket of her lime color dress. Teresa listed her wristwatch, her neckchain with a medal of Saint Joseph and her engagement ring with five little diamonds, and she hid a ring with a turquoise in the pocket of her dress. Carlos only had his gold wristwatch and his plain gold wedding band to declare. They stood in line before the table again to submit their statement and the clerk that took it approved everything on it except Ana's pearl ring.

"You can't take this, miss", he told her, crossing it out. "You'll have to leave it with whoever came to see you off." He handed the statement back to Méndez. Ana turned away from the table with the ring in her hand and followed her mother. It was the ring her grandmother Eva had given her when she had graduated from eighth grade; she had worn it for ten years. The pearl had originally been in a hatpin and then in her grandfather José's tiepin. She hesitated and looked back at the clerk. He was already busy with the line of passengers and not looking her way, and she impulsively slid the ring into her handbag. She sat down next to her father, trying to calm herself. She was afraid.

Gustavo and Blanca were standing outside the glass wall, with their aunt Cristina, Marcos, their uncle Guillermo and Beatriz. Cristina had one cheek pressed against the glass, while tears trickled down her face, like a child. Apparently, they hadn't called their aunt Esperanza, or Blanca's parents. They'd be offended. She felt tense.

An official stood before the table and, his arms extended to command attention, he threatened, "If anything is found on anybody, the flight is cancelled."

They looked at each other with suspicion anticipating a reason to turn into accusation.

After a while, a civilian clerk by the gate to the field called, "Juan Carlos Méndez Miranda,... María Teresa Bermúdez Trejo,... Ana

María Méndez Bermúdez. Go out to have your baggage inspected."

They walked out on a ledge, where their suitcases already lay lined up on the floor, and inspectors asked them for the keys to open them. The man opening Ana's felt through the clothes, spilled the costume jewelry, the locket and filigree bracelet among them, missed the four unopened bottles of perfume and the two towels, but came instead upon a newspaper page. Only then did Ana notice that the page she had kept for ten years showed a photograph of ex-President Carlos Prío and she was surprised.

"The only reason I k- kept that page", she stammered, "is because it has my picture on it", and she turned the page over for the man to see her graduation photograph on the other side. He didn't look at it.

"We have nothing against Prío", he said slowly, smiling a little sarcastically. "He's not a bad man, only a man who wanted to protect his money", and he smiled more broadly. Ana only half-smiled back, timidly. He dug his hands into the clothes, pulled out a few pieces which he pushed back in, closed and locked the suitcase, put an inspection sticker on it, stood it on its side and handed the key back to Ana. She stood by her up-ended suitcase and saw that her mother's had already been closed and the boy who had inspected it was very young and was still talking to her.

"How hot! Have you noticed", he wiped the perspiration from his forehead with his handkerchief, "the heat hasn't let up, since early July? And we still have about three more weeks like this."

"It's going to be worse in Miami", Teresa commented, maybe to show sympathy. Ana looked at her mother's face with interest and could see from her expression that she was sorry she had said that the very moment the words were out of her mouth. The boy looked at her too, but indifferently, lighting a cigarette.

A man was still inspecting her father's suitcase. He was frowning at an unlit cigar. He finally looked up at him, shrugged and suddenly slammed the lid back on the suitcase, locked it, straightened up with a groan and gave the key back to Méndez.

They went back to the glassed-in section and sat down again. The relatives who had come to see the passengers off were bringing them sodas to ease the long wait, which were taken by the guard at the door and given to the parties. Her uncle Marcos brought them Cawy lemon sodas. They thanked him by signs. Blanca had apparently not heard Dany's phone number; she was still standing with Gustavo by the glass wall. Inside, a few children were running around. Ana tried to read, but gave up; she couldn't concentrate. Two strikingly beautiful girls she thought she had once seen at her clinic were sitting with their parents and two younger brothers, reading, oblivious to their surroundings. Ana wondered if they weren't nervous. At that moment she didn't feel any emotion at leaving behind her relatives, her country, her love, everything she had known; she was numb, she could feel only anxiety to be free.

A few at random were taken down a corridor to the right to cubicles similar to nurses' examining rooms, where they were searched individually, the women by a militia woman and the men by a militia man. The woman, heavy, rough, felt Ana's ribs on her sides, her waist, her thighs. It was degrading. She shook the magazine she was carrying. Ana sat once again. They waited. They talked in monosyllables. They leafed through the magazines. And fidgeted. Restlessness became unbearable.

At 5:30 they started calling the passengers of the flight. Their names were read. She felt relief. They stretched. They waved goodby to Gustavo and the others through the glass. Her brother looked older, sick. Her aunt Cristina was pressing her hands against the glass wall, crying inconsolably. Marcos had put his arm around her shoulders and was offering her a handkerchief. Her uncle Guillermo, thin and stooped, his hair gray, wore a sad look. Beatriz hung on his arm, leaning her cheek against his shoulder. Blanca had a sad expression. And for the first time, it all hit her, the scene was driven into Ana's mind; she felt terribly afraid she'd never see them again and she realized the magnitude of what they were doing, her heart shrank in her chest and her tears spilled. Her mother was crying too, and Carlos took her arm and led her out the gate to the field.

A small table had been set up just outside the gate and, as they stepped out on the ledge, a militiaman took their handbags, canvas bags and any parcels to search them, and emptied the contents of some onto the table. They hadn't known this would be done. Ana thought, too late, of the pearl ring in her handbag — she could have hidden it in her pocket, — and remembered the $1.53 in change she had in a little manila envelope, and she felt her stomach flip. She had gathered one coin of each denomination, *"quilo"*[60], two cents, *medio*, *"real"*[61], *peseta* and two *pesetas* with the traditional national

[60] one cent coin, slang
[61] ten-cent coin

coat of arms on the heads and a star with their value in Roman numerals on the tails, as a memento of their official currency, and twenty-five and fifty-cent coins minted in 1953 in commemoration of the centennial of Martí's birthday with his profile on the heads and a Phrygian cap on a fagot of twigs on the tails.

Her mother had thirty-five cents in American coins in her handbag, which the man now took and gave her two nickels in exchange. "This is all you need, for a call from the airport", he told her.

Ana handed her handbag to the man, who rummaged through it and was just about to close it when something caught his eye, he reached in and brought out the ring. He looked at it and asked her, "Did you declare this?"

"Eh,... well,... yes" He kept looking in her eyes. "Well,... I was told to leave it. I forgot to leave it with m..."

"Did somebody come to see you off?", he cut her babbling.

"Yes, my brother", she answered fast.

"Well, leave this with him, if you don't want to lose it because we confiscate it. What's his name?"

"Gustavo Méndez."

"Rojas!", he yelled. "Give this to Gustavo Méndez outside", and he handed the ring to another militiaman. Ana tried to follow the man with her eyes, but lost him in the crowd, and she made a mental note of the last name to ask Gustavo about the ring when they wrote to him. The man now turned the rest of the contents of her handbag on the table and Ana watched the Cuban coins spill out of the little manila envelope and roll on the top. "We'll have to confiscate this money", he said firmly. "You can't take money out of the country."

"I thought that applied to American currency", Ana alleged stubbornly and uselessly.

"And Cuban silver", the militiaman answered curtly, sweeping the coins into the open drawer with one motion of his arm and stuffing the rest of her things back into her handbag. He didn't look in her wallet, where she had put an American dollar bill and a quarter. She followed her parents out to the field.

Méndez suddenly stopped, remembering the liquor bottles, and turned back to the wheelcart to claim them. When Teresa, already at the foot of the rolling stairs, saw him turn back, she screamed at him almost hysterically, "Leave that! Do you want to stay behind? The plane is leaving."

An airplane attendant by the stairs said jokingly, "It seems he

On Leaving the Homeland Behind

doesn't want to leave, doesn't it?"

Carlos got the bottles and ran to the plane. He was the last passenger to board. Ana sat next to the window in front of her parents. The stairs were rolled away.

The lookout terrace had been closed to the public in the last ten months. They could no longer see Gustavo, Guillermo, Cristina and the others through the windows.

The engines started. The plane taxied up the runway. It picked up speed and got off the ground. As it gained altitude, they saw the green land sprinkled with royal palms rush away below, the Malecón hugging the shore of the capital, which receded fast to their right as the plane flew out over the blue water of the Straits bound Northnortheast. Their dear, dear land. The land they were leaving behind. She didn't want to leave! She strangled a scream in her throat and gripped the armrests of her seat to regain control.

After a couple of minutes of tense silence, the pilot's voice was heard unexpectedly over the intercom announcing deliberately, "We are now outside the Cuban three-mile limit, and flying over international waters." A relieved murmur instantly spread and grew down the length of the plane; somebody started to applaud and most of the passengers joined in.

The heavy, older man sitting next to Ana suddenly burst out, as if he had been holding his breath, "Now that I can talk, I hope a steam roller flattens Fidel out!" He sounded like a child, and Ana had to laugh at his outburst. He *had* been quiet; she had barely been aware of him. "A pleasure to meet you, miss", he proffered his hand. "Ulises Peraza."

"Same here", she answered him, taking it. "Ana Méndez."

She leaned back, closed her eyes and breathed more deeply.

After a while, an attendant went by spraying with a mist that enveloped them in a cloud. Peraza coughed.

"They're fumigating the plane", he said surprised.

"In tourist flights they don't fumigate", said Ana, "at least until a year ago."

"It may be that we who emigrate are a different type."

"Contagious?"

"Maybe."

After a moment, Ana went to the washroom, pulled her gold bracelet out of her pocket and put it on. She washed her hands, fixed her hair and touched up her powder and lipstick.

As she headed back to her seat, one of the beautiful girls who had been reading, now sitting to the rear, observed, "Ah, you hid that!" She sounded admiring and Ana was surprised that the girl had noticed. She held out her wrist and noticed that the girl was also now wearing a string of pearls, earrings, a bracelet, a ring, a pin. "It's very nice", she complimented.

"Thank you. I see you did too", Ana smiled.

"I hid it in my underwear", she explained deprecatingly.

"They made me leave a ring", Ana expanded. She didn't know why she felt so outgoing, but she wanted to talk. "Pearl. I didn't dare hide it." Perhaps she had been quiet too long that day.

"What a pity!", the girl sympathized.

Ana went on forward to her seat. Small consolation!, she thought, intent on smuggling a few pieces of jewelry when the most important things stayed behind.

Teresa, by the window, was leafing through the mid-June issue of The Saturday Evening Post which Ana had brought, and next to the aisle, Méndez was leaning back, his eyes closed, his fingers drumming on the armrest of his seat, the newspaper folded on his lap. Ana took it, her father opened his eyes and she sat in front.

The Ministry of Social Welfare was being dissolved and a new Minister of Transport was named. Two consolidated enterprises were being created and their directors named. Guevara would head the Cuban Delegation to the Inter-American Economic Conference at Punta del Este. An ambassador to Poland was accredited. A reorganization of the syndical system was disposed; a worker's syndicate would be identified with his basic labor unit. Two property registrars were resigning. More rebels had been arrested in the countryside. **"COUNTER-REVOLUTIONARIES CAPTURED.** <u>Remedios</u> - The official spokesman for the Ministry of the Interior announced today the arrest of six terrorist members of the counter-revolution, carried out in the southeast of the Bamburanao Range near Buena Vista yesterday by members of the country militia, commanded by responsible comrades Estanislao and Hermenegildo García Soa, who received information that the agitators were gathered in the Hacienda San Alfonso, on the Loma de Centeno, where they were surprised in subversive activities. Weapons and munitions were seized. Those arrested have been identified as Francisco Pérez Hernández, age 22, resident of Cabaiguán; José González Díaz, 29 years old, from Placetas; Manuel Fernández Pérez, 21, Trinidad; Juan Rodríguez Sánchez,

On Leaving the Homeland Behind

24, from Camajuaní; Alejandro Dávila Rodríguez, 25, native of Caibarién and Ant..." Alejandro Dávila? Alejandro! He'd been gone only a month and a half. And he'd already been caught. She continued reading, "Antonio López Martínez, 28, resident of Sancti Spíritus. The malcontents have been temporarily transferred to this city." She looked at the heading of the news again. Remedios. Malcontents, subversive, agitators, terrorists. Alejandro, so gentle. What would happen to him now?

"Miss, miss." She became aware of an elbow nudging her arm. It was the man sitting next to her. The stewardess was bending forward over a tray smilingly offering them *daiquirís* or orange juice.

"Daiquirí, please", Ana asked her, folding the newspaper.

Her seat neighbor took the glass from the stewardess to pass it to Ana. He hit his elbow on the armrest and spilled the daiquirí over her skirt. Ana reached silently for the other glass and the napkin the stewardess was holding out to her.

"Oh!, I'm sorry", Peraza said, visibly embarrassed. "Here, take my napkin."

"Don't worry", Ana answered him, taking the napkin he was placing on her lap, while the icy liquid soaked her Arnel skirt and ran down her thigh. "It's not important. It won't show on the lime by the time we arrive."

"I'm sorry", he repeated, genuinely upset.

Ana smiled at him. And she turned to stare out the window into space. She fingered the newspaper at her side, but didn't open it again. Were these the men Alejandro had mentioned over the phone that evening? What was to be of him?

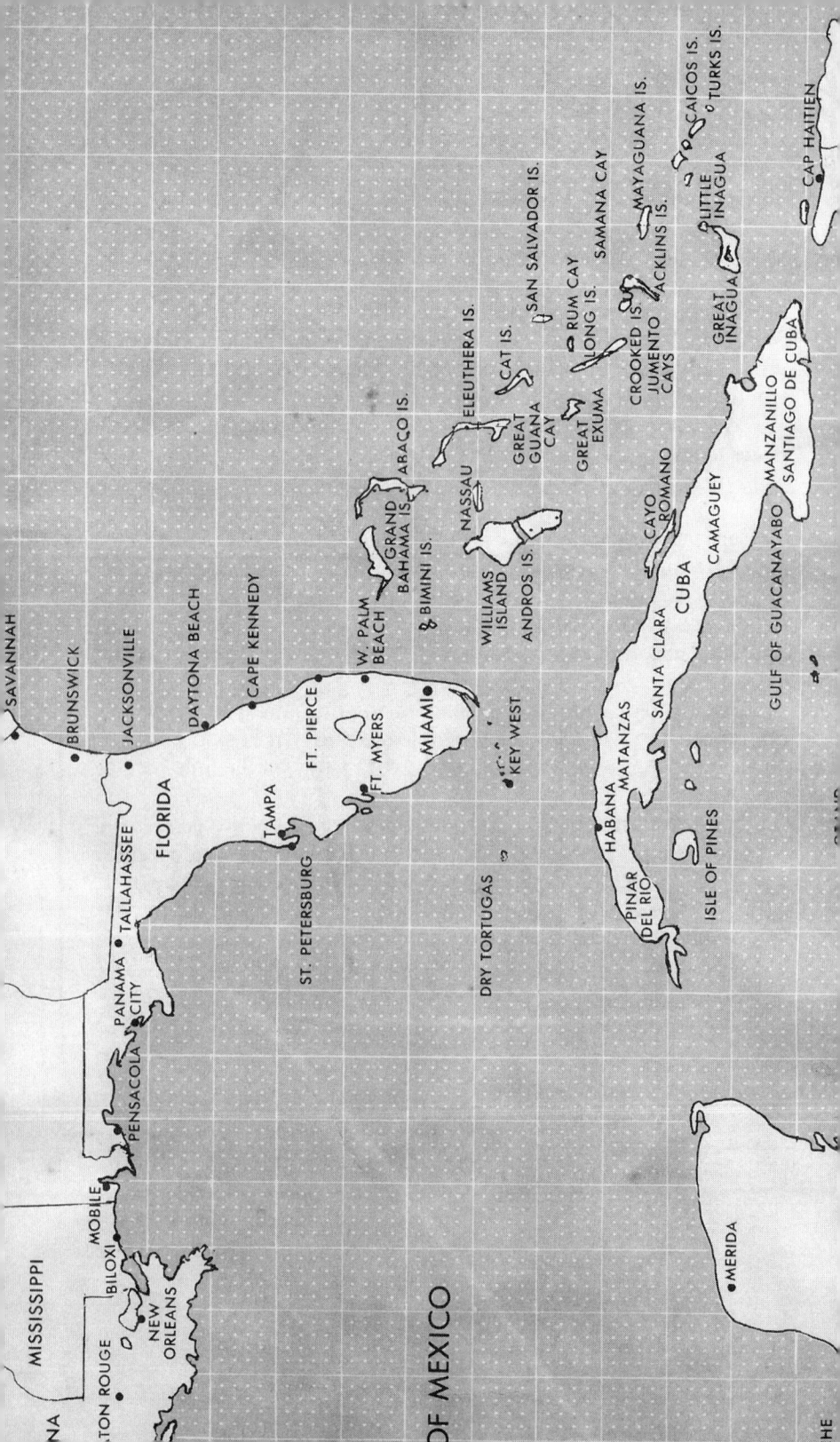

PART II

EXILE

CHAPTER 11

LANDING ON FREE SOIL

> *"Donde la guerra taló*
> *todo el monte y todo el llano*
> *y ni una cruz se elevó,*
> *donde descansa el hermano*
> *que por su fé sucumbió.*
> *De allí fue donde, a pedir*
> *un albergue al extranjero,*
> *me hizo el déspota venir*
> *¡y es allí donde yo quiero*
> *ser libre, amar y morir!..."*[11]
> *("Connais tu le pais?",*
> Isaac Carrillo y O'Farrill)

After twenty minutes' flight, the pilot's voice was heard again, "We're now flying over Key West. If you look out the left-hand side windows, you can see the city."

> [11] Where the war ravaged
> the whole mount and the whole plain
> and not even a cross was raised,
> where the brother
> who succumbed for his faith rests.
> It was whence that the despot
> made me come to ask a lodging
> in foreign land,
> and it is there I want
> to be free, to love and to die!...

People scrambled to look out the windows. They could see the lattice-work of street lights starting to come on far below in the foreign land. Ana had seen it three times before, but it now seemed alien.

The flight lasted fifty-five minutes. They landed in Miami at five minutes to seven.

As they went down the rolling stairs from the plane, they noticed television cameras were filming the arrival of the flight, a floodlight bathed them and a reporter was recording the statements of the passengers who wished to talk. A few seemed anxious to unburden themselves. Ana evaded the cameras. For some reason they made her throat clamp, and her eyes filled with tears. She wasn't sure whether it was emotion at being taken in by this country or realization of the loss of her own. She raised her arm and held it before her eyes, in part to protect them from the floodlight that blinded her, in part to hide her face from the prying camera that inspired modesty in her. The three followed other passengers to the escalator that took them upstairs, where they sat until an Immigration Service officer appeared with a uniformed girl.

The man announced matter-of-factly, in Spanish, "Those of you who have fraudulent visas, please form a separate line."

It seemed an absurd request, but a few people got up hesitantly at first, and then more followed and they lined up to a side, eight or nine persons. That settled, the woman then proceeded to call the names of those with legitimate visas from a list.

The man, wearing a silver badge, looked at their passports as the line moved, stamped on them, "ADMITTED" and the date of their entry, and kept Méndez's visa waiver.

"Welcome to the United States", he repeated to each one mechanically, and yet it made them feel a little comforted.

"Thank you", they smiled back half-heartedly.

A woman who had been claimed by her minor American-born son was instructed to stay behind until they decided on her migratory status.

"But I'm already here", they heard the woman say in a low voice, settling back in a seat with a sigh of relief.

They went down to Customs, where their luggage was inspected. Many passengers who had become friends during the ordeal of the day were exchanging addresses at the exit. Heavy Peraza sought them out and jotted down his address and phone number for Méndez.

"We don't know yet where we'll be staying", Carlos told him. Peraza shook hands with all with wishes of "Good luck". And they never saw him again.

Ana asked a man where there was a telephone, and he directed her to one by the stairs.

They dodged the redcaps and made their way among people who were embracing emotionally, and they carried their own suitcases to the phone booth. Ana took out the quarter that the militiaman had missed. She had forgotten about her mother's two nickels. She looked around and spotted a young photographer, camera poised, near the doors. She approached him and asked him in English, "Could you please give me change for a quarter?"

"Glad to." He reached into his pocket, the subject of focus momentarily neglected, and produced two dimes and a nickel. She thanked him and went to the telephone booth to call Ernesto at the number he had sent her. She wondered if he'd be home on a weekday, but it was late. Would he be surprised?

"Don't move!", he said. "I'm leaving right away to pick you up."

They sat on their suitcases by the stairs. The photographer eyed them discreetly. An American woman emerged from Customs and several reporters stepped in front of her. The photographer's camera flashed.

Ernesto arrived shortly, with a friend. He walked to them and hugged them all effusively and kissed Ana on the cheek. He seemed genuinely excited and Ana was surprised at his display of affection, especially to her father. She realized he had been away from home, family and friends for two months. As they were leaving, Ana turned to wave good-by at the photographer. In the parking lot before the terminal, Ernesto introduced them, "This is a friend. He's living in the same rooming house."

The tall boy shook Méndez's hand, "Pleased to meet you. Javier Zubieta, to serve you." He had light brown hair.

"A pleasure. Carlos Méndez."

"Pleased to meet you", said the women.

The two boys loaded the three suitcases in the trunk of a rusty 1951 maroon Pontiac, amidst a loud rapid chatter.

Once in the car, Ernesto turned around in the front seat to face them. "We were together at Belén school for nine years."

"Until we were fifteen, right?", said Javier, at the wheel, turning also. His eyes were very green, Ana noticed, like elm leaves.

"How long have you been here?", Teresa asked him.

"Three months. No,... less. It'll be three months on Wednesday. I'd been here a week when I heard Fidel propose to exchange the prisoners from the invasion for tractors."

"Are you working?", Méndez asked.

"I haven't found anything", said Ernesto.

"I'm working at a restaurant next to the 'Park Edge' hotel", said Javier, "but I think I'm going to have to go on north. It's easier to find a better-paying job up there."

"He's an agronomic engineer", Ernesto explained.

"I didn't graduate", Javier corrected him. "I only finished third year."

"And can't you find a job in that field here?", Ana asked.

"I don't speak English well, only what I learned in baccalaureate, and it's not enough."

"You can go to the Refugee Center", said Ernesto, now addressing Méndez.

"What's that?"

"An Emergency Center the State has opened for Cuban refugees on First Avenue."

"'Refugees'?", Carlos repeated. "That sounds of..."

"War", Teresa finished.

"Or hunger", said Ana.

"They give free medical attention, and free tuition and books at the vocational centers", Javier explained.

He stopped at the "Dog House" restaurant on Flagler Street, and he and Ernesto went in to buy them sandwiches to go.

"We're going to take you to the hotel where I stayed when I arrived", Ernesto told them when they came back to the car. "It's inexpensive, and quiet."

They turned right and entered the southwest section. They soon stopped before a three-story building, the "Dolley Madison" hotel, old, but dignified, with tall wood-framed windows and a side entrance.

"I'm going to talk to the manager and ask him to give you a little time until you find your way."

Ernesto talked, with difficulty, with the American behind the desk, a Mr. Jameson. The rent was thirty dollars a week, the three in one room. The men carried the three suitcases, preceded by Mr. Jameson, up a carpeted, wooden staircase which creaked under their feet,

Landing on Free Soil

to a room with varnished doors — Mr. Jameson turned the light on, — a double bed and a twin one, and a bathroom. It was a big difference from the Colonial of their vacations. As soon as they had set their suitcases on the beds, Ernesto promised, "I'll be by on Saturday to see how you are."

Javier wished them good luck and they both were gone, and the three were on their own.

A landscape of outlined coconut trees leaning over the beach against an orange sunset and a mirror with etched flamingos hung from the wall, and on the wooden floor there was a multi-color braided rug. A sash window with varnished wooden frame looked out over the back of the building, where a golden shower tree shaded a wooden table with two benches. It was hot and there was no air conditioning.

They unpacked lingering, clumsily, and hung their clothes in the damp closet with varnished louvered door. They showered. After they ate their sandwiches sitting on the edge of the beds, Teresa grinned and surprised them slowly pulling a folded ten dollar bill she had hidden in her compact.

"And you hadn't said anything!", her husband marvelled.

"You were braver than I", said Ana.

Their total cash on hand now amounted to eleven dollars and twenty-five cents.

They felt depleted after the exhausting day and they went to sleep early.

The next day, Friday, they first walked to the Western Union office on 3rd Street before 9:00 and sent a cable to Gustavo. Then they asked which bus took them to the Justice building and went to the Immigration Service office on Biscayne Boulevard across from a field near the Bay Point development, where they stood in line for almost two hours. There were about eighty or ninety immigrants there, mostly Cubans. In a small inner cubicle, the official cancelled Ana's tourist visa, placed a stamp on her passport reading,

"INDEFINITE VOLUNTARY DEPARTURE,
AUTHORIZED —
UNDER DOCKET CONTROL",

with the date, and stapled a parole admission ticket to it. She asked him, "Can I go out of the country?"

"Sure you can", he answered her without looking up.

She realized he had been sarcastic and rephrased her question, "I mean, may I leave the country and come back in?"

"No. You're admitted on parole only once. If you leave, you can't come back in again, except as a resident."

They went next to the Social Security office on Miami Avenue and in an hour and three quarters they obtained their retirement account cards. Ana agreed with her father not to apply to the Refugee Center unless they had absolutely no other choice. They were now ready to set out to make the rounds, Ana of the openings for office personnel, her father of the ones for restaurant, hotel and factory work. Their first step would be to go to the State Employment Service Office. They went out of the building, on the sidewalk they squinted over their directions, Teresa walked back to the hotel and, with mutual words of encouragement and armed with Cities Service street maps, Ana and her father went their separate ways. She walked the four blocks to the State Employment Service commercial office on 1st Avenue.

"Are you a resident?", the woman behind the information counter asked her.

"No, I'm not."

"Then we can't place you. The Refugee Center will help you."

"But I'm not registered at the Refugee Center", Ana protested.

"You're not?" She looked lost. "Do you have the admission stamp on your passport?", she asked hissing the esses.

Ana produced her passport, the woman looked at the stamp and handed her an application card to fill out. She did so, at a table, returned it and sat down in a stiff chair with wooden seat to wait. After a while, a man at a desk behind the wooden railing called her name.

"How do you do, ... Ana?", he said, standing, her card in his hand, and indicated the chair by his desk. As soon as they had sat, he asked her, "How long have you been here?"

"One day."

He looked at her surprised and scribbled something in pencil on the card.

"Haven't you registered at the Refugee Center?"

"No."

"Because, if you are", he explained, "we can't place you. The Center has to help you."

"I understand. I'm not. I want to try not to resort to them." She thought he'd admire her dignity; he couldn't care less. She wondered into what troubles her father might be running, and speaking no English.

He looked back down at her application and read half to himself. "Twenty-four, five and a half years' experience, bilingual, single. We do have a demand for bilingual secretaries. But the firms might be reluctant to hire somebody who's been here only a short time. No local references, you know." He shuffled with two fingers through some upright index cards in a wooden bin on his desk. "Make them believe you plan to stay here."

"But I do."

"But be sure to make them believe it", he smiled. "Would you take a shorthand and typing test?"

"Sure."

"Be here Monday at eight thirty for the test." He handed her a slip and stood up. "My name is Mister Greene."

Ana took the slip from him and stood up. "Thank you. Good afternoon." It seemed odd to her how Americans called themselves *"mister"* as part of their names. It was three minutes before four.

That afternoon Ana went to Rosa Izquierdo's address, which was within walking distance. It was a wooden house set back away from the sidewalk. There was nobody home, so she left her a note on the door with the address of the hotel. She was anxious to see a familiar face.

And Rosa came to the hotel that evening to see them, an American boy with her. After kissing Ana, she introduced him in English, "This is Tim." She sat down on the edge of the twin bed. "We're engaged to be married in two months." She was bubbling.

"I'm very glad to meet you", said Ana. "Congratulations!" Tim sat down in the only chair.

"How did you leave all that?", Rosa asked in Spanish.

"Getting worse by the day", Ana answered, sitting next to her. She didn't want to elaborate on the subject and she got the impression that Rosa wouldn't be too interested. "Does he understand Spanish?"

"A little", Tim answered holding up his index and thumb.

Rosa asked about Olga.

"Integrated", Ana informed her.

"Stupid!", was their friend's opinion.

"And what became of Mirta?"

"Mirta has been here two months now. She lives nearby."

"I should have guessed. Are you working?"

"I'm still at the five-and-ten store. Ah!, come over to my house so you'll see my parents, won't you? Papi loves to talk to the people who've just arrived."

Ana couldn't imagine her quiet father loving to talk to anybody. Fortunately, hers, sitting on the double bed, excused them, "Not yet, after a few days, when we've gotten settled. We're not up to it yet. Still a little confused." Ana was glad to be let out of the obligation.

Ernesto came to the hotel on Saturday, and he and Ana went by bus to Bayfront Park. They strolled along the edge of the water, he put a coin in some binoculars and they looked at the green little Dodge isles, in the bay, and at the beach, blurred, on the other side. Ana forgot, for a while, the difficulties that rose before her, and she pretended she felt as she had when they came out of classes, in Cuba, in more stable conditions. They walked among the coconut trees and around the Dade County War Monument. The band shell was empty and in the metal chairs of its amphitheater rested an occasional man. They took photographs by the statue of Christopher Columbus, the busts of Simón Bolívar, José Martí and Rubén Darío, and in the cool coral rock garden, on the little bridge over the pond where waxy water lilies floated on their cleft pads. Later they sat on the grass in front of the white marble library, near the peeling cajeput trees before a cluster of areca palms facing Flagler Street, the pigeons which had induced the Cubans to nickname this "the Park of the Pigeons" fluttering or leisurely waddling around them. A large Bible rested open in a glass case on a stand under the shade of a huge strangler fig.

"I applied at the Refugee Center for help", Ernesto told her. "I haven't been able to find a job yet, so I'll probably have to leave for Chicago the beginning of October."

"Oh, don't tell me that, Ernesto!", Ana lamented. "I'm going to miss you. We don't have anybody we know here."

"There's that girl who used to work with you at Wayne. What's her name?"

"Rosa. But she's so juvenile. I was never so open with her as I am with you. Besides, she's getting married in two months."

Flanking the foot of Flagler Street were the single-story Pan American Airways office and another airline on the ground floor of the McAllister Hotel. A sign over a restaurant further south, displayed between two jesters, advised, "Keep your eye on the doughnut, not on the hole", and across the street, the First National Bank. Further north was the Columbus Hotel with the Eastern Air Lines office on the ground floor.

"There's something that pulls me from Chicago, ... Adelaida, the girl who..."

"Who used to work with you in the electric company, with whom you used to go out", she finished for him. She remembered when he'd told her he wanted to leave the country the day they had studied at the Habana Hilton, he had mentioned the girl.

"She's up there."

"I didn't know she was in the States." She didn't want him to leave Miami. She felt he was deserting her.

"How has it gone looking for a job?", Ernesto asked her.

"Nothing yesterday. I went to the Employment Service. I have a test Monday. Afterwards, I'll go to the agencies."

"You'll find one, because you speak English better."

"We'll see. Ernesto, do you remember coming out of classes? And that little fat girl who used to sing on the bus?"

"And how I used to annoy Dany saying I was going to call you on the phone at twelve... Did you say good-by to him?"

"I didn't dare. Can you believe I didn't dare?! The day we were leaving I tried to tell him over the phone and he didn't understand me."

"How was that?"

"I told him I was leaving and he thought I meant I was going to hang up."

"Oh... Is he still with the government?"

"Yes", she tilted a hand to indicate ambiguity, "but he left the militia."

"Well, that's a step. That's where Javier works", Ernesto pointed toward the north corner, across the street from the Columbus Hotel.

"Your friend who went with you to the airport?"

"Uh-huh."

"The Cubana de Aviación used to be around there, didn't it?"

"I think on the corner." He stood up and held out his hand to help her up.

On their way back, crossing Biscayne Boulevard, with its three rows of royal palms, their straight gray spindle-shaped trunks like cement pillars, two women passed them and Ernesto observed, "Did you notice how those two women were holding hands? Not like this", he took her hand to show her, surprised, "but like this." He entwined her five fingers with his and dropped her hand again.

They passed three of the tropical fruit juice counters typical of Miami. A dress in the window of a small store near the Town theater caught Ana's attention. She stopped to admire it. It had a skirt and three-quarter sleeve jacket in natural linen, with white polka dot blouse and belt on brown background, the jacket lined in the same fabric. When I have money, she thought, I'm going to buy it. She didn't voice her vain thought.

That afternoon, the newspapers carried disturbing news. During the Inter-American Conference, Castro had declared all paper money void after midnight Sunday, August 6 and forced the exchange of old *pesos* for newly printed currency with revolution scenes, to avoid the exchange of money in Miami by "worms". The arrival of planes and ships was suspended during the exchange. Only $200. in cash per family would be permitted to be exchanged between Sunday and Monday. Each person could exchange money only once, he would receive 200 new *pesos* and an explanation would have to be submitted for any amount over that as to how he happened to have more, and the rest, up to a total of $10,000., would have to be deposited in a special savings account, which would be held in escrow until the explanation were investigated. Up to $1,000. could be drawn initially, and then the rest at 100 *pesos* a month for ninety months. All above that would be confiscated and taken out of circulation to be applied against the national debt; $497.6 million was withdrawn from circulation.

They thought of the money they had left with Gustavo. Would he be able to deposit it and draw it out for them? But he would also have his own money about which to worry. It would take him almost four years and it wouldn't be any good to them there anyway, so it was best not to dwell on that.

Méndez and Ana spent the better part of Sunday making a list of all the employment agencies in the city arranged by address from the yellow pages of the telephone book in the hotel lobby.

Early Monday morning, Ana walked the 16 blocks to the Employment Service office to take the test. There were two other girls, one of them Cuban. Ana noticed the last name Cruz on her application. She passed the test, but, after flicking through his cards again, Mr. Greene told her he didn't have anything for her.

She went to the local office of Wayne Motor Company, on Bayshore Drive, where the tall, thin receptionist, older, dyed blonde, gave her an employment application, the name of the personnel director and an envelope in which to mail it back. She sent the completed application, but never received a reply.

She filled out applications and took tests in every conceivable place during the next few days. She also answered classified ads in The Miami Herald.

She hadn't known Flagler Street beyond the railroad tracks at 1st Avenue, or Miami City outside of the tourist section. She was now surprised to find that many streets didn't have paved sidewalks.

She had an interview with an electrical equipment distributor on Lincoln Road in the Beach. She walked into the air conditioned office and completed the application the receptionist gave her. The man who took it, standing, looked at it and up at her.

"Are you a citizen?", he asked her.

"No."

"Then I'm afraid we couldn't hire you. We get contracts for government work and all our employees must be citizens." He hadn't even asked her to sit down.

"I understand", she said helplessly. "Well, good day."

In a lawyers' office on Flagler Street, a stout woman with dyed black hair interviewed her for a secretarial position. She explained that it was for some clients in Richmond and she would have to move there.

"To Virginia? But it must be very cold there."

"No, not so much. And the salary is higher than they would pay here. Here the climate compensates for the lower salary."

"I don't know. My parents are here and... I don't know, we hadn't thought of moving north."

"Richmond is nice. There are three universities. I remember I used to go there a lot when I was young, to the football games. I was at the State U in Petersburg, twenty-five miles away, and used to go see Virginia's Cavaliers play Richmond's Spiders." Ana smiled, not knowing about what she was talking, and didn't answer. "Well", the lady concluded, "think it over and let me know." They stood up, the woman walked her to the door and told her, "Give me an answer the day after tomorrow."

Ana hoped to get a job in Florida.

In answer to a newspaper ad, she went to an address on 1st Avenue. It was a small printing shop. The manager, a high-strung middle-aged man with a lisp and bad breath, dictated a letter to her in English with atrocious grammatical construction. Standing over her shoulder, he instructed her at length about the setting of the margins and the centering of the letter before she typed it – she got the impression he'd really feel better typing them himself – and, when she handed it to him, he asked her, "Do you smoke?"

"No, I don't."

"Well,... we pay sixty dollars a week, Monday and Tuesday, and Thursday to Saturday, with Wednesday off, from nine to six. I interviewed another girl this morning – Canadian – and I haven't made up my mind yet. I'll call you one way or the other." He never did.

Tuesday they went to the bank where Teresa had opened the savings account eleven months before. The three had written down the number of the account in their address books. They walked up to a clerk sitting at a desk and Ana explained to her that they wanted to withdraw money, but had destroyed the passbook.

"Then you have to complete a form, the account you had will be cancelled and a new one opened with another number, and you can withdraw." She had silver white, very short, straight hair; she looked elegant. "It takes thirty days."

"Thirty days!", Ana exclaimed, dismayed. "But... we need the money."

"Yes, thirty days. In case the passbook shows up, you know."

"The passbook can't show up. We burned it in Cuba before we left."

"Yes, I understand, but it's the policy. It's for your own protection."

"But...", Ana started to insist, but realized the futility of it, and sighed. Teresa completed the form and they left the bank.

In a small office in the Aviation building on 27th Avenue, Ana told the secretary that she wanted to see the personnel manager. The girl looked up at her and barely nodded. There were papers piled up on the two chairs.

"Do you mind if I sit down?", Ana asked the sullen girl. She'd need to move the papers.

"Yes."

"Excuse me?"

"You may not."

She stayed standing for a moment. She didn't know whether the personnel manager would come out. Frustrated, tired, she left. The secretary didn't look up from the typewriter. Maybe she was being replaced.

The heat was unbearable. It was nothing like what they had ever

Landing on Free Soil

known in Havana. The asphalt of the street softened, Ana's high heels dug into it leaving tiny prints, and the sun burned to peel. The temperature sometimes soared to 92 degrees, and it was very humid. In the afternoons, after a shower, beads of perspiration broke out even before she had finished drying herself with the towel.

In the evenings they watched television in the hotel lobby. Suntanned, young newscasters with damp, sunbleached hair gave the impression of having just come in from the beach. Cubans continued to arrive on the daily flights.

Sitting in the lobby, Méndez struck up a friendship with another Cuban guest, Peñalver, a dentist. He lent them the newspaper. The middle class in Cuba, it said, had kept part of their savings in socks, boxes, mattresses and buried in the ground. Housewives had found messages hidden in Polish canned ham which read, "Cubans, wake up. Act before it's too late. Otherwise, you'll be slaves as we are." Similar messages had been found on paper slips in flour sacks from Russia; in some cases they had been discovered on the outside of the sacks. If they would listen...

Ana talked the Richmond position over with Peñalver. "The lady says it's nice."

"What I remember of it", he said, "is a lot of fog, smoke and soot... But she has to find a secretary for their clients."

"Have you been there?"

"On my way back from New York, six years ago, in my drifter days." The dentist seemed to have been everywhere.

"I've noticed", Teresa commented to him, "the water doesn't seem to leave my teeth as clean."

"It is different. You should get a hard toothbrush", he advised. He bought the bottles of rum and cream of cocoa from Méndez for six dollars.

A hum started, it grew, a plane engine approached, it was near, it was going to bomb, it zoomed by, a bomb exploded. Ana screamed.

"What's the matter?" Her father turned the light on.

Ana was sitting on the bed.

"You had a nightmare", her mother said.

"The explosion?"

"It was a plane", said Méndez.

"They fly low here", Teresa said. "Do you want water?"

Her father brought her a glass from the bathroom.

"Did it pass?"

"Yes." She lay in bed, shaken, her eyes staring in the dark, her heart still pounding fast.

At one employment agency they gave her an introduction slip for a poultry export firm near the airport. She took a bus and had to transfer. When she got off at LeJeune Road, she saw a solitary bus bench on a deserted corner by a vacant lot. It was only a few minutes after noon and the sun was shining perpendicularly over the street. She sat on the corner and stared at another vacant lot across the street in front of her and at a restaurant across the other street to her right, where a wooden framed screen door banged once in a while. Her shoulders below her sleeveless dress felt dry and her skin smarted. Surely a bus would be by. Diagonally across the intersection was a service station and further west what appeared to be a hospital. Her shoulders were red. There must be a bus by *some*time. Three quarters of an hour went by. The bus finally arrived and she boarded. She watched the street signs going by fast, afraid to miss her stop, and she rang the bell one block too soon. She got off, walked the block north to the right street and turned right looking for the number. It was a block and a half away.

A man in a cluttered small office raised his flat face from a stack of invoices as she came in, and asked her before she opened her mouth, "The agency sent you?"

"Yes", she answered, extending the introductory slip. He took it without looking at it and placed it on his desk.

"Are you Cuban?"

"Yes."

"I'm Mister Rivera", he told her in English. "I'm Puerto Rican. Can you take dictation in English?"

"Yes, in English and in Spanish."

"Can't you talk any louder? I can hardly hear you."

"Not much louder", Ana replied.

"Try." He handed her a shorthand pad and a thin pencil. "I'll dictate two letters to you, one in English and one in Spanish." When he was through, he indicated a typewriter on a desk near his. "There's paper in the drawer."

Ana typed the letters and gave them to Rivera, who looked them over and nodded.

"Good. Are you familiar with the phone?"

"Not much", she answered honestly, imagining legions of Americans calling, spelling names fast, slurring words.

"How much were you expecting per week?" He didn't linger on one subject long.

"Seventy dollars."

"We only pay sixty-five to start. There's a lot of work this time of the year, but then it tapers off to almost nothing. I'm sure you could handle it. The only misgiving I have is you talk too low. Mister Shapiro, the president, calls long distance from the main office in Atlanta every morning and he likes to hear his girl's voice clearly over the phone, no mumbling."

"I've never had any trouble making myself heard before." She was feeling offended now and reacted by rebelling.

Rivera smiled for the first time, lopsidedly. "Leave your phone number", he told her in Spanish, and handed her the introductory slip. She wrote the hotel telephone number on the back and returned it to him. "We'll call you as soon as we decide." She never heard from him again.

When she walked out of the air conditioned little office, she felt the sun again strong on her shoulders and looked down to see tiny bubbles forming. The sunshine had blistered them in the time she had sat on the bus bench. When she got off the bus, she saw a clear liquid starting to trickle from them.

When Ana came out of the Employment Service office Thursday, it was raining. She tied her scarf over her hair. The hood of her plastic raincoat had gotten lost in packing. She waited at the bus stop holding the raincoat over her head. Two cars with men at the wheel slowed down and stopped to offer her a ride, and she didn't dare even to look at them. An old man standing next to her egged her on, "Get in. Don't get wet, don't be a fool. What the heck!"

She ignored him and moved away from the curb. By the time the bus arrived, she was feeling sorry for herself. She had never found herself so forsaken.

They had been at the hotel for a week. Méndez had laboriously promised Mr. Jameson that he'd pay him as soon as either of them got a job, and the man had seemed sympathetic and agreed to wait, but how long could he wait? Teresa spent most of the day in the room, embarrassed to face him.

They had been trying to stretch their money with fourteen-cent square hamburgers with three drilled holes and nine-cent cups of coffee at the White Castle, eleven blocks away, and the root beer, for which they hadn't developed a taste yet and Méndez insisted tasted like liniment, but seventeen dollars could be stretched only so far and no more. The bus fares especially, over double that in Havana, even when they tried to walk as much as they could, were biting into their pockets and hunger pangs were beginning to gnaw at them.

There was no time for missing Dany.

"How did it go today, Papá?", Ana asked Méndez that afternoon, when he came in taking his wet shirt off. "Did you find something?" Although it was still drizzling, the heat had forced them to open the window. Somebody had removed the screen.

"Nothing", he answered, dropping in the chair, his back to the window. "I've already gone to seven restaurants and seven hotels. Today I went to the 'Everglades'." He took his wet shoes off and wiggled his toes inside his socks. "I've gone to that office on Twelfth Avenue five times. Today they sent me to a window factory. But the interviewer explained that they try to give preference to those who're collecting unemployment insurance." In a gesture of discouragement, he tossed a shoe over his shoulder. "Tomorrow I'm going to an airplane parts factory." The shoe sailed out the window. Méndez didn't realize the course of his shoe.

Without saying anything, Ana went to look out. It had landed on the table in the yard. It provoked her laughter. Her mother started laughing also. Her father, surprised, turned and appraised what had happened.

"I have to go down to get it", he said, laughing too. "I can't afford to lose a shoe now."

"I'll go", said Ana. "Jameson might think you're crazy."

"No, he'll think we're tossing our clothes out the window little by little to sneak out without paying."

The three burst out laughing. The tension had eased. They had forgotten, for the moment, their somber situation.

That night, before going to bed, Teresa suggested, "Carlos, why don't we apply for help at the Refugee Center?"

"No, I want to try not to. It'd depress me terribly to have to beg for charity."

"Everybody gets it."

"Yes, but we don't have to be 'everybody' if we can help it."

"We can't hold out much longer."

"I think we can hold out a little. What do you think, Anita?"

"I agree we should try to wait until there's no other alternative." She actually felt less optimism than she tried to let on.

"Well, I'm getting panicky", her mother confessed.

"No, Tera!", Carlos walked over to her and squeezed her arm. "Remember, it's always there. It's not as if we had a time limit to apply. If we see we don't have another choice, then we can always resort to it."

It seemed to Ana she saw her mother shudder, but she knew she'd get a hold of herself, she had much control. And they were together.

She called Ernesto once from the lobby phone. "You never come to see us", she reproached him.

"Ana", he confided, "the truth is I don't have the money for the bus fare. I live near the City cemetery."

She was embarrassed at having recriminated him.

Friday she had an interview with a lawyer on 2nd Avenue, set up by an agency. After the customary dictation, he said, "I hope you're not sensitive to off-color jokes." This surprised her and she only stared at him not knowing what to answer. "Sometimes I get clients who enjoy telling the secretary a joke a bit off-color, but you can just let it go in one ear and out the other, not get offended and fly off the handle. They don't mean any harm by it."

"Right. What's the salary?", she asked him to get him off the subject, "and the hours?"

"Seventy dollars a week, from eight forty-five to five fifteen, Monday through Friday, with one hour for lunch. If you want to start Monday, the job is yours."

She nodded, relieved. She had been looking morning and afternoon for six days, she had gone on fourteen interviews and this was the only concrete offer she had received. Her stomach growled.

As she walked out of the office, he felt her arm. "You look very healthy and have a nice, wholesome tan."

She wriggled out of his grip and walked to the elevator. "See you Monday."

He walked ahead and pressed the button for her. She felt afraid of him. She wouldn't mention anything to her parents. As she walked out of the building into the blinding sunlight of the early afternoon, she noticed she had no money for bus fare. She had to go to the employment office and it was 27 blocks from where she was. She couldn't walk that much, not in these high heels. And she hadn't put stockings on this morning, it had been so hot, so now her feet felt sore. But she had to go, she had to see Mr. Greene today. Maybe he could place her and she wouldn't have to take the job with the lawyer.

She took the side streets where there were a few trees that gave some shade and started walking. She was over two thirds of the way there when she thought that the pain in her feet wouldn't let her go on. She had blisters on her heels. She looked up at the street signs on the corner. Only seven more blocks to go. There was a grocery store on the corner, the soda refrigerator at the open door by the sidewalk. She leaned against it, pulled her feet half out of her shoes and looked into her handbag again, hopefully. Nine cents. A soda would be eleven. She felt a surge of self-pity and indulging tears came to her eyes. But she couldn't afford that emotion at this time. She took her shoes off and went the rest of the way barefoot. It was the first time she had ever walked barefoot except on the sand in the beach. The pavement and the asphalt were hot, there were no more trees in this area. Nobody was looking at her. When she arrived at the Dundee building, her feet were dirty and swollen. In the elevator, she struggled with her shoes and felt a moment's panic that she wouldn't be able to squeeze her feet back in them.

Mr. Greene asked her to call him again before 4:00. He had something for her, he told her, in a bank, but he needed to set up the appointment first.

She walked back to the hotel hopeful, slowly now that the hour didn't matter any longer, her shoes digging into her swollen insteps. Perspiration made her half slip stick to her hips and she felt it tug uncomfortably at her waist with each step. Vultures hovered around the pyramidal top of the County Courthouse.

In the newspaper borrowed from Peñalver that afternoon, there was an ad for an apartment for rent in the northwest section.

"Let's go see it", Ana asked her parents.

"We'd better wait until one of us gets a job first", Méndez reasoned sensibly.

"Just to get an idea about rents", Teresa argued.

"You two go", her father resisted.

"No, Carlos, you come also", her mother urged.

"We don't lose anything by looking", Ana insisted.

"Well", Carlos gave in, "we have nothing better to do."

Ana put on flat shoes after she took her shower, and they walked to the address. Many streets had no curb and the grass and the pavement ran together. Cars parked on the dirt at the side of the street, and the grass showed dry patches. It was near the Orange Bowl, an old wooden cottage at the rear of a larger house. There were a few

scattered clumps of gaillardias, but the yard was mostly dirt, sandspurs and crabgrass. The fat woman who came to the door of the front house in a print house dress and thongs asked them over the bark of a dog, "Any children?"
"No children", Ana answered.
"Pets?"
"No."
"I'll go get the key." She had a hacking cough.
She was back presently, the dog at her heels. She shooed it inside.
"How many are you?", she asked as they crossed the yard.
"Three."
A live oak rose between the two houses.
"It's a nice place", the woman said, walking ahead, "cool."
Inside, a musty odor assailed them. The woman turned the light on and rushed to open a jalousie window. The furniture was rattan painted a cream color with faded flowered cushions. The worn linoleum in a gray spiral design with red roses was cracked. In two bedrooms there were more chipped cream color furniture and two twin beds in each. Faded landscapes in glass-less plastic frames and pictures made of tinted seashells decorated the dirty rose walls. The kitchen had a small gas stove, a chipped old refrigerator, a deep enameled sink with a flowered curtain gathered on a string hung around the bottom, a chipped enameled table, open shelves and a bare bulb with a string hanging from it. The bathroom had the same lighting, an old tub on claw feet and the paint blistered and peeling off the tileless walls. They walked silently through the cottage, the woman ahead, chattering. The place was depressing.
When they were again out in the yard, Ana asked her, "How much is the rent?"
"Fifty-five. Do you have a car?" Before anybody answered, she went on, "Because if you do, during stadium events, you can't park here, because I rent out the parking spaces. I'm a widow, you know, and I need the money."
"We don't have a car."
"Well, what do you say, *señor, señora*? No speak English, eh?" She smiled. "You been here long?"
"No, not long", Ana answered.
"Nice girl you have here."
Teresa smiled, Méndez thanked her and Ana hurried to say, "We'll let you know."

"Well, I can't hold it unless you leave me a deposit." Gone was the smile. "If somebody else comes in the meantime, I'll have to rent it, you know."

"Yes, we understand." They all said "Good night", and they walked away from the house. It was a shack and not even this could they afford.

So preoccupied were they, a meteor shower that spectacularly reached its peak Saturday failed to draw their attention particularly.

Mr. Greene sent Ana on an interview late Monday morning at the Commercial Credit Department of the Burlingame Commercial Bank in the southeast section. She didn't go to the fresh lawyer's office. She turned south and walked two blocks, passing a supermarket, a cafeteria, a solid-looking hotel with polished cut oolitic limestone façade and a long porch, and an apartment hotel with balustered balconies and a central courtyard with a fountain. It was a three-story building with several Jamaica thatch palms in the grass strip in front, and a weathered brick and tinted glass façade with blue and gold drapes. The river was about 220 yards further down. Inside, the place was small and cozy. The paneled or papered walls, the thick carpeting and the drapes muffled the traffic noise. The furniture was wooden and there were bookcases, hutches and credenzas. There was about it the air of a resort where vacationers had had the need to transact some deals and had reluctantly improvised a business place, but tried to keep it as homey as possible. It retained the charm and flavor of the Miami of six or eight years before, still prevalent in other smaller towns of Florida, as they had known it on their vacation trips, when permanent resident women still wore gloves and hats.

After the usual dictation and typing, there was also an aptitude test. Mr. Mitchell, the suntanned man with the Southern drawl who interviewed Ana, seemed favorably impressed with her, and he explained the work would consist mostly of taking dictation and typing letters of credit. He talked in a very low voice and Ana had a little trouble hearing him. Her hopes rose. When she left the bank, she noticed a natural foods store, an old hotel, a sandwich shop. Walking to the bus stop behind the "five and ten" store, she felt even like smiling to herself a little. Beating her fingernails rhythmically on the bus window frame, it seemed to her the bus was moving slowly.

She arrived at the hotel excited. Her father was still out.

"I just had an interview at a bank today", she told her mother, "and it looks promising." She was afraid of getting too enthusiastic. The

agency that had sent her to the lawyer's had called. "Where's Papá?"
"He went to apply at a tomato plant."
"To pick them?"
"No, packing them."
She returned the call from the agency and as an explanation for her absence, in a candid impulse, she confided rapidly to the lady, "What that man is looking for is not a secretary. I would advise you not to send any decent girl there." After she hung up, she wondered if she should have said that.
She took a shower. Tired though she was, she felt too restless to sit quietly.
Tuesday few classified ads appeared in Peñalver's newspaper, and not one was new. Ana didn't have anywhere to go.
Mr. Mitchell, from the bank, called her. "It seems you're the one elected. I'd like to talk to you a little more. Could you come by this afternoon, after lunch?"
"Sure, I'll be there." Another bus fare meant skipping lunch today, but she didn't want to show up perspiring. "At one fifteen?"
Mr. Mitchell showed her into his office toward the rear of the ground floor. Ana positioned herself, ankles crossed, arms loose over those of the chair, for yet another interview, as she had for countless others in the past.
"There were three other applicants", he told her, "but you were my favorite. I only have one question: Will you be staying in the country?"
Would she? How was she honestly to know? But only one reply fit.
"Yes", she answered him firmly.
He looked at her for a moment. "Well, I guess all the Cubans say that they'll stay, but, if they later can, they'll go back."
"I believe the opposite", Ana differed. "Even many of those who now think they'll return will be staying." She found her English flowed more fluently than she'd have expected, now that the job offer made her feel more self-assured.
Mr. Mitchell cocked his head slightly considering this. "You mean they might have settled...", and then, dismissing the subject, "Well,... the job pays two sixty-five a month. I see you wrote 'sixty-five dollars a week' on your application, but we pay semi-monthly and it comes to a little less than that."
Quite less. – "All right." It was actually almost four dollars less,

but she would have as well accepted sixty a week.

"Okay, then. You'll be working in the Commercial Credit Department on the main floor. You'll be taking dictation from me and the head of the Latin American Department, Mister Tamargo – he's Cuban too, – and typing some letters of credit which will be given to you hand-written in pencil. The hours are from eight thirty to five, an hour for lunch, two ten-minute coffee breaks. So it comes out to about seven and a quarter hours a day, a five-day week. We pay on the fifteenth and the last of the month. Do you have any questions?"

"No, I don't think so. Probably tonight a lot of them will come to my mind."

"That's always the case. Do you have a Social Security card? You will start... tomorrow. That'll be the sixteenth, the beginning of a pay period."

"Fine." She felt like shouting, singing.

"Then, will you fill out these forms for Personnel?"

When she returned the completed forms to him, Mr. Mitchell stood up, Ana said good-by and he walked her to the door. The two tellers were closed, balancing.

She walked the 18 blocks back to the hotel with a quick pace, feeling exhilarated. Some twelve blocks away, she saw a sign before a pink building, "Apartment for rent". She stormed into the hotel room and hugged her mother. "Mamá, I got the job!"

"Finally!"

"Two hundred and sixty-five a month."

"Oh, that's good, Ana María!"

"Papá?"

"He was going to the Robert Clay Hotel, and I don't know if the Towers."

"There's an apartment for rent on the way to the bank. I think the location would be perfect for us."

She took a shower and waited impatiently. When Méndez arrived, downcast, she told him the good news.

"Thank God! I went to a printing press on Tenth Street and to two hotels. Then I met a man who used to work as waiter in a restaurant in Havana where Velázquez and I used to have lunch, and he suggested I go to a hotel on Second Street, where they needed an elevator man. But they had a college student who works during vacation. They said they'd call me when school starts."

"But then they gave you hope", Teresa told him.

"They always say they'll call. If they called me from every place they've told me that, I'd already be working, Tera. By the time school starts, others will have applied."

"You have to be optimistic, Papá. Do you want to go see an apartment for rent about nine blocks from here?"

"What for, Anita, if I haven't found a job yet?", he protested wearily.

"But I did, and they gave you hope, Papá", she pleaded.

Teresa didn't interfere this time.

"All right", her father gave in.

After he took his shower, they walked to the apartment, Méndez despondent, Teresa skeptic.

When they approached the place, they noticed that the red sign hanging on links from a post in front instructed to inquire around the corner. In the building around the corner was an optical shop. When they walked in, a bell rang over the door and a girl in a white smock came out.

"We'd like to see the apartment for rent", Ana told her.

"Oh!" The girl seemed a little disoriented. "I'll call Doctor Knowles."

After a few minutes, Dr. Knowles appeared, his white duster open, a polite smile on his face. He was a handsome man of around forty.

"You want to see the apartment?" He jiggled the keys in his hand. "Come with me, please."

They walked around the side yard to the rear of the building and cut across the backyard to the pink building on the side street to the left. There were no fences. "I was just getting ready to leave." Outdoor wooden stairs in back led to the upper floor. They walked around this side yard to the front of the building.

He opened a screen door and a wooden one to the right-hand side apartment on the ground floor, and let them into the living room, which had a large steel corner window to the southwest, opening over the front lawn, and an archway to the hall. The two bedrooms had closets, and casement windows overlooking the yard on the south side. The modern Danish furniture looked inexpensive and sort of spindly, almost fragile, but it seemed fairly new and cared for. The hardwood floors were partly covered with area rugs and there were venetian blinds on the windows. The kitchen had wooden wall cabinets, vinyl tile floor, a gas stove and an old refrigerator. There were several pictures of orange blossoms, mockingbirds and cabbage palms hung on the walls, which intrigued them. The bathroom tiles were pink. The whole apartment was painted white, but the walls were dirty and had nail holes, and the doors were yellowish and badly in need of paint.

"Do you like it?", Méndez asked Teresa.

"It's nice." She seemed to have perked up a little.

They walked back out the front door to the stoop. Four mailboxes were encased in the wall. Yellow allamanda formed an arc over the entrance of the building, which looked about twenty years old, with wooden awnings over the windows and a tar paper roof. There was a row of aralias along either side. An Indian almond tree stood in one corner of the lot by the sidewalk on the south side, its base surrounded by lantana. A blue mahoe tree in the other corner of the lot near the sidewalk shaded the north side of the building from the sun, now setting. There were four parking spaces in front. The houses on either side were wooden bungalows.

"How much is the rent?", Ana asked Dr. Knowles.

"Eighty, first and last month", he said, setting a foot on the higher step and resting his forearm on his knee.

Ana wasn't sure what the phrase meant, but she translated it to her father literally.

"The one upstairs on the other side is also vacant, if you'd like to see it. It's a little bigger, it has a dining room. That one's eighty-five."

"No, this is fine", Ana said. "We don't need a dining room." She paused. "I just got a job. I start tomorrow."

"Ah! Where do you come from?"

"Cuba."

"Recently?"

"Twelve days ago."

"Well, do you want to think it over? When will you know?"

"Day after tomorrow, Thursday?"

"Fine. I'll wait for your call." He pulled out a business card from the front pocket of his duster and handed it to Méndez with a smile.

"Sank you vetty mush", Carlos thanked him in his Commercial school English.

Teresa had hoped for an unfurnished house, so they could pick out their own furniture, but they found out, from Peñalver and Ernesto, that they wouldn't be granted credit at the stores without local references, so they'd have to settle for a furnished apartment.

Wednesday before going in to work, Ana turned the near corner and walked east. She saw an old-fashioned Atlanta-plantation antebellum style wooden structure, housing an insurance agency that advertised itself as the oldest one in the city, and another three-story office building. She was still early.

Two girls were sitting on the edges of desks talking about where they had gone on their dates the night before when Ana walked into the inner office. She felt shy, the only foreigner there. One of them, a thin freckled girl with blond hair and gray eyes, walked to her smiling.

"You're the new girl? I'm Jennie. I work in the Loan Department. This is Kathy." People didn't seem to shake hands much.

"I'm Ana", she said, and wished she could be more outgoing.

"Hello", Kathy smiled, it seemed to Ana, condescendingly.

"She's the secretary to the vice-president in the Trust Department", Jennie offered amiably. She had long, straight hair.

A man walked in, Jennie silently formed the words "her boss" with her lips, and the group dispersed. Ana walked back to her department, at the rear of the building, and stood while a few young men walked in and settled down. Blue and gold drapes partly let the sunlight in through the large windows on the street to the north. Mr. Mitchell walked in with a trim Spanish man and introduced her to him.

"Raúl, this is Ana Méndez, our new stenographer — she's Cuban also. — She'll be taking your correspondence."

"How do you do?", Ana said in English.

"Welcome aboard!", said Tamargo in Spanish, shaking her hand briefly, and went into his office, next to Mr. Mitchell's.

"This will be your desk", Mr. Mitchell told her. Familiarize yourself with things and I'll be having some dictation in a while."

She felt giddy. She sat at her desk between the doors of the two men's offices and opened the drawers. There were several types of commercial letter of credit forms which she had sometimes seen at Wayne's and the import company, letterhead, lists of correspondents and envelopes. After a while, a buzzer startled her and she hesitated for a few seconds looking at the local line light on the instrument before she picked up the receiver.

Mr. Mitchell's voice asked her, "Will you come in with your note pad?"

She found a note pad and pencils in a drawer and went into his office. He dictated several short letters and then said, "I sign 'Stanley P. Mitchell, Manager, Commercial Credit Department'."

She sat at her desk and started typing the letters.

It seemed only a little while had elapsed when Jennie stood in front of her desk. It was ten fifteen.

"Do you want to go get some coffee?"

"I'll be glad to."

Jennie led the way out of the building and down the block, saying, "There's a lunchroom in the bank that I'll show you later, and we have free coffee, but I like to get out for a little while. Don't you?"

"Sure." She would have preferred not to spend the dime.

On the stools at the small luncheonette over coffee, Jennie asked her, "Do you think you'll like it?" She talked barely above a whisper.

"Oh, I'm sure." How could she know, her first day on the job, her first job in a foreign country? She felt dizzy. She put cream and one lump of sugar into her coffee. She really didn't have much choice but to like it. She had really been lucky to find the job so fast.

"The work load is not very heavy", Jennie told her. She had her coffee black. "Where are you from?"

"Havana... Cuba."

Jennie nodded. "There was another Spanish girl in that job before, but she was Puerto Rican." Her nails were short, unpolished. They smiled awkwardly at each other. "Do you like Miami?"

Ana didn't much like anything she had seen, now that she was living there, but she answered politely, "Yes, it's nice."

"I'm from Pensacola, in the panhandle, but I've been here four years. I like it, especially the beaches; it's warmer." Her fingertips were pink and so was the base of her nose. "Is your family here?"

"My parents came with me."

"Spanish girls live with their parents", Jennie observed.

"Yes... My brother stayed back home."

"I'm here by myself. I share an apartment with another girl, Debbie, the redheaded teller. Holidays I go home."

They couldn't think of anything else to say, so they drank their coffee in silence.

After lunch, consisting of coffee and toast, in a little sandwich shop nearby, away from any co-workers' prying eyes, Ana called Mr. Greene from a drugstore to let him know she had been hired. He congratulated her.

She walked back to the office feeling for some reason a little mopish. Knowing Mr. Greene was there to resort to had given her a certain sense of protection that now, severing the contact, she lost. An American boy approached her.

"Would you have a dime for... a nickel and five pennies?" He pointed to a dispenser. "For the newspaper."

She looked in her wallet, produced a dime and took the change he handed her. She was ready to walk on when he asked her, "Did you get here two weeks ago?"

She looked at him surprised. "Yes, thirteen days", she answered slowly. "Why?" Who was he?, from Immigration?

"I was at the airport the day you arrived." She looked in his eyes and smiled faintly, and he went on, "I'm a photographer and happened to be there covering a story, and you asked me for change for the phone."

"Ah!", she smiled at the tall, thin man with rust color hair, recognition coming slowly. "I recall now." How had he remembered?

"You looked so lost, lugging your suitcase. And I was surprised that you spoke English."

"I'm glad to see you again. I'm due back at work."

"Oh!, you already found a job? Nearby?" She indicated the bank on the next corner. "Would you have a cup of coffee with me after work? My name is Irving", he extended his hand and she answered his gesture, "and I'm staying at a hotel down there." He pointed down the street.

"Mine is Ana. Some time after work", she promised vaguely, and rushed off.

She answered a few telephone calls and, as she had feared, she had difficulty understanding the names and getting the numbers. The local slow drawl and low tone were not like those of the Michiganders, to which she had gotten accustomed.

After work, she wandered up the street, past a twelve-story hotel with a bar, and came to a tiny park, perhaps 100 by 160 feet, on the next block. Beyond it was the river. This was a quiet, light-trafficked section filled with sedate hotels of the type where the older, wealthier Northern tourists came to spend the whole winter.

In their evening conversations in the lobby while they watched television with the dentist and other guests, they talked about Cuba. Food was scarce and meat was rationed. Canned lobster and beef from the Soviet Union, hams and strawberry jams from Poland, and rice from China were found in the grocery stores.

"Did you read", Méndez asked Peñalver, "that, according to Herbert Matthews, Mexico, Brazil, Chile, Uruguay, Costa Rica and Venezuela are 'genuine democracies', but are shaky?"

"He says that? He writes all the editorials about Cuba in The New York Times."

"That's right. And he says that Mexico, Brazil, Chile and Argentina are rich and developed. According to him, there are two 'social revolutions' in Mexico and Bolivia. And two other revolutions are in Uruguay and Costa Rica."

"That contradicts itself", observed an ex-reporter.

"That is what the American people read", said Teresa.

"And what we read too", said Méndez, "when he interviewed Castro in February of fifty-seven."

"Have you found a job?", Peñalver asked Méndez.

"Not yet."

"Maybe I can find you something with a friend of mine. I'm going to talk to him. Are you willing to do anything?"

"Yes, I'd do anything."

Thursday afternoon, when Ana was leaving the bank, Irving was walking by in front of the building. He pretended surprise, "Hello."

"Hello."

"Would you like to have that cup of coffee with me today?" He was persistent.

"All right."

They walked to the coffee shop on the next block.

Over coffee, he confided, "When I saw you coming down the street yesterday, I had to think fast of how I could stop you without appearing fresh, and the only excuse I could come up with was the change for the paper."

"Do you mean you had recognized me before you stopped me?"

"Of course", he smiled. "I didn't even need a dime, the dispenser was on the honor system." Her pride received a boost. "You're Cuban, aren't you?" She nodded. "I'm learning Spanish and wish you'd help me. Could I practice my Spanish on you and you correct me?"

"I'll be glad to", she answered him in English.

"Where are you staying?"

"At the Dolley Madison Hotel."

"Is it nearby?"

"In the southwest section."

"I thought it was so sweet of you to turn to wave at me at the airport as you were leaving."

She smiled. He asked her the telephone number of the hotel and she gave it to him.

And then she started to long for Dany.

The Alliance for Progress was signed on August 17.

Walking to the sandwich shop for lunch on Monday, she heard a man's voice call her name. She turned and was startled to see Salvador Conde in the doorway of a camera shop.

"Well, well", he said, visibly glad. "How long have you been here?"

"Less than three weeks. And you?"

"Almost seven months."

She felt genuinely happy to see him. They talked animatedly, fast, interrupting each other, about their co-workers, the ones who had stayed behind, those who had left, the ones who were there. He was working in a kitchen cabinet factory. They exchanged telephone numbers.

Ana and her parents walked eleven blocks to have the hamburger and the root beer, sitting on stools at the high counter facing the street, which cost them twenty-four cents a head.

Tuesday afternoon Irving called her at the hotel.

"I'm off tomorrow. Would you go to dinner with me?"

"All right", she agreed unenthusiastically.

When she told her parents, her father was upset. "You can't go out with a man you don't know, Anita."

"He seems nice, Papá."

"How do you know?"

"Carlos, Ana María doesn't have any friends here", her mother interceded. "She needs friends."

"She'll make friends at work. Going out alone with a stranger!"

"I used to go out alone with Dany in Cuba."

"That was completely different. We knew him, he visited the house, we knew where he worked. We don't know this guy. You don't know what kind of a man he is."

"She's not a child", said Teresa. "She can judge for herself and can make herself be respected. We'll meet the boy when he comes to pick her up. And you can inspire respect, assert discipline."

Irving picked her up Wednesday evening at 7:00 in a rented car. In the lobby, Méndez indeed inspired respect and Teresa displayed a cautious politeness.

"Let's go to the 'Pub', on Coral Way."

"Isn't Coral Gables far?"

"No, it isn't far, but it's not Coral Gables, the neighborhood, but Coral Way, the street."

It was a nice street planted with false banyan trees down the median. He ordered a martini, she a dry vermouth on the rocks.

"This restaurant was recommended to me", he said.

"What's your descent?", Ana asked him after he'd ordered for them, London broil, medium. She felt curiosity about nationalities.

"Hungarian."

"You're not married, are you?", she asked him suddenly. The possibility had just occurred to her.

"Oh, no! What would I be doing asking you out if I were?"

"You wouldn't be the first married man who ever asked a girl out."

"Well, I'm not. It didn't even cross my mind that you'd think I was. You're not either, are you?"

"No!", she laughed. The American medium felt rare to her.

"There's never been a divorce in my family... Is that a Cuban custom? Having vermouth for an aperitif, I mean."

"Well, I don't know whether it's Cuban, but it's a custom. Perhaps Spanish, or Italian."

"I was surprised, but it must be common, because the waitress didn't bat an eyelash when you asked for it."

Ana ate slowly, afraid to let the full meal hit her empty stomach too fast. Her conscience bothered her that her parents would be eating a square hamburger with three holes and drinking root beer with a smell of liniment while she was here worrying about getting indigestion.

"I'm twenty-seven", Irving said in Spanish. "Why don't you speak Spanish to me too? To get used to understanding it. I hope you don't mind my asking how old you are."

"Twenty-four. Do you work for a newspaper?", she asked him in Spanish. He looked lost.

"Would you repeat it very slowly?" She repeated it. "No, for Consolidated Press. An agency. I'm from New York. Latin America is where history is being made. That's why I'm learning Spanish. Are you Catholic?"

"Yes. I'd rather not speak Spanish to you." She didn't want all the effort of speaking slowly, using simple words, repeating, translating, but she fibbed piously, "I want to practice my English too. You go ahead and speak Spanish to me." She'd go through only half the torture.

"My parents are Jewish." He pushed the food on his plate with his fork for a moment. "But I consider myself more of an atheist."

She was shocked to hear him say that. She remembered somebody — had it been Duarte? — who said he didn't trust an atheist.

"My grandparents came from Miskolc at the turn of the century. They've always lived on Eldridge Street." This didn't mean a thing to Ana.

She was stunned when he asked for a doggy bag to take what he hadn't eaten.

After dinner, Irving asked her whether there was a theater that showed Spanish movies and she suggested the "Tívoli", which she passed daily. They arrived in the middle of the first movie, Mexican, and stood in the dark in the back near the door until their eyes grew used to the darkness. Later, sitting, by the middle of the second movie, afraid she'd be too late and knowing he wasn't understanding a word of the films anyway, Ana suggested they leave.

When he left her in front of the hotel, Irving told her, "I'll be off again next Wednesday. Could we go out again?"

"All right." She was afraid he'd try to kiss her good-night and retreated to the lobby door. Her parents were waiting up for her.

The FORD (Democratic Revolutionary Labor Front), on 1st Street, belonged to the FRDC, headed by Dr. Manuel A. de Varona.

In Havana a three-day conference of cooperative managers was held, closing on August 28.

Next Wednesday, when Irving came for her, Ana suggested the club in the Beach where she'd been in the spring of the year before, as a tourist, with César Villaamil. She recalled the refined atmosphere of the first wealthy Cuban exiles from Batista's time loaded with the money they had taken out of the country and the buxom blonde who sang from inside the bar. All that, she found, was gone. They sat at a small table and had one drink. A Jewish stand-up comedian told jokes from a stage, non-sequitur, some Jewish, most off-color.

"Two compact cars locked bumpers", the comedian said, "and an old lady came out on the street and threw a bucket of cold water on them."

Ana felt embarrassed.

The show over, Irv told her, "You know, you puzzle me. You were so confident." It seemed to her he alluded to a contrast with her shyness at the jokes. He had given up trying to speak Spanish, and she was grateful. "You never had a doubt that you'd find a job, or anything."

"Sure I had doubts."

"I think you're very sure of yourself."

"I'm not really."

"Do you live with your parents? I mean, normally."

"Yes, almost all single girls in Cuba live with their parents."

"Here if a girl of twenty-four still lives at home, people wonder if there's something wrong with her."

"I know." She shrugged.

"I noticed you didn't thank me for the evening last Wednesday."

"It wouldn't occur to me to thank a man for taking me out."

"Would you like to go to the beach Sunday?"

"All right."

On the way back, Irv parked the car a few blocks before the hotel and kissed her. She let him kiss her several times; she didn't dislike it. He suddenly covered her breast with his hand and Ana pulled away from him with a jerk, feeling insulted more than shocked.

"What's the matter?", he asked.

"I'm not going to let you... feel me."

"Why not? I'm not asking you to... well, to go to bed with me, but what's wrong with a little petting? Don't tell me you don't feel excited."

"Even if I did, I won't let you. *Every*thing is wrong with it." The faint sensation his kisses had started to stir in her had vanished as soon as his hand touched her.

"I can tell you're not a virgin, by the way you talk and act, even how you walk", he said, apparently by way of justification. She was surprised and wondered if he really could tell.

"Even if I weren't, there's no reason to let your feelings go unrestrained. There's such a thing as self-control."

"What's the purpose of going against what comes naturally?"

"What's the purpose! Is something wrong with you? I feel satisfaction in knowing I have enough control of myself to do what I know is right, not just whatever I feel like."

"You find satisfaction in frustration? That doesn't make any sense to me." He sounded to her honestly puzzled. Could he be just pretending, to get his way with her? She felt she had to apologize. She remembered a saying her grandmother Eva had quoted sometimes which she'd heard among the Spanish people in New York when she'd been there over thirty years before, when Teresa had just started working. "If an American girl over fifteen and still a virgin ever walked under the Statue of Liberty, the statue would bring down her arm with the torch", and Ana wondered how much truth the cynical saying might hold. She would still be a virgin if she hadn't fallen in love with Dany and, even so, she still thought it was wrong and it wouldn't have happened if she hadn't had so much to drink that evening.

When Irving left her in front of the hotel, he told her, "I'm not dropping you in any way, shape or form." But he didn't call her Sunday. That was the end of their friendship.

That scared her of American boys. She didn't know whether she could risk going out with another one. A Cuban boy wouldn't make any attempt at intimacy until he had repeatedly professed to love the girl, whether sincere or not, and even then, he felt she had to be conquered because she wouldn't do it of her own will, and he cautiously felt his way around to find out whether she'd consent to it. And, however more hypocritical that approach might be, Ana thought she still preferred it to the coarse way of this boy. She didn't mention it to anybody, or her mother would be alarmed and her father wouldn't let her go out with anybody else.

On Thursday, her first pay day, Ana took 65 dollars from her check to pay on account at the hotel.

"I had better start looking for a job, Carlos", Ana heard her mother from the bathroom say to her father that evening.

"You?"

"Yes, it has been a month now and you haven't found anything yet."

"But you going to work before I do?"

"We need another income besides Ana María's."

"Let's wait a little longer. I've gone everywhere and talked to everybody."

"I know, I know. But the poor girl is giving her whole salary and not keeping anything. And it's not enough."

"Yes, I realize that. Maybe Peñalver can get me something."

"If she can work, so can I."

"But Anita can work sitting in an air-conditioned office. What kind of job could you get without speaking English? Working your kidneys off at a sewing machine in a hot factory?"

"We need to move."

"I'm sure I'll find something soon."

Ana came out of the bathroom.

"When she gets married", Méndez went on, "then you can go out to work to help me, but not yet. At least not while I can work."

Monday was Labor Day and, contradictorily, there was no work. The bank held a picnic for the employees at the beach to see the summer off, but Ana excused herself. She couldn't get there by bus, and she wasn't familiar with the employees.

Thursday, having been counting, the thirty-day term over, Teresa and Ana went back to the savings bank, where they were issued a new passbook and were able to withdraw another 85 dollars to pay off the past-due bill at the hotel, and they thanked Mr. Jameson for being patient.

They received a letter from Gustavo that afternoon. It was the first news they had from him since they had arrived. It was dated August 30 and he reported that Norma had delivered Ana's resignation letter to a girl who worked with Betancourt on Monday, after he had received their cable, and that he had retrieved her pearl ring from Rojas, the militiaman at the airport. Blanca added a note saying that she missed them and sending the children's love and regards from her parents. It seemed so short!

Carlos walked into the room at dusk, humming and grinning. "Good luck today", he announced to them, beaming.

"Did you find a job?", Teresa asked him, hopefully.

"Yes. As elevator man at the Fort Dallas Hotel downtown. All I need to know there is the numbers, greetings, thanks and very little else. The college student went back on Tuesday. Fifty-two a week. I have Fridays off and half a day Thursday."

Ana threw her arms around him. "Oh, that's wonderful, Papá! You see? I knew it wouldn't take you long." She looked at her father, proud of having found a job as elevator man in a foreign country working week-ends, and thought of the office he had given up back home and the pride he'd taken in his work as an accountant. And she felt a weight in her heart. He suddenly seemed so old to her for the first time, and she wanted to bawl so badly, that she went to hide away in the bathroom.

Landing on Free Soil

It was announced that five prisoners from the invasion, Ramón Calviño, Rafael Soler, Jorge King, Roberto Pérez and Antonio Padrón, had been shot in El Polvorín, in Las Villas, and nine, among them José Franco, sentenced to thirty-year terms in the Isle of Pines prison.

The Cuban government prohibited the procession of the Virgin of Charity. Four thousand Catholics gathered in front of and around the Church of La Caridad on September 10, shouting for freedom. The crowd yelled, "Hail Christ the King!, Down with communism!" for three hours. G-2 troops dissolved the mob with gunshots and machine-gun fire.

On the 11th, Castro deported 132 Cuban priests, including Auxiliary Bishop and rector of Villanueva University, Monsignor Eduardo Boza Masvidal, who was shipped to Spain with 45 other priests.

The heat continued still as terrible all through the early half of September.

CHAPTER 12

GETTING SETTLED

> *"Aún habrá corazones en Cuba*
> *que me envidien de mártir la suerte,*
> *y prefieran espléndida muerte*
> *a su amargo azaroso vivir."*[12]
> *("Himno del Desterrado",*
> José María Heredia)

Thursday afternoon Méndez walked into the room waving the little manila envelope in his hand. His first pay. He kissed Teresa's cheek and put an arm around Ana's shoulders.
"We're going to survive this, Anita." It seemed he was believing it for the first time.
"God tightens, but He doesn't choke", said Teresa.
The three walked to the vacant apartment, and the red sign was still hanging outside.
"Let's rent it, Papá", Ana pleaded with him.
"We don't have enough yet", her mother argued. "We need a hundred and sixty. Let's wait until next Thursday."
"They'll have rented it by then", Ana protested. No one noticed that the sign was hung from a post firmly driven into the ground. "And you saw how the other one looked."
"That hotel is also costing us fifty dollars more a month", Méndez reasoned.
They went in to see Dr. Knowles.
"My father got a job", Ana told him. "I'm sorry we didn't answer you before, but we couldn't. Could we still rent the apartment?"
"Sure you can. I'd thought you weren't coming back."
"Well, he... he got paid today", she said a little embarrassedly.
"When would you like to move in?"

[12] There might still be hearts in Cuba
that may envy my fate of martyr
and may prefer a splendid death
to their bitter unfortunate life.

Getting Settled

"Could we pay you the first month tomorrow and the last one on the twenty-eighth?"

"That'll be fine."

She asked her father in Spanish.

"Tomorrow", he said.

"Then I'll draw a lease for a year. I'll date it back to the first." Ana first thought that would be an advantage, then realized they'd be losing half a month, but it seemed to have escaped her father's accountant mind and she didn't want to raise any objection.

Jennie O'Hara continued to be friendly, but they only got together at coffee breaks and lunch; they didn't socialize after working hours. In the afternoon break, on the little terrace of the employee lounge on the third floor, with a view of the river to the south, Jennie, a bottle of Coca-Cola in her hand, told her about her boyfriend, whom she had been dating for over two years. It gave Ana the impression that Jennie talked — they all did — as if they were asking questions.

"Last night he took U S One south without saying where he was going?, and, when I asked him?, he told me, 'I'm going to kidnap you'? and I kept saying, 'But I don't even have my toothbrush'?, and Jeff said, 'We'll buy you one'." Jennie was partial to long-sleeve dresses.

"And where was he going?" A fishing boat was coming up the river.

"To Florida City, to have root beer at an A and W." The bell rang. The Miami Avenue drawbridge started to go up.

Ana recalled the night that Dany had taken her through Marianao to end up at Ward's. She told Jennie about the dear brunet boyfriend of almost three years that she'd left behind. They got along very well.

Friday Méndez gave Dr. Knowles the first eighty dollars and he gave him the key. They paid the last 35 dollars at the hotel and said good-by to Mr. Jameson and Peñalver. They hauled the three suitcases the nine blocks to the apartment and hung their few clothes in the closets. Her parents insisted Ana take the front bedroom.

"You had the rear one in Cuba", Teresa reasoned. "We're old now."

"Fifty-three isn't old", Ana argued.

"Now it's your turn", her mother insisted.

Ana set her shoes and slippers on the floor of the closet, hung her belts, put her underwear and stockings, the camera and her jewelry in the drawers of the dresser, placed her costume jewelry and the bottles of perfume on top, her mass book and her rosary in the night stand, set her three books and pens on the table, and put the photograph albums on the closet shelf. The unpacking had been finished and all her possessions lay arranged.

They realized then that they had no pots, pans, dishes, silverware, glasses, sheets or pillowcases. They had packed six towels.

The deposits for the electricity and gas would have to be made Thursday. The water was included in the rent. And they wouldn't have a telephone.

They noticed the lyrics of "Swanee River" printed over a landscape of cabbage palms hung on the hallway wall between the doors of the two bedrooms. There was a Seventh Day Adventist temple nearby.

"We can paint it", said Carlos.

"Yes, it'll look much better when it's painted", Teresa agreed.

"Maybe Doctor Knowles will give us the paint", Ana ventured.

The only things they bought were soap and a pot. They ate with their fingers and drank water cupping their hands under the faucet, and they slept on the bare mattresses and pillows for almost three weeks. There was a small Cuban grocery store, "Varona", three blocks away. Chicken was cheap. Méndez had given up smoking since they had arrived.

Ana wrote a short letter to Dany right away sending him their new address. She didn't know how to apologize for the way she had left and only hoped that he'd understand. Teresa wrote to Gustavo, and to Guillermo, Cristina and Esperanza.

Ana called Ernesto from the red-framed glass telephone booth to give him their new address. "Why don't you come over to see the place? We haven't seen you in over a month and a half."

"Okay. I'll go over tomorrow."

Ana now went to see Rosa with her parents. They lived near a United Methodist Church. Teresa and Carlos met Rosa's quiet father and fat mother. Ana gave her their address. They were served the customary black coffee. She was hoping they wouldn't, but the dreaded words came, "Come, so you'll see the house." And they were taken apologetically on the inevitable tour. "The backyard floods when it rains hard", Rosa's mother complained.

Rosa asked her to accompany her to the bus stop on 8th Street to wait for Tim to come home from work. He worked as checker in a supermarket. She seemed to be in love with Tim more than she'd

Getting Settled

been with that blond boyfriend she'd had in Cuba, even a little obsessively. They sat on the bench in the quiet evening, talking, Rosa impatient.

"You know Mirta's cousin Wilfredo, don't you?", she asked, looking toward the east, from where the bus would appear. Ana remembered having danced with him at Olga's house on New Year's Eve. "He's here too. But Tim can't stand him."

Further down, there was a drive-in restaurant, and two blocks away were the "Eight-O-Nine" steak house with a taxi stand in front and James City drugstore, with a sign angled high over the corner of the roof and a soda fountain, but aside from that, 8th Street was mostly dark and deserted while they waited for Tim's bus.

Once Ernesto had seen the apartment Sunday, he asked Ana to go down to the city yacht basins. They took the bus downtown.

They walked down North Bayshore Drive past the piers where sightseeing boats, a glass-bottomed one, were tied. A few booths sold tickets carnival-style. She told him about her job.

"You were lucky. Javier left for Chicago on Monday. And I'm leaving on the first."

"I'm sorry."

"I have to, Ana, I can't find anything here... Have you heard from Dany?"

"Not yet. I only wrote to him day before yesterday... Maybe Javier can help you find a job up there."

"That's what I think."

"You're old friends, aren't you?"

"Yes, we went to school together at Belén since first grade and we became good friends."

They walked down the wooden pier, where there were fishing boats for hire, to where the larger yachts were anchored. A soft sea breeze blew.

"The summer after we finished eighth grade – we used to live in La Ceiba then, when my Old Man was still living, – his parents invited me to spend the summer vacation at their *finca* in Cienfuegos. His father, Sebastián, is the son of Basques, *Guipúzcoans*, and his mother, Merced Puig, the daughter of Catalonians, *Barceloneses*, and they had a big *finca* named 'San Ignacio en Montserrat' in Palmira, on the highway to Ariza near the Salado river. We used to pass an inactive mill on the way – I'll never forget the name, *'Tumbacazuela'*." He laughed. – "They had a sign at the entrance by the road carved in wood with the motto 'Neither slave nor tyrant' – the house was reminiscent of the Alpine chalets... – and a shield with a *botonée* cross. There were palmettos around, and 'satin leaves and cashews', as the song goes. His mother's parents, the Catalonians, short, broad-headed and bulgy-eyed, from Tarrasa, lived on the *finca* and had a shrimp processing plant nearby, in O'Bourke. I liked his sister, Llivia, but she was two years older and never even looked at me. His father's parents, the Basques, narrow-faced, round-headed and broad-shouldered, from Tolosa, were energetic, athletic and compact, resistant to physical effort, big eaters and drinkers. His paternal grandfather worked at the 'Portugalete'[62] mill, nearby. And on weekends they all got together in the *finca* from Friday afternoon until Monday morning."

On their way back, Ernesto wanted to go into the "Trade Winds" restaurant by Pier 5 for sodas.

"The way they ate!", he said when they had sat in a booth. "You know how we tend to think that Spaniards only have Galician broth and *cocido*? Hah! You should have seen those dinners: codfish *al 'pil pil'*, baby eels, clams marinara, squid, spider crab, seafood *zarzuela*, lobster à la Catalonian, octopus, *'suquet de peix'*, fish soup, rabbit *al 'alli oli'*, *'carn d'olla'*, *pulpeta* à la Catalonian, red beans with sausage, black sausage, rice à la Catalonian, mushrooms, *tostones* with the white Chacolí wine, Priorato red or Alella wine and 'gray' wine, and then white *manjar*, and chufa nut *horchata*." To Ana, who hadn't eaten well in so long, this, with a carbonated soda before her, was a torture, and she guessed that for Ernesto, who couldn't be feeding himself any better, it must be masochism. "You've had almond orgeat?"

"Yes, at El Naranjal restaurant on San Miguel. Delicious."

"Well, with chufa nuts it's even better." He visibly quenched a burp that seemed to be fighting its way up. "That was during Prío's time; they could import anything. I remember the big blue and white tile kitchen, Basque style. They had a redheaded *Majorcan* cook, and his wife, a *Ceutí*, was the housekeeper. And on July thirty-first, the name day of Javier's grandfather Iñigo, they threw a big party and his robust grandfather, who worked in the sugar mill, always wearing his beret, did the *Aurresku*, the goblet dance, the Basque leap, the

---

[62] Two sugar mills bore the same name, one in San José de las Lajas and the other in Palmira

Getting Settled

farandole and all those fierce dances, and his grandmother on his mother's side − I think her name was Eulalia, − with a big behind, did the Catalonian *sardana* and the *contrapás* with Javier. They sang the *zortzico*. We took pictures that day. And you know Javier brought some of them with him?"

"That's the first thing I packed", emphasized Ana enthusiastically, identifying with his sentimental instinct.

"His grandmother used to make lace with bobbins. His Catalonian grandfather, bald − Jorge I think, − the one with the shrimp plant, used to talk to us of his town in the Vallés Occidental and the *masía* with its vestibule; they spoke *Catalán* between themselves. And his Basque grandmother, wiry − I don't remember if her name was Gixane, − talked about her town on the Oria river and the *caserío* with its big porch, the Monte Adarra and the Sierra de Aralar and of the *pastorales* and *mascarades*; they spoke *Euskera*. The Basques and the Catalonians were always arguing about which region was better. You know how sectionalist they are. They had a large reproduction of monk Fra Juan Andrea Rizzi's original Seventeenth Century painting of Saint Ignatius in the Holy Cave which is in the pinacotheca of the Benedictine Monastery, in the living room hanging over the sofa. I didn't want to go back home that year..." His look was absent, reminiscing. "Then I felt bad for my old folks." He brought himself back to the present. "That was in nineteen forty-nine. In fifty-four Javier entered Marta Abreu Central University and we hadn't seen each other again. But he could only finish third year, because he had to lose some time during the last of Batista's office."

Ana was listening to him fascinated. It awoke in her the same interest that Alejandro inspired when he talked about the mill and his town, and about his grandfather.

"And his family's still there?"

"Yes. They took most of their *finca* away, left them four *'caballerías'*."

"But that's still quite big."

"Well, over seven blocks, almost seven and a half, on each side, but that's not a shadow of what they had. His sister married a Frenchman, a Gasçon by the name of D'Armagnac" − a note of spitefulness could be detected in his voice, − "and they have a daughter. They took his grandparents' shrimp plant too. The 'Portugalete' central was renamed 'Elpidio Gómez'."

"Then he's here by himself?"

"Yes. What puzzles me is that his father would accept that, because he was so independent, individualist... Unless he wouldn't want to leave his parents behind, or his daughter."

"Javier doesn't say why they stayed?"

"No, he doesn't talk about that. He was in hiding for seven or eight months, wanted, before coming here, and he never talks about that either."

They took the bus back. Ernesto went in to say good-by to her parents and at the door, he promised Ana, "I'll write to you as soon as I have an address."

"Good luck", Ana wished him. "And give my regards to Javier." It saddened her to see him go.

Teresa was annoyed at being requested to sign her husband's last name.

"After being Teresa Bermúdez all my life", she complained, "now I'm expected to give up the name my father gave me, of which I've always been proud, and suddenly become María Méndez. What's that about 'married name', 'maiden name'? That a woman should lose her own identity, and precisely in a country where women are supposed to be so independent!..."

Ana had never heard her mother referred to as María Teresa except on legal documents. Everybody knew her as Teresa. Close friends called her Tera, as did Carlos often.

"Go on using your maiden name then", he told her simply now, unfazed.

"But people will think we're not married", she protested.

"And what do you care? Our relatives and friends saw us get married, and Ana and Gustavo have seen our marriage certificate. That's all that should matter to us."

So she affixed her maiden name on the mail box. And she let the neighbors speculate what they chose. The idea of provoking their shock amused Ana. She personally had had her own brand of rebellion since she was very young. When she heard old-fashioned women say a woman needed a man "to represent her", she, not over 17 then, felt indignant and demanded, "Why should one human being need another human being to represent her? Are there women who think so little of themselves that they need somebody else to represent them?" And she couldn't understand it when her mother told her, at 14, that if a boy stood her up she shouldn't ask him why he hadn't shown up, she should pretend she didn't care. It didn't make any

Getting Settled 423

sense to her to let him stand her up without asking for an explanation and pretend she hadn't noticed he hadn't shown up. Méndez compromised by identifying himself as J. Carlos.

They went to the Colonial Hotel, but found that the Carvajals had moved to an apartment and the desk didn't have their forwarding address.

At work, Kathy Clark was very aloof. Mitchell and Tamargo were courteous. Ana noticed in Tamargo's speech a certain inflection she had known among many of the employees at Wayne and Rina's friends, and expressions like "It doesn't exist!" when he meant "Impossible", and "There's no torment" for "Don't worry", about which she hadn't thought much then and had almost forgotten since. Paula Monroe, the president's secretary, who had been with the bank for many years, was sometimes very friendly and very distant at others. Ana hadn't made any personal friends. She realized she sounded peculiar to them with her Sorzano grammar. She found their business was mainly with their correspondent banks in Barranquilla, Maracaibo, Veracruz, Santo Domingo and Colón, and she had to deal with Colombian importers.

An air raid alarm siren went off over the city on Saturdays at 1:00 in the afternoon. Shortly after, Ana left for Rosa's house. Mirta was there. Rosa and Tim were getting married next Sunday afternoon. They were being married at the house of a justice of the peace. Ana found it so typically American! The wedding would be intimate, with only her parents, her sister and the witnesses, and Ana was a little glad, since she had neither appropriate clothes nor the mood to go to a social event yet. Tim's family was in Tallahassee. He pulled out his wallet and showed pictures of them. Mirta was leaving for Los Angeles soon to join some relatives.

Rosa and Tim took Ana with them to look at a furnished apartment for rent. It was on Glen Royal Parkway near a post office station. Tim went up the steps to ring the doorbell, Rosa stayed a few steps behind in the walkway and Ana waited on the sidewalk. A woman came to the omnipresent screen door and Tim told her, "We'd like to see the apartment for rent."

"Oh, yeah. How many?"

"Two, my wife and I. My wife-to-be. We're getting married in eight days."

"Oh, congratulations!", she said cordially. Then she looked past him at Rosa and squinted to see through the screen. "Is your wife

Cuban?", she asked sharply.

"Yes", Tim answered, a little guardedly.

"I don't rent to Cubans", the woman said tartly. "I had a Cuban woman living here and she spat at me."

"Lady", Tim snapped, "maybe you had it coming." He spun on his heel, flushed, took Rosa's arm, who had stood for a moment at the foot of the steps, humiliated, and walked away. Ana, confused, followed them through the service station and across Flagler Street.

At their insistent invitation, she went along to the movies with them. From the record player of a Royal Castle nearby, came "A Hundred Pounds of Clay". They stopped at an open fruit stand on their way and Tim bought "Yoo-Hoo" for them, which tasted to Ana surprisingly like *"Nao Capitana"*. At the "Tower" theater they saw "The Savage Innocents" with Anthony Quinn. Back outside, Tim sounded fascinated for the isolation of a couple in the Arctic. The Royal Castle jukebox was playing "Hang Down Your Head, Tom Dooley". On the street, Tim, in a feigned high, thin voice, cried, "Stop, you fool, I'm only twelve!... Besides,... the zipper's on the other side." The movie inspired them to talk about night picnics on Haulover Beach, sleeping on the sand under an army blanket and in the Everglades, roasting frankfurters and marshmallows over a campfire, daubing on insect repellent, and about alligators in the creeks.

The Méndezes met their upstairs neighbors, a Cuban couple in their mid-forties who had been in the country two years. Oscar had been a policeman and was now a security guard, and his wife worked in a clothes factory. Aida, a heavy woman with oily, straight, black hair in a bun, thick eyeglasses, in pants, told them at the front steps, "We had to leave in September of the first year. Well, you know, policemen didn't have a chance. Although he was only a beat cop... We have a boy, but he just got married and is living in Hialeah. The doctor's mother lives downstairs, on that side."

"The lady is very quiet", said Teresa.

"The other upstairs apartment next to us has had three tenants since we've been here. It gets the sun in summer and nobody lasts there more than seven months. As soon as summer starts, they move out. You have the shady side."

"Yes, our side is cool", Teresa agreed. Ana inwardly congratulated herself that they hadn't rented the other one.

"That other apartment downstairs is cooler because it's in the shadow of the house next door and that blue mahoe tree in front shades the living room. Our side gets the sun in winter." In the garden of the bungalow next door their American neighbor was watering his lawn. "How long have you been here?"

"A little less than two months."

"Less than two months and you've already rented an apartment? Well, your daughter speaks English, so she had no trouble finding a job, did she? You don't have any relatives here?'

"No, none."

"This house had only one large six-room flat on each floor and the doctor used to live upstairs. He has three children. But a few years ago he bought a house in Kendall and then, when his father died a couple of years ago, he divided each floor into two four-room apartments." They guessed she must know this second hand. "It was too big for the little old woman by herself. And she stayed on there."

The temperature stayed warm until the first week in October.

On her next payday, Ana gave her father 45 dollars. And she could finally write to Octavio Guillén in Nassau, sending him a money order for 52 dollars, thanking him for having lent her the fare and telling him he could now let everybody know she was in Miami. She told him she had run into Salvador.

Rosa came to their house Sunday afternoon with Tim, both still in their wedding clothes, to invite them to a toast they were having at her parents' house. Ana alone went with them. A table had been trimmed in the kitchen and there was a small cake and champagne. They had photographs taken with a home camera. Ana took some of them cutting the cake and drinking champagne. They talked about what they would buy when they had money.

"Tim says that our children are going to be 'half-breeds'," Rosa said laughing.

"But you're white", said Ana.

"Well, that's what he says."

They didn't go away for a honeymoon, but moved right into a rented trailer in a park on 8th Street near a cemetery with what was left of the champagne.

Ana and her parents bought the indispensable pots and pans, dishes, silverware and glasses, bedsheets and pillowcases, a broom, and more towels. And the harder toothbrushes Peñalver had recommended.

The three had lost weight. Teresa and Ana couldn't get used to the lack of a bidet. Teresa felt distressed at ruining her hands, having to wash so much by hand. Carlos' first haircut was at the barbers' college.

Ana wrote to Olga Salazar, Gloria Serrano, Carmen Zayas and Ofelia Barquet, who had all stayed behind in Cuba, to Leonardo Vidal and Graciela, who were in Nassau, and to Yolanda Solís to the address she had sent her from Caracas; to Idalia, her childhood nexrdoor neighbor, and to schoolmates. Her mother wrote to their relatives in Cuba, and to Alicia, Carolina and other friends. Her father wrote to Velázquez in Puerto Rico and Peláez in New York.

Ana repeatedly dreamed about Dany. In her dreams they had broken up and went back together, but he acted indifferent. She woke up concerned, dispirited. She pulled out her album then to look at the photographs.

On October 7 Fidelito, eleven years old, visited Russia with a group of other children.

Without television in the house, not even a radio or telephone, walking downtown to window-shop became their evening pastime.

"That, after working all day, me on my feet", complained Carlos, "we should walk seventeen blocks each way to look at windows is crazy."

"But if we stay within those four walls looking at each other", said Teresa, "we're going to grow mold. And you two at least go out and see your co-workers. Most of the days I don't see even Aida."

The evenings were no longer hot, so they walked down Flagler Street. Ana noticed there was always a light blue 1954 Mercury with a continental kit parked on the north side of the one-way street between 1st and 2nd Avenues, and she secretly wished she could find its owner and buy it from him. Beck's, on the corner, almost as big as "La Isla", displayed a large selection of shoes in its windows. McCrory's five-and-ten store was open late also on Thursday evenings, besides the usual Monday and Friday late hours of most other stores, and Jackson's-Byrons stayed open late every night. They went into large, four-story Walgreen's, the tourists' drugstore, where they had often shopped before, looked at the window of Duval Jewelers and walked as far as Drug City, on 3rd Avenue, known to Cubans as "the drugstore of the flags", because of the international ones displayed along its marquee.

Starting back from an auction shop on the north side, they passed three theaters on one block, the "Town", the "Paramount" and the

"Florida"; on the next one, the "Olympia" and the "Miami". Two sandwich shops offered papa, mama and baby beers. The main post office, out of their way on 3rd Street, was open until 12 midnight and there they bought the 10-cent airmail stamps and mailed their letters to Cuba. Back on Flagler, in front of the long, narrow drugstore on the corner, closed at this hour, a Salvation Army group sang with a tambourine. They walked past the Industrial National Bank, now still, and Benjee's restaurant. Once they passed the silent County Courthouse building with its ample stairs, which marked the last sign of the commercial section, and crossed the Florida East Coast Railway tracks, they abruptly entered the quiet section of low buildings, particularly dormant before the winter season. The Tamiami Hotel, on 2nd Avenue, sheltered the latest arrived Cubans; old, small "Flagler Theater" served the neighborhood; "The Village Barn" nightclub opened its cavernous mouth on the sidewalk, a bandstand to the left side, from where the singer sometimes beckoned to the curious passers-by who stood at the door to go on in. At the intersection of North River Drive, there was a Standard service station on the near corner, Exotic Gardens florists on another, and on the other East Coast Fisheries. Aida said that there had once been a hotel on the upper floors, but no sign of it was left.

They crossed over the Miami river on the rusty steel sidewalks of the old waffle-iron bridge, the rickety wooden planks rattling noisily under the weight of the occasional cars. On the other side, a boat was tied to a dock, its captain sitting in a deck chair, his feet up, watching television, waving back at anybody who called to him, "Skipper!" from the bridge, as many did. The Del Rio Apartments stood on the near corner at the intersection of South River Drive, Schuberth's Sea Food Grill extended to the bank of the river on the other, with outdoor tables set to the water's edge, triangular Apparel Outlet, now closed, was on another, and on the far one an Atlantic service station. Robert's all-night drugstore was lit on 6th Avenue, a television set in a wooden cabinet on its parking lot across the street with outdoor wooden benches where the retired old men watched their favorite shows free under the stars. Harvey's restaurant, a hotel. Colonial Finance offered automobile loans, the Veterans' Administration followed. Many stores were still closed for the summer. Riverside Cadillac Service Station advertised specialized service and Storkland displayed juvenile furniture.

The city of 300,000 people seemed to them like a sleepy, small town.

Black people sat only in the very rear seats of the buses. They had separate restrooms in bus terminals and some other public places, specifically marked "Colored". Also marked were the water fountains. "Colored Town" extended roughly north of N.W. 5th Street.

Some Americans walked barefoot on the streets.

Dr. Knowles paid for the paint, and they painted the apartment, between Thursday and Sunday, Teresa also helping this time. The living room became green, Ana's bedroom blue, her parents' yellow, the kitchen aqua and the bathroom pink, and the doors white.

On Sunday Oscar, in thongs and untrimmed shorts low under his big stomach, helped Carlos finish painting the kitchen and the living room, while drinking iced tea.

"Ah, you have them also!", Aida cried out over their pictures. "My son says that Doctor Knowles is a Florida fanatic. And those are the state bird, flower, tree and song." That answered the puzzle for them. "We have them all over our apartment too. He's from Sanford."

The place looked different now, cleaner, newer and more cheerful.

Teresa ran into the Carvajals on the street, who gave her their address in the southeast section, and she gave them theirs.

Friday Ana received a letter from Octavio Guillén dated October 5 from Nassau, letting her know he had received her money order. He congratulated her, said they were all glad she was in Miami. He wrote, "I see from your money order that you're one of those people who 'don't fade' because you included the 7-dollar difference between what your mother passed and the check I brought among the files." He said he was glad to have been able to help her in some way and offered to help her in all he could. He asked whether she knew of the rest of their co-workers, especially Danilo and Ramiro, told her his wife and children were well, asked her to write soon and closed with "a hug". The letter moved her.

On the 15th of October, 15,000 Rebel Pioneers were sworn in.

They found a coin laundromat nearby, where they could wash their clothes for a quarter and dry them for a dime, and discovered that the large American chain supermarket six blocks away offered lower prices than Fermín's closer small Cuban grocery store, but the latter did sell fresher meat. They gained back the weight they had lost. Méndez started reading the local Spanish newspaper, *"Diario*

Getting Settled

Las Américas", founded eight years before by a Nicaraguan. And Teresa started saving the market's Triple-S blue trading stamps.

Ana sat at the kitchen table and watched her mother go through the morning chores. Since she had a bad memory, Teresa set up a routine for herself to follow mechanically. If she broke the sequence and left it to memory, she would forget something. Teresa took out from the refrigerator a can of grapefruit juice and one of tomato, a container of milk and three biscuits in a cellophane bag – she always kept the bread in the refrigerator, – and placed this on the countertop by the sink and the margarine on the table. From the wall cabinet she took three glasses, cups, saucers and paper napkins and the sugar bowl, and three teaspoons and the butter knife from the drawer, and set all this on the table. She turned the flame on under the percolator, which had been filled with ground coffee and water and left ready on the burner, and put the biscuits in the oven. She emptied the cans of juice into big glass jars and placed them on the table. She took two sandwiches already in waxed bags from the refrigerator, slipped them into brown paper bags and set them on the table also. She heaved a sigh and walked out of the kitchen to knock on the bathroom door, "Carlos!", as she used to do to Ana in Cuba. Sometimes she checked off the mental list out loud as she went about her tasks, which never failed to bring a grin to her husband's face.

She came back and, with another sigh, sat at the table and finally smiled at Ana, "Is it going well for you at the bank?"

"Yes, I can't complain."

Teresa knocked on wood. "Anything special today?"

"No, the same as everyday."

Near the corner, a squirrel ran up the trunk of a tree. A stock clerk before the closed door of the furniture store waited for it to open. The Cuban service station attendant exclaimed with a dramatic sigh, rolling up his eyes, "Today the brownette has looked at me, today I believe in God!" Ana thought of the office building elevator boy in Vedado and smiled.

A mounted policeman was talking to Kathy at the curb in front of the bank. Ana had noticed Americans didn't answer a greeting when they were in conversation with somebody else; they seemed to consider it an interruption or a distraction. So she had taught herself to ignore them when she saw them talking, and she now walked around the horse and into the bank.

They had free instant coffee in paper cups at the bank with non-

dairy powder cream, artificial saccharin tablets and plastic stirrers. On pay day there were doughnuts.

A blue chambray was in fashion, and backless shoes, and the hemline was shorter than in Cuba. Office girls favored white blouses.

Instinct told Ana her acquaintances didn't want to hear about her experiences coming out of the country − American people seemed to have built a cocoon around themselves and not want to find out what went on outside it, − so she never referred to anything that had happened to her, her family or her friends, not even to any specific incident for that matter. Only seldom did she refer to general conditions and then she always thought she sensed a tensing in her audience − as if it embarrassed them, − and she rushed on to finish what she had intended to say, lest the person think she was trying to play for sympathy. She vaguely thought of herself as being considered by her American acquaintances as stoic and discreet, somebody who didn't want to burden anybody with her own problems.

They went to visit Enrique Carvajal and Estela, now in a nice apartment near a fire station, who met Méndez and were very glad to see them.

The first reply from her friends, aside from Guillén's, that the mailman on his bicycle brought to Ana, on Saturday, was Carmen Zayas' letter dated October 14. She wrote that Miguel had been in Miami since early September and she was planning also to go soon, she asked Ana where she could go to look for a job and said she hadn't received an answer from Rosa. Carmen also asked for her telephone number! The next one was Yolanda Solís', dated the 15th, from Caracas, in which she said she had been very happy to learn Ana was now out of Cuba, that the day before she had left she had been calling Ana's and Duarte's houses, but there was no answer in either one and she hadn't been able to say good-by, and she hadn't been able to write to Duarte because Eladio hadn't sent her the address. Then Ofelia Barquet answered her and said she would have liked Ana to tell her she was leaving, but she had done the right thing, that all her girl friends had left, she had hopes of seeing her again soon and that Betancourt had a secretary very different from Ana as far as ideas were concerned. Olga Salazar answered her saying that she had been very glad to have news from her because, since she had left without saying anything, it had hurt her very much to think that it was because Ana didn't want to continue her friendship with her,

Getting Settled

that she got bored and she now had a salary. She wrote that she hardly ever talked with Mirta – "Hardly ever"? Apparently she didn't know that Mirta was already in the States. – Leonardo Vidal told her that Nassau was very much like Cuba in landscape, that he had been given a promotion and a raise, the weather was very hot and he had air conditioning in his bedroom. A classmate and another friend also answered. And they started corresponding fairly regularly. But, surprisingly, Graciela never answered her. The first reply from their relatives that her mother received was from Guillermo, who said that Betancourt had called Blanca on Wednesday and had later seen Gustavo and told him that "he had guessed it". Then Esperanza wrote and Cristina, sending a photograph of Norma's wedding.

Hallowmas Eve was celebrated by the children going around the neighborhood from house to house dressed in allegoric costumes, as witches, ghosts, vampires, mummies, monsters, skeletons, black cats, jack-o'-lanterns, scarecrows and werewolves, asking for candy with the traditional threatening phrase "Trick or treat".

Rosa and Tim came by the house in shorts, to tell them they were moving to Tallahassee, where he was going to work for his brother.

One afternoon in November there was an unexpected ring at the door and, when Teresa opened it, they were surprised to see Laura, Esperanza's daughter, her husband, Adrián, and their four-year-old daughter Lourdes.

"Laura!", Teresa cried, kissing her. "I can't believe it!"

"What a surprise!", said Ana, hugging them excitedly. "When did you arrive?"

"Two days ago."

"Two days ago? Come in, sit down."

"Why didn't you come before?"

"We wanted to get settled first, Aunt. We didn't want to bother anybody."

"We knew you were still finding your own way yourselves", Adrián said.

"We've already registered at the Refugee Center", said Laura when they had sat down.

"We're staying at a hotel on them."

"We're so glad to see you!", said Ana.

"How are Esperanza and Augusto?", Teresa asked.

"They're fine. Papi retired."

"And your parents, Adrián?"

"Everybody's well."
"How did you come?"
"With a visa waiver", Laura said.
"From my uncle in Pennsylvania", said Adrián.
They asked about Guillermo and Beatriz, Cristina and Marcos, Elena and Mateo, Norma, Jorge, Lorenzo and Pilar.
"Carlos should get home any moment", said Teresa. "I didn't know you were coming so soon. Esperanza didn't say anything to me in her letter."
"We didn't tell anybody", said Laura. "You didn't say it either when you came."
"You're right", Teresa admitted.
"How did you leave all that?", Ana asked.
"Well, everything is scarce", said Adrián. "And there is no freedom."
"Betancourt called Blanca at home on Wednesday", Laura told them. "Norma took your resignation letter to the Ministry on Monday, after Gustavo received your cable, and she left it with another man's secretary there."
"Ofelia."
"Norma mentioned the name, but to tell the truth, I can't remember it. And she slipped out without waiting for a reply from him."
"Blanca didn't tell me Betancourt had called her."
"I know. Gustavo told her not to."
"But Guillermo had already written us that", said Teresa.
"So you're working in a bank and Carlos in a hotel?", Adrián said to Ana.
Teresa offered them coffee.
"Come in and see the apartment."
"Did you go to Norma's wedding?", Ana asked.
"Yes, it was very nice. In Saint Anthony of Padua. Marcos was the *'padrino'* and Víctor's mother the *'madrina'*. She looked very pretty."
Méndez arrived and the exclamations started over. Carlos and Adrián vigorously slapped each other on the back.
"A man with an arm in a cast got to the airport", Adrián told them, "and they got an anonymous phone call saying the man's arm wasn't broken and he had money hidden in the cast. So they took the cast apart and they found that there was no money and the man's arm really was fractured. Then, imagine!, the man demanded they let him

call his doctor to have him reset his arm in a cast. Well, he called him, the doctor came and set his arm in a cast again", he made a dramatic pause, "only he was in on the deal with the man and this time he stuck all the money in the cast!"

"Did they build anything where 'El Encanto' used to be?"

"No. And after they deducted one day's wages to rebuild it", said Laura. "They made a park and named it after the militia woman who died in the fire, Fe Del Valle."

Laura had been a fourth-grade teacher, and Adrián a linotypist in a press. They now had their first relatives in the country.

From the first week in October until the first one in December the temperature was cool, pleasant and some days cold.

Ana was surprised to receive a very nice letter from Berta Penabad in Nassau, to whom she had only sent her regards. Berta told her she knew about her from Guillén, and Leonardo Vidal added a note to her letter.

On November 11 Armistice Day was celebrated and there was no work. Red poppies were sold.

When Ana got home from work Thursday afternoon, Aida was waiting for her by the arc of allamanda at the entrance of the building.

"Ana, I need to ask a favor of you." She pulled her to a side by Mrs. Knowles' apartment. "I'm pregnant and I can't have another child. I have to get an abortion. I found a man who'll do it, but I'm afraid to go by myself and Oscar is working. Would you go with me?"

"Eh, would... uh... Why don't you ask my mother?"

"No, I'm embarrassed to tell your mother. Ana, I'm forty-five, my son is twenty-three; *he*'s ready to have children. I can't have a child now. You understand?"

"But I can't even drive you."

"No, the man will pick us up and bring us back. It's just to go and come back with me."

"Well,... Okay", she agreed reluctantly. "When is it?"

"He's going to call me today to give me the appointment."

That evening she sat in Aida's living room while she gave the man the address. It seemed he was suspicious. Aida told her he would pick them up on Flagler Street and 10th Avenue Saturday morning at 8:00.

Saturday morning they stood on the corner in front of the Cities

Service station and a fat, middle-aged man with a woman in a modest car picked them up. He drove west and turned south, and stopped in front of an old two-story four-apartment building. They walked up the stairs and another woman came out to meet them. There was a fireplace in the living room and Ana was surprised there'd be a fireplace in an upstairs apartment. A boy was leaving. The man put out his hand and Aida paid him 250 dollars. The women were the man's wife and sister-in-law. They let Ana go into the kitchen with Aida. She wished they hadn't. Aida was helped onto a wooden kitchen table, about three feet long, her neck resting over the back of a chair and her legs draped over the backs of another two. When one of the women pressed a terrycloth soaked in some liquid on Aida's face, Ana had to leave the kitchen. She sat on a sofa in the living room.

Aida screamed horribly. What if something happened to her? After close to an hour, when she was already biting her cuticles, Ana was led into the bedroom. Aida was sitting up on the low bed trying to reach for her shoes. The woman behind Ana said, annoyed, "She's already getting up. She should still be out." The man rushed in after them.

"You screamed", he recriminated her. "The neighbors must have heard you. They'll report me. The police will find me."

Aida didn't answer him. She held her arms out to Ana, who helped her put her shoes on and stand up. The man drove them back, complaining all the way about Aida's yells. He left them off in front of their building. Aida wanted to stop at the mailbox for her mail. Ana walked her up to her apartment. When she sat on her bed, there was a large blood stain on her skirt. Ana helped her lie back, brought her a glass of cold water from the kitchen, pulled the telephone close to her on the night stand and rushed out of the apartment. She went down into her own bathroom and retched until her ribs hurt.

There was no work on Thanksgiving Day, the fourth Thursday in November, but the Méndezes didn't celebrate.

On December 2 Fidel declared publicly in a five-hour speech, "I am a Marxist-Leninist and will be until the last day of my life." He conceded he had hidden his communist goals, said he had never made a declaration because most of the people who had helped him gain power would have turned against him, and he admitted having lied to the people. He said the new program of the party would be Marxist-Leninist.

Ana received a letter from Yolanda Solís, surprisingly from Chicago, where she had been living for over a month, and working in a bank. She and Eladio hadn't gotten married yet.

Ana got to know her co-workers better. Tamargo lived in Brickell Estates. The smell of Mitchell's cigarettes became familiar to her; he smoked 'Parliaments'. There were three other men in her department. One, Ted Miller, was very affected, acted as if he were on stage, said everything out loud, talked six minutes non-stop. Another, Jim Davis, was very cynical, mocked everything, snorted often. The third, Dave Harris, still new, trying to find his way, didn't always follow what they discussed. Kathy Clark had a tactic of coming in early, turning on her typewriter, adding machine and the light and scattering papers over her desk, giving it a busy look, and then going up to the employees' lounge for coffee. Wilson, the vice-president, Kathy's boss, referred to any plan as "exciting, fascinating, stimulating, a thrill."

She found it was very common among many of them to have misspellings. And they had gotten used to printing because their cursive handwriting wasn't legible. Most insisted on spelling her name with two N's.

She heard new American slang expressions with which she hadn't been familiar. "Hang-up", "up-tight", "with it", "be in", "hip", "stay loose" and "groovy" seemed to come up often in the Americans' speech.

One afternoon, sitting in the crowded bus on her way home from work, Ana noticed a woman standing in the aisle holding on with one hand, while she balanced three packages in her other one and under her arm. Feeling sorry for her, she asked the American woman, "May I hold the packages for you?"

The woman, a scowl on her face, snapped, "No!"

Embarrassed, and hoping nobody had noticed, Ana fixed her eyes on the back of the seat in front for the rest of the trip. That'd teach her to play good Samaritan!

Tinsel garlands were hung over Flagler Street. Christmas carols were played in stores over the amplifiers. But at home they didn't have a tree that year.

Ana sent Christmas cards to Octavio Guillén, Leonardo Vidal and Berta Penabad, in Nassau, to Gloria Serrano, Carmen Zayas, Ofelia Barquet, Olga Salazar and Idalia, back in Cuba, and to Yolanda Solís, now in Chicago. And one to Dany, hoping. She tried once again, sending a card to Graciela. And she ventured sending one to Reynaldo Duarte, but she didn't receive an answer from him or from Graciela. She considered writing a letter to Betancourt — he had been so nice to her, — but she never quite got around to doing it.

From the first week of December it started to get cold.

Ana was eligible for group health insurance coverage since the beginning of the month and her payroll deductions now started. They didn't like the idea of having an out-of-pocket deductible amount and having to lay the money up front to be reimbursed weeks later.

Laura and Adrián found a one-bedroom apartment in an old big building in the southwest section near the Ada Merritt Junior High School. There was a musty smell in the stairway and the sofa cushions had an odor of mildew that pervaded the whole living room and could be smelled from the front door. They continued receiving help from the Refugee Center, consisting of 100 dollars a month, and surplus food from the Department of Agriculture, which they went to pick up monthly at 2nd Avenue, typically canned meat, peanut butter, powdered milk, powdered egg and processed cheddar cheese. Laura fried slices of the meat, scrambled the powdered eggs, and made milk shakes with the powdered milk and the peanut butter.

Leonardo Vidal went by unexpectedly one afternoon in December. He told them he was in Miami to meet his older brother, who was coming from Puerto Rico to spend Christmas with him. He brought Ana up on news about Wayne and their friends in Nassau. She learned that Mr. Kent was in Wayne Motors' office in Caracas. She called their local office to get its address and wrote a letter to him. He never answered.

On Flagler Street the Lions, Rotary and Kiwanis Clubs posted Santa Clauses on the sidewalk ringing bells by kettles, asking for donations. Wilson volunteered.

At the bank they trimmed a tree in the lobby by the front entrance, in the inner office they hung greeting cards on the windows. Friday they had an office party. The employees gathered in the Commercial Credit Department because it was out of the sight of the people walking by the drape-less front doors. Ana liked cognac and ginger ale, brandy or rum and cola, but there was only whiskey — Scotch, bourbon, rye and blended, Debbie, the redhead, informed her, — so she mixed it with Coke. Jennie had left at lunch time to get an early start on her drive upstate. Her boyfriend was going with her to meet her family. Ana sat on the edge of a desk by the wall.

Kathy sat holding her cigarette away from her own face and

Getting Settled

touching the tip of her ring finger with the fingernail of her thumb, talking about the European Common Market. "... That's what the so-called 'continental'" – she traced imaginary quotation marks in the air with her index and middle fingers – "authorities claim." Not a hair was out of place in her "flip". She rubbed her hand on the nape of her neck, reflectively.

A man who had been closing a business deal in the Trust Department was invited to join them. He sat in a chair facing Mr. Mitchell, his back to Ana. Paula was sitting to a side. Tamargo was in the Loan Department. The client seemed to have started celebrating early.

"How's business?", he asked Mitchell, his tongue a little garbled.

"Fine, fine."

"Fine bunch of people you have here. A pleasure doing business with such fine people."

"Thank you", Mitchell said, and Paula echoed. "That's what we like to hear", he added trying to sound jovial.

"Growing, eh? Growing."

"Yes."

"But the Cubans... We're having trouble with the Cubans."

Mr. Mitchell coughed uncomfortably. Paula leaned forward in her chair. Did she think she was going to stop him? Ana leaned back against the wall, without making a noise, and smiled slightly. Her pride wouldn't have let her do anything else. At least he would make a fool of himself. Let him gather rope.

"Aren't you having problems with the Cubans?", the man insisted.

Mr. Mitchell was stupefied. "No, we aren't at all", he stammered.

"Oh, those Cubans...!"

"As a matter of fact", Paula interrupted him nervously, "we have a Cuban secretary and we're very happy with her", indicating Ana.

The man whirled around, noticing Ana for the first time. "Oh!, I'm sorry."

"Our assistant manager is Cuban", Mitchell pointed out, sounding a little frantic.

"I don't mean all Cubans. But some Cubans." His eyes were glazed.

"It's all right", said Ana.

"You know what I mean", he said, leaning toward her.

Ana nodded, got up from the desk and walked away from him.

A teller, a thin man wearing a wedding band whom Ana heard being called Fred, kept refilling her glass and, after her third drink, she had to run to the ladies' room, sick. Paula followed her.

"Splash water on your face", she advised.

"Whiskey doesn't agree with me", Ana explained, looking at her pale reflection in the mirror over the basin. It reminded her of the mirrors over the basins in the ladies' rooms in Cuba.

"Young people don't know when to stop. When you get older you know when you've had enough. I could drink any man under the table. But I can hold my liquor. How old do you think I am?"

Ana was steady enough to know to underestimate it. "Thirty."

"Ah, you're sweet!", said Paula.

"Have some black coffee", advised Debbie from the door.

"That's a fallacy", said Paula.

When she recovered, Ana repaired her make-up and went home.

For Christmas Eve supper, Méndez bought roast suckling pig by the pound and almond nougat at the Varona market, Teresa made white rice and black beans, and they accompanied it with "Roma" red wine.

In Cuba they celebrated the first Socialist Christmas.

In the latter half of December the cold weather already turned harsh. December 30 was the coldest day of the year, the temperature dropping to 39 degrees. That Saturday evening her cousin Laura came with Adrián to get them. They all went to Flagler Street and 5th Avenue, where the Orange Bowl parade ended, hoping to glimpse something of it. They stood shivering in the cold wind in their inadequate clothes, but it was already breaking up and they only got to see the last few floats dispersing. They grew closer to Laura and Adrián than they had been in Cuba, where months had gone by without seeing each other.

On New Year's Eve, Laura and Adrián appeared around 10:15, a new friend of Adrián's in tow.

"You have to come with us, Ana. No excuses", Laura announced. "We're going to the DiLido."

"With whom did you leave Lourdes?", asked Teresa.

"Our next door neighbor stayed with her."

"This is a friend of mine", Adrián introduced the man, pulling him into the living room. "He was staying at the same hotel we were."

The young man took Ana's hand timidly. "It's a pleasure. Rogelio", he mumbled. If he said his last name, Ana didn't catch it. He was homely, his toothy smile made him appear stupid, and she was willing to bet he couldn't dance.

"Go ahead, Ana María", her mother encouraged her when she saw her hesitate.

She did want to do anything rather than stay to greet the New Year sitting at home, so she smiled with an effort. "Well, will you wait until I change?"

"Sure, go ahead and change. We'll wait", said Rogelio, more confident now that he had roped a date.

"Sit down", Méndez asked them, as Ana ran into her room. She could hear them making small talk. Rogelio sounded much better than he looked. She changed into an orange faille dress with a plunging neckline and went back out. On the street, she was shoved into a car where a couple was waiting, the man behind the wheel.

"This is a friend of ours", Adrián again introduced, "and his wife."

The man leaned forward over the wheel. "Rafael Arroyo", he said with a South American accent, "at your feet."

"A pleasure. Librada", his wife said smiling, and leaned back again.

Adrián explained, settling in the back seat between Laura and Rogelio, "They are Colombian, from Manizales."

"Oh!, yes? Nice!", Ana exclaimed, dutifully holding her smile.

At the DiLido, in the Beach, a trio that seemed Israeli, a woman singer with two male musicians who played the tambourine and a drum, sang Hebrew songs. Laura said they were the Yemenite Trio, but Arroyo said they were "Míriam and the Sons of Paraguay". New to Ana, she thought it lovely music. The woman, dark, almost like an Indian, wore a white Roman robe-like dress that contrasted with her skin. They played *"Hava Nagilah"*.

There were no grapes. After the show, the band played dance music. Twist. None of them knew how to do it. "It's as if you were putting a cigarette out with your foot", Ana had heard Dave Harris say at work.

"Does your mercy wish to dance?", the Colombian asked his wife. He was a thin, stooped, yellowish pale man with nervous movements. They went out on the dance floor. Librada had shiny, smooth, reddish, dark skin, flat, wide, high cheekbones, slanted eyes and very sparse lashes; she had no waist.

Rogelio, as Ana had guessed, was especially lost, so she insisted they sit it out and listen to the music.

"I think you don't know how to dance", he declared at the table.

And Ana had to burst out laughing.

When the club closed, Arroyo urged them to go on to the "Habana Madrid" on Biscayne Boulevard.

"Wouldn't you like to, *Doña* Laura?"

Adrián didn't want to go. The Colombian called him aside. When they joined them again, the man said decisively, "Let's go", and Adrián now reluctantly agreed.

At the Habana Madrid, near the bay, the music was Cuban. Laura and Adrián headed straight for the dance floor, Ana suspected, to avoid the uncomfortable position. Arroyo led the others to a table.

"Sit down, your mercy", he said to his wife, and to Ana, "Allow me", pulling the chair out for her, and he ordered a round of drinks for all six, bridging the delicate situation.

When the Cuban waitress had served them, he asked her, "Old lady, bring me the check."

As soon as the woman had left the table, Librada, fast as lightning, raised her hand and slapped her husband noisily across the cheek. Ana was appalled.

The man laughed embarrassedly, trying to minimize it. "What was that for?"

"You didn't have to treat her that way."

Ana thought the Colombian woman was referring to his use of the *"tú"* familiar pronoun form.

"What do you mean?"

"You didn't have to call her 'old lady'," said his wife, indignant.

"But the girl is Cuban and that's accepted among Cubans."

"But you're not Cuban", the woman said hoarsely, "and in Colombia you don't address a strange woman that way."

Ana wouldn't have dared point out that in Cuba you didn't address a strange woman that way either. Rogelio asked her to dance and now she welcomed it gratefully. He stepped on her feet and bumped into her, but she took it bravely. By the time they went back to the table for their drinks, Laura and Adrián with them, the couple were talking animatedly, the spat evidently forgotten.

When they were leaving, Ana noticed nobody had left a tip for the waitress. So did Librada, who said in the car, "I feel bad that we didn't leave the old lady a tip." Apparently it was acceptable for *her* to refer to the woman that way.

Rogelio took advantage of the confusion in the car to try to kiss Ana's neck!

Getting Settled   441

When she arrived home after 3:00, Ana still thought it had at least been better than having stayed sitting at home all night and gone to bed early. Fortunately, nonetheless, she never saw Rogelio again.

The "United Party of the Cuban Socialist Revolution" resulting from the ORI was of the communist wing.

There was a shortage of meat, milk, butter, eggs, chickens, beans, vegetables and fruits in Cuba. The people formed queues outside stores. Former President Dr. Ramón Grau San Martín said, "General *'NoHay'* (There's None) will defeat the Reds."

Before 1961 ended, food was scarce, rationing was established, and machinery and equipment were deteriorating, since no replacement parts were being received.

The firing squads continued in action month after month. It was estimated that almost 5,000 had been shot by December 31, 1961.

There were 50,000 rebel army troops. Militia was becoming compulsory. There were 300,000 militia-men and -women. And thousands in the Rebel Youth, the Juvenile Patrol and the Youth Labor Brigade.

Workers were under military orders, working when, where and how much they were told.

Education, culture and entertainment were turned into indoctrination. Pictures of Lenin and Khrushchev were displayed in stores. Newsstands were filled with Soviet newspapers and magazines. Cigar stores sold lighters with communist symbols. Small boys waved red flags.

There were in Cuba suppression of freedom, regimentation of spirit, sordid political terror and a complete political and economic dependence on the Soviet bloc.

CHAPTER 13

PLANNING CAMPAIGN

> *"Patria... ¡Nombre cual triste delicioso*
> *al peregrino mísero, que vaga*
> *lejos del suelo que nacer lo viera!*
> *...*
> *¡Cuántas dulzuras, ay, se desconocen*
> *hasta perderse! No: nunca los campos*
> *de Cuba parecieron a mis ojos*
> *de mas beldad y gentileza ornados,*
> *que hoy a mi congojada fantasía."*[13]
> *("Patria",* José María Heredia*)*

Ana met several people she knew from Cuba on the street; neighbors, schoolmates, salesclerks; she found others in the telephone book. She counted over 35. One evening she met Mestre on a bus sitting in the seat in front of her!

Letters from Cuba bore postage stamps proclaiming 1962 as the "Year of Planning".

The cold wave crested on Wednesday the 3rd, the coldest day of the season, when the temperature dropped to 38 degrees. Aida and Oscar gave them two quilts.

Ana received a letter from Ernesto: "I'm working in a machinery factory near Union Station", he wrote, "and I live near Columbus Park. The pay is good and I'm working like a Negro and saving like a Jew. Now I see what the lure of the North is: money. With a little

---

[13] Fatherland... Name delicious as well as sad
to the miserable pilgrim who wanders
far from the soil that saw him be born!
...
Oh, how many sweetnesses are unknown
until they are lost! No: the fields
of Cuba never seemed to my eyes
more ornate with beauty and gentleness
than today in my anguished fantasy.

luck, I'll have saved enough in less than seven years to go back to Miami with enough money to open my own business. Javier is working as shipping clerk in a paper mill near the stadium and lives further out, in Oak Park. He was active with an anti-communist group here for a while, but they all seem to dissolve. There isn't much talk about Cuba here. I've made up my mind to make this country my home. There doesn't seem to be any hope of our ever going back to ours and the less we think about it, the less we'll torture ourselves. Don't you agree? It's horribly cold here, very windy, and the snow is awful. Are you still working at the bank? Give my regards to your parents and write me a long letter. Did Rosa get married after all? Sincere regards," He didn't mention Adelaida.

Ana's attitude toward exile *had* changed. She now tried to push the thoughts of home out of her mind, they hurt so much. She felt actual physical pain when she thought she'd never walk around the streets of her Vedado with which she had ben so familiar, or see her relatives back home, and friends, schoolmates, neighbors. She thought of parks, buildings, restaurants, clubs, schools, houses and streets with real love, and her heart caught in her throat at the thought of their loss. Ernesto was right that it was a torture to think about home. But she was pushing the thoughts away from her mind only until the time when she could go back. She hadn't lost hope of returning. And she didn't want to lose it. That would be giving up. Seven years! There were many groups right now making efforts. But work there was limited to the men; there was less that women could do than in Cuba, save take up collections or distribute flyers.

She realized that disagreement in politics stirred in her a violent urge that she had to quench by rapidly changing the subject.

Ana ran into Casimiro Abreu, her pock-marked co-worker from the Ministry, at a five-and-ten store. When they met, the first reaction of the thin man in his early forties with thinning, curly hair, was, "And I wàs *so* sure you were with the revolution!"

"And I was so sure that *you* were!", she laughed.

"We were impressing each other. Are you here by yourself?"

"No, with my parents. And you?"

"I came ahead alone to make my way. My family will follow later by way of Mexico." Ana knew he was married and had a daughter.

"What made you think I would be with the revolution?"

"Well, I recall that during the invasion of April, when you heard that they were landing, you said very confidently, 'They don't even stand a chance', and I said to myself, 'There's a true revolutionary'."

"Did I actually say that? Well, I must have been regretting that they didn't. But that must have slipped out, because I wouldn't have dared say anything like that if I had realized it. It's a good think it was taken that way."

"And why did you think I was?"

"Because I once heard you call Morejón 'comrade'."

"I don't remember. I must have been making fun. Are you working?"

"Yes, at the Burlingame Bank, in the southeast section. And you?"

"Not yet. I'm going to start taking drafting in the evenings to try to get a job in that."

"Drafting?"

"Yes, architectural. Why don't you take it too? It's only two nights a week, and tuition is only two dollars."

"Well, maybe. I might."

"Why did they arrest you the day of the invasion?"

"I think they had me mixed up with Betancourt's former secretary."

"Ah, yes, Ana..." His shirttail was always untucked from his pants on one side. "Do you have a telephone?"

"No, not yet. But here's my address," she wrote it on a slip of paper, "and, since you're alone now, whenever you have nothing to do, come over to our house in the evening, to have a chat with my parents about Cuba and we'll lament the tribulations of exile."

"All right. Here's my sister's telephone." He jotted it on a piece off the sheet she had given him, with a NEwton exchange.

Abreu soon started coming by sometimes in the evening, he met her parents and they talked for hours. Teresa made coffee and sometimes he brought a pound cake. He had a good sense of humor. "Well, I've become a pest in exile", he'd say apologetically when leaving, putting himself down. He kept encouraging Ana to take drafting.

She started taking architectural drafting on Tuesday and Thursday evenings. It gave her something to do. The street of the high school where the classes were held, Ana noticed, was a good two feet lower than the sidewalk.

On January 11 Juan Marinello, president of the old Popular Socialist Party, was named rector of the University of Havana.

Teresa received a letter from Alicia, in La Sierra. She and her older son, Marvin, planned to leave Cuba.

There was a bus strike that lasted over three weeks, during which Jennie and Tamargo took turns driving Ana to work and home. Méndez made similar arrangements with a co-worker, and sometimes he had to walk to and from work.

They started hearing Sunday Mass at Sts. Peter and Paul's Catholic Church.

They became members of a medical clinic, the Spanish-American United Society, recently founded, where, as in those in Cuba, they received unlimited medical attention for a fixed monthly family quota, which here was $12.

Teresa wrote to Cristina offering her to claim them if she wanted.

On Groundhog Day, February 2, Phil, the squat, furry groundchuck of Punxsutawney, Pennsylvania, came out of his burrow on Gobbler's Knob in Jefferson County and saw the deep black shadow he cast, which, according to the legend, predicted another six weeks of winter weather. They found out that from the first week in January the weather was sometimes icy cold and it lasted until the first week in March. It was much colder than it got in Havana, they needed flannel nightwear and blankets, and in many houses people used electric heaters.

Ana read Paar's "I Kid You Not" and Nye's "Stay Loose". She spent a lot of time reading. She got a card at the city library.

They became familiar with milk in cartons, Lifebuoy and Woodbury soaps, flat cardboard matches in books, coin boxes by the bus drivers, string mops, chain link fences, state sales tax, one hour lunches, newspaper dispensers, efficiency apartments and cottages, Fahrenheit degrees, miles, yellow school buses, policemen in short sleeve shirts, notaries public, the Goodyear blimp in the sky instead of Castro's helicopter, plastic fumigating tents for termites, football, baby sitters by the hour, osteopaths and chiropractors, doughnuts. Until one became used to the buildings, they didn't look much different from a humble Cuban *"pasaje"*, but one later realized that the type of construction had been so widely adopted because it enjoyed more sunlight and ventilation than the conventional enclosed buildings offered.

They started going once in a while to the movies downtown, where there were six to choose from, and they saw "Friendly Persuasion" with Gary Cooper, "The Great Impostor" with Tony Curtis, "Never on Sunday" with Melina Mercouri, "The Pit and the Pendulum" with Vincent Price, "The World of Suzie Wong" with William Holden, "Snow White and the Three Stooges" with Patricia Medina.

Ana shopped at modest Mangel's, at Three Sisters and Darling Shop in the Arcade, and Lynn's on 1st Street. While back home she had been considered on the thin side, here she was often complimented on her beautiful figure.

On February 11 rationing of medicines began in Cuba.

On Saint Valentine's Day the bank gave all the female employees red carnations, and Fred's wife sent home-baked red-frosted heart-shaped cookies.

Thursday as they came out of class, Abreu told her, "I'll treat you to an ice cream soda, today's my birthday."

They went to a nearby soda fountain. Ana wished him a happy birthday, he thanked her and she thanked him for the ice cream soda; she felt awkward alone with him sitting at a counter.

The population of Greater Miami reached one million on February 20, the same day John H. Glenn Jr. blasted off from Cape Canaveral in Friendship 7 to circle the earth. The State of Florida was 32% larger than the island of Cuba.

Washington's birthday was celebrated on February 22, and there was no work.

They approached the task of filing their first federal income tax returns with apprehension. It fortunately didn't turn out to be such an overwhelming ordeal as they had been intimidated by everybody into thinking it would be. They gathered their salary statements, Ana translated the instructions to her father at the kitchen table, and he completed the forms both for himself and Teresa jointly, and for Ana.

Ana received a letter from Gloria Serrano, her first, dated February 18 and, strangely, unsigned. She wrote that she was still working in the Accounting Department of the Corporation. Ana knew that was where Dany was working. She told Ana she wished very much to see her, asked about work in Miami, complained about her nerves. But no mention of Dany. Ana answered her right away, and asked her about everybody who had stayed behind, being careful to list everybody's name in more or less the same order as degree of friendship she had had with them. She only cared what Gloria would answer about Dany, but she didn't want to ask only about him right out. She found it somehow humiliating.

In a letter dated March 5, Leonardo told her his brother was working, but they hadn't given up the idea of moving to Miami too.

Elvira surprised her by adding a note to his letter, where she referred to him as "this fatso", but Ana impassively ignored it; she couldn't bring herself to answer her.

She also received a reply from Idalia, her former neighbor from 24th Street.

A letter from Gustavo brought them photographs of Gustavito with Lorenzo, his godfather, and of Blanquita with the Pomeranian dog. He wrote little and when he did, he didn't say much. Gustavito had started kindergarten in September. Their uncle Guillermo and Beatriz had visited them Sunday. Blanca always added notes, but hers were superficial and light – Blanquita weighed 38 pounds, Elena and Mateo sent them their regards, – and always ended sending the children's love.

A communist-type collective leadership was announced March 9 consisting of a 25-member directorate headed by Castro and including ten acknowledged communists. On March 12 the ration book was created in Cuba.

At work Ana received a $7^{1}/_{2}$ percent raise in salary. They had a telephone installed, with a FRanklyn exchange.

Méndez opened a joint special checking account with Teresa at a nearby bank, to have a record of their payments.

The cold weather still continued strong until the latter half of March. And until the first week in April the temperature remained cool.

The invasion prisoners were tried *en masse* like war criminals on March 29 in the courtyard of El Príncipe Castle. They had been in jail eleven months. They wore bright yellow tee-shirts and were nicknamed yellow worms. When asked whether they had any statement, Luis González Lalondry, a tall mulatto, raised his hand and said he wanted to go to the bathroom. The brigade burst into laughter.

Boatloads of people fleeing from the communist rule continued to risk their lives in **the Corridor of Death** to land on the beaches of the Florida Keys. The end of Batista's government had left a closing balance reported as 19,000 murdered and 20,000 in exile. By the beginning of 1962 the total of Cubans who had escaped from Castro's regime and were living just in the United States alone had reached 150,000.

On April 1st, April Fools' Day was celebrated with pranks.

Jorge Alonso Bermúdez, Guillermo Alonso Pujol's son, made a

declaration and his father bought his freedom. There were 1,179 prisoners left. On April 8 the Girón prisoners were sentenced to thirty-year terms. A ransom of 62 million dollars was fixed.

Anti-Castro Cubans bombed the Rosita de Hornedo hotel in Miramar from the sea, where Russian technicians were staying.

Sixty wounded prisoners went to the United States on April 14, among them Enrique Ruiz-Williams, second in command of the Heavy Gun Battalion.

Sixteen people on a bus threw the vehicle against the fences of the Embassy of Brazil in Havana, and took asylum.

Abreu went by to say good-by. His family had arrived via Mexico and they were moving to Atlanta. Ernesto had moved, so had Rosa, and now Abreu was leaving.

The bank was open on Good Friday. Ana asked for the day off without pay to observe the Crucifixion. As she was leaving Thursday, Paula, a Pentecostal, wished her "a happy Good Friday". And Saturday she finally went to confession again.

They went with Laura, Adrián and Lourdes to Biscayne Boulevard on Sunday to watch the Easter Twins' Parade roll down the seven blocks alongside Bayfront Park.

From the first week in April until the first one in June, the temperature was warm, mostly pleasant, and some days hot.

They learned that Miami in summer was a quiet, off-season tourist resort resting morosely, populated by its few permanent residents, mostly old, retired and poor. And in winter it was invaded by the tourists down from the North, mostly rich, retired and old, its beach a glittering, illusory floating community. The young didn't get as far south; college students stayed further north in newer, cleaner Fort Lauderdale.

One thousand one hundred nineteen men remained in prison. The prisoners had been at the Sports City twenty days, until May 13, when they had been taken to the Naval Hospital for over two months. On July 17, 1961, nine hundred had been transferred to El Príncipe Carlos Castle, a fort completed in 1779, where they would remain over seventeen months, first at the *"bartolinas"*[64], later at the *"leoneras"*[65] and the *"sanatorio"*[66]. There was hepatitis and dysen-

---

[64] dark, narrow calabooses, dungeons
[65] lion dens
[66] sanatorium

tery. Now on May 28 the rest were taken to the Presidio Modelo on Isle of Pines, where they were to stay for almost seven months. The Cuban Families Committee raised $2.9 million for their exchange.

Memorial Day was celebrated on May 30, and there was no work.

In June Ana saw a small item in the local Spanish newspaper, reprinted from a Cuban one: "**HAVANA**, June 9 - A Prensa Latina report today disclosed that a Revolutionary Tribunal at La Cabaña Fortress integrated by five members, in case of the current year, for a felony against the stability, integrity and powers of the State, sanctioned to thirty-year prison terms: José González Díaz, Antonio López Martínez, Francisco Pérez Hernández, Manuel Fernández Pérez, Alejandro Dávila Rodríguez and Juan Rodríguez Sánchez." Thirty years! A whole lifetime! A shudder ran through her body. It seemed impossible to her that somebody she had known could have met such a fate, Alejandro, somebody for whom she felt such affection. It hurt. If they had gotten involved, would he not have left?, not gotten caught? Could she have prevented it? She talked to her parents about him. But they had never known how she had met him, only that he was a friend of Duarte's.

From the first week in June it started to get hot.

There was only one bus that took her to the bank and, if she missed the 8:14, she was late for work. Ana started taking driving lessons. First there was a written test to get a restricted license. Her instructor, Héctor, a young Cuban man, picked her up at the bank after work. She took nine lessons, and learned to drive on a Mercury Comet. Héctor took her to the Orange Bowl lot to teach her parallel parking between two stanchions; and he took her to the skill test. And she got her driver's license. It didn't have her picture on it.

On the day of her last lesson, Héctor asked her out. It would be the first time she would go out on a real date since that photographer. He picked her up smelling strongly of "Old Spice" in a large Plymouth and took her to the "Painted Horse" on 8th Street for Swedish *smörgasbord*. They had one drink. He was very attentive, an active, very cheerful, thin, dark-haired man. He was from Alquízar, he said, but had been in Florida five years, since before Castro. They talked and laughed a lot. He was divorced, he told her, and had a little daughter.

After dinner, he took her to his home near Parrot Paradise, to meet his parents and his brother, simple people who immediately made her feel at ease. The family also owned the house across the street, Héctor told her. His father mentioned, "They are showing a Mexican movie about karate", and Ana was surprised to find herself going to the movies with the whole family. Héctor left her with imprecise promises to call her again.

Thursday and Friday, June 21 and 22, torrential rains fell registering three inches, the record for the season. There were no adequate storm sewers in the city and streets flooded, the water reaching over the sidewalks up to the doorways, and cars stalled. The water came up to their ankles crossing some streets, and they got soaked waiting for the bus.

On the Fourth of July, Independence Day, there was no work, the people raised the flag and celebrated by shooting firecrackers, and there were displays of fireworks.

From the latter half of June the heat already became scorching. Just moving bathed one in perspiration and any effort became exhausting. Many people found electric fans a necessity in their homes. It was a terrible summer even by Miami standards. On Thursday, July 26, as an unpretentious early celebration of the sixty-sixth anniversary of the founding of the City of Miami was held by the Women's Club, the temperature rose to a sweltering 93 degrees. Nobody, not even Ana herself, remembered it was her name day. Meanwhile, in Cuba they ostentatiously celebrated the anniversary of the attack on Moncada. Because of the heat, that evening Ana had inadvertently put on a pair of red shorts and a black blouse, and Oscar advised, "You had better not wear that today. People might think you're celebrating. It could be taken for taunting." The mercury climbed up to that level on nine days during that season. It was the hottest summer they had ever lived through.

On July 29 four invasion prisoners arrived in Miami, their ransoms paid, one of them Fabio Freyre Aguilera, the cattleman from Oriente.

CHAPTER 14

HOPE OF RETURN

*"Y luego mas ferviente
por Tu pueblo rogando,
¡alza, diré, Tu brazo omnipotente!
¡Que el enemigo su poder destruya
y a Tu culpable grey mira clemente,
según la gran misericordia Tuya!"*[14]
*("Miserere",
    Gertrudis Gómez de Avellaneda)*

Bossa nova was created in Brazil, and "The Girl from Ipanema" by Sergio Mendes became popular in the States.

The Méndez family were introduced to chicken and dumplings, chopped steak, catfish, hushpuppies, hominy grits, rutabaga, hot open face sandwiches with gravy, corned beef, barbecue, *chile con carne*, corn bread, peanut butter on white bread, rhubarb, cream cheese and jelly sandwiches, pancakes with maple syrup, waffles, blueberry and pecan pies, jelly beans, pistachio ice cream. They adapted easily to the weak American coffee, with which they had become familiar on their former vacation trips.

Laura was working as an operator in a handbag factory. They had enrolled Lourdes in a nursery school. Adrián hadn't yet found a job. He complained that there was no help to orient refugees. Carlos and Ana got into drawn-out arguments with him.

"I look at it this way, Adrián", Carlos said. "If we were back in ... say, as late as nineteen twenty-seven...:"

"In nineteen twenty-seven, I wasn't born", Adrián debated.

"What I mean is before Welfare existed, when a man had no

[14] And I will later say more fervently
praying for Thy people,
"Raise Thy almighty arm!
May its power destroy the enemy
and look Thou on Thy guilty herd leniently,
according to Thy great mercy!"

choice but to work in order to eat...", Carlos went on, "and you moved to this country, you would still have to go out and work if you wanted to eat, just as you would if you were back in your own country, wouldn't you?" He waited for an agreement from Adrián, which didn't come. "Without help. So, when we come to a foreign country now, why shouldn't we work for a living just as we would if we were back in our own?"

"Oh, but we're not cavemen, Carlos. That's a very primitive way of reasoning, and it doesn't apply to the complexities of our present day."

"It still holds true", Ana said.

"Now society protects the people. They invited us to come...", Adrián started.

"No, they didn't invite us", Carlos interrupted him. "They admitted us."

Adrián ignored it. "If I had known what this was like, I wouldn't have come."

"No, you would have gone on working for communism, without freedom?", Ana asked him.

He didn't answer her. "The type of work that's available to us here is nothing like the type of work for which we had trained in our country."

"You can't expect it to be, Adrián", Carlos argued. "Do you think I like running an elevator? On weekends! But we're lucky we found a country to which to come."

"And what about the language?"

"There are many jobs you can do while you're learning it", Ana said, knowing that was not so easy as she wanted to pretend. She had had an advantage.

"Like what? Washing dishes? Picking tomatoes? Mopping floors?"

"Why not, if that's the only thing you can do?" She knew she was being inflexible now.

"Oh, Ana... And I suppose after six months, I'd have learned enough English to be a speaker and... and give lectures. About the Linotype!"

"No, but you could have learned enough to become a waiter."

"Step promotion", Adrián said sarcastically.

"It's better than living off public charity", said Carlos. And Teresa, overhearing the argument from the kitchen, came out with cups of coffee to interrupt it, for fear Adrián would get offended and their relationship with Laura would be ruined.

Ana, who'd never even so much as warmed a meal, now learned to cook. Teresa taught her the basics and she ventured into elaborate dishes on her own, consulting a cookbook.

And, never having bought more than a bottle of soda at a grocery store, she now sometimes did the weekly grocery shopping. Usually, her mother would go to the market on Friday, while her father minded the wash at the laundromat. But this Saturday Teresa gave her their usual fifteen-dollar weekly grocery allotment and Ana headed for the supermarket nearby glancing at the list in her hand, which varied only slightly: juice, grapefruit and tomato; coffee, Cuban and American; milk, with cream and skimmed; whole wheat bread and biscuits; cheese, ham; enough meat and fish, rice, vegetables, soap – these were constant. – Then the variables: eggs, carrots, cucumbers, tubers, fruits, sugar, margarine, sardines, soup, detergent.

She knew the procedure well now and followed it methodically. First to the meat counter. There were, let's see, one meal a day each for everybody, seven days, one more per day for her mother five days, two for her mother and herself on Saturday and Sunday, plus an extra one for her father on Friday, thirty-one. She got cube steaks, minute steaks, chicken steaks, ground beef – pork was cheap and so was liver, – keeping count of the portions. She picked up a package of chicken breasts, and dropped it; thighs were cheaper. She went through them looking for one with six pieces. She found one; it was too much. If she changed the price for a lower one, would they notice? She found a package of wings and slid the sticker off the damp cellophane with a swift sweep of her hand. She looked up at the convex circular mirror high on the wall. From where were they watching? Who could see her? Were those slits blinds? Was that an office? Maybe the clerk stamping prices would notice. Or perhaps the manager was right behind her this very moment. But, if she paid that much for the chicken, she wouldn't be able to get enough meat for the whole week. She'd risk it. Partly from the cold in the refrigerated counter and partly from fear, the flesh on her arms rose in goose pimples. She reached in, slid the sticker off the package of thighs, stuck the lower one on and tossed the package into her cart. She looked longingly at the sirloin, Porterhouse and chuck for a moment, then decided to splurge on a shoulder steak. On to the seafood section; shrimp was out of the question; flounder was abundant. She counted the portions: thirty-one. No lamb or veal. Then came the bread, juice, "Home" milk, coffee, enough cheese and ham for eleven sandwiches, rice, margarine and the soap. She stopped then and wrote on the list the price next to each item she'd gotten, added it. What was left would have to do for the rest. And she went down the aisles picking cans, boxes, packages, bags and bottles from the shelves while she added in her mind. Eggs, vegetables, tubers, sardines. Fruit? Six bananas. One can of beer? The cheapest brand, 15 cents. Three cans of soda? The market's brand. Some cookies? The smallest box. She added up the prices again before she approached the check-out counter, $14.51. She'd allow the forty-nine cents for taxes and deposits. When she was already in the line she remembered. Condiments! Her mother always complained that she forgot them. Garlic? But there was no money left. She hoped there'd be some left from last week, when her mother had done the shopping.

When she got home, she found Aida in the kitchen, standing while Teresa folded the clean wash on top of the table. She set the two bags of groceries on the table next to the wash. It seemed Aida was in their house more every day.

"There are 'possums in the attic", Aida announced.

"Possums?", echoed Teresa.

"Yes, they're like ... like a ferret ... no, like a *hutía*. They live in the trees and hang by their tails, and they come down at night. We can hear them. And, if they're caught, they roll over and play dead."

"And they are in the city?"

"Yes, the couple next to us", she pointed upstairs, "saw two on the back stairs. She had put food out for their cat and they chased him away and stole it. He set up a trap, but they don't fall in, they just eat the bait and get away. Some carry rabies, but some country people eat it with yams."

"Well, there are cockroaches, mice, gnats, lizards, frogs, mosquitoes, snails, fleas, grasshoppers, snakes and rats", said Teresa, finishing folding the wash.

"That's why there are screens on all the windows", said Aida.

"The screens are so the bugs won't carry us away flying", said Oscar through the back door, on his way up the rear wooden stairs.

"That's because of all the dirt around the houses", said Teresa, starting to put the groceries away in the cabinets.

"I buy our milk at the gas station. 'Puritan'. It's cheaper", said Aida. "I once stepped on a scorpion in the closet, and on a second floor too."

"And the termites!", said Teresa.

"That's because they use so much wood to build the houses", said Ana.

"My son once found a turtle in his backyard in Hialeah", Aida commented, "and on the beach there are raccoons and they steal the food."

"Well, yes", observed Ana, "but raccoons are cute..."

"Yes, but some of them have rabies", Aida inserted.

"... and there are also bluebirds and woodpeckers, and squirrels".

The summer heat rendered them exhausted. Giant water bugs appeared by the dozen on the sidewalks of Flagler Street. Perhaps from a river overflow.

Ana spent that summer reading. She read Orwell's "Animal Farm", Remarque's "Heaven Has No Favorites", Françoise Sagan's "Those Without Shadows" and *"Aimez-Vous Brahms?"* in English, Wilson's "A Summer Place", Hawley's "The Lincoln Lords" and Mergendahl's "The Bramble Bush".

The bank employees brought fruit from the trees in their yards in bags and placed them in the lounge for their co-workers to take. Ted Miller brought mangoes, Paula avocados, Jim Davis grapefruit, Mitchell carambola and Fred Taylor Natal plums or *carissa*, a scarlet, papery-skinned fruit Ana had never seen before.

Cuban girls were strongly criticized for wearing tapered skirts narrower at the knees than at the hips, and for kissing each other on the cheek when they met on the street and in the stores.

A Friday in late August Ana received another letter from Gloria Serrano. She said it seemed like a very short time since she'd last seen her, she told her Elsa Toledo had left for Detroit four months before and she hadn't heard from her again, nor from any of their other co-workers, except for Dalia, who was now working in INRA and, Gloria added, it was hard to believe was the same person. She wrote that half of Arroyo Arenas was in Miami, she complained about her Chinese pen. Still no mention of Dany. Ana again answered her promptly and again asked her, a little impatiently, about everybody she had mentioned in her previous letter.

"Alma", the first tropical depression of storm intensity that developed that season, started as a weak disturbance and hit the Keys, moving at some ten knots. They taped the window panes with gummed paper. It began to intensify slowly on Sunday, August 26 and hit Miami that day. Ana remembered a cyclone in Havana when she'd been seven years old. She had been afraid to go to bed by herself and had gotten into Gustavo's. When he'd gone to bed, he'd tickled her until she'd ended falling on the floor. Some time during the night her father had carried her, asleep, to her room, and she had been surprised to wake up in her own bed in the morning. Through their windows they had seen the balusters of the banister on the roof across the street fall in sequence like so many playing cards.

Alejandro had also told her about a hurricane. "We almost spent a cyclone on Guayo Cay when I was about ten", he'd told her. "A mistake. We'd gone swimming, five of us, at Bocas de Antón, and the gusts took us by surprise. Some lobster fishermen finally saw us from the shore and went in a rowboat to bring us in. You can imagine how our parents were."

Ana dreamed about Dany often. In the recurring dream, they were in Cuba and she saw him come to visit his godfather, who lived in an apartment diagonally across the hall from hers in the same building, similar to their real one in Vedado, and she supposed he'd come to see her when he came out, but, after waiting for him for several hours, she realized that he had already left and hadn't come to see her. Sometimes she dreamed that *she got up the next day and went on waiting for him!* She woke up troubled, disheartened.

One Tuesday afternoon late in August, when she got home from work, her mother told her, "Go see, you have a mysterious letter there."

She found the letter on her bed with just an address but no name on the return flap of the white envelope. She didn't immediately recognize the handwriting on the front or the address on the back. She didn't dare even hope it would be from Dany.

It was! "Dear Ana," it read, "I received your short note and then your Christmas card, but you know it's quite a chore for me to write a couple of lines. From your letter I could see that you're well. I'm working in the Accounting Section. I'm practicing some sports Saturdays or Sundays. Some evenings I play chess. In parenthesis, I played a game of chess", he wrote sarcastically, "with your idol, Major Guevara. I was recently in the Habana Libre a Sunday night to have a few drinks and, logically, that atmosphere makes me think of you and one might say long for you. Also when I go by your old neighborhood, our moments renew themselves for me. I'll always remember you," No mention about the way she had left. No "love" in

Hope of Return

so many words.

A spark of hope lit in her. The letter was short and not loving, but he couldn't well say more in it without knowing what her situation was now one year later, and it *was* affectionate. He even said he thought of her and he would always remember her, that he had *longed* for her. What was he doing around her old neighborhood? She answered him the next day with a long letter, telling him in detail about her job, the apartment, her parents, their mutual friends. She reminisced about Graciela's birthday party, their lunch at the Mandarín, their evening at the Havana Riviera. She mentioned the song *"Añorado Encuentro"*, and his gray and brown suits. She listed a few places back home where they had gone in the last few weeks, Kimbo, Karabalí and the corner cafe across from Vaillant Motors. A cardinal lit on her windowsill while she wrote and she paused to watch it. Her letter was cautious. She rewrote it twice. She told him, "There have been moments that have made me think of you and times when I would have wanted you to share a moment with me, and sometimes I have missed you", and ended it, "Love". She didn't tell him she missed him so much, that her chest ached.

She told Jennie. "I don't understand it", she tried to explain. "While I hadn't heard from him, I was a little calmer ... as if asleep, but once I received his letter, I got such anxiety, I had to answer him right away."

"I know what you mean. It's happened to me when Jeff and I have broken up. While your mind is made up you're not going to make up with him, you're all right, but once you decide you're going to call him, then you can't dial fast enough." It felt so good to have somebody understand her.

Ana saw Salvador again. This time he called to her from a telephone booth as she went by with her father one evening on their way to McCrory's to buy spackling compound.

She introduced them and he told them, "My wife just arrived with our children. Imagine!, I hadn't seen them in twenty-two months."

"Congratulations", said Méndez.

"I'm so glad!", said Ana. She was anxious to ask him if he'd heard anything from Dany, now that he'd written to her, but didn't know how to bring it up in front of her father. Salvador seemed to have read her mind. Well, after all, didn't he say he could read her eyes?

"My younger brother, Ricardo, came with her. And he says he saw Gutierrito on Avenida de Coyula in front of the San Carlos theater a few days before he left. He didn't tell him he was coming, my brother,... but Danilo mentioned he was disgusted and said he'd like to leave."

"Dany?, Danilo?", Ana asked stupidly.

"Yes, Danilo Gutiérrez. He's fed up with voluntary work and indoctrination."

She didn't know whether to believe him. "But he just wrote to me that he played chess with Che."

"Oh!, he wrote to you? Well,... he may have played chess with him, but he'd like to leave just the same. Believe me."

"Come over some evening, with your wife. I haven't seen her since your son was born." She could ask him more about Dany then. "How old are they now?"

"Five and three. I don't have your address. Here, give it to me. I live in Westchester." He pulled out a note pad and Ana dictated. He went on as he wrote, "If you saw the girl, Ana,... she's very affectionate, and wants to follow me around the house wherever I go."

"Bring them over", said Méndez.

"I will, some evening."

"Nice meeting you."

They went on their way and he want back to the telephone, and Ana couldn't help wondering whom he was calling from a booth downtown at night.

Ana attended the picnic that the bank held at Crandon Park on Labor Day for its eighteen employees and their husbands or wives. Jennie drove her there. There was fried chicken, frankfurters, baked beans, potato salad, Coke and beer. Paula drank beer. Ana met the men's wives, Mitchell's, Tamargo's, Jim Davis', Ted Miller's. They took a dip in the sea. Kathy only modeled her bathing suit, holding her stomach in, and didn't get her hair wet.

Ana's parents started attending the County English Center recently opened on 3rd Avenue, reconverted back into a school after temporarily serving as a court. "If we don't know how long we'll have to stay here", Méndez reasoned, "we might as well put our time to good use."

O

Méndez arrived home from work one afternoon and, instead of heading straight for the shower, he sat in the living room. The unusual act merited his wife's and daughter's imitation.

"Anita, what would you think of buying a car?"

"Oh, Papá!, I had been thinking about it for a while now, but I thought you wouldn't want to."

"Nothing fancy, I was just thinking of a nineteen fifty-nine Rambler. I think with a hundred and seventy-five down we can get it."

"But how much will the monthly payments be?", Teresa asked.

"I don't know. Maybe about fifty dollars. I think we can manage it."

"Carlos, I don't think we should go into more debt than we absolutely have to."

"Oh, Mamá!, everybody manages", Ana interceded. "Everybody we know has a car. It's so necessary here!"

"The bus service here is very sparse", Carlos said. "And the other day Anita got home soaked from waiting for the bus in the rain because nobody gave her a lift from the office. And there was that strike in January and the three of us had to walk around the city so much."

"Oh, I know how convenient it would be, but..."

"Do you want to, Anita?"

"Yes, Papá, count on me."

"Well, let's figure it out." Carlos pulled pen and paper from his pocket and went to sit at the kitchen table. Teresa and Ana followed him. He multiplied, added, subtracted and divided for a while, as the women watched, and announced, "I think we can do it."

Carvajal took them to a dealer he knew on 7th Avenue and they bought the car. It was an aqua blue square block that prompted Teresa, used to Gustavo's blue 1957 Chevrolet, to remark, "What an ugly sight!" They got two years' financing, with payments of $54.87 a month.

Since Méndez started work earlier than Ana did, he drove the car to the hotel with her and she then took it over to go on to the bank, where she parked free in a lot around the corner. In the afternoon, she went to the hotel after work and picked her father up, he took over the wheel and drove home.

They found out that besides the monthly installment, there were also collision and liability insurance, license tag and semi-annual inspections. Carvajal advised them to get the insurance policy on their own.

Ana set the buttons on the car radio to WMIE, which broadcast in Spanish, for her father's sake, and her four favorite stations, WIOD, WGBS, WINZ and WQAM. On her two weeks' vacation, she drove to the beach daily and spent the time on the sand near 13th Street before the *bas-relief*ed Art Déco hotels, reading Jackson's "East 57th Street" and Howells' "The Big Company Look".

A call to Gustavo was an occasion of nervous tension and awkward frustration.

Teresa asked, "How are you? And Blanca and the children?" She paused, listening. "Ah!, we're all fine. Your father and Ana María working. It's still hot here. How are Cristina and Marcos? They are? And Guillermo, Beatriz and Jorge? Esperanza and Augusto?" Another pause. "Yes, I know. Take care of yourself, Gustavo. Are you working hard?" She started to cry, but she asked one more question, "How are Elena, Mateo, Lorenzo and Pilar?", before breaking in sobs, and Méndez took the receiver from her.

He asked, "How is everybody? How's the job? Yes, I know... Ah, I'm fine, strong and healthy. I don't even get a cold. No, it's not too hard. Really. And Anita is doing well at the bank. She got her two weeks' vacation last month. They gave her a raise in March. Your mother told you? Don't worry about us. Your mother is fine. Take care of yourself." He listened for a while, his expression growing serious, then said in a lower voice, "Have you taken him to any other doctor? What does he say? Do you need medicines?... No, we can't do that. But have the doctor prescribe the patent for him and you send us the name and we'll send it to you from here right away. We'll take care of that here." From his conversation they could tell that Blanca had taken the phone, while Teresa continued to sob. Ana couldn't think of what to say. Many topics were taboo over the phone. What could Gustavo say about his job? She reached for the receiver and her father handed it to her. Gustavo was on again, asking her how she was.

"Gustavo, who's sick?"

"Tavito". She could hear his voice clearly. He sounded tired. "Something in his respiratory system."

"Like Papá said, we can send you the medicine. With no problem. Just send us the name." She wondered how many hours he had worked that day. What could he say? That he was working fourteen hours a day? That his mail was opened and half the letters never reached him? That they didn't make it to the groceries when they were received at the market before they ran out? Had he had to join the militia? It wasn't likely, since he had such long working hours. He probably did have to keep post at work overnight often.

"I'm trying to draw the money out", he was saying. But Ana wasn't paying attention to that. She wanted to plead with him to go through Canada or Mexico. He could leave Blanca and the children behind and they could follow later. There would be nothing against them to hold them back. But she couldn't say any of that over the telephone.

"Take care of yourself", she said instead. "Write often. Send us photographs. Give my love to Blanca."

Teresa, now fairly calm, took the telephone again and talked to Gustavito now. "Did it fall? Yes, you did right. And the Little Mouse left you a *peseta*?" And then she hung up. "Gustavito lost his first baby tooth", she announced, "and he put it under the pillow." Her eyes watered again.

"Gustavo wanted me to go to a doctor here and explain to him Gustavito's symptoms", Carlos said, "so he could prescribe for him, but I told him that wasn't possible. He's going to send us the name..."

A let-down feeling hovered over the living room. They sat in silence for a while. Darkness was falling. Telephone calls to Cuba depressed Ana. Was she trying to withdraw from the reality of the difficulties that those who had stayed behind were going through?

There had been news lately, backed by photographs, that there were missile bases back home. On October 4 the United States forbade American ships to call on Cuban ports.

Ana's aunt Esperanza and her husband Augusto, Laura's parents, arrived on a Saturday. Augusto had retired from Crusellas a year before. They moved with Laura and Adrián into their small apartment.

"The ceilings of the houses are caving in", Augusto reported. "And there are no building materials to repair them. The porches and balconies of the houses in Havana are propped up with posts. They took Mateo's drugstore."

"Yes, Xiqués had to retire", said Esperanza. "The neighborhood committee watches one's every move."

On October 22, President Kennedy declared a military blockade on Cuba by air and sea, he demanded the dismantling of the bases and the withdrawal of nuclear weapons, and the so-called "Missile Crisis" started. Ships were sent to halt and search all other ships going to the Island. In Cuba two medium-range missiles were ready to operate.

An attack was feared. Many people, and particularly most of the Cubans, formed lines to buy emergency supplies to entrench themselves at home. Supermarkets were sold out of mineral water and toilet tissue.

On the 23rd, the Pan American and K.L.M. flights were suspended.

Twelve Russian ships on their way to Cuba were halted at high sea. On November 9 the rockets were shipped back to Russia. It was said that, when Castro learned that Khrushchev was retrieving the missiles, he had smashed a mirror with his fist. A meeting at the University where Castro spoke ended with the students chanting, "Nikita, Nikita!,/ what you give you don't take back".

That year they celebrated the American Thanksgiving Day. Teresa especially liked to adopt the traditions of the country which didn't infringe on their own, particularly where it concerned food. They invited Laura, Adrián, Esperanza, Augusto and Lourdes to dinner. She and Ana shared the work in preparing the traditional dishes, stuffed roast turkey with cranberry sauce, corn on the cob, yams, and pumpkin and mincemeat pies. They had "Roma" white wine, because it was inexpensive. The eight didn't fit in the kitchen, and they had to sit out on the back porch.

"We watched Macy's parade on television", Laura told them.

Aida and Oscar came down to the backyard after dinner and had white wine with them.

With the approach of winter, the air smelled differently, something they hadn't noticed the first year.

Ernesto, in Miami for his vacation, visited them.

"Javier sends you his regards. Remember him?"

"Of course", said Ana.

After some wine, he told them, "You know what I find there ... here? A lot of discrimination. A country that should be used to immigration more than any other. And they discriminate awfully. I feel it at work."

"Well, put yourself in their place, Ernesto", Ana said. "In a way, you can't blame them for discriminating against us. You have to realize we have invaded their country, taken over a whole city. How would we have reacted to something similar? In fact, how *have* we reacted through the generations?: How did we react to the Spaniards, the Chinese, the Poles and the Jamaicans? Didn't we call all the Spaniards *'gallegos'* and make fun of their dirt, and the Chinese *'narra'* and poke fun at their weakness? And we called all the Jews 'Poles' and all the Poles 'Jews' as if they were the same and made fun of their stinginess; and we called the Negroes *'niche'* and considered them inferior, and we had nicknames for every race, the mulattoes *'mulañé'*. And we had the saying, 'Cuba for the Cubans', deprecatory enough."

"But there wasn't that xenophobia. Why, we used to go out of our way for any foreigner. There was no real prejudice in Cuba, not cruel."

"Maybe not as bitter as here, you're right about that. We tended not to get so hot under the collar, to be more relaxed about it. But hasn't the whole human race always been prejudiced against somebody else? People have always found somebody they've considered inferior from the beginning of time, and there will be prejudice until the end of time. It has always been like that. Maybe that's the way it was meant to be. Why should we resent – I mean *really* resent – their discrimination? Let's take it in stride."

"Oh, Ana", he smiled, "you and your philosophy. They've opened their doors and practically beckoned to us..."

"But they haven't", Ana interrupted him, "we practically begged their hospitality."

"'Send these, the homeless, tempest-tost to me', says Liberty. We come here very grateful and all that, but we need jobs and we're going to take what we find and at the wages we can get and, if we have to work for less than the ones who were holding the jobs and they get unemployed in the deal, it's only the law of survival."

"So we've done, so we'll do", said Méndez. "But you can't blame them for resenting us. We're like a tidal wave that was washed them away in their own ..."

"Resent us yes, the reaction to being displaced – here in Miami, because in Chicago we're by far not the largest immigration group, – but not discriminate against us. Why should they try to make us feel inferior? Why do they think they are superior at all in the first place?"

"Why does anybody think he's superior to anybody else?", said Ana. "Did you consider yourself the same as, say, the boy who parked your boss' car in front of the Electric company and washed it for him?"

"No, of course not, that was different, Ana, we weren't on the same level."

"Well, that's what the Americans think of us", said Teresa, "that we're not the same."

"First, what basis do they have?; and second, what do we mean by Americans, the first generation who was born here? Where did *their* parents come from?, Germany, Italy, Ireland, Russia, Hungary, Austria, Poland, Greece? They're not native Indians."

"No, the Indians were here and they've been discriminated against more than anybody", Teresa put in.

"Don't they realize their parents were just as foreign as we are?", Ernesto asked.

"No, they don't", said Ana. "They didn't live it, so they don't feel it. Now they're the Americans, so now they discriminate. When their parents came over, others discriminated against them. And the sad, sad part is", her voice dropped, contemplating it for the first time, "when our children grow up, they'll discriminate against others. And they won't feel what *we*'ve suffered."

"I see exile has turned you very articulate. Well, let's drop the subject or we could go on arguing forever. Javier's sister Llivia and the Gasçon have been in Tarbes about nine months now. They may come over. The air here now", he observed, "smells like up north at Easter time."

"What ever became of Adelaida?", Ana dared ask him.

"We still see each other, but she's become very independent, materialistic."

So have you changed, Ana thought. Have you turned unreasonable, insensitive? He left soon; he was going with some friends to the Vizcaya Palace, about which Ana had heard.

Carlos and Teresa celebrated their thirty-second wedding anniversary. Carlos brought Teresa a bunch of fresh daisies and gave her a glass canister set, and Ana got them a small yellow cake.

On December 5 the Cuban government confiscated over 5,000 small businesses dealing in clothes, shoes and hardware. Ana guessed the hardware store of Gutiérrez, Dany's father, would have fallen among them. Would this be what Dany needed to push him over?

That year they put up a small artificial Christmas tree on the corner table in the living room.

They braced themselves for the century's coldest spell and out-of-fashion heavy coats, gloves and mothball-smelling wool stockings surfaced, and on Thursday the 13th the temperature dropped to a befuddling 32 degrees, as people hurried, bundled up, heads bowed, faces hidden, butting against the stinging wind, too cold to window-shop.

Ana saw a dress in the window of Holly Shop on Flagler Street near 1st Avenue, nevertheless, Friday at lunch time. It had a black velvet bodice and a white tulle full skirt, and was lying spread out on the bottom of the case. She wanted it badly for New Year's Eve. It didn't have a price. She went inside to ask. She was surprised to find Sandra, the owner of the little shop on San Rafael, working as a salesclerk, her eyes deeper set than ever. She couldn't afford it. She went back three times to look at it. She got a charge account at Lerner's across the street near Miami Avenue instead, and finally had to settle on Tuesday for a less expensive frosted jade green woolly dress. She told herself it would be too cold for the other one anyway. She never bought it, as she never got to buy either the one with the natural jacket and polka dot blouse that she'd seen near the Town theater.

Two other cousins arrived, Carlos' nephew Diego Miranda with his wife, Xiomara, who was expecting a baby in five months, and Teresa's godson Sergio Trejo and his wife, Magaly, with their seven-year-old daughter Haydée. They had not seen either of them for five years. Diego had been a civil engineer, and he and Xiomara, an Episcopalian, lived in Nogueira. Sergio had been a lawyer, and he and Magaly lived in Aranguren development. They brought news of the worsened situation.

"The ration book system is terrible", said Magaly. "They allow you twelve ounces of beef per week. But, when the meat arrives at the butcher shop, the long lines form early and by the time you reach the counter, there may be none left. Two pounds of chicken per month. And a liter of milk per day only for children under seven and old folks. For adults, one-fifth of a liter[67]. Blanca is very unhappy there."

"That's the gateway to hell", said Xiomara.

"A boy asks his father, 'Papi, how far is Florida?'," Diego told, "and his father tells him, 'Shut up and keep swimming'."

It became customary for the exiles who had been there longer to take their newly arrived kin to huge Shell City on 7th Avenue, where the poor newcomers' eyes all but popped out of their sockets at the maze of shelves stacked high with products which were no longer available in Cuba. Adrián now took upon himself the sadistic task of

---

[67] 6.76 ounces or 0.211 quart

taking the relatives on the tour of the market, where they oh'ed and ah'ed mesmerized, their eyes bulging at the sight of the stock. They came away with only two cans of whole kernel corn.

"I read that when Fidel was here", said Sergio, "he stayed at the coral rock house on Northwest Twenty-second Avenue."

"Oh, yes, that one on the corner of Seventh Street", said Adrián.

In mid-December, Ana received a letter from Olga Salazar asking her to send her a latex girdle and Roux hair tint.

The days became shorter. At the bank Ana helped trim the Christmas tree and some of the men got token gifts for the girls. Mitchell gave Ana a potted arrowhead for her desk and an Argentinean grain shipper from Rosario, a leather wallet. Monday they stopped work at noon and had a small party in the employees' lounge on the third floor. Management limited the liquor this year, since so many employees had gotten tipsy the year before. Debbie hung mistletoe over the doorway. Jennie was going to her boyfriend's parents' for the holidays. Ana noticed Dave Harris watching her. She chatted with Ted Miller.

"I was impressed by Orwell's 'Nineteen Eighty-Four'," she commented. "I must have read it about six years ago. That part when they hear the voice that says, 'You are the dead'... And this summer I read 'Animal Farm'."

"Have you read 'Catalonia' by him? Fantastic. About the Spanish Civil War. You'd like it." They served themselves cookies on napkins.

"Have you ever thought of modeling?", Dave asked her.

"No, I haven't."

"The Iberian 'Lady of Elche' is Artemis of Ephesus", Tamargo was saying to Mitchell. Was Mitchell interested?

"Is the art in the Altamira caves really paleolithic?", asked Fred Taylor instead.

"Yes, but that's in Old Castile, in the north", said Tamargo, "and this is in Valencia, in the south, and it shows a Greek influence."

Ana had one brandy. "Four of my great-grandparents were Spanish."

"Then you're Spanish." Ted licked the crumbs off his fingertips.

"No, no. In Cuba, if you were born there, you were Cuban whether the child of Spaniards, Chinese or Poles. We didn't call ourselves what our parents were." Tamargo smiled, nodding.

"I'd think you'd be glad to be Spanish."

"Not more than Cuban."

The remaining 1,113 prisoners of Assault Brigade 2506 arrived in ten planes between Sunday, December 23 at 6:06 in the afternoon at Homestead and 9:45 at night on Christmas Eve at Miami, exchanged for 60 million dollars in food and medicines. They had been in prison a total of one year and eight months.

In the Méndez household, they celebrated Christmas Eve the traditional Cuban way, but on a small scale. They had Sergio, Magaly and Haydée over. After supper, Aida and Oscar came down with a bottle of rum. Ana recalled their last Midnight Mass at Saint John Lateran's Church two years before and, now with two glasses of wine and a shot of rum in her, told the joke about the drunk who walked into church with his hat on.

"Everybody was whispering to him, 'The hat', 'The hat' as he went down the aisle, so when he reached the altar, he turned around to face the congregation and said, 'And at the audience's request, it's my pleasure to render "The Hat"'."

This prompted Oscar to sing the *pasodoble "El Sombrero"*. Sergio and Magaly danced. Haydée had fallen asleep curled up on the sofa.

On Christmas Day, they exchanged modest presents. They roasted another turkey, and bought fruit cake and eggnog. Ana had found steamed plum pudding in a supermarket to be just heated in the oven and served. They invited Diego and Xiomara and had an early dinner. Aida and Oscar had gone to their son's in Hialeah.

Ana received two more letters from Dany in those four months. She wrote to him mentioning "La Gruta", the "Habana 1900", the "Johnny 88", the "Pigalle", "El Roco" and "Johnny's Dream"; she wanted to make him think about their times together. His third letter arrived on a Thursday in the latter half of December. He told her he loved her, he missed her, he had felt lost since they had parted. Nothing about going, though. But, of course, she reasoned, he wouldn't be mentioning anything like that in his letters. Salvador Conde had never gone by or called.

On December 29 at the Orange Bowl, Erneido Oliva presented the gold-and-blue flag of the Brigade to President Kennedy, "for safe-keeping", said Kennedy, and promised it would be returned to fly again over "a free Havana".

"What an incredible fawning gesture!", Méndez expressed.

"And what an act of hypocrisy on Kennedy's part!", Ana said.

"After the way they deserted them!", Teresa agreed.

"We can't deny Cubans have a short memory", said Méndez.

"Well, it must be they're so grateful to be free", Ana reflected, "they're not reasoning clearly yet."

Carvajal called Méndez to ask them over to a little gathering at their house on New Year's Eve. Some friends from home would be there.

Laura and Adrián went by early, with Esperanza and Augusto.

"We're going to Third Avenue to see the parade", said Lourdes enthusiastically. "There are floats."

An ambulance wailed by.

"This year we're going earlier", said Laura.

"The Shriners drive miniature cars around", said Adrián.

Ana wore her new green woolly dress and they went to the Carvajals' comfortable apartment. They were surprised to find Peñalver, the dentist from the hotel, there. By coincidence he and Carvajal were old friends from Cuba. Ana sat most of the night.

"Let me have a 'little lie'," Peñalver asked Estela.

"What's that?", asked Teresa.

"A *'Cuba libre'*," Carlos answered.

"Listen", Carvajal said, "Fidel's there while this country wants. These people have their plan. The day they want to topple him, believe me, he doesn't last one day. He's there only until this country wants."

"Yes", Estela said, "it's too bad they want him to stay there."

Ana danced once with Carvajal, another time with Peñalver and once with a boy who kept talking about his recent trip to Spain, and, Carvajal later informed her, was supposed to be the date of a round-faced plump girl with gold hair who sulked all night by the refrigerator in the kitchen. Estela snapped a couple of pictures.

A man said, "I had to leave. If I'd stayed, now I'd be either in prison or dead, I can't keep my mouth shut."

A woman occasionally gave a cackling laugh and seemed to wind it down, ending with a sigh.

"For New Year's in fifty-five I was in New York", said Peñalver, "and I went down to Times Square to see the ball drop. What a crowd! Now that's real gaiety. And then I went into a bar on West Forty-first Street near Seventh Avenue. For some reason I recall a life-size cut-out they had of Barbara Nichols dressed in a waitress costume."

Hope of Return

Those who had arrived during the first three years of emigration and had been there longer started to feel superior to the ones who had arrived during 1962, like pioneers. Having gone through hardships became a symbol of superiority, and they told stories of how hard life was at the beginning and how little employment there was, exaggerating the difficulties they had gone through. They competed in exceeding privations suffered and they took turns in topping each other. The conversations usually started with "When I arrived here".

"When I arrived here", a man said now, "this was a country village, there was no work anywhere and I used to walk from Southeast Ninth Street to Twentieth looking for a job."

"Ah!, me from Southwest Seventh to the factories on Northwest Twenty-ninth everyday."

"Well, I used to go from Southwest Fourth to Hialeah."

"I used up a pair of shoes walking."

"They gave me a pair of shoes that were tight."

"And me, some pants that were too short, and I felt very happy."

"And me, a tight blouse", said the woman with the cackle, "and tears of happiness came to my eyes."

"I used to eat a hamburger a day with a cola."

"You were lucky you could eat everyday, I ate every other day."

"I should have been so lucky to have a hamburger, I used to eat the bun by itself."

The more a person had prospered, the more he talked about the difficulties he'd suffered, apparently inviting admiration. Ana and her parents didn't talk about what they had gone through. There was always somebody who would have left them behind.

"We were four living in an 'efficiency'."

"Well, you were well off, we were five in one room."

"*Compadre*, we were six in the kitchen at my brother-in-law's house."

"I used to sleep on a table and considered myself fortunate."

"Well, I slept under the table."

"And me, in a bathtub."

"Yes", Méndez now remarked between his teeth, "and this one inside a *car*, that one *under* the car, that one under a bicycle and the other one under a roller skate."

Teresa bit her lip discreetly, but Ana couldn't contain a burst of laughter.

All the other men were married and they apparently didn't dare ask Ana to dance. So she sat and drank cognac and ginger ale until her parents decided to go home.

Cubans were being relocated to other parts of the country away from Florida by the Cuban Refugee Emergency Center, which paid their fare and relocation costs. But these Cubans, not used to the cold weather of the Northern states, as soon as they earned enough money, moved back to Florida, now on their own, without any further aid from the Center, to look for jobs in the warmer climate, earning themselves the nickname of "boomerangs".

CHAPTER 15

ORGANIZATION CAMPAIGN

> *"¡Cuba!, al fin te verás libre y pura*
> *como el aire de luz que respiras,*
> *cual las ondas hirvientes que miras*
> *de tus playas la arena besar."*[15]
> *("Himno del Desterrado",*
> José María Heredia*)*

Dr. Knowles had told them it was a Southern custom to eat black-eyed peas on New Year's Day for good luck. So, with Teresa's enthusiasm, they now followed it.

Gradually, the apartments and houses around the center of the city were occupied by Cuban families. Americans who didn't want to live next to the Cubans sold their old houses that other Americans wouldn't buy to the Cubans for much more than they were really worth, pocketed the profit and moved to newer houses across the Broward County line, where, they claimed, "the schools are better".

Cuban labor took over jobs at hotels and restaurants at lower wages than had been paid until then, and the colored population who had held those jobs complained publicly of being displaced by the refugees. The percentage of Cuban children in the public schools around the center of the city increased to make up most of the enrollment. Slowly at first, Cuban commerce sprang up along Flagler Street, S.W. 8th Street, 12th Avenue and the other main streets just west and south of the downtown area: Cuban coffee stands that sold tiny paper cups of black coffee at seven cents, restaurants that served Cuban dishes, bakeries that sold Cuban crackers, bread and pastries, many jewelry stores that sold 18-karat gold jewelry, fabric stores that sold material by the yard, *"notarías"* which handled residence visas, new bookstores with Spanish books, record shops, nightclubs that

[15] Cuba!, you will in the end see yourself free and pure
like the air of light that you breathe,
like the seething waves that you watch
kiss the sand of your beaches.

played Cuban music and presented Cuban performers, medical clinics, drugstores that sold Spanish patent medicines, grocery stores, meat markets, used automobile part shops, ironworks that made Sevillian window grilles, driving schools, drycleaners, seamstresses, beauty parlors, barber shops, clothes and shoe stores, tailors, photographers, cigar and cigarette factories, ceramic floor tile factories, service stations with Cuban mechanics, offices that dealt in "Cuban affairs", accounting offices, many auto dealers, travel agencies, repair shops, hardware stores, lumber yards, florists, religious article stores, home food delivery services, a couple of *frita* stands and a few cane juice stands.

Professional associations were formed. Private schools started operating, pioneered by Loyola. A new Catholic church opened in the midst of the largest Cuban concentration where a car dealer had been. Municipalities in-exile organized. Many industries opened with trade names familiar to them back home, Kirby soups, Teresa, Ancel and Delicias preserves, Pinos Nuevos bread, Wajay crackers, Balear cookies, Pilón coffee, Ironbeer, Cawy and Nehi sodas, Miño sausages, Ingelmo shoes, Perro and Once-Once undershirts, Trinidad and El Cuño cigarettes, Defensol and Mejoral analgesic tablets, Gravi toothpaste and hair pomade, Sol de Oro hairdressing, Hatuey beer and malt, Bacardí rum, Mirta de Perales cosmetics, banana chips, pork rinds, meringues. Cuban magazines, *Vanidades, Bohemia, Romances, Bandera, Foto-Impresiones, Aquí, Farándula*, and newspapers, *Patria, Zig-Zag*, sprang up at the newsstands. Men wearing *guayaberas* became a common sight and also a new short-sleeve Miami version adapted to the stronger heat. And the winter-resort town that closed down in summer for its long nap woke up and took on a year-round life.

Three radio stations broadcast in Spanish, three theaters showed Spanish movies, a playhouse presented Spanish shows and two television channels transmitted Spanish programs and newscasts. Cuban singers were there, Blanca Gil, Luisito Bravo, Pedrito Román, Manolo Fernández; Orlando Vallejo, Ñico Membiela, composer Arsenio Rodríguez; dancers Nancy and Rolando, and Blanquita Amaro; *bongó* player Manteca; comedians Leopoldo Fernández, Rolando Ochoa, Rosendo Rosell, Federico Piñero, Alberto Garrido, Guillermo Alvarez, Mimí Cal, Luis Echegoyen, Jesús Alvariño, Nobel Vega; actors Otto Sirgo, Dinorah Ayala, Lupe Suárez, Augusto Borges. Traffic signs in Spanish went up on street corners. It became a common practice for the driver of one car to stick his head out the window and shout, sometimes colorfully, at that of another in Spanish, taking it for granted that he would be Cuban too. Doctors and dentists who were not licensed to practice lawfully in the States worked illegally at their patients' homes. Little Havana had been born.

Cuban Jews were nicknamed "Jewbans". *Santería*, a practice looked down on and disclaimed back home, all of a sudden became fashionable and *santería* shops sprang up euphemistically calling themselves *"botánicas"*.

Many anti-communist groups organized to fight Castro: Artime's M.R.R., Oliva's R.E.C.E., the Brigade 2506 Veterans, Masip's F.O.R.D.C., Ray's J.U.R.E., Cancio's A.R.E.C., de Varona's Democratic Rescue, Carrillo's Montecristi, Barrero's 30th of November, Revolutionary Student Directorate, Omega Plan (a merger of the Second Front of Escambray, Alpha 66 and MRP), Seiglie's Revolutionary Unit, Conte's Anti-Communist Front, Alberti's Pro-Constitutional Government, Miller's Feminine Crusade, Gómez's Pledged Rebels, Manrara's Truth Committee, Olba's Pro-Human Commission, M.I.R.R., M.D.C., Revolutionary Council, 17th of April, Anti-Communist Women's Association, Democratic Revolutionary Alliance, Martian Democratic Movement, L Commandos, Freedom Sentinels, New Pines, the Maceo Battalion, Frank País, Revolutionary Teachers' Directorate, Teachers' Front, Transport Revolutionary Organization, Petroleum Revolutionary Front, Resistance Aid Committee, Cuban Economic Corporations, *etcetera, etcetera*. Far too many.

A major accomplishment was achieved. Sugar mills opened, Talismán and Serrallés in South Bay, Palm Beach County; U.S. Sugar Corporation in Clewiston, Hendry County; Glades County Sugar Growers in Moore Haven, two in Belle Glade, one in Pahokee. They were by far not the size of those back home, which were veritable towns, but they gave work to Cubans experienced in different facets of the sugar cane industry.

A bartender in the lounge of a downtown hotel leaned over the bar to ask an American patron, "What's the shortest distance between Cuba and Israel?" and, at the latter's 'Don't know', closed with a broad grin, "The MacArthur Causeway."

A crop of children emerged named Jacqueline, Kimberly, Alexander, Andrew and Kevin, called by parents who didn't speak English, with last names like Rodríguez, González, Fernández, García and Pérez. Ana wondered if back home new-borns were being named Ivan,

Dmitri, Boris, Natasha and Tatiana.

The stamps on letters from Cuba proclaimed 1963 as the "Year of Organization".

At work Ana repeatedly heard names renowned in Batista's time mentioned; Collado, Conill, Cossío, Cueto, Mena, Mendoza, Menocal.

She paid a five-dollar service fee with the admission application card at the Dade County Junior college, not yet three years old, on 95th Street, and registered to take an advertising course in the evening. It was almost seven miles from her home, by Little River. She took 17th Avenue north and turned left on 95th Street west to 18th Avenue.

In the classes she made friends with another Cuban girl. Silvia Cárdenas was about 24, thin, and had light brown eyes with yellow glints; her hair was curly and blond like Olga's, but she was taller and had a shy smile. She lived with her mother and worked in an export company, tending to the mail and filing. She felt bashful speaking English, and Ana suspected taking advertising wouldn't help her advance much in her work.

Costa Rica, Venezuela, Colombia, Ecuador, Panamá, Argentina and West Germany had broken diplomatic relations with Cuba by January 13

On the 24th of January, 1170 Cubans aboard the "Shirley Lykes" bound for the States sought asylum.

A Saturday afternoon in February the telephone rang and Jennie O'Hara asked her, "What are you doing?"

"I was just going to wash my hair", said Ana.

"Why don't you come over and wash it here?"

"No, I couldn't do that." Why would she be asking her something so odd?

"Oh, come on", Jennie insisted.

"I'll hurry up and wash it, and go over afterwards. Okay?"

"Okay,... but hurry. Jeff's here and there's a friend of his, and we wanted to make it a foursome."

"Oh!" So that was it. He'd surely be American. She didn't find anything in common with them.

After washing her hair and towel-drying it, she couldn't find any other choice but to head for Jennie's home. She lived in an apartment building near St. Michael the Archangel's Church. Her roommate, Debbie, the teller, had recently moved out.

Organization Campaign

A tall boy with a square jaw opened the door with a glass of water in his hand. Another boy was lying on the couch.

Jennie came out of the kitchen, in a sun dress, and shook the boy's arm, "Jeff, get up. I don't want people coming in here and seeing you lying there." He sat up with a reluctant stretch. "This is Ana", Jennie introduced her. "She works with me. Jeff and Don", she gestured to the boy with the square jaw on the second name. "Don's an ambulance driver and lives across the street."

"Hello", Ana smiled a little hesitantly.

"Hello. Gee!, you're sure nice", said Don.

"Thank you."

The apartment was modern. It was clean, but disorderly.

"D'you want a drink?", Jennie asked her. "I have Scotch, vodka, soda and orange juice."

"I'll have a screwdriver, please."

"I don't drink", Don excused himself, taking a gulp of water from the glass he was holding.

"Give me a Scotch on the rocks, baby", asked Jeff. He hadn't stood up.

Jennie poured Scotch and soda for herself. Ana picked her drink from the kitchen counter.

"Bring the pretzels", Jennie asked her. They sat in the living room.

"You Cuban?", Don asked her the usual question.

"Yes."

"How long you been here?", Jeff wanted to know.

"A year and a half."

"How do you like America?", asked Don.

Here we go again! Don't they realize Cuba is also in America? She didn't want to sound pedantic. "It's nice. I like it."

"I'm surprised you know the name 'screwdriver' for vodka and orange juice."

She had known the term back home, but now replied, "I've had time to learn it in a year and a half."

"You speak good English", said Jeff. "Did you learn it here?"

"I had taken it in school in Cuba."

"Ana's a stenographer", Jennie put in. "In English", she specified.

"Really? I thought they only spoke Cuban down there", said Don.

"Well, the official language is Spanish, but some schools teach English, if you want to take it."

There was a wire rack filled with records on the floor in a corner of the living room. More records were stacked on the floor next to it.

"How big is Cuba?", Jeff asked her. He seemed sharper than Don. She knew from Jennie that he was a physical therapist.

"It's forty-four thousand two hundred twenty square miles, a little larger than the state of Tennessee, a little smaller than Pennsylvania."

"Oh, it's bigger than Tennessee?", said Jeff. "I didn't know." Ana hadn't known the size of Tennessee until seven or eight months before, when she had been consulting an atlas.

"There are a lot of Cubans here now", said Don. "I guess Castro's grabbing everything there, isn't he?"

"Yes." She didn't want to talk about it to Americans. They didn't understand what it was like.

"Hey!, why don't we all go out tonight?", Jeff suggested. She had passed. Had there been a signal?

"Okay with you, Ana?", Jennie asked her. Ana wondered if Jennie had asked Jeff to get her a date. Jennie didn't need her along. Maybe Jeff had asked her to get Don a date. Dany hadn't written in almost two months. Ana nodded.

When the boys had left to shower, Jennie insisted on cooking for themselves, so Ana called home and stayed for supper. Jennie took her shoes off and made lamb chops, mashed potatoes and green peas. They lingered on at the kitchen table after eating, talking about the bank and discussing their co-workers.

"Kathy likes to put on airs", said Jennie. "I think she's a phony."

"She's not friendly to me", said Ana. "And I don't understand Paula. Sometimes she's very nice and others very withdrawn."

"Yes, she blows hot and cold. But I admire her. After working all day long, she always looks neat and collected, ready for a good time. Do you know she was in the WAVES? I guess she must be about thirty-seven, thirty-eight, wouldn't you say?"

"Is she divorced?"

"Yes, but she doesn't tell anybody. Did you know she likes Jim?"

"I hadn't noticed. Are you sure? How do you know?"

"Yes, because once I saw a note she had left him on his desk asking him if he was going by her house that afternoon..." She paused, then confided, "Ted came after me."

"Ted?"

"Yes, one day that I stayed out he showed up here at lunch time, he got very insistent and wouldn't leave until I gave him an answer, and I had to throw him out."

What intrigue! It seemed unreal to Ana. It all took her especially by surprise because she didn't sense the currents of the Americans at work. She *had* noticed Ted "had loose hands". Fred had been married three times. Of Wilson, Jennie said, "He's been educated beyond his intelligence." Jim's wife had had a hysterectomy. "I think that Debbie's thinking of moving in with a boy", Jennie said picking her teeth with a match. "Would you shack up with a guy?"

Move in with a man! "No", Ana answered without sounding shocked, trying to appear very sensible, "because, if I fell in love with him and he left, I'd get hurt." She wouldn't be living with him if she weren't already in love with him to begin with, but that would sound prudish.

"Well, you could want to leave yourself and, even if you were married, he could still leave the same." How could she want to leave herself?

"And Tamargo?"

"Do you like him?"

"No, he's nice to work for, but I don't care about him. I only felt curiosity to know what he's like."

"He keeps his private life separate from the bank. Nobody knows anything about him other than that he's married and lives in the Roads."

Jennie brought out a photograph of her younger sister. "That's Cindy at her prom. She's eighteen." It showed a girl in a royal blue lace formal gown wearing a corsage; her date in a tuxedo behind her had his arms around her waist, and she was holding his hands in front of her. It struck her as quite a private pose to preserve for posterity.

Ana cleared the table and stacked the dishes in the sink.

"Leave them", Jennie said. "I'll do them later."

Ana didn't listen to her — after all, Jennie had cooked, — and started to wash them directly under the faucet.

"Ah!, I use this", Jennie said, holding up a plastic dishpan.

They freshened up, Jennie changed clothes, and they put on makeup. Jennie wore no lipstick, only eye shadow.

"Ah! My only new stockings have heels", Jennie complained, "and the shoes I'm going to wear are backless."

Jeff came with Don to pick them up and took them to the "Swanee" on the Trail, where a Negro combo played blaring music, and later to the "TePee Club". Don had a soda, the others drank beer, and they danced.

Ana felt obligated to apologize, "I don't do American dances well."

"You're doing fine", Don assured her, "really." He was trying to be nice.

She knew she wasn't. "Thank you."

"I'm crazy." – A loud burp interrupted him. "Sorry. – Just a crazy American."

When they parked at Jennie's building, Jeff embraced Jennie by the car and kissed her, and Ana discreetly walked away. When they reached the apartment door, he grabbed her by the waist and pulled her to him, while Don and Ana looked away.

As soon as they walked in, Jennie kicked her shoes off. "Why don't you stay overnight?"

Ana again called home. Her mother answered and Ana was surprised she didn't raise any objections. She had almost hoped she would. She stayed, feeling a little awkward. There were twin beds. Jennie lent her baby doll pajamas to wear. Having had no problem sleeping on a bare mattress at home, here it took her long to fall asleep in the strange bed. In the morning, she took a shower and washed the pajamas. The boys came by before they had even had breakfast.

"Let's go to the beach", said Don.

"No, I have to go home now", said Ana.

"Are you going to church?", Jeff asked.

"Not this week", said Jennie. "Are you sure you don't want to go to the beach?", she asked Ana. She didn't sound very enthusiastic herself.

"No, after staying out overnight, I have to go home now."

"Party-pooper", Jeff reproached her.

"Oh, chucks!", said Don. "Will I see you again?"

"Sure, she'll be by", Jennie answered for her.

Ana received a letter from Leonardo Vidal from Nassau telling her he was being transferred to the home office of Wayne Motor Company in Detroit.

A letter from Octavio Guillén in Nassau told her his wife had had another baby. A "conch", he joked. When Wayne had moved its offices from Nassau, he had changed jobs.

She received a letter from Carmen Zayas from Marion, Ohio,

where she and her husband had been relocated. She told her she and Miguel were both working in the office of a metal products company, it was very cold and they planned to move back to Miami the beginning of September. She asked her to check the job opportunities for them there. Ana clipped a few classified want ads from the newspaper and sent them to her with a copy of her well-worn list of local employment agencies.

In March, incited by Jennie, they gathered at Ana's house and held a party. Jeff, Jennie, Debbie, who had moved back with her, and Brad, a friend of theirs, arrived together, late, with a bottle of whiskey and a bag of potato chips. Silvia Cárdenas brought along a girl friend, Maritza. Laura and Adrián were there, and Aida and Oscar. And two firemen from the nearby firehouse that Aida had invited. Ana provided rum, cola, crackers, anchovies and cherries.

Debbie was to be Brad's date, but, when he opened the back kitchen door, he found her in the backyard kissing one of the firemen, a burly fellow. Ana was in the kitchen pouring a drink for the other fireman, a quiet sort, who, embarrassed, almost pushed Ana out of the kitchen to the hallway. Brad then asked Silvia to dance, but she, in her excessive shyness, unloaded him on Ana. The other, quiet fireman then spent the evening talking with Silvia.

Jeff, in the kitchen before the refrigerator, his bottle of whiskey under his arm, announced, speech-style, "We're members of the Presidium and are going to a meeting."

Carlos spent most of the time talking with Oscar, and Laura with Aida.

"Sometimes I get laid off during the summer", Oscar was saying. "But then I just take it easy and collect unemployment insurance for a month and a half or so. Thirty dollars a week."

"I've seen dresses in the windows of Burdine's for sixty dollars, and I come home and can make them myself", Aida declared.

Debbie got drunk and Ana had to take her to lie down in her room, where Adrián solicitously went to sit on the bed by the redhead's side, while Teresa brewed coffee for her, at Jennie's request. Ana went into the room to get Adrián out; Laura was sitting just on the other side of the wall in the living room. The burly fireman, now finding himself idle, turned his attention to Silvia's friend Maritza. About her, the other fireman, Jason, had a quiet observation for Ana, "That girl's hippy. She's young now, but when she gets older, she's going to be big."

Ana got thoroughly bored with Brad. Her father fortunately had seemed absorbed in conversation with Oscar all evening.

Just before leaving, Jason, the quiet fireman, said to Ana, "I think there was too much liquor, and that always brings problems."

As Teresa closed the door on the last guest, she widened her eyes at Ana. Ana knew they wouldn't be having another party.

On March 14 four men in a stolen jeep hurled themselves against the fence of the Embassy of Uruguay in Havana. One of them was killed, one wounded and the other two taken prisoner. Other people drove trucks and buses into the fences of other embassies to seek asylum.

Ana got a $20. a month salary increase at the bank. Monday she and Jennie went to lunch at Jim's bar on Miami Avenue, where they were serving green beer in celebration of Saint Patrick's Day, and they had thick corned beef sandwiches.

Manuel Cardinal Arteaga Betancourt died in Havana on March 20.

One Saturday in March Teresa came home with a used vacuum cleaner, and Ana with a full-length mirror she'd bought, and her father hung it in the hallway.

They received a letter from Gustavo telling them they had received the medicine they had sent them, but the beef bullion cubes they had included with it had been taken out.

In April, the Cuban Revolutionary Council dissolved, and its leader, José Miró, published his resignation in the newspaper in Miami, which made headlines, with a multi-page account of his charges against government officials.

Fighters of Alpha 66 and the Second Front of Escambray were reportedly operating in Cuba, including Gutiérrez Menoyo, on the north coast of Las Villas province, and in the Escambray mountains in the south, under Antonio Veciana and Cecilio Vázquez. Mobile movie units, their director admitted, had been attacked by counter-revolutionaries in Matanzas province.

Méndez said, "Much as I hate to admit it, I think there's only one man who can oust Fidel, and that's Batista."

"I think you're right, Uncle", agreed Diego. "He's the only one strong enough. 'Others will come who'll make me seem good', as they say."

Many photographs taken inside Cuba were published in several newspapers and magazines. Méndez came home with the April 3 edition of the Miami News. "Maybe, just maybe", he said wistfully. Diego brought him the April 9 issue of "Look" and Sergio, the April 15 issue of "Life" in Spanish. Photographs also appeared in the English edition of Life and The Saturday Evening Post. There were over thirty of anti-communist soldiers in the underbrush, Menoyo among them, of naked prisoners taken inside Príncipe Castle by a Cochinos Bay invader jailed there, a Cuban citizen begging to be allowed aboard the "African Pilot" to escape, Russian ships, some of the people taken in the streets, two dozen in Havana, one inside La Cabaña prison, others at the Banco Industrial, the docks, a sugar mill, a sugar cane cutting, a "culture center", the ballet studios, a beauty parlor, the Carnival Queen pageant, the Country Club and a TASS press conference; an interview with Che Guevara was also published.

The ship "American Surveyor" left Havana with 675 exiles for Fort Lauderdale.

Adrián and Sergio took piles of paper to a waste paper company on 14th Avenue, which bought it by the hundred pounds. The Episcopalian Church helped Diego and Xiomara giving them clothes.

Adrián finally found a job in a pillow and cushion factory.

Ana got a letter from Berta Penabad, still in Nassau, where she was now working in a hotel and shared an apartment with a girl friend. Graciela was working for an insurance company, she told her, and living with her mother. Elvira had quit her job at Wayne.

Driving to work Wednesday after leaving her father off at the hotel, Ana turned the radio on and heard the police officer warn the drivers of the heavy traffic condition. She wasn't far, but she'd be late again. Maybe Dany would go via Mexico, she thought. She knew some people who had gone that way, or through Jamaica. Everything would be all right, she dreamed. They could get married. In church. St. Michael's Church. She could wear a lace waltz-length gown. She loved *torchon* lace. And gray gloves and shoes. That would be different. Gray stockings. She could wear a little gray head ornament with little flowers and a veil over her forehead. She liked drop pearls. She wondered if she could get a gray one. She would carry a Mass book covered in gray with a flower marker. And a gray pearl rosary. Her father could give her away. It had rained and a beautiful rainbow rose from the river behind the buildings, arched before her over the southeast and seemed to fade into the sky. Rainbows could be seen more often here than in Havana. Would Dany have any problem being admitted because his British visa had been revoked? He spoke enough English to get by. He could work as accounting clerk in some export company. Or maybe even in the local office of Wayne Motor Company. Until they went back home. They could move to a furnished apartment in the southwest section. She had seen some cute houses there. Around 16th Avenue, near the Jewish Community Center. Until it were all well again back home. Everything would be all right.

Silvia Cárdenas was friendly and became as close a friend of Ana's as Olga had been back home. Her grandmother, gray hair rinsed a faint shade of blue, stiff-girdled from ribs to thighs, and bedecked in string of pearls and gold bracelets, lived at the Spaniard Valcarce's Royalton hotel − probably come out in the first few weeks of the revolution, − chatted on the porch and ate in restaurants. Ana went shopping with Silvia on Saturdays. Sundays they went to the movies together; they saw "Doctor No" with Sean Connery and "Rome Adventure" with Troy Donahue. They went to Lummus Park on 3rd Avenue and watched the elderly people do the polka, to see the Hootenanny at the Crossways Inn, once on a ride in a glass-bottom boat around the bay, to the Vizcaya Palace and to the Coconut Grove Playhouse to see the comedy *"Irma La Douce"* with Genevieve, and sometimes to a dance at the P.B.A. or the Hungarian-American Club. Or to the "Old folks' dance" at Pier Park on Sundays and afterwards to the Lum's. Without dates. Ana had met several boys at the dances, but, perhaps because she didn't seem to put her heart into the friendships, they soon stopped calling her.

Herb Alpert and the Tijuana Brass played "Spanish Flea". The Cuban and Spanish singers sang about "the curl I have lost and cannot find it...", "clock, do not mark the hours, because I'm going to go insane...", "with your glance you sent me a telegram...", "the little telephone, ring, ring, a little call...", "in your mouth you will bear a taste of me...", "then I will do an about-face...", "that damned wall, I'm going to tear it down someday..." and "the bed is to be of stone, the headboard of stone..."

And it had been over four months since Ana had heard from Dany.

Ana and Silvia sometimes double-dated. They went dancing at the "Rinconcito" in the Springs, or to the "Ocean Ranch" by the bay, to the "Aloha", to have broiled lobster at the "Edith & Fritz", to the "Carino" for Italian cuisine, to the "Shrimp Place" near the railroad station, or to the "Jade Pagoda" for Chinese food.

Organization Campaign

Ana read a lot. She became a member of a book club and she bought paperback editions of best-sellers. She read Rona Jaffe's "The Best of Everything", Shute's "On the Beach", Pearl Buck's "Letter from Peking" and "Peony", Auchincloss' "Portrait in Brownstone" and Boland's "They All Discovered America". Debbie lent her Kathleen Windsor's "Forever Amber" and Jim Davis, "Wanderers Eastward, Wanderers West". And magazines filled the gaps between books. Until her eyes burned and stung. Sometimes boredom bent her to the point of depression. Silvia was in the same situation and referred to her despondency as *'surmenage'*. She read even more, almost constantly, everywhere. Letters from Ana's friends, and even some of their relatives, were becoming scarcer. Ana herself felt less like writing.

Pant suits for women, with long jackets, went into fashion.

As soon as it warmed up, Ana spent many Saturdays and Sundays with her parents at Crandon Park, from morning until late afternoon, and they barbecued chicken on the grills among the coconut trees and ate on the tables under the seagrapes. During Daylight Saving Time, her father now had alternate Saturdays and Sundays off at the hotel. Silvia often joined them. It had become a favorite spot of the Cuban families. Some groups played the guitar in the shade of the seagrapes and a few louder ones, the *bongó* or the *tumbadora*. Sergio or Diego sometimes joined them with his family.

It was difficult to get used to the idea. They were so close to their country – 250 miles – and yet so far, in a place so similar and yet so different.

"To think that two years ago we were in our own country", said Méndez, "in familiar surroundings leading a stable life, and now we are in a foreign country struggling to make a living and adapt to a strange way of life. Sometimes I think, 'What are we doing away from our country?'"

"There are those less fortunate than we", Teresa said. "Think of Marcos' nephew, who's in jail."

"And Alejandro Dávila", said Ana.

Magaly voiced her feelings, "Crane, to your homeland, even on one leg."

Sunday morning Ana noticed the wild orchid tree on the corner. Its branches bearing small orchids reached down low near the ground. She picked a few orchids and took them to her mother for Mother's Day. Teresa was surprised and touched.

On a Friday night after Ana had bought a beach robe at Richards and Silvia a bathing suit, they walked into a drug store for sodas. At the entrance they met Héctor, the driving instructor, who came up to them. After greetings, the introduction and small talk, he asked them, "Could I invite you to a soda?"

They accepted, and the three sat on stools at the counter in a pattern of tiny boomerangs.

"What have you been doing?", he asked her.

"Working." They noticed that a group of blacks were assembling outside.

He addressed Silvia. "Having fun?"

Silvia nodded, "A little." The blacks were protesting the Cubans' taking jobs from them.

He turned back to Ana, "Do you go dancing?"

She had been looking at his ear in the mirror behind the counter and now turned to face him. "Sometimes. To the P B A or the Hungarian Club."

"Do you have a phone?"

"Uh-huh."

"May I call you some time?" He pulled a little address book and pen from his pocket and handed them to her. He had vanished for almost a year, but she wrote the number anyway and handed it back to him, not expecting him to call her. Yesterday had been Dany's birthday. "May I call you tomorrow?"

The blacks had dispersed.

"Why not."

When they walked out of the drugstore, two homosexuals crossed the street running in front of them, tight pants hugging their slim hips. "Moraima!", one called to the other.

Héctor called her the next afternoon. "Will you go out with me tonight, if you don't already have other plans?"

"I was planning to go to the P B A with Silvia and another friend."

"You're nowhere."

"Why don't you come along?"

"I was thinking of the Café d'Artists, where Olga Guillot is singing."

"Well, okay. Is it all right with you if I tell them to meet us there after the P B A dance is over?"

"Sure. I'll pick you up at nine."

The place was crowded. They got a table pretty close to the

dance floor. Héctor ordered Seven and Seven. He was a very good dancer. Olga Guillot sang that she "had been enjoying that calm that a love that has already passed leaves us". Some comedians did a routine. Héctor joked. Silvia and Maritza showed up at 1:30 with two dance partners.

Diego Miranda, Carlos' nephew, started to work pumping gas in a service station, and he and Xiomara moved to a cottage at the rear of a stucco mission-style house in the northwest section near Henderson Park. They did their grocery shopping at the Twelfth Avenue Community Market, open all around the clock. That spring, Xiomara had a baby boy. They named him Eric. The mechanic at Diego's service station lent them his daughter's bassinet and the family made him layette gifts.

The christening was on a Sunday, and, although Xiomara was an Episcopalian, at Gesu Catholic Church. Ana and her parents attended. There was a buffet at the house afterwards, and Xiomara's family, with whom they were not very familiar, were all in the cramped cottage. Their landlady brought a present for the baby. They hadn't had lunch yet, and were close to fainting when refreshments were finally served at 5:00. Xiomara would stay home taking care of the baby.

They bought a used television set and their evening outings now ended. After dinner, Teresa and Carlos spent their evenings watching "Leave It to Beaver", "What's My Line?", "Candid Camera", "Hawaiian Eye", "77 Sunset Strip" and "Route 66". On the few occasions when Ana sat down to watch it, she preferred "Surfside 6" with Troy Donahue, because it was filmed in Miami Beach, and reruns of "Life of Riley" with William Bendix. She liked the American humor. It was subtler, not overdone.

As Ana was walking home from the drugstore late Saturday morning, a Jehovah's Witness approached her in Spanish with a batch of Watchtower's rolled up, covers inward, in her hand. Ana only shook her head without looking directly at the woman, who followed her accusing her, "It's our duty to learn the Word of the Lord." She raised her voice, "The world can only be saved if we listen to His teachings." She yelled after her, "Now, there's an article in this month's issue...", and Ana walked on looking straight ahead.

Ana went out with Héctor again. He stopped at the S & S Sandwich Shop on 2nd Avenue for blueberry pie and coffee, on their way to "Raul's 21" on the Beach. Rolando Lasserie sang,

> *"Mi Habana, mi tierra querida,*
> *¿cuándo yo te volveré a ver?*
> *Habana,*
> *¡cómo extraño el sol indiano de tus tardes!*
> *Habana,*
> *a pesar de la distancia no te olvido.*
> *Habana,*
> *¡cómo siento la nostalgia de volver!"*[(88)]

It was torture.

Sergio Trejo, Teresa's godson, got a job running errands for a lawyer who had Spanish-speaking clients, and his wife Magaly started making dresses for the higher-income immigrants. They moved to a wood frame house near a synagogue. "Come see, we have loquat in the backyard", Sergio told them.

"And there's a Geiger tree", said Magaly, "come look". Their daughter Haydée was attending the parochial school. They began sending money home through the offices that had opened for the unofficial exchange and transfers.

Shortly after, Haydée took her First Holy Communion at Saints Peter and Paul's Church. Eight relatives attended, and later they all had the hot chocolate breakfast together at the Rancho Luna restaurant. Their American next-door neighbor gave the girl Easter lilies.

Ana had another date with Héctor the next Saturday, when he took her to the Trio Diner for key lime pie and then to Roy's Bar on 8th Street, where a record player showed a screen video as the music played. "Diana" by Paul Anka, "Yellow Polka-Dot Bikini" and *"Dime Quando Tu Verrai"* were very popular. When he left her off at her house, Héctor told her he was going back with his girlfriend, with whom he had temporarily broken up, because she was pregnant.

Girls all across the country pressed their hair straight with an iron.

"Lorenzo, Blanca's brother, and his wife are in Zaragoza", said Teresa.

"Is he working?", Méndez asked from the stepladder. He was changing a light bulb in the hallway.

"As paymaster in Aragón's, his father-in-law's, winery in Cariñena. Elena is depressed."

Ana now heard the word *"machismo"* here often with reference to the Latins. She had never heard it before in Cuba. More than male-dominated, their society had been rather parent-influenced. The wife didn't always feel obligated to follow the husband. Because she didn't want to separate from her parents, the man often found himself acceding to follow in his father-in-law's footsteps, a pattern later perpetuated on his own sons-in-law.

Ana came out of the shower and went into her room. Her parents were talking in the living room.

"She's always coming over here when you're home from work", her mother was saying and Ana knew she was referring to Aida. "And she's always calling you and asking you to do her favors."

"What would you have me do?"

"She has a husband."

"I doubt she does it with any intention."

"Oh, Carlos!, don't give me that. At that party here she asked you to dance." And Ana had thought she'd been too busy to notice.

"That's because she was drunk. And I said I didn't know how and went on talking with Oscar."

"Oscar is not an idiot."

"But I haven't done anything, Tera."

"She flirts with you openly."

"But what you should care about is what I do, not she. And I don't pay any attention to the woman. I don't stop to talk to her outside. When she's here, I only answer if she talks to me first. I don't go into her house unless Oscar is there, or you're along. What more can I do?" Ana had noticed Aida too, and had been annoyed by the fat woman's hoarse laughter and silly giggle. She wondered why her mother welcomed her in the house.

"The way she walks! And those pants she wears!"

"She's knockkneed."

"Ah!, so you've noticed that. And the language she uses! I've heard her say cuss words that I had only heard from truckers before."

"But, Tera, I repeat it. What you have to care about is what I do. Have I ever acted disrespectful to you?"

"I know you haven't."

"Then forget about what she does. A vulgar woman like that would never appeal to me."

"Aha!", Teresa said, but in a different tone now. "Then if she weren't vulgar, she'd appeal to you."

"I'm too old to be enticed into anything like that."

Ana breathed easier. Her father was a sensible, decent man. She finished dressing and walked out into the living room.

On her way to work, Ana saw Rosa from a distance getting off near the bank from a truck Tim was driving. She heard from somebody that they had a son of over a year.

Sixteen buildings all alike from S.W. 34th Avenue west to 36th Court and from S.W. 9th Street south to 11th filled with Cubans and gained the nickname *"Pastorita"*, after the buildings of the Savings and Housing Institute in Cuba. Another 26 buildings all alike around S.W. 5th Street and 6th Avenue were said to have been built by ex-Senator Anselmo Alliegro.

Méndez drove down S.W. 13th Avenue, recently renamed "Cuban Boulevard", on their way home from the "Parkway" theater. They passed a huge silk-cotton tree in the median, its tall roots forming coves on the ground, the trunk tapering off as it reached up to the heights. "They say that's the only silk-cotton tree in Dade County", he said.

"It was so revered in Cuba, with the tradition of the first Mass", said Ana.

"People also claimed it brought disgrace", Teresa said.

Méndez agreed, "Some people wouldn't live in a house that had one."

A map of the island of Cuba had been recently sculpted in the median. And on the corner of 8th Street a hexagonal monument had been dedicated to Assault Brigade 2506, with a burning torch on top.

"I think there's another silk-cotton tree in Colombia park in front of Miami Senior High School."

●

At El Carmelo restaurant on 8th Street they met Carvajal. "I came to Lindsley Lumber on Twelfth for some mahogany shelving", he said before an enormous red-wax *pâte grasse* or Edam wheel cheese on the counter. Later, in the course of the conversation over coffee, he told them, "I wouldn't become an American citizen. I'm a legal resident, and I pay my taxes and obey the laws, but to renounce my citizenship of birth to... If I lived in another country where I weren't considered inferior, I'd take on their citizenship, but... to take on the citizenship of a country where they consider us inferior, no, I have some pride. We're still not considered their equals."

"They chew us, but they don't swallow us", agreed Méndez.

"People tell me, 'But then you'd be able to vote', 'But then you could work for the federal government'. No, my dignity is worth more than that."

In front of a luggage shop on Flagler Street, Ana ran into a short, stocky man she and Silvia had met on the beach. He had told them he was 33. "I wish I'd gotten married. If I had children, I could... project my love on them", he said. "After thirty you don't fall in love, because you see the other person's faults." Later she couldn't recall the man's name – they had nicknamed him "the Shrewd One", – but his words stayed with her more than she'd have expected at the moment.

Writing the date every day made Ana aware of the passage of time. "The hours crawl, the years fly", said her aunt Esperanza.

Some children were playing in the yard of the house in back, singing "Mother Goose" songs, "Mary had a little lamb..." Ana was lying on her bed on her stomach. A parakeet periodically gave a wolf's whistle. It reminded her of the canary in the next building in Havana. She tried to remember in detail the coffee shop near the Publicity school, the day that she had deliberately resolved to remember it. And she couldn't, not the details, not the way she had thought she'd be able to. After a while, she was mortified to find herself humming "London Bridge is falling down". She was surprised to hear the children's voices suddenly burst in a rush of Spanish. They spoke Spanish, but sang in English. The coming generation in the States would be American, the one in Cuba would be Russian subjects, the present generation would vanish in a few years and Cubans would cease to be. Jews had survived because Judaism was not only a nationality, but also a religion, a race, a tradition, a way of life. But Cubans would be wiped off the face of the earth and a whole way of life, a good life – "Under the Cuban sky life is good and it's beautiful", – would be lost forever. She recalled a wry joke of Diego's, "Our grandchildren will be told, 'Cuba was a country that used to be on this little island in the Gulf of Mexico'." The joke wasn't funny at all.

"We'll be the lost generation", Méndez prophesied fatalistically. "The new Cubans stayed behind in Cuba, the coming generation born there will only know communism and will like it because they'll have never known anything else. The children of the old Cubans, the exiles, will be born here, or in other countries, and will be native Americans or whatever and they'll be loyal to their country. And we, the exiled Cubans, who knew Cuba as it once was, we will disappear entirely, we're doomed to be a lost generation."

In bed that night Ana thought of the time when she wouldn't be there, after her death, and the familiar fear grabbed her heart. A fear that was coming more and more often lately. It had started suddenly recently, and she had felt it like a cold wave that washed over her being inside her chest. It had been mild at first, and she had tried to ignore it, refusing to acknowledge it. But lately it had become increasingly stronger and more and more frequent until she couldn't ignore it any longer. She tried to force it out of her mind, but she never succeeded in getting completely rid of it. It was the thought of just not being there, to stop breathing — nothing, to dissolve into nothing, stop being. — Her head felt as if it were stuffed with cotton, the fear turned into terrible panic and she felt a cold hand grip her heart. She wanted to scream and the feeling jerked her up in bed. Stop! She turned on her stomach, got hold of herself with an effort, and again pushed the thought to the back of her mind and buried it. Did everyone else have this same fear of death? Everybody seemed to accept it... or they pretended. She took the St. Anne card from the nightstand and prayed for calm, comfort, acceptance. She fell asleep gripping the card under her pillow.

As she came down the front steps of the building Tuesday, she saw Aida talking with the fat, gray-haired American neighbor with a crew cut from the bungalow next door, a dangerous-looking saguaro at his back. When Aida saw Ana, she called to her, "What's he saying to me, *chica*?"

"She doesn't understand you", Ana told the man.

"I was telling her that when my friends ask me why I live in 'Cuban Town'," he repeated for her, "I tell them that I know, as long as the Cubans are here, the darkies aren't going to move in."

She interpreted for Aida unsmiling, while the man nodded his head. He thought he was being very witty. They had just been told they were the lesser of two evils. Aida laughed her throaty laugh and Ana went on her way.

First thing in the morning they had a boring meeting at the bank. Kathy passed her desk, saw Ana frowning over her shorthand notes and paused to ask her, "Do you take it down in Spanish?"

Ana stared up at her and her mouth opened slightly at the absurdity of the thought. Could she be joking?

"How could I translate it in my mind as he's talking?" — the first words had come out too fast and loud, and she now continued more softly and slowly, — "write it in Spanish and then translate it back again as I read it to type it in English? It could never go back to exactly what he said." The logic of her explanation was lost in the blank smile with which Kathy received it. Ana turned around and rolled her eyes and puffed her cheeks because it felt an outlet.

Ted Miller asked her, "Don't they teach proportions in..." — he yawned loudly, — "Aaah... in the Cuban schools?"

She chuckled. Who did he think he was! As a matter of fact, no, they did not teach proportions any longer. It had gone out of style almost twenty years before, because it was considered too old-fashioned.

Magaly complained, "Do you know that schools here don't teach children penmanship until they're in the fifth grade? Children don't learn to write in cursive hand. Our neighbors' son is ten, he's in fourth grade and he still prints. And they allow them to cross out."

Sometimes Jim Davis would make a derogatory remark against the Cubans and would quickly explain, "Now, this is no reflection on you, of course." How could there *ever* be no reflection on her?

Or Paula Monroe said, "They shouldn't judge you all alike. You're so different!" But Ana didn't want to be "different". She considered herself typically Cuban.

Or Dave Harris would say about somebody, "She's Cuban, *but* she's very nice", or "*but* he has a college education."

Ted Miller asked her, "Do you have rice and beans for breakfast?"

Mitchell went to a Cuban restaurant with Tamargo and came back telling that "they had tablecloths".

About Cuban coffee, Mitchell said, "It's too rich for my blood"; Jim Davis, "It tastes like sour sugar", and Dave Harris, "I'll try anything once." Ana remembered when Kent had dictated to her that he had already learned not to load it in his fountain pen.

There was a phone call early before Paula had come in and Ana took it. Fred's wife told her he was sick and wouldn't be in. Paula drove in almost 29 miles from Florida City, where she lived near the Farmers' Market, and she sometimes arrived complaining about the traffic.

Ana passed the message on to Debbie. "Mister Taylor won't be in. His wife called, he's in bed with phlebitis in a leg."

"And what's that?", Debbie asked her as she stretched noisily.

"Inflammation of the veins. A swollen leg."

Paula had once asked her what a "hemorrhage" was.

Walking to the parking lot Wednesday afternoon, Ana said to Kathy, "In many places they don't hire Cubans, they don't rent to them." She said it matter-of-factly, she didn't know why. She saw Kathy swallow and avert her eyes. She stopped then and suddenly realized she enjoyed embarrassing them, reveled as she saw her words make them uncomfortable.

At the corner sundries store, where they were having cherry Cokes, Ana stood before the magazine rack with Silvia. There was a lizard perched on top of it. Ana moved to the jukebox.

"Look", she called to Silvia, "*'Llorar'* by Carlos Díaz."

"Oh, I didn't know that record was still around, that's old. 'The Theme from Summer Place'?"

"That reminds me of the last New Year's Eve I spent in Cuba. *'El Son se Fue de Cuba'* by Fernando Albuerne", Ana said, pushing the buttons.

> "*...Rompieron sus guitarras,
> callaron sus pregones
> y en vez de oir canciones,
> sólo hay llanto y soledad.
> El son se fue de Cuba
> llorando de tristeza...*"(89)

Ana felt her heart shrink.

"No", said Silvia, "that makes me so sad I don't like to hear it."

"'Picnic'?"

"*'Cuando Salí de Cuba'*,... Luis Aguilé's."

> "*...cuando salí de Cuba
> dejé mi vida, dejé mi amor.
> Cuando salí de Cuba
> dejé enterrado mi corazón...*"(90)

"No", complained Ana, "that's the same thing."

A policeman who had been having coffee at the counter came with his cup to stand by them. A young boy tagged behind him.

"'Nights of Moscow'," said the policeman and he turned to Silvia. "Don't you like jazz?", he asked when he saw she didn't recognize it.

"I never hoid that before."

"Where did you pick up that Yankee accent?", he asked her, surprised.

"Why?", asked Silvia uncertainly, "because it came out 'bofore'?"

"No, because you said 'hoid'."

The young boy laughed. "A Cuban with a Yankee accent", he said, amused. The policeman grinned. "That's a riot!", the boy said.

Ana was embarrassed and wanted them to shut up. Silvia's face was turning red. The other Cubans seated were now looking at them. Silvia looked confused and on the verge of tears. The young boy roared with laughter. Ana laid the 31 cents on the counter and they walked out.

When Paula spoke, things were never nice, good, beautiful or even wonderful. Everything was always, "the most exquisite thing I have ever, ever seen in my whole, entire life." It made you think she didn't know modesty. And she never asked anybody to do her a favor. It was always, "the biggest favor in the whole, wide world."

When Wilson went on about a plan as "exciting, fascinating, stimulating, a thrill", Ana thought, "Bore!".

Clichés irritated her, like "bend over backwards trying to please", "when the chips are down", "want to touch bases with", "at this point in time", "a ballpark figure", "by the same token", "the whole nine yards", "be that as it may", "as it were".

Thursday Dave Harris asked her out for a drink after work. Ana hesitated. He insisted. She accepted. He took her to Betty's Lobo Lounge on Biscayne Boulevard.

They sat at the bar, Ana had a brandy Alexander, and Dave started talking about Spanish women. He knew them. He knew how they acted. He knew how to act with them.

"In Spain a *señorita* walks on the street with her mother on one side and her *dueña*", Dave lifted his forefinger at this point to demand attention, "who is her oldest aunt", he raised his eyebrows to emphasize his knowledge, "on the other." − '*Dueña*'? Where had he gotten that information? − "And a married Spanish woman doesn't waste time in nonsense. You have to know the right moment." He narrowed his eyes in mundane experience. Ana looked at him in disbelief. Could he be serious? He was deadly serious. "When she gives a little wiggle" − this was punctuated by a wriggling shake, − "she expects a little pinch. And when she's ready..." The corners of his mouth went down and he nodded until his double chin stuck out further than his very chin, then he moved his forearms to indicate the raising of a body, pulling it to himself and then pushing it away, accompanying the motion with a suction sound. Ana thought she was going to be sick. Her mouth had dropped open and she stared at him aghast. This man honestly thought he knew what he was talking about!

She changed the conversation. Talked inanely about the weather, the sea, the sun, the heat. She fought between frequent yawns and an uncomfortable restlessness. She finally said she had to get home.

Out on 14th Street, still light in the spring afternoon, by his car,

Dave asked her, "Are you going to let me kiss you?" Ana shook her head. He opened the car door for her. As he got in behind the wheel, he asked her, "Aren't you curious?"

"No, why?, are you a Martian?"

"You're impenetrable."

"Me?"

"Yes. Do you know what that means?"

"I *know* what it means. I just don't see myself that way."

"I can never begin to guess what you're thinking."

She remembered when Salvador had told her her eyes could be read like a book. Had she changed that much? She thought. She guessed she must have started changing when she'd started working at the Ministry. A defense against people like Valdés. Dave still asked her out again, but she turned him down.

"I don't think Cubans should be treated any different from whites", Jennie said on Friday at lunch carrying her plastic tray in the Polly Davis cafeteria.

"But it's the ingrained discrimination." Ana set her tray down. "Do you hear what you've said?, 'Cubans or whites'."

"Well, I mean Caucasians or Spanish-Americans."

"Before I came here, I never considered myself anything other than white. Never noticed a green hue. There are whites, black, yellow and copper. Caucasian means originating in the Caucasus Mountains. What do you consider the Germans and Italians?"

"White."

"What about the Spaniards?"

"Well..."

"Do you consider the French white?"

"Yes."

"Then why, when you get to the Pyrénées, are Europeans all of a sudden not white?"

"Many Latin-Americans are Indian."

"There are no Indians left in Cuba." Ana felt the cords in her neck harden. Her anger had been pent up. "Cubans are white or black, or maybe yellow." She was taking her frustration out on Jennie and couldn't help it.

Jennie was at a loss for words. "... Not everybody's a bigot."

"I just feel offended."

"But you're generalizing... Have I ever treated you as if I considered you different?", Jennie protested.

Organization Campaign

Ana brusquely said, "Forget it. It's not your fault. You have all been brought up considering yourselves superior to the rest of America. In fact, you only think of the United States as 'America'. Don said it at your own house. Not even Mexico, being in *North* America, is considered part of the continent. To a European, an Argentine is just as American as a Canadian."

Maybe Ernesto was not so wrong after all.

Ana noticed herself turning vengeful, bitter. She felt herself faltering and was afraid she might lose her mind. She resolved not to take things to heart so much, but more shallowly, reason with the philosophy she'd had at the beginning. And she forced herself to calm down.

"Our greatest enemies are the CIA and the State Department", Sergio said. "The Girón Beach invasion? It was lucky that the invaders of Cochinos Bay were only taken prisoner. The CIA hadn't planned Fidel would do that. They had carefully gathered all the young male Cubans who wished to fight in one group and sent them all to Cuba together, to wipe out the drive to fight communism. They had no idea they were going to be sent back to them again."

Ana remembered Alejandro saying something very similar.

The personal ads in the classified section of the Sunday newspaper were overflowing with "redheaded, petite, vivacious, financially independent widowed Jewish ladies" living in the Kendall area, who loved to cook. These ladies, in white slacks and cashmere sweaters embroidered in pearls and tube, round and glass beads, with lacquered hair, filled Dadeland mall and Lincoln Road.

Sergio had mentioned that the owner of the Benigno's Restaurant had belonged to a group in Cuba and was active here now, but he didn't tell her his last name. Ana went to the library Friday evening and pulled out the thick city directory down from the shelf. At the table, she ran her finger down the page: Bencomo, Bender, Bendix, Benedict, Beneficial, Bengochea, Benítez, Benjamin... no Benigno's. The restaurant was probably new. She tapped her forefinger absently where it had stopped and looked up, sucking her lower lip pensively. Should she ask Sergio the last name? No, she didn't want him to know that she intended to contact the man. He would tell her father and her father would worry. She looked down at the page again. Benítez. Benítez, Alvaro. Alvaro Benítez. Alvaro Benítez!, her old boyfriend. But he had been in New York. His occupation was listed as "silver pltr" — it *was* him — and his employer, as "New Era Silversmiths". It didn't indicate a wife's name in parenthesis. His address was in the northeast. She felt curious. She looked up New Era Silversmiths. It was located in Perrine. She looked up the address and wrote down their telephone number. She had forgotten, for the moment, about the owner of the Benigno's. She returned the heavy directory to the shelf and walked down the wide stairs of the library building smiling, past the huge strangler fig, to her car on Biscayne Boulevard.

She called the New Era Silversmiths Saturday morning. She asked the telephone operator if she could leave a message for Alvaro and asked her to tell him Ana called, and she left her phone number. At 1:00 that afternoon, the phone rang and she answered herself.

"Ana?", he asked. His voice hadn't changed.

"Yes."

"How are you?"

"Fine. And you? How did you know who it was? I didn't leave my last name."

"Ah, because I only know two Anas. The only other Ana I know works for a sheet metal supplier and we don't get along too well. She wouldn't be leaving me a message saying just, 'Ana called'. And..."

"Weren't you surprised I'm here?", she interrupted him.

"... I knew you were here", he continued. "I saw you waiting for the bus once about a year ago, in front of a furniture store. I went around the block to stop, but you must have gotten on the bus in that time." She suppressed an impulse to ask him why he hadn't looked her up in the phone book. "How are you doing? Are you working?"

"Yes, I'm working in a bank", she said. "And how have you been?"

"I've been working for this firm for over three years now. Could you believe me — what a coincidence!, — yesterday I was singing '¿Quién Será la que Me Quiere a Mí?' all day and you were on my mind? Do you remember it?"

"Of course I remember it", she said warmly.

"It was too cold for me in New York, I couldn't take the snow any longer. I lived there almost three years, you know?... You know that I tried to look you up in the phone book,... Méndez, but I couldn't remember your father's first name."

"Well, a year ago we probably weren't in the phone book yet, anyway."

"Is he here too?"
"Yes, he's here."
"How long have you been here?"
"Over a year and a half, almost two years."
"Is your family with you?"
"Yes, well, my mother. Gustavo stayed in Cuba."
"Did you get married?"
"No, I haven't."
"I did. I have a two-year old daughter."

It came as a surprise. She hadn't thought he'd be married. She hadn't heard from him in about six years. That changed everything. She hoped her disappointment didn't show in her voice. "I'm glad you're well."

"I'd like to see you, partner. Maybe we could meet for a drink after work some time for old times' sake. There's a bar near where I work." He sounded merry, too merry. 'Partner'? "Or maybe on a Saturday."

"Sure. On a Saturday."
"I'll call you up again. Give my regards to your parents."
"Thank you."

Well, that was that.

Ana called the John Birch Society at the phone number Fred Taylor, the teller, gave her. She'd learned he was a staunch Republican. They mailed her sample literature. But she found out she couldn't afford to join.

She opened the door of the *Nacionalismo Democrático*, in a store-front office in the northwest section, past the York Rite Temple, and entered a small room with a desk, four straight chairs and two book-cases. She had found their propaganda in the door handle of her car on the college parking lot several times. A tall, heavy man with a tuft of unruly straight black hair and sunglasses – indoors, in the evening, – Gregorio Nogueira Serrats, was standing behind the desk with some papers in his hand, which he set down on the desk when she came in. She recognized him from the building on Monserrate where she had worked, but she didn't acknowledge it. She closed the door behind her as two men sitting in the chairs looked curiously at her.

"Good evening. I was given your address by a member of your group in Cuba and am interested in joining your organization." The man nodded slowly, cautiously. "I could answer the telephone, distribute propaganda, get addresses, type, translate, run a mimeograph... anything."

"Sit down." She did. "Well, we have a recorded reply on the telephone."

"I know. I'd been trying to get through for two days now. Maybe I could answer the telephone personally for a few hours in the evening."

"Now, you'd have to fill out an application and we'll investigate you." She nodded. "We'd give you a booklet on our regulations and doctrine which you can read in the meantime, to get an idea of our purpose and intentions. We want our members" − the man seemed to perk up − "to share an organized principle and instructions. We don't want just to hand out rifles and say, 'Let's go fight' without an idea behind it. Do you follow me?" She nodded again. "Then, if you still believe you'd like to join us, we'll accept you. Can you draw? We distribute these cartoons with political themes."

"I know, I've seen them. But I am interested in something more active than drawing."

"Don't put down drawing. It's a good medium to reach the people."

"I know, but I want to have a faster and more direct effect on the people I approach. I have use of a car and know the streets of Miami. I could distribute literature."

"Here's the application. Fill it out. Manolo, hand me a booklet." Nogueira pointed to the bookcase and held the application to her. One of the men sitting reached in back of him and gave her a booklet.

Maybe he expected her to take it home with her. "Could you let me use a pen?" He handed her one.

She leaned forward, fanned away cigarette ashes and, resting on the desk, filled out the mimeographed application. Name, address, telephone number, age, occupation, local place of work, last place of work in Cuba, religion, political connections in Cuba and in the States, name of person referring her, aptitudes which could be useful to the group. Did she know how to use a weapon? − It was intended for men − She completed it and handed it back to Nogueira, who took it and looked at it briefly.

"Well, Ana, we'll call you."

"I'm interested in taking a first-aid course. I heard the M R R had one. Do you?"

"Yes, we're making them available."

The man called Manolo scribbled an address on a piece of paper, handed it to her and spoke for the first time. "We're meeting there every Wednesday evening for a first-aid course coincidentally starting next Wednesday at seven thirty. One of us could pick you up and take you."

She looked at the address. "It's not necessary, thank you. It's only three blocks from my house. I'll be there Wednesday."

"We'll see you there."

"Good night."

Drawing! She read the booklet. She attended the six classes they offered, and learned how to take the temperature and blood pressure, apply several ointments and unctions, shave, cleanse and bandage a wound, set a limb on a splint, apply a tourniquet to a wound, give an injection and (only in theory) an enema. There were a few women, wives and fiancées of the members. Nogueira wasn't there. When she was leaving, the men would try to hang around her and make conversation.

But the group never called her. Instead, from the address she'd listed on her application as a reference, they contacted her cousin Diego.

Ana received a letter from Ofelia Barquet, who told her she had quit her job and gotten married, but they hadn't been able to find a house. Betancourt had requested a transfer to Canada and was now in Saudi Arabia. Ana's successor had resigned for "personal reasons" – even though she had been "very different from Ana as far as ideas"!

The school year ended and for her twenty-sixth birthday her parents took Ana to the Schuberth's Sea Food Grill Friday for dinner at a river-side outdoor table.

Their neighbor's lawn-mower woke Ana up Saturday morning – it reminded her of the deaf woman's television set in Havana – and she thought she heard sobbing. She propped herself up on an elbow and heard Magaly's low voice. She somehow felt she shouldn't intrude. She got up and went into the bathroom, brushed her teeth and washed her face, and went back into her room to get dressed. When she finally walked into the kitchen for breakfast, she found Magaly hunched over the table, head lowered, Teresa patting her arm. Ana felt awkward. Magaly looked up, eyes red, cheeks tear-stained, and sobbed. Ana's eyes widened. Teresa raised the question with her eyebrows and Magaly nodded her consent.

"Sergio left on a mission to Cuba on a boat with three other men", her mother told her.

"When?"

"I'm not sure", said Magaly. "I had known they intended to do it, but he didn't want to tell me when because he knew I'd be pleading with him not to go. He left the house last Saturday morning to go fishing with these three other men from the barber shop and hasn't come back. I called his friends' wives Monday morning and they knew they were going."

"Why didn't you tell us before?"

"I didn't know if I should. You know, for his safety's sake. I thought it would be only a matter of a couple of days. But he's not back yet. I'm afraid they may have been discovered."

"May God not allow it!", said Teresa.

"How long has he been involved with these people?", Ana asked.

"They started coming around the house about four months ago. And I guess he let them talk him into it."

"What were they going to do? Shoot at a target? Blow up something? Smuggle weapons? Infiltrate themselves? Smuggle somebody out?"

"I don't know. He didn't tell me. He knows I worry."

"With whom did you leave Haydée?"

"With the wife of one of the other men. They live on the same block near Eleventh." She paused, heaved a sigh and went on, addressing Ana, "You know he'd been involved in the underground in Cuba in 'sixty, but he'd left that. Until he became friends with these men. And with a seven-year old daughter! Doesn't he think of what would become of her if something happened to him?"

"He's young", Teresa said, "and doesn't think anything is going to happen to him. He wants to take his family back to a free country. You yourself have often said, 'Crane, to your homeland, even on one leg'. There's nothing you can do but pray that he'll be back safe."

"Teresa, I want you to talk to him. If he comes back. He doesn't have any other family here. I think he'd listen to you."

"I don't think he would, Magaly. He loves you. If you haven't been able to make him give it up, he isn't going to listen to me."

"I understand... He's only a second cousin, you don't want to interfere. He's not your son."

"Magaly", Teresa shot at her, as if slapped, "my own son is in Cuba and I don't know if I'll ever see him again!"

Organization Campaign 501

"Forgive me, Teresa." Magaly got up and hugged her. "I don't know what I'm saying. I'm so, so afraid...!"

"Let us know if we can help in any way", Ana said. "If you need money. Take you anywhere? Anything. Papá or I can take you. Need something for the girl? Mamá or I can stay with you in the evening."

Magaly straightened up, evidently disappointed that Teresa wouldn't try to talk to Sergio, and composed herself.

D

Silvia had gotten her driver's license Wednesday and was driving her mother's three-year old red Falcon. She came to pick Ana up Sunday evening.

"Let's go for a drive up Eighth Street", she said. "Maybe to Uncle Tom's Barbecue." On the windshield was a decal of a worm holding a Cuban flag. "Maritza was a bridesmaid at a wedding and they had the photographs taken at the Prado Entrance."

Across Red Road in West Miami was the TePee Package Store, the first place outside the city limits where liquor could be bought on Sundays. A white egret looked out of place on the north side of the Trail. Silvia drove west for over five miles and then decided to turn back and go to a Burger King for shakes. She turned right on a side avenue. Their attention was caught by a group of men in the porch of an old house on the east side. Another car was coming in the opposite direction on the narrow avenue. They approached each other slowly. When it was near, they could see the driver was a Cuban boy.

"What's that?", Silvia surprised her by asking him. "A birthday?"

"Or a funeral?", asked Ana.

"They're going to overthrow Castro", the boy answered satirically. "They have the boat anchored at Dinner Key."

"Oh, good!", they followed his joking.

The pale boy tried to continue the conversation, but Silvia drove on past him. They were still curious, so she drove around the block again. As they reached the house once more, the group was dispersing and young Cuban men were coming out. Silvia turned right at the corner and got next to the curb. One was passing by the car and she asked him, "Was that a meeting?"

"That's an anti-communist organization." The boy had been right. "You might be interested in our information." He called to another man walking near. "Pepe, do you have some literature with you?"

The other came up to the car too. "No, I'm sorry."

"Well, if you're interested, come by any time", said the first one. He rested his arm on the roof of the car. "You can ask for me, Edmundo Ferro, or any of the other men will help you." He was being earnest. "We have a meeting next Thursday. Why don't you come around then?"

"We may", Ana said. She knew Silvia wasn't too interested in that. The men headed for their own cars.

Silvia was going to pull away. Two other boys were getting into the car behind them. Silvia backed out into the street in front of the other car. The one driving asked her, "Do you want me to park it for you?"

"No, I'm not trying to park", she yelled back. "I'm trying to leave."

"She just got her driver's license today", Ana said, exaggerating the situation.

The driver called out something to them. Silvia cut through a gas station and got back on 8th Street heading east. The car followed them and then got alongside of them. The man driving yelled across the other one, "May we invite you for a drink?"

"No, not a drink", answered Silvia, very confident, "but coffee we will accept."

"Where?"

"'Toby's'?"

"Where's that?"

"Follow us." Driving seemed to give Silvia more self-assurance.

They drove into the parking lot of the restaurant on 27th Avenue, followed closely by the other car, a light green '53 Dodge. They got a good look at the boys and got out of the car. When they walked into the cafeteria, Ana got into one of the booths and scooted to the wall − a wooden pepper mill rested before her, − and Silvia sat across from her. The man who had been driving sat next to Silvia − they got cups of coffee − and the other one, next to Ana. He had crooked teeth, she saw now. She could see the other one in front better. He had light brown hair and hazel eyes, his teeth were slightly separated, and he was wearing a tan and brown plaid shirt.

Where are you from?", he asked the usual question.

"From Marianao", said Silvia, "Reparto de Hornos."

"Havana", Ana answered.

"I'm from Sancti Spíritus, the land of the *guayabera*", said the man next to Ana. It had become customary to ask where one was from before even exchanging names.

"And you?", Silvia asked the other boy next to her.

"From Dividivi del Cupey."

"Where's that?"

"In Las Villas, south of Placetas, 'neal' the Agabama Range." He substituted L sounds for most of the R's, in the countrymen's way, said "neal".

"I never heard of it."

"It's not on the map", said the other next to her. "It has fifty-two people."

"Fifty-one, now that I'm here", said the man across from Ana.

"There are fourteen houses, seven on each side of the road", said the one sitting next to her.

"They are pulling our leg", Ana said to Silvia.

"There's no mail delivery", said the one with the spaced teeth. "When a letter arrives, the mailman stands at the door of the post office and yells." He had a low, choked laugh that came out almost like a cough.

"Ah, but you have a post office?", said Silvia.

"And the last one to go to bed...", the other one started.

"Yes, I know", Ana finished, "turns out the light."

"My name is Evelio", the countryman offered after a while.

"Leonel", said the one from Sancti Spíritus.

The girls didn't offer their names.

"Do you go to the beach?", Leonel asked.

"Sometimes."

"I'm not used to it", said Evelio. "We swam in the Jagüeyes River. We lived so far inland, that we had to take a horse and then a cart, and by the time we got to the seashore, we were too tired to swim."

His exaggerations made them laugh loudly. They enjoyed his sense of humor.

"Crafty", said Leonel. "Where do you work?", he asked Ana.

"In a bank", she answered vaguely.

"And you?", the countryman asked Silvia.

"In an export company. Do you belong to that group?"

"First time we had been there." What a coincidence!, Ana thought.

After more small talk and a few more jokes, Ana suggested leaving. Out on the parking lot, a thin boy walked across, eyes half-closed, a cigarette in his mouth. Ana felt a powdery sweet smell and swung her head to look at him. "Is it?", she asked and Evelio nodded.

"Yes."

"What?", Silvia asked.

"Marijuana", Leonel answered.

By Silvia's car, they asked them for their telephone numbers. Silvia wrote her name and number on the flap off an envelope and passed it to Ana. Ana wrote her own phone number, but the name Julia. She felt curious to see whether they would actually call them, but didn't want to give them her name. Evelio took the paper and read, "Silvia and Julia. May we call you tomorrow?"

"All right", said Silvia.

Monday morning Magaly called them. Sergio had come back in the middle of the night.

"Dirty, with a beard", she said, half laughing, half crying, "and stinking, but sound."

"Thank God!", said Teresa. "I had been praying."

That afternoon after work, when Ana was coming out of the shower, the telephone was ringing and Teresa answered.

"No, you have the wrong number", she heard her mother answer in Spanish. "There is no Julia here." When she had hung up, Teresa commented, "That's the second time today they call asking for Julia." Ana grinned.

Tuesday after dinner, Silvia called. "That boy called me. Evelio. He says he called the number you gave them yesterday and they told him there was no Julia there."

"I heard Mamá answer."

"They want to go out with us", she said, mimicking his country accent and Ana got the impression that she was trying to put it down to conceal her interest. "Tomorrow."

"Ah, Silvia... I don't feel like going out with them."

"Oh, Ana! We end up going to the movies by ourselves. I would much rather go out with two boys. Let's go."

"Who goes with whom?"

"It seems that I go with Evelio and Leonel goes with you."

"Evelio called me first."

"You liked Evelio?"

"No, I'm kidding." But Leonel did have crooked teeth, she thought. "Are they going to call you?"

"Yes, Evelio said he would call me tomorrow."

Organization Campaign

Wednesday afternoon Silvia called her again to let her know they would pick Ana up first — she had already given them her address, — and they would then go pick Silvia up. They shared an apartment. She had suggested going to the movies. At 8:00.

At 7:35 they were ringing her doorbell. She had dressed nicely, in peach color. Her parents met them. Evelio drove and she sat in front between the two. They went on to pick up Silvia near the State Highway Patrol. Ana moved to the back seat with Leonel, and Silvia sat in front with Evelio.

"Where are we going?", he asked her.

"To the movies", Silvia answered. "The 'Trail'?"

"Let's go dancing", said Evelio.

"It's too early to go dancing", said Ana.

"Silvia said eight o'clock", argued Evelio.

"Because I thought we were going to the movies", alleged Silvia.

"You can't talk in the movies", he protested.

"And he doesn't understand English", added Leonel.

"Where can we go dancing? You pick a place", Evelio said to Silvia. "Tonight you will be 'Queen for a Day'."

"To 'Les Violins'."

"How do we get there?"

"Don't you know your way in Miami?"

"No, I just came from New York a few days ago."

Silvia led them up 1st Avenue around the downtown district, avoiding the traffic lights, but hitting all the stop signs instead, while Leonel complained, Evelio kept encouraging her to be 'Queen for a Day', and Ana was amused.

"How long have you been in the country?", she asked Evelio.

"Nine and a half months, almost ten."

"Ana, is that the name?", Leonel asked her.

She nodded and grinned guiltily.

"I was wrong. When you gave us your names", Evelio said addressing Silvia, "I was sure you were the one who had given us the wrong name."

"So Julia, eh!", Leonel grumbled. He then asked Silvia, "Do you have any brothers or sisters?"

"No, I'm an only child."

"Did you hear that, Evelio? So is he, two only children, you're going to get along well."

The nightclub was deserted so early. They picked a table near the dance floor next to the wall by a column. Ana ordered cognac and ginger ale, Silvia a pink lady, and the men Scotch and soda.

Evelio took a sip of Silvia's drink and complimented her on her taste. Leonel couldn't dance, and he and Ana didn't find much to talk about. Silvia and Evelio danced most of the night.

> *"Total, si no tengo tus besos,*
> *no me muero por eso,*
> *ya yo estoy cansada de tanto besar.*
> *Viví sin conocerte..."*[91]

Leonel attempted to talk a little about Sancti Spíritus, the cheese and butter factory where he'd worked, the Main Church and the colonial arched stone bridge over the Yayabo river, and Ana paid polite attention pretending interest. He then tried asking her about herself and she dutifully gave him a brief account.

Violinists strolled around the floor. The singing waiters burst out in song as they served the customers, and the show took place among the tables.

During the short intervals Silvia and Evelio sat at the table, Ana overheard snatches of their conversation. Silvia asked him for change for the phone to call her mother. Evelio mentioned he had cut sugar cane, he had wounded his finger. New York was too cold for him. He later talked about his father. He laughed his choked laugh.

"You're not married?", Silvia asked him.

"No. Why?"

"I don't know. You look married." Silvia changed to the *"tú"* familiar pronoun form.

"Do you think, if I were married, I would be so free?"

"Your wife could be in Cuba."

"If she had stayed in Cuba, I would have brought her."

Silvia inclined her head, doubtful. "No, because maybe she hasn't been able to leave."

Evelio shook his head. "In nine months, she would have already been able."

Ana and Silvia went to the ladies' room.

"I wonder if he's married", said Silvia.

"Why?", Ana asked. The idle attendant was listening.

"He's of a married age."

"Well, he looks married." They were giggly, unstable and silly.

"Do you think so?"

The attendant joined in their giggles and nonsense.
Later Ana saw them kissing on the dance floor.
When Ana called her Sunday, Silvia told her she was going to Pier 1 with Evelio. Thursday they had gone to the Wakamba, Friday dancing at the Raul's 21 and Saturday to El Toledo for dinner.

Tuesday there was a dance at the DiLido Hotel, and Silvia insisted Ana go along with her and Evelio. They had expected Leonel to meet them there. He didn't show up. A boy younger than she, and shorter, asked Ana to dance, and he didn't say a word.

Wednesday Silvia said she was going to eat at the Dahla Horse with Evelio.

Ana called Silvia Saturday to go to the beach.

"Ana, you're going to be surprised. Thursday when I was going home for lunch, I met Evelio in front of a stationery store on Seventh Street. He was waiting outside for a friend who works there who had invited him for lunch at his house. He didn't know where I worked. He walked me home and had lunch with me, and then he walked me back to work. I suppose he went to see his friend then." The noise of the planes flying low over the northwest section made it difficult to hear her. "Last night we went to the Minerva for dinner and we had *'sangria'*, and he called me this morning. Do you mind if he comes along with us?"

"No, Silvia, you two go. I'm going to feel like a fifth wheel."

"I can ask him to bring Leonel along."

"No, no, Leonel and I didn't like each other much. I'm not going."

On Sunday she went with her parents to Crandon Park, to avoid having Silvia think she should take her along. Silvia was going to the Tívoli Theater with Evelio to see a movie featuring Sandro. Laura, Adrián and Lourdes joined Ana and her parents.

Tuesday evening Silvia called her and insisted Ana go out with them. She was being loyal. Evelio drove to the organization where they had first met them, parked the car across the street from it, turned the radio on for them and told them, "I won't be long. I just have to introduce some guys I brought."

Ana had subconsciously registered he had a sexually attractive way of walking, but she couldn't quite put her finger on the reason.

"He told me he does belong to this group", said Silvia, "but hadn't wanted to tell us because he didn't know who we were; we could have been sent by somebody to find out something from them. In fact, that was the reason he came down from New York, not the cold weather. I told him, even if we had been sent by somebody, how could we know that he had any information that would be useful? He said that maybe we knew who he was" − that smacked to Ana of conceit on his part, − "and I had to remind him that *he* followed *us* that evening."

"Right."

"He says he arrived by boat in late August of last year with two other men."

"How old is he?"

"Thirty-three. My mother is always saying he's a drifter, he doesn't have a job. His parents owned a *finca* in Las Charcas, and they're still living there. He was telling me how he and his father installed a shower."

They watched him walk around the porch of the old house, as they listened to the radio. Míriam and the Sons of Paraguay sang "The Blue Lake of Ypacaraí". It suddenly hit Ana what the characteristic of his walk was. He walked like a typical countryman, shoulders hunched, head lowered, body bent forward at the waist. And she had found that attractive. She yearned for Dany. She felt lonely.

"Last night we went to eat at the Mesón de Gaviria", Silvia told her.

Evelio was back after a while. "I heard you laughing."

"Oh, the mosquitoes are big as helicopters. We were listening to the radio", said Silvia. "Are you through?"

"Yes. I told you, I just had to take some guys in." He started the car. A man was jaywalking.

"He's walking down the middle of the street", Silvia observed.

"Like a countryman?", asked Evelio. They didn't answer him. "People say that. Countrymen don't walk down the middle of the street", he said. "Inland there are no streets and, if they walked down the middle of the highway, they'd be run over by a truck."

Saturday Silvia insisted Ana go to the beach with them.

Ana was reluctant. "Look, the eleventh commandment is 'Thou shalt not be in the way'."

"No, Ana, you won't be in the way. Let's all go together."

"Well,... all right."

She put on a shirt and slacks over her orange striped one-piece bathing suit, and they went to Indian Beach, on 46th Street. Silvia and Evelio went into the water right away and waded to the south, away from the crowd, by themselves. After swimming a little and floating for a while, Ana got out of the water and sat by herself with a Pearl Buck book Silvia had lent her on a towel on the sand, where she dozed off. When she woke up, there were hardly any bathers left on the beach, the sun was red and low over the bay to her back. She spotted Silvia and Evelio near the Eden Roc Hotel, got up, walked to the edge of the water and waved at them with both arms. She gathered her bag and towel and "The Good Earth", which she hadn't opened, and went to sit on the rock wall before the snack counter, closed now, to wait for them. Silvia wore an apologetic smile. Ana smiled back shaking her head. She understood.

As they were leaving, Evelio met an acquaintance and offered him a ride to the city. The boy, Honduran, thin, with pimply sallow skin, sunglasses atop his head, introduced himself as "Ferrera", then asked them, "Call me Chema. I'm from San Francisco de Patuca", he told them. "My father owns a banana plantation. They got leaf blight there now." They were amused to see a crab crossing Alton Road. "I'm very sympathetic with the Cuban cause. I met the leader of this movement at the Peace Monument in Comayagüela on my trip home last February, when the revolutionary was requesting contributions from sympathetic owners of banana plantations and silver mines." As they approached the city on the MacArthur Causeway, the sun was tinting the sky a strawberry hue behind the skyline of buildings. "Beautiful person", Chema said constantly. When he got off on Biscayne Boulevard before the Berni Hotel, Evelio pronounced, "He talks too much."

Sunday the family went to Crandon Park, and Diego and Xiomara took chubby, seven-week Eric with them and set him in the shade of a seagrape. The temperature soared to an incredible 95 degrees.

"Sometimes we don't allow ourselves to enjoy the happiness we already have", Diego said, "because we consider ourselves obligated to set others' goals for us that won't make us happy. Happiness consists of knowing how to enjoy the small pleasures we find on the path we trace for ourselves to reach the goal we've considered ourselves obligated to set. Violets, pansies and daisies, cardinals, bluejays and woodpeckers, butterflies, ladybugs and dragonflies help sweeten the spring afternoons of exile."

"We're in summer, Diego", said Xiomara. "it's ninety-five degrees and we're blistering."

> *"Cuando calienta el sol aquí en la playa,*
> *siento tu cuerpo vibrar cerca de mí..."*[(92)]

"I think you have sunstroke."

"Seagrape, coconut trees, the sand, the sun, the sea foam", he continued, "drums and beer help us forget we're in exile."

"I think it's the beer."

Eric woke up crying and Ana went to pick him up. He needed changing. "Xiomara!", she cried.

Another Cuban girl, Alina, a typist, started working at the bank. She had lived in Tampa the last seven years, was about 29, from Holguín, fat, dark and unrefined. She was somewhat reserved and Ana wondered if the adage would prove true that there was no worse wedge than that from the same wood.

Wednesday on their break, Jennie told her, "I've remembered something you told me a while ago, 'Don't change for anybody, because, if you change for him, you'll spend your life hating him for having made you change'."

She'd said that? Ana didn't remember. "I wouldn't have thought you'd remember that", she told Jennie.

"No, I know. Forgive me, Ana, but... you think you have a monopoly on feeling."

"You're right" — as with her brother, being always surprised when he expressed his feelings, and Olga — "I realize I believe I'm the only one who thinks. I'm sorry."

Silvia was seeing Evelio Estévez often. They went to eat at Topp's and Harvey's, to the Trojan Lounge. Evelio sent her flowers when she had a cold. The only singer Evelio liked was Nat King Cole. Evelio left the radio on in his car when he turned the ignition off so he wouldn't forget to turn it on when it started again. Evelio liked fried pork and steak. Evelio joked to her mother that Silvia ate a lot. Evelio liked salty food. Evelio didn't like sweets — Then he couldn't really have liked the pink lady. — Evelio had very good table manners. Evelio didn't wear sunglasses. Evelio didn't like her to wear makeup. Evelio read *Arsène Lupin* detective stories. Evelio liked her to wear black. Evelio was romantic. Evelio wouldn't admit he liked poems. Evelio had kept the two nickels she gave him. Evelio was going to buy a white Buick Invicta. Evelio, Evelio...

"Didn't you say today was Silvia's birthday?", her mother asked Ana Saturday. "Did you get her something?"

"Yes, a mother-of-pearl perfume atomizer. She'll be twenty-five."

"Are you going out with her?"

"No, I'm sure she's going out with Evelio. She was going to see

'Tom Jones' with him last night."

◀

In the afternoon the phone rang and Teresa answered. "Happy birthday. It's Silvia", she said, surprised. "You must be having a nice time with Evelio today... You're not?... You're alone? You're surely kidding... She wants to talk with you", she said, handing the phone to Ana. "She sounds upset."

Silvia's voice was, in fact, close to breaking. "What happened?", Ana asked her.

"I'm not sure, but I think Evelio has left."

"Left?, Miami? For where?"

"For a training camp."

"Why?"

"I've been calling his apartment and there's no answer."

"But didn't he say anything to you?"

"No, nothing."

"Didn't you see him last night?"

"Yes, we went to the 'Radiocentro' and afterwards − we hadn't had time to eat dinner before − to have a sandwich at that 'J and S' sundries nearby."

"And he didn't tell you he was leaving?"

"No."

"Did he know today was your birthday?"

"Yes, he knew."

"But maybe he hasn't left."

"I drove by his house and the car he had been driving is parked across the street."

"Come over. Mamá is saying she doesn't think he would leave like that. Come over. Don't be alone today."

She arrived shortly afterwards. Méndez was still at work. She told them, "Last night when he left me home, he had told me, 'Happy birthday' − it was after midnight, − 'and now let somebody else try to beat me to wishing it to you.' He said he'd call me at noon today. 'If you wake up before twelve', he said, 'don't call me, force yourself to stay in bed' − that struck me as strange, − 'it's late now and you need to rest.' But, when by a quarter to one he hadn't called, I called him and there was no answer. I called several times and about three or so I drove by his house and saw that green car he had been driving parked across the street."

"But that doesn't mean he has left."

"Where is he, then?"

"I don't know, but he wouldn't leave without saying good-by to you, especially not on your birthday. Did you have a fight?"

"No, not last night. We had had arguments about this before, about his going away to the camp, up to several days ago, but not in the last few days. I thought he had given up the idea."

"When you said you were alone", Teresa said, "I thought you were kidding."

Ana gave her the atomizer.

"Ana, will you go with me by his house?"

"What are you going to do?"

"I'm not sure, but I hope I can find out where he is."

"All right. Let's go."

Silvia drove by Evelio's apartment building near Citrus Grove Elementary School. A black man was selling a truckful of watermelons from the back of a pick-up. Silvia parked behind the Dodge. "Do you have a pen?", she asked Ana.

Ana hadn't brought a handbag. "No."

Silvia took a little piece of cardboard from her wallet, scratched something on it with her car key and went to stick it in the frame of the apartment door. With her legs shaking visibly, she walked to the other car. The door wasn't locked. She opened it and Ana saw her look at some papers she took out of the glove compartment, she closed the car door, and rushed back to her own to lean against the steering wheel, shaking.

"There is a window envelope with something, a bill, inside that says 'Roberto Rodríguez', but no address."

"So?"

"Well, if it had an address, I would go to see the man and ask him where Evelio is." She was obsessed.

"I think you should wait, Silvia. Keep calling the house, and wait until you hear from him. Leonel will tell you something. You'll hear from him." She wasn't at all sure she would. This all seemed very strange.

"Ana, I feel sick. I think I'm going to lose my mind. I've never felt like this in my life." She started crying, sobbing convulsively. Ana patted her shoulder.

"I know how you must feel, but calm down." She held her right forearm. "You won't gain anything by breaking down. Let's go back to my house."

"No, I'm going home. My mother must be back by now. When I left for your house, she went to see my grandmother at the hotel. She gave me a skirt. I'll try to calm down."

She drove Ana home. When she let her off, she told her, "I'll go on calling his house."

Mrs. Knowles' black kitten scuttled up the front steps and let Ana pick him up. A firefly flew around. She cuddled the kitten for a moment, staring after Silvia's red Falcon, then put him down on the grass before going in.

CHAPTER 16

ACCEPTANCE OF EXPATRIATION

> *"¡Me lo dijeron; y, por un instante,*
> *apagóse la luz de mi razón,*
> *helóseme la sangre, y su latido*
> *detuvo el corazón!*
> ...
> *¡El cáliz del dolor, gota por gota,*
> *mi labio, hasta las heces, apuró,*
> *y el raudal de mi abundoso llanto,*
> *al cabo se agotó!*
> *¡Y proseguí el camino de la vida*
> *por la suerte dejándome arrastrar,*
> *cual náufrago infeliz que se abandona*
> *a las olas del mar!"*[16]
>
> *("....",* Nieves Xenés Duarte*)*

Ana called Silvia early Sunday, and encouraged her to go with her to the beach — it was 90 degrees, — but Silvia was steadfast in her refusal. So Ana went to Crandon Park with her parents, and Sergio and Magaly joined them with Haydée. They roasted chicken on a barbecue grill. Looking over the skyline inspired Sergio, leaning

> [16] They told me; and, for an instant,
> the light of my sanity went out,
> my blood froze and
> my heart stopped its beat!
> ...
> My lips drained the chalice of pain,
> drop by drop, to the dregs,
> and the abundant torrent of my tears
> at last dried out!
> And I went on the path of life
> letting myself be dragged by fate,
> like a wretched castaway who abandons himself
> to the waves of the sea!

Acceptance of Expatriation

back against a coconut tree, to sing,
> "*Mirando lejos sobre el azul del horizonte,*
> *mirando fijo, veo tu rostro aparecer...*
> *Por eso ahora, cuando yo miro al horizonte,*
> *recuerdo siempre aquellos días junto a ti...*"[93]

"Laura invited us to dinner tonight", said Teresa.

"She's going to serve *'ropa vieja'* for me", said Carlos, "because I mentioned I hadn't eaten it in a long time."

Ana called Silvia again Monday afternoon. "Did you hear anything?", she asked her.

Silvia's voice was low and shaky. "I went on calling his house and after twelve o'clock last night Leonel finally answered. He said he had just gotten home and 'it looked as if Evelio had left' because he had found a note on the kitchen table saying, 'I'll see you soon. Good luck to you', and it seemed he had remembered to take my picture from his drawer." She started crying. "Why did he do this to me?"

"What are you going to do now?"

"Leonel said I should call him today; he was going to find out for me the address where I can write to him. He noticed I was very nervous. He said that for the time being I could write to him at their address and he would see that it's forwarded to him. He's being very nice. He was in a Christian seminar."

"Where's the training camp?"

"Somewhere in Central America, I think." There was a pause, then she said in a low, tired voice, "Evelio had said when we were on Young Circle in Hollywood one evening two weeks ago that he wanted to get married on August twenty-third, because that was the date he had arrived..."

"Well, Silvia, don't go on torturing yourself thinking about that, because you can't do anything. Maybe he had to leave, couldn't help it, had no other choice. Write to him. Wait until he writes to you and explains what happened."

"Yes, I'm going to wait."

"Try to rest."

Tuesday Silvia wrote her first letter to Evelio, and one every three days for the next twelve days. When she saw her again Saturday, Silvia confessed to her that Sunday she had looked up all the Roberto Rodríguezes in the telephone book and driven past the houses of most of them. Ana hesitated, but felt she had to ask her. "You and Evelio didn't...? You didn't let him...? You didn't...?"

"No, Ana, it's just that I fell so much in love with him."

Friday it was 90 degrees again.

"We've been here two years today", Carlos said Saturday, setting on the back porch three orange webbed aluminum chairs he had bought. Mrs. Knowles' cat was climbing the kitchen screen door, clawing at it. He would probably be the first one to use the chairs.

After she had mailed him five letters, when she took solace in writing to him, Silvia seemed to calm down somewhat and in a way accept Evelio's absence. Now she only lived to wait for his first letter. But now Ana insisted that she go out with her. Evelio might never write. And off they went to the movies, to see "The Cabinet of Caligari" with Glynis Johns, *"Irma la Douce"* with Jack Lemmon, "The Birds" with Rod Taylor, "The Sins of Rachel Cade" with Angie Dickinson, "The Thrill of It All" with James Gardner, "For Love or Money" with Kirk Douglas; to the Golden Point for a hamburger or to the Toddle House for pecan pie, to a *jai-alai* game, or on occasional double-dates, to the "Wreck Bar" in the Castaways, the Club Capri on 8th Street, the Sands in the Beach, the "1800" on Bayshore Drive, the Jamaica Inn in Key Biscayne, "The Apartment" in North Miami Beach, the new "Club Intimo", recently opened where Raul's 21 had been, the "Centro Español" by the river, or the Copa Lounge. And, although Silvia acted aloof and often distraught, and Ana herself was cool and sometimes distant, she at least felt better that Silvia was not staying at home. Ana's mind was on the absence of letters from Dany, who had been silent now for eight months. Once they went to the Machu Picchu, where the Café d'Artists had been, with a couple of men they knew, and chatting by the bar, Ana discovered that one of them knew Danilo from Cuba.

"He wears his hair falling over his forehead", the boy said – That wasn't like Dany. – It had been less time since this man had come from Cuba than Ana.

Silvia's date, a diver, recommended, "You should see the Argentinean movie *'El Rufián'*. Fantastic! It's about a surgeon's wife who has clairvoyant powers. It's playing at the 'Tower'. I wouldn't mind seeing it a second time."

While they danced, Ana kept taking the conversation back to Dany, asking about him and interrogating the boy, until he got tired, shut up and wanted to leave.

... A month went by.

Monday they went to Representative Dante Fascell's thirteenth Labor Day picnic at Crandon Park, even though he was a Democrat. He had criticized the Latin American nations that did not act against communism in Cuba.

When Ana walked into the office Tuesday morning, Jennie was talking on the telephone. As she passed her desk, Ana overheard part of the conversation. In the morning break, Jennie went to get her.

"I have some news to give you", she said in the employees' lounge. Ana had realized what it was, but didn't want to spoil her surprise. "I'm getting married."

"Congratulations! When?"

"November sixteenth."

"Here?" At another table, Paula was peeling an orange with her fingernails.

"No, we're going to have it in Pensacola. That way all my family can attend. My sister Cindy's going to be my maid of honor and my dad's going to give me away. And Jeff's family is in Saint Augustine and it's closer for them. His younger brother who's at State U is going to be his best man. Saturday night we went to the beach and he took me down to the lifeguard's stand. I was wondering what he was up to. And he gave me the ring." She held out her hand to Ana. It was one diamond in a Tiffany setting on white gold. "That's where we used to go at the beginning to make out. He said he wanted to give it to me right there."

"How romantic!"

"And last night we went to the 'Top O'the Columbus' for dinner."

"How glad I am for you! You look so happy."

"We had frog legs. I didn't like them, but I didn't want to hurt Jeff's feelings. They tasted to me as if they were hot and salty on the outside?, and cold and bland in the inside?"

"Where are you going for your honeymoon?"

"To Bimini. I'd like you to go to the wedding. It's on a Saturday. Do you think you'll be able?"

"Let's see. I may. I could go by bus. Is there a train?"

Norma, Carmen, Ofelia, Rosa and Natalia had all gotten married. Jennie was getting married, and so were Yolanda, Lydia and Berta. She wondered if Duarte and "the Country Girl" had gotten married.

Carmen Zayas had moved to Miami with her husband. Ana went to visit her in the rear apartment in the southwest section near the Southside Park where they were living with her mother, a heavy lady with her hair in a bun, whom Ana had met at Carmen's bachelorette party.

"I had nosebleeds up there", said Carmen. She was working as secretary in the office of a paint company. Her husband Miguel's features resembled Dany's, but he had light brown hair and green eyes. They talked for a long time. Carmen told her Rina had been in Cuba – again? – and was now in Miami working in an insurance company. Nelia was now living in Kansas. Eugenia was also in Miami. Mr. Batten's and Mario's wives had recently had babies. Lydia Dennis had finally married an American and was living in Puerto Rico.

Ana bought a new blue and green striped bathing suit. She took her two weeks' vacation and went down the MacArthur Causeway to the beach by herself almost every day.

She read Burdick's "The Ninth Wave", Grace Metalious' "The Tight White Collar", Hunter's "Mothers and Daughters", Shirley Deane's "On the Road to Andorra", and four books by retired Air Force Major Donald E. Keyhoe about unidentified flying objects. Fred Taylor lent her Lederer's "A Nation of Sheep".

Ana got an unexpected call from Yolanda Solís. She was in Miami on vacation; she and Eladio had finally married; they were moving to the Virgin Islands; she thought she was pregnant; Aurora was here!; she would try to call her once more before she left. She didn't call again.

Ana had been at the bank over two years and was now making $310. a month. Her co-workers were nice people to work with, but, other than Jennie, she didn't have close friendships with any of them outside the bank. Alina hadn't become her friend. Ana had finished her two-semester advertising course in August — she did have a knack for picking courses that she couldn't put to use, — and her parents, their first year of English at the Center. Méndez took a tax course at Lindsey Hopkins Center on 2nd Avenue and started preparing federal income tax return forms for acquaintances. He had been at the hotel almost two years and was making $60. a week.

"We should start thinking about getting our residence visas", said Méndez.

"We'll have to go to a Consul outside the country", said Ana.

"We could go to Toronto next year", said her father.

"Why do we have to go out of the country?", asked Teresa.

"Because the visas are given by Consuls, and the Consulates are outside the country", said Carlos.

"We can do the paperwork ourselves", said Ana.

Acceptance of Expatriation

"We could visit the World Fair in New York at the same time", said her mother.

"It's going to be set up at Flushing", said Ana.

"We can visit Peláez", said her father. "He's living in Astoria."

When Americans heard Spanish being spoken, they went paranoid and imagined they were being talked about.

Magaly told them she was in the supermarket talking to Haydée in Spanish and a Jewish elderly lady in the line to the check-out counter told her, "Why don't you speak to her in English so she'll learn? You're in America now."

"I was going to answer", said Magaly, "but decided to laugh instead, and go on talking to her however I wanted. I thought of so many Chinese on the bus and Poles on the beach in Cuba talking in Chinese and in Polish, and nobody would have thought of telling them not speak their language."

Laura told them of another Jewish lady in the supermarket who saw Lourdes carrying a plastic milk bottle with a nipple and asked Laura, "Why do you let that girl drink from a bottle? She's too big."

"Imagine what impudence!", fumed Laura.

The few Cubans who had at the beginning been interesting, exotic and novel, in four and a half years turned into a plague of thousands, and they were no longer novel, exotic or interesting. As long as they were only a few, they didn't represent a typical specimen in which to recognize idiosyncrasies of the nationality, but when they constituted a considerable segment of the population — 258,500 Cubans had entered the States, 190,000 into Miami — and the characteristics revealed themselves, the ways were observed to which the locals were not accustomed and faults surfaced which irritated them. At first businesses displayed little signs that said *"Se habla español"* to attract the new growing Spanish clientele. In time there came to be signs that read "English spoken" to call the attention of the decreasing old American patronage. While at the beginning Americans said, "Let's go to that little Cuban restaurant to have *'picadillo'* and ripe plantains", with time they came to say, "Can't you find an American restaurant any more where you can eat a club steak?"

"We're becoming an amusing attraction for the Americans", said Sergio. "They come down to Miami to see us in 'Cuban Town'."

"Yes, they have Monkey Jungle, Parrot Jungle", said Diego, "and now Cuban Jungle."

"Where the Cubans 'roam free in their natural habitat'," contributed Ana.

The Americans who discriminated against the Cubans openly were labeled by these as "rednecks". They seemed to perceive the Cuban as a dark, short, loud man wearing a gold neckchain and medal, who smoked a cigar, ate rice and beans, drove a white Buick, paved over his lawn and bet at *jai-alai* games. They in turn were seen by the Cubans as rude, rough, big, beer-guzzling football fans in denim shorts and tee-shirts who chewed bubble gum, liked to live outside the city limits, went barefoot in the house, drove pick-up trucks and hosed them down in their yards. If he had had the means, Oscar would have come closest to epitomizing the stereotype that the Americans had of the Cubans.

Mrs. Knowles moved out of the downstairs apartment next to them to the Kendall area near her son. A young Pakistani couple by the name of Gonçalves da Silva moved in.

A few Americans stayed on among the Cubans. They were mostly the lower class, looked down on by others. They disliked Cubans more than anybody, but living among them gave them somebody on whom to take out their hate.

Carmen went by one evening with her husband, Miguel, and her mother. The women exchanged kisses in greeting.

After serving them the obligatory coffee, Teresa said, "We've become fairly accustomed, but it's not easy to adapt to this way of life."

"You have to struggle to make a living", said Méndez.

"We couldn't get used to Ohio", said Carmen. "It's too gloomy."

"Here at least it's bright", said Carmen's mother. She had had her teeth fixed.

"There's a more familiar atmosphere", said Miguel. He was wearing a brown herringbone sports jacket with suède elbow patches.

"Carlos' sister Esperanza is also here with her husband", Teresa told them, "and her daughter Laura with her family. They live close by. But you know our son Gustavo stayed back home with his family." It was unusual for her mother to go into that subject. "He's working in a ministry. There was no other choice, you know. I still miss them so much, especially the children!" Her eyes watered.

"Don't, Tera", Carlos stopped her.

"I know how it is", Carmen's mother said. "My sister's back there too and we were very close." Carmen shook her head and smiled sympathetically.

Augusto dropped in. "Hello."

Acceptance of Expatriation

"Speak of the King of Rome", said Teresa.

"I went to buy bread at Adler's and just stopped by on my way back." The introductions were made. "I live four blocks from here", he explained to Carmen and her family.

"Teresa was just talking about you", said Méndez.

"No wonder I felt my flesh was raw. I like flute bread better than this", Augusto held up the white bread, "but Esperanza insists this yields more." To Méndez he said, "I got The Miami News. Did you read it?"

"No, I have the *Diario Las Américas*. Do you want to trade?"

"All right. I find English difficult."

"The pronunciation is confusing", agreed Miguel. "Take the ending 'ough'. There are seven ways to pronounce it: 'bou', 'kôf', 'dō', 'lŏkh', 'rŭf', 'trôf', 'thrōō'."

Carmen laughed. She didn't find it confusing; she'd attended the American Dominicans' Academy.

"You saw the car when you came in, didn't you?", Ana asked Carmen, "the aqua one."

"Yes, we noticed it", Miguel said. "Nice. We bought the Oldsmobile as soon as we came back from Ohio – you need a car here; – on time of course, and we owe more than two thirds on it."

"Ah!, we bought the Rambler on time too", said Méndez. "Two years, and we've only paid less than one."

"That's the way it is here", said Carmen's mother. "Like the houses with twenty-five year mortgages."

"They are never yours", said Augusto. "They belong to the bank."

"Well, it's better than paying rent", said Miguel.

"At least you have something when you move out", said Teresa.

"A friend of ours is after us to buy a house", said Méndez. "He has a friend who's a real estate salesman. He says there's one now he insists we go see in the next few days."

"But buying a house here...", said Carmen's mother. "What if the problem in Cuba is solved?"

"You could always sell it", said Carmen.

"If the problem in Cuba is solved, there won't be anybody left here to whom to sell it", said Augusto.

"This house is for rent with an option to buy", said Ana.

"Oh, that's better", said Miguel. "It'll give you time to see how things go."

"Construction here is hollow", said Carmen's mother. "Hardboard. In Cuba they built with cement block."

"And before that with clay bricks", said Augusto. "Stretcher, laid flat for the outside walls and rowlock, on edge for the inside walls. That was solid."

"We became members of a medical clinic, Cuban style", said Teresa. "Carlos and Ana María have insurance at work, but this is like back home, the Spanish-American United Society. It's near the Dade County Auditorium."

"We'd like to become members of one too", said Miguel.

"Carlos can get you the application", said Teresa. "Couldn't you?"

"Sure. Getting sick here costs a bundle", said Carlos.

"In Cuba there were so many free hospitals", said Teresa.

"And the Spanish regional centers for two seventy-five a month", said Méndez.

"And the doctors were better", said Carmen's mother.

"Cuba was in the lead in everything", said Augusto. And added pointlessly, since the seven persons present were all Cubans, "The Cuban *peso* was at par with the American dollar." Older people bragged about it so much, that they detracted credibility from their arguments.

"I wish we could have star apples", said Teresa, passing plantain chips around. "That was my favorite fruit. I haven't seen it here."

"A bellhop at the hotel says he knows of a place on Milam Dairy Road that has them", said Carlos.

"Where?", asked Ana,

"Northwest Seventy-second Avenue, past Miami Springs."

"The fruits here may be bigger, but they don't taste the same", said Augusto.

"Those apple bananas!", said Carmen's mother.

"My godson, Sergio, has loquat in his yard,... and a Geiger tree with orange flowers. He's also here with his family. And Carlos has a nephew, Diego, with his family", Teresa returned to the subject. "But my sister Cristina and my brother Guillermo are still back home. He's retired..." Ana smiled embarrassed. "I get carried away when I start talking about the family", her mother apologized. Carlos patted his wife's arm before getting up to serve them wine.

"It happens to all of us", Carmen's mother offered sensitively.

"I've been reading about flying saucers", commented Ana.

"I find the subject interesting", said Miguel. "I also saw a book about the North Pole advertised in TV Guide that I want to buy, by a member of Byrd's crew."

"I want to try to write a book", said Carmen, "about exile."

"What type?", Ana asked her.

"A historical novel." Her short jet-black hair swung and her face came alive.

"I could never write a novel", said Miguel. "If I ever wrote anything, it would have to be non-fiction. I guess I just have no imagination."

"I would base it on facts, but would create some fictional main characters", Carmen explained.

"What ever gave you the idea?", asked Ana.

"I don't know exactly..." Méndez came back with the wine. "... I was sitting on a bench one morning waiting for the bus to go to work — I had had my license suspended for driving without my glasses – and I started to think about writing and to compose a paragraph in my mind, and I haven't stopped thinking about it since."

"Have you ever written anything before", Ana asked her, "... a story?"

"I just wrote one short story when we went to visit my cousins on my father's side in Sagua la Grande before coming here. But that was only three pages long, and I never sent it anywhere."

"You should pursue that idea", said Carlos.

Ana listened to her with admiration. She'd never have the patience or the perseverance to write a book. The thought of the research involved overwhelmed her. "Are you going to carry it out?", she asked her.

"I'm going to try."

Their next purchase was a set of aqua plastic dishes for four.

A building for federal offices was being constructed on 1st Avenue, across from the railroad tracks.

Silvia called her Thursday afternoon. "Ana", she cried excitedly, "I got a letter!"

"Oh, I'm so glad! When?"

"Today. I wanted to tell you right away. It's a very warm letter, a page and a half. I'm so happy! Finally! I'm going to answer him tonight."

Ana, who had harbored doubts that Evelio would ever write, was genuinely relieved. "You see? I'm very glad."

Now Silvia sent him books, Orwell's "1984" in Spanish, Remarque's *"Der Funke Leben"*, magazines and photographs. She copied poems for him. She sent him "Andy Capp" comics, "Mad" cartoons, the horoscope and greeting cards. There was censorship of the mail. He sent José Angel Buesa's "The Lady of the Pearls" and Darío's "Love Your Rhythm" to her.

Hurricane "Flora" struck Cuba and made an unusual turn in its path, hitting the provinces of Camagüey and Oriente three separate times between Friday and Tuesday. Torrential rains poured on the area, causing floods. It was the first time a hurricane ever behaved that way. Ex-tensive damage was suffered, particularly in Baracoa, and casualties were reported.

Paula Monroe was going to organize a "kitchen" shower for Jennie. People were the same all over, basically good everywhere.

Thursday the 10th the Spanish-American United Society held a dinner in their hall in commemoration of the Yara War Cry. The proceeds would go to help support the training camps. The family reserved a long table and twelve relatives attended. There were newspapermen, radio announcers, speakers, singers and reciters. They talked, they remembered the lost homeland. The speakers sobbed. They sang the *"Himno Invasor"*, which Ana hadn't heard in twelve years, since she was in eighth grade, and *"La Bayamesa"*. They recited poems invoking the enslaved island. They sang *"Yo Volveré"*[103]. Tears brimmed in Ana's eyes. She looked around her at the table. Her father was there, her mother, her cousin Laura, Adrián, her aunt Esperanza, Augusto, Diego, Xiomara, Sergio, Magaly, Haydée. The women were wiping their tears, the men wore sorrowful expressions, her uncle Augusto blew his nose, Haydée sniffled.

This was sick, she thought suddenly, a group of people of one nationality gathered together in a place working themselves up to the point of tears, boundless nostalgia, a contest in suffering, a study in masochism, as if they felt they deserved this penance for not having known how to defend their sovereignty and were showing others they were taking their punishment. In the future she'd make donations, but wouldn't attend.

*

On Friday Méndez took them to see the house that Carvajal had told him about. It was further west and south, on 15th Street, in a quieter neighborhood, near an Orthodox Church. It was a duplex for rent with an option to buy. It would be available on the 1st of November. A narrow concrete walk led from the sidewalk. A hedge of yellow ixora went around the front half and a Lombardy poplar graced each front corner. Three steps led up to the little porch at either side of the houses. A little curved iron railing painted white ran down one side of each group of steps. A little clump of monkey-face huddled by the whirl of the railing and a violet-blue dawn flower vine clung to it before the porch. It had a weathered brick façade, white flat tile roof, carport, and a small white colonial door with a broken pediment and a brass doorknocker in an eagle design. The black house numbers were affixed to the wall by the door at eye level. There were white louvered shutters by the colonial pane awning windows. Carvajal had told them that the Argentinean couple who lived in the other apartment had the key, but when they rang the doorbell, nobody answered. Their mailbox said "Mauricio Milano". Through the large front window, which looked into the living room, they could see the beige terrazzo floors and a fireplace with a brick mantle. There were a very few pieces of furniture left. In a planter under the window of the front bedroom grew blue plumbago and there was a hedge of Surinam cherry around the rear half. Another look through the kitchen window showed them mica kitchen cabinets in a wood design, plastic countertops in a marble pattern and an electric stove. The house was nice. They would have to buy furniture. A key lime tree grew in the backyard and there was a brick barbecue. The grass was overgrown in some places and bare patches of dirt sprinkled with sand showed in others. A lavender-blue fern tree and a yellow poui stood before the house across the sidewalk.

"Why don't the Milanos have the option to buy?", Teresa asked.

"Carvajal says they're here only for six years."

Saturday Ana saw in the window of a frame store on Lincoln Road a charcoal drawing of a couple that attracted her. The young man was sitting on the floor, one knee raised, and the girl sitting in front of him, with her back to him, leaning back against his chest. They seemed so comfortable together. She felt she *had* to have it. She went in and put it on lay-away.

In the afternoon, Silvia asked her over the phone in a very quiet voice, "Are you going out? May I come over?'

"Of course", Ana answered. "Is something wrong?"

"Evelio is married."

"What! Married? How did you find out?"

"What's wrong?", Teresa was asking.

"That friend of his who works at the stationery store", Silvia answered.

"Come over", Ana said to Silvia. And to her mother, "Silvia says Evelio is married." Her father was just getting home from work.

When Silvia arrived, Aida was there. Ana realized Silvia was trying to put off talking in front of her, but she finally started, "Remember that friend of his I told you about who works in the stationery store near my house? Evelio had told me about it less than two weeks after we met him. I knew him from Marianao, around the Normal School, but had never talked to him in the stationery store. I had intended to mention to him that I knew Evelio, but hadn't gotten around to it. Well, my mother told me yesterday that a friend of Evelio's who had left with him and had a girlfriend here is married in Cuba and has two children. And I started thinking, if they're friends, about the same age and from the same province, couldn't Evelio be married also? I recalled one day we had met this friend in front of the Western Union office and they had gone aside to talk. And I remembered this other friend of his in the stationery store. And I had to ask him. I should have gone by myself, but I mentioned it to my mother and she went with me. When I got there, I almost didn't dare ask him anything and left. But my mother wouldn't leave. I was sure, wanted to be sure, that he would say he wasn't. So I said, 'I wanted to ask you something' and he said, 'Yes, I know, you're going to tell me you know me from somewhere. I know you too.' I said, 'No, I know you from Marianao, but what I want to ask you is, do you know Evelio Estévez?' and he said, 'Yes.' I asked him, 'Is he married?' and he said, 'Since you ask me directly, I have to tell you. Yes, he is; he has two children.' I felt my chin start quivering right away. I just said, 'Thank you' and left."

She wasn't crying now.

"Maybe he's divorced", Teresa ventured.

"No. If he were divorced", Silvia said very assuredly, "he would have told me."

"Maybe it's just a concubine he has", Aida butted in.

"But, even if he were only living with her, if he has two children, he has just as much responsibility."

Carlos, reading Tony Solar's Spanish column in The Miami News in the chair by the window, had been listening in silence.

"What does your mother say?", Teresa asked her.

"That she suspected it. I'm afraid she might go back to the stationery store and talk to him more."

"What are you going to do?", Ana asked her. She regretted sounding so practical lately.

"I'm just not going to write to him any more."

"But there could be an explanation", Teresa tried to justify. "He seemed to be genuinely in love with you."

"Well, that's not the kind of thing you can write about in a letter", said Aida.

"Especially since there's mail censorship", Ana put in.

"Yes", Aida went on. "You should go on writing to him as if nothing were wrong."

"I can't. How long could I keep that up?"

"He may come up and then you ask him about it in person", said Teresa.

"I'm not going to write to him any more." She sounded very firm. "I'd have to make a big effort to write to him pretending there's nothing wrong, and I don't know for how long."

"I understand you", Ana said. When Aida had gone, she asked Silvia, "Do you want to go some place?"

"No, Ana, where would we go?", said Silvia defeated.

When Silvia had left, Ana expressed, "I feel so bad about this."

Her father put his newspaper down and spoke for the first time. "You're misleading the girl. She's right. If the guy's married, what explanation could there be? He deceived her. He's a cunning countryman. He could have told her before he left. And that's another thing, the *way* he left."

"He had told her he wanted to get married on August twenty-third", Ana said. "I wonder what he intended to do."

"But he left on July twenty-seventh. What angers me is they do that to her because she doesn't have a father. They don't find a man in the house and they take advantage. Hope that she not be pregnant."

"She isn't", said Ana.

Sunday Ana called Silvia and she agreed to go out. On her way to pick her up, Ana listened to the radio — she enjoyed Casey Kasem's unique deep voice. — It was actually too late in the year for the beach, but she drove to 14th Street. On Ocean Drive a Cuban boy who'd just parked his car in front of the Sea Horse Hotel, opposite, crossed the street to theirs and introduced himself. Ana talked to him. Silvia sat in silence. The boy, leaning over the car, looked at Silvia's hair closely. "Your hair is so light!", he said admiringly.

"You lighten it, don't you?"

"You see, Silvia?, and you thought if you lightened it, it wouldn't even make a difference", Ana said, trying to cheer her up.

"I didn't get to lightening it", Silvia said curtly.

"Oh!"

Silvia got out of the car, walked over the grass to the sand, dropped her shirt and slacks at the foot of a coconut tree, and walked into the water. Ana followed her. The boy walked away. Silvia waded out into the sea. Ana was afraid; she swam around – the water was cool, – keeping Silvia within sight. She hadn't cried. It was frightening. She was alarmingly impermeable. The next day she developed a severe toxic condition.

▶

Ana received another surprise call. Octavio Guillén was in Miami on his way to Washington.

"I want to see you", he said. "I'm staying at the Bristol Hotel, downtown. You know where it is, don't you? I guess you must be ancient." It had been three years since they had last seen each other.

When she left the bank that afternoon, she picked up her father at work, he left her off at the Bristol Hotel and she visited Guillén in the lobby. His wife had stayed behind in Nassau with their three children until he got a job. He had an offer. He went up and brought down the letter to show it to her. They talked incredibly for two and a half hours. Graciela had been on the same flight as he, coming to marry an American boy. Guillén thought Graciela was very confused. Berta Penabad, apparently finally over Ramiro, had married a Venezuelan man. Mario was working in an office Wayne had left in Nassau. Rina had gotten married. Raquel Weiss had gone to Philadelphia. Ramiro had answered his Christmas card. Ana told him Carmen was in Miami and Leonardo Vidal had written to her from Detroit. Ana didn't want to tell him she hadn't heard from Danilo in nine months. He seemed to sense it, and didn't mention him.

Walking down the street for the Sunday newspaper after Mass, Ana saw a boy at the corner bus stop making a squirrel run up an electric post with a stick. The squirrel ran along the wire over the street to the other side.

A few children were playing in a yard nearby in the afternoon and their voices buzzed,

> "... la media vuelta,
> ésta la vuelta entera,

> *éste un pasito a'lante,*
> *éste un pasito atrás,*
> *ésta es la de un costado,*
> *ésta la de ...* "[101]
>
> *"... y canela.*
> *Dáme un besito*
> *y véte pa' la escuela*
> *y si no ...* "[102]

A mother was calling her daughter in to dinner, "Caruca!" They all spoke Spanish. Sometimes Ana could hear a Cuban lady somewhere nearby, a grandmother, trying to teach her grandchildren the Cuban National Anthem. A dog was barking a few houses away. An ashy brown mockingbird with white markings on its wings lit on her windowsill for a moment, it trilled just for an instant, turning its head nervously, then flew away. Ana went to the window to look out. It had taken a short flight to light on an aralia. The last rays of sun painted the edges of the clouds pink over the houses to the west outside her window. The large leaves on the tropical almond tree in the yard of the house next door, beyond the aralias, had taken on a dark flaming red color in the cool weather that made it look, when it caught the sunlight, as if it were on fire. The tropical almond in Dany's house in Buena Vista must have looked like that, she thought, and instantly, "Stop torturing yourself, this has no purpose." It would be almost ten years since that. Why would she have thought of it? Probably not even Dany remembered it any longer.

Ana dreamed about Dany. In her dream she was in Cuba and they worked in ministries. She called him on the telephone at work, the one who answered transferred the call to his department, somebody grabbed the phone and the receiver was left off the hook. Ana could hear his voice at a distance, but he didn't come to the telephone. She didn't know his direct extension, she couldn't get through and she couldn't call again because the phone had stayed off the hook. She woke up frustrated, depressed. She was sure her dream had some meaning that would be very obvious to a psychologist, but she didn't understand it.

Carmen called Ana on the phone Tuesday. "Miguel got some star apples, and he has some for your mother."

"Oh, thank you... Carmen, did you ever start that book that you intended?"

"As a matter of fact, I have. I'm exhausted, tense. It drains me.

There's so much research to do and so many notes to take! I have to read a lot. I had no idea that you had to look up so much data. I thought I'd just sit at the typewriter and clever sentences would flow."

"I remember from second year Spanish, that somebody, perhaps Villaverde, said, 'Writing is like tying beasts to the cart'."

"I spend hours at the library on Saturdays. Miguel gets mad at me. Says I neglect everything."

"Yes, an Eighteenth Century British writer, Samuel Johnson, said, 'A man will turn over half a library to make one book'."

"I drive friends, relatives, co-workers and acquaintances crazy asking questions about Cuba. And I don't tell many people why I ask. I find the hardest chore is trying to recall the sequence of events. Somebody, I *think* it was a physicist, said, 'An author never finishes a book, he merely abandons it.' And another physicist added, 'I have come to appreciate vividly the truth of this statement and dread to see the day when, looking at the manuscript in print, I am sure to realize that so many things could have been done better and explained more clearly.' I write until after one, sleep six hours. Luckily Mami does the housework. She says this is a very long term proposition and warns me about an acquaintance who went crazy. I don't know how long it will take me."

"What are you going to title it?"

"I'm not sure yet, but I've been thinking of 'Song of the Mockingbird' or 'Goodby, Homeland'. I don't know if I'll ever finish it, Ana."

"Oh, I hope you do!"

"A man in a book store on Flagler Street told me the other day a woman should never write a book before she's forty. I'm not going to wait thirteen years!"

"Tai T'Ung in the Thirteenth Century said, 'Were I to await perfection, my book would never be finished'..." Ana felt interested. "By whom would you say you've been influenced, Carmen?"

"Well, I guess Betty Smith,... James Joyce with his stream of consciousness... and Herman Wouk."

■

Wednesday going home from work, despite the overcast skies, Ana was in high spirits. She had bought a black sweater and a pair of gray flannel pants on Miami Avenue in her lunch hour. She had also bought Wouk's "Marjorie Morningstar" in the drug store at lunch time and was going to start reading it. Silvia had called her in the afternoon; it had been eleven days since her discovery and she

Acceptance of Expatriation

seemed to be starting to come out of her shock. Something good was going to happen. A boy Silvia had dated some five months before had recommended Stormer's "None Dare Call It Treason" to Ana. And today Fred Taylor had told her he had it and was going to lend it to her the next day. Her father stopped at the market to buy plums, peaches and apricots.

"Hurricane Ginny has eighty miles-per-hour winds", Méndez said, dropping the newspaper on the car seat, "and it's taking aim at Stuart tonight."

"That's in Martin County."

"About a hundred miles from here."

Ana picked up the newspaper. At 6:30 there was "Americanism vs. Communism" on Channel 7; then on Channel 10, "Ozzie and Harriet", the Patty Duke Show and "Ben Casey", and at 9:30 Dick Van Dyke on Channel 4. She might write to Ernesto tonight.

Ana walked into her room and found a letter from Gloria Serrano on her bed. She was optimistic. She had the premonition this time Gloria was answering her questions about Dany. Maybe he'd confided in her as he had in Salvador's brother. She tore the envelope open anxiously. Gloria told her about her job at the Corporation of Transport, about her nervous condition, the shortages they were going through, the rationing of everything, her father's financial difficulties, a boy younger than she with whom she had been going out, the dances at the social circle, her father's car, her cousin, her cousin's husband. And then came the paragraph, like a slap. It was the first time she wrote about him: "Danilo got married to a girl accountant, revolutionarily integrated, very homely and very dull. I think they expect a baby by mid-March."

She had read in novels that the meaning of a shocking piece of news wasn't grasped immediately, it took a moment. But it didn't take her any time. As soon as she had read the first sentence, the desolation hit her. She read it over before she'd allow herself to believe her eyes. She was numb. Married? And to a revolutionary girl! Had Gloria tried at all to soften the news for her? Probably not, since Ana hadn't told her that he'd written to her, and he probably wouldn't have mentioned it either. Why did she tell her that the girl was homely and dull? Her dreams came tumbling down. She had **known** he loved her, she had been *positive* about it. How could he have married somebody *else*? He had actually *chosen* somebody else! Could it be out of hopelessness? No! She had dated several boys, but she hadn't cared about them. She couldn't have fallen in love with them. She loved only him. She had really been only filling her time until he could again be with her. In the back of her mind her love for him had always been latent, keeping her from caring for any other man. It was him she dreamed about, him she wanted. How long ago had he stopped loving her? How long had it been since he had written to her? Ten months! Of course he could have stopped loving her in ten months! Or could he really have stopped loving her? After they had been so close!, so... so spiritually close! But, if they were going to have a baby by mid-March, they would have gotten married, when?, in mid-June? That was over four months ago, only six months after his last letter. She forgot Silvia's disillusion to give herself wholly to her own.

Thursday morning she called Jennie to the ladies' room, leaned back against the green tiled wall for support and forced out, "He got married."

"Dany?", Jennie asked, surprised. "I'm sorry. I don't know what to say", she said awkwardly. She couldn't comprehend so much emotion.

Ana was shaking. Her teeth chattered. "It's cold", she said.

"The air conditioning *is* cold", Jennie agreed. After a moment, she asked her, "Are you all right?" Ana nodded.

She went through the following days in a stupor. She was drowsy. She slept a lot and had a feeling of fogginess. She went to bed early and fell asleep right away, but she woke up before dawn, her heart pounding, and she tossed and turned in her bed, her thoughts spinning around in her head, and could not fall asleep again, waiting impatiently for it to be time to get up. This wasn't like the fight in Cuba when he'd told her it was the last time they'd see each other. That was different. There had been hope then. This was definite. Her chest hurt from some pressure inside; her temples throbbed from the constant headache. She felt empty. She didn't feel hungry; she felt very tired, her arms heavy to lift. She hadn't known heartbreak could inflict such physical pain.

She locked everybody out. She alternated between desperation, when she could barely control herself from screaming, and despair, when she cried silently for long whiles. She didn't want to get *over* him. She wanted *him*. It was Tuesday. She looked up at the Ryan building. A single light was on in an upper floor. She sat on the little concrete bench by the 2nd Avenue bridge for a little while, staring at the light traffic going by. After a few minutes, she crossed the bridge, glancing absently at the dark still waters below, and came upon 6th Terrace and the Art-Déco style Miami Shipyards. When she saw the tiny wooden grocery store on the corner, she realized she had wandered eleven blocks from home. She turned west on 7th Street up the slight slope and headed home.

She got through the days somehow, working, in a haze. He had actually chosen somebody else! This was final. And a week had gone by. It was Thursday. She had taken a shower and mechanically eaten supper early. It was Halloween. From her bedroom she could hear the children running up and down the block yelling, "Trick or treat!" She caught a glimpse of herself in the mirror over the dresser. And she walked over to it and inspected her face closely. She saw her hands go up to her cheeks and had a feeling of detachment, as if she had no control over them. She had never thought she would experience such a sensation. It was as if she were looking at her reflection in the mirror in the restroom of some nightclub. She looked at her eyes − they had red veins, − her nose − the pores around it were enlarged, − her lips. She was twenty-six. She thought of the happiness she had known with Dany, of the dreams she had had for the future, now gone, her ties with the homeland severed, and she threw herself across the bed and couldn't stop the tears that came in a torrent. She must have been crying for close to an hour when the telephone rang. She was lying on her bed face down. She blew her nose. It was 7:35. Her parents had been watching "The FBI Story" with James Stewart on Channel 4. The phone continued to ring. They didn't answer it. Ana walked out of her room to answer.

She held her voice steady. "Hello."

"Ana, please", asked an unfamiliar male voice.

"Speaking", she said warily.

"Ana? This is Javier. Javier Zubieta... Ernesto's friend."

"Yes."

"How are you?"

"Fine, thanks." She was surprised. She hadn't seen him in over two years. "And you?"

"Fine. I got in town yesterday. I had asked Ernesto for your phone number."

"How is Ernesto?"

"Fine, but desperate to come to the warm weather. He sends you his regards. And to your parents. He says he still has about five more years up there."

"Are you here on vacation?"

"No, I came down to stay. It's too cold up there. And windy. I quit my job nine days ago, got my two weeks' vacation pay and left Chicago Friday."

"Did you drive?", she forced herself to ask.

"Yes. I bought a sixty-two Chevrolet three weeks ago and I stopped off in Jacksonville to see my sister Llivia. They settled there over five months ago. She didn't want to stay in France. I spent three days with them. I hadn't seen them since they came from Tarbes. Do you have a cold?"

"No... Yes."

"How are your parents?"

"They're fine, thank you. My father's working in a hotel... And Adelaida?"

"Adelaida got tired of waiting for Ernesto and she got married. Denis, my sister's husband, is working as a technician in metal processing. They have a little daughter, you know? Bernadette."

"Yes. My brother has two children. Are you going to look for a job here?"

"Well, I have an offer as agronomist from the Robinsol sugar mill, south of Okeelanta. I have an interview Monday."

"Where is that?"

"About sixty miles north on U S Twenty-seven, in Palm Beach County, past Alligator Alley, near Andytown."

"Is it small?"

"Tiny. A hundred people... I have the appointment with a Piedrahita. I'm staying at a motel near the Shenandoah elementary school now, but later I'd like to get an efficiency apartment in Miami Springs."

"It's quiet around there. What color is the car you bought?", she asked him, she didn't know why.

"A green Biscayne. Ah!, Denis' mother met your sister-in-law's broth... ther's wife, Pilar's father. Did I get that right?"

"Ah, Aragón?"

"Yes, at Lourdes." He paused for a moment, then asked her, "Would you like to go out with me tonight? I heard there's a Halloween dance at the Hungarian Club."

"I don't know..."

"Or we could go to the movies, if you prefer. At the Florida they're showing Hitchcock's 'Vertigo' with James Stewart and 'To Catch a Thief' with Cary Gant. The Casino Deportivo *'comparsa'* is going to parade at the Saxony Hotel on the Beach."

"Well..."

"Or for a soda or coffee", he said with momentum, without giving her much time. "I would like to see your parents... Or is it late?"

"No." She had absolutely nothing to do, except drown in her sorrow. And she didn't want to lie on her bed any longer, thinking. "All right."

"All right to what?", he laughed. "The dance, the movie, the soda?"

"Anything... The dance? Do you have to wear a costume?"

"I'm not going to. I'm wearing a suit. Should I pick you up in thirty-five, forty minutes?"

"Fine. Do you know the address?"

"Yes, I have it."

She found her parents in the kitchen and announced, "Javier Zubieta's coming."

"Ernesto's friend?", her mother asked.

"The boy from Cienfuegos who went to pick us up at the airport?", asked her father.

"That one."

She wondered if she would have recognized him had she met him on the street. She would wear her bronze color Arnel. She started to dress. They were well into the Fall and the temperature was cool, pleasant. She would have to buy a couple of dresses. The birds were chirping in front of her window before turning into the trees for the night. The trees were outlined against the darkening sky. It was a nice view. Some children were going up to the sagging porch of the bungalow next door. She saw the life around her for the first time in a week. It was turning dark fast inside. She turned the light on. She bent down to pick up her brown shoes from the floor of the closet. She needed a board across the bottom part of her closet on which to put her shoes. Maybe her father could put it up for her next Friday. Unless they were going to move to the new house soon. She straightened up and looked across the room. From the mirror above her dresser her red-rimmed eyes in her tear-stained face looked back at her. Her stomach was flatter still than usual. If they moved to the other house, next spring she would plant some pansies, petunias and cream colored roses in the yard. She didn't know yet if she could find love again. But she could find a will to live. They had a lot in common they could talk about. She went to wash her face, looked at her puffy eyes in the mirror over the washbasin and rubbed the tear streaks from her cheeks. She would need a lot of face powder around those red rims. Silvia's mother had mentioned rose water and almond milk for enlarged pores. The door bell rang. She heard her parents' familiar voices and Javier's new one rise in greeting in the living room.

"Good evening. How are you?"

"Fine, boy", said Méndez. "Come in. How are you?"

"Sit down", Teresa invited.

"How Miami has grown in the two years I was away!"

"Yes, it has been fast", agreed her mother. "Is it cold up there yet?"

"It was just starting when I left."

"I was just reading in today's paper that Fidel says a hundred fifty-foot Rex patrol craft attacked Cuba", her father said, "and claims it was a CIA raider. He says he captured two Canadians, CIA agents."

"Up there we didn't get much news about Cuba", said Javier. "I'm moving back here."

"It's more like home", said Teresa.

"This apartment is comfortable."

"Yes, it's not bad", said Carlos. "When we arrived here..."

∞∞∞ **The End** ∞∞∞

CHARACTERS

Ana María Méndez Bermúdez - Secretary in automobile internat'l. sales company, 21 years old, Advertising student
Danilo U. Gutiérrez Núñez - Ana's fiancé, accounting assistant
J. Carlos Méndez Miranda - Ana's father, accountant
M. Teresa Bermúdez Trejo - Ana's mother
Carmen Zayas - Co-worker, order clerk
Silvia J. Cárdenas - Classmate Miami, export clerk
Ernesto Crespo - Classmate, Publicity school, Electric Co. clerk
Javier Zubieta Puig - Friend, agronomic engineer, in Miami
Alejandro Dávila Rodríguez - Friend, counter-revolutionary
Gustavo J. Méndez Bermúdez - Ana's brother, age 26, accountant
Blanca C. Xiqués Monzón - Gustavo's wife, Electric Co. clerk
Octavio Guillén - Co-worker, Assistant Sales Manager
Reynaldo Duarte - Co-worker, Ministry
Jennifer O'Hara - Co-worker in Miami, Loan Departm.
Gloria Serrano - Co-worker, file clerk
Rosa Izquierdo - Co-worker, mail clerk
Leonardo Vidal - Co-worker, Quotations clerk
Casimiro Abreu - Co-worker, Ministry
Salvador Conde - Co-worker, Quotations clerk
Yolanda Solís - Co-worker, Ministry, secretary to Mestre
Olga Salazar - Friend, Rosa's neighbor, volunteer Ministry Agricult.
Ofelia Barquet - Co-worker, Ministry, of Lebanese descent
Berta Penabad - Co-worker, pool typist
Nelia - Co-worker, secretary to Palacios
Guillermo Bermúdez - Ana's uncle, retired from sugar mill
Cristina Bermúdez - Ana's aunt and godmother
Esperanza Méndez - Ana's aunt
Laura - Esperanza's daughter, elementary school teacher
Norma - Cristina's daughter, Pedagogy student
Beatriz - Guillermo's wife
Marcos - Cristina's husband, druggists clerk
Jorge Bermúdez - Guillermo's son, sugar chemist
Augusto - Esperanza's husband, soap factory clerk
Diego Miranda Cabrera - Carlos' nephew, civil engineer
Sergio Trejo Aguilar - Teresa's godson, lawyer
Adrián - Laura's husband, typesetter
Gustavito Méndez Xiqués - Gustavo' son
Blanquita Méndez Xiqués - Gustavo's daughter, toddler

Víctor - Norma's fiancé
Xiomara - Diego's wife, Episcopalian
Magaly - Sergio's wife, seamstress
Rina - Co-worker, secretary to Palmer
Elsa Toledo - Co-worker, receptionist, Colombian mother
Mr. Kent - Supervisor in automobile comp. in Havana, Sales Mgr.
Mestre - Supervisor in Ministry, Head of Section
Betancourt - Supervisor in Ministry, Division Director
Stanley P. Mitchell - Supervisor in Miami, Mgr.Comm.Credit Dep.
Raúl Tamargo - Supervisor in Miami, Mgr.Latin-American Depart.
Folgueira - Acquaintance from building, paper represent., Spanish
Aida - Upstairs neighbor in Miami, apparel factory operator
Fred Taylor - Co-worker in Miami, teller, Republican
Alvaro Benítez - Ana's former boyfriend, silverplater
Miguel - Carmen's boyfriend, tire-factory clerk
Evelio Estévez - Silvia's boyfriend, countryman
Enrique Carvajal - Friend in Miami, acquaint. from hotel, builder
Estela - Carvajal's wife
Peñalver - Friend in Miami, acquaint. from hotel, dentist
Oscar - Aida's husband, security guard
Irving - Acquaintance in Miami, photographer, NewYorker, Jewish
César Villaamil - Blanca's former neighbor, car salesman in Miami
Dave Harris - Co-worker in Miami, bank
Azucena - Laundress, Nigerian grandfather
Dr. Knowles - Optician, landlord
Paula Monroe - Co-worker in Miami, secretary to President
Lourdes - Laura's daughter, nursery school
Haydée Trejo - Sergio's daughter, parochial elementary school
Eric Miranda - Diego's son, infant
Ovidio Medina - Countryman in San Antonio de las Vegas
Juana Guzmán - Ovidio's wife

☺ ☹ ☺

POPULAR DISHES

ajiaco -	Créole boiled meat and tuber stew
aporreado -	shredded veal
caldereta -	fish caldron
capuchino -	syrupy conical egg confection
casabe -	cassava, yucca flour
cazuela -	grouper pot
cocido -	Spanish chickpea and boiled meat
congrí oriental -	rice and red beans *à la* Oriente province
churros -	sweet yucca flour crullers
fabada -	Asturian butter beans and pork
frita -	fried meat patty
fufú -	mashed plantain
guacamole -	avocado salad
horchata -	chufa nut drink, orgeat
huesitos de santos -	molded marzipan confections
majarete -	sweet corn pudding
malanga -	a tuber, arum
manjar blanco -	*blancmange* - cornstarch pudding
media-noche -	sandwich in an oval bun
mojo -	sour orange sauce
moros y cristianos -	rice and black beans
paella -	Valencian rice and shellfish
picadillo -	ground beef
ponche romano -	almond torte
pote -	Madrilenian white bean pot
pru -	Indian reed drink *à la* Oriente province
puchero -	boiled meat stew
pulpeta -	Catalonian meat loaf slice
ropa vieja -	shredded loin
salpicón -	veal loaf
tamal en cazuela -	pot corn meal
tamal en hojas -	husk corn meal
tatianoff -	chocolate torte
tostones -	toasted chickpeas
zarzuela -	seafood medley in sauce

§

EPILOGUE

I have tried to stay factual, be objective, even play down the events a little, as if seen through rather indolent eyes, and not to be emotional or editorialize. I have kept away from the overused names of "hyena", "satrap", "beast" or "tyrant" for Castro, or calling Batista an assassin. I wanted to let the readers draw their own conclusions, and alert them to a pattern of action that can envelop any country.

I've shown an average middle-class young woman, the shared love within the limited circle, the selfishness, the veiled prejudice, the faults, the ignorance, the indifference and the indolence, against the background of the political disintegration, trying blindly to hold on to a way of life that was fast disappearing, desperately hoping that they could go on as always, stubbornly pretending nothing was amiss, as developments unfold and everything around her toppled, and finally the acceptance that their life style had changed and there was no choice but to leave it all behind, and the harsh uprooting from their homeland. I hope to have cleared many misconceptions about Cuba and the Cubans by narrating our customs and presenting us candidly with our virtues and faults, but our own, not others'.

Once in exile, I've taken the young woman and her family through the severing of the love ties, first the relief of finding themselves free and the gratefulness for the hospitality, then the rebellion against the discrimination encountered, the difficulties in adapting, the gradual revelation of the imperfections unfamiliar to them, then the realization of the lost identity, the magnified nostalgia, then facing their own faults and in the end, after the devastating love disappointment, the acceptance.

§

ABOUT THE AUTHOR

Zilia L. Laje was born in a suburb to the west of Havana, is an only child, and her father, a medical polyclinic monthly quota collector, died when she was five. She grew up in a suburb to the south of the city, where she attended a girls' municipal school. She knew her maternal grandmother, a second-generation Cuban. Her paternal grandmother's ancestors had arrived in Cuba in the 1580's. She studied shorthand in Spanish. Then she and her mother went to live in New York for over five years. In Manhattan, she attended junior high school and took shorthand in English at a business school, and in early 1957 they moved back to Havana. She worked in the personnel office of a glass bottle factory in a little nearby town to the southeast for over a year and a half, and as export documentation clerk in a plate-glass international sales company on the eastern edge of Vedado for over a year and a half. She attended the Vedado Professional School of Commerce for two years of Business Accounting.

She came to Miami with her mother in July of 1961, and she worked in the branch office of a life insurance company nearby in the southwest section for almost four and a half years. Here she took bookkeeping in a high school, and got her Associate in Arts degree in Business Administration at Miami-Dade Community College, New World Center campus. She worked as property management coordinator in a banking corporation for about four years. She has a son, who earned his Master of Science degree in Physics at FIU. She has traveled to Europe and South America.

She started writing this novel in November of 1963, but had to set it aside for over sixteen years, while she raised her child and worked full-time... and studied. "Your Memory" and three other poems were written when she'd just turned all of fourteen, still in junior high. She has written several short stories, the last one titled "The Award".

≈ ≈ ≈ ≈

BIBLIOGRAPHIC REFERENCE

Bibliography used for the data, from which all the news were taken to which the public figures involved are linked, mainly political, artistic and international, all mentioned in the historical background

PHILLIPS, Ruby Hart - The Cuban Dilemma - 1962
RIVERO, Nicolás - Castro's Cuba, an American Dilemma 1962
WEYL, Nathaniel - Red Star Over Cuba - 1960
THOMAS, Hugh - Cuba: the Pursuit of Freedom - 1971
RUIZ, Leovigildo - *Diario de una Traición, 1959, '61* - 1965, '72
JOHNSON, Haynes B. - The Bay of Pigs - 1964
ROLDAN Oliarte, Esteban - *Cuba en la Mano* - 1940
MARRERO, Leví - *Geografía de Cuba* - 1966
SANTOVENIA, Emeterio & Raúl Shelton - *Cuba y Su Historia* 1966
YOUNGBLOOD, Jack - The Devil to Pay - 1961
BRENNAN, Ray - Castro, Cuba and Justice - 1959
RIERA Hernández, Mario - *Cuba Libre, 1895-1958* - 1968
BARBA, Antonio - *Cuba, el País que Fue* - 1964
VILLA, Salvador - *Cuba: Cénit y Eclipse* - 1976
BOURNE, Peter G. - Fidel: a biography of Fidel Castro - 1986
ADAM y Silva, Ricardo - *Cuba, el Fin de la República* - 1973
BARQUIN, Ramón M. -
 El Día que Fidel Castro se Apoderó de Cuba - 1978
CHADWICK, Lee - Cuba Today - 1975
BARNET, Miguel - *Biografía de un Cimarrón* - 1968
CARBAJO, Antonio - *Un Catauro de Folklore Cubano* - 1968
BALASCH, Enric - *Rumbo a Cuba* - 1989
MATTHEWS, Herbert - The Cuban Story - 1961
McGAFFEY, W. & C. Barnett - Survey of World Cultures - 1962
HUBERMAN, Leo & Paul Sweezy -
 Cuba, Anatomy of a Revolution - 1960
COBO S., Manuel - *El Cielo Será Nuestro* - 1965
JORGE V., José & Guillermo Zalamea A. - *Exilio* - 1967
GARCIA, José H. - Liborio Speaks in English - 1968
LACHATENERE, Rómulo - *Manual de Santería* - 1942
WYDEN, Peter H. - Bay of Pigs: the untold story - 1979
The Woman's Club of Havana -
 Flowering Plants from Cuban Gardens - 1958
CHACON y Calvo, José María -
 Las Cien Mejores Poesías Cubanas - 1958

STANZAS of Poems Quoted:

Chapter(s)	Poets	Nationality	Lived
1	Manuel Acuña	Mexican	1849-1873
2	Ricardo Miró	Panamanian	1883-1940
3, 8	Antonio Médiz Bolio	Mexican	1884-1957
4,12,13,15	José María de Heredia Heredia	Cuban	1803-1839
5	Leonardo da Vinci	Italian	1452-1519
6	Bartolomé Leonardo de Argensola	Spanish	1562-1631
7	Juan Clemente Zenea	Cuban	1832-1871
9	José Agustín Quintero	Cuban	1829-1885
10	Concepción Trillanes y Arrillaga	?	?
11	Isaac Carrillo y O'Farrill	Cuban	1844-1901
14	Gertrudis Gómez de Avellaneda	Cuban	1814-1873
16	Nieves Xenés Duarte	Cuban	1859-1915

WORKS QUOTED

REF.		AUTHOR	LIVED

POEMS

68	Recuerdos	Juan Clemente Zenea	1832-1871
69	Tu Recuerdo	Zilia L. Laje	-
70	Rondeles	Julián del Casal	1863-1893

SONGS

71	La Cita	Gabriel Ruiz	1912
72	Guateque Campesino	Celia Romero	
73	Camino Verde	Carmelo Larrea	
74	Cadete Constitucional	Jacinto Rubalcava	1895-1960
75	montuno of "Lágrimas Negras"	Miguel Matamoros	1894-1971
76	Tenía que Ser Así	Bobby Collazo	1916-1989
77	El Madrugador (guajira)	- José Ramón Sánchez	1901
78	Domingo Pantoja	Eliseo Grenet y Sánchez	1893-1950
79	Se acabó lo que se daba, se acabó	- (Anonymous?)	
80	Añorado Encuentro	Giraldo Piloto and Alberto Vera	1929
81	¿Dónde Vas con Mantón de Manila?	Tomás Bretón	1850-1923
82	Hymn of Alfredo M. Aguayo School	- Sara Estrada	
83	Amalia Mayombe	Rodrigo Prats	1909-1980
84	Ay, Mora	Eliseo Grenet y Sánchez	1893-1950
85	Yo Te Daré Café	(Spanish) (Anonymous?)	
86	Santa Bárbara bendita	Celina Rodríguez & Reutilio Domínguez	
87	Mata Siguaraya	Lino Frías	
88	Nostalgia Habanera	Bobby Collazo	1916-1989
89	El Son Se Fue de Cuba	Billo Frómeta (Dominic.)	1915-1988
90	Cuando Salí de Cuba	Luisito Aguilé (Argentin.)	
91	Total, si no tengo tus besos	- Ricardo Perdomo	
92	Cuando Calienta el Sol	Bros. Carlos, Mayo & Pituco Rigual	
93	Horizonte	Heriberto O. Costales	
103	Note: Yo Volveré	by Eduardo Davidson	(1929-1994)

had not actually been composed yet in October, 1963

Continued

Works quoted - Continued

CHILDREN'S PLAY CHANTS AND NURSERY RHYMES
(Anonymous, in the public domain)

94 Viola (A la 1 mi mula, a las 2 mi reloj, a las 3 mi café, a las...)
95 Por la carretera sube ¿quién? Isidro con su farol en busca de los civiles...
96 La gallina jabada puso un huevo en la canal, puso dos, puso tres, puso...
97 Tengo una muñeca vestida de azul (Dos y dos son cuatro, cuatro y dos...)
98 A B C, la cartilla se me fué por la calle de la Merced, mamaíta no...
99 Un chino cayó en un pozo, las tripas se hicieron agua, arre, pote, arre...
100 A Marlborough Chateau, yo quería un paje, ¿qué paje quería usted?
101 Estaba la pájara pinta posada en su verde limón, con el pico recoge...
102 A la rueda de pan y canela, dáme un besito y véte pa' la escuela y si...

Discounts: 10 copies or more: 30%
Book stores: 40%
Distributors: 50%

✂= Mail to: =====================================

Ms. Zilia L. Laje

P.O. Box 45-1732
Shenandoah Station
Miami, Florida 33245-1732   Telephone: (305) 856-9314

Please send me _____ ( ) cop(y/ies) of **"The Sugar Cane Curtain"** at $19.95 plus $2.^{05} postage. I am enclosing my check or money order issued **to the author** for $22. for each copy.

Name: _____

Address: _____

City: _____, State: _____ ZIP Code: _____

✂= Mail to: =====================================

Ms. Zilia L. Laje

P.O. Box 45-1732
Shenandoah Station
Miami, Florida 33245-1732   Telephone: (305) 856-9314

Please send me _____ ( ) cop(y/ies) of **"The Sugar Cane Curtain"** at $19.95 plus $2.^{05} postage. I am enclosing my check or money order issued **to the author** for $22. for each copy.

Name: _____

Address: _____

City: _____, State: _____ ZIP Code: _____